FALLEN CREST

Mason
Fallen Crest High
Fallen Crest Family
Fallen Crest Public

TIJAN

TABLE OF CONTENTS

MASON
Book 0.5

TIJAN

CHAPTER ONE

HE BROUGHT HER HERE

I got shit done. That was my job. That, and football, were the two things I excelled at. Each person in my family had their own set of skills. My dad was good at making money and sleeping with women. My mom was good at pretending no one knew her husband was cheating. Her other skill was drinking to help her keep pretending. My little brother, Logan's, was doing everything possible to get attention from me. Like now, as I looked for my textbook, I already knew it was gone.

I needed my science book.

My brother was so hilarious, *so* hilarious that he'd be crying from laughing so hard when I would pound him for taking it. I sighed. I didn't have the hour it would take to get the book back from him. We lived in a mausoleum. It wasn't a home and it was too big to be called a mansion. He could've hidden the book anywhere, but he wouldn't tell me and he would laugh when I pretended to look for it. Every time.

"LOGAN!"

He laughed and bolted past my doorway. The little shit had been waiting.

I yelled after him, "I don't have time for this. I have to go to Nate's." Then I waited. I had said the secret words. He knew I was leaving for my friend's house. He'd do anything to come with, but I couldn't blame him. Who the hell would want to stick around in this fucked-up home we had?

My phone buzzed at that moment. It was from Nate. **We up for night bball? Fischer said he could get us beer if we went to his place. Parents gone.**

I cursed, but typed back. **Trying. I need to do my homework before I can come.**

K. How long?

How long? I was tempted to make Logan do my homework. I typed back instead, **I will let you know when I find out. Logan hid my book again.**

Haha.

Haha, my ass.

We'll get him back. Don't worry.

Damn straight we would. I typed back, **Be over as soon as I can. Gotta kill the punk first.** Then I tossed my phone on the bed and shoved back from my desk. "LOGAN! You punk-ass bitch. Where's my book?"

He sprinted past my door, laughing, and headed downstairs. I couldn't stop a grin. I knew he had come back. I shook my head and tore after him. I could hear him going down the east stairs. That'd take him through the east wing and past Dad's library. I went to the north stairs to cut him off. He still didn't know about the short-cut through the second pantry. The back wall swung open to another room.

Hearing him hit the ground floor, I grabbed the handrail and launched over it, skipping over an entire section of stairs. I hit the ground in a smooth landing and pushed forward. The pantry was the second door. I went through it, pushed the back wall open, and paused on the other side. Logan's feet were pressed against the door from the hallway. He was waiting for me.

He was hunched down. Then he moved. His feet disappeared from the door and his little pinkie slipped under the door as he waited for me.

I grinned. The little fucker. I started to reach for the doorknob. I was planning on shoving it open, hitting him with it, and then pounding on him when he'd try to run away. I started to turn the handle when I heard Logan gasp from the other side. I froze. My head lifted. I had left the back wall open so I could hear what Logan was hearing.

Our mom was crying.

Letting go of the handle, I went back through the wall and out through the second pantry. Trailing down the hallway, all the lights were off in the north hallway. A lone light was on in the dining room, but the kitchen was dark. The crying had turned to a soft weeping. It was coming from the kitchen.

I caught movement coming around the corner. It was Logan. His eyes were big as he came up to me and whispered, "Mom's crying in there."

I pushed him back slightly. "Go upstairs."

"No."

"Logan," I hissed, frowning. He was just a kid, he didn't need to deal with this crap. "Go upstairs and find my fucking book. I still have to do my homework."

He rolled his eyes, wearing his own frown. His hair was sticking up all over. "I already did your homework. Don't worry about it."

"You did?"

"Yeah, it's why I took your book." Then the tiny frown turned into a smirk. "And to use as collateral so you'd take me with you tonight."

I laughed. I had to. "You're such a pain in the ass."

"Yeah, but I'm a smart pain in the ass."

"You are." I pulled him close and thumped him on the back, ruffling his hair at the same time. "But you're not coming."

"Why? I heard Nate and Ethan talking about beer at school. Is it because you guys are drinking tonight?"

"Maybe." My eyes narrowed down at him. How the hell did he know everything? "You're too young to drink beer."

He rolled his eyes and pushed me back. Tried. He *tried* to push me back. When I didn't move, even an inch, he let out a disgusted sound and mumbled, "Whatever. I'm only a year younger than you."

"So?"

"I did your homework."

"No one asked you to. I can do my own homework."

"I get better grades than you."

"I'm number one in my class."

Logan opened his mouth, ready with a retort, but didn't have one. His mouth closed and he cursed at me. "Whatever."

I was laughing on the inside. Logan was probably number one in his class too, but I knew he didn't know. Gotcha, punk-ass bitch. As he continued to glare at me, I tried to hold back my smirk. I lost. It slipped out and Logan started grinning too.

He hit me. "You're lying."

"I'm not."

"You are." He lifted his arm to hit me again, but I swooped in. Grabbing his arm and waist, I lifted him in the air like he was a case of beer. Then I hoisted him around my waist, holding onto his legs and under his bottom arm. I started to turn in a circle, then went faster and faster.

"Oh my god. Mason." He clutched my leg. "Stop."

"This is for taking my book." I went faster.

"I'm going to puke."

I felt him laughing and went even faster. "This is for doing my homework when I didn't ask and trying to use it as blackmail so you could come with us tonight."

His hand dug deeper into my leg. "I mean it, Mase. I'm going to puke."

His body convulsed and I stopped, dropping him immediately. He fell to the floor and rolled onto his back. His cheeks were flushed and he had a sour look on his face. "Shit." I bent down and nudged his shoulder. "Roll over. If you puke, you won't choke on it."

His hand flew up to cover his mouth. He started arching up from the floor, his eyes closed, and I knew it was coming. I started to back away, but then he burst out laughing.

Wait.

Logan flipped his legs in the air and jumped to his feet in one smooth motion. He pointed at me, still laughing. "The look on your face." He bent over and more laughter spilled out. As he slapped his knee, he shook his head. "That was awesome. I know what to do next time, just puke on you. Best prank ever."

I hit him on the back of his head. "That's the dumbest prank ever." I rolled my eyes, but he kept laughing and I couldn't stop myself from grinning with him. His laugh was so damn contagious. "Okay. Enough."

He kept laughing.

"You can't come tonight, but if you want to in the future, get my book right now."

He stopped. "Really?"

"Really." As he started to go, I repeated, "But you can't come tonight. No way am I letting you drink; I don't want to hear about it from Mom later."

He shrugged. "Fine, but she wouldn't know. I'm a fucking Kade, Mason. I know how to be discreet." Then he was off. He disappeared down the hallway and I heard him sprinting up the north stairs. That was when I saw the flash of car lights and remembered our mom.

Peeking around the doorway, I saw her standing at the sink. The window overlooked the driveway. The car's lights were still on and trained on the house, flooding the kitchen before they were cut. The room plunged back into darkness.

As I moved closer to my mom, I noticed her shoulders were shaking. She was so damn skinny. I was starting not to like skinny girls. They needed meat on them. I liked the healthier-looking girls at school. Nate and Ethan liked the other girls, the skinny ones, but they were nuts. Those girls were weak.

My stomach twisted as my mom dropped her hand to the counter. I watched as she bent down, her sobs coming from deep inside her now. She sounded like a dying animal. The pain was too much to hear.

"What'd he do now?"

She froze. Her fingers had a death-like grasp on the counter. Then she let out her breath and sucked in another before she shot back up and ran a hand through her hair.

5

As she started to turn to me, I shook my head. "Don't." It came out harsher than I intended. I cringed. I hadn't meant to yell at my mother. "Sorry, but don't. I know you're crying, Mom. Don't turn around and pretend that you weren't." Lies. The whole house was full of lies, except Logan. He was the only one who had never lied to me.

"Mason." Her voice trembled. "I thought you were going to your friend's house tonight."

I frowned. "I have to do my homework before I go."

"Oh." Her head bent down and she tightened the silk robe around her. "I suppose I should've known that. I didn't." Her voice dropped to a whisper. "I'm so sorry, honey. I've not been a proper mother to you lately."

I snorted. Lately? She'd been absent for years. "Whatever. You're crying about Dad?" *Again?* I wanted to say, but I held back. She would've started lying to me again. She always lied for him, but I caught her this time. She couldn't lie.

Every nerve in my body was stretched thin. I was so sick of being lied to.

"Yeah."

The tension left me, but anger filled its spot. She cried every night. She just didn't know we knew about it. I glanced back and saw that Logan was peeking around the corner. Yes, he knew too. Motioning him back, I glared at him. He stuck his tongue out at me, but disappeared from the doorway. I knew he was listening, but he wouldn't be able to hear everything.

Moving closer to her, I ignored the mascara running down her face and looked out the window. I saw them too. My dad had a woman pressed against her car. Her arms were wound around his neck. One of her legs had lifted to his waist. He caught it and lifted it higher, pressing her body further against the car. He was almost on top of her.

"He doesn't even take them somewhere else anymore." My mom's voice sounded hollow. "He brought this one here. They came in through the basement doors. I was swimming in the pool, but they didn't notice me. They were down there for two hours and she's just now leaving."

"Why didn't you say something?" As I asked, I knew her answer.

She laughed, the sound was mixed with pain, grief, and defeat. "What's the point? Your father's been cheating on me for years, honey. He's not going to stop." She began wheezing slightly. "I've tried to protect you guys from it, but I can't. I won't. You deserve to know the truth. This is what your father does. He won't ever stop."

She turned to me, more tears brimming in her eyes. As they fell, she whispered, "I have to leave your father, Mason. I can't stay here anymore and be in this marriage. I just can't."

My eyes narrowed. I heard the pain in her voice, but I shook my head. Anger jolted me and I growled, "Whatever. Fucking leave him if you want." I turned to leave.

"Where are you going?"

"Out. What do you care?"

"Mason," she gasped.

I ignored her, left the kitchen, and threw open the back patio doors. I could hear Logan trailing behind me. Ignoring him, knowing I shouldn't be doing this in front of him, I circled around to the parking area where my dad was. He was still on top of that bitch, their mouths fused together.

I hollered at him, "Hey! When you're done macking on your newest whore, you might want to book a vacation for Mom."

He whipped around and looked at me. "Mason?" The blood drained from his face. "What are you doing here?"

I snorted. "My homework. That's what I'm doing, or what I was trying to do before I heard Mom sobbing." He stiffened. I laughed. "Yeah, she saw the whole show, Dad. Not that it's a big surprise. The new fucking shocker is that you're bringing them here." I lifted a hand. "No offense to you, lady, but he's my dad and there's a whole family factor here that you're helping to break up." I turned my hand around and gave her a thumbs up. "But good for you. I'm sure my dad will pay you with lots of dinners and diamonds. If you don't get the private jet ride while you're sleeping with him, you're doing something wrong."

"MASON!"

I ignored my dad. "Oh, and just so you know, I'm leaving for Ethan's now. I'll be staying at his or Nate's place all weekend." I turned to go, but twisted back around. "And I'm going to be drinking beer. I'm telling you now, considering that you've got no leg to stand on with your parenting skills."

Logan was right behind me. He held two bags in his hands, mine and his. As I bypassed him, he held mine out. "Can I come?" he asked.

"Yes," I ground out. I'd never leave him alone again. No way in fucking hell.

He trailed past me. Helen was gone, but I didn't care where she had disappeared to. This was normally the time she took a pill or started drinking.

As we went out to the sidewalk, he asked, "Can I drink beer too?"

"No."

"Oh."

Hearing his disappointment, I sighed and tugged him close. My arm went around his shoulders and we walked to Ethan's like that. They'd be fighting tonight. I already knew it. Our mom witnessed it. We witnessed it and I called him out. I tightened my arm around Logan. He had heard too much already.

CHAPTER TWO

THE WAKE-UP CALL

We stayed at Ethan's that night and then went to my best friend's house for the rest of the weekend. The sad part was Nate never asked if we would. We all waited on the curb and when his parents' driver came to get him, he told him to open the trunk. He said, "Mason and Logan are coming with." When we got to his house, Nate walked inside and we followed. When his mom came out from the kitchen, her smile dimmed when she saw me. Then Logan popped out from behind me and it stretched again.

She asked, "How was it, honey?"

Nate reached up and kissed her cheek. "It was good." He gestured to me. "Mason and Logan are staying the weekend."

"Okay. I'm making pizza for tonight."

Nate hit my shoulder and laughed. "Last one downstairs doesn't get any pizza."

Logan took off first. Nate wasn't far behind. I waited until they were down there and turned around.

Nate's mom was watching me warily, biting the corner of her lip. I knew she was a busy woman; both of Nate's parents directed movies. In that moment, I was jealous of him. His mom was home, but she wasn't crying. She wasn't drinking. She didn't look like a made-up Barbie doll. She was wearing jeans, an apron, and a normal t-shirt. She wasn't like my mom, who always dressed like she was going out to a socialite party. My mom even wore big huge necklaces and her hair always looked perfect. Nate's mom was so far from mine in every way. She cooked for him. Our chef prepared every meal. If we ran out, food was ordered in. His parents were as wealthy as mine, but they were more down-to-earth.

Her eyes narrowed now. "What's up, Mason?"

I heard the wariness in her tone and knew she didn't like me. That was part of the reason I wanted to speak to her. "I know we stay here a lot. Thank you."

She nodded. "Yeah, well, your dad's good friends with us, and I know you mean the world to Nate."

"I know, but I know you don't like me."

Her eyes widened and her hand went to her chest in an absentminded gesture. "No, Mason. I don't want you to thi—"

I shook my head. "It doesn't matter. I know you don't and you shouldn't." What the hell was I doing? I wasn't a great kid. I knew that. I smarted off to my dad all the time. I cursed around Logan every other minute. I was disappointed in my own mother, but this was Nate's mom. She used to like me, but I wasn't stupid. I knew when she stopped; it was when my dad's cheating started to be more obvious. All that crap at my house pissed me off. Logan handled it differently than me. He didn't seem as angry as me. I said to her, "You're a good mom to Nate. I know you're worried I'll get him in trouble or something."

"Mason, really—"

"I won't." *Well...* "I'll try not to. I just want to say thanks for always letting us stay here and for letting Logan come with me."

Genuine warmth sparked in her eyes and her hand fell from her chest. As a fond smile lit up her face, a dimple appeared on one cheek. "He's a sweet boy. You take good care of him. I know you do."

I nodded. I wasn't there to talk about Logan so I said, "Anyway, I wanted you to know that I will never purposely get Nate in trouble." I turned away, then turned back. "Thank you." Then I took off. When I got downstairs, Nate and Logan were both on the couch. Neither said anything about me being last and when the pizza was done, nothing was said about not eating it. As we ate and watched a movie,

Nate's mom came down to check on us, and again when we were getting ready for bed. And she cooked breakfast for us in the morning. Every time I felt her gaze on me, I couldn't tell what she was thinking. I assumed she thought the worst of me, but I didn't know what to do. I owed Nate's family. When our house was full of fights or painful silence, we could always go there. One of his parents was always there. That felt good, for some reason.

When we walked home later that Sunday night, Logan glanced up at me. "Nate's mom helped me with my homework."

I frowned. "I thought you didn't need help with it."

"I didn't. It was nice, though, so I didn't tell her that."

Anger blasted me. My kid brother enjoyed doing his homework with an adult. I wasn't wise or old, but fuck, I knew there was something wrong with that picture. When we got to the house and went inside. I ignored the cold feeling in our own home, but I couldn't stop myself from tensing up. There'd be fighting later. I saw a note on the table and read that my dad had been in the cities all weekend; I knew the fight would be more explosive than normal.

When we went upstairs, Logan asked me, "Are you going to tell Mom we're home?"

"Yeah." I pointed to his room. "Get ready for bed. It's late."

"Okay." He took off, but turned around. "Thanks for taking me with you this weekend."

I nodded. "Go to bed, punk."

"Yeah, yeah," he grumbled, but shot me a grin before darting into his room down the hallway.

I went into my own room. I had no intention of telling her we were home. Nate's mom usually called and left messages, giving them updates; I knew she would've this time. I didn't want to see my mom. I didn't want to see if she was wasted or passed out. I went to bed instead.

"You can't bring them here anymore."

I sat up and ran a hand over my face, groaning. Again. This was fucking happening again. I glanced at my phone and saw it was three in the morning.

My dad yelled back, "This is ridiculous, Helen. Our marriage is not working. We need to stop this charade."

"Charade?" She laughed. Her voice was muffled through the floor, so I threw on a shirt and headed to the hallway. Her voice became clearer as I did, so I knew they were in the front entrance, right below my stairs. "There's no charade. I'm telling you the facts. Your children are being affected by this. Stop bringing your women here. I mean it. I won't say it again."

"Helen."

"I mean it. No more. You saw how Mason reacted."

I padded barefoot down the hallway until I was above them. The lights were still off in the hallway and when I got there, I saw Logan already sitting there. His knees were pulled up and his head was pressed against them. I sat down and nudged him. "When did you wake up?"

He didn't lift his head. His voice was muffled by his knees. "They've been fighting for an hour. I heard them when I went to the bathroom."

They couldn't hear us or see us, but we could hear them too well. I could hear the emotion in our mom's voice as she said, "We need to go to counseling. James, you need to go to counseling."

"No." He was calm.

I frowned. Logan lifted his head and held his breath.

Our dad continued, "No, Helen. Our marriage is over. It was over before it even started."

"No."

"Yes."

Hearing that, I closed my eyes. Relief, sadness, and anger all blasted me. Logan stirred next to me. "You think it's for real?"

I nodded. I heard the finality in our dad's voice. "Yeah."

Then he said, "Finally."

I shook my head. This was too messed up. "Come on. Let's go downstairs to the media room and watch a movie."

"Okay."

We stood and left. They never knew we were there; we left through the north stairs, at the opposite end of the house. Neither of us slept the rest of the night. A movie played on the television screen. Logan picked it out, but I never focused on what it was. I didn't think he did either. Their voices kept going for the rest of the night, but they were muffled since we were further away. I glanced at Logan, he was looking back at me. We didn't need to hear the rest.

The family was done.

CHAPTER THREE

POOL BREAK-IN AND CHOICES

I had to get out of that house, so I waited until Logan had fallen asleep. It was a few days later, but for once, the house was quiet. Our dad took off and Mom was around, but once she handed me the keys to my new Escalade, she packed a bag and went to my aunt's. She asked if we wanted to come along and Logan thought about it, then asked if our cousins could swap with her. She would go there and they would come to our house. She laughed, but I hadn't. I knew what Logan was thinking. Our mom would cry. She would drink wine, lots of it, and would talk shit about our dad the whole time to our aunt. There'd be lots of 'I told you so' and 'Amen. Just like all the other men' and other phrases women liked to say. It was uncomfortable. He wanted to avoid being around that, but he wanted to see our cousins. In the end, our mom kept laughing softly to herself as she pressed a kiss to both of our foreheads, then told us to call Mousteff if we needed something.

A rock was thrown and landed on the sidewalk in front of me. I looked up, seeing Nate wave from behind the gate, and darted over. When I slipped over the gate, Nate had stuffed his hands in his pockets and his shoulders hunched forward. He asked, "Are you sure about this?"

I paused. "Yeah. Why?" He couldn't have had cold feet. We had done worse things.

He lifted a shoulder and nodded to the house. "Aren't your parents gone? Will Logan be okay in there?"

"Yeah." I turned, just to make sure, but his window was still dark and his curtains never moved. "Mousteff is staying so if anything happens, he'll call."

"Your chef is your chaperone?"

I smirked. "I know. My mom's idea to soothe her guilty conscience." Wait. We started down the sidewalk, but I stopped. "How'd you know both my parents are gone? I only told you about my mom."

Guilt flared over his face. "Sorry. Your dad's at our house."

"Really?"

He nodded and grimaced. "I'm sure he's doing the same thing as your mom. There's lots of drinking, lots and lots of it. I think Mom's getting sick of it. I caught her glaring out the kitchen window at our dads on the patio."

"What'd they do?"

He laughed, following me further down the sidewalk. "Nothing. They were both wasted. I think my dad's kind of happy yours are splitting. He's got his old drinking buddy back. I heard him telling my mom last night that it was like his old college days."

"What'd your mom say?"

"To grow up. He's too old and fat to be in a fraternity again." He grinned. "My dad wore his old fraternity shirt for the rest of the day yesterday. I knew it was to get back at my mom."

"What'd my dad do?"

"I think he found his old one too. I swear, I wouldn't be surprised if I found a game of beer pong going on in the garage when I get home."

It was hard to hear that. My parents were getting a divorce. Hoo-fucking-rah. No more fighting, wait—who was I kidding?—they would always fight, no matter if they were together or not. Man, though, my parents were getting a divorce. No more Mom in the house. No more Mom and Dad together in the house. I couldn't say my parents were together, but shit, I haven't been able to say that for a long time anyway. I couldn't remember a time when we had a real sense of family, of Mom being Mom and Dad being Dad. They'd been cold roommates for so long.

Nate sensed the turmoil in me and grew silent. When I told him I wanted to get out of the house, he knew of a party. The rich pricks from Fallen Crest Academy were having one. I wasn't sure about being social tonight. We'd be allowed in, no matter our age. I was Mason Kade. My dad owned half the town and my reputation on the football field gave me an advantage. Even the seniors knew to let me do what I wanted, but when we got there, I stopped on the sidewalk.

Nate looked over. "What's wrong?"

I shook my head. "I'm not feeling all that social." I gave him a grin. "Sorry, I know you snuck out."

He shrugged. "It's fine. Mase, your family is dunzo. I'll do whatever shit you want me to do."

"I know." He was a good friend, my best one besides Logan. The house was filled with lights, loud music, and drunken laughter, but I saw the pool in the backyard. It was gated off so no one was using it. I gestured to it. "If we climb the fence, we could hang out down there."

"You want me to sneak into the party and grab some booze?"

"Nah." I indicated my backpack. "I stole beer from the garage. It's the good shit too."

Getting over the fence was easy, and we headed to the far corner of the pool. Neighboring trees gave us some camouflage so we were able to put our feet in the pool and watch the festivities in the house. The music and laughter was still loud, but it wasn't as bad. I handed a bottle to Nate.

We didn't talk. We sat, listened to the party, and drank. After we both finished half the bottles I brought, Nate let out a belch. Then he laughed, looking at me in shock. "Sorry. I don't know where that came from."

I lifted my bottle in the air. "From this. It's supposed to be the good stuff."

He continued to chuckle, shaking his head, then bent over and pressed his face to his legs. "I don't think this is the good stuff. Your dad brought over a truckload of booze to the house. Wait." He held a hand up, his head still pressed to the tops of his legs, his shoulders shaking. "I take that back. I saw some cheap shit on their table last night. Yeah, you're right. This is the good stuff. Your dad would have left it behind to save it."

He kept laughing, the sound was muffled, but it got worse. "Your dad. He looked so ridiculous in his shirt. It was a size too small for him."

I grinned, finishing my fourth beer and reached for another. "He probably shrunk it on purpose, to show off his physique."

"Not my dad." Nate lifted up. A silly grin was still there, but the laughter had lessened. One or two chuckles still slipped out and he started laughing all over again. "My dad's shirt is so small, there's a little pooch hanging out."

I grinned. "As long as my dad's not holed up with some other woman. I don't know. That makes me feel better." I sighed. Not my mom; she would've been hurt either way. I stopped thinking about it. That shit didn't matter. It was done with. We got our lives back. Still, it was a hard fucking pill to swallow.

Nate must've sensed my thoughts. Growing quiet, he asked, "So how's Logan handling it?"

I snorted. Finishing my fifth beer, I tossed the bottle in the pool. I shrugged. "He's been a bigger pain in my ass than normal, so I guess that means he's not handling it well. I don't know. He doesn't talk about it much. We're just glad it's over." It felt as if there was a knot in my gut, and it never went away. I didn't know how to explain it.

"You're staying, right?" He sounded anxious. "With your dad? He told my parents that your mom will probably go back to L.A."

"Yeah, she will."

"So you're staying then?"

I nodded. "Yeah, coach is here."

"Did your mom even ask?"

17

I shrugged. "Yeah, she said something once. I don't know if she'll ask again, but she knows I'm staying. We could go back with her, but this is home. Fucked-up as it is, this is home." Nate was there. I didn't have to deal with city driving. Coach was there. I could make sure Logan was fine here. He'd have different friends and a different school if we went to the city. I could watch him better this way.

"Hey!" A large guy was heading down from the house, squinting at us, with a couple others behind him. "Who's out there?"

A smaller guy tugged on his arm. "I told you I heard voices out here. They broke in."

Some girls were with them, but it was obvious the bigger guy was the leader. He came to the fence and stuck his hand through it, pointing at us. "This is my house. Get the fuck off our land. PJ, call the cops."

"On it."

I snorted. PJ. He could've been called BJ for the way he was acting, on his knees and at the guy's beck and call.

The guy heard me and barked out, "What was that? You're laughing?"

"Yeah." I stood up and grabbed my backpack. The emptied beer bottles stayed where they were and I left the other ones in the pool. Nate stood with me, walking beside me as I walked out of the shadowed area. When he could see me better, I said, "I'm laughing because your friend is a wuss. I saw him earlier." I was on my second beer when he came out, saw us, and headed back inside. I smirked at him now. "It took two beers to tattle on us."

The bigger guy relaxed when he saw me. "Oh. Kade. Why didn't you just say something?"

"Hey, Graham." Going to the fence, I reached through and he slapped my hand. "We weren't up for being social tonight."

"Nah. That's fine. I heard about your parents. Sorry to hear that."

Yeah. Everyone in this town had heard about my parents. Graham was a starting running back for Fallen Crest Academy's football team. We trained at summer camp together. His friend was looking between us, his eyebrows bunched together, and he frowned. "Kade?"

"Yeah." Graham shifted on his feet and gestured to me as he turned to his friend. "Why didn't you tell me it was him? I wouldn't have cared. Kade, you can hang out here anytime you want."

"Thanks."

"I mean that." He placed his arm around a girl next to him and pulled her into his side. Leaning on her, he turned to his friend. "PJ, this is the guy who's going to demolish you when wc play FCP."

PJ swallowed, glaring at me.

I smirked. "I think he'd like to try and demolish me now."

Graham laughed, shaking his head. "No way, PJ. Don't do it. You'll lose. This guy's going pro. All the scouts came early to see him. He's too young, but the rumors are already spreading." He sobered. "I am really sorry, man. My parents split last summer too. They got back together, but it sucked. Please tell me you're sticking around? My dad knows yours and he said something about your mom leaving."

I shook my head. "No, we're sticking around. My little brother knows this place."

"Your parents won't have a custody battle?" one of the girls asked.

"No, they both said I get to choose."

Both of them had come to my bedroom. It was the day after it had been decided. My mom sat on the couch and my dad stood in the doorway. They had a fucking speech prepared. It was nice, neat, and articulate. I knew neither of them had written it. No doubt their lawyer had drafted it for them, but the gist was that I made most of my own decisions already so I could choose. I did. I chose for Logan too and for a second I thought they were going to fight me. I wouldn't let them decide. Not for him. He was mine. They lost their chance to be his parent when they decided to let me raise him.

Fuck them. Fuck them both.

"That's good, then." Graham nodded, rubbing his hand up and down his girl's arm. When he caught her hand and laced their fingers, she sent me a coy smile. There was a reason the guy was being possessive.

I fought against rolling my eyes. Dealing with another guy's girlfriend was the last thing I wanted to deal with.

"Anyway," Graham gestured to the house, "we're pretty sure the cops were called because of the noise. We have some whiny old hags that live down the road. So we're relocating. You both are welcome to join."

I glanced to Nate. "What do you think?"

He finished his beer and said to me, "Whatever you want. I'm being the friend tonight, remember?"

I chuckled, then shrugged. "Sure. Logan's sleeping. We can sneak away for a bit longer."

"Awesome." Graham clapped his hands together and rubbed them. He gave us a wicked grin. "Hop your asses over the fence and let's get going."

When they headed back to the house, as I climbed over the fence first, Nate asked, "I thought you weren't being social."

"I wasn't." As he climbed next and landed beside me, I said, "But all this talk is making me want to forget." I pounded him on the shoulder. "Let's get drunk tonight. Mousteff can handle Logan for one morning."

Nate lifted an eyebrow. "Are you kidding me? Your brother is more likely to wake up, find you're gone, and then come hunt you down. I doubt your chef will have a clue you're both gone."

"Yeah." I sighed. I should go back, in case Logan woke up, but I wanted one night away. I'd go back to handling everything tomorrow. For now, I wanted to forget that my life was a mess.

CHAPTER FOUR

HELEN LEAVES

"Mason."

It was a month later. I knew it was coming. She had returned to pack her things. Her personal luggage was the last to go, but those had been taken an hour ago. It was only her and a purse now. I sighed deeply and pushed my notebook away. Tossing my pen, I looked at her. My mom stood in the doorway of my bedroom. She gave me a soft smile as a tear slipped down her cheek. Holding onto her bag, she readjusted her sunglasses before giving me a forced smile. As she spoke, her tone hitched on a sob. "I'm ready."

Fuck that. I closed my eyes, wanting to yell, wanting to throw shit, wanting to burn this fucking house down. Instead, I shoved back in my chair and shook my head. I pointed at her bag. "That's the goddamn dumbest thing ever."

She laughed. I heard the pain in her voice, but she tried to tease me back. "It's a purse."

I took it from her. "It's a picnic basket."

She laughed again, but I heard the sadness in it. She led the way down the hallway to the front door. When we got there, she turned. I handed over her bag and she placed it on the floor next to her. I didn't have to look to know she had a car waiting for her. The rest of her belongings had gone the day before. She sighed. "Logan's on another date?"

I nodded and looked away. "I told him to go."

"Does he know?"

I nodded again. "He was here when all your shit was going. I'll bring him to your hotel tonight."

"Oh," she paused, and sighed softly, "I suppose it's for the best. It might be traumatic for a child to see one of their parents leave." She took another pause as she looked at me. Then she lifted a hand and cupped the side of my face. I didn't move. I didn't flinch. I didn't look at her. She rubbed a thumb over my cheek. It was one of the gestures that a mom did. She said, "I'm so sorry, Mason. You'll be sixteen soon and you have to deal with this."

I refused to cry. I didn't think I had the capability anymore. My voice was rough as I shrugged out of her hold. "Whatever. As long as you and Dad are happy." I tried to smile, but fuck it. I couldn't. "It'd make my life easier."

She nodded, taking a step back. "I am sorry, Mason. I did try, but your father..."

I couldn't hold it in. "My father is an asshole who thinks with his dick. Trust me," I bit out, meeting her gaze. I ignored how my own mother flinched when she saw the hatred in my gaze. "He's losing you. It's going to affect him for the rest of his life. I hope he'll never be happy again."

"Oh, Mason."

I turned away, hearing that sympathetic tone. I hated hearing that from her. I didn't need sympathy. I was the fucking strong one. I was there. I fought for her. I was always on her side. Turning a heated look on her, I wanted to lash out at her. I wanted to tell her not to feel that shit for me. I didn't need to be pitied, but she was crying again, wiping those damn tears away.

She shook her head. "Your father was a horrible husband. I will admit that, but he's not a horrible father. I think I was the horrible mother. I should've shielded you from this, protected you so that you didn't know what was going on."

"He came *here* with them."

She stopped, stepping back when she saw the fierceness from me.

I said again, "He fucked those women here. He didn't hide. He didn't even lie. That's not a father. That's a stud looking for his new whore to fill. He's nothing, Mom. Stop making excuses for him."

Another tear slipped down her cheek and she flicked it away. "I am so sorry, Mason. This will change you forever. I know it and I am so very sorry. I should've protected you more."

I rolled my eyes. Picking up her bag, I shoved it at her. "Just go. He's with that woman for the weekend."

She nodded. "You'll bring Logan tonight?"

"I will."

"Okay." She shed more tears, but she never cared if I saw them. She never brushed them away. Pressing another soft kiss to my forehead, she whispered, "I love you. I will always love you. You will never lose your mother. I promise that." Then she pulled back, gave me another reassuring smile as those tears kept falling, and left.

When the door closed behind her, I waited. It wasn't long before the car left the driveway and she was gone. That was the end.

"Why didn't you say anything?"

Turning, I glanced to the second floor above me. Logan was watching me, but pulled back immediately. I couldn't see him anymore so I went up there instead. When I got there he was huddled against the wall. His arms were crossed over each other, resting on his knees, covering his head. I sat beside him. Some of his hair was sticking up so I pressed it down. Ignoring how he flinched, I said, "Why didn't you just say something? I thought you were going out with that girl again."

"Fuck off," he growled, still sheltering himself with his arms closed over his knees. "Get off me."

I sighed and moved away. "You could've just come down and said goodbye." But he didn't want to. That's what the big brother voice was telling me in my head. I told the voice to shut the fuck up, although he was right. Logan wasn't looking at me. Smiling at him, I said, "I told her that I'd drive you over tonight. You can say your proper goodbyes tonight and then..."

He lifted his head. "And then...we can drink beer tonight?"

"No."

He rolled his eyes and brushed some of his tears away. "Come on, Mase. I'm dating now."

"You're dating?" I scoffed, grinning at him. I wanted to ruffle his hair, but he always got mad at that. "What's her name again?"

He glared at me. "Tate."

"Shit," I sighed, "you like her, don't you?"

"Yeah, she's cool. She's in your grade too."

"You got an older woman. You like cougars?" I flashed him a grin.

"Shut up." I relaxed a little when I saw that his anger was gone. He added, "Our mom just left, for real. They're done. It's you and me now."

"I know." I threw an arm around his shoulder and pulled him into my side. "Dad's going to go nuts, now that he doesn't have to hide all those women. It's you and me." It had been for a long time. My own anger started to stir inside me. It was always there when I thought about our dad and the hell he'd put us through. It had gone on for too damn long.

"Why'd she stay with him for so long?" he asked softly.

I glanced down at him. "What do you mean?"

He wasn't looking at me. Instead, he was picking at his pants. "I can't remember a time they were ever happy. Why'd she stay?"

He was almost fifteen. My little brother was in eighth grade, and he was asking those questions. Rage crashed through me. He shouldn't have to deal with this.

"Mase?"

I shrugged. "Who knows? Us, maybe? I don't know how chicks think."

"If any girl cheats on me, that's it," Logan said fiercely. "I'm not putting up with that shit. No way. That girl is done."

"You can't cheat either."

"Never." He looked up at me.

The adoration on his face pushed some of my anger away. Shit. He was looking at me like I was his parent. Who was I kidding? I was. Our stuff might've been paid for by Dad, but I've taken care of everything else for so long. I hugged him tight again. "So you're not going on that date tonight?"

The adoration disappeared. He shoved my arm off and a scowl quickly formed when he scooted against the wall, putting an inch of space between us. I was half tempted to crowd him again. He liked this girl. I could see it, and I was surprised. Girls always liked Logan. He never cared about them until a year ago, but to actually like one girl. That was a new thing for him. I frowned at him. Chicks could be crazy. I hadn't seen a lot that weren't. If he liked this girl, I only hoped she was a good one.

He said, "I thought we had to go see Mom and do the goodbye crap."

"We don't have to. She'll be around for a while."

"She's not going to L.A.?"

I shook my head. "The divorce is final, but I think she wanted to stick around town for a few more months. Transition away from us or something."

He made a disgusted sound. "Why aren't we going with her? We could go to L.A. and leave Dad. That's what he wants, anyway. He just wants to live his own life."

"Logan."

He rolled his eyes, and his scowl deepened. "Yeah, yeah. I know. You want to stay because of the football team. What's so great about the team anyways?"

"The coach knows scouts."

"Whatever." He stood up. "I'm not going to see Mom tonight. I'm going to call Tate and have her come over here."

I frowned. "You better not be having sex with her."

He had started down the stairs, but froze and turned around. He made an exasperated sound. "Mason!"

"I mean it. No sex. If I find condoms in your room, heads are going to roll."

"Oh my god. What's it to you?"

"I'm your brother and I'm in charge. You stick that prick in her, I will know."

His eyes narrowed. He didn't believe me.

"You're a bad fucking liar. I can tell. Don't do it. You're way too young."

"Fuck off." He started to leave again.

"Logan," I rose my voice. When he didn't stop, I said, "I'll tell Mom and Dad."

He whipped around. His eyes were heated and his cheeks were flushed again. "You wouldn't. You'd narc on me? You pansy."

"I would about that. I mean it. Keep your prick out of her."

"This sucks." He threw his hands in the air. "This fucking sucks. How old were you when you started having sex? I know you've had girlfriends before."

"Yes and they cheated. I'm too young to deal with that shit. No dating for me and as for the sex part, none of your damn business. But I was too young."

"You're only a year older than me." He rolled his eyes and clarified, "Sorry. A year and a few months older. You're not dad."

That last comment was a parting shot as he stormed off. He went upstairs and slammed his door. I wasn't his dad, and I muttered under my breath, "I'm the closest thing you got to one, though." Then my phone buzzed. It was a text was from Nate; he wanted to go drinking tonight. I didn't even think about it. I typed back, **I'm in. Where and when.**

Now. Fischer wants to take us to his cabin tonight. Meeting there now.

I looked up towards Logan's room. I knew what he was going to do. He was going to screw her tonight, just to go against me. Decision made. I typed back to Nate, **I'm bringing Logan.**

He's going to drink then.

I sighed. **Rather have him do that then something else.**

Ok. I don't know what that means, but ok. Need a ride?

Nah. I'll drive. See you at Fischer's. I tucked my phone in my pocket and hollered, "Logan! You're going to a party instead. Cancel your date."

The door opened within a second. "Can I drink?"

Fuck my life. "Yes, but not too much."

"Fine." He slammed the door again.

I waited.

It opened again. "When are we going?"

"Now. Pack a bag."

"Okay," he said, his tone cool, calm. The door shut and I heard, "Hell yeah! This is going to be awesome."

I grinned, and went to pack my own bag. I would text my mom later and let her know the plans had changed. She'd be hurt, but I didn't care. She was gone. The responsibility for Logan landed on me. I might not be doing the best, but I was only sixteen-years-old. This was all I knew. It wasn't until we were already in the van and heading for his cabin that I realized, I never considered letting James know.

I shrugged. He didn't matter anyway.

CHAPTER FIVE

THE CABIN

When we got to the cabin, Logan jumped out of the van and headed off with a friend. We'd been there before so he knew where to stash his bag and head off for their own fun.

Nate rounded the van from the other side and saw that I was watching Logan round the corner and disappear from eyesight. He asked, "You worried about him?"

I sighed. "Always." Then I frowned. "Who's that kid with him? I don't know if I've seen him before."

"I think that's Derek Smythe. He's in the same grade as Logan. Why?"

"Is he a punk?"

Nate laughed, scratching his head. "Aren't they all? Aren't *we* punks?"

"I need to know if he's a punk that's going to get Logan in trouble."

He laughed again. "Besides the trouble we get him in?"

I shot him a dark look.

"Sorry. If you're thinking drugs and crap like that, I don't think so. Derek's older brother is Jared Smythe."

"He's in the grade above us?"

Nate nodded, watching as another car pulled up to the cabin. "He seems like a legit guy. His ego is normal sized, like the rest of us."

We shared a grin and leaned back to watch more and more people arrive. They were older than us, juniors and seniors. Recognizing Jared Smythe as he parked his car, I felt a little more reassured. "We play football with him."

Nate barked out another laugh and shook his head. "No, *you* play football with him. You're both on varsity. Us, minions, aren't deemed good enough. We're on the normal teams for our grade."

"Shut up."

"Kade." Jared Smythe came over and held out his fist.

I met it with mine and he nodded, stepping back. He nodded to Nate and shoved his hands in his pockets. Then he glanced around. "I saw your little brother's here."

I narrowed my eyes. He slighted Nate just now and if he was going to start on Logan, we'd have problems. I raised my head in a challenge. "Yeah?"

He grinned, shaking his head. "Relax. I'm not going to start with you. I'm just saying because he's friends with my brother."

"Yeah." Since he was in front of me, I asked, "Do I need to worry about your brother?"

"What's that mean?" His tone cooled and he frowned.

"Does he do drugs?"

He laughed. "That's rich. You brought your own brother to a party. You know he's going to drink here and you're questioning my kid brother?"

"Does he?"

"No." He raked a hand through his hair and rolled his eyes. "Shit. This is hilarious. You and your friends were invited—"

"Fischer's my friend."

"Yeah and his brother is throwing the party. This is an older party. You little shits were invited because of Ethan and because you're on varsity with us. Come at me with this attitude and I'll get you banned from every single party for the rest of the year."

I laughed. "You're forgetting one goddamn thing, Smythe."

"What?"

"You fuck with me off the field, and I will fuck with you on the field." My threat held weight and he knew it. I was better than him. That meant I held more power than him and there was nothing he could do about it.

A harsh-sounding laugh came from him and he began backing up. "This year's going to be fun. Let's see who wins, Kade."

Nate burst out, "Come on, Jared. He's just looking out for his kid brother. That's all. He doesn't know your brother."

Jared wasn't listening. He came back, his eyes flashing with anger. "For the record, it's your brother that I'm worried about. I love my kid brother too, but yours got him grounded the other night. Derek's been sneaking out past curfew, taking off to who knows where, and he came home stoned. Sorry, Kade, but your little brother is the reason for all that. He's the leader in his grade. Mine's not. You do the fucking math."

I scowled. "I will. If your brother's getting stoned, it's not Logan's fault. If mine is doing drugs, he'll have me to answer to. No way is my brother getting into drugs."

Jared still frowned, but it lessened. He sighed. "Fine. Fine. Okay. Whatever. Truce?"

I didn't say anything.

He laughed. "You're a trip, Kade. A part of me is glad you're on the team and the other part of me hates it." He took off, still shaking his head.

Nate cursed when he was out of earshot. He shot me a look. "What are you doing? Smythe is one of the top guys in his grade. He's a senior. I'd like to keep partying and getting laid this year."

"Whatever. I'm better than him on the field. We'll be fine."

"I hope so." Then he nudged me with his elbow. "Kate's been looking your way a lot lately."

I glanced over. She was standing with her group of friends, and she grinned when she saw me looking. I told Nate, "It's because we started hooking up this summer."

"You did? You never told me."

I turned to him, hearing the surprise. "Are you hooking up with her too?"

He flushed, but shook his head. "No, but I am with her friend. Parker."

"I think Ethan hooks up with the other one."

Nate nodded. "Yeah, I saw them leave the group the other night."

I was getting restless. Smythe's accusations were in my head, and they were pissing me off. If Logan was into drugs, I wasn't sure what I was going to do, but I would have to do something. "Come on. I want to talk to Logan real quick."

When we headed to where I knew Logan usually slept, Kate stepped in front of me. "Hey, Mason." She turned to the side, but she lost some of the seductive tone. "Nate."

He jerked his head in a nod and said to me, "I'll go get Logan."

I nodded. As soon as he walked away, Kate stepped closer to me. Her friends were right next to us, watching and whispering to each other. Kate didn't seem to care. She trailed a hand down my chest and lingered when she got to my jeans. She moved a step closer, and murmured softly, "You and me tonight?"

I took her hand and lifted it from my jeans, but I didn't let it go. "I don't like girlfriends." A quick frown appeared on her face, and she tried to pull her hand away. I didn't let it go and I tugged her close again. "If you're okay with those terms, then yes."

"You're such an asshole."

I moved her away from her friends, but kept her close to me. I moved so we were touching, lowering my own voice so no one close by could hear. "I have too much shit going on in my life. I won't be a whore with other girls, but I don't want to be tied down. I told you this last time and you were fine with it." I shot her friends a look. "Did they change your mind?"

"I changed my mind because I'm not a whore."

"You can have your freedom. You can do whatever you want. I will have no claim to you either."

31

She flushed. "You're too young to be this big of a douche."

I flashed her a cocky grin. "Yeah, well, there's a reason you keep coming around." Then I let her go and started to walk away. I said over my shoulder, "Find me later if you're okay with the agreement. I won't change my mind and I won't be manipulated into being your boyfriend."

"Asshole," she yelled at me.

I shrugged, grinning. She'd come. She had all summer. I had a brother to handle now. When I headed inside the cabin, I noticed there was alcohol everywhere. A video game was on the television and the living room was crowded. People were talking, laughing, touching, and others were waiting for their turn with the video controllers. When I headed upstairs, the music turned on, filling the entire house. Fischer's cabin wasn't really a cabin. It was a huge house and it was isolated, making it the perfect place for a big party. Passing by a couple already heading into a room, I saw Nate in the hallway. He was knocking on a closed door and I heard him say, "Logan, Mason needs to talk to you. Come out."

"Hey."

He looked up, and gestured to the room. "I told him about Smythe and he freaked."

Shit. My gut tightened up. I nodded. "I'll handle it." Raising my voice, I yelled, "LOGAN. Let me in." I waited. Nothing happened. I added, "Now."

The door burst open and Logan glared at me. "What? So you can accuse me of doing drugs? I'm not an idiot. I know not to touch that shit."

He moved to slam the door shut, but I blocked it and went inside. Nate followed, but when I saw no one was in there, I told him, "Give us a minute?"

"For real?"

I nodded. "Yeah, just a minute."

"Okay." He shrugged and gestured outside. "I'm going to start getting wasted."

As soon as he was gone, I shut the door. Logan was sitting on the bed, his arms crossed over his chest, scowling at me. When I locked the door, he started, "Not cool, douchebag."

I fought back a grin. He's a year younger than me, but he looked like a little boy at that moment. "You have any friends hiding in here?"

"No."

He said it too quickly. "I mean it. I'm going to get real personal here. You want our shit exposed to your buddies?"

The scowl disappeared and he rolled his eyes. "Are you serious?" Letting out a big huff, he went to the closet and opened the door. "Get lost, guys." Two of his friends, one was the younger Smythe, scrambled from behind a pile of blankets. They darted around me and out the door, slamming it behind them.

I locked it again and wasted no time. Logan had returned back to the bed, but he dropped his attitude. I asked, "Who's doing the drugs?"

He shrugged. "I don't know."

"Logan."

"I don't. I don't touch that shit."

"You're the leader in your grade. You would know. Who does them?"

"I don't know. I really don't. I mean, there's a few guys, but we don't hang out with them."

"Little Smythe is going home stoned. His brother is blaming you. Is this going to be a problem? I need to know so I know how to handle Jared when he comes at me again."

"It's not me. It's really not. Derek has other friends. He doesn't hang out with just me and the guys."

"His other friends are shady?"

"Yeah." He nodded. "I don't hang out with him, but I can't tell Derek not to hang out with them either."

"What are their names?"

He squirmed on the bed and rolled his eyes. "Come on. I can't do that."

"I'm not going to narc to the cops or anything, but Jared's going to ask for names. I have to give him something. He can handle it from there."

"That's the same thing. Derek's brother will go after them. He's like you," he frowned, "but nicer."

I grinned at that. "Give me the names, Logan. I'd want to know if it was you."

He groaned. "You're killing me."

"Then handle it yourself."

"Yeah, right. And do what? I can't tell people who aren't my friends not to do drugs."

"No, but you can tell your friend not to do drugs. If he hangs out with them, he doesn't hang out with you. What your friends do comes back onto you. You'll have to deal with it at some point. There's nothing wrong with protecting yourself. That's all you're doing."

He lifted his hand and swept it through his hair, messing it up. Then it dropped and his shoulders slumped down. "Really? You're going to make me do this?"

"Either you handle it or I will. I don't want you anywhere around that crap and I won't let some prick say you are."

Logan gazed up at me, seeing I meant what I was saying. He sighed and looked back down to his lap. "I'll do it. I will."

"Good." I went to the door, but turned back. "It's you and me, Logan. You got that, right?"

"I do. Yeah."

When I saw that he did and he wasn't fighting me, I sighed in relief. We dealt with so much shit at home. We couldn't control that, but dealing with school and our friends—that was something we *could* control. I was determined not to let anyone else push us around. One way or another, I was going to protect us.

CHAPTER SIX

DINNER WITH HELEN

I was at dinner with my mom when my phone buzzed. It was from Nate. **Good to go, but come through the basement door. Mom's pissy 'cause of her party.**

I responded back, **With my mom. Be there soon.**

Is Logan coming?

No. Out with that girl.

Shit. That's been going on for a long time now.

Yeah. Too serious for Logan. I laughed to myself.

Ha. Hurry. I got beer.

"Is that Nathaniel?" Helen asked as she folded her cloth napkin, brushing the corner of her mouth, giving me a warm smile.

I shook my head, putting my phone away. "Why the hell do you call him Nathaniel? His name's Nate."

She grimaced. "Mason, language. Do you always have to curse in my presence?"

I nodded and flashed her a smile. "Don't worry, Helen dearest, I don't discriminate. I curse outside of your presence too."

She groaned. "Well," she glanced around at the other diners around us. It was an early dinner, but the restaurant was known for its expensive cuisine. Even though we were a safe distance from the other tables from hearing, they were curious anyway. She added, "People in our circle don't need more material to gossip about us. Can you refrain from cursing when you're around your mother? Please?"

I rolled my eyes. "I don't think a few swear words from your son is going to add more fuel to the fire. Dad's cheating and your divorce is plenty to keep the old hags going."

Noticing one old hag in particular watching us steadily, I narrowed my eyes at her, leaned forward, and raised my voice, "She just asked me to stop swearing, in case you wanted to know what's going on."

"Mason," Helen hissed next to me, "lower your voice."

I ignored her and said to the lady, "She really hates it when I say the word FUCK all the time." Her eyes got big and she sat up straight. When I saw the same movements as all the others, when they lifted their noses to look down them, I yelled again, "In case you're confused about that word, it's like having sex, but fucking. You know? I like to mix it up, use it with other words like 'I'm fucking talking to you'." The lady looked horrified. When she began looking around for the server, I lifted my hand. "I'll get them for you." Then I extended my middle finger in the air, pointing it right at her. "That lady there wants some help. Right there."

"Good god, Mason." My mom shoved my finger down and held hers out towards the lady. "I am so very sorry. He and his brother aren't handling the divorce that well."

I snorted. "Good one, Mom. That's the best lie all year."

"Stop it." The server came over and Helen reassured him, "He will quiet down. I promise. I am so sorry."

He didn't look comforted, but I stared him down. We both knew they weren't going to kick Helen Malbourne-Kade out of the restaurant. She owned shares in the restaurant as did a bunch of my other relatives. When he left and my mother paid for the old lady's dinner, plus her guest, Helen settled back in her chair. She shot me a dark look. "You could act properly. I know you know how. What is with you lately?"

"You mean besides the divorce, hearing you cry every fucking night, raising Logan, and Dad's affairs?" I shrugged, reaching for my water to take a drink. "Nothing, Mother dearest, but you might want to try raising your other son. I'm a lost cause. Logan's not."

"Not yet, but I don't think he wants me around. He won't talk to me anymore."

I frowned. "What do you mean?"

"He called me the other night and informed me that he was happy I was divorcing Dad because he was tired of the fighting and the 'shit storm'. His words."

"When was this?"

"Sometime this week. I hoped he would come for dinner."

The timing of his date made more sense.

Helen sighed and pushed her plate away. "He doesn't want to have a relationship with me. He said it's pointless because you're the only one who's there." I saw pain flash in her eyes before she lowered her head. I could hear the regret in her voice. "He was calling to inform me of his decision." Looking back up, she gave me a wry grin, but she couldn't hide the hurt. "That's my other son for you, and this, spending time with you is pointless. Every time I try to spend quality time with you, something happens. I can't spend time with you alone. I never know what you're going to do. Last week, the cops called me and told me to reign in my child. I enjoyed that phone call immensely."

I shrugged. "Cops are assholes."

"This week it's this. You're flipping off the elderly and using coarse language on purpose?" She leaned forward and lowered her tone. "That lady wasn't doing anything to you."

"She was judging us." I stared right back at her. "She was judging you, Mom. I don't give a shit what she says about me. Bad reputations aren't a bad thing for guys like me, but you," I tsked at her, shaking my head. "Trust me, she would've been on the phone with her biddies and all their daughters about *that woman* James Kade is leaving."

Helen sucked in her breath and her fingers curled on the table, holding onto it for support. She realized that I was right.

I said, "Now she'll talk about what a horrible son James Kade has." I finished my water and gave my mother a polite smile. "That was a win-win for us. No gossip on you and my badass rep continues to grow."

A soft curse slipped from her lips, and she leaned back in her chair. Her hands lifted to rub her forehead, massaging it in circles. "You're right, except I wish your reputation was *only* a reputation."

"Yeah." I shrugged. My phone buzzed again, and I said to her, "I have to go. Nate's waiting."

"Mason—"

I got up and shot from the table, ignoring the rest of whatever she was going to lecture me about. I didn't want to sit there and hear what I knew she'd say. She would ask questions about who would be at Nate's house, but it would only torture her further. Nate's parents were having a party. I was fully aware of who would be in attendance, lots and lots of my father's mistresses. Nate thought I was going to hang out with him in the basement. Nope. I was going to have some fun tonight. Logan was off having a nice, normal date so the coast was clear. I was going to rip into a few people tonight, whether Nate's parents kicked me out or not.

Nate saw the fight in me the second I walked through the basement patio door. He put the video controller aside and cursed, raking his hand through his hair. "You're going to cause a problem tonight, aren't you?"

There were four other people sitting on the couches and chairs in the room. I didn't recognize any of them, but at Nate's words they all looked at me. I said to them, "Who are you people?"

"They're friends. Their parents are friends with my parents." Nate pointed to a guy. "That's Nick."

A lanky guy, wearing a polo and trendy jeans nodded to me. "Yo."

Nate continued, pointing to the girl next to him. "That's Maria."

"Hi." She gave me a nervous smile. Brushing some of her blonde hair back, she moved away from Nick's hand and her eyes grew more welcoming. He frowned at her, then it turned into scowl as he turned to me. I shot him a warning look. I wasn't going to take any crap from him. At that, it went back to a frown, but there was still heat in his eyes. He could be a problem later.

Nate kept on with the introductions. He gestured to the opposite couch where a girl sat. She had black hair and could've been a model. He said, "That's Wren and the guy next to her is Wayne. They're twins." The guy said hello, but I ignored him and lingered on Wren. Her lips pressed together in a smug smirk, and she adjusted her legs, opening them for a second before she swung them back underneath her bottom. She wore a shirt that looked like a corset with a black bra underneath. Her breasts were full and I imagined cupping them later. They'd be a good handful.

When my gaze snapped up to hers, the invitation was there and I nodded. If I didn't get thrown out of the party or arrested, I knew what I'd be doing later. I gave the other guy a nod and headed for the bar in the basement. "Did you guys start drinking?"

Nate followed me. He hopped on a bar stool when I went behind the counter and poured rum into a glass. As he watched me, he said, "Yeah, but we were waiting for you to start doing shots."

The others got up and stood around the bar. I skimmed them again and grunted. Nate's parents were rich movie directors. That meant they had rich friends, who had rich kids, and since Nate's parents directed major motion pictures, I knew the who's-who were upstairs. I was a rich kid. I was aware of this, but I wasn't an entitled prick like these four were. And the people upstairs were worse. Even now, glancing towards the ceiling, I could list the people up there.

I finished mixing my drink and asked Nate, "Is my dad up there?"

He tensed and shook his head. "No."

"Is he?"

"Come on, Mason. Don't do this."

I flashed him a hard grin. He was up there. "Is there food up there? I think I'm hungry."

"Mason. Seriously. Don't."

Nick frowned. "What's going on?"

Maria and Wren shared a look, both smiling at each other. Wayne frowned at them, then at me, and swung to Nate. "What's going on?"

I slammed my drink back and started for the stairs.

"Mason." Nate got in front of me and tried to block me from the stairs. "Think about this. This is my parents' house."

I stopped and flashed him a heated look. "Move, Monson."

He shook his head. "My parents already don't like you. They threatened me the last time we got into trouble. They want to move from Fallen Crest and take me with them."

A voice in the back of my head was telling me to listen to him. He was my best friend. He was always by my side. He did whatever I needed and he took a lot of crap because of it. The other part of me wasn't a voice. It was the need to pummel someone. The voice got silenced and a calm came over me. I needed to do this. "My dad is up there."

Nate was holding his hands up to me, but they lowered. An air of acceptance came over him and he said, "I know he is."

"You know who else is up there?" My voice grew rough, hardening. My jaw clenched and I lowered my head, as if I was going to charge right through him.

He nodded. "I do."

"I'm going up there, Nate. I'm sorry, but I am. All his colleagues are up there. All those women he's slept with. He keeps them around. He works with them. He introduces them to his friends. They're all in the same social circle."

He gazed at me, studying me.

I let him see me. I let him see the gnawing ache inside of me. It had been there forever. I couldn't remember a time it wasn't, and the person who put it there was with his friends.

My dad was doing his thing. He was acting like he was perfect. He was pretending that he had never hurt anyone and he was getting away with it.

"Nate," I softened my tone, "I have to make him hurt. Just a little bit."

"He's outside on the patio." Then he stepped aside, and I didn't wait another second. I charged the stairs.

When I burst through the door, conversation stopped. It was like they sensed trouble coming and I smirked, seeing alarm come over more than a few. Some of them scattered away, and I knew it wouldn't be long before someone told Nate's mom I was out here. She'd come and try to intervene, but it wouldn't matter. As I passed the buffet table, I grabbed a drink and headed to the patio. When I got there, Nate's dad had his head bent close to my dad's. They turned as one to me. I flashed them a grin. That hadn't taken long at all. With mirroring guarded expressions coming over them, I headed their way, then skimmed the woman next to my dad up and down. She wore a black dress, high heels, and a shiny bracelet on her wrist.

I pointed to it. "When did he get that for you?"

"Mason." My dad moved forward. He lifted a hand to me, but I dodged around him.

I said again, "When did he get that for you?" I gestured around the room. "Because you know he's gotten a lot of women here the same gift."

She looked at my dad. "Who is this?"

I laughed. "She doesn't even know. You must be one of his short-term girls." I swung around to my dad. "Or are you still with that bitch? What was her name? I didn't like her, Dad." As I stressed that word, I threw the woman a pointed look. She flushed, registering the insult and moved back a step. I turned back to him. "Or are you cheating on her with her." I pointed to the woman and looked around the room exaggeratedly. "I don't see the other one, so this must be the one in your bed tonight."

She clenched her drink tighter. "Dear god."

I shook my head. "Not god, honey. His son." I flashed her a hateful smirk. "But close. I'm sure my father thinks he is a god. He plays with people's lives like he is one. Right, Dad?" I swung around.

He was standing there, just watching me with pity in his gaze. Nate's dad was beside him, so was Nate's mom. She held a hand to her mouth and horror filled her gaze. I hated that. It set me on edge and I gritted my teeth. They had no idea. They were horrified because of me? Because I was going to ruin their party? A burst of fury like I had never experienced shot through me. I lunged for him.

Nate's dad tried to catch me, but I ducked, avoided him, and kept going. My dad fell back and Nate's mom stepped in front of him, like she was going to protect him. I laughed; this was ridiculous. Another guy stepped in and caught me. Both of them wrapped their arms around me. I wasn't really fighting, but I wanted to. I wanted to hurt him. Nate's dad and the rest were reacting to my threat, but my anger wasn't at them.

I yelled at him, "You screw women like they're snacks for you. You always have. You'll never change."

Seeing that I was restrained, even though I wasn't really fighting them, he shook his head. "Mason, things happened in my marriage that you won't understand."

"Fuck you."

He stopped, a glimmer of his own anger flared, and I waited. I wanted him to fight. I wanted him to react. *God yes*, I thought, but then he backed down.

I laughed. They tightened their holds around me, but I wasn't fighting. I was standing there, shaking my head. I hated him. In that moment, I hated my father like I had never allowed myself to feel. A strangled sound came from me and I said, "You ruin lives and you don't give a shit."

I stopped.

Everything stopped. This wasn't me being a smartass or

some punk kid. This was me speaking the truth. Everyone sensed it and they stopped pretending to hold me back. Nate's mother dropped the hand she had pressed to her chest. Even the woman I had insulted paused. My dad had an arm around her waist to comfort her, but she moved away, out of his reach.

I said further, "Logan doesn't want to have a relationship with Mom. Who do you think is to blame for that?"

He started to retort.

I shook my head. I knew what he was going to say. My mother. Everything was her fault except it wasn't. "Stop, Dad. Just stop. This is you. This is all on you."

"Mason." He started for me.

I jerked back. Their arms went back up, but it wasn't to hold me back. Now it was to protect me, and they had no idea they did it. They just reacted to what was going on. I shook my head. "There's no way you can justify what you've done. You screwed her." I pointed to the woman. Her face reddened and she jerked away, but she didn't leave. I knew it was true then. She didn't want to leave, in case he wanted her later. Knowing that, knowing it wouldn't matter, caused something to die inside of me. He would do it. He would keep doing this and nothing I said or did would matter. He would get away with it. I didn't matter. I was just his son. I was collateral damage. I was something that was swept up and tossed away with the garbage.

Feeling that and knowing that was the truth stopped me. It would never matter. I was just a kid. I wasn't more. Feeling that and digesting that sent a new wave of rage through me. I *would* matter. I wouldn't be tossed away.

I wanted to kill him.

He saw it in me and moved back. Nate's dad and the other guy locked hands. They reacted to the change in me and it switched back to where they were holding me back. I wanted to rip through them. I wanted to lunge for him. I wanted to hurt him how he hurt me, how he hurt Logan, how he had hurt his wife.

I couldn't, though. Anything I said wouldn't be taken seriously among these adults. They would laugh me off. They would say something to discredit everything I said and none of this would do a damn thing. At that, accepting that, I stood there and an anchor dropped in my gut. He won. He would get away with it. No one would care that his own son showed up to ruin his life. This wasn't abnormal in their world.

So instead I said, "I hate you."

"Mason."

I shook my head. "I *will* continue to hate you."

"Stop, son."

"Don't call me that. I may be your blood, but you haven't raised me. You don't care." I gestured around the crowd. "*They* don't care. You'll get away with this. You can sleep with any woman and they won't care about the damage they're a part of."

I couldn't hit him. They were holding me back, but I needed to hurt something, anything. I scanned the crowd and my gaze zeroed in on a lady. I smirked. Her eyes got big and she took a step back. Too late. I called out to her, "I remember you. You were the car girl. He had you up against the car in our driveway."

The man next to her whipped around to face her. "Is that true?"

She stood frozen. "No, uh—" She glanced at my dad.

The guy saw it and asked, "Why are you looking at him?"

She looked away. "I'm not."

"You did. I just saw you." The man looked at me for confirmation.

I nodded to him. "It's true. And my mom saw the whole thing."

"Mason," my dad hissed, stepping closer, "stop it. You're going to hurt people."

This was it. This was how I could hurt him, by hurting them. That couple was already gone. The guy had taken off and she ran after him, but this room was full of targets. I started looking again and moved to a lady who had been standing next to the car girl. Of course. They must've been friends, but this one I remembered from the pool. Her mouth dropped when she saw I wasn't looking away. I was only looking at her.

I pointed to her. "Red dress." The rest of her friends turned to her. They were waiting for what I was going to spill. "You were in the pool with him."

The guy next to her grabbed her arm. "You better tell me that's not true, Vivienne."

"I—" she began to look at my dad, but stopped.

I said further, "She had on a hot pink bikini. I remember because my friends and I went through the backyard to go into the basement and one of them grabbed her top. I think he still has it."

The guy was shaking his head. His teeth were clenched together. "You did say you lost that top."

"Dean, no—" She stopped. Her date was already backing away from her. With a disgusted sound, he turned and shoved through the crowd. She started after him, but stopped as she went past my dad and hissed at him, "Stop your son. He's going to ruin everything!"

There was more. I could feel it. They could feel it too and the air in the room changed. Women started leaving; they didn't want to be the next target. But people were looking around to see who was leaving. Who would leave? Who was guilty?

"Mason." My dad reached past Nate's dad and the other guy still holding me back. He grabbed my arm and started to pull me after him. "Stop this. Now."

I shoved his arm off me. "You touch me again and we're going to fight." I was bigger. The coach had me on a weight training schedule, and I had begun to fill out more. I was bigger than him. My dad registered all of this and paused, cautious now. When he didn't do or say anything, I laughed and looked for the next target.

I saw her. There was a couple in the corner by the bar. I pointed at her. "Yellow dress."

She lifted her drink to me in a salute. "I'm single, kid. You're not going to hurt me."

"Good to know." I moved to the next one. A woman in another black dress was inching into the house, away from the patio. "You. Black dress."

She hurried into the house.

It wouldn't matter. I glanced to where she had been standing. A group was there, waiting for what I was going to say next. I knew which one was the husband right away. He was glaring at James, his jaw clenched, with the same look of violence in his eyes that I was feeling. He turned to me, waiting. I told him, "In his office. He was supposed to give me a ride to an away game and I heard them. When she left, her dress wasn't zipped up all the way."

The husband was seething. He didn't go after his wife. He went for my dad. His fist was already formed. I watched it happen. My dad was focused on me. He was trying to figure out how to shut me up. He wasn't looking at who was coming at him and then a woman screamed. The husband didn't say anything. He was a foot from my dad when he threw the first punch.

It connected with his jaw, square in the middle, and my dad went down.

It was chaos after that.

The husband hit him again, but Nate's dad went from holding me back to holding the husband back. He yelled in his ear, "Patrick, stop this."

The husband shook his head. "It wasn't your wife, Dom. It was mine and that bastard has been with her more than the time the kid saw. I know it. I've known it for a while." He lunged for my dad again, but two other men joined in and held him back.

I wasn't being held back anymore. I met my dad's gaze. He was still on the ground, holding the side of his face.

Nate's mom was kneeling at his side, yelling for them to take the husband out. In that moment, all the yelling and chaos melted away.

It was just him and me.

He asked, "Are you done?"

No. "Not by a long shot."

My dad wasn't sorry. I could see that. He was going to continue to do what he wanted. There was an arrogance to him. Standing there, seeing him on the ground and bleeding, didn't make me feel better. Instead of the need to hurt someone, I was empty. The gnawing ache in my stomach was still there, but it was worse. I closed my eyes and hung my head. The gnawing feeling would never go away.

"Mason."

Nate's mom was in front of me. She pointed to the house. "Leave my house. Now."

I nodded. "Yeah. Okay."

As I left, I realized that the only people paying attention to me were the ones I hadn't called out. As I went past them, each one turned away or stood behind a person, hiding from me. The rest were buzzing about what had happened, and I could hear shouts from outside still. I never minded when people were fearful of me, but this time it left me empty. I had joined them. I had sunk to their level and I felt dirty because of it. When I got to the door, Nate was there. His prick friends were too. I didn't give a shit what they were thinking, but Nate folded his arms over his chest. He gestured towards the patio area. "My mom kicked you out?"

"Yeah. You're probably going to be banned from being my friend."

"They've already tried." He shrugged. "I won't listen. I never do."

"I'm sorry."

"For what?"

"I put my dad shit above our friendship just now. I'm sorry, Nate." And I was. It had been the wrong thing to do.

He'd be hurt by it. I wouldn't. That was the sad thing. My dad would come home and pretend I wasn't there. It's how he dealt with life. He would continue to do his own thing and pretend there were no consequences.

"Mason."

I had started out the door, but turned back to Nate again. "Yeah?"

"Spend time with Logan tonight. Just the two of you do something together."

"Why?"

"Because being around your brother always seems to help you."

Guilt and shame shot through me, and the hole in me grew bigger. "You're a good friend."

"So are you." He flashed me a half-grin. "Maybe not today, but you are. I'll sneak over tomorrow."

"Sounds good."

"See you."

He shut the door behind me and I walked away. I didn't feel better at all.

CHAPTER SEVEN

AN AGENDA

A girl in a tight shirt and jeans came over with a beer. I skimmed an eye over her—she looked fine—tight body, decent rack for our age. Her bra was showing; girls did that shit on purpose. They wanted us to see it. When Nate saw my approval, he flashed me a grin and took off. We were at one of Fischer's parties, but it was still early in the evening. Logan insisted on coming, but he was in the corner with his girlfriend draped all over him.

A grin teased the corners of her lips. "Do you know who I am?" She placed the top of her bottle between her lips, sucking on it lightly.

Did it matter? That thought flashed in my mind, but they never liked it when I called them on their bullshit. I slowly skimmed her up and down, and this time, I tried to place her. When I couldn't, her grin fell and she straightened to her fullest height, frowning instead.

Kate came over, her own frown on her face. They were dressed the same, but Kate's pants were ripped around the crotch and her shirt exposed a lot more of her rack than this girl. As she stopped at our little group, she glared at the girl. "Sarah Cast."

I grinned. "Your name is Sarah." I nodded at Kate, but said to Sarah. "Cast. Sarah Cast."

She snorted and grinned again. She turned to Kate. "Do you mind? I was hoping to talk to Mason alone."

Kate moved so she was closer to me, her back brushing against my arms. It was a gesture for boyfriends to put their arms around their girlfriend, but I didn't. I kept my hand in my pocket and never moved from the counter that I was leaning against. Kate shot me a dark look, but I flashed her a grin. We weren't a couple. We'd have to have the same conversation again, but she wouldn't want it to happen in front of the new chick. She said that was embarrassing. A sound of disgust came from her. "Are you kidding me?"

Sarah glanced between the two of us.

I lifted an eyebrow. I wasn't in the mood for Kate today. "I'll be in the mood tomorrow."

Anger flared in her eyes, and she stormed off. "Whatever. I won't."

She would. She always was. I turned to the new girl and kept that information to myself. "You go to FCP?"

She nodded, but glanced down for a moment. When she looked back up, she was biting her bottom lip. I frowned, wondering if this was the same sexy appeal she was going for. She seemed cautious, not sultry now. "My mom works for your dad."

"A lot of people do."

"Yeah. True."

She started looking around. When she saw her friends, they gave her a thumbs-up sign and she rolled her shoulders back, lifting her gaze back to mine again. What was going on?

"What do you want?"

She tensed. "What do you mean?"

"You came over here looking like you wanted one thing and now you're playing at something else." I didn't like games, and this girl was throwing out too many different signals. She was a head trip. "Look," I started. I shook my head. "I don't know what you're playing at, but girls don't come over to me unless they have one thing in mind. I don't date. Girls know not to even try with me. So…" I drew out the last word and let it linger between us.

She didn't react. She knew what she was doing. Realizing that, I narrowed my eyes. Then I asked, "Did they put you up to this?"

She looked too and frowned. Her friends realized we were talking about them and squealed, turning around so their backs were to us. All their heads went together and Sarah sighed. "You saw that before?"

"Was this like a dare? I dare you to go up to Mason Kade and what? Kiss me or something? What's the end goal?"

Her eyebrows shot up. "Jeezus. You're straight to business, aren't you?" She went back to biting on her lip, but she rolled it out so it looked like she was pouting. "This was a mistake. I should've never listened to her."

I grinned. Now we were getting somewhere. "Who's her?"

"What?"

"You said you never should've listened to her. Who's her?"

"My mom."

"Your mom?"

She nodded. "She works for your dad."

"A lot of people work for my dad." As I said that, I already knew the angle. The mom wanted an introduction to my dad. She heard about the divorce and sent her kid as bait. My stomach clenched. I let out a disgusted sound. "Bit of advice."

She paused, listening. Her eyes narrowed.

"If a guy has a reputation for being an asshole and doesn't date, he's not fairytale material. He's not going to change so don't go over to waste his time."

Her mouth fell open. "Jeezus, you're blunt."

"Are you here to screw me?"

She turned away and crossed her arms. I thought she was leaving, but she didn't. She stood there, as if thinking it over. When she turned back, there was a tentative look in her eyes. I said, "You heard me. I don't date. I don't hold hands. I don't do nice things for girls. I have sex and that's it. Your mom put you up to this, right?"

She nodded. "Yeah, I know, but my god. You're so 'in your face' about it."

I frowned. "I don't know why you're so shocked. You know my reputation. Your mom wants an 'in'. How do you think this would happen?" I made a show of looking her up and down. "Think about it. I would have to like you. I would have to keep you around. I would have to develop feelings for you. All that would have to happen before we'd think about inviting your mom over—" I saw that she was speculative. That didn't make sense, and I paused, thinking about a different angle. When it hit, I had to laugh.

"What?"

"Shit." I shook my head. "No. Your mom wasn't going to wait around for that to happen. She was going to wait for us to screw a few times and then what? You'd pretend to get pregnant? Your mom would sue us for money?" Seeing the surprise in her eyes, I watched as it turned to being suspicious and realized she hadn't thought about that either. Then it clicked and a storm filled her gaze. I smirked and shook my head. "Your mom is a piece of work."

She muttered, "I was just hoping to hang out. None of that crap."

I began to look around, but Kate was gone. No. I saw her. She was grinding against a different guy. When she saw me looking, she gave me a smug smirk, but I didn't care. She could do whatever she wanted and thanks to this girl's appearance, I was in a certain mood now. Feeling the old restlessness and anger in me, it was all boiling together. I needed to get laid or I'd end up getting in a fight. As if sensing my mood, Logan lifted his head from Tate's neck and frowned at me. I narrowed my eyes at him, but turned away when he began to lift his girlfriend off of his lap.

As he approached us, he looked her up and down, throwing an arm around my shoulder. "Who's this, brother?"

I shrugged his arm off. "Sarah Cast."

"Hey guys."

I tensed when Tate came over to the group. Her tone was friendly, but she was trying to dissect the girl with her eyes. Logan cast me a questionable look. He had felt me stiffen next to him, but he didn't say anything.

Logan frowned, leaning back against the counter beside me. Tate laughed softly. "What's going on?"

I said to Tate, "Why'd you come over here? We were fine." Tate had been doing that shit a lot lately. If a girl was talking to me, she came over. The only time she didn't was if it was Kate. Those two had started to pretend they were friends. They weren't. They only thought they were fooling the other.

"Mason."

Tate's head reared back. "Fuck, Mason. Do you always have to be an asshole?"

"Yes. Why do you always have to poke your nose where it's not needed?"

"My boyfriend is over here." She gestured to Logan. "Excuse me if I wanted to know what was going on. He left me over there for you."

"Yeah," I shot back at her. "He left you over there for a reason. He didn't bring you with him." Then I remembered the girl was still there and said to her, "Go. None of it's going to happen, even if you're interested. I'm not anymore."

She hurried off. Then Tate started, "Mason."

I rounded on her. "You're not wanted here."

She looked at Logan. "That's your brother."

He started to say something and didn't. Instead, he lifted his shoulders up and let them fall. "You're butting in, Tate."

"You always butt in. Butt out." I glared at her. "Go away."

"Logan." She pointed at me. "Are you going to let him talk to me like that? Really?"

He started again, but I cut him off this time. "I didn't come to you. You came to me. Go. Away."

"Unfuckingbelievable," she hissed out, and left, shoving through the crowd. They scattered at the sight of Tate, her jaw clenched, her eyes enraged, as she passed through without hitting anyone. Like a flock of birds, they moved back together in her wake and turned back to watch us.

I looked at Logan. "Your girlfriend's pissed."

"Uh yeah. With good reason." He shook his head, but he didn't seem too concerned. "Why do you talk to her like that? It's been getting worse lately."

Because she'd been more of a whore lately. I hadn't told him about the times when I was in the gym at home and she would come in to use the treadmill. The speed was so low, she barely moved. She just watched me, but there were others. She would come in my room when he was sleeping; there were times when she would ask if I would make food for her; or if I was in the pool, she would come out to race laps. My friendliness waned the more frequent those occasions happened and it had turned into hostility when I saw her outside my bedroom door the other night. She waited, listened through the door, and lifted her hand to turn the knob. I watched from down the hallway when I was coming back from the kitchen. Kate was in my room, and when she said something on the phone, Tate hurried away. She went back to Logan's room and shut the door, but her whole demeanor had been guilty. Her shoulders tightened. She never looked around. She fled.

She was a migraine waiting to happen. I had no idea how to stop it from coming. Logan wouldn't believe me, not unless I had proof. He loved her.

"She's not my girlfriend. She doesn't have to involve herself when I'm around," I said

Logan let out a short laugh. "Are you kidding? She practically lives with us."

That was the problem. Tate wanted something. I was starting to think every chick wanted something. Glancing over, my gaze lingered on Sarah. She was with her friends. She paused, watching me back and then tilted her head to the side and grinned at me. It was an invitation for more. My stomach clenched from anger. Even now, even after I laid it out how her mother wanted to use her, the girl was actually interested.

I was beginning to believe no girl was trustworthy.

CHAPTER EIGHT

CAUGHT

I could hear Logan and Tate in the hallway. She was giggling, then she shrieked, and his door shut a second later. His room was down the hall, but when his music switched on, I grinned. He was getting it on.

My phone buzzed. It was a text from Kate. **Want me to come over?**

I leaned back from my desk. I'd been trying to do homework. Fischer had a party tonight, but I opted out. Coach wanted me to come in for extra training in the morning so I chose to stay in and be responsible.

Where are you?

Horny. That's where I am.

I grinned, but typed back, **I'm good. Talk to you tomorrow.** Then I waited. Kate hated being rejected and I'd been rejecting her a lot lately. It was a while before my phone buzzed again.

F U.

Yep. I laughed. She was pissed. Logan kept telling me to hook up with other girls; that it would put Kate back in her place. To be honest, I didn't mind other girls, but I wasn't a whore and Kate was good in bed. She knew me. I knew her. It was comfortable and easy. The clingy shit was getting old though. I debated my next move. I could text back a smart-ass comment or leave it alone.

I sighed and tossed my phone in my drawer. I left it alone. Sometimes it was fun to see how pissed I could make her, but I didn't want to deal with her anymore. She'd find another guy tonight and think I would care. I hoped she wouldn't bring it up because I *wouldn't* care. If another guy was dealing with her, good for him. She hated being reminded how little I gave a shit.

I had other things to deal with. With a plan set in my mind, I went downstairs for a quick mile sprint in the gym. When I came back, the hallway was dark and the music in Logan's room had been turned off. When I passed his door, I didn't hear a sound, so I figured they had passed out. Because of that, I didn't lock my door. I had started to when Tate was around. She liked trying to spend time in my room. One time she brought her textbook and spread out on the couch before I even realized what she was doing. I had been about to kick her out, but Logan came in and lifted her feet so he could sit on the other end of the couch.

I hadn't liked it and asked Logan the next day why he had his girlfriend hanging out in my room. He was startled and responded with, "Why not? I'm in there all the time anyway."

I wanted to tell him his girlfriend was a skank, but I kept quiet. She hadn't done anything wrong. My gut told me she would. It was only a matter of time. When I mentioned to him about seeing her outside of my room one night when Kate was inside, he laughed. He said, "Oh yeah. She told me about that. She wanted to talk to you about my birthday, but didn't want to deal with Kate. Can you blame her?"

That told me two things: one, she was smart and she covered her bases; and two, he wouldn't have believed me. He wouldn't want to hear what my gut said about her; he was in love with her. So since that night, I kept my door locked. Logan questioned me about it and I told him the truth, "I don't want to deal with the skanks in this house." He assumed I meant our dad's women. I let him. I wasn't sure if I wanted to tackle a fight with him. It would've been because of a girl, and I didn't like letting a girl have that power over my relationship with my brother.

When I went to take a shower and came back out, I saw that fight had come to me instead. I was glad that I pulled my boxers on inside the bathroom. Tate was sitting on my couch. The room was dark, but I wasn't an idiot. I knew what was going to happen so I grabbed my phone and pressed two on my speed dial for Logan without hesitation. This was her move, and she was doing it even though I never gave her any encouragement. Fine. So be it. I was going to record her. I silenced the phone so she wouldn't hear and kept it hidden in my hand. Then I went and flipped the light on.

"Man, that's bright."

Ignoring her, I went to my desk and hit the webcam button. When it came up on screen, I hit record then hid the window right away. As I did, I turned it around so it was on Tate. Then I asked, "What are you doing here?"

She blinked, startled by my harsh tone, but smoothed it over with a grin. "Logan passed out. We were having sex."

"I'm aware."

She paused. I was cold to her, but she'd been trying to get close for months now, she was used to my attitude. She wasn't going to stop. I saw the determination flash in her eyes. She gave me a seductive smile, turned her head so it was slanted, and said softly, "I didn't cum with him, you know."

"How's that my problem?"

Her head went down. Then her hand went to her waist. She was only wearing a long t-shirt. It was obvious she wasn't wearing a bra and I doubted she had on anything else. She stood and her hand slid down to the edge of her shirt and she touched between her legs. "I was hoping you would help me out." Her voice went low and throaty. She started to walk towards me. One slow step at a time. Her mouth curved up at one side and she licked her lips, holding my gaze. "I've been hoping for a long time, Mason."

"Stay by the couch."

I didn't want her near me. She mistook it as a different command. Her eyes lit up and her mouth fell open. She was panting. "I think about you, when he's in me."

I closed my eyes. Shit. He was going to hear that.

"I love Logan. I do, but he's not you. I think about touching you all the time. I think about being with you." As she talked, her finger slid inside her. Her hand moved and I knew she was going in and out in rhythm with her words. Her voice dropped to a whisper, "I get so jealous when Kate's with you." She grimaced, a flash of pain came over her face, and she groaned a little. "When I hear her voice in here, it takes everything in me not to come in and drag her out." Her hand began moving again, harder this time. "Mason, come over here."

Disgust rolled over me in waves. She was a spectacle for me to watch and knowing how this would hurt Logan stripped any normal response a guy would have watching a girl finger herself. It left me angry and the need to make sure she paid for this. She was trying to come between us. She wouldn't.

"Mason?" A small note of confusion intermingled with her lust. Her other hand reached up and she grasped onto her hair, pulling at it until she let her hand drop to her throat, then to her chest. Her hand lingered between her breasts. They were erect against her shirt. As she held my gaze, a small smirk formed, although I'm sure she meant for it to be teasing and alluring. Her hand slid over and covered her breast. Her thumb moved in circles over the tip. She was doing this for me. She wanted to see that I wanted her, that I was enjoying this.

I cleared my throat, unsure how far to take this. This was enough. It would tear Logan up. She moaned. "Mason." Her head went back, exposing her throat and she reached for her shirt. She pulled it off and let it fall to the floor. Her hand was going faster now, her breasts were moving in rhythm, her breathing was speeding up. "Please," she whimpered. Her hand went back to her breast, now touching it without a barrier. She wasn't even looking at me anymore. "Please, Mason. Come touch me. I want you in me instead of my hand."

I glanced down at my phone. The call had been picked up; Logan was still listening. The door swung open silently. His phone was pressed to his ear as he came inside. She had no idea he was there. When he looked at me, there was no emotion. I shook my head and gestured to my computer.

Logan frowned, but soon realized. I was pointing to the webcam. His phone dropped from his hand, landing with a thud on the floor.

Tate's head snapped back and she saw him. She gasped, and she scrambled for her shirt. "Logan!"

He was seething. There was rage in his eyes and his hands were in fists. He jerked forward a step. "Get. Out."

"Logan." She glanced at me.

I held my phone up. "I called him."

He ground out, "I heard everything."

"Oh." She paled. "Oh my god." Pulling her shirt on, she wavered on her feet like she was going to fall down. Her hand pressed to her stomach. "I think I'm going to be sick."

"Welcome to the fucking club." Logan never looked away from her. The rage was there, but it was held in control. Barely.

I stood from my chair. Casting a concerned gaze over my brother, I said to her, "Get out. Now."

"Mason—" She started walking toward to me.

"STOP!"

She jumped back, her eyes large and horrified as she watched Logan with caution now. Her jaw started trembling. "Logan," she whispered, "please—"

"GET OUT OF MY HOUSE!"

She choked out, "Oh my god." Then she fled. When she turned to go to his room, he went after her.

"Logan." I caught him and held him back.

"GET OUT OF THIS HOUSE! NOW!"

She froze, then a strangled gasp ripped from her. "My clothes."

"Fuck your clothes. I tossed 'em."

Her eyes got even bigger. "What?"

A bitter laugh came from him; it was harsh and ugly sounding. "Why do you think it took me so long to get here? Your clothes are gone, bitch. Get the fuck out of this house. Now!" He jerked forward against my arm again, but I felt the control in him. He was still holding it back. She just didn't know it.

She stumbled back a step. "I have to go out like this—"

"GET THE FUCK OUT!"

A hallway light switched on from the third floor. I cursed. Our dad was up. Then I snapped at her, "Get the fuck out of here or I'm calling the cops."

"But—"

"NOW!"

"What the hell is going on down here?" Our dad was coming down the stairs. As he got to the last step, he tightened his robe and gazed around the group. He frowned. "Why doesn't this girl have pants on? Why don't you have a shirt on, Mason? Logan? What is going on?"

I stepped forward. Logan was close to snapping so I pushed him inside.

He resisted. "No."

"I'll take care of it," I told him. "You're going to lose it soon."

He bit out another harsh-sounding laugh, but leaned around me. "He recorded you."

"Oh no." Her mouth fell open again, and she fell against the wall. "Oh god no."

"Every fucking thing. He recorded it from the beginning and he called me. I heard the entire thing, not part of it, not a little bit of it. The whole fucking thing. You're done, Tate. You're goddamn done. No one will want to be your friend."

"Go." I shoved him inside and pulled the door shut. Logan tried to open it again, but I held it firm and waited until he let go.

He continued to yell through the door, "You want to fuck my brother? You think you can play us? You have got another think coming, Tate! I know you. I know all your goddamn secrets. I know how to make you suffe—" He cut himself off and a sick laugh came next. "FUCK! You went after my brother, that's my family. He's my blood, and if you'd—you bitch!"

She started whimpering. "What am I going to do?"

I whipped around and got in her face. She backed up, a startled gasp in her throat, and slammed against the wall. I leaned close, keeping only an inch between us. I'd been holding it back. I wanted her to show her real self and she had. All of my contempt and my own anger had been kept in check. It was about Logan then, but not anymore. Logan was in my room. He wasn't coming out. It was her and me, so I let my mask fall. When she saw my loathing, the near hatred I had for her, she began crying. Large tears gathered in her eyes and they fell. She didn't stop them. She gasped for air instead, but kept quiet, watching me as if her life depended on it.

"You will leave this house. You will leave my brother alone. You won't email him, Facebook him, text him, tweet him, you won't do anything except wait until he chooses to talk to you again. If he's walking down a hallway, you leave. If he enters a room, you leave the room or you stay in the farthest corner away from him that you can. Now," I paused, "I won't say it again. Leave this house."

James beckoned for her. "Come on. I'll call a driver for you."

When she edged away from me and went to him, I shook my head. "You'll call a cab. Not a driver."

He took hold of her arm and frowned at her. "Does she have clothes?"

She was sobbing, but said around them, "Logan did something to them."

He sighed. "Of course." Then he said to me, "I am not going to call for a cab. If she's hurt somehow on her way home, she could sue us. I won't have her damaging this family any more than she has." He pointed to my room. "And whatever you have recorded, you will delete it immediately. She could sue for that as well."

"Dad—"

"Delete it, Mason." His eyes flashed a warning. "You're thinking short-term. I'm thinking long-term. I have no doubt she will hurt within her social groups. I know both of you have power among your friends at school, but those are both items that tread into a different system, one that you could get hurt from. I might be an asshole father, but I'm still a father and that's what I'm doing right now. Delete it. Now."

He didn't wait for a response. He went forward and led a sobbing Tate with him. It wasn't long before the front door opened and they were outside. In some way, I was happy that she didn't wait for a car inside. Then I went back to my room. Logan was sitting in front of my computer. The video was up and I saw that he had watched it. He was pale, calm, and there were tears sliding down his face.

"Dad said—"

"I heard." He sounded defeated now. His voice was soft as he stared at the screen. The last image on it was of her. She was naked. Her head was back. She was holding her breast and her other hand was pressed between her legs, moving inside herself.

He shook his head. "I will. I'll delete it. Dad's right, but..."

"What do you want me to do?"

He turned around. His eyes held mine and I saw the stark need in them. She'd broken him. Then he said, "Hurt her. Hurt her even when I've forgiven her."

"I will." The pain in his gaze sealed her fate.

CHAPTER NINE

MARISSA AND THE PROMISE TO TATE

It had been three months since we threw Tate out of the house. She apologized to Logan for the first week, but he ignored every message and every apology. She was nothing to him now. Then she began with me, but she only apologized a few times. I warned her to get the fuck away from me. She heeded the warning and had kept a safe distance since. Neither Logan nor I talked about what happened, but everyone knew he and Tate had a nasty ending. Like sensing a weaker prey, Kate turned on her. Her friends all tormented Tate, who took it for a while before she started fighting back.

Getting to class late one day, I stopped in the doorway and saw my usual seat was filled. The guy in it saw me looking at him, but turned away. His neck grew red as I continued to stare at him. The teacher stopped writing on the board. "Mr. Kade, you weren't here when I had everyone pick their new seat for the rest of the year."

I frowned. "We're in the middle of a semester."

"Your point?"

"I don't have a great attitude, but I'm never late and I'm not a bad student." I gestured around the room, ignoring how everyone was staring. They always stared. "Did you do this because I was late this one time?"

He barked out a laugh and shook his head. "Mason Kade. Of course, this whole thing was about you." He rolled his eyes. "I like when my students are confident, but you're to the point of arrogant. No, this had nothing to do with you." He sent a pointed look to the back where Kate was sitting. She flashed him a smile and flicked her hair back, behind her shoulder. Then he sighed and looked in the opposite

64

corner, to the front of the room. Tate lowered her head and slumped down in her seat. He continued, "Due to the history of heated exchanges these past few months, these are the seats you will have for the rest of the year and there will be no talking amongst the tables."

I saw the open seat. It was in the front row, but on the opposite side of Tate with a table between us.

The teacher pointed to it and said, "You will be sitting with Miss Hooper for the year. Be nice, Mason. She's the only one you can talk to for the rest of the year."

As she was named, my table mate glanced up. I recognized her from other classes, and remembered we had been assigned to work on a different project at the beginning of the year. She hadn't been excited to deal with me then either, but I hadn't cared. I hadn't paid her any attention. I did now, though, considering the circumstances. Then I tensed. Kate was always jealous when I spoke to other girls. I glanced back at her, but she wasn't paying attention. Then I gritted my teeth. She needed to stop acting like my girlfriend and I needed to stop caring.

As I sat next to her, she scooted her chair back. Her eyes were filled with fear and awe. She was tiny with dark hair that was pulled in a ponytail. I scanned her over, but there wasn't much to her. When I nodded hello, she jerked her head away and hunched over her notebook.

I frowned. Shit. I knew I was scary, but I didn't know I was that scary. "Relax. I only screw with people who fuck me over."

She made a choking sound, but she didn't look up.

"Don't fuck me over and we'll be fine."

"Mr. Kade," the teacher glared at me, "I told you to be nice to Marissa."

"I am. I'm laying the ground rules." I leaned back in my chair and gestured for him to continue. "You can keep teaching. I won't interrupt anymore."

He pinched the top of his nose and looked in pain. Shaking his head as he turned back to the board, he muttered to himself, "I retire in five years. Five years. I have to get through five more years."

I frowned. I didn't think I deserved that reaction. My table mate slid a piece of paper to me. She gave me a shy smile and said softly, "He wants us to start working on these."

I nodded. "I didn't mean to scare you."

Her eyes got big again and she retracted her hand as if she'd been burned. The slight smile vanished. Then she jerked her head in a nod. "I know. I...you're a lot."

I narrowed my eyes. I knew what she meant, but this wasn't a girl that I was used to dealing with. Taking the worksheet, I saw she had started on the first question. When I began to fill out the second question, I said to her, "We worked together before. Do you remember that?" She didn't answer so I added, "You're not a normal chick, are you?"

"Oh god." Her cheeks turned red and she closed her eyes for a moment. "Do you know the answer to question three? I couldn't find that one."

She was one of those girls that hugged the wall. I saw them in the hallways. They stayed by their locker or their friends' lockers and never said anything. When I walked by, they watched me, but they never said a word. I had never dealt with one up close and personal. I was used to girls coming onto me. "Do you date?"

"Um." She was biting her lip and her hands slid from the table to her lap. She grabbed fistfuls of her pants and held onto it. Her head hung down.

"Relax. I'm not asking if you want to date me. I don't date girls like you." I didn't date at all, but she looked ready to pee her pants and sit in it even if it formed a puddle on the floor. "You're not like other girls I deal with. I'm curious, that's all."

She began counting to herself.

What the fuck? She'd been more normal the first time we worked together.

"Mr. Kade."

I glanced to the teacher. "Yeah?" He was frowning at us.

"Maybe less talking with Miss Hooper. You can hand in the worksheet on your own."

I shrugged. "Fine with me." As I opened my textbook, I looked back over at her. She had stopped counting, but a look of relief was evident on her face. We didn't talk for the rest of the day. After class, the teacher called me to his desk, and I was instructed not to talk to that girl. He added, "Maybe I should change the assigned seating."

"She'll be fine. I'll back off."

He gave me a dirty look then and said, "Do not touch that girl, Mason. She's not like you. She's innocent."

I smirked at that, but replied, "I'm not planning on it. She's a refreshing break from the rest of the chicks."

Kate popped her head in the doorway at that moment. She stared at us, then jerked her head to the hallway. "I need to talk to you."

Whatever. "Meet me in the south stairs." She nodded and disappeared. I turned to the teacher. "The assigned seat is fine. Trust me." I gestured to where Kate had gone. "I have to deal with her. My new table mate is like getting cake during class. I doubt I'll have to deal with any drama from her."

He shook his head. "You're perplexing. Are you aware of that?"

"Do I care? That's the question you should be asking and no, I don't." When I left, I headed to my locker and saw Logan was already there. He was leaning against my neighbor's locker with his arms crossed. A few girls were watching him from across the hall. As I got there, he flashed them a grin and a few of them began laughing.

I stopped. Shit. He was flirting with them.

He saw my reaction and tensed. "What?"

"Nothing."

"What?"

"You're flirting." He hadn't flirted in months.

"Yeah. I'm a dude."

I frowned at him. "You haven't flirted in a long time."

"What are you talking about? You were lecturing me this morning on not becoming a man whore."

"Hooking up and flirting are different." It was easy to grab a girl and have sex with her. It took work to flirt. I didn't flirt. Girls got the wrong idea then, but Logan was doing it again. That meant he was getting better.

"So what? Maybe I like flirting?"

I narrowed my eyes at him. "Just don't get a girlfriend right now."

"Maybe I want regular sex? Is something wrong with that?"

"You get regular sex already. You don't need a girlfriend for that."

"What's your problem?"

What *was* my problem? I was on edge and then I glanced at the girls beside us. It was them. It was their games, even now I felt it. They had moved closer to listen in. "I'm sick of this shit." Gesturing to them and around the hallway. "If I want them, I'll pick one at a party, but they cling during the day. They're annoying. They think they're funny when they're not and they try to manipulate you, like if I say hi to them, then that means I want them. I don't. I might've said hi because, for once, I didn't feel like being an ass."

I didn't want another one to hurt Logan. Studying him now, I saw it happening. He wanted to cover the pain up. So far he had only used sex to do it, but he was considering dating again. I saw it in his eyes. It wouldn't work. I knew my brother too well. He had loved Tate and she had shattered him. I didn't want him to depend on another girl, be used, and get hurt all over again.

The entire group of girls was now listening to us, not just the few who'd been flirting with Logan. They all wanted something. I could feel it. I always felt it. The more my status grew in school, the worse it got. I said to them, "Yes, I know I'm being an ass again, but it's true. You all just want something from us. You want to be our girlfriends. You want the attention we can give you. You want to be powerful and popular." They were like pigeons, just waiting to see if I would throw them some breadcrumbs. "Go away. Find me at a party and I'll be nicer, but not in school. I don't have the patience in school to deal with this."

I skimmed over Logan. He'd been flirting, maybe I shouldn't stop that? Fuck. I didn't know what to do. He couldn't get hurt again. All I knew was that enough damage had been done.

Ethan came down the hallway and pointed at me. As he went past us, he said, "Supposed to tell you that Kate's waiting for you."

"See. That shit." I shook my head. "I'm not her boyfriend. I don't come when *she* barks."

Logan asked, "Does she want a quickie?"

"Who the fuck knows." I grabbed my bag from the locker, then shut it. The girls were still there. They didn't go away. They would scatter at times, but they never went far. "I'm not in the mood."

He asked, "Are you going?"

"No." I gestured to the parking lot. They weren't leaving so we'd have to go. "Let's get some food before practice. We got an hour to wait and I don't want to deal with Kate." She'd come looking. She would want something, demand something, and I'd have to be an asshole yet again to get her to back off. It was tiring.

Logan laughed and as we headed for our cars, I saw Marissa at her locker. She was different and perplexing. She didn't want anything from me. She didn't even want me to sit with her. She wasn't like the rest. Even now, she stood out from the others. There were cliques all around her. Girls were giggling, whispering together, but she wasn't. She stood alone with her back turned to us. She wasn't even paying attention to us. She was focused on a book she was holding, but she wasn't putting it in the locker. She wasn't reading it. She was staring at it with her head down.

Logan saw her too. "Who's that?"

"Mr. Rooney assigned seats today." I pointed at her. "She's my table mate, but I'm not supposed to talk to her."

He snorted. "You were talking? To a stranger?"

"She's different."

As we headed farther down the hallway, we glanced back. She saw us, then gasped, turned red, and whipped back around. Her head hit her opened locker door, but she didn't do anything. She buried her head inside her locker as if she hadn't hit it. Then we turned the corner and Logan nodded at me. "Yep, she is. That's for sure."

I was okay with that. When we were almost to the door, we saw Tate was coming back in. Her path came across us and she stopped. The blood drained from her face, and she jerked back as if she'd been hit. We stopped and I glanced at Logan. Pain flashed over his face. I'd been right. He was covering it up. He looked away and walked around her. Nothing was said. The encounter was filled with tension and hurt. At seeing that, at seeing how much it still hurt him just to see her, I gritted my teeth. She had hurt my brother. It was time for her to know.

She spoke first. "What do you want, Mason?"

"He loved you."

She flinched again and turned away. "Yeah, well—"

"You don't get to talk right now."

She flushed, but she didn't leave.

I added, "You're like all the other girls. You used my brother and you wanted to use me too."

"It wasn't like that."

I snorted. "Yes, it was. You were friends with Kate. I saw you guys. You're the popular girls in our grade and what? You wanted more, didn't you? You didn't even like me, Tate. You wanted the power that I could give you, but you didn't think it through."

"MASON!"

Hearing Kate yelling my name, I turned to make sure she couldn't see me. I wasn't hiding, but I didn't want to hear her crap at that moment. I told Tate, "Logan asked me today if I sicced Kate and her friends on you." She met my gaze then, waiting for the answer. "I didn't, but I'm glad they're making your life hell." Logan acted normal today. He was getting better, but it had taken months. "When Kate is done with you, that's when I'll start. I will break you just like you broke him."

CHAPTER TEN

THE SURPRISING CONNECTION

The next week, Mr. Rooney sent half the class to the library. We were assigned a project to work on, but the same instructions that he enforced in his classroom were applied there. No talking. Period. The only person you could talk to was your table mate. Glancing to where mine had gone, she scooted around the group and walked to the very back of the library.

As I followed her through the book cases, she went to a table set in its own section. It was away from the main lobby and isolated with bookshelves all around it.

I put my notebook on the table and took a seat. "I'm not a typical dumb jock, but I had no idea this was back here."

She paused, her fingers stopped flipping through her pages, and she studied me for a moment.

I narrowed my eyes. She still hadn't talked to me. When Mr. Rooney announced the project, he pulled me aside at the door and said that I would have to talk to Marissa. Then he added, "Be nice. Be respectful and then back away from her. I mean it, Mason."

I rolled my eyes. "I don't care about deflowering virgins, Mr. Rooney. I have enough headaches in my life because of women. Your warnings are insulting now."

"You heard what I said."

I did. I didn't care. I'd talk to her, but I had no intention of anything else. Focusing on her again now, I frowned. "You have to talk. I'm not doing a presentation all on my own to prove that I did the work."

She frowned. She had stopped becoming flustered after the first few days. Now she was hostile instead. I was starting to get sick of it. If I had done something to her, then yeah, I deserved it. Unlike most of my run-ins, I'd been nice to her.

Then she said, "I don't want to be held back by you. This is important to me."

I laughed.

She looked ready to piss her pants, but that made me laugh even more. "So you do think I'm a dumb jock?"

"No…" She did. I could see it in her eyes.

"I'm number one in our grade. If anyone holds anyone back, it won't be me."

Her mouth fell open an inch. She became flustered again. "You're in the number one spot?"

I nodded. "Yep." I flashed her a grin. "See. I'm not the typical dumb jock."

"Oh."

Then I reached for the worksheet with the instructions. "Hand it over. Let's get this bitch done with."

We worked the entire week together. Every day Marissa relaxed and by the end of the week, she was a chatterbox. I didn't talk, but that was fine with me. I didn't want to talk. Everyone else wanted me to talk. They wanted to know what I was thinking. They wanted to know an 'in' to get with me. Not her. Marissa did most of the talking for our presentation. She surprised everyone. I could tell no one expected her to be as enthusiastic or as confident as she was. A few of the guys were looking at her with interest.

She wasn't bad to look at. A heart-shaped face, cute lips, a decent body underneath her baggy clothes. A few of them were giving her lewd looks and I knew they were imagining her naked. For some reason, that ticked me off. I blocked the view of one of the guys and he glanced up. He moved back, seeing the warning in my gaze, then he lifted his hands in the air. He didn't lift them high, just off the table, but enough to show me he would back off. The others caught the motion. Marissa kept rambling on about the effects of desertification, but a new spark of interest went around the room. The others saw that I was protective of her. I glanced towards Kate. She was staring straight at me. She was dissecting me. Her eyes were clear and filled with interest. I frowned. I shouldn't have done anything. There was a target on this girl now. Kate wasn't going to forget the look I gave that guy.

Shifting back into place, Marissa paused, but I leaned against the wall and let her finish the speech. When she was done, Mr. Rooney asked, "Marissa, please tell me that you didn't work alone on this project."

"No." She frowned, her hands grasping tighter onto her paper. "Why?"

He indicated me. "Because your partner didn't say a word through the entire presentation."

"That's because he hates speeches." She didn't blink an eye. "He's shy."

The room burst out laughing. Marissa fell back a step, taken aback by their response, and then turned to me. She was confused.

"Why do you think I'm shy?"

Mr. Rooney came to the front of the class, shaking his head, chuckling. "Uh, Miss Hooper, I can think of a lot of words to call Mason Kade, but shy is not one of them. It's not even close to any of them."

"Tread lightly."

He kept laughing, but held his hands up. "No offense intended." The class continued to laugh except Kate. She was staring Marissa down like she wanted to tackle her. I tensed. That would be a battle.

When we took our seat, Marissa leaned close and whispered, "Why are they all laughing at me?"

"Because I'm not shy at all. If I was, that'd probably help me in life, but I'm not. Why do you think I'm shy?"

"Because you never talk." She said it louder than she had intended and another roar went through the class. Her cheeks grew red and she ducked her head down. "Oh god."

I glanced at Kate and saw her chewing the corner of her lip. If I didn't talk, that meant I didn't care for them. She knew that about me. The problem was that wasn't true for Marissa. I enjoyed her presence, but for her own safety, I didn't want Kate to catch onto that.

I sent Marissa an apologetic look before I cleared my throat. I made sure people could overhear me, "Why would I talk? You don't need encouragement to talk more." It wasn't that hurtful, but I knew people would take it as that. I was throwing her under the bus. As hurt flared in the depths of her eyes, I wanted to explain it to her. But I couldn't. Then I snuck a look back again. Kate had gone back to flirting with a guy.

Damage was done.

Marissa went back to not talking to me. After class, she fled to the hallway and the next month was strained between us. It wasn't until one day when I stayed for extra training and had showered. It was late, around six in the evening. I was heading for the parking lot when she turned the corner. When she saw me, she squeaked. Her hands clenched around her book, but she lost her footing and fell to the floor. I could've caught her. My hand had started to reach out, but I kept it held back. She didn't need my help. I'd only be damning her.

"Oh ugh." She moaned, standing up, brushing off the back of her pants. "That was embarrassing. Ouch." She looked up, and then hung her head again. "You're still there."

I glanced around. There was no one else around so I grinned. "Were you expecting me to leave?"

"That's your reputation. You're an asshole, right?"

I winced, but she had a point. "When was I an ass to you?"

She scowled at me. "You know."

"That was for your own good."

She rolled her eyes and scoffed. "Please."

"It was."

"Right. Because I'm in danger, right? You have a reputation for being an ass, but not for screwing with someone's mind and feelings. You're known for saying it how it is."

"I am."

She shook her head and began to turn away. "You're just screwing with me. You're like those other guys."

She started to walk away, but I caught up with her and grabbed her arm. "What other guys?"

Jerking her arm away, anger flashed across her face. "Back off, buddy. All those other girls may fall all over you, but that doesn't mean you can touch just anybody." Rubbing where I had grasped her arm, she scowled at me. "I'm not one of those girls. I don't care about you. Not at all."

A firm look came over her. I tried to hold back a grin. She looked like a pissed off Chihuahua.

"You think this is funny?"

"Sorry." My grin vanished. "Look, I had to be mean. Kate was noticing you."

"Noticing me? She used to pick on me, but that stopped."

"She did?"

"Yeah, from the first time we worked together on a project..." Her voice trailed off when she saw my reaction. "What?"

"It was because of me?"

She nodded. A stark note appeared in her gaze. "Yeah. It's been on and off all year. Tate too—"

"What?"

"Yeah." She was becoming scared again. "Don't tell them I said anything. Don't say anything to them at all. It'll get worse. I know it. I—" She cursed.

My eyebrows shot up when I heard words from my daily vocabulary.

When she saw the surprise, she rolled her eyes. "Right. Like you're the only one with a potty-mouth. I don't think so."

A chuckle slipped out. At the sound of it, she froze again and her head jerked back down. Then she was muttering, "I should get going. I shouldn't be here. You're right. I'm sorry."

She was about to slip away, when I blocked her. "Hey." I frowned.

"Stop, Mason." Agony was in her voice now. The sound of it had me wincing. Dropping to a whisper, she added, "You're right. You were right to be mean. I didn't think about that. I thought they had stopped, but if you say that she noticed," she stopped. "I can't handle that again."

How bad had it been?

"I have to go." Then she rushed off. I was left in the hallway, wondering what had really happened just now.

CHAPTER ELEVEN

PSYCHO AND THE BROUDOUS

The girl beneath me groaned as I continued thrusting in her. Her hands fell to my hip and her eyes were closed. Her head was tipped back, exposing her neck to me and she moaned again. I thrust deeper, closing my own eyes, as I felt it coming. The build-up was the best. I was almost there and I went deeper, harder, then it was there. It was so close. Fuck. I thrust one last time, going as deep as I could, her legs lifted up from the force. They wound around my waist. Her hips rose from the bed, but then I felt her own climax shooting through her. Her walls were trembling and she collapsed. I collapsed with her, feeling my own climax ripping through me.

Her legs were still wound around me. They slipped from my waist and rested against the backs of my legs. Her hands were still clamped onto me, but as I pulled out, she let go. She opened her eyes and raked a hand through her hair. She gave me a smile and murmured, "Fuck. That was good."

I nodded. "Sex is usually good."

She chuckled and sat up when I went into the bathroom. As she watched me wash myself off, she said, "Sex isn't always good with everyone." A seductive glimmer appeared in her eyes and she smiled at me, trying to draw me in. "But it is with you."

I snorted, coming back into the room. "Jenny, you're good at sex. You know it. Own it."

A genuine laugh came from her and she scooted to the edge of the bed. I sat on the corner, but she wrapped her legs around me and wound her arms around my waist, propping her head on my shoulder. Then she nipped my skin, brushing her tongue there in a swirl, one meant to be a caress. She murmured, "I'm not a whore, Mason, but I'm not inexperienced and trust me," her legs wound tighter and she rubbed against me. Her eyes closed and a small whimper left her lips. "You're very, very, very good in bed. I can see why Kate's so nuts about you."

I had been tempted to turn her around and slide back into her, but that feeling stopped cold at those words. She felt me stiffen and lifted her head from my shoulder. "What's wrong?"

"Nothing." I tapped her foot. "Release."

She did and when I started to dress, she frowned at me. She lifted her hands, trying to smooth down her red hair, but wariness filtered in her dark eyes. She stuck her lip out, trying to figure me out. But I kept my face blank. Pulling my jeans on, I left them unzipped and grabbed my shirt. Slipping my feet into my shoes, I headed for the door still holding my shirt. I lifted it in a salute to her. "Thanks for the fun time."

"Wait." She scooted forward, making no move to cover herself. Her breasts were still perked up but she didn't care.

I grinned. Jenny wasn't a new kid around the block. She was the head of the drill team and she had a sexual appetite like me. It was there, it liked to be satisfied, but she didn't pick just any guy. We had hooked up before, but when she brought up Kate's name, all the shit from the past few months came back. I enjoyed forgetting it, forgetting Kate, forgetting Tate, Logan's pain, and my family drama. At her one statement about Kate, it opened a door and the real world filtered back in. Getting away for a nice lay had been fun, but the old emptiness took root in me. It knocked inside, reminding me it was there.

I asked, "What?"

"That's it? You've stuck around in the past for another round."

"Not this time." I flashed her a half-grin. "Thanks."

She sighed. "Okay. Just wait. I'll dress and leave with you." She stood and reached for her bra, giving me a good view of her tight ass. After she pulled her skirt on, she wiggled her underwear up and grinned. Her bra wasn't hooked, just pulled over her arms so I knew she left her tits out for one last little dance for me. "Like it?"

"I do." I grinned. "Don't people pull their panties on first?"

She laughed. "I don't know why, but it's hilarious when someone says panties to me. It's a thong. It's what women should be wearing." She became speculative. "What does Kate wear? Somehow I see her not wearing anything."

I shook my head. "I'm not stepping into that one."

She pretended to groan, shaking her head, as she continued to hold my gaze. She reached around, hooked her bra and slipped her shirt over her head, still watching me. Then she licked her lips and drew close to me. Her hands went to my waist and she moved so she was lightly rubbing against me. Her hand went to the front of my pants and cupped me. "I like this guy. He's welcome any time he wants in my home."

I smirked down at her, but pulled her shirt down and rubbed my thumb over one of her tips. A slight tremor went through her. I said, "As long as your home remains drama free, my guy will keep that in mind."

She laughed, and I opened the door. Jenny went out first, running her hands through her hair again, but stopped abruptly. I had lifted to slip my arms through my shirt and bumped into her. Pulling my shirt over my head, I saw the problem.

Kate was there. She was leaning against the other side of the hallway with her arms crossed and a snarl on her mouth. "Really?" There was so much condescension in her tone.

Jenny cried out, "Really? He's not yours, Kathryn. Get it through your fucking crazy head."

Kate reacted. Her eyes turned feral and she reached up, grabbed Jenny's hair, and started to pull her head down.

I didn't think. I reacted and caught Kate's arm, stopping her. It happened in the blink of an eye, no warning, nothing.

Jenny's head was two inches from the wall. She hadn't prepared to fight, but when I held Kate's arm suspended and she saw what had been about to happen, her eyes got big and she wrestled out of Kate's hold.

"You're a fucking psycho!" She leapt at Kate, but I caught her around the waist and held her back.

When Kate looked ready to hit her, I shot a hand out to stop her and warned, "Don't you fucking dare."

She moved back with a huff. "You're going to regret this."

I wasn't sure who she was talking to, but Jenny responded first. She laughed, still trying to claw at her. "Are you sure about that? You and your friends are bullies in school, but I've got the numbers."

Kate had moved down the hallway, but stopped. She listened.

Jenny kept going, flicking her off. "I'm the captain of the drill team. Guess how many girls want to be on my squad? Guess how many girls want to be me?"

"Whatever."

"Take your fight elsewhere, Kate. You'll lose against me."

"Stop."

She struggled against my hold, but Kate had turned the corner. Lowering her to the floor, as soon as her feet were touching, she shoved my arm off her and raked her hands through her hair. Her eyes were wild. "Holy shit, she's psychotic."

I frowned. I was realizing just how psychotic she was now.

Jenny shook her head and a hollow laugh came from her. "You have a major problem on your hands. Keep messing around with her and she's going to get worse and worse. She's going to do major damage to someone." She swept a palm over her face, wiping at her eyes. "My god. I can't believe that just happened." Then she slashed a hand across her throat. "You and me, no more. I'm not ready to battle that crazy, not for a guy I screw every now and then. If you were my boyfriend, yeah, I might battle her, but not for what you're offering." She started down the hallway, but glanced back before turning the corner. "You know that little friend from your class? Heads up, Kate's got her eyes on her. You know what Kate would do to a sweet girl like that? It wouldn't be pretty. That's all I can say."

Kate was a fucking headache and I had no idea how to defuse her. When I went downstairs, she was outside with her friends. When she saw me coming, she looked ready to bolt, but thought better of it and held her ground.

My patience was up. I wasn't going to deal with her anymore. Grabbing her arm, I dragged her around the side of the house. There were people there, but I didn't care. I was fed up. Pushing her against the house, she shoved me back. "Watch it. You wouldn't want to hurt a girl."

"Shut up." I barely touched her and she knew it. "I don't need to use force to hurt someone. If you push me far enough, I will fight back and it won't be physically. I'm *not* that type of guy so *do not* insult me again." I stressed my words and let her see the warning in my gaze. It was real. She needed to heed it. I meant what I was about to say.

The conversations around us quieted when they heard us, and they moved closer.

Kate was watching them. Her unease was clear, but she kept quiet. For once. I rolled my eyes. "You listen to me because this was the last straw."

She snorted, folding her arms over her chest. She was trying to be brave, but I saw the fear in her eyes.

I kept going, this wasn't her time to smart off to me. "I don't care about you. I might have at one point, but the farther you push things, the less I give a shit about you. You did this. You trampled our friendship into the ground. You and I are done. Do you hear me?"

"Good luck trying to get with someone—"

I shook my head in a forceful clip. She stopped talking and I finished for her, "There will always be someone else. Always. You don't have the power to keep girls away from me so don't use that card. Don't even try to use it. It won't work. You're scary, but not nearly as scary as I can be. Trust me."

The fight was in her gaze. She wanted to fight back, threaten me, use her fists, but she didn't. She kept it reined in. As I stepped back from her, she hissed at me, "We're through."

"Good."

"I mean it, Mason." I almost rolled my eyes, but I refrained. I'd let her have her say. She added, "You can screw whoever you want. I'm done. I won't give a shit anymore because I don't give a shit about you."

Then she swept a cold look at the crowd that had formed. "Do you hear that? He's fair game. I'm out. Go ahead and deal with him, but I feel sorry for whoever does." She ended with a last hateful look at me. "You're broken inside. I don't know what broke you, but they did a goddamn good job. You'll never love anyone. Only Logan. That's all you'll let in. I feel sorry for whoever falls in love with you. It's not a mistake I'll be making."

She left, stalking around the house. I heard her snap out, "Let's go, you guys!"

"Why? What just happened?"

"LET'S GO!"

There was a little bit of silence after they took off and then someone started laughing. "Finally. She's been on that high horse for too long." Others joined in laughing and I glanced over. Her friend was there, the one that hooked up with Nate. He had his arm around her waist, but he dropped it when he saw me looking. He jerked his head in an abrupt nod and moved back a step. Parker? I think. She twisted around, fixing him with an accusing look. He never met her eyes. Then she cursed. "Are you serious?"

She stormed away, but bypassed me on her way. As she went past me, she muttered, "You turned Kate into a laughing stock just now. Don't think for one second that I won't tell her."

I didn't care. Maybe I should've, but it was becoming hard for me to care about anything at that moment. Kate. Other girls. Maybe I should've cared, but I didn't. Then Nate came up to me. He said, "Logan called. He needs a ride. He's at Quickie's."

"What?"

He shrugged. "I have no idea. You want me to go?"

"No." I shook my head. "I'll go. Stay here and have fun."

"You sure?"

"Didn't your hook-up just leave?"

Nate shrugged. "My dick's not dipped in gold like yours, but I don't have a problem getting girls either." He flashed me a grin. "But if you want to go and pick him up, I wouldn't mind sticking around and finding a new hook-up."

"Yeah. Have fun. I'll get him."

"All right." He paused. "You okay?"

Was I? I shrugged. The Kate thing was a problem that I didn't know how to reign in.

I didn't answer him. I didn't know how and I didn't want to lie. When I pulled into Quickie's, I didn't see Logan. Sending him a quick text, I waited, but there was no answer so I got out. When I went inside, there was still no Logan, but I saw Marissa behind the counter.

She was biting her lip as she waited for my reaction.

"What are you doing here?"

Her hand shot up in an awkward wave before her cheeks grew red. She looked down and her hand slammed to the counter, spilling her water. "Oh shit." She lunged for the napkins, knocking over another glass of liquid and then groaned. "Oh my god." The second glass tipped onto the register and she began repeating, "Oh my god, oh my god, oh my god," over and over again as she looked around. "There's no towel. Nothing. My uncle will kill me. I swear."

I grabbed a bunch of napkins and began piling them on top of each other, absorbing the first pile of liquid. When I had enough, I slid it over. She was still jumping in a circle, frantic, so I started wiping up the second spill. Leaning over the counter, I was finishing off the register when she squealed, grabbed her coat from under the counter, and pivoted back to me. She was ready to use her coat to absorb it, but she froze when she saw the spills were already cleaned up.

Her hands dropped. "Oh."

I grinned. "It's done. No damage."

"That's so embarrassing."

I checked my phone. Still no reply from Logan, but I asked again, "What are you doing here?" After sending another text to him, I added, "Working a gas station at night is dangerous. You shouldn't be here."

"I know. He knows."

"Who?"

She was picking up the soaked napkins now. A few slipped from her fingers and fell back with a splat. When she tried picking them up again, they broke in half. "Dammit."

"Marissa."

"What?" she looked up. "Oh yeah. My uncle runs this gas station. I don't normally work, but there was a family emergency and he asked if I would fill in. I'm only here for a little bit. He's on his way back."

"Your uncle owns Quickie's?"

She nodded. "Yeah." She gave up trying to pick up the napkins by hand and grabbed a trash can. Holding it beneath the counter, she swiped all the napkins into it, then groaned when she saw the puddle of liquid that hadn't been absorbed. "These are cheap napkins."

I frowned. "I guess." There was still no answer from Logan. "Have you seen my brother? I'm supposed to pick him up from here."

"What?"

"My brother." She was still focused on cleaning the counter. "You know Logan? My brother. An inch shorter and leaner than me. Is this ringing a bell?"

85

She flushed. "I'm sorry. Yes. He's in the back."

"In the back?"

"He was really wasted so I told him he could lay down in the back."

"He's passed out?"

She nodded, her cheeks were red, but it spread to cover her entire face. She tucked a strand of hair behind her ear, looking nervous again. "I'm sorry. I texted Nate. Logan told me not to text you before he passed out. He said you needed to get laid so, um, I texted Nate instead. I'm sorry. I should've texted you or called you or I don't know."

"Is he okay?"

"Yeah. Yeah." She started to leave the counter, but cursed and stopped. "I can't leave. I'm sorry or I would show you. It's just through the back door. He's on the couch back there."

"Okay." I frowned at her.

She waved at me. "Go. Take care of your brother. My uncle is coming back now." A sweep of headlights flashed in the window as a car pulled into the lot. "See. That's him."

"Okay." I waited until I saw a guy hurrying inside. A harassed look was on his face, but it morphed into alarm when he saw me.

"What are you doing here?" he started forward.

Marissa hurried around the counter and held him back. "He's a friend, Uncle Ben. He's a friend. That's it. His brother is sleeping in the back."

"I know you." He pointed at me. "You leave her alone. She's a good girl."

At the warning, the slight concern I had felt for Marissa left. In its place, the old emptiness and anger settled back in. They were like a second layer of skin, and it wasn't until then that I realized they had lifted for a moment. It was because of Marissa. They didn't press so hard on me when I was around her, but they were back and I'd gone back to being the bad guy.

"No, no. He's going. He's getting his brother and he's going." She waved at me. "Go."

When I ducked into the back office, Logan was sitting up, cradling his head with his phone in the other hand. He saw me and blinked, dazed at me. "Mason? Did you just text me a bunch of times?"

"I'm surprised you heard them. Marissa said you were wasted when you got here."

He groaned, then looked ready to puke. "I feel like shit."

"What happened? I thought you were at that party." Hearing Marissa's uncle begin to yell, I took his arm. "Come on. Let's go. We have to get out of here."

Logan clutched his stomach. "Shit. What the fuck did I do?"

"I have no idea, but we need to go. The owner is going to call the cops." When I helped him through the door and saw his face in the light, I almost dropped him. "Shit. What happened to your face?"

"What?" Logan touched his cheek and cursed. "It was throbbing in there, but it's killing me now."

His cheek and jawline were swollen. I touched the corner of his eye and Logan sucked in his breath. "Man. You're going to have a black eye."

Before I could fully comprehend that someone had done this to my little brother, Marissa's uncle descended on us. He was pointing and shouting at the same time. "You! Get out. Get out of here! Now."

Logan flinched from the harsh tone. When the guy got closer and closer and didn't look like he was stopping, I moved Logan behind me and shoved the guy backwards. "Back off."

He paused, taking in my size and height, but shook his head again. "Him. I want him gone."

"Uncle?" Marissa was standing behind the aisle. She looked confused. "What's going on?"

"That's what I'd like to know," I bit out. "Logan?"

He shook his head. "I have no idea. I can't remember a thing."

"Him!" The uncle started again. His hand was up once more. He advanced again, his tone was irate. "He started this. Someone dropped him off."

Logan groaned then. "I think I got laid. I can't remember."

The owner kept going as if he hadn't said anything, "Then the Broudous showed up and they all started fighting."

"Wait. What?"

"The Broudous. Budd and Brett Broudou, and their slob of a sister," he spat out. His chest was heaving and the veins in his neck bulged out. "My son was here and he went to stop the fight. They started to hit this one, but *this one* hit my son. I had to take him to the hospital."

"Oh my god," Marissa muttered. She had paled. "I never saw the side of his face. He was sitting on the curb when I told him to go inside." She raised horrified eyes to me. "I wasn't looking at him close. I'm sorry, Mason. I would've called for an ambulance if I had known. I was more concerned about calling you and letting you know and then taking care of the store."

"And your cousin."

She turned to her uncle. "What?"

"You should've been concerned about your cousin. If he was okay or not."

Her hands were twisting around each other and she gulped. "I was, but you called and told me he was fine. I'm sorry."

I didn't care. I didn't give one iota about her cousin, about the owner, or anything else. I turned so my back was to them. I asked Logan, "You remember anything?"

He shook his head, frowning with his eyes narrowed. "Not really. Wait...something about their sister? They were saying you slept with her?"

"Their sister? I don't even know who she is." It didn't

matter. My decision was made. I was taking Logan home. I was calling Nate. I was calling anyone who wanted to come along and we were going to find the Broudous. This was going to be handled tonight. They hurt my brother. I was going to hurt them.

"Wait."

I looked at Logan. "What?"

He cleared his throat, wincing from the pain. "Wait. Whatever you're planning, I want in. Wait until I'm healed. You'd want in too, if it had been you."

I gritted my teeth. He had a point, but fuck, I hated it. "Fine."

"I don't want you guys back here," the uncle started in as I helped Logan out. He kept following us but I tuned him out. As soon as Logan was in the car, I shut his door and went to the other side of the Escalade. Marissa's uncle was there, tapping on the window, and I scanned a look over Marissa. She was standing inside the gas station, her hands pressed against her mouth. I tried to apologize to her, but didn't know if she got it. Then I stopped caring. Her uncle began yelling again through the window at Logan. I had enough.

I grabbed him by the throat and pushed him backwards. This was the second time that night I had physically moved another person. I was a lot rougher with him, but not enough to hurt him. It was just enough to remind him I was bigger and stronger. When he shut up, I glared down at him, but removed my hand. He started to open his mouth, but I shook my head, stopping him.

I said, "I'm sorry Logan punched your son. I can tell you that he didn't mean to. Now, I am taking my brother and I'm going home. We will stay away from your gas station, but if you even think about suing my family, we'll counter sue." I gestured to the camera in the corner. "My brother was attacked here and no cops were called. I don't know, but there might be room for negligence on your end."

I could tell it was hurting him to hold back.

"You might want to ask your niece who our father is. He's a rich asshole. Those pricks always seem to win, one way or another." Then I got in and started the engine.

I shot away from there, but hadn't gone far before Logan said, "I don't like that one."

"We'll use a different station."

"No." He was in pain, but he wanted me to hear him. "I don't like her."

"What do you mean?" I was trying to quell the anger in me, the need to protect my brother, but I tried to stuff it down. "Who are you talking about? Marissa?"

He nodded, swallowing and groaning at the same time. "I was out of it, Mason, but I noticed that she's not right. There's something wrong with her."

I frowned, but didn't say anything. Logan was still out of it, but I couldn't tell how out of it he was. When he didn't say any more, I didn't question him on it. I took him home and I took care of my brother.

CHAPTER TWELVE

THE CAFETERIA

I was tired.

It'd been months since Logan was attacked by the Broudous. They were angry at me, saying I used their sister for sex. When I realized who it was, I laughed. She had come onto me months ago, but I rejected her advances. She had come onto all of us, Nate first, then Logan, and then me. None of us wanted anything to do with her. I didn't know why she waited so long to say anything, but her brothers didn't want to hear the explanation and a war was launched between our schools. We retaliated for Logan's attack by burning down their barn. It was their turn now, but they weren't the only problems on the horizon. I hadn't forgotten my promise to Tate, but Kate seemed to have started taking her anger from me out on Tate even more. I didn't understand the logic, but I wasn't arguing. As long as both of them were hurting each other and I didn't have to deal with them, I wasn't going to stop them. The fighting was becoming hostile between them and after another explosive confrontation in the hallway broke out between them, I ducked into the cafeteria. I needed a breather. Logan acted like he didn't care about what Tate had done anymore and maybe he didn't. He had gone back to his laughing, smart-ass ways and he seemed to be fine. That meant I was fine too, but if Tate tried to get back in with Logan, she'd have to deal with me. She had done enough damage to my brother. She wasn't going to do more, or even have the opportunity to do more.

As the door shut behind me, conversations halted. I saw Logan sitting on a table, his feet on the seat. He was smiling down at a girl, looking down her shirt. When I glanced at her,

I saw her adjust it to give him a better view. He glanced up at me and narrowed his eyes. I saw the silent question from him. He wanted to know if I was fine, so I gave him a short nod. He flashed a grin and went back to flirting. As I moved through the room, a few of the juniors nodded their hellos. They were the top dogs in school during lunch since most of the seniors were allowed to leave campus. Sometimes I sat with them, but the door opened and Kate strolled in. She headed for their table, folding into the lap of one of the guys. Her friends followed her except the one that Nate was hooking up with; she went to his table instead. He was sitting with Ethan and a couple other guys from our table.

I didn't want to deal with any of them. After grabbing some food, I skimmed the room. I could sit at any table, but then Tate came in. She was followed by a group of girls and I watched as they took the table next to where Kate was sitting with the guys. Shit. The fighting would start all over again. I was tempted to leave and eat in my Escalade, but then I spotted my table mate in the back corner, hidden behind a post. Logan never repeated his comment about Marissa so I started to wonder if he had ever meant it. At that moment, I didn't care. I wanted to get away from the tension. As I started towards her, I saw there were two other girls with her. I grinned. They all looked the same. Two of them had books out and were reading them while the third was staring off into space.

I stood beside the table and waited. They didn't notice me at first. When one did, it was one of the girls reading a book. I had shifted on my feet and my shadow hit her book. She looked up and then gasped. Marissa looked up from her book. Her eyes got big. The third one was still staring off into space, oblivious.

Marissa asked, "What do you want?"

A grin formed. Shit. This was refreshing. "Can I sit?"

"No." She looked horrified.

"Marissa," her friend said, a note of alarm in her voice.

"I know. I know," she reassured her.

The third girl still had no clue.

"You can't sit here, Mason. No way," Marissa said firmly. She was looking around.

Her friend whispered, "Oh my god."

I frowned. I thought we were okay. I hadn't talked to her in a while. This wasn't the reception I had expected. "Look, I'm sick to death of dealing with bitchy girls. You don't have to talk to me. Just let me sit. I'm looking for a spot away from the drama right now. That's it."

"Oh dear lord!" The third girl saw me and physically jumped off her seat. She landed on the floor. There was a moment of silence from the tables around us and then people started laughing.

"Shut up," I barked at them. I had sought this table out to get away from that shit. Another hush fell over the tables, but it was from surprise. I could sense the interest. All eyes turned to the table and a few girls in our class recognized Marissa. They started whispering to each other, and I was beyond caring what would happen because of this. I turned back to Marissa. "I really just want to sit. I don't want to talk. There's no drama at our table in class. I didn't think there would be drama at your table during lunch either."

"Oh." Concern filled her eyes, and she bit her lip. "Oh man."

The third girl had crawled back onto her seat. She was watching me like I was a lion ready to tear into her. She was cowering. The other girl was just watching me. Her eyes kept darting from Marissa to me. After another few minutes, she was the one who broke the silence. She cried out, "Oh god, Marissa. Let him sit."

"Paige, I don't know."

The friend leaned across the table and whispered, "Damage is already done. People are already looking."

Marissa gazed around the room and sighed, nodding to me. "You can sit."

I frowned at them. Did they really think I would hurt them that bad? I didn't take the seat next to them. Marissa was on the end. Her two friends were across from her. I sat at the other end of their table, keeping three chairs between Marissa and myself. All three of them watched me but they didn't talk to me. After a few more minutes, I realized they had taken me literally. They really weren't going to talk to me, so I turned and began eating. When I was done, I glanced up and was surprised again. They were still watching me. As I thanked them for letting me sit there, I took my tray and stood up. People turned away and I realized they had all been watching. It wasn't just those three.

When I put the tray away and turned for the exit, that's when I glanced at the other side of the cafeteria. All my friends were on that side. They were confused, but I saw Kate standing, glaring across the room. Her arms were folded across her chest as she pinned Marissa down with near-hate in her gaze.

Walking over to her, I stood in front of her.

Kate looked up. The dark look in eyes didn't leave. "Why were you sitting over there?"

"Because I can." I narrowed my eyes. "Stop looking over there."

"You're lunch friends with her now?"

"You don't get to have an opinion. Remember?"

She moved to the side and the glare was directed back to them.

I moved to block her again. "Stop it, Kate."

She gave me a tight smile, but her eyes were cold. "You don't get to have an opinion."

I glanced to Logan and saw him watching. He was frowning, gazing at where I had been sitting too. When his gaze caught mine, he nodded and stood from his table. Walking to us, he stood next to me, blocking Kate's view again.

She let out a disgusted sound. "So because the big bad Kade brothers are standing up to me, you think you can tell me what to do?" She turned that chilly smile to me. "All you do is preach about how I have no claim on you. Every time I'm dumb enough to fuck you, you leave me with the same message. Message received, Mason, but it goes both ways." She glanced to the guy whose lap she vacated. "I'm with Tim now and I won't be coming around anymore."

I didn't care. "Yeah, okay. Whatever makes you feel better."

Tim didn't stand up. As Logan and I looked at him, his Adam's apple bobbed up and down as he swallowed. When he wiped his palms on his pants, I told him, "Relax, Cosello. I have no beef with you." Then I lowered my voice, "Kate, leave the girl alone. All I did was sit with her at lunch."

She lifted her chin up. "Like I said before, you have no business telling me what to do. I'll do what I please."

I sighed. Tate was standing too, but she remained at her table. Recognizing the gleam in her eye, I suppressed a curse. If I said anything more, I'd make it worse. Tate saw a new victim. Kate was distracted. As I stood there, my jaw clenched. I hadn't realized this would happen, but both groups were looking at Marissa like she was prey they could both enjoy.

I turned around. Marissa was watching us, her face pale.

Kate started laughing. "Christ, look at you. What's wrong? Don't tell me you actually care about the girl?" I thought the only person you care about is standing next to you. He's all you protect. Even Monson gets the shaft sometimes. She gestured to the side where Nate had stood, but he was waiting for my call. I shook my head. If he came over, it would be worse. Kate would become even more determined and Tate would be even more relentless, seeing a distraction from her own torment. Then Kate distracted me when she said, "Don't beat yourself up, Mason. It's not the first time that girl's stepped out of place. We had a little round with her at the beginning of school."

"Stop this, Kate."

She laughed and shook her head. "Not your problem. Remember? Those are the terms you've always set. What I do is none of your business." Then she walked away.

A sick feeling took root in me, but I didn't know what to do. Kate controlled the girls. She had for a long time and I knew things went down that the guys never knew about. When I glanced to Tate, she was smug. Her gaze collided with mine and I knew she was remembering my promise. I was going to break her how she had broken Logan, but still I hadn't done anything.

Logan was following my train of thought. "She doesn't care."

"What?"

He glanced at Marissa too and frowned, then turned back to me. "Tate. You told her that you'd hurt her. She's going after that girl because of that now, to hurt you back."

"I haven't done anything to her."

"Yeah, you have. Kate wouldn't have gone after Tate if it wasn't for you. People know what happened, Mason. They know she came onto you. It was obvious even though we didn't say anything. They figured it out. Tate blames you for what Kate's been doing to her." He nodded in Marissa's direction. "If you want to help her, distance yourself from her. The girls will do what they always do. You can't stop them."

He was right.

Then he said, "Mom called last night."

I stopped thinking about Marissa. "What?"

He nodded, becoming closed off again. "She wants us to stay with her before she moves to L.A. permanently."

"Mom's already there. She's going to stay there the whole time now?"

He frowned. "She hadn't told you?"

"No." She always told me things first.

Logan shrugged. "She's been calling me a lot lately. I don't know why, but yeah, I'm giving you a heads up."

Even the thought of Mom wanting us to stay with her brought the old weight back on my shoulders. Our dad would fight that. Things were tense at home anyway, but it would get worse.

"Mase?"

Hearing the concern in his voice, I flashed him a grin and shoved all that shit down. Fuck it. I didn't give a damn what happened. "Yeah."

"You okay?"

"I'm fine." I nodded at him. "You?"

"Yeah."

We weren't. Being at home was a nightmare. Dealing with our dad and his women, and now our mom wanted us to stay with her more often? The nightmare was going to get worse. I could feel it in my gut. I shook my head. I couldn't worry about anyone else. Football. Logan. Me. That was all I could deal with. I was going to sit where I wanted. No one was going to control that. Marissa would be fine. Kate couldn't do much to her anyway. I'd sit with them if I wanted, but glancing around the cafeteria and sensing the change in the air, I was tempted not to even come to the cafeteria anymore.

Life was just hard sometimes.

CHAPTER THIRTEEN

ANOTHER YEAR

Things didn't get better. They got worse. I sat with Marissa a few more times at lunch and then stopped. Those times were a breather for me. Her friends didn't have an agenda, but the tension in the cafeteria was always too much. After a while, one of her friends told me to stop.

"Paige," Marissa hissed, "it's not his fault."

Her friend turned to her with a hard expression on her face. "He's not stopping it either."

"It's that bad?"

Her friend snorted. "Look at her. She's lost twenty pounds. She didn't have twenty pounds to lose. She's a stick."

I gazed around and saw that Kate was acting normal. She and Tim had broken up, but she was already flirting with someone else. Then I glanced where Tate was sitting. She was watching Logan with a wistful look on her face. Fuck no. She couldn't have him, not again. I didn't know what to do to help Marissa, though. I didn't know if I could do anything. They were girls. This was a girl fight. I asked her friend, "Did you talk to the principal or the counselor at all?"

"Yes." Near hatred flashed in her gaze. "They can't do anything unless there's evidence. So far, we don't have enough."

"Mason, just go." Marissa smiled at me. She wore a brave front. "I'll be fine."

She wasn't. I stopped sitting with them after that, but it didn't matter. Over the next few months, Marissa began to look unhealthy. She stopped coming to school towards the end of the year and when I heard she was transferring, I was relieved. Her friends blamed me. Paige told me when she passed me in the hallway one day. She held onto her books tightly and she glared at me. "Don't call her. Don't email her. Leave her alone. That's the only thing you can do to help her." She started to walk off, but turned back around immediately. "She's going to email you. She's going to try and keep a friendship with you, but if you really want what's best for her, don't answer any of those emails. Let her think you don't care. Trust me. She's better off that way."

I stood there and took it. I deserved that. People were watching and somehow, because I didn't handle her after being told off, that girl gained some credibility in school. I was glad. Nate told me that Marissa's friends had become targets during the year as well, but Kate and her friends had backed off.

I asked him, "You've been hooking up with Parker this whole time?"

He grew guarded. "Was I not supposed to?"

I didn't know. Most days I just wanted to get away from my dad. My phone buzzed then and I silenced it. When he saw it was my mom, he asked again, "Are you avoiding her?"

I shook my head. "I feel like I'm avoiding everyone right now." Shit. The battles were coming. I felt it. My dad had stopped bringing women around, but I knew what that meant. There was one woman. I only hoped it wasn't the one I remembered catching him with a long time ago. She was cold, but my gut told me we hadn't heard the last from her.

"Yo." Logan came over and held his fist up. Nate bumped it. My brother turned it to me and I gave him a look. He lowered it. "Right. So school's over after tomorrow. What are we doing to celebrate?"

Tate headed down the hallway at that moment. As she saw our group, she paused, staring at Logan. His back was to her. Then she saw me watching and jerked her gaze away. She hurried down the hallway then, her little friends enveloping her on both sides as they walked away.

I asked Nate, "Do you know if Parker's said anything about them going after Tate?"

He frowned.

Logan stiffened, but didn't say anything.

Nate scratched his head. "I think there was a truce called for a while. Why?"

I met Logan's gaze and a look passed between us. He was still hurting. Whether he admitted it or not. I knew he was and we both remembered what he asked me to do that night. Even if he forgave her, he still wanted her to hurt. He looked away, his lips pressing together.

Tate had suffered, but she broke him. She needed to suffer more.

***

There was a party at Fischer's cabin again. We drove ourselves this time. As I pulled up and got out, I waited at the front of my Escalade. The cabin was lit up. People were everywhere. We could hear girls shrieking, like always. Guys were laughing. There were people drunk on the front lawn and I heard a moan from a car around us. As Logan circled the front of the Escalade to stand beside me, he flashed me a grin. "Another year."

I nodded. "Another year." It was a shitty year, too. "Let's hope next year's better."

He laughed. "Nate coming with Parker?"

"Yeah." I didn't want to go in there. I frowned to myself. "Why don't I want to go in there?"

"Because our school is full of douchebags and bitches?" Logan shrugged, crossing his arms over his chest, leaning against the front of my vehicle. "Just a thought."

I grinned at him. "I think most people would call us the same thing."

He snorted. "Who the fuck cares?" He held a fist up. "Us against the world, big brother."

I hit his fist with mine and sighed. "Us against the world, little brother."

We shared a look, remembering all the shitty things that had happened over the past few years. I had a feeling we had shittier years coming. Then I shook my head. "It'll get better. It has to get better."

"Whatever." He pushed up from the Escalade. "I want to get wasted and laid tonight. I wish those two things rhymed." He paused, frowning at me. "Ripped and dicked? Does that work?"

I shook my head. "You're not a poet. Don't even try."

"Wait, wait, wait." He began following me towards the cabin. "Get my drink on and then my fuck on? No. That doesn't sound right."

"Shut up."

"Wait. I got it." His hand came down on my shoulder and he tugged me to a stop. His smirk widened. "Shagged and bagged?"

"That's the same thing."

"Shit. You're right."

Ignoring his hand, I started forward again.

He snapped his fingers behind me. "I'd like to get fucked faced and then fuck someone's face."

"You still suck."

"I'm better than you."

I grinned, but didn't turn around. Someone yelled our name, "Kade!" Looking around, I saw it was Jared Smythe.

He was coming from the bonfire, a case of beer hanging from his hand. With a wide smile, he was shaking his head as he got closer. He tossed each of us a beer, then pounded me on the chest. "Hey, man. We made it through the year. Me in college and you in school." He pointed at Logan. "You. I remember when you were a little shit. I thought you got my brother into drugs."

The humor disappeared from Logan's face and he stood at his tallest height. He was an inch shorter than me, but he had grown so he was Smythe's equal now. Then he smirked at him. "You should thank me. Because I kicked your brother's ass, he's not a stoner this year."

"Yeah, yeah." Jared rolled his eyes.

Logan narrowed his. I grinned, feeling proud. Smythe had gotten weak over the last year. He had graduated a year ago so he didn't know not to mess with Logan anymore. He said now, "You want to say that again?"

"Say what?" Jared looked between us. "Huh?"

Logan moved forward a step, closing the distance between them. He was eye to eye with Jared now. "Be more disrespectful. Please."

Jared glanced at me. "Kade?"

I did nothing. I shook my head. "Smythe, I did't help you two years ago. Why would I now?"

His face clouded over and he looked around. People were watching. No one was coming to his aid. Realizing his mistake, he moved back a step and laughed, his tone on edge. "Guess I'm behind on some things. No disrespect meant, Logan."

"Yeah, yeah." Logan turned away, gave me a half-grin, and headed off. "I'm going to get my drink-on so I can get my fuck-on later. Bye, bitches."

I waited. Jared didn't say anything. He stared at me, half dazed, and then nodded to me. "Okay. Well. I'll talk to you later. It's good to see you again, Mason."

As he left, Nate bypassed him. I looked over and saw Parker heading towards her friends. When Nate got to me, I gestured to her. "I don't like what they did to Marissa."

He frowned. "What do you want to do about it?"

"I don't know." And that was the truth. There'd been guys who challenged me a year ago. I had been a freshman on the varsity team, and I was a starter. Not a lot of them had taken that lightly, but when they realized they couldn't beat me, most of them backed off. There'd been no problems this year either, but that was all with guys. Things were different when girls fought. "I have absolutely no idea."

"They'll probably do that crap again, but to a different girl."

"They're probably doing it now." I frowned. I didn't know how I felt about that.

"Mason?"

I had turned to watch Parker and Kate. They had gone to the keg right away and had their cups already. Laughing, talking loudly, I realized they were like us. They were at the top of the social chain. Kate glared at another group of girls and I realized they weren't. They were the top in our grade. The girls in the grade above us didn't fear Kate. For some reason, I was happy about that.

"Mason."

"What?" I turned back to Nate. "What'd you say?"

"What do you want to do about them?"

"I have no idea. I don't know what we can do." A gnawing feeling was in my gut. It would be a problem in the future. "Marissa's transferring."

"Yeah." His tone softened. I heard the regret there. "You kind of liked her, didn't you?"

I shrugged. "Not like that. She was innocent. There was no agenda with her." Everyone seemed to have an agenda now. "Want to get wasted tonight?"

"No girls. It's a guys' night tonight."

I nodded. "Sounds good to me." As we headed to find Logan, I caught the look Kate sent my way. I shook my head. Fuck no. She'd hurt my friend. It'd be a long time before I would talk to her again. As she got my message, she rolled her eyes and turned away. Her voice raised and she went back to laughing louder. It was like nothing happened.

As we headed inside, I stopped in my tracks. Tate was draped all over Logan. Her arms were around his neck and her head was nestled against his shoulder. His arms were stuffed in his pockets, but he wasn't pushing her off him. A growl ripped from my throat and everyone stopped.

Logan stiffened, straightening to his tallest height.

Tate lifted her head, growing cautious.

Someone cut the music and I heard a whisper, "This is going to be good."

I ignored them as I advanced on Logan and Tate. As I stepped closer, Logan moved away from her. Her arms dropped from him, but she didn't look at me. She was looking at the corner of the room when I stopped in front of her. Instead of talking to her, I said to my brother, "She wanted to fuck me."

"I knew it!" someone hissed from the crowd.

Another person muttered, "Yep. Called that shit."

Logan flinched, but met my gaze. He said, "She's a good lay."

She shook her head. "I can't do this. Not again."

She started to slip away. I nodded at Nate, who caught her arm and held her in place. She tried to jerk her arm away, scowling at him, but he ignored her. He was waiting for me. I said, "Stop fighting, Tate."

She did, but glared at me. "What are you going to do to me, Mason? Huh? If your brother wants to spend time with me, what business is it of yours to butt in?"

All I could do was laugh. "Are you fucking with me?" I grinned. "Wait. Wrong choice of words. Do you want to fuck with me? That's the right way to say it. You wanted to before. You kept trying, even though I gave you no encouragement. Are you going to repeat history?"

"Shut up." She tried to sound threatening, but she glanced around. Her cheeks were red and her head was lowered. Nate still had her by the arm; it was obvious she wanted to run.

I shook my head. "This is unbelievable." Turning to Logan, I said, "Really? What are you doing?"

He sighed. "She's good in bed. What do you want from me?"

"Logan."

He looked at me and I saw the pain in his gaze. He was still holding onto her. I shook my head. "She left you in bed. She came to my room, and she took her clothes off." The crowd began to murmur around us. It grew louder as I divulged more details. I added, "She masturbated in front of me. She wanted to turn me on. She thought she was."

"Slut."

I glanced at the crowd. No one was even pretending not to listen. We were the entertainment. We were front and center. I shook my head. I looked at Tate and said, "I don't want to humiliate you."

Tate laughed. "Not really getting that feeling right now."

I kept going as if she hadn't spoken, "But I will. If I have to do that to remind my brother the hell you've put him through, I will record myself, telling everything, then play it over the local radio." I looked at Logan. "You watched the tape."

"Fuck," someone cried out. "There was a tape?!"

"She came to me. She touched herself. She was making herself come. She was doing that for me."

Logan clamped his eyes shut and turned away. "Stop."

I wouldn't. "Us against the world? That's what you just said."

He shook his head, but a mangled cry tore from his throat. "Stop, Mason."

I moved closer and lowered my voice. "She said that she thought about me when you were in her."

"Oh my god." Tate fell. Her knees folded, but Nate kept her upright.

I studied her. She wasn't weak. She could handle a lot more. I told Nate, "Don't let her go anywhere."

He nodded. "I wasn't planning on it."

Then I turned back to my brother. "Logan, don't do this with her again."

"I was going to fuck her. That was it. I was going to fuck her and drop her." He met my gaze, but I saw his pain. The haunted look was back.

I shook my head. He wouldn't have had the strength. "You would've fallen back in love with her." When my words hit him, he turned away and I realized the truth. He was still in love with her. I thought he was only still hurting, not loving. "Maybe you should go?"

"I'm sorry."

I nodded. "I know."

Then Logan left. He grabbed a case of beer on his way out and I knew he'd find a different girl to be with for the rest of the night. It was how he dealt.

I turned to Tate. My full attention focused on her now. This was how I dealt. "Really? You thought that would work?"

She lashed out at me. "Shut up." Suddenly she was standing on her own. She wasn't backing down. Nate didn't have to hold her up anymore. Her eyes were clear. Her shoulders were back, and she raised her chin up. "I still love him—"

"You never fucking loved him."

She stopped.

"You wanted me."

She looked away and I saw that she still did. I laughed. That was rich. "Are you serious? You were hoping to fuck my brother when you still think about me?"

She didn't answer. When she remained turned away, I knew it was true.

"You're unbelievable." I shook my head. I had more to say, but none of it would've made a difference. She was going to keep going after him and I wondered if she thought she could still keep trying for me. Then I glanced over and saw Kate. She'd been watching and listening the whole time. When my gaze met hers, she straightened from the wall. I saw the hunger in her eyes. She wanted me too. I asked her, "You want me?"

There were no pretenses. Kate didn't care who heard. She was like me in that way. She nodded. "Yes."

"Make her life hell and we can talk."

Kate nodded. "I will."

I looked at Tate, saw the wariness in her eyes, and shook my head. "You should've stayed away from my brother."

She knew what was coming her way, but she held my gaze for a moment.

In that second, I realized I would never understand Tate. I had no idea why she wanted me, why she tried to be with Logan, why she endured Kate and had put herself in a position to endure her again. Then I stopped caring. I remembered Logan as he sat at my computer and had watched the tape of her. I remembered the broken look in his gaze.

I said to her, "I want you gone. If they don't push you to leave, I will. I don't care what I have to do. I want you out of our lives."

I left. Kate took over and for once, I was thankful to her. Then I went to get drunk. Nate went with me. It was guys' night now.

CHAPTER FOURTEEN

MASON MEETS ANALISE FOR THE FIRST TIME

"Mason," the girl moaned as I kissed down her throat. Sweeping a hand up her shirt, I grabbed her breast and felt her body buck under me. I grinned. One touch, one little caress, and this girl was ready to unzip her pants for me again. When my hand curved around her hip and slid underneath her jeans, her elbow jerked and slammed against the horn.

"Shit!" she gasped and looked at me with wild eyes. Her hair was messed up. Her top lip was curved up in a lustful grin. "Hey." She reached for me, to pull me back down.

I shook my head and straightened away. We were in her car. We'd been at a party and she wanted to hook up so I left with her, but I hadn't felt in the mood to go back to the party so I had her bring me home instead. I flashed her a grin. "I'm going to head in." I paused, frowning. "I had fun, though."

Her eyes narrowed to slits. The daze she'd been in left immediately and she snapped, "Do you even know my name?"

I laughed. "How cliché is that?" I didn't remember her name, but I knew her reputation. She didn't sleep around. That was important to me whether I explained that to them or not.

She folded her arms over her chest. "I mean it. What's my name?"

I rolled my eyes, then tapped her work identification tag that she had hung from her rearview mirror. "You mean it's not Pam?"

She flushed. "Oh." Her bottom lip stuck out in a pout. "That's all I get? A wham bam thank you ma'am thing?"

"What else did you want?"

"How about some protection at school? Do you know what your girlfriend's going to do to me?"

I snorted. "That's your problem and she's not my girlfriend."

"She's still sniffing around you."

Flashing her a cocky smirk, I got out of the car. "I can't help being irresistible. Thanks for the ride. Both of them." I heard a groan from her. "God, why he's so hot—" Then the door was shut and I waved goodbye before heading inside. I had her drop me off in the back so I went inside through the basement. I hadn't gone far when I heard my dad.

I stopped on the stairs.

It was years later, but it didn't matter. My stomach still rolled over itself when I heard him bring his women here. It would always churn. This had been my mom's home. Every time he brought one home, it was like he was spitting on their memory. She had given him the house in the divorce settlement, but fuck that, this was my home. Logan's home too. But he never cared. As I headed up the stairs, more and more anger built and then I saw them at the door. She was saying goodnight, then laughed as my dad kissed her again. I heard a husky moan next and my jaw tightened. Thank god Logan was still at the party. He'd been getting lippier lately and I knew he would've wanted to launch into an attack. As I went up the stairs and through the dining room, past the kitchen, and stood at the end of their hallway, I stopped.

Shit. They were right there. No lights were on and I wasn't hiding. Her head went back with another moan, exposing her throat, and my dad placed kisses there. Her dress had been pulled down and he was cupping her breast with one hand. As he kissed his way down to her breast, his other pushed her against the wall and she groaned again.

For fuck's sake. I was going to go upstairs.

"Analise." James grabbed her around the waist and hoisted her up.

Her legs wound around his and her hands went to his pants. As I watched, she started to undo them and I couldn't hold it in any longer. A long laugh came out of me. I couldn't stop it. It was harsh and filled with disbelief. They froze and looked over at me.

"Mason."

I kept laughing and pointed at them. "Look at you. You're about to screw a different one right here in the front doorway. Shit. This couldn't be any funnier."

"Mason." His hair stood up from where she had been running her hands through it. As he dropped her, he moved towards me, shielding her so she could fix her dress.

I gestured to his pants. "Your dick's out. You might want to readjust, Pops."

He flinched as I called him that. I rarely called him any name except James to his face. Pops was meant to be condescending. I smirked, knowing that it hit the target.

"Mason, this isn't—"

"What?" A genuine laugh came now. "What are you going to say? You can screw now, Dad, not that anything stopped you before."

He sucked in his breath, as if I had punched him, and turned away.

The woman tried to smooth her hair back and plastered a fake smile on her face. "You are?"

I rolled my eyes. I knew this bitch. She'd been sniffing around my dad for a while now. "Don't play that game."

"Mason," my dad hissed at me.

I ignored him. "You've been calling him, sending him letters, showing up at his company for a goddamn year. You fucking knew he was married. Don't act ignorant, not for me. If you want to do it for your sake, go ahead, but it's a worthless cause. You can't brainwash yourself into believing you're not what you are."

My dad's head hung down and his shoulders drooped. She was silent behind him. I was waiting. I knew the lengths she could lie. Hell, Logan wanted to sic a private detective on her because this one stuck around. All the others came and went, but this one was sticking like a parasite. Then she stepped around him. Her hair was in place. Her dress was smoothed down. Even her face had lost the dumb-fucked look they always got on their faces. She was cold and as my gaze collided with hers, I saw the crazy mixed with intelligence. That only confirmed my suspicion. She was ruthless and cunning.

My dad was a goner, whether he realized it or not.

She said now, "They're divorced."

I grinned. "There you are. Show your true colors. Admit to everything. You don't have to fool anyone in this room."

"Mason, stop it." James stepped forward and took her arm. "Analise, can I have a minute with my son?"

Her eyes flashed at me with hatred, but she murmured to him with a soft smile, "Of course. I'll be outside."

Before she went out, her eyes narrowed one last time at me before the door shut behind her. I snorted. "She have a glass in that purse? You know she's listening through the door."

"Enough," he ground out.

I laughed again. "You say that to me? Enough? Really? Am I supposed to walk past you and pretend I didn't see my dad pressing his latest whore against the wall? Shit, James. We live here, Logan and me. This is our home too."

His head whipped back. "You will watch how you talk to me. I am still your father—"

I turned away, shaking my head and laughing. "That's priceless. It really is. You're as much of a father as you were faithful to Mom. When you're getting that bitch off, let that simmer in the back of your mind. Hope it brings you pleasure."

He cursed behind me. "You've got so much anger in you."

"No shit, Sherlock." As I headed up the stairs, I gave him a mock-salute. "That's what happens watching my dad bring home woman after woman and watching Mom cry about it every night. You ruined this family. You, Dad, and it was because of women like that." I stopped. Rage and pain were in me, like always. Fuck. Would it ever leave? I was starting to think I'd never be normal. "I know Mom wasn't perfect, but she didn't cheat on you. She was here. She was in the house. That's a lot more than you. You were off working or with those women. You weren't around to be her husband, to be my father, and certainly not Logan's father—" I stopped myself, my chest was tight. "This shit's been going on forever." Another laugh came from me, but this one was hollow. I flinched, hearing it myself and went to my room. It was pointless. He'd never care.

I couldn't hear the door close from my room, but I went to the window. His car left the driveway a moment later, but she turned around as he drove away. She must have known where my room was because she saw me. There was no reaction on her face, but I listened to my gut. This one was going to be a problem.

CHAPTER FIFTEEN

KATE AND THE COPS

Kate was sprawled over me and she grinned, panting slightly. "So, that was amazing."

I grunted. This was my last time with Kate. She was done after this. I had wrestled with myself when she was hurting Marissa. I hadn't done enough, but I was going to do something now. Lifting my leg up, I started to push her off of me. I wasn't rough, but it wasn't a gentle shove either. Kate complied and laid beside me on the bed. She grabbed for one of the blankets and wrapped it around her chest, tucking it under her arms. Running a hand through her hair, she gave me another lopsided grin. Then she sighed and turned on her side, facing me.

I ignored her and reached for my phone. This was coming to an end.

"Are you expecting a call?" Anger stirred in her tone. "Another girl?"

I sighed. "Stop, Kate. It makes you look pathetic."

She laughed, it was harsh and biting. "Are you kidding me?"

I sent a text to Logan. **Where are you?** Then I glanced at Kate. "We're friends and we screw. That's it."

"You're an asshole."

"That's already been established." I pointed to the door. "I've told you enough times you're not my girlfriend. Maybe it's time you finally start accepting that."

A strangled scream ripped from her throat, but she squashed it right away and scrambled off the bed. When she was dressed, she stood there and glared. I waited, trying not to laugh. Her hands were balled into fists and she had crazy eyes. Then I couldn't stop myself. I grinned at her and asked, "Planning my murder?" She would be in a few hours. I knew that much.

"Yes." Her eyes flashed with rage. "So far I have a shovel, rope, and a knife in mind."

I laughed. "That's weak. Plan a better one."

She rolled with it and leaned back on her heels, crossing her arms over her chest. The rage dimmed, but it was still there. The craziness faded too. That's what always worried me. Kate had it in her to go nuts. She was the toughest chick I knew. Some of the things she could come up with amazed me. I hadn't met another girl who thought like she did.

She said, "I would drug you because I can't overpower you. Then I'd have my way with you one last time before rolling you in plastic and burying you alive."

I flashed her a grin. "As long as I went happy."

She snorted, rolling her eyes. "Why are you such an asshole and so freaking hot at the same time?"

"Kate, I'm hot *because* I'm an asshole. You girls are stupid."

"No." She shook her head, her eyes darkening from lust as she looked me up and down. A slow grin curved at the corner of her mouth again. "You're hot anyway. You could have a dork personality and you'd still be hot. You being an asshole just makes you even hotter, that's all." She groaned, raking her hands through her hair before letting them fall back down. "You drive me crazy."

My phone buzzed at that moment. It was from Logan, **With a girl. Eating.**

I frowned.

Kate asked, "Who was that?"

"Logan." Sitting up, I typed back, **Where?**

The Chinese buffet.

"What's he saying?"

I responded to him, **Where are you going after that?**

Why?

I want to know.

"Mason." Kate snapped her fingers to get my attention. She waved at me. "Hello. Person here. Talking. It's rude to ignore."

I ignored her and typed to Logan, **Done with Kate. Up for being crazy tonight.**

Done? Giving her the boot?

Yeah. She's planning to kill me. I need to do something crazy tonight.

Good. I'm in. Tell me where and I'm there.

"Asshole," Kate barked at me. Then she lunged at me, reaching for my phone, but I'd been waiting for her to react. Wrapping my arm around her waist, I ducked to avoid her fist when she tried to hit me, and threw her on the other side of the bed. She gasped, but I heard the excitement and felt her body stiffen. She was going to lunge for me again so I laid down on her. When she was completely underneath me and couldn't do a thing, she tried wiggling out. She couldn't. Then a hoarse gasp came from her, but she was already softening. It'd take another moment before she'd be turned on. A small moan came next and I grinned, but pulled my phone back out. I typed to Logan, **One more time and then I'll drop Kate at home and pick you up. Be ready in an hour.** Then I tossed my phone on the ground and looked down at her.

She was already breathing heavy. The lust was unmistakable in her gaze. "Are you going to do something or not?"

"Are you baiting me now?" I grinned at her.

She groaned, biting down on her bottom lip. Then she pushed up against me. Her legs tried to slip out, and she began rubbing against me. She hadn't fastened her pants and I reached in them. She was already wet. Her arms were still squished by me, but she pulled them up. As I lifted up, her arms and legs wound around me. She pulled me back down and then began doing all the work.

I rolled us over so she was on top me. This was why I indulged in Kate. She was tough. She was a spitfire, but she was always down for whatever I wanted, whether I did all the work or she did, like today. I closed my eyes when she bent down and felt her mouth close over me.

***

An hour later, I dropped her off. As she shut the door and started for her house, I opened the passenger door's window and called through it, "Kate."

She turned, flashed a grin, and propped her hands on the door. I got a good view of her rack as her shirt was baggy and fell low from her neckline. She was cocky as she asked, "Yeah?"

"We're done."

She straightened abruptly. Her hands shot from the door as if she was burned. "What?"

"This. You and me. Your jealousy crap. It's over."

"What are you talking about?"

"You hurt a friend of mine."

"Are you kidding me?" A storm was brewing in her eyes. I was giving her the boot and she knew it. "We just screwed, you asshole."

Yeah, I was. I was a complete and utter dick, but Kate was a problem I didn't want to deal with anymore. "You got rid of Tate. That was my thank you."

She began shaking her head. If steam could've left through her ears, it would've. She was flashing back to our conversation before. I grinned. *Yes, honey, that was my foreshadowing.*

"I'm going to make you pay."

"You can try, but if you hurt anyone I care about again, you and I are going to have problems."

"Really? What are you going to do about it?"

116

"I don't know." She saw I was being honest and paused. "But I'll figure out what I can do and I'll do that."

I laughed. "You can't do a damn thing to me."

"Well, I can stop fucking you. That seems to be a good way to punish you since you always come back, panting after me."

Another anguished scream came from her, but she clamped her mouth shut and flipped her middle finger in the air. "I'm going to finish you one day."

I laughed. "You can try. I don't think you'll get it done, but it'll be fun to watch you try."

"AH!" She kicked at my door. As she fell back and I saw that she was winding her leg up to kick at my mirror, I sped off. She kept screaming, but I drove away. I never looked back and I knew I wouldn't. As I went to pick Logan up, it felt right. Kate was behind me now. As I sat there and sent him a text, my phone buzzed. Assuming it was him, I read it absentmindedly, but the name startled me.

It was from Marissa. **Paige told me what she said to you. I'm sorry. You weren't to blame for what happened.**

A weight fell back on me. I was to blame. It happened all because of me and because I hadn't reigned Kate in a long time ago. I typed back, **I'm sorry. I'm finished with Kate.** I didn't know what else to say so I just typed again, **I'm sorry.**

There wasn't even a second before she replied. **It's not your fault, but thank you.**

"Yo." Logan jumped in the car and he frowned, looking from the phone to me. His eyebrow curved up. "Not Kate still?"

"No." I shook my head and tucked my phone away. Marissa would keep texting. I knew she liked me, and we were friends. Somehow I would make it up to her. I didn't know how, but I would try. "You cut it short with whoever's house this is?"

He laughed, glancing back at the house. "That chick is pissed. I told her it was a guys' night tonight. She threatened to find Kate and the girls and have their own girls' night."

I swore. "They can do whatever they want." I shot from the curb and peeled through traffic, taking a wide turn into the next lane.

Logan cursed and reached for hand strap on the door. "What's your problem?"

"Nothing." I careened over two lanes, cut off a car, and took a quick right turn down the road to Nate's house. When we got there, I told him, "You stay. I'm just going in to grab Nate real quick."

Logan looked at me as if my head fell off. "Are you nuts? Nate's mom hates you, but she loves me. I should go in and you should stay here."

"Good point." I clapped him on the shoulder and pointed to the door. "You go. I'll text Nate quick so he knows what's going on."

"Wait." Logan had opened the door, but he shut it. "What *is* going on?"

"Just grab him. We'll figure it out as we go." I leaned over and shoved him out. He sighed, shaking his head, but went inside. I sent Nate a quick text, telling him Logan was there to get him. I didn't say anything else, but it was then I saw the missed call from our dad. I was calling my voicemail when Nate texted back, **K. Be out soon.** Then I heard my dad's voice, "Mason, I know you've met Analise before, but I would like for you and Logan to officially meet her." He paused. "Please be polite this time. She'll be staying at the house the whole weekend. Again, I am aware that you don't like her, but this one is different. We'd like to have dinner brought in tonight. I know this is short notice, but what are you and Logan doing tonight? Could you please come home and spend an hour with us? It would mean a lot to me."

I tossed the phone as anger rolled over me. He wanted me to play nice? He wanted Logan to meet her now? She'd be at the house the whole weekend? When Logan and Nate came out, they both took one look at me and grew cautious.

Logan got in the front seat. "What's wrong?"

"Dad wants us to meet her."

His eyebrows shot up.

Nate said from the back, "Whoa."

"That bitch you told me about?"

I nodded, my jaw was clenched tight. "Yeah."

"She's married."

"I know."

Nate said again, "Whoa." He leaned forward and his head popped in the space between our seats. "This is the one you caught him with at the house?"

I nodded. I couldn't talk. I was so pissed.

He glanced at Logan. "You've never met her?"

He shook his head, watching me the whole time. I felt his own tension as he continued to wait for what I was going to do.

Nate asked again, "How do you know she's married?"

Logan smirked at him. "We googled her. Mason knew her name and get this, her husband's the football coach at Academy."

"For real? No way."

"She's got a kid too." Logan looked back at me, and we shared a look. A kid was a weakness. It was one we could exploit.

I frowned, knowing what he was thinking.

Nate looked in between us. "What are you guys thinking? You're doing the silent conversation thing again."

I shook my head. I said to Logan, "I don't know. We don't know who she is."

"Wouldn't be hard to find out, just ask a couple people."

"It's a daughter? Your dad's married girlfriend has a daughter?" Nate kept looking between us. "I'm playing catch-up here. You never told me that before."

I said to him, "Because we don't know how old the daughter is."

"She's in my grade," Logan informed us. We both turned to him. He had been watching me the whole time. "I don't know what she looks like, but I asked Decraw and he told me."

"Who's Decraw?"

I told Nate, "Mark Decraw. He played league baseball with Logan this summer."

He asked Logan, "He didn't tell you what she looked like or a name?"

"It was in passing, but he said she was in his grade. I didn't have time to question him about anything else and I forgot to later."

"Well, whatever she is, we can't do anything about her now." I started the engine and turned around.

Nate leaned back, asking, "So what are we doing again?"

I glanced at Logan. He understood. James would be at the house the entire weekend. She would be there with him and they expected us to act like good little boys? We weren't going home this weekend. As if reading my mind, Logan nodded, giving me the go-ahead. Then he flashed me a grin. "I've always wanted to steal a cop car."

"Wait. What?" Nate shot forward again.

I returned my brother's grin. "You could be the decoy. They'll get out, I'll rush in and take the car."

Logan nodded. His wheels were turning and his eyes lit up. "I'll be naked. They'll get out, thinking I'm drunk. They won't draw their weapons and then I'll take off through the alley."

"No, wait. You have to stumble to the alley so they will follow you. I'll get the car then."

He nodded. "As soon as I'm in the alley, I'll take off. You better fucking pick me up on the other side."

"I will."

Nate groaned from behind us, "Oh my god, you guys. My parents are going to flip out. I can't get arrested. They'll move. I'm telling you right now. They hate you, Mason, and with this last thing, if you get me arrested, it's over. I'm out of here. I just know it."

As I turned towards the main street, where we knew the cops lingered, I told him, "You can take this car and just meet us later. You don't have to be a part of it."

He groaned, shaking his head back and forth. "You don't get it. I'm here. There's no way I can't *not* go with you guys." A resolved look came over him. "I'm all in with you guys."

"All-for-one-and-one-for-all type of shit?" Logan grinned back at him.

"Oh my god. I guess."

I laughed, then slowed the Escalade when we saw a cop car parked outside of a taco shop. Pulling into the parking lot, I parked and we waited. When Logan started taking his clothes off, I asked, "Why do you have to be naked?"

"Are you kidding me? We're going to steal a cop car. How could I not be naked for this story? It's going to be epic."

CHAPTER SIXTEEN

THE THREAT

It was the next morning when we were bailed out. As we went to the front of the station, James was there. Logan muttered next to me, "He looks pissed."

I grunted. "Good. Let's do this every weekend."

He sent me a grin and then our dad was in front of us, shaking his head. "Get in the car. Now." He stormed out, leading the way.

Logan followed first, but turned around to walk backwards. He flashed me a smirk. "Mission accomplished, huh?"

I nodded, watching our dad as we went outside and towards the car waiting for us. When we got into the back, he told the driver to go, but turned around to us. "Are you kidding me?" He was looking right at me. "I call you and tell you that Analise would be at the house; that we wanted to have dinner with you two, and you get arrested instead?" He glanced at Logan, then looked back at me. His nostrils flared from anger. His lips pressed tight together with disappointment. "And you get him arrested too?"

I rolled my eyes. "How much did you spend to make it go away?"

He drew in an angry breath. "I will ignore that last comment, Mason—"

I shot back, "I don't give a shit what you ignore. Yes, we got arrested, and yes, I know you paid off a nice judge to let us off."

"You did this because of her."

"Damn straight I did."

"You endangered his future." He pointed at Logan.

"You endangered both of us every time you stuck your dick into some other woman that wasn't your wife."

His eyes grew heated and he leaned away from the seat, as if putting space between us would calm him. I waited, watching for his next move. When he didn't make one and kept quiet, I taunted him. "What are you going to do, Dad? Ground us? Send us to Mom?" I laughed, and even I flinched when I heard the resentment in my own voice. "We both know you don't want Mom to have us. Fuck the football scouts. I'll get them to watch me on another team. I don't give a shit."

"You are so angry."

I snorted and turned away to watch out the window. "I'm angry? Are you kidding me? Of course I'm angry—"

"She's married," Logan spoke up, and we both looked at him. His mouth was pressed in a flat line and he was glaring at our dad.

"What did you say?" James' voice grew quiet.

He said again, "She's married, Dad. We looked her up. Her husband is the football coach at Academy."

He didn't react. I was waiting for something, surprise, shame, or even guilt, but nothing flashed in his eyes. He didn't move one damn bit. I shook my head and a disgusted sound came from me. He looked to me now, growing cautious as he did. I said, "You knew and you don't give a shit, do you?"

"Mason—"

"Don't start," I cut him off. "Don't even fucking start. She's a married woman."

"She's unhappy in her marriage."

I scoffed, shutting him up again. "I'm sure she is because she's cheating on him. What if she didn't cheat? Maybe she'd be happy? Why her? Pick another one. Pick someone who's not fucking married. Don't screw up *another* family."

"He didn't pick her." Logan's soft voice got our attention again.

"What?" James asked.

His voice grew louder. "She picked you, didn't she?"

"What are you talking about?"

Logan looked at me. "I was at his office a long time ago, and she was there. They had lunch together or that's what he said. He said it ran long. Dad was supposed to give me a ride somewhere, but he spent the whole afternoon somewhere else. His secretary had to call and remind him that I was there. She was with him when he got off the elevator." He paused and then added, "And I saw her another time before that. She was at the gym. I was there with Dad, but he didn't notice her then. She noticed him. When we went into the weight room, she followed us around." He gestured to James. "He didn't notice her at all. I think he had another girlfriend at that time."

His words triggered a memory of the first time I met her. She had stared at me from the car when they left, after I caught them in the front entrance. I shook my head. My gut had been right. This one was going to be a problem. "I had no idea it'd been going on that long." I looked at our dad again. "How long?"

He flushed. "It is none of your business."

"She's in our house too. That makes it our business."

He shook his head. His anger rose and he lifted a hand over the seat to point at me. "Let's get one thing straight, Mason. You will stop with this rebellious shit you're pulling. You will stop being disrespectful to me. You will begin to cooperate with me, and you will set a better example for your brother." Then he pointed to Logan, who started laughing. James turned to him and snapped, "Shut up. I won't hear any more smartass comments from either of you. You will grow up and you will put on fake smiles when we get there."

"Are you kidding me?" My mouth dropped open. "She's still there?"

He was becoming more hostile. He clipped out icily, "Mason, you and I will have a private conversation later, but right now you will act like loving and respectful sons. She is waiting for us."

"At the house?"

He turned to Logan. "What?"

Logan gestured out the window. "We're not going home. Where are we going?"

I shook my head and said, "Unbelievable. You're taking us to eat somewhere?" I glanced at Logan. "He doesn't trust us in private at the house and he thinks we'll act appropriately in public."

Logan grinned. "It's like he doesn't know us at all."

I grunted. This was all becoming ridiculous. I hadn't said two words to this woman, but I was already beginning to hate her. "Do you love her?"

James grew still at my question.

I saw the answer in his eyes. "You do. Shit. You love her." He was standing up for her. He was reprimanding his children for her. He was still going through with this meeting. My gut twisted as I realized that this was the love he should've had for our mom. "Are you kidding me?"

Logan looked over. "What?"

James was watching me. He saw that I saw it and he grew guarded. A warning note flashed in his gaze. He shook his head at me, telling me not to share that detail with Logan. I scoffed. Logan was going to know. Logan knew everything anyway. Then the car was pulling over and Logan asked again, "Mason? What? What's he kidding about?"

The car stopped then and James pointed to the door. "Go inside, Logan."

"But—"

"Now."

Logan glanced at me. I nodded, giving my approval. He went, but he waited outside the door of the restaurant.

"You love her." I said it. I hated saying it. "You love her how you should've loved Mom. Don't you?"

He wasn't even ashamed of it either. James glanced at Logan before looking back at me. "You won't say a word about this to Logan. Do you understand?"

"Why? You're going to ask her to move in, aren't you? That's what this is all about."

He shook his head. "Not yet. She's not going to move in yet, but yes, eventually. She's not quite ready to leave her husband yet."

I rolled my eyes. That was ridiculous. "What game is she playing? She targeted you, Dad. I have a hard time believing she doesn't want to leave her husband yet." Unless...I watched him and saw how a mask fell over him. Then I knew. "It's the daughter, isn't it?"

His eyes widened. "How did you—never mind. I don't even want to know, but what I do want to say is this," he stopped, an ominous cloud formed over him and he scowled at me, "you will stop all of this bullshit you're doing, Mason. You lead him." We both knew he was referring to Logan. "He will do anything you want him to do. He worships you so you will stop with your games right now. Being arrested is the last straw."

I laughed. "Yeah? What are you going to do—"

"I will send him away."

I stopped. A chill went through me and I saw he was being serious. "You wouldn't."

"I would. You are both underage. Nate's parents called me this morning. They're taking him away too."

Shit. I closed my eyes. He had warned me, but fuck, I hadn't thought it was true.

James added, "I will send Logan away, and it won't be to your mother's where you can follow him. It'll be overseas and in a private boarding school. He'll go and he'll stay, and you'll stay here, stuck with me."

I couldn't lose Logan. "You can't do that."

"I can and I will. I've already contacted three schools this morning. Everything is set up. They're just waiting for the final paperwork. Logan will pick which school he wants, and he will have to pick one. Then he'll go and you won't see your brother for a long time."

"You're a dick."

"Yeah, well, you get some of your qualities from me." Then he opened the door. "Now, you will get out of this car, you will pretend that you love me, and you will be polite when you meet Analise. She's important to me. And you will not say a word of this to your brother. You got it?"

I was cursing inside. A wave of fury crashed over me, but I clamped it down and jerked my head in a nod. When we got out of the car, Logan narrowed his eyes at me, but I walked past him. This was going to be the longest meal of my life, but I would play nice. There was no chance in hell he was going to take Logan from me.

CHAPTER SEVENTEEN

THE MEAL

She stood up when we got to the table. Smoothing the bottom of her dress, she held out her hand. "Hello, Mason."

I sat, then gestured to Logan. "Shake his hand. He's nicer than me most of the time."

James cursed.

Logan scoffed, sitting next to me. "Whatever." He said to her, "I'm not. I'm just the youngest so I'm always underestimated." He flashed a smile at her, baring his teeth in the same gesture. "I'm the one you'll need to look out for in a couple years. Here's the warning right now. Don't forget this." A warning flared in his eyes. "We know you have a daughter."

Her eyes got big and she turned, gasping at the same time. "James?"

"They're joking." He flashed us a similar warning as Logan's. "Right?" He emphasized that word as he glared at me, but held his hand out. "Please, sit, Analise. They're pranksters." Forcing a laugh out, he sat at the same time she did. "As you're well aware from the phone calls last night."

"Yeah." A small frown appeared on her face. "Samantha's never been in trouble. She runs a lot, and she doesn't have the greatest friends, but I can't complain. My daughter really doesn't have many problems."

"Right now."

She turned to me. Anger flashed in her gaze for a second and I grinned. Got you, bitch. That was the real Analise, not this articulate and kind-spoken woman.

She cleared her throat, the anger gone instantly. "Excuse me?"

I opened my mouth, but Logan beat me to it. He said, "You're married."

She choked on a gasp, turning to James again. The blood drained from her face.

"Mason," he hissed at me.

"I know. You threatened to send Logan to a boarding school if I didn't play nice."

"What?"

The fury rose in him; I watched as it filled his gaze. He reached forward, but he grabbed onto his fork and held it tightly. His knuckles turned white from his hold. He said through clenched teeth, "You will play nice now."

"Or what, Dad? I thought about it in the two seconds from the front door to here and I'm calling your bluff. You're not sending Logan away. You have shared custody with Mom and there's no way she'd agree to that."

"Dad was going to send me away?" Logan was mystified. "Dad?"

He ignored Logan. "Mason, do not test me on this."

"Or what?" I leaned forward again, staring right at him. I never looked away. I never blinked. I wasn't backing down. "I'm not even being mean right now. I'm just saying it how it is. She's choosing to be ignorant if she thinks her daughter won't have problems." I turned to her now. She froze at my words, but she blinked, catching up with the conversation. "You're married. What's your end goal here?" I pointed to my dad. "To marry him? You're going to have to leave your husband. What then? You're going to uproot your daughter? Take her from her father? If you think she's going to handle that well, you either want to act delusional or you don't give a shit. If that's the case, I pity your daughter. Take it from me, coming from a destroyed family, it's one of the hardest goddamn things I've gone through, and with our family, it was probably the best ending we could hope for." I fixed her with a cold stare. "Walk away from him. Find a way to love your husband again and don't fuck up your daughter's life. Take my advice. Please."

She held my gaze. No doubt. No regret. No emotion. She stared right back at me and she never wavered. My gut had been right. I laughed, shaking my head. "I wanted to be wrong. I'm not, though. That is your goal, isn't it? You want to marry him."

"Or she wants his money," Logan joined in. His tone was bitter. He turned to our dad again. "You were going to send me away?"

"Logan," James started. "That's not how it was said."

"Bullshit." I stopped him. He wasn't going to do this.

"Mason doesn't lie and he wouldn't make that up." Logan shook his head, leaning back in his chair. As he did, he looked down at his lap, a frown appearing. "I can't believe you, Dad. I'm always with Mason, but man, to threaten that? That's just cold. And you did it to control him. You were trying to control both of us."

"Because you're both so goddamn out of control," James burst out. He began drawing attention from the other diners and Analise leaned forward. She hissed, "Keep your voice down, James." He didn't. He was shaking his head and his voice rose. "Why do you two do this? Why? What have I done so wrong to have both of my sons turn against me?"

"James." She touched his arm, looking around. "Lower your voice. We're drawing too much attention."

"Yeah," Logan spoke up, disdain dripping from his tone. "You wouldn't want this to get back to your husband, would you?"

I threw him a grin. I was proud of my brother in that moment.

As he sat up and his shoulders rolled back, he added, "Your daughter's in my grade, isn't she?"

The air changed. It had been hostile, but it dropped to a more intense level. Everyone was silent for a moment. Then she clipped out, "What does that mean?"

Logan was holding her gaze steadily. He lifted a shoulder. "Nothing. I'm just checking my facts. She's my age. She's a year younger than Mason." He paused, drawing out his message. "We might know people in common. She might even start to hang out with us, be our friends." He gestured to me. "All the girls are crazy about Mason. Who knows? Maybe living with us could help her reputation? Is she popular in her school?"

Logan wasn't offering to help her social standing. Everyone read the threat correctly.

Her face grew pale again. "You had better stay away from my daughter. You hear me?"

Logan threw me a triumphant grin. I nodded. There she was. The real her came back out again. She had come out earlier, but pulled back in. Her mask shielded her, but he got it to fall away. I leaned forward, signaling to Logan that I would take over. He leaned back in response and she turned to me, reacting to the undercurrents between us. I narrowed my eyes and spoke clearly, "We're not threatening anything against your daughter. We're reminding you what we could do if we choose."

"Mason." James looked at Logan. "You too. Stop this. Both of you. This is ridiculous."

"Maybe, Dad." Logan shook his head. "Or maybe you should listen to us." He pointed at Analise. "She's not a good person. We both know that. Why can't you see it?"

Because he loved her. Our dad glanced at me, and we both remembered what I had said in the car. He loved her and if Logan knew the extent of it, I shook my head. I wasn't sure how my brother would react. Clearing my throat, I stood up. So did Logan. I said to our dad, "We'll get home by ourselves." I glanced at her. When she held my gaze, I knew she wasn't going anywhere. She'd been one of the women to help destroy our family, and she had every intention of trying to become the new Mrs. James Kade.

She was crazy, cunning, and ruthless.

I had no idea how to handle her so I didn't say anything and left. Logan followed me. We never went home that weekend. We drove to see our mom in L.A. and didn't come back until late Sunday night. We never did tell her about Analise or getting arrested.

CHAPTER EIGHTEEN

THE HEADS-UP

There was a knock on my door, but I already knew who it was. Logan always yelled my name on his way inside. He wasn't home and there was only one other person who lived with us. "Yeah?"

My dad came inside. I saw the tension on his face and knew what he was there for. It'd been six months since we were arrested, since Nate's parents shipped him off, and the disastrous meeting with Analise. At first there'd been nothing. It was like my dad's girlfriend went away and I had hoped she was gone for good, but when he didn't bring any other women home, I knew Analise wasn't out of the picture. That stopped three months ago and she was over more and more lately. I sighed, shaking my head. "I suppose I should just be happy you haven't force-fed her down our throats."

He stopped, the grim look doubled, and he sat on my couch. Leaning forward, he rested his elbows on his knees. Still dressed in his business suit, the top three buttons were undone and he reached up now, tugging at the collar. My dad looked in pain, but I doubted it had anything to do with the shirt. He cupped his hands together. "I don't know where to start."

I tossed my pen on the desk. "I'll do it for you. She's moving in, isn't she?"

He opened his mouth, ready to say something and then closed it. He nodded slowly.

Fuck. "I don't like her."

He held my gaze, flinching a bit, but let out a sigh. "I'm aware."

"Logan won't be happy."

133

"Logan hasn't been happy for a while."

We shared a look. We were thinking the same thing. It'd been a year ago when Logan's girlfriend came in here. My lips pressed tight at the memory. Logan was still working through those issues. He had loved Tate.

I said, "She's just like her."

"No." He shook his head.

I leaned forward on my chair. "Yes."

"No, Mason. You have this irrational anger at women—"

"They're both cheaters," I stopped him. "They're both manipulators. They're both liars. They both don't care who they hurt."

"That's not fair."

"Does she cry when she thinks of leaving her husband?" I didn't need to wait to hear the answer. I knew she didn't. "Or is she the one pressuring you to let her move in? Because she'll be so happy to be with you? I've met her husband, Dad. He's not that bad of a guy. He's a good coach too." I paused a beat. He looked away. "He could've been my coach."

"Stop."

I was getting to him, but I knew it wouldn't do any good. I shook my head. "Why this woman?"

"What do you mean?"

"She has you wrapped around her finger. Why her? Does she have magical lube or something?" I channeled Logan. "Is her vagina some fairyland for your prick?"

"Stop it. My god. You and Logan. You're both so crude sometimes."

I shrugged. "I say it how I see it. Sometimes."

He shot me a look, tugging at his collar again. "I'm aware. You've been barely tolerable since the divorce."

I snorted. "You mean since you started cheating. Wait, that'd be your entire marriage, wouldn't it?" Even thinking about it was making me angrier. "Why'd you marry her? It's obvious you didn't love Mom. Did you think you did at some point?"

He closed his eyes and hung his head. His shoulders slumped downwards. "I tried. I really did, Mason. It just wasn't meant to be."

"You didn't even try."

"I did too. You have no idea. You don't remember the beginning, dealing with her family, dealing with her father's threats."

"Right. Because Grandpa's such a controlling asshole."

"He was." The intensity in his eyes made me pause. He softened his tone and ran a hand through his hair. "He was before he died. Your mother never listened to me. It was their way before us. We were doomed from the start." He grew bitter. "You don't put someone else's wishes before your partner's. You don't do that. When you marry, that's your first priority. It should've been. I tried, but your mother didn't see her loyalties like I did."

"You thought you loved her?"

He grimaced. "I tried to love her."

I grunted. He never answered the question.

Then he said, softly, "She got pregnant, Mason. That's why we got married."

She had been just another one of his women. A hollow laugh ripped from me. Fuck. I'd been the doom of them. I'd been the reason for all the pain for everyone. A lump formed in my throat and I swallowed it down. "That's a hard pill to swallow. Shit."

He shook his head. "I tried. I really did, Mason. Your mother wouldn't take my side in things. She wouldn't listen to me. It was about what her family wanted. To give Helen some credit, she's the oldest daughter and they're old money. They have a lot of expectations for her to live up to. I know that's part of the reason she held onto our marriage as long as she did." A soft curse slipped from him. "She'd still be here if I hadn't ended it. I am sorry for how things worked out."

"You gave up."

"Mason," he sighed.

"Were you ever faithful to her?"

He pressed his lips together and glanced away.

He couldn't look me in the eyes. I was so tired of the lies and the manipulation. I was sick of everything.

Then he murmured, "I did try."

"Not hard enough. What? A month?" I was disgusted. "That's not a marriage. I don't blame Mom for not giving up her loyalties to Grandpa. I wouldn't either if my wife had another dick in her after a month of marriage." I laughed. "What a riot. You tried. That might be one of the biggest lies I've heard from you." It was killing me because he wouldn't cheat on this new one. I had sensed it in him for a long time. He would be the husband to her that he hadn't been for my mom.

"I am sorry for putting you guys through all of this. We should've been more discreet, your mother and I."

"Just stop." I sneered at him. I sneered at my own father. That was wrong, but somehow it seemed so acceptable in our lives. "I don't want to hear about your failed marriage. I lived it. Say what you came to say."

"She's moving in."

"When?"

"Next weekend."

I felt sucker punched. We had less than a week.

"Do you want me to tell Logan or—"

I didn't even let him finish. "No. I will." He had to hear it from me. "I'll tell him."

He stood, nodding to himself. As he went to the door, he wiped his hands down the front of his pants and I had to laugh. He looked up. "What?"

It was like he'd been nervous, but that was the irony. It didn't matter what we wanted or what was best for us, he was going to do whatever he wanted. We never mattered. For him to be nervous now? It didn't make sense.

"What?" he asked again.

"I think you're a coward."

He took a step back, looking like I had sucker punched him instead.

I didn't care. "After all the stuff you've done and now you give me a week's heads up that some new woman is moving in? Should I thank you for the consideration of even telling me?" I gestured to his hands. "You were sweating. That means you were nervous and that means you cared how this would go. Why? You haven't cared this whole time."

Pain and regret flashed over his face and he didn't answer for a moment. I didn't think he would. His throat jerked up and down as he cleared his throat. When he spoke, his voice was hoarse, "I'm sorry for threatening to send Logan away. I'm not a great father. I know that. I wasn't a good husband at all, but this is a new beginning. That's what I'm hoping for."

He started for the door, but I stopped him again. "Were you with her the whole time?"

"What?"

"Logan saw her around years ago, but I know you were with other women. Have you been with her this whole time?"

"No." He shook his head. "I didn't want to leave a marriage and jump into another serious relationship, but you're right. Analise has been around. She's been patient. She waited for me. I love her, Mason. I love her a lot."

I knew he did. I hated that he did. "What about her kid?"

"She's coming too."

I narrowed my eyes.

So did he. He hesitated and then said, "I'm quite aware of what you are capable of, Mason. I've watched you grow up."

"What's that supposed to mean?"

"You will leave Samantha alone. If you have any idea of pursuing her to hurt me or hurt Analise, let it go now. That girl has no idea about any of this. Her entire world is going to be turned upside down in five days. You let her be when they move in."

I laughed again. "I don't have to hurt that girl. You and her mother have already done enough. If I did anything, it'd be to help her."

He studied me for a long minute. "You just let her be. Logan too. I don't want either of you to even talk to her."

Of course. As he left, I had to appreciate even more irony. He was telling me to be a stranger to his old mistress/ new girlfriend's child when they became our roommates. Only in our lives would that make perfect sense.

Then my phone buzzed and Logan's name appeared on the screen. He needed to be told too.

CHAPTER NINETEEN

TELLING LOGAN

We were at a party, but I couldn't hold it in. Nodding to Logan, I gestured away from everyone. This had nothing to do with them. This was family business. This was private. When Ethan and Strauss started to come with him, I shook my head. They fell back immediately. They never questioned me, but Logan saw the exchange and he frowned.

We went to a back room. Once we were there, he said, "What's going on? You're acting weird."

Shit. I didn't want to say it, but he had to know. "She's moving in."

Logan was silent.

I waited. He was my kid brother and I was scared. What would he say? How would he react? Then he shrugged. "Okay."

I frowned. "Next weekend."

He hung his head.

There he was. He was my little brother again. We didn't talk about our parents' relationship or lack of one. We talked about people who were trying to hurt us or use us. We were a united front against them, but this was different. Logan had always clammed up when it came to Mom and Dad. He needed to talk about it, but fuck. I had no idea what to say.

I tried, "I'm sorry."

"Why?" He bit out a bitter laugh. "You didn't force Dad to sleep with all those women. You didn't make him give up on their marriage or Mom to put up with his shit. You fucking raised me. That's what you did." He wiped at his eyes, swallowing for a moment. "Shit. For real?"

I nodded. "Dad told me today."

"Christ. My god. FUCK." He closed his eyes and turned away. His shoulders shook.

"Logan."

"Stop, Mason." He turned to me.

The sight of his tears silenced me. He had cried in front of me before, but this was deep. This had been going on for so long. My own emotions were coming up in me. I didn't want to deal with it.

He asked, his voice hoarse, "Why the fuck can't we have normal parents? You know, where the dad and mom don't lie all the time? Maybe some of the time, but they fight, make up, and the family pretends everything's fine. Why'd we have to have ours?" He shook his head. "We're not even a family. It's you and me. Who the hell is Dad to us? He's not a father." His arm jerked up to me. "You're my father. You raised me. He didn't. She didn't. FUCK."

He turned back away, but it didn't matter. He hurt. I hurt. No one could deny it or ignore it anymore. Everything he said was true. It was us against the world. It had been for a long time.

"He loves that bitch, doesn't he?"

I nodded. "Yeah."

"He's going to marry her."

"Probably."

"She already hates us."

"Yeah." I closed my eyes. I'd been protecting him for so long, but I couldn't anymore. "I have no idea what she'll do, but I'm assuming she'll want us out eventually."

Another harsh laugh came from him. "So it's over."

It was. A resounding ache was in my gut. It was worse than ever before. "Yeah. It's over between Mom and Dad."

"They've been divorced for a while. She moved out years ago." He sighed. "Why is this still hurting? It's like the pain will never go away."

"Yeah." The ache deepened as he spoke.

His voice dropped to a whisper. "Why do I feel like I'm that little kid again, listening to Mom cry as he ignores her?"

We were both there, reliving that moment. I was on the stairway with him, hearing their argument from our floor. Logan said, "We shouldn't have had to go through that."

"We're not the first."

"I know." I wouldn't do that, not to my own child. "It hurts because it's done, for real this time. He moved on."

"Mom hasn't."

"She will." She would have to. "He left her alone a long time ago, she just didn't let him go."

Logan cursed again. "This sucks."

"I know." The ache was still embedded in my chest. It wasn't going anywhere. I'd have to live with it. I already had been. "I want to get drunk tonight."

He flashed me a grin, brushing at his eyes at the same time. "I thought you stopped drinking for football."

"Really?"

He laughed. "Coach says you can't drink, remember? It'll screw up your training."

"Fuck my training." I shook my head. "Fuck this night."

"Fuck our life."

I nodded. "Fuck our family."

Logan stopped grinning. The sadness appeared over his face again. Sometimes I didn't think it ever left him. He said softly, "You and me."

"You and me." It always had been. It always would be. "Let's forget what's going on for tonight, just one night. Let's have fun. Then we'll deal with whatever happens."

He nodded. "Okay." He cursed then. "We're going to have a stepsister. Shit. How's that going to go?"

I grinned.

"What if she's ugly?"

I frowned. "Does it matter?"

"What if she's hot? Would that be worse?"

I didn't know. In that moment, I didn't care. Logan knew she was moving in with us. He had handled it better than I thought. Then I said, "I love you, brother."

He murmured back, "I love you too, big brother."

We didn't leave the room, not at first. We didn't say anything else either. It was a comfortable silence between us. Our lives were changing again. We'd deal. We always did. I didn't want to go back to the party. For a moment, just one moment, I sat in that room and I wasn't the Mason Kade everyone expected to deal with. I was hurting. I was angry. I felt like we had no parents, but I did have a brother. Logan met my gaze. He was thinking the same thing. We had each other. We would continue to have each other, but at that moment, we were still the little boys who were hearing their parents break up a family.

I could've sat in that room for the rest of the night.

CHAPTER TWENTY

MEETING SAMANTHA

"Mason, we have a problem."

It was the night before they moved in. I gripped the wheel tighter when Logan started laughing like a hyena beside me. Our buddy, Strauss, was dissecting the exchange we witnessed twenty minutes earlier between Kate and Jasmine so I adjusted the rearview mirror to see Ethan better. "What?"

"We have a problem."

"Then Kate whipped out that bottle and Jasmine pissed her pants, I almost lost it," Strauss continued to say as Logan kept laughing.

"Shut the fuck up." I punched my brother. He was drunk, he'd just gotten laid by two girls, and he loved hearing Strauss' commentary on any chick fight we saw, but I couldn't take anymore.

"Mase!" Ethan hit my seat. "I told you. I have a problem."

Logan glared at him. "Shut the fuck up, Fischer. Strauss is talking."

"You shut the fuck up. Now. I have a problem."

We were all silent. Waiting. When Ethan didn't comment right away, Logan reached over and punched his leg. "No follow through, man. That's your problem. On and off the field."

"I forgot my problem."

"Fucker."

"Yeah." Strauss shook his head. "We were all quiet, but you lost your turn. You didn't perform. You gotta think quick on your feet, Fischer."

"You guys are pissing me off."

Logan started laughing again. When I heard his voice starting to rise again, I spotted Quickie's and turned into the parking lot. I'd had enough. As I wheeled next to a gas pump, I turned the engine off and twisted back around. "Logan, go inside and get something to sober up. I'm not taking you home like this."

He smirked at me as his eyes glazed over. "We're not going home. You heard Ethan. He's got a problem." Then he clambered outside.

When Fischer didn't follow him right away, I shot him a glare. "Go with him. Calm him the fuck down."

He grunted, but did as I told him. Logan waited at the front of the car, and when Ethan joined him, I heard him say something about Molly's pussy.

Strauss started laughing. "I know your brother isn't high as a kite, but man, he's acting like it."

"What do you expect? Two girls blew him." And he was trying not to think about tomorrow, but I didn't share that information with him.

I lifted the gas handle and put the nozzle in my car. I knew Logan wanted to fight someone; he kept asking if we could go after the Broudous tonight. I kept saying no. When we fought them, we were going to make sure they wouldn't come around for a long time, but I felt the itch inside of me too. I wanted to fight someone. I wanted to do physical damage.

I sighed and leaned against my car, waiting for the gas to fill up. We were supposed to help them move in the next day. There was no way we were going to, and there was no way we'd take his money to help move them. The bitch and her spawn would have to move themselves, even though I knew James would end up paying for movers if we didn't go.

Then I saw her.

It felt as if someone had punched me in the stomach. It was the same girl Logan had googled. Samantha Strattan. It was her.

She was waiting by her car. Her arms were crossed over her chest, hugging herself. She was staring at Logan, who was now inside of the gas station. She had long black hair. It whipped around her from the wind, but it was like she didn't even feel it. No. She didn't give a damn. That look punched me in the gut.

She was strong. I saw it in her. She had dark eyes, petite lips, and high cheekbones. Her rack was decent. Her body was long and thin, and her legs were strong. Shit. She was tiny, but her eyes were dead.

This was the bitch's kid?

Then her shoulders tensed. She'd been studying Logan. Her eyes were eating him up, but not like the two chicks who had just been with him. She looked at him with loathing.

I narrowed my eyes.

I saw her turning—here she came—and her gaze locked with mine. Her eyes widened. She moved away from her car, just a step. It was the same look I got from wide receivers after I sent them to the ground with one touch. They were always shocked by the force and they'd reassess me. Every time. I had shaken her, but she had shaken me too.

Strauss came to stand beside me. He studied her a second before he commented, "Kate's going to shit her pants by the looks of that one."

I wanted her. And he was right. Then I smirked at her. This was going to be interesting.

She saw the exchange. Her eyes narrowed and she lowered them for a second.

I couldn't stop watching her. What was she going to do? She knew we were talking about her, but then her jaw hardened. She jerked her head back up and there was that same loathing, but it had doubled. She stared right at me. Her shoulders squared as she faced me and then her chin lowered. Whether she realized it or not, her stance was challenging me.

I fought against smiling at her. She was hot. I knew Logan was going to think so too, but damn, I didn't know if I could pass this one up.

Logan and Ethan came back. My brother said my name, but I didn't hear him. He said something else to me, but I wasn't paying him attention. All of it was directed on her.

"Who is she?" Strauss asked as she went inside to pay. "You know her, don't you?"

I wasn't sure what to say. He'd say something and I didn't want the guys to dissect her like they normally did. I shrugged and said, "I'm going to pay." As I did, she was coming back. The challenge was back in her gaze. I couldn't help myself. Veering towards her, I purposefully walked right at her. At the last second, I moved away an inch so my jacket brushed against her. I wanted to brush against her. Shit. I wanted to do more than that to her already, but I glanced back, watching her the entire time as I passed by.

She never wavered. She held her ground and stared right back.

She had balls, whether they were real or not, the girl had balls. After I paid, I was itching to test her some more. I wanted to see what she'd say, but when I went back outside, I could hear her friends giggling behind me. I didn't want to deal with them, but still... I paused by her car. She straightened, expecting me now. I started turning towards her without thinking, but the sound of screeching brakes pushed everything out of my head.

"What the hell?" It was the Broudous. Two cars had pulled into the lot and one of their buddies jumped out with a smoke bomb.

Everything else was forgotten. I rushed past her. I knew Logan and the guys were behind me, but I didn't care. I grabbed the first guy to pound. After that, it was game on. Logan took the smoke bomb from the guy and handed it to me. I launched it. If they wanted to fight, they were going to pay for it. A second car emptied and we were all fighting.

"Mason!" Logan shouted from somewhere, but I lifted my fist for another hit. I kept ramming it at the guy and then moved onto another when he couldn't fight back.

It was later, after the guys were tugging on me that I realized the cops were coming. As we headed for my car, I remembered her. Our eyes caught and held for a second, but then Logan pounded on the car again and we peeled out of there.

We never went to Molly's that night so Ethan could get laid. We went somewhere else, but I couldn't lie to myself. James had asked us to help move Analise and her kid in the next day. We both refused and we already had other plans, but I changed my mind. I found myself wanting to help them move in. I wanted to be around this one. I wanted to study her. She was different. I wanted to know how different.

"Mason." Logan distracted me and I stopped thinking about it. He tossed me a beer. "Time to get lit, big brother."

I flashed him a grin. "Sounds good to me."

He never asked why the change of heart and I didn't know if I wanted to tell him or not, but there was a shift in the air. My gut felt it and I knew something was going to happen. I could feel that change was going to happen.

I was looking forward to it.

FALLEN CREST HIGH

Book 1

TIJAN

CHAPTER ONE

It was a Friday night, two in the morning, and my two best friends were shrieking in drunken laughter behind me. I sighed as I pulled into the gas station. My little Corolla had been chugging near empty for the last few miles. And I'll admit that I'd been worried we would've broken down on the side of the road, not for my car's sake, for my sake. I didn't know if I could've handled walking with Lydia and Jessica. And on cue, Lydia rammed her elbow in the back of my head.

"Oh, Sam!" Muffled laughter. "I'm sorry. I didn't mean—" She dissolved in laughter once more.

Jessica wrapped her hands around the passenger seat and leaned forward. "Can we go to another party?"

"Puh-leaze?"

"No." I unclipped my seat belt and started to get out.

They scrambled out, or tried. Lydia tripped and was nearly clocked by my side mirror. Jessica tumbled after and leaned her weight on Lydia's shoulders so she wouldn't fall while she sidestepped over her.

What a friend.

"Why not? It's our last Friday night before school. Come on, Sam!"

Lydia stood and straightened out her skirt and top. When her boobs were back in place and the skirt barely covered her ass, she turned her pleading eyes on me too. "It'll be fun. Come on! I know where a public party is."

Jessica whirled to her. "Oh! That sounds awesome."

They bounced together. Both wore flowing skirts, tight tops, and brown curls that flung everywhere. When one hit me in the face, I swatted it away.

"I'm taking you guys home. You're both drunk."

"Come on, you're such a loser tonight," Lydia moaned.

Jessica frowned and flipped her hair over her shoulder. "Yeah, you are. What's going on with you?"

"Did you and Jeffrey have a fight?" Lydia's eyebrows wiggled up and down. She peeled over in laughter once more.

I gave them my polite fuck off smile and each rolled their eyes. Then Lydia lifted her nose and got a whiff of gas station pizza. Her stomach growled and off they went. As I watched them skip together, holding hands, and giggling over the fact they were drunk, I leaned back against my car.

While the gas was guzzling into my car, I heard Jessica's question again. Was something wrong with me? And I sighed. Only my whole world had changed that afternoon. I could see my mother's face when I had left Jessica's house and went home for the afternoon. We'd all been so happy to go out that night. Even me. Yes, Jeffrey was usually an ass, but a small part of me had wondered if tonight was going to be the night we slept together. He'd been my boyfriend for three years now. He was nice, well, he was a douche at times, but he still seemed to like me. And I liked him too, but while my mother had been happy jumping from bed to bed before she got knocked up with me, I didn't want to end up like that. So I had taken everything slow with Jeff, but when I got home to get ready for the party that night, little butterflies were in my stomach.

They died and burned in flames when I opened my front door. Boxes upon boxes were lined inside and in the middle of them sat my mother. A bottle of wine was half empty beside her as she sat in her silk bathrobe. Tears coated her face, but when she saw me a bright smile was forced out.

"Hey, honey." Hiccup. "How are you?"

I let the door go and it slammed shut behind me. "What happened?"

"Oh." She gave me a dismissive wave. "Nothing. You don't need to worry about a thing."

"Worry about what?"

"We're going to be fine."

I hadn't moved. My purse still hung from my arm. "Mom, what happened?" Boxes were everywhere, even in the kitchen. I saw two empty wine bottles in the sink.

"You and me, honey. We're going to be just fine."

"Where's dad?"

Her hands froze. She'd been taping up a box, but she sucked in her breath and held still.

"Mom?"

She finished the rest of her wine and she almost fell backwards from the effort. When she set the bottle aside, I asked again, "Mom, what's going on?"

She started sobbing. "Oh honey. I'm so sorry about this. I really am."

"Mom! What's going on?"

"Ifellinlovewithsomeoneelseandwe'releavingyourfather." She hiccupped again and swiped at some of her tears.

"What?"

She took a deep breath. "I...we're leaving your father."

My insides screamed at her. My hands curled into fists and I wanted to launch myself at her. I wanted to pound the hell out of her, but I didn't do any of that. Instead, I collapsed on one of the couches and I listened to everything she said. She'd fallen in love with someone else. She wanted to be with him. She told dad, he kicked us out, and tomorrow we were going to move in with this boyfriend of hers.

"Who?"

"Huh?" She lifted tear-stained eyes to me.

"Who?"

A soft sob and she whispered, "James Kade."

"James Kade?"

She nodded and wiped her arm over her face. "He has two boys your age, honey. You might know them."

Know them? Everyone knew them. Mason and Logan Kade. While they were rich, their dad owned five of the factories that our town thrived on, they chose to go to public school. Everyone knew the Kade brothers. They could've gone to the private school, where most of the rich kids went, or where I went because my dad was the football coach, but they'd shaken everything up when they chose public school.

And now I was going to be living with them?

As I watched my mom, who sobbed as if she'd been the one cheated on, something shriveled up inside of me. I would never be like my mother. Never. And sorry, Jeff, but that meant he wasn't going to be getting laid by me for a very very long time.

However, after I had spent most of the afternoon and evening packing my things, he wasn't excited to hear my change of plans when Lydia and Jessica waited for me to go to the party that night. In fact, he'd been a jerk. Not surprising. A few choice curse words, a few beers guzzled, and he wiped his mouth clean of me.

"I'll get someone better, bitch. You're not the only hot chick here." And off he went. His jeans rode low, a beer in hand, and his hair gelled into badass spikes.

I rolled my eyes and went in search for my friends.

Heaven help me, but Jeff would be back. I was at the point where I wasn't sure if I cared or not.

An Escalade wheeled into the slot beside mine. At first I didn't pay attention, lost in my world-ending daydreams, but when someone shouted all my attention snapped back to reality.

Four boys spilled out of the vehicle and two passed by me.

I sucked in my breath.

"Fuck that, man. Let's go to Molly's instead," one boy laughed as he hung on his friend. He threw his head back and laughed on a carefree note. His brown curls danced and he seemed invigorated. "You'll get pussy there. Promise."

He laughed another maniacal laugh before the two disappeared inside.

My hands clenched the gas nozzle tightly and I couldn't take my eyes off of him.

Logan Kade, my soon-to-be-roommate. While I watched through the window, he laughed at something his friend said. Lydia and Jessica saw who was in the other aisle and quickly went to flirt with them. The friend looked interested, but Logan skimmed a bored eye over them and went back for something more inside the store.

I hadn't seen the Kade brothers up close, not in a long time, but I'd heard plenty about them. Logan was a junior, like me. Mason was a year older. Both were good looking and Mason was rumored to be six foot one with a muscular build. He played defensive lineman for a reason on his football team. Logan had the leaner build, but he was an inch shorter.

I snorted to myself. I couldn't believe I even knew these details. As I cursed my friends inside for their gossiping ways, I glanced back at the Escalade and froze once more. Two green eyes stared back at me.

Mason had been filling up his vehicle and watching me the whole time.

I swallowed painfully and was barely aware that my gas was done. I couldn't look away from him.

Logan was handsome. There was no doubt about that, but he had nothing against his older brother. Now I understood why so many gossiped and whispered about the Kade brothers. The hairs on the back of my neck stood straight up and my eyes were locked with his in some sort of battle.

I couldn't look away. I just knew that.

His friend rounded the vehicle and leaned beside him. Both watched me and I saw the grin come to his friend. He crossed his feet and looked like he was at the movies, popcorn and all.

Then he said something and Mason smirked at me.

"Mase, dude. Candy flavored condoms." Logan leapt across the lot and did a small dance when he handed a box to his brother.

I knew I shouldn't have been watching, but I couldn't stop myself. I was riveted by both brothers. Logan was bobbing his head in rhythm with the music that blared from the gas station's speakers while Mason hadn't taken his eyes from mine.

That's when I knew without a doubt that he knew who I was.

I sucked in my breath and my knees trembled for a moment. What'd I do? Did I do something? Then I remembered my mom sitting in between all those boxes, tears down her face, and an empty bottle of wine beside her.

Fuck them. And fuck their dad.

My mom wasn't a saint. I knew that for sure, but she'd been with my dad for the last seventeen years. Now she cheated? Now she decided we should move in with her new boyfriend and his family?

Fuck them all.

My eyes hardened. Mason's narrowed. And I sneered at him before I went inside to pay. When I came back out, Lydia and Jessica were still in the bathroom; Mason passed me to pay inside. He wore a black leather jacket over a black shirt and jeans. His black hair was cut short and his eyes held mine in some form of trance as he passed by me. His jacket rubbed against me, he passed so close, and we both turned to watch the other.

My heart faltered for a moment.

The same hatred I felt for him was in his eyes.

Fuck him.

I lifted my lip to sneer at him and I knew he read the message because he narrowed his eyes, but shouldered inside the store.

I sighed and went to my car to wait. Logan and their friends were inside the Escalade, laughing about something. Then the door pinged its exit and I stiffened. I knew who'd be coming again.

I looked, I couldn't help it, and met Mason's gaze as he neared me. He paused close to my car and looked like he was going to stop. I lifted my head up, ready for whatever he was going to lay on me, but two cars screeched to a halt not far from us.

His eyes snapped up. "What the hell?"

"Hey losers!" a guy yelled and cursed at them as he ran from the car with something smoking in his hand.

"Oh hell!"

"Mason!"

Logan and their friends were out of the car in an instant. Mason rushed past me and I stood there, shocked, as all four dragged the guys from the other cars. Logan grabbed the smoking thing from the guy's hand and gave it to his brother. Mason took it and threw it in the first car. And the rest of the doors were flung open. Guys from that car poured out. Then another smoking thing was produced and Logan flung it into the other car.

Their two friends were still punching some of the other guys. Mason and Logan started punching the rest. It wasn't long before the cars were filling up with smoke and I got the first whiff of fire.

"Oh no," I muttered to myself and dashed to the store. After I flung open the door, I screamed, "Lydia, Jessica, get out here now!"

They rushed from the back section and stared, dumbfounded at me. "Sam, what's going on?"

I latched onto Lydia's arm and dragged her out with me. "We're leaving. Now."

Jessica followed behind, but braked in the middle of the lot. Her eyes were wide as she took in the sight before her.

I shoved Lydia inside the car and twisted around. "Get lost! The cars are going to explode."

Mason and Logan's friends heard me and stopped. They grabbed Logan first, but all of them dragged Mason away from the guy he was punching. Fury lit up his face, but when Logan said something in his ear, he turned and leapt for his Escalade. As he climbed inside, his eyes met mine for a second.

I shrugged and shoved Jessica behind Lydia inside mine. Then I hurried into my car and we were out of there in a flash.

Everything happened so fast.

Lydia and Jessica were bowled over in the back. "I can't believe that happened!"

"What did happen?"

"Logan Kade is so hot."

Jessica snorted. "Logan is? Didn't you see Mason? I'd do him in a heartbeat."

Lydia moaned. "Let me go to bed with my dreams right now. Why can't they go to our school?"

Jessica grinned again. "I heard it's because public school is tougher. They didn't want a pansy school."

Lydia fanned herself. "Whatever. I don't care. I'm transferring."

Then Jessica grew serious. "You think that'll be on the news?"

Lydia lifted her shoulders. "All I know is, how are we supposed to go home now? Sam, please, please, please can we go to another party? I bet I know where they're going."

I dropped them off at the party and left for home.

CHAPTER TWO

My weekend was spent packing and moving. The Kade house wasn't a house at all. It was a mansion, one that had pillars on their front patio. A fountain was in the foyer with a spiral staircase behind. Then there was the kitchen. It looked like it could've been built for a restaurant, with a chef that went with it. His name was Mousteff and he had a twitchy mustache and meaty hands. My mom introduced us, but it was with a hand waving in the air as if she was the first lady giving a tour. When we moved beyond the kitchen I glanced back. Moustefff was sharpening a meat cleaver. He winked before I turned the corner.

As for the actual moving, James Kade paid for a moving company, but he and his sons still helped with some things. Mason and Logan moved past me, grabbed boxes, and took them inside. I didn't look at them. They didn't look at me. And not once did anybody say a thing. The only two who talked were my mother and James. He was a tall, slender man with graying white hair. There was a kindness in his blue eyes, but he never met my gaze, not even when he walked behind my mother with a hand at the small of her back.

"Analise," he murmured in her ear. "I have friends who've invited us out for drinks tonight."

She gave him a bright smile and whirled around, her hands raised in a clap. "Oh, that'd be wonderful. I'm excited to meet some of your friends."

"Mitchell and Malaya Smith. He owns Smith Telephones, the local company."

As they turned a corner, I heard my mother ask in a breathless voice, "Do you think Malaya would be interested in meeting for tea one afternoon? I'd love to meet some of the other ladies."

I snorted to myself, like my mother would be welcomed among that club. Then my phone vibrated in my pocket. Lydia wanted to go to a party that night. Jessica sent me another text not long after. Then Jeff sent me one an hour later with an apology for his behavior.

I ignored them all and slid down the wall in my room. It was covered with boxes, a bed that five people could've slept in, and two couches on the far side. I had my own apartment. Maybe I wouldn't have to see anybody any longer.

Here's hoping.

I ventured out once during that night. My stomach had started to cramp so I figured I needed something to calm it down. As I tried to find my way to the kitchen a large television boomed from inside some room. The local news was on and I heard the news anchor report on a local car bombing incident.

"Two cars were on fire outside a gas station in the town of Fallen Crest. Each of them was owned by two teenage boys who attend Roussou High School. This incident is believed to be one of many in a long list of vandalisms between two schools, Fallen Crest Public High School and Roussou High School. Their football teams are arch enemies. An upcoming game is scheduled between the two and officials fear this is only the beginning of what seems to be an ongoing rivalry between the two schools. Sidney?"

Logan stood up from a couch and turned off the television. As he turned, he saw me in the hallway. I skirted ahead, but not before I noticed another head on the couch beside him. When I found the hallway for the kitchen, I glanced back. Mason and Logan both walked the opposite way, dressed in low riding jeans and tee shirts.

That was my only human interaction for the rest of the night; even Mousteff was gone. When Sunday dawned bright and early, I rolled over and checked my phone. Lydia and Jessica had called throughout the night. Jeff tried a few times, but he stopped texting at five that morning. My phone rang again and I saw it was nine in the morning. I figured Jessica and Lydia never went home if they were still trying so I turned it off, then yawned as I sat up.

I headed home that afternoon to make sure we'd gotten everything we'd need, or my mom would need. I knew she'd send me back and forth for any little item and it would've been the end of the world until she'd gotten it. Not that I would've minded, but her timing was never at decent hours.

When I had checked the upstairs and entered the kitchen, I heard the front door open.

"Dad?"

He paused in the doorway. He wore his coach's jacket for the football team, red and black. "Hey, honey..."

I gestured around. "I'm just making sure we didn't forget anything."

He grimaced. "You mean if Analise forgot anything."

"Yeah..."

He winced again and I bit my lip.

"Uh, dad...You weren't around this weekend."

"Yeah." He ran a hand over his face. "Your mother thought that would be for the best, if I cleared out. She didn't want any awkward run-ins."

"Oh."

His smile was painful. "Do you like your new home?"

"My new home?" I frowned. "This is still my home."

He looked away.

"Isn't it?"

His jaw clenched. "Your mother feels it's best if you stay with her, permanently."

"But...what? You're still my dad."

"I'll get to see you at school, honey."

"Dad!"

"I should get going. We're starting our Sunday practices. FC Public is going to be tough this Friday. We play them, you know, your new..."

I narrowed my eyes and spat out, "My new what? Roommates? My mom's boyfriend's sons? They aren't anything to me."

"Yes, well, it never hurt to make friends, Samantha."

I flinched at the sound of my full name. It was only used when I had disappointed him, once in seventeen years.

"I'll see you at school, honey." He moved past, and then hesitated for a moment. His hand patted my shoulder before he left. When the door shut, I released a ragged breath and sagged in a chair.

My life was screwed.

When I returned to the mausoleum, my mom was in the back patio area. I had to pass by to get to the stairs that were right next to my room. She saw me and called out, "Hi, honey. What'd you do today?"

James sat with her, but when I stepped outside he stood. "You can have my seat, Samantha."

I knew my mouth twisted into a scowl, but he waved a hand to the chair and gave me a polite smile before he disappeared inside.

Analise beamed at me. "Sit, sit. Let's chat."

I sat and glared.

She pushed a cup to me. "James didn't touch his coffee. You can have it. I know you like those coffee drinks."

It went ignored. "I went home today."

"Honey, this is your new home." She frowned and glanced towards the ocean. A divider wall sectioned off their backyard, but a small trail led from behind a door in the divider to the beach. "Isn't it beautiful here?"

"I saw dad."

She picked up her cup. "I just love tea."

"Since when?"

"Oh, Samantha. You're too funny sometimes. I've always liked tea."

"You've been a caffeine addict since I was little."

"Yes, well, I'm trying to wean myself from that. Tea is much better for you."

"And is James better for you too?"

She turned and set the cup down.

"Is he, Mom?"

"So you saw your father?" Her voice hardened. "He wasn't supposed to be there."

"At his own house?"

"I asked him to stay away. I knew you'd go back today to make sure we had remembered everything."

"You didn't want me to see him?"

"It's for the best, Samantha."

"For who? You? He's my father."

She patted my arm once and leaned back, tea back in hand. "You'll see him at school. Your tuition is still going to be paid."

"Why wouldn't it?"

"We're getting a divorce, honey. You do know that certain things in life change during these times."

"Yeah," I bit out. "Like families."

The corner of her mouth curved down and she set the tea down. Her hands were gentle as she placed it back on the cup holder. "I am your family, Samantha. It'll always be you and me, but now I have James. You should get to know Mason and Logan. They're very nice boys."

"And you've gotten to know them?"

"I have." She watched me. "A few times."

"When?" My stomach churned inside. My hands clasped onto the back of my seat.

"Over the last year, I've had dinner with them."

"Over the last year?"

"I did tell you that I left your father. We've been struggling for a long time, Sam. I know you noticed, though you never say anything. You should talk more, honey. It's healthier for you."

"You cheated on dad for a year?"

She sighed. "I didn't cheat—"

"You said a year. You've been cheating on dad for a year?" I leaned forward in the chair. "Did dad know?"

She rolled her eyes. "Like your father was a saint. It takes two to keep a marriage. David hasn't been around for years. You might want to ask him why he's been so absent too. Or didn't you notice?"

"He coaches a football team. He's gone a lot."

"Football season doesn't last a year, honey. You might want to wake up if you're going to start casting blame." Her voice was like whiplash.

I shoved back the chair. "It takes long hours, sometimes two practices a night. They're already starting their Sunday practices. They have training that lasts all year, mom. It's a private school. Their football program is a big deal there. I know all the hours it takes. Jeff's been on the team for three years."

She sighed again. "You and that Jeffrey boy, he isn't good for you either, Sam. His father's a mechanic and his mother works as a cashier at the grocery store. There isn't a future with him."

I reared back. "I'm not marrying him."

"I know you, Samantha. You've been dating him since before you were freshmen. And even I noticed that he cheats on you."

A cruel smile came to me. "You're right, mom. You would notice. Cheaters can always tell when they've met another cheater. Congrats on being in that special club."

I sailed inside, but stopped short. Mason and Logan both sat at a table. They watched me. I watched them and then I darted upstairs. It didn't take me long to change clothes and grab my iPod. When I went back downstairs, they were gone. It didn't matter. Nothing mattered.

I hit the driveway running and kept going. Running had always been an escape for me and it still was. I didn't return until it'd grown dark and my body could barely stay upright. When I walked back inside, the whole place was silent. Eerie. My footsteps echoed in the hallways.

When I went past the dining room, my mom spoke from the table, "You've taken up running again?"

I took out my headphones and stood there. Sweat dripped off of me and I wondered if she'd make some comment how I dirtied the floor.

She sighed to herself and stood. "I guess I shouldn't be surprised."

I mopped some of the sweat off my face.

"I had dinner with James and the boys. They asked about you, but I told them you were upset with me. And do me a favor, Sam, eat something tonight? I don't want to start worrying that your eating disorder is back."

When she went down a hall, I saluted her back and then extended my middle finger. Then I rolled my eyes and went to my room. After I showered, I sat down and turned my phone on. It beeped continuously. Jessica and Lydia were at a bonfire. There was no word from Jeff. Then I shut it back off and crawled in bed.

My first day of the school year was going to be exhausting. I knew the whole year would be. The weekend had just started it off with a bang.

CHAPTER THREE

It was the first day back and I was a junior this year. Before last weekend happened, I'd been ecstatic for the year. We were juniors, one year away from being seniors. Then IT happened and I had no idea how the day would go.

My dad was their varsity football coach. He was beloved by many rich fathers and even a few mothers. The guys respected him. And my mother had left him high and dry. As I walked towards my locker, I wasn't sure what reception I'd get. If people would sympathize with me or label me a whore, like mother like daughter and so on. But when a few of the football captains rushed past me without a second glance, I wondered if no one knew...

Then Jeffrey fell against the locker beside me. His hair was filled with mousse and he gave me a crooked grin.

Oh, those dimples, how they used to work on me.

He grunted. "You no showed all weekend. What's up with that?"

"After that great farewell you gave me on Friday?" I reached inside for my books. "I have no idea what you mean."

He rolled his eyes. "Come on, Sam. I texted you a ton and I apologized. You didn't text me back at all."

I shrugged.

"Jess and Lydia were hurt. They thought you'd show."

I shrugged again.

He sighed, "What's with the act, huh? What's wrong with you?"

My eyes snapped to his. "What are you talking about?"

"You've been weird since Friday. It's like someone died in your family or something. What's going on?"

"How was the party and bonfire?"

He sighed again. "Whatever. They were fine."

"Did you find another hot chick there?"

His jaw stiffened. "You're playing that card?"

"I'm playing a card? Why don't you tell which one it is because I'm not aware of the hand you've dealt me."

He pushed off from the locker, rolled his eyes, and strutted away.

I didn't do anything. I didn't curse, sigh, or feel like crying. What I did do was roll back my shoulders and put my bag in the locker. Another day, another adventure. I took two steps towards my English class before Jessica and Lydia bounded up to me, literally.

We all wore uniforms, but their skirts barely covered the bottom of their ass cheeks. A lot of girls had the same. My friends had their shirts unbuttoned to show off their cleavage, complete with the red and black lacy bras each of them wore.

"Hey..."

Lydia readjusted her shirt so more of her right boob showed. "You totally were absent this entire weekend. What's up with that?"

Jessica nodded with a solemn look on her. "We were worried about you."

"Really?" I arched my eyebrow up.

They both nodded, and then someone walked past us and down the hallway. Their expressions changed immediately. They went from seriousness to exuberance.

Jessica clamped onto my arm and leaned forward. "Ashley DeCortts and Adam Quinn broke up this weekend."

Lydia nodded. "We heard that Ashley slept with one of the Kade brothers. Adam found out and dumped her. It was real and public, at Kara's bonfire last night. I was front and center."

"She was."

"You were?"

"I was. It was awesome. Adam was all grrr and 'I thought we meant something to you,' and she was all, 'I did, but a girl can only do what a girl can do.' It was awesome. Totally. I wish that happened at every bonfire."

"You should've been there."

"Yeah," I deadpanned. "I should've been."

"So where were you?" Jessica asked, but both of their faces turned to blank masks as they stared at me.

"What?"

"Where were you? We went to your house, but no one was there. Lincoln said that your dad was at some conference over the weekend. Did you go with?"

"I had family commitments this weekend." I lifted my shoulders. "I wasn't supposed to say anything."

Lydia leaned closer. "It's football confidential?"

"Yeah."

Jessica frowned. "Really?"

"Really. My dad would get mad. I wasn't even supposed to say anything."

"Oh." Lydia looked at Jessica. "They do play Public this week. He might've gone to a conference for more pointers. That team is good, really good."

I clenched my jaw and my fingers tightened around my books. "What are you talking about?"

"Mason Kade." Lydia gave me a 'duh' look. "He's the star of that team. I heard Adam Quinn talking to Mark Decraw that he thought Kade can go pro some day. I'm not sure about Logan, but they were mainly focused on Mason. I think he's scared of him. He's the one that tackles, right? He can sack Adam the whole game, right?"

Jessica and I frowned at her.

Lydia rolled her eyes. "That's what I heard anyway, that Adam's scared of Mason Kade."

My fingers clenched tighter around the books and my knuckles went white. I was so sick of hearing about the Kade brothers, either of them. And I tried to remember if it'd always been like this, but I had never cared.

I was grateful when my class started and I tried to avoid Lydia and Jess the rest of the day. Bonus, no one else seemed interested in me. I didn't pick up any extra buzz about my dad so I was safe to bet that he hadn't spilled the beans. Everybody was more interested in the Double A break up, Ashley and Adam.

The week passed uneventfully. Lydia informed me on Wednesday that the Double A team was still broken up and Adam had been spotted by Nancy Burgess's locker that morning. Jessica made a disgusted sound and stomped away. I thought I heard a few curse words, but wasn't sure. Probably.

And I met Jeff for pizza that night. He liked the buffet, I liked the salad bar.

"You need a ride home?" he asked as we went back to the parking lot.

"Nope. I drove, remember?"

A look passed over him. "Yeah, about that—why did you drive? I usually pick you up."

I shrugged as we came to my car. "I'm going to Lydia's after this. It makes sense."

"Oh. Okay..." His frown never left and then he leaned in for a kiss.

I breathed out as our lips touched and felt his hand cup my cheek. His lips were soft and he didn't apply pressure. As his thumb stroked my cheek, I let out a soft moan.

Jeff smiled and rested his forehead against mine. "That was nice, huh?"

"We've been doing this for three years. It should feel nice."

He chuckled and kissed me again. This time he was more insistent, harder. I leaned back against my car and Jeff pressed against me. His hand tilted my head up and his kiss grew more demanding. When his tongue swept in, I pulled away.

"What?"

169

"What do you mean 'what'?" I pushed him back. "I don't want to make out on the street."

He rolled his eyes. "What do you expect? Is this why you drove here, so you wouldn't have to kiss me?"

"What are you talking about?"

"Come on, Sam. We used to be hot and heavy, but the last couple months you're ice cold."

"I didn't think you cared. You've been so distracted lately." I bit my tongue.

His mouth clamped shut. "What are you talking about?"

I took in the storm in his eyes, how his jaw was clenched and the stiffness of his shoulders. And something gave way in me. This wasn't a fight I wanted right now. At least, this wasn't the fight that I wanted.

I glanced away. "Nothing. It doesn't matter."

He touched the back of my elbow. "Hey, what doesn't matter?"

I didn't look back, but some tension left me at the softness of his voice.

"You think I'm cheating on you?"

I met his gaze now. "It's nothing, Jeff. I've got a lot on my mind."

"Like what?"

"Like how I need to get going. My mom's been on a rampage about family time. The longer I'm at Lydia's the later I'll be. You know what she's like."

He still frowned, but nodded. "Yeah, okay. You want me to pick you up for school tomorrow?"

"I'm good. I've got a car."

"That's not the point, Sam."

"I know." I didn't care.

He sighed and turned away. "You're kinda being a bitch, you know."

As I watched him go, I stood there. I knew I was being a bitch, that wasn't the problem. Then I sighed when my phone vibrated. Lydia wanted me to hurry so I got in the car and drove over.

When I got there, she was bouncing like a rabbit on meth. She squealed as she pulled me to her room. "Jessica told me today that Adam Quinn asked about you!"

My insides snapped to attention. "What?"

"Yeah." She grinned and nodded her head up and down. "Can you believe it?"

I watched as some drool slipped down her chin. "Why would he ask about me?"

"Who cares! He did. Aren't you excited?"

"What did he say?"

"Are you kidding me? I think he asked how you were doing. You want a soda?"

"You've had enough for both of us."

"Huh?" She stopped bouncing and stared at me.

"Nothing."

Then she grabbed my arm again. "Get excited, Samantha. You can dump Jeff, finally."

"Dump him? Why?"

She snorted and threw herself backward on the bed. As she landed with her arms spread out, she rolled her eyes. "Like you really care about the guy. When was the last time you went out with him?"

"Tonight. We just had dinner."

She stopped short and jerked upright. "Really?"

"Yeah." I sat at her desk. "Why?"

"You and Jeff had dinner tonight? As in right before you came here?"

"What's with the twenty questions? Yes. I had dinner. With my boyfriend. Who I have been dating for three years."

"Oh." Her mouth shut, though her eyes were still wide.

"I get interrogated for this?" I stood up and started for the door.

"Don't go!" she called out and caught my arm. Then she sat me down with a serious expression on her face. "So if Adam Quinn asked you out, you'd say...?"

"No. I have a boyfriend." I frowned. "What's going on with you? You're acting like Jeff and I broke up."

She lifted her shoulders weakly. "Well...you two don't act together."

"That's crap. What's really going on? You always ask me about Jeff, if I've seen him at the parties or whatever." I folded my arms over my chest.

Then I stared her down. Hard.

Lydia swallowed. "I, just, I, nothing. Adam Quinn would make a way better boyfriend than Jeff. He was faithful to Ashley when they were together. She wasn't, but that's beside the point. Come on, you can't turn Adam Quinn down because of Jeff."

"Uh, yeah I can."

"Jeff cheats on you every weekend." She jumped to her feet.

"So I've heard." I grabbed my bag and headed out the door.

"Wait, Sam. Don't go like this. I'm sorry."

"For what?" I whirled around to her.

She stopped an inch from running into me and her mouth opened, closed, and then opened again. Her eyes looked to the ceiling. "Uh, for...hoping you'll dump Jeff because he's a scumbag?"

"Thanks, Lydia." I headed for my car. When I shut the door behind me, she had stopped following. I saw she had the phone to her ear so I turned mine off. Jess would be calling in a minute, after she'd heard the whole story from Lydia first.

I didn't care. As I drove away, I sat back. I really didn't care, about any of it. And I knew in the back of my mind, far far in the back of my mind, that this wasn't the healthiest feeling. But then again, I didn't care.

When I walked inside, it was dark. No one was around, but a plate was left on the kitchen table with a sandwich wrapped in saran wrap. My name was posted next to it, but I bypassed it and headed upstairs for my running gear. Five minutes later and I was back out the door. This time, I only stayed away an hour. However, sweat still ran down me as I went into the kitchen for a glass of water.

I sat at the kitchen table to finish it because I knew I'd need a refill before I headed upstairs to shower and crawl in bed for the night.

I was almost done when the door burst open and laughter filled the room. The smell of perfume and booze followed behind. I slumped further down in my chair and watched when Mason came into the kitchen. He turned for the fridge and stuck his head inside. Logan came next with a blonde wrapped around his arm. Her top barely hung on her and it exposed the side of her breast.

He laughed and pressed her back against a counter. As his head sunk to her neck, Mason glanced up and stopped. He saw me in the darkness.

Neither of us said a thing. Neither of us looked away.

The girl shrieked when Logan nuzzled further down her top.

Then he drew back, grinning. "Mase, man, you think I should bang her here? You think Momma-Wannabe would be upset? My stuff next to her teacups? Oh, a sandwich." He unwrapped the one left for me and ate it in three bites. When he was done, he gulped down a glass of water Mason held out for him and then turned back for the girl.

She started laughing again, followed by a quick moan.

Mason leaned against the sink. He never broke eye contact with me and he folded his arms over his chest. "You can do her wherever you want."

Logan tickled the underside of her breast and the girl giggled. Then she looked up, panting. Her eyes roamed up and down Mason as she asked in a husky voice, "You want in, Mason? You can have me too."

Logan burst out laughing, and then clamped a hand on her arm. "I think not. I don't share like that. You're mine for the night, girl."

When he dragged her away, she reached out and trailed a finger across the top of Mason's bicep. As they went up the stairs, she was still squealing and it wasn't long before he told her to shut up or Momma Wannabe might wake up and no one would get laid that night. Then it was quiet in the kitchen.

I hadn't moved a muscle, but I did now. I pushed back the chair, crossed to the fridge and refilled my glass. The hair on the back of my neck stood up. With stiff movements, I turned, ignored the scalding burn from his gaze, and headed upstairs. As I got to my room, I shut the door behind me and let loose a long breath of relief.

I was surprised to find my fingers were frozen around my glass. It took a few moments before I was able to loosen them back up.

CHAPTER FOUR

Friday night came and went. I stayed in, but Fallen Crest Public won against Fallen Crest Academy by a landslide, 32 to seven. I knew my dad would be heartbroken, but I still felt as if he had kicked me out of the house. My sympathy scale was in the negatives. The only high point was that Jessica and Lydia were both so hyped about the parties; they forgot to harass me into going. Jeff did the same, though I knew he was always sore after a loss. Even if he didn't play since he's second string, I knew he'd be grumpier than normal.

Apparently, my new roommates were the highlights of the game. Mason sacked Adam seventy percent of the time and Logan ran in for three of the touchdowns. I got all that from Lydia's text messages.

"Honey, are you going out tonight?" My mom found me the next afternoon. She came into my room and took a seat on one of the couches with a cup of tea in her hand.

I was in the bathroom and had just gotten out of the shower. When I saw her curl her legs underneath and tuck them away, as if she were sitting with the Queen of England, I snorted in disbelief. Then I let loose the towel I had wrapped around me and walked into the room.

"Samantha!" she gasped and glanced at the door. It'd been left open.

I stood and perused my closet. Ignoring the shiver that ran over my naked body, I pulled out a pair of black skinny jeans with a black tank top.

"Honey, I wish you'd put some clothes on."

I pulled out a black lacy bra and a pair of black thongs.

She sighed behind me. "I suppose this is you trying to get back at me, hmmm?" She took a sip. "I should expect this. Malaya said this is what teenagers do when they've been displaced from their homes, especially girls. I can only wonder what else you have in store for me."

I threw the thong to the side and pulled the jeans on. Then I glanced in the mirror. Analise's mouth twisted in a frown, but she took another sip.

"Are you sleeping with that Jeffrey? Is this why you're dressing like some..."

I turned around, slowly. "Like what, mother?"

Her lips shut for a moment and then she exhaled, "Like a whore."

One of my eyebrows shot up. "You think I'm a whore?"

She set the tea cup aside and smoothed out her skirt. "I think you're dressing like one because you want to get back at me. You never used to dress like that."

"Yeah, well, I used to have a family." I ducked my head and pulled the top on. When it fit like a glove, just above my jeans, I leaned forward to inspect my face in the mirror. I wasn't anything great, long black hair, thin with a runner's build, and eyes that were bleak.

"Samantha, honey, I worry about you. You're so beautiful and I know that other boys can tell."

I looked back at her. "What are you talking about?"

"Jeffrey." Her hand raised in a helpless motion. "I worry that you're wasting your high school years on him. He is clearly not good for you. Look at you; you're thin as a rail."

My mouth twisted.

"He obviously cheats on you. Even your friends have told me this."

"You've talked to Jessica and Lydia?"

"Of course, I have. They're your friends."

"When?"

"What?"

"When did you talk to them?"

"Oh, I don't know, maybe a month ago."

As a breath of relief left me, I turned back to the mirror and did up my hair in some braid. Jessica taught me how to do it so I tried. It didn't look the same, but it'd do. It was swept up and some strands fell free. I knew Lydia would croon in approval. Then I toed on my sandals.

"Where are you going, Samantha?"

I'd been prepared to walk out and ignore whatever else she was going to say, hell, I would've enjoyed it, but her soft voice made me stop. I cursed inside as I turned. "I'm going to some party with Lydia and Jessica."

"Oh."

I wanted to roll my eyes. I wanted so badly. "Why?" I didn't.

"I think Mason and Logan are going to a friend's get together. Maybe you could go with them? You can't keep ignoring them."

Her idea of a 'get together' was their idea of a 200+ house party. I wasn't sure if my mom chose to be dense or if this came from the new relationship.

"Sure, mom. I'll get right on that."

She sighed, "Honey, at least try for me, please. It's important to me if you get along with them."

I stopped what I was doing and watched her in the mirror. If I hadn't known her all my life, I would've wavered at the broken look on her face. It was like she'd lost her puppy. Then I cursed myself. I knew I was wavering anyway.

"I'll see if Jess and Lydia know about any Public parties. I'm sure Mason and Logan will be there."

She brightened and flashed me a smile before she picked up her tea again. "It means a lot to me, honey." Then she pressed a kiss to my forehead and sashayed out of my room with her skirt swinging around her hips.

I'd been sucker punched by my own mother. She'd gotten me to fold.

Then I looked in the mirror again and changed everything. The black was thrown to the side and instead I pulled on a pair of pink skintight pants with a flesh-colored sparkly top that molded to my body. I grinned as I turned and headed out. My mom would've had a heart attack if she'd seen the new outfit.

Instead, I was content with Jessica and Lydia's reactions.

Jessica frowned and twisted her shirt in her hands. Lydia's eyes popped out and her mouth kept opening and closing like a fish. Finally she remarked, "You look good, Sam."

"Hot damn," one guy remarked as he and his friends moved past.

Another one gave me a wolf whistle while a third asked if he could feel me up. The last one asked if I'd go to dinner, but I grinned until I felt a pair of hands snake around my waist. I was pulled back against a body and a pair of lips started on my neck. I heard the chuckle and relaxed, slightly.

Jeff whispered in my ear, "Can we please go somewhere? You walked in that door and I got hard."

"Sweet nothings. That's what I look forward to from you." I patted his cheek and walked away.

He groaned behind, but followed. His hand curved around my waist and he pulled me close again. "Seriously, Sam. I've got an itch that I really want you to scratch."

At that moment, a guy burst through the crowd and landed beside us, against the counter. He glanced over with glazed eyes, but threw his head back and started howling. Some guys' answered and Jeff's hand tightened on my arm. When it increased and became painful I started to say something, but the crowd parted at that moment.

My words died in my throat.

Mason and Logan walked through the crowd with a few of their friends beside them. They strode forward as if they owned the party, which it felt like they did. It was a Public party. Jeff and I were next to the drinks so they stopped close. Logan skimmed an eye over us and grinned, but turned and grabbed a bottle. He started pouring drinks while Mason took one that was offered from someone. His eyes were locked with mine.

After a moment, Jeff nudged me. "You know Kade?"

"No," I clipped out and shoved through the crowd.

The group howled again as Jeff followed behind.

Lydia found us in a back room later on. She gripped a cup in her hand with a drunken haze over her eyes. "Did you see them?"

Jeff groaned. He had a hand curled around my waist and he'd been kissing my neck for the last hour. He pulled away and fell back against the couch now.

"Them?"

"Mason and Logan Kade."

My frown was quick. I couldn't block it.

Jeff noticed. "You sure you don't know them?"

"I don't need to know them to not like them."

Lydia swooned, "Mason is so gorgeous. Maybe I should tell them I was at the gas station that night. I bet he'd talk to me then. Maybe I will." She looked hopeful as she scanned the room.

"Pretty sure he went upstairs half an hour ago with some blonde," Jeff clipped out.

She frowned. "Oh."

"Where's Jessica?"

The excitement burst forth again as Lydia turned back. "She's in the back playing pool with Logan Kade."

"Really?"

Jeff shifted beside me on the couch. "I'm going to get something to drink. Sam?"

I held out my cup, but he left without it.

As I frowned after him, Lydia took his seat. "She's not playing with just him, but a bunch of others. I'm sure he doesn't even notice her, but maybe. Maybe they'll start to date. Could you imagine that? Being Logan Kade's girlfriend?"

"He's not that great, Lydia."

She frowned. Some of the drunken haze tried to clear up. "What do you mean? Have you talked to him?" Then she nodded to herself. "That'd make sense. You were out there. You saw the whole thing. Did they threaten you? You've never said a word about the car bombs. People don't know that you witnessed the whole thing. I bet they told you to shut up about it, didn't they?"

I gripped her arm tight.

She kept on, "Can you imagine being threatened by them? I'd have a hard time trying not to jump in their arms. Mason's so dreamy..."

Some people near us started to pay attention to the conversation. I saw their glances and as she rambled on, I felt more and more attention. My hand squeezed harder. "Lydia."

"Huh?" She tried again to focus on me.

"Shut up." I had a death grip on her now.

She gave me a silly smile. "Or did you get it on with them? I wouldn't blame you, especially with Jeff. Who cares about him, right?"

I snapped and stood up. "Would you give it a rest? They're not that great and my love life, if it is one or not, isn't your business."

When I whirled to stalk out of the room, I stopped short. Logan stood in the doorway with a cup in hand and a pool stick in the other. Some of his friends were around, but Jessica had a hand on his arm. She frowned when she saw me, but glanced up to Logan with a small smile on her lips.

Logan narrowed his eyes with his mouth in a firm line. I watched how his hands gripped the cup tighter. And then I stormed out. I didn't care if I pissed him off or not. Hell, I would've enjoyed that.

I tried to head for the front door, but there were so many people. I kept getting lost and so I headed up the stairs. It was empty and it was somewhere I could gather my sanity again. However, as I pushed into a bedroom, I hadn't expected to find Jeff in the bed with another girl.

He glanced over his shoulder with a scowl, but his eyes went wide. The girl twisted out from underneath him and tried to pull down her black tube top. Lipstick was smeared over both of their faces.

I gutted out in a laugh, "Are you kidding me?"

"Sam, wait." He scrambled off the bed. I turned to bolt, but he caught my arm in the hallway. "Wait. Please."

"I'm not even surprised." I spoke in a calm voice. My heart was racing. I knew my face must've been red because I felt my blood boiling. My arms, legs, knees, everything trembled and shook, but my voice sounded like I had asked if it was raining.

He paused and watched me.

"Isn't this the cliché ending to us?"

"Ending?" His Adam's apple moved up and down.

"Yeah," I laughed outright now and swept a hand towards the bedroom. "You were making out with another girl."

He narrowed his eyes and pulled up his pants.

A door opened behind him. It was quiet, so quiet that if I hadn't seen it, I wouldn't have sensed his presence. Mason came out with a skinny blonde on his arm. She looked unable to stand, but I saw his hand grip underneath her legs and he lifted her against him. She hung on around his neck and leaned a head against his chest with a contented smile on her face. He narrowed his eyes when he saw me.

Then Jeff broke the spell. "I know it looks bad."

"Looks bad?" I spat out. "Are you dense?"

"Yeah, well, you had me going so hard all night." He gestured at me. "Look at you, Sam. You're hot, hella hot. And I get nothing. I've been your boyfriend for three years. It's taken me a damn year and half to see your tits."

My eyes turned to a glare.

He ran a hand through his haphazard hair. "I'll change, Sam. I've gotta. I love you."

"You don't love me." I said it quietly.

"Three years. That's gotta mean something. Please, Sam."

"You don't love me."

He looked ready to argue, then something flashed over his face, and a snarl came out instead. "Why don't you get off your high horse? Fine, we're done. I'm not even going to kiss your ass. It hasn't done me a damn thing in the three years we've been dating or the two it took me to get you. I can be half the nice guy I am to you and I've got no problem getting panties to drop."

I geared myself.

He spat out, "You're just some high class bitch that ain't high class, Sam."

Mason lifted his head. His eyes remained narrowed to slits, but no other reaction came from him. His face was a blank mask.

I tore my eyes from his and found my soon to be ex boyfriend's in a glower. "Don't you want to know who I've been with? You don't have any inkling?"

"I know that you've been cheating on me. Even my mother knew."

"That makes you look like a fool." A cruel smirk came to him. He stuck his hands in his pockets and a prideful look came over him.

"Maybe. Or maybe I didn't give a crap."

He grew quiet. "Yeah, you're screwed up, Sam. I've never known another girl who'd stay with a guy if he cheated the whole time."

My heart skipped a beat. The whole time?

He laughed again. The sound sent shivers up my spine. "You've got no clue who with, do you? You've got piss poor taste in friends."

"Friends?" I wrung out. My eyes gleamed with an ugly feeling.

He was so smug. "Jess has been giving it to me for two years now."

"Jess."

"And Lydia knew. She's known the whole time. She's helped us cover it up too."

"Lydia knew?" I parroted like a fool.

Jeff chuckled and shook his head. "I'd be up here with her now if she wasn't so obsessed with Kade. Ever since the car bombing, it's all either of them talk about. I told her to get straight. The Kade brothers are going down. They set fire to those cars. The cops have to know—"

Mason started to step forward.

I cried out, "Shut up. You don't know a thing about it!"

Jeff frowned.

"I was there. I was outside and you don't know anything. Jessica and Lydia were inside. They didn't see a thing. They were wasted that night."

Mason moved back a step. The girl on his arm looked up with concern, but settled back against his chest a moment later.

"It don't matter. They'll get what's coming to them." His mouth curled up in an ugly smile.

I slapped him. When it was done, his head snapped back and he stared at me, his eyes wide. The air had grown thick, tense. I found it hard to breathe. Then I turned and left. This time I found the front door and I drove off. The hand I slapped him with shook even after I got home and crawled in bed. I tucked it under me and tried to go to sleep.

I never fell asleep that night.

CHAPTER FIVE

When the morning came, I rolled out of bed and went for a run. I didn't last long, four or five miles, but I slowed to a walk and I didn't return home till noon. When I did, I was surprised to find a bunch of cars parked in the driveway and on the road. Then I rounded to the back patio and saw a ton of people by the pool area. The door in the divider wall was open and more people were on the beach.

The Kades were having a party. Joy.

Then I checked my phone after I had showered and ate a few crackers. Lydia and Jessica both wanted to know where I'd gone from the party and why I hadn't said goodbye. I turned my phone back off. There was no one else I cared about who would call.

As I headed to the kitchen, Mousteff was there in his chef's white apron and he wore a hat too. He brandished a cutting knife and gestured to the table in front of him.

"Sit," he grunted.

I sat.

He sliced up some meat and put it between two pieces of homemade bread. A parsley and tomato were placed on the side before he set the plate in front of me. A knife and fork were plunked beside it, along with a glass of water.

"Eat," he grunted again.

An apple was cut up next. He put the bowl beside me, turned his back, and left. I didn't see him for the rest of the day.

Later in the afternoon, I headed back to the kitchen for some water. When I went past the patio, I peeked out again and saw the group hadn't left. A bonfire had been lit on the beach and most of the people were around that now. Loud bass blared through the windows. It got louder when a door opened and closed.

I didn't glance up, but Mason stepped next to me. He reached around me and pulled out a pitcher. When he moved back to pull out a glass, I let out my breath. I hadn't known I'd been holding it.

I didn't turn around. No way.

Suddenly the door flew open again. Logan's voice carried through as he howled and ran through the house. Then a car door was slammed shut in the front of the house. When I looked over I saw Mason watching through the kitchen window. A small smile was on his face. He looked softer, just a bit.

My stomach kicked a notch.

I spread a hand against it and frowned. What the hell was I doing?

Then the front door was thrown open and we heard Logan holler, "Finally! Dude!"

Male laughter responded. When Mason left the kitchen window, I took his place and saw Logan trying to dry hump some guy. I didn't recognize him, but they had so many friends. He was tall, over six feet and his jet black hair matched with Mason's. The two almost looked like twins. While he went out to greet the new arrival, both gave each other a hug with a smile on their faces. It was so genuine, that I clenched my hands around my glass and turned away.

I didn't come out of my room for the rest of the day. When I did, it was past ten in the evening. The party was still full force outside by the beach. No one was beside the pool and I was surprised by that. Then I checked my phone and regretted it. Lydia sent me a text: **Jeff said you guys broke up. CALL ME!**

I turned it off and put on a movie.

My body was tired so I did nothing on Sunday, except for the little homework I already had. I heard my mom's voice once when I ventured downstairs, but Mousteff told me, "Mr. and Other are gone for day. Cooking in cities is better than cooking at home. No one cares. You eat." And he dumped a bowl of soup in front of me with some crackers on the side. When he went back to the kitchen I heard him muttering to himself.

It was late when I heard Mason and Logan in the hallway. A third male's voice was with them so I assumed that it was the guy from before.

"Nah, man. That's her room. You're parked in the east wing." Logan's voice carried down the hall.

Two doors shut after that and it was silent for the rest of the night.

When I left for school, Mousteff stuck his hand out as I passed by. He held a brown bag to me and barked, "Eat. Lunch."

I took it and there was more muttering as I left. I couldn't hold back a small grin, but it was gone when Lydia and Jessica caught me at my locker.

"What happened with Jeff?" Lydia sounded breathless.

Jessica frowned and readjusted her hold on her books. "You never reply to my calls anymore. You're not a very good friend."

I slammed my locker shut. "Get away from me you whores."

Lydia gasped, "Me?"

Jessica got red in the face and hurried away.

I watched her go, but when Lydia stayed I snapped, "You covered for them. A disloyal bitch is the same as any other disloyal bitch. Shove off, Lydia. I don't want anything to do with you."

She hung her head, but glanced up quickly. Her feet shuffled in place and she said in a hush before she scampered away, "Adam Quinn is going to ask you out. Everybody's talking about it."

I closed my eyes, not something I wanted to deal with.

When I went to my last class, my lab partner kept glancing at me. After the twelfth time, I sat back. "You got something to say?"

She looked around and then pulled back her red curls from her face. It didn't matter. The frizzy hair clung to her skin. She didn't seem to mind. Her excitement couldn't be contained when she leaned forward. Her pudgy elbow rammed mine off the table. "You and Jeff Sallaway broke up, right?"

I nodded and crossed my arms over my chest.

"Is it true that Adam Quinn asked you out?"

I lifted an eyebrow.

A high-pitched squeal left her. It sounded like laughter. "He was asking your friends about you this weekend."

"They're not my friends."

"Oh." Her eyes kept darting around. "So are you gonna say yes?"

"Who are you?"

"My name's Becky Sallaway."

My mouth quirked up. "You're Jeff's cousin?"

She shifted in her seat. "Only through marriage. My mom married his dad's brother. Are you going to go out with Adam Quinn?"

"Why are you asking me? Did Jeff ask you to?"

Her mouth gaped open a second before her pasty white cheeks matched the color of her hair. "That pipsqueak? He's a loser. Not like Adam Quinn."

And she wasn't one? I rolled my eyes. "Why do you care so much?"

She shrugged. "Maybe I want to be friends."

"Friends are overrated."

"Not if you've got good ones."

"And you're going to be a good one?"

"Better than those two. Jessica Larsen's been jealous of you since sixth grade when Forrest Adams thought you were cute and Lydia Thompson doesn't have the backbone to be a good friend. She always does what Jessica tells her. Everyone knows that. I've always wondered why you didn't know that."

I sighed. "He hasn't asked, but the word is that he's going to."

"Are you going to say yes?"

The bell rang and I scooted my chair back. "Why don't you say yes for me?"

She hurried to catch up as I started to shoulder my way out the door and to my locker. The day had been long and I was in need of a good tiring run.

Panting, she tried to mop back her hair again. "Do you really want me to? I'll go find him right now."

"Sure."

When she stopped and headed one way, I kept going. The girl was a freak. But then a different freak planted herself in my path.

I groaned on the inside while I couldn't hold back a snarl. "Jill."

She tilted her chin up and her blue eyes flashed. As she flipped her bleach blonde hair over her shoulder, she responded, "Samantha."

I started to move around.

She blocked me.

"What do you want?"

"I'm dating Jeff."

Nothing surprised me anymore. "That was quick. You two been scooting and booting for a while?" Then I gave her a smile. "Are you my homewrecker?"

She narrowed her eyes. "Jeff asked me out last night. I've decided to date him."

"And you're going to make him change?"

The bottom of her uniform top started to ride up her waist. She reached down to pull it down, but stopped. A satisfied grin came to her and she let it up even further. One of her hands moved to the bottom of her skirt. She pulled it down an inch so her hipbones showed, along with the black thong she wore.

"Look at you," I purred. "You wanna be Britney Spears? Wear the pigtails tomorrow. I'm sure Jeff would love it."

She moved closer. "Only when I give him head."

"That's the spirit."

Her smug smile slipped a bit. I knew she was a cheerleader, she'd forgotten that.

"You do know he cheated on me with my best friend for two years, right?"

"He won't with me."

I laughed. "He won't cheat with you or he won't cheat on you? I'm sure both will happen."

"Jessica Larsen won't be sleeping with him anymore. She only did it to get back at you and from what I've heard; she's close to getting Logan Kade to date her."

"Yeah." I threw my head back and laughed. "You'll be luckier thinking Jeff won't cheat on you."

"He's wanted me for years." She pulled the other side of her skirt down as well, readjusted her hold on her books, and arched her back slightly. Her breasts were on display as people went past; the guys had stopped a while ago and were watching. I heard the whispers and knew this'd be all over school, probably already was.

"And you're the Mecca for his dating daydreams?" I caught sight of Becky on the sidelines. Her cheeks were inflamed and she pointed to the corner. When I looked over, I saw a confused Adam Quinn against the wall with some of his football teammates. He pushed some of his blonde hair out of his eyes and scratched his forehead.

Then Ashley DeCortts pushed through the crowd. She sidled next to Jill and touched her on the arm. "What are you doing, Jill?"

"I'm making my stand." Her eyes drilled into me.

I rolled my eyes and snorted. "Are you kidding me? You can have Jeff. I don't want him back." Then I thought about it again. "I haven't wanted Jeff for a couple years now."

Someone gasped. Someone laughed. And I turned to leave, but I stopped when I saw him right behind me. A look of hurt was evident when he met my gaze for a second.

My jaw hardened and I pushed through the crowd.

When I saw the men's locker room door was open and no one was inside, I went without thinking. My dad's office was in the back and his door was open. I paused in the doorway. I'd rarely come to his office because of where it was, but I took a deep breath. I was there now.

The small bathroom that attached to his office had the door closed. The toilet flushed and a moment later he came out, drying his hands.

He froze for a brief moment. "Samantha."

"Hi." I glanced over my shoulder. Male voices carried through the room and I heard them coming closer so I closed the door and sat in one of his chairs.

"What are you doing here?"

I hugged my books on my lap. "I haven't seen you since we moved out."

"Yeah...I know." He sounded tired as he sat behind his desk. His body was tense and his finger started to tap on his chair. I watched as it continued to tap, a habit I knew he did whenever he was nervous.

"How are you?"

A small grin appeared. "I'm okay. I'm the one who's supposed to ask you how you are."

One of my shoulders shrugged. "I'm not the one who's getting a divorce."

"Yeah, there's that."

"Jeff and I broke up."

"Oh?"

"He was cheating on me."

My dad's face remained void of any reaction.

My hands twisted together in front of my books and I looked down at my lap. "With Jessica. You remember her, right?"

There was silence.

I ploughed on, "For two years and Lydia knew. She helped them lie about it."

I waited and then after a minute, he asked in a quiet voice, "Why are you telling me this, Samantha?"

"What do you mean?" I looked up now. I needed something; I was looking for it in him. I didn't know quite what, though.

"I'm sorry that Jeffrey cheated on you. That's a horrible thing to find out."

"Like you and mom?" I swallowed thickly.

He froze again. His finger stopped tapping. And then a deep breath left him and he hung his head a moment. When he looked up again, I reeled back. The pain was so clear, so evident in his eyes. I was speechless for a moment.

He choked out, "I can't keep lying to you, Samantha."

Lying? "Dad?"

He closed his eyes and looked away. "I'm not your father."

I laughed.

"I mean it, Sam. I'm not your biological father." He caught my gaze again.

He was serious. I saw it in them and a flare of pain stabbed me in the gut. I almost bowled over, but my fingers caught my chair's sides and dug in. My books fell to the floor, one of them thumped on top of my toe. I didn't feel it. I was caught in his eyes and I felt seared by them and by his words.

Something cracked. I lifted my hand and saw blood trickling down from underneath my nails.

"Sam, let go of the chair."

"What?" I jerked my chin upright. I couldn't see him. He had blurred and there was two of him. They were starting to swim around.

"Let go."

I opened my mouth. No sound came out.

Then he got up and rounded my chair. He forcibly lifted my other hand and there was more blood from that one. Two of my nails were gone.

He cursed under his breath and left.

My head slammed to my lap and I gasped for breath. No way. There was no way...

Footsteps were heard coming back and hands lifted me in the air. There were more faces now, but I didn't pay them attention.

"Put her on the trainer's couch. Quinn, get the nurse."

I was placed on my back and both of my hands were lifted in the air. I felt some cool liquid poured on them as they poked and prodded. I looked at the ceiling. The white tiles above me looked like they were mocking me.

"Sam. I'm sorry." His voice was muffled close to me. His hand brushed some of my hair from my forehead. "She made me keep that secret all your life. I should've told you a long time ago. Analise didn't want—"

The footsteps were coming back. They were louder this time. My head rolled to the side and I saw a nurse and another man hurrying to me, they looked like they were moving through the air. Some guys were behind them.

"Get 'em all out, Quinn," my dad barked.

I frowned. Not my dad. David.

"What, honey?" He bent low to me.

"You're just David now."

He frowned and closed his eyes. He seemed to struggle with something and then when he opened them, they looked bleak. He looked how I did now. "Yes, Samantha. I guess I am."

CHAPTER SIX

Becky sat next to me where the sidewalk dipped to the parking lot. I'd been there after the school's nurse had tended to my hands and after my da—David took the football team to the field for practice. That'd been around four. It was six now.

"I don't understand why you won't let me drive you home," Becky grumbled.

I stared straight ahead.

"You want something to eat? Let's get something to eat. I'll drive."

I jerked my head in a nod and stood up. When we got to her car, I winced as I tried to open the door. Becky hissed and moved me out of the way. She opened the door for me, and then climbed on her side. As she started the car, she muttered, "And you expect to be able to drive home like that? You can't even open a door. You're crazy."

I grinned. "I thought you were going to be a good friend."

"I am and I'm telling the truth. You're crazy."

That shut me up.

Her voice took on a giddy note. "Did you see how Adam was hovering over you? It was so romantic."

I hadn't. I'd been distracted.

"You guys are going to make a great couple. I can already tell."

"How?"

"What?"

"How can you tell? You don't even know me."

"Well... Okay, I'm being honest here, but you weren't all fabulous before. I mean, I've always known who you are.

We're lab partners, seriously, but I didn't care. But something changed with you this year. I have no idea what, but it's like you don't care anymore." When we pulled into a coffee shop, she laughed. "Then you showed up at that party in that outfit. It sounds stupid, I know, but there's just something about you, like you're a mystery or something. Everyone knew Jeff wanted you hardcore that night. And everyone knows he's been cheating on you. Then you showed up today and you told off those pathetic excuses for friends."

"Are you obsessed with me?" My hands were starting to throb. I sucked in a breath when I tried to flex one hand, but stopped right away. What the hell had I done?

She laughed another one of those high-pitched squeals and flipped the red curls over again.

I cringed.

"Um, no. Are you crazy? I mean, you are, but are you?" Her laugh weakened. She turned to face me in the car. "I've known Adam all my life. He's my neighbor and he's a good guy. He's one of *the* good guys. I was thrilled when he broke up with Ashley."

"So why don't you date him?"

Her cheeks got red again and her hands started to fidget in her lap before she tugged her skirt further over her knees. She mumbled something then.

"What?"

When she looked back up, her whole face was red. "I'm not good enough for him. I'm fat. I know it. Everyone knows it. Your friends used to call me hippo every day until—they still do."

I frowned.

"Anyways, I'm happy that he likes you. Last year I wouldn't think you had any balls. I mean, look at who you were. You had two sleazy best friends and an even sleazier boyfriend. They were all sleazy together behind your back. Some people thought you were stupid or had special needs or something."

"Thanks," I said dryly.

She brightened. "Now you're awesome. Jill Flatten tried to decimate you and you got away from her, easy as pie. No one does that. And you made her look stupid too."

"Is that hard to do?"

"Ashley DeCortts is afraid of her. That says something."

I grinned. "Are you going to buy me dinner now? All this flattery, then you drove me, now's the food part? What's next? A movie and a drink?"

She went back to tugging her skirt down again.

"Relax." I caught one of her hands, but grimaced from the contact. My hands were going to be in rare form for a while. I swallowed the pain down. "I'm sorry I'm not as excited about Adam Quinn. I don't know him. I've never cared to know him either."

She turned to the window and mumbled under her breath, "He's only the best guy in school. That's all who he is."

"I think you should try for him."

A corner of her mouth twitched up. "He doesn't like me like that. He's interested in you."

"Okay, well, we'll have to wait and see, hmmm?" I elbowed my door. "Can you help me out over here?"

"Oh." She scrambled around the car and opened my door. As we walked inside, she started to bounce up and down. "I picked up an application here for a job. I'm hoping to work here. I think it'd be awesome. Everyone cool comes here, you know."

"When'd you turn your application in?"

"A month ago."

"Have they called for an interview?"

Her smile dimmed when we approached the counter. "The girl said they were fully staffed, but they'd call when they had some openings."

A Help Wanted sign hung underneath the cash register.

"Can I help you?" A brightly smiling petite girl waited for our orders.

I shook my head. "No."

"What? I like this place." Becky hurried after me towards the door.

"You tore into me how I let people walk over me last year. If we're friends, then take my advice. Don't let this place walk over you." I pushed open the door and started to step out, but a wall slammed into me from the side.

I cried out and blinked past tears from the sudden pain. It speared through me, but hands caught my shoulders and set me to the side.

"Oh....hi..." Becky had become a third grade little girl.

I sucked in my breath through my teeth and tried to numb down the pain. It felt like fire as it bolted up my arms and through my legs. I couldn't see for a moment when more tears kept threatening to spill out.

A voice asked, "What happened to her hands?"

Becky shuffled around on the sidewalk. I could hear her blushing. "She had an accident."

"Did she scratch some girl's eyeballs out or something?" The same voice laughed and another male voice joined in.

"I dunno. She won't tell me." Becky's voice had grown soft, even weak.

Enough of my tears had cleared and I was able to see who was in front of us.

My heart stopped. Of course. My luck.

Mason was in front with Logan beside him and their friend on his other side. Logan had been the one asking. Their friend still snickered. And Mason watched me with impenetrable eyes.

I scowled.

Then the friend asked, "Can she drive home with those?"

Becky had been watching the sidewalk, but her head whipped up. "No. I know. I've been trying to reason with her so I could drive her home, but she won't let me—"

I shook off Mason's hand. He'd been holding my elbow and I surged away. "I'm fine."

"Sam, wait." Becky jogged to catch up.

I bypassed her car.

"I drove you here."

"I'm fine," I repeated through gritted teeth and when I rounded a corner, I started to run. Forget my iPod or running shoes; I was grateful that I'd worn sneakers to school that day. I'd just run home.

And I did, or I tried. At mile ten, I slowed to a walk. My legs hurt from the different sneakers and my back hurt from my bag. When a car slowed beside me, I snarled when I looked over. I was ready for anybody, but David stopped beside me.

The fight left me in that instant.

He reached over and unlocked the passenger door and I climbed in, though my body was stiff.

He blasted the air conditioner and started off again. Then he turned the radio off and leaned back. His voice was weary. "I saw your car still in the lot and I wondered how you'd get home."

I let out a breath. I had nothing to say.

"Then I remembered what you said about Jeff and Jessica and Lydia. Do people know you're staying with the Kades?"

I shook my head. My throat was too thick to talk.

"Yeah, I imagined that." He watched the road and his voice grew distant. "You were always so stubborn and proud. I used to worry about your pride, even when you were three. I always told Analise that it'd either make you or break you. I'm not sure which it is."

I closed my eyes.

The car turned at an intersection. "I know you might have questions for me, but I'm not sure they're questions that I can answer. Analise always wanted me to keep quiet so I did. I loved her. And now..."

"You raised me all my life."

He stopped the car somewhere and held my gaze.

My heart thumped, it was so loud in my ears.

He looked emotionless, but then he turned away and pressed a hand to his mouth. "I did." He was choked up. "I did, Sammy." And he took a deep breath. "Listen, if you'd like I can give you a ride to school tomorrow. I know you won't ask anyone and you don't have your car right now."

I realized we were a block from the Kade mansion.

"I will be here at seven tomorrow morning, on the dot. You don't need to call or anything. Actually, don't call. I'll be waiting for you."

I jerked my head in a nod. He reached across me and opened my door. As I got out and used my elbow to shut it, he called out, "See you tomorrow, Samantha. Get some sleep tonight."

Like that was going to happen.

He sped away and I walked up the mansion's driveway. There was only one car parked in front, my mom's new convertible she'd gotten the week we moved in. My heart started to pound again when I went inside. And then I heard her voice. It grew louder until I found her in a library-like room with her back to me. She had a phone pressed to her ear.

"Yes, honey. I know that." Pause. "Oh, I'm sure they'll be fine. Samantha's adjusting just fine—well—no." She sighed. "I'm sure he's not that bad of a boy. Mason seems very sure of himself. No, I know. Yes. Okay, honey. I'd like that a lot too." She listened to the other end for a minute. "Everything will work out wonderfully. I promise you."

Then she laughed. The sound peeled through the room and it jarred me. I jumped back and tried to block the pain from the movement.

"Okay. Yes. I love you too. Bye."

I opened my eyes in time to see her turn around. Her eyes widened a fraction of an inch. "Honey, I didn't know you were there. How are you?"

I waited.

She gasped.

She saw my hands.

"What did you do?"

When she came over and started to reach for one of them, I jerked away. "I'm fine. It's nothing."

"Were you in a fight?"

I fought against the urge to puke. All accusations, all questions I had went down my throat then. I didn't want to hear her lies. I wasn't sure if I could stomach more fake promises coming out of her mouth either.

"I was trying to open this door, it was stuck, and someone banged it shut from the other side. They didn't see my hands."

"That's it?" my mother asked flatly.

"What do you mean?"

"Nothing." She shook her head and plastered on a smile. "The boys are coming home soon. They had practice that ran late, but James and I wanted to have a family dinner. What do you think?"

"It'll suck."

She sailed past me. "Do you think they'd like meatloaf? They seem like the kind to like meat, maybe pasta? Chicken and pasta? The chef went home, I asked him to go. I wanted to cook this dinner by myself."

I scowled and followed her down the hallway.

She turned into the kitchen. "You want to help, honey? You could make your famous green bean dish. You always made that for Jeffrey."

"Can I invite him?"

Her laughter bounced off the walls. "Oh, honey. You're so funny. You must get that from your dad. David could be funny at times."

As she went into the kitchen, I went to my room. My skin felt like it was stretching off of me. My feet wouldn't stop moving. Dinner or no dinner, I had to get out of there or I'd be bouncing off the walls too.

When I had changed into my running shoes with my iPod on my arm, I hit the sidewalk. As I ran down the driveway, Mason's black Escalade pulled in. Logan's yellow one came behind, but I didn't look at either of them and started running.

I'd have to go back. I knew that. I couldn't keep running from my mom or what she'd done to our lives, but for now this was how I was going to deal with the storm that was happening inside of me.

At that point, I didn't care when I went back home. It could be long past midnight before I returned, preferably when everyone was asleep. I'd slip in, sleep, and sneak back out. I took a deep breath and pumped my arms higher in the air. This was going to be my life, until everything would crash underneath our feet.

It was only a matter of time.

CHAPTER SEVEN

It was late when I hobbled inside. At this point with my bloody hands, the weak legs, and how much I've been running, it was time to admit that I needed to cut back. Making myself numb might not have been the healthiest way to handle recent changes in my life, but I wasn't sure if I dared any other option. Talking had never been my strong suit.

As I passed a room, the light switched on.

I could feel Analise's anger from where I was and I hadn't looked yet.

So I did.

Her face was white, eyes strained, mouth pinched, and her arms were folded over her chest. My mother never folded her arms, it was deemed unladylike and too confrontational. Then her foot started to tap on the floor.

Guess I pissed her off.

"Do you know what time it is?" she clipped out.

No clock was in sight. I shrugged.

"It's one in the morning. One in the morning, Samantha." Her leg moved off the other and both feet were now on the floor. They stopped tapping.

She still remained on her chair.

I tilted my chin up. "Do you know what's happened to my life?"

She made a disgusted sound and hissed at the same time. "Are we back to this? You knew my marriage wasn't working out. You should be happy for me, Samantha."

"Happy?" My voice cooled. "It happened a week ago."

"Would you rather I were in an unhappy marriage?"

"How could I tell? You were fake all the time."

Her eyes threatened to bulge out and she sucked in a dramatic breath. When she talked, it was forcibly controlled, "What are you talking about?"

"You're the fakest person I know. Why are you really pissed off? Is it because I missed your precious *family* dinner?"

"I'm fake?" She started to stand up.

My eyes went flat. "So much that I can't stand being fake. I'm real all the time. Congratulations. I have no friends because of it."

"I'm fake?"

"This is news to you?" I laughed as she drew closer.

There was a stillness to my mother. Her anger was so vivid, but I was past caring. My body ached. My hands hurt. And I was tired, so tired of everything.

She stopped in front of me.

I met her gaze and my hands formed into fists. "What do you want? Tell me what you want me to say so I can go to sleep."

Her voice grew soft. "You missed dinner tonight."

"We're back to this?" I mocked her. "Your precious dinner?"

"It was an important dinner."

"I highly doubt it." I started to leave, but she caught my arm.

She hissed, "I am talking to you."

"Not anymore. I'm moving out as soon as I'm eighteen. That's all you need to hear from me."

"What?" she gasped.

"Reality check, . This is your life. This is your boyfriend. I don't want any part of it. I want to be home with dad again. I want to move in with him."

"You. Will. Not. Live. With. Him." She had to take breaths to calm down. Her arms started to tremble, her chin was rattled. Her eyes clung to mine in a beseeching manner, torn between pleading and commanding.

"Why not?" I tested her. "He *is* my father, right?"

Her mouth shut in a firm line.

"Doesn't he have some right to see me? Don't I have a right to see him? Why is it always your way? You didn't give me any choice. You said we're moving and we did, just like that. We moved because you said so. Well I don't want to be here. I don't want to be a part of your boyfriend's family. This is your thing, not mine."

"You are my daughter."

"Am I? Are you sure? How many nights have we eaten together since the move?"

"I wanted—"

"It would've been once, tonight. And that's because it's what you wanted, not me. You've stopped being my second we moved in here. The only role you fulfill is his girlfriend as the wannabe wife of James Kade."

Analise went white around her mouth. Her arms jerked up in balls, but she forced them back down. Her arms shook and her hands started to tremble. She choked out, "You will respect me—"

"Where's my respect? As your daughter, don't I get respect?"

"I am your mother—"

"I wish you weren't—"

She slapped me. The force of her palm pushed me back a few steps and I cradled my cheek as I whirled back to her. She stood there, ashen in the face and with her hand still in the air. The palm was spread out and she looked from her hand to me in disbelief.

The pain was numbing. And a part of me wanted more, but I said, "If you slap me again, I'll hit you back."

"Samantha..." She darted towards me.

I jerked away and retreated to a far wall.

"I..." Her eyes kept spinning around the room, from me to her, to her hand, and back to her feet. "I..." Then her face cleared and she looked back up. She spoke in a calmed voice, too calm. "The dinner tonight was important to me."

I narrowed my eyes.

She swallowed and hung her head again. "I wanted you there."

"You want to know where I was?" I didn't wait for her answer. "Running. I've gone running almost every day since we got here. I run until my body can't take anymore and then I go to sleep and I get up, go to school, and I can't wait until I can do it all again. I don't want to feel anything, mom, because sooner or later, we're going to be out of here. Have you thought about that? What happens when he breaks up with you?"

"We're getting married."

I hesitated for a beat. "And I repeat, what happens when he breaks up with you?"

"Didn't you hear me? James proposed to me. We announced it tonight at dinner."

"Oh," I bit out. "Well, then I'm so sorry your daughter wasn't there to represent your side of the family. He had his two sons, right? Their friend too?"

Her eyes narrowed again and she was still, so still.

I laughed, mocking. "And you looked at your side of the table and there was my empty chair. You were humiliated, weren't you?"

"Yes." Her teeth were gritted together.

"I'm humiliated every day we're here. I'm humiliated you left dad for this—"

"You will watch your words."

"I won't. Why should I? You don't watch yours." I pressed a fist into the side of my face. My hand had grown numb and I laughed. It rumbled from the bottom of my stomach and gurgled out. The sound sent chills down my own spine. "I love you. I'm divorcing you." A pause. I glanced up and held her eyes. "Your father loves you."

Her eyes went wide and she paled again. This time she was as white as a sheet.

I let out a deep breath, one to calm me, but the storm started to take over. "Your father will always love you. I'll always love you. I'll protect you. I'll put you first in my life." My mouth twisted into an ugly smile. "It was all lies, wasn't it, Analise?"

"You know," she breathed out. She looked horrified.

"Why are you marrying him? You just want to find a new daddy for me? David couldn't keep lying to me anymore?"

"That wasn't....this isn't...Oh, Samantha..." A sob came from her.

"Stop it," I snapped out.

Her mouth clenched shut and she watched me. A tear came to her eye.

"You don't get to feel bad for yourself." My whole body started to shake. "I wish I'd never been born from yo—"

She swung her hand wide and it smacked against my cheek. This time it hit across my nose and as my head was thrown to the side, I tasted blood. I glanced up, felt my insides churning, and fisted my hand. I threw my whole body behind.

I watched her in slow motion. She looked from my face to my hand and her mouth formed a small o. Her eyes widened, but then something caught me. I was hauled backwards in the air and against something. I tried kicking free, but an arm held on tight around my waist.

"Samantha!"

"Let me go." I kept kicking, until I heard laughter from behind.

"You could help," a male voice reverberated from behind my ear.

"I think you got it under control."

I was swung around and I saw Logan, James, and the friend in the doorway. Logan wiped a hand over his face as he continued to laugh. The friend was fighting back a smile and James gave me an emotionless expression.

I doubled my struggle.

Mason's arms tightened around me.

"Let me go. I won't hit her."

He grunted and dropped me.

I swung around and he watched me with caution.

Then I swiveled on my heel and went to bed. Not a word was spoken behind me and when I left the next day, Mousteff gave me a sheepish smile as he handed out his brown bag. I took it as I passed and met my da—David a block away. He was quiet when I got in the car, but I felt his attention. His eyes raked over my face, but he didn't say a word. I breathed out in thanks when we pulled into the parking lot. I hurried from the car before he got out of his side and I was in the school early enough so no one was in the hallways.

The rest of the day passed in a similar fashion.

Jessica and Lydia kept their distance. Jill Flatten sneered as she passed by once. Her arm was curled around Jeff's. He avoided my gaze and stared straight ahead. Then there was Becky. She gushed about the Kade brothers and how they had talked to her. She asked once about my hands and I lifted them. It was funny. I'd forgotten about their pain until she asked, but then she started to gush about Adam Quinn in the next breath.

Apparently, he told her that he did want to ask me out.

My hands had started to hurt again, but I listened to her story and tried to block the pain out. I asked her when he said he wanted to ask me out. She looked the other way while one of her shoulders jerked up in a shrug.

Adam Quinn never said a word.

Over the next week, things were at a bypass at home. Analise avoided me. I avoided her. And the boys seemed to have disappeared.

It was perfect.

When I got to school on Thursday, the rumors started.

I was a whore.

Jeff dumped me because I had herpes.

Lydia and Jessica were my friends because my mother bribed them.

My own dad hated me, he barely talked to me.

Then I cornered Becky at her car one day and demanded to know where the rumors had come from.

She squealed as she got red in the face, "Lydia."

My eyebrow rose up.

"And Jessica."

I waited.

"And Jill Flatten. She really hates you."

"I knew it."

Then Becky said in a small voice, "And Ashley DeCortts."

"Wait—what? Why does she hate me?"

"Because Adam likes you."

I rolled my eyes. The guy didn't give a damn. When would she drop this obsession of hers?

"What else could go wrong?" I muttered under my breath.

The back door burst open at that moment and the football team jogged across the parking lot on the way to the field. Their spikes clattered against the tar and the sound was soon deafening.

"Hi," Becky squeaked with a small wave.

I turned to see that Adam Quinn had fallen to a walk as he drew close. He stopped with his helmet in one hand and a water bottle in the other. Up close, I saw why so many girls wanted to love him. Striking blue eyes, golden curls with streaks from the sun, and a square jaw that would've sent romantics swooning. Hell, they already did.

He towered over us with shoulder pads that made his already muscular shoulders larger. His chest tapered down to a slender waist and he grinned at Becky. His eyes scanned to me. "You need a ride home, Becky?"

"No." She sounded breathless. "My mom let me use her car this week."

"Good old Nancy." His grin brightened. "Am I still invited for chili and cornbread this weekend?"

Becky's foot started to push a rock back and forth on the ground. She didn't look up. "Yeah, of course. I know Eddie might come home this weekend."

"That's great. I've missed your brother." He cast me another questioning look.

I sighed and held out my hand. "I'm Samantha."

His hand enveloped mine. They were rough, slightly calloused, probably from throwing the football, but they weren't so rough to the touch. I could see why he dated Ashley DeCortts, the girl that seemed to reign over the cheerleaders. I suppose she daydreamed about the Ken Barbie he reminded me of, how he must've been the prince to her damsel in distress fairytale.

"I know. Adam Quinn."

"I know."

We grinned at each other.

"How're your hands?"

A faint scowl came to me. I remembered that he'd been there. "Oh, they're..." I lifted them up and shrugged. "I guess they're okay. They'll heal."

"You can drive home today?"

"What?"

"I saw your car here that night. Then I saw coach take off. I figured maybe you didn't have a ride or something."

"Oh, yeah. No, I'm fine. I've been driving all week."

"That's good."

"Yeah."

Becky continued to hang her head and I arched an eyebrow.

"So," he watched her too. "Are you guys going to the beach party tomorrow night?"

Her head snapped up and her cheeks were in flames.

Not surprised.

Then she mumbled out, "I' dlove to, butIdon't know whereit's at."

"There's a party?" I asked with a frown at my redheaded friend.

"Yeah." His teeth were blinding. "You could both go with me?"

Becky whirled to me. Her eyes were fervent with hope.

"I..." I wanted to say no, but a stricken look came to her eyes. I crumbled. "Sure. You can pick us up at Becky's."

"Great."

"Great."

Becky breathed out, "Great!"

"I'll—uh—I'll see you then, I guess?"

I nodded. "See you then."

He jogged after the team, but glanced back with a small wave before he got onto the field.

Becky whooshed out, "I can't believe I'm going to a party with Adam Quinn."

My shoulder nudged her. "Maybe there's hope for you after all."

"What do you mean?"

"Here's your big chance." I gave her a duh look. "He's going to be drinking. You're going to be drinking. I can drive us home..."

Then she squeaked again and clamped her mouth shut. Her cheeks got big and her whole body was soon red, even her hands and fingers.

I laughed. "Now you just have to figure out what you're going to wear."

As I headed to my car, I heard her groan behind me. Somehow, things didn't seem so bad when I had a friend to distract me. Too bad it wouldn't keep. I wanted something to keep.

CHAPTER EIGHT

Becky was bouncing off the wall when I got to her house the next afternoon. I was dressed in a see-through white summer dress that tied behind my neck. My black bikini was visible underneath and I had on simple black flip flops. While I was going for comfort, Becky wanted sexy.

She let out a dramatic groan and collapsed on her bed when I went to her room. One of her arms had been pulled through a black tube top, or that's what it looked like. A blinding rainbow colored bikini top had been pushed up. When she rolled over, she cried out, "I can't fit into anything."

"What are you talking about?"

"I have nothing, nothing! I'm so fat, Sam."

I frowned and grabbed her hand to pull her up. When she looked at me, I shrugged. "What do you want me to say? If you're trying to be a model, you need to lose weight. I think you're fine just how you are."

"Thanks a lot," she grumbled.

"I thought friends were honest." I flashed a grin.

She stood back up and struggled to pull the rest of her tube top over her left boob. Then she started to hop around. "Yeah, but it'd be easier to take if you didn't look how you did."

I scowled and crossed my arms over my chest.

She paused mid-hop. "That's a compliment."

"Oh." I loosened my arms. "My mom's always on me about my weight."

"You could gain some. You want mine?"

I chuckled and watched as she continued to hop around, sometimes skip around the room. After an hour, when

Becky stopped to pant with beads of sweat on her forehead, I gestured to a dress in her closet. "Why don't you just wear that?"

"Ugh." She let out another drawn-out groan. "That makes me look like a tan marshmallow."

"It does not. You wore it to the first day of school. I thought you looked nice."

Her eyebrows arched high. "I didn't know you knew who I was back then?"

I shrugged. "I didn't, but I still thought you looked nice."

"Your besty Jessica called me fatso that day."

I rolled my eyes. "If she went out of her way to call you a name that meant you looked good. And I bet some guy she wanted to flirt with was looking at you instead."

"You think?"

"I know so."

"It's my last option anyway. I need to lose weight, or buy new clothes and I refuse to buy new clothes." She grimaced. "My bank account won't allow it and I can't live down the fact that I'm a size larger since last year."

"You could go running with me."

She shot me a dark look. "I'm not that desperate. I'll try walking first."

When she pulled on the black dress, it fit her. It was snug in places it was supposed to be and loose in places that she was embarrassed about. After a few twirls in the mirror, I gave her the thumbs up and waited until she finished her make-up.

I called to her in the bathroom, "This is a beach party, right?"

"Hmmm mmm." Her voice was muffled from the bathroom.

"So why are you putting make-up on?"

Then she came into the room. "Because it's waterproof and because Adam's taking us."

I frowned at that logic. "He's picking us up?"

"Yeah, in thirty minutes."

"Why'd you have me come over two hours earlier?"

She posed with an arm on her hip and rolled her eyes. "Are you serious? You're my girlfriend. Aren't we supposed to get ready together?"

"I'm ready."

"Yeah, well, I needed the moral support. And besides," she flashed me a smile and a wink. "My mom has wine. I thought we could raid her cabinet."

"Oh." I surged upright on the bed. "Why didn't you say so in the beginning?"

Becky giggled as she led me downstairs and we both had a glass. We'd had our second when her phone vibrated and she continued to giggle as she knocked over her mother's lamp. "Adam's outside."

When she stood, her knees buckled and I caught her arm. "Are you okay?"

She gave me a weak wave. "Oh, no worries. This has more to do with Adam than the wine, but I didn't eat all day. Oops." She giggled again and her face was lobster red.

When we got outside, the silliness was gone and her limbs became rigid. Her back was stiff, her chin down, and she walked like a robot. Adam gave her a small frown, but shook his head slightly. When we climbed in, he asked, "Are you guys ready?"

Becky giggled into her lap.

I sighed from the back. "What party is this?"

"It's a Public party. Is that okay?"

Her head popped back up. "They're only the best kind."

Adam chuckled and rested an arm on the back of their front seat. His fingers scraped her shoulder before they fell against the headrest. I saw her almost faint.

"I guess so. More people, right?"

"And the Kades."

My scowl was back.

Adam mimicked my reaction.

Becky was clueless as she bobbed her head up and down. "I heard it's their party. They're actually inviting people at our school."

"Wait, what?" I shot forward and clasped onto their seat.

"Yeah." She was a grinning idiot. "They're usually so exclusive. I mean, I heard no one's allowed in their house, but I guess they live on the beach. It's in front of their home."

Every tendon in me wanted to snap. By the time we got to my house, the tension suffocated me and was weighing me down. Becky hot-footed it out of the car, but my legs couldn't move.

A party. At my house. By my soon-to-be-stepbrothers.

Adam had grown silent too as he glanced back. "You okay?"

Becky shoved her head next to his. "Yeah, you look pale, really pale."

"I'm fine." My voice was calm, but my body trembled. My knees buckled an inch when I got out of the car, but Adam caught me and held me upright. I flashed him a smile in thanks and then turned to see Becky's grin falter a bit.

My stomach dropped. That wasn't good.

A crowd of people had congregated at the bottom of the driveway, but they started to head around the hill and down to the beach. I let out a small breath in relief. I remembered their other party. No one had entered the house then and I hoped no one would this time.

When we bypassed the gate around the pool, Becky grabbed one of the bars. "Look at that. They have their own pool and a hot tub." Her eyes were wide as she took the rest in, the sand volleyball and basketball courts.

Adam touched her shoulder. "I think they have a bonfire started down here."

"Oh, wow..." Becky was lost in stardust as she followed the line downwards.

I breathed another sigh of relief when I saw the divider door was still closed, not to mention locked.

Then we were on the beach and there were three bonfires. A keg had been hidden in some bushes towards the back of the beach with coolers placed all over. When people quickly congregated to them, I figured they had alcohol inside.

"Oh, look!" Becky pointed to the farthest bonfire.

Logan and their friend were there with others grilling over the fire. Soon music blared from speakers placed by the pool.

Adam suggested we sit around one of the smaller bonfires and after we snagged some lawn chairs, Becky jumped back up. She was all smiles. "I'm going to get something more to drink. You guys want?"

She hot-footed it away before we could answer and Adam looked over with a hesitant smile. "More?"

"We got into her mom's wine."

"Ah, I see. Nancy. She does love her Moscato."

I grinned. "My mom's decided she loves tea, not the coffee she's been drinking since I was born, but tea now."

The small smile disappeared. "Yeah, uh...I heard your dad that night..." He seemed to be choosing his words.

"No one knows. Please don't say anything."

He nodded quickly. "I won't. I wouldn't—I mean—I know what that's like, to have your personal life on display, you know?"

I nodded. "Yeah..."

"So," he sat forward and leaned closer. "You and Sallaway, huh? You two were together for a while."

"We were."

His eyes seemed to be watching me intently. "And you don't think there's any chance...?"

It took a moment before I realized what he was asking and my eyes went wide. "He cheated on me for two years with my best friend. Some girls might tolerate that, but I have self-esteem."

His shoulders loosened and he grinned. "That's good, I mean, you deserve better."

"Any girl deserves better."

"You're right. No one deserves a cheater."

From the dark look on his face, something relaxed inside of me. He understood. "I heard DeCortts cheated on you?"

He looked startled for a moment and then cleared his throat. "Yeah, uh, she did."

I lifted a shoulder. "It was all over school."

"I know, I just...hearing it from a stranger is different, you know..."

"I was informed the two of you were the 'hottest couple ever'." I thought those were Lydia's exact words.

He stiffened in his chair. "I guess so. She's—she threw herself at one of the Kades, of all people." He laughed and gestured around.

"Which one?"

"Logan, I think." He frowned, and then shook his head. "It doesn't matter. She said he turned her down, but I still knew what she'd done. I heard the whole thing at some stupid party. Then Peter told me she'd been sleeping around for the last six months."

"Peter Glasburg?" His best friend.

Adam nodded. "Yeah, I don't know who with, but I trust him. Peter doesn't say much and if he said it, then it's worse than he let on."

I grew silent and turned to watch for Becky. She'd been gone a while, but I couldn't squash an inkling of jealousy. He had a friend who looked out for him and that friend wasn't the one to sleep with his girlfriend. My mouth clamped shut and my chest grew tight as something burned inside of me.

But then Mason and Logan's friend walked towards us from the beach. He had gone past at some point and he was now going back to the other bonfire. A couple of beers were in his hands and as he started to bypass us, he stopped, backed up, and frowned at us.

Adam lifted a hand. "Hey, man."

The friend shot him a look and glanced at my hands. The gauze I had used to wrap my fingers was gone. I scowled up at him, waiting for what he was going to say, but then he held out a beer to me.

"Thanks." The word felt awkward on my lips.

He rolled his eyes and kept going.

Adam twisted around to watch him. "Do you know him?"

I shrugged.

"That was...odd. Do you know who that was?"

Again, I shrugged.

"That was Nate Monson. He's best friends with Mason Kade. He moved away last year, but I guess he comes back to visit." Adam continued to look at me strangely. "I have never seen him do something like that. That was weird."

"Do something like what?"

His eyes seemed to be inspecting me. "Be nice to a random girl that he or his buddies aren't sleeping with."

I shifted in my seat. "I'm not sleeping with anybody, if that's what you're getting at."

His hands shot in the air in surrender. "I didn't mean that. I've just—do you know him?"

I sneered at him. "His name's Nate?"

"Yeah." Adam leaned forward and rested his elbows on his legs. "He's bad news, like really bad news. I heard him and Kade are not a good team together."

I snorted, "Which Kade?"

"Mason." He frowned at me. "What'd you mean by that?"

I fought the urge to roll my eyes and popped open the beer. "I just meant that the Kade brothers seem close, it'd made sense if he was friends with both."

"Oh." Adam leaned back again and stretched out his legs. "I don't know about that, but I heard when he and Mason Kade get together, it's not good."

"You're scared of them?"

"No, but they played football together against me last year. I'm happy that I only get sacked by Kade this year and not both. Anyway, whatever. I'm sounding stupid, aren't I?" He gave me a grin.

I sipped the beer, but it tasted flat.

"Maybe I should go find Becky and get something to drink?" His blues sparked in good humor and another knot in my stomach unraveled.

When he left, I watched him go. My hands were curled into my chair and I jerked a hand up to finish my beer. Another was handed to me and I looked up. This one was from Logan. He had a sober look on his face, but he wasn't watching me. I shifted and saw that he was staring in the direction Adam had just gone.

When I took the cold can from him, it slipped from my hold. He caught it and sat in Adam's seat as he held it to me again.

I held my breath, but I didn't say a word. Something in me wouldn't allow it, but I opened the beer and put it in the chair's cup holder.

He stretched out his legs and lounged back for a moment. Then he sighed.

I heard the small sound escape his lips and was confused. It was a sound that I'd make.

Laughter rang clear not far from us. I realized that Adam and I had picked seats farther away from the party. I didn't know if it was for privacy or because of the loud music, but I was suddenly aware of the looks we were getting now. Had Adam and I gotten the same interest?

"They went to the city this weekend." Logan's voice sounded rough.

I glanced over and he lifted his head up.

"Mase went to go see our mom tonight."

We had both been watching the crowd and when two figures separated themselves from the rest and were headed towards us, he grimaced before he stood.

He didn't look at me. I didn't look at him, but he held out a second beer. I took it and then he sauntered away. The party-boy air was back with him when Logan neared the crowd. Some girls eyed him with sultry poses and his friends made way for his arrival.

When Adam and Becky stopped by the chairs, neither sat nor said a word.

Then Becky said in a rush, "Was that Logan Kade?"

I gripped the beer tighter and kept my voice neutral. "I wanted to ask about Jessica, if he was going to date her or not."

Something flashed in her eyes and she clipped out, "I heard that he told her to get lost. She's back to rubbing herself all over my cousin again. I just walked past them."

My hand gripped the can tight and I chugged the rest of it.

Adam shot her a look.

Becky's mouth opened and hung there. "I mean...she's not good enough for Kade. That's what I think. And my cousin's a loser, a first class loser."

Adam grunted.

She bit her lip and pulled a chair over. "Are you okay, Sam?"

I finished the beer and put it away. It was the last bit of alcohol that I'd consume that night or heaven help me, I would do something I'd regret later. I almost hit my mom once, I wouldn't be held back a second time with Jessica.

CHAPTER NINE

The party went late, but not late enough. Becky was stumbling drunk by the time Adam parked his car outside the two houses. He had to help get her inside and then asked if I needed a ride home. After he asked, he gave me a rueful grin. "Sorry, you're sober, aren't you?"

"I only had those two beers."

"Yeah." He scratched his head and Becky's snores soon thundered down to where we stood in front of her door. He laughed and shook his head. "She's something else, isn't she?"

"She likes you." I watched him carefully.

He stood still for a second and closed his eyes a fraction.

It was enough. I knew where he stood. "Stop being nice to her. You won't hurt her so much then."

He nodded and ran a hand through his hair. "I know. I do. I like Becky, just not that way."

I shrugged and started towards my car. "She's not Ashley DeCortts, but I think that's a good thing."

"Hey." He hurried to walk beside me. "Do you—would you want to meet for dinner tonight?"

I opened my car door and turned around to look where Becky's room was. "That's my only friend right now."

"She's my friend too and I could be another friend."

My laugh was genuine. "That's what you say now, but when I don't put out it's going to be a different story." My eyes narrowed on his. "Because I won't, you know. I never had sex with Jeff and I'm not going to start again with you. My first and only time was a mistake I will never make again."

"I know. That's okay. I respect you for that."

Another one of those knots unraveled in my stomach again. Why did it happen with him? And at times when I felt he was being honest?

I tilted my head to the side and studied him. "Are you really this nice guy or is this an act?"

He grimaced. "I'm nice. I am, but I'm not being that nice to Becky."

"No, you're not."

"She's the only person that you talk to. I didn't know how else to approach you without looking like a complete loser."

I rolled my eyes, but couldn't shake the slight smile. "Try not going through the friend that likes you next time."

"Next time?" His hand caught my car door and held it open.

I looked at it, saw he wasn't going anywhere anytime soon, and stared him straight in the eyes. "What do you want, Adam Quinn?"

His eyes widened an inch, but he didn't miss a beat. "Dinner. Just dinner."

"And if I don't want dinner? If I want to bail? If I bring Becky with?"

His smile looked painful. "Then I think you're not being a good friend either."

"Maybe." I got inside and shut the door, but I rolled the window down. "Or maybe I don't believe in friends anymore."

He leaned down. "For what it's worth, Becky's the best friend you could get. Those other two were jokes."

I gave him a small wave and started home, but I muttered under my breath, "You don't say."

When I pulled into the driveway, I had to key in the code for the gate. It wasn't usually closed, but I figured the party was still in full gear. After I made sure my car was in the garage and the front gate had been closed again, I headed inside and towards the kitchen.

A peak of sunlight was starting outside and I saw it was five in the morning. When I'd gone to all-night parties with

Jessica and Lydia it was a tradition to go for breakfast in the morning and on cue, my stomach rumbled. However, as I opened the fridge, the bright light filled the room and I screamed.

Mason stood behind me, leaning against the kitchen counter with one foot crossed idly over the other. He looked relaxed and carefree, but everything in me went on alert. The hairs on the back of my neck stood straight up and I knew he was anything besides relaxed.

When he didn't say anything, my insides clenched even further. So this is how we were going to be? Fine. I reached inside and pulled out some slices of meat. I was determined to ignore him or, at least, not let him bother me anymore than he already had. My stomach wanted a sandwich and I wasn't leaving the kitchen until I got one.

An arm reached around me and I jumped. My heart doubled in pace and I bumped against his chest as Mason reached for the water pitcher. He caught me from moving back into him with one hand on my arm. I held my breath as he held me in place. When his arm moved clear of me, I sagged in relief. Then my fingers deftly plucked out the tomatoes and a head of lettuce.

When I pulled out a cutting board and a knife to start on the lettuce, Mason placed a glass of water into my hands.

I stood there, dumbfounded, as he nudged me over with his hip. Then he picked up the knife and I watched in almost sick fascination as he started to cut the lettuce and tomatoes. A moment later, he pulled out cheese and arranged all of them with the meat between two slices of bread.

He put the sandwich on a plate and pushed it into my other hand.

I stood there, water in my left and the sandwich in my right. My mouth was open. I knew I needed to close it, but I couldn't.

He reached into a corner cabinet and pulled out some rum. After he mixed himself a drink, he sat at the kitchen table and kicked out a chair for me. I sat, but I didn't remember doing it.

He leaned back and sipped his drink. It was early in the morning so the sunrise peaked into the room more. The bass from the music was muffled through the windows and then the air conditioner kicked in. We could barely hear the party still going strong outside.

He raked a hand over his face. "They're going to be out there all weekend."

I didn't hide the grimace that came to my face.

"Logan said you went down there."

I gulped down half of my water. "You went to see your mom?"

He jerked a shoulder up. "It's not her fault my dad's a prick. I'd want to know."

"She didn't know?"

He gave me the first grin I'd ever received from him. It was soft and I knew it had more to do with his mom than me. "They divorced last year and haven't talked since. James probably didn't feel she was worthy of this information."

My eyes went wide. I couldn't stop them. When I realized I was staring, I shoved the sandwich in my mouth. Then chewed.

His eyes narrowed, a gleam of anger glittered in them. His mouth drew shut and his jaw tightened.

My stomach clenched again and something burst in my body. I shifted, uncomfortable, on the seat. I shouldn't be there. I shouldn't be hearing this, talking to him. It wasn't right. When a full blown alarm started to sound in my head, he shoved back his chair and stood.

He took my now-empty plate and glass to the sink. As he passed, he tapped my shoulder lightly. "You should come down. I think Nate got some jet skis." Then he was up the stairs and gone.

It was like he'd never been there. I still sat at the kitchen table.

I never went down to the beach. I didn't want to chance a run-in with Jessica, Lydia, or Jeff. I didn't care about the others, but a headache had started. It grew as the day progressed. When the evening came around, it had lessened dramatically. I felt a bit more human and checked my phone.

There was a text from Becky: **Adam likes you. You should go out with him**.

You like him.

I waited a minute. **He doesn't like me and I'd rather he were with you than someone else. No one's good enough for him**.

Oh Becky. I groaned, but replied: **Maybe**.

Good. I gave him your number.

And sure enough, I saw an unknown number had texted me: **This is Adam. Dinner?**

I stared at it. What the hell was I doing?

He sent another: **Please? I'm being a loser here**.

I smacked my forehead with my palm. **I'll meet you at Mastoni's, 830**.

It wasn't even thirty seconds before I got back: **See you then!**

Again, what the hell was I doing?

Mastoni's was a nice restaurant. I'd been there once with my parents, or my mom and my fake father. Analise wanted to dress up so we did. I wore a simple dress while hers was blaring red. David wore a dress shirt and khakis. It'd been good enough for me, not for her. As I walked inside the cool interior, heard the fountain gurgling, and saw all the foliage around, I remembered the fight that had happened that night.

It'd been my first two-hour run.

This time I wore jeans and a black top, nothing special. This wasn't going to be special. When I spotted Adam at the bar, he waved, and I saw he must've felt the same. He had on khaki cargo shorts and a blue polo. He looked good, but not the dressy that my mom had wanted so long ago.

I preferred this night already.

He held out a drink for me as he drew near. "Hey, I got this for you."

"You're twenty one?"

Perfect white teeth flashed me. "The manager's a friend of the family, plus, I used to work here a while ago."

Oh. I took the drink from him. Great.

"I already got a booth for us; it's kinda in the back if that's okay?"

It was. Privacy was always good, but it wasn't long before a group of girls took the booth beside ours. When we waited for our food to come, they sent flirty looks and smiles Adam's way. I was sure they talked louder for his benefit too.

When the food came, I heard one of the girls exclaim, "I didn't know Nate was in town."

"Oh yeah!" Another shrieked in laughter. "You didn't know? He's been here for a week."

"Whatever, Natalie."

A third offered up, "I heard they're going down the beach to Roussou tonight."

The girls grew quiet for a moment.

"What are they going to do?"

"What do you mean?"

"They always do something. When Nate and Mason team up, they always do something. Last year they stole some police cars and then they went on a bender."

"I heard that too. Mason's dad paid off the cops. They vandalized some of the bars. He must've paid the owners off too."

Then the first girl spoke up with authority in her voice, "Well, they're doing something tonight. They disappeared from the beach an hour ago."

"How do you know?"

"Duh. Summer texted me. She's still there."

"Hey." Adam's hand jolted me back to our booth. He gave me a gentle grin. "You okay?"

"Actually…" I looked down at my plate of pasta. "I'm not hungry."

His smile stretched a bit. "You're not bailing, are you?"

I gave him a weak one in return. "I think I am. I'm sorry. I…I have to do something."

When I got to the house, Mason's Escalade was just starting to leave. I raced towards it and waved my arms in the air. He braked and rolled down his window. "Yeah?"

Nate grinned at me from the passenger seat, but I felt he was laughing at me.

I was breathless from my hurry and panted, "You're going to Roussou? I know where the coach lives."

Mason frowned. "What are you doing?"

"I want to go with you?"

Logan howled from the back seat and a fourth guy started to laugh with him.

"No."

"Yes." I grabbed his window when he started to let the vehicle roll forward. "Let me come."

Nate elbowed him. "Let her come."

"What?" Logan popped his head forward. "No way. No way in hell, Mase."

Mason jerked a thumb towards the back. "Get in." He popped open the back trunk area and I crawled in. My heart was pounding. I knew my face was red, but as soon as I heaved the door shut the Escalade shot forward.

It was an hour drive down the beach. Logan grumbled and sent me a glare every now and then. The fourth friend ignored him and after a while, started to give me a few grins. He offered me a soda too. Mason and Nate talked with each other and Logan would lean forward to join in.

Something told me that Logan was trying to persuade them to drop me on the side of the road. When they didn't, I relaxed a little. I figured we were too far for them to do that and then we were in the town of Roussou. It was small, but it was rich. A lot of wealthy men owned stock in internet companies, which helped their football program be competitive against Fallen Crest High and it was the reason why an extra sense of rivalry sparked between the two schools. I remembered hearing a rumor that the Roussou team had heavily recruited Mason and Logan for their team.

They'd given them a resounding middle finger.

"Where's the coach's place?" Logan glared at me.

I jerked forward to recite the directions. It wasn't long before we were outside the three-story house I knew where David played poker on Saturday nights. And then I saw his car. My hands curled into small balls and everything inside of me went cold.

My chest started to heave up and down at a rapid pace. But I only saw my father's car, not my father's car. David's car.

"What the hell?" Logan cursed and shot me a look. "There're people here."

"Does it matter?" I asked idly as I spied some fireworks in the back with me. Then I heard a door open and loud voices came across the yard. I snagged a couple of them and a lighter before I started to get out of the car.

"Are you crazy? He's going to tell."

He wasn't. I got out, but left the door open. David had started down the sidewalk to where his car was parked, but he stopped when he saw me.

"Samantha?"

I lit the fireworks and strolled to his car.

"Samantha! Don't!"

I keyed in his code, opened his door, and threw them in.

"Oh my god!" He rushed past me, but I locked the door. It'd take him a moment before he could get it open.

The fireworks started to sizzle and they exploded in the next second.

David threw himself away from the car, shaking and cursing.

My face was blank. I didn't feel a thing. My hands didn't shake. My back was straight. My shoulders were square and then I turned back for the Escalade.

"Samantha, what did you just do?" David reached for my elbow.

I whipped away and seethed, "Get away from me."

"Get in!" Mason cursed and pounded the side of his door.

I whirled and threw myself in the back as he started to pull away from the curb. I heaved the door shut. It was silent in the car for a moment and then Logan and his friend threw their heads back and howled in laughter. I curled into a ball and stayed there. I didn't care about the smirk on Nate's face or how Mason seemed to look through me in the rear view mirror. He could try, he'd only see emptiness. The guys stopped a few times, left, and returned to do the same thing. I didn't know what they were doing. I didn't care. I'd done what I wanted.

CHAPTER TEN

They dropped off the fourth friend and the rest of us traipsed into the house. Logan picked up a phone and ordered a pizza. Nate snagged a cooler of beer and brought it downstairs to the media room. I followed behind. I didn't know why, I just did. When Mason turned on the news, I curled into a ball in one of the leather recliners and after a while I tugged a blanket on top.

When the news came on and there was no word of my vandalism or whatever the guys had done, I uncurled my legs and headed to bed.

Mason followed me.

"What?" I went to brush my teeth in my bathroom.

He perched on my bed, studying me with an impenetrable gaze. He barely blinked. "That car thing should've been on the news. Cops would've been called."

"It wasn't." I moved back to the room after rinsing my mouth.

"You seemed sure of it."

"I was." I pulled off my top, then my bra.

He still didn't blink and he sounded bored. "How'd you know that guy?"

"He's the coach at my school." I pulled on a tight tank and then shimmied out of my pants. The light hadn't been turned on so the room was dark except for a small amount of light that shone through my windows from behind a clump of clouds.

"That was your dad."

I hesitated and held my breath. He looked like a statue, a god made of stone with the light's shadow on him. His eyes were intense as he seemed to stare through me, into me.

"Yeah," I spoke in a small voice.

He nodded. "I got it."

As he moved past, his hand brushed my leg and lingered on the curve of my thigh.

I closed my eyes as a stab of desire flared in me. This wasn't supposed to be. I hadn't expected this.

Then he moved past and out the door. My hands and legs were a bit shaky when I crawled under the sheets.

It was past midnight, but I lay in bed. My mind was reeling from the look on David's face. There was a haunted feel to him, then when he saw the firecrackers in my hand a look of disappointment came next. For a second, I'd been ashamed but then I remembered the lie he had been a part of and everything hardened, it all became clear again.

He deserved it. He deserved more.

That was your dad. I got it.

Mason's voice floated in there too. My chest tightened each time I heard it. His face was unreadable, he was always unreadable, but something softened when he spoke those words. Heat flared all over my body and I threw back the sheets. I gasped as the cool air hit my skin, but another need pulsated between my legs. I clamped them together and hoped it would pass. It was an annoyance and not something I needed right now.

The sound of my phone woke me the next morning. When I answered, Becky greeted me with a chirpy voice, "Morning! Whatchadointoday?"

"Huh?"

"Come over. My family's grilling this afternoon and Adam's family is coming too. It'll be fun."

I grimaced against how sunshiney her voice sounded. My head pounded. "Yeah, maybe."

"Oh, come on, Sam. What else are you going to do today? Homework? You can do it here."

"Why do I feel like there's no other option here?"

"Because there's not. Be here in an hour or I'm coming to get you."

I grinned at that threat. "It'll be more than an hour. I'm going to go for a run first."

"Okay. Just come. We start grilling after church."

The clock said it was nine. "When is that?"

"After noon."

"You told me to come in an hour, but you're going to church?"

"My mom goes to church. The rest of us stay home."

"Oh. Okay."

"Just come. Okay, Sammm?"

"Yeah, okay. Be there in a couple of hours."

"See ya!" There she went away, chirping, as she ended the call.

It didn't take me long to get ready for my run and when I headed downstairs, the guys were in the kitchen. Coffee had been made and each had their own mugs. Mason lounged against a counter while Nate had hopped up on the counter. As I came closer, Logan was skirting around the kitchen. He seemed to be bouncing around with too much energy, but he stopped when he saw me first.

"Should we take bets? An hour? Two?"

Mason narrowed his eyes over his coffee cup. "I say an hour."

Nate grunted and dropped to the floor. He busied himself inside the fridge.

Logan draped an arm over his brother's shoulders and grinned at me.

My back straightened. His smile seemed more of a leer and I heard the mocking tone in his voice.

"She did see her dad last night so I'm guessing two hours, maybe more? Sound right, wannabe sister?"

My mouth tightened and I grabbed a water bottle from the pantry. "Don't be stupid."

When I moved to the door, Logan was in front of me in a flash. He laughed at me. "Did I hit a nerve? Your claws are showing."

I shoved him out of the way. "What do you think?"

He opened his mouth for a retort, but I slammed the door shut behind me. I hadn't taken two steps away before I heard his high-pitched laughter on the other side. Mason barked something and it stopped.

I sighed, but tried to clear my mind. That was what running was for. My head needed to be clear. I needed to quiet the storm in me and after an hour, it was successfully subsided. Sweat dropped from me as I made my way back into the house and I hadn't made it to the stairs before I heard my mother's voice.

"Really, Samantha. Can you dry off a bit before coming inside after your runs?"

I gritted my teeth and wanted to go right back for another run.

She came from one of the side rooms dressed in a yellow dress and a white sunhat. Her make-up was done flawlessly with bright red lipstick. Pink lipstick had been her favorite until a month ago.

She stopped in front of me and her hands perched on her hips. "David called me last night. We came back earlier because of it. What were you thinking, honey?"

I knew my eyes were either heated or they looked dead. It was one or the other because both emotions twisted inside of me. "You're a calculated woman. Figure it out."

"Sam—" She started to follow when I went up the stairs, but James' voice pulled her back.

"Analise?" he called from the hallway.

She sighed with a dark frown, but went to him.

I hurried upstairs and got ready for Becky's. Thirty minutes later and I was back out the door. It was a welcoming feeling with the mansion in my rearview mirror and when I went inside of Becky's house, the two places contrasted sharply. One was homey and welcoming and the other had a stranger's coldness.

An older woman, probably in her mid-forties, welcomed me at the door. Her dark brown hair was pulled up in a ponytail and freckles covered her face. It made her look tanned and healthy as her eyes sparkled in warmth. "You must be Samantha. Rebecca has told me so much about you."

"Yeah..."

She gestured inside. "Come in, come in. I'm Laura, her mother."

"Sam!" Becky hollered from somewhere inside. "Tell her to come out here, mom."

Laura patted me on the back. "Make yourself at home. Pretend this is your home from now on. Everyone's in the backyard. I was grabbing some fruit platters on my way back."

"Do you want some help?" I watched as she started to lift two giant silver trays of meat and fruit.

"Oh, no. Go and have fun. We're not going to get these nice summer days for long."

"Hi, Sam!" Becky waved from a small pool in her backyard. The raft slipped from underneath her and she screamed as she fell into the water.

Adam shook his head and came over with a can of soda. He had a lopsided grin on and sunglasses in place, dressed in only red swim trunks. "She can never stay on those things on a sober day."

I took the can from him. "She's drinking?"

"Wine coolers, nothing hard."

"But." I saw Laura at a picnic table where the food had been compiled. Another older lady was with her. She had blonde hair and wore a similar dress like my mother's. Something told me this was Adam's mother. "Her parents are here."

He shrugged and gestured to two recliners by the pool. "They're pretty lax about it. My folks aren't. If my mom saw a beer in my hand, I'd be running killers at five in the morning for a month."

"She doesn't say anything to Becky's parents?"

"They have different parenting styles, but they're old friends. They respect each other."

"Oh." For some reason I felt weird as I sat beside him. Becky came over a moment later with a towel wrapped around her. She perched on the end of my seat and water dripped off of her.

"Did you hear about the Roussou players last night?"

Everything snapped to attention in me, but I drawled out, "What do you mean?"

She leaned forward with an eager grin. "I heard the Kades went there with their friends. They wrecked your dad's car at the Roussou's coach's house and slashed a bunch of their football players' tires. Can you believe that?"

Adam frowned.

"Did your dad say anything?"

I felt Adam watching me, but gave her a casual look. "Oh, no. He didn't say anything about it."

"That's probably because he won't press charges. Your dad's nice like that, but I would if it were my car. I can't believe they did that. I wish they played for our team. We'd go to state for sure."

Laura called out, "Rebecca, go and get your brothers from the basement."

She frowned and stood up. "My stupid little brothers." And off she went, muttering under her breath.

"You haven't told her?"

I shot him a look and remembered he knew about my situation. My shoulders stiffened and the chair became uncomfortable to sit on. "It's no one's business."

"She's your friend."

"She's been someone I talk to for the last week. That's all."

"Really?" His eyes mocked me.

"It's none of your business either."

"Except that Coach Strattan's my coach and he's the best coach I've ever met."

"You've only been on his team."

"I do football camps in the summer, Sam. He's the best coach I've met and that's including FC Public's coaches. They

233

got lucky that the Kades didn't go to our school. They didn't develop their talent at all."

I studied him underneath my eyelashes. "You sound a little jealous?"

He grimaced and stood up. "The Kades are some talented sons of bitches, that's all I'm saying. Your dad would've made them better than they are, they might be more respectful too. All they are is rich a-holes right now."

"Sam, Adam." Becky waved us over to the food table. "We need to grab our food first before my little brothers and all their friends get out here. They're like bugs; their saliva will be crawling all over the food."

And after we sat at a far table with our plates; eight boys who looked like they were in seventh grade burst through the back door. They swarmed around the table. Becky was right. As the afternoon passed, the guys never left the food for long. They were different heights, but all were skinny except for one that looked on the pudgy side. When Becky got up and got us some more beverages, her brothers and their friends took over the pool too.

She sighed as she popped open a beer. "There goes my tanning today. Little rodents."

Adam laughed and stole the water she had nabbed. "Come off it. You love your brothers and you know it. You dote on Jake and Greg."

She scowled. "I'm going to make their lives hell. JAKE!"

A boy popped his head out of the water. "What?"

"If you don't get your little friends out of the pool, I'm going to tell mom and dad what's under your TV."

He froze and his eyes got wide.

Then Adam laughed and stood up. "Don't worry about her, Jake. She won't do that to you. Come on, Becks." He tugged her from the table. "Let's you and me take Sam to the movies."

A pink flush came over her cheeks, but she pretended to pull against his hold on her. "I wanted to tan today, Adam."

He laughed again and swatted her butt. "Go get cute. We can make a matinee and it'll be my treat."

I watched as she tried not to make it look like she was hurrying inside. Then I frowned when he sat back down. "You're not being nice again."

His eyebrows lifted slightly. "I thought I was being really nice."

"You're not and you know it. What's your game?"

He let out a deep breath and glanced at his lap. A moment later he peeked over and I followed his gaze. Two older men were in a heated conversation. Their hands were in the air and each had a can of beer. "I don't feel like being here. My dad just got here."

"Which one?"

"The tall guy. He got here from a meeting ten minutes ago."

From the way he said that and how he was scowling at him, I figured Adam knew something I couldn't discern. His dad was handsome. He was an older version of Adam and he was dressed in custom fitted shorts with a white shirt. He could've been a model for a summer GQ edition.

Becky's dad was the opposite. His white wife beater had stains from the grill and his beer belly hung over his board shorts. He had a slight worshipful look on his face as he debated something with Adam's dad.

"Did he really have a meeting?"

Adam's mother had grown silent next to Laura where they sat underneath a patio umbrella.

He sighed. "What do you think?"

Understanding dawned. "This is why I've kept quiet about my situation."

"Yeah, well, that's not going to happen to me. He'll never leave her."

I heard the bitterness and asked, "You want him to?"

"I want her to."

I fell quiet. I didn't know what to say.

Then Adam surprised me when he tapped my arm gently. "My mom works for James Kade, you know. She's the assistant to his junior assistant."

I shot him a dark look. "So?"

He shrugged. "So nothing. She talks about how nice he is to her."

Relief flooded me and my shoulders sagged forward. Then I gave him a wicked grin. "Oh, so are you saying you could be stepbrothers with Mason and Logan Kade."

He grinned. "Yeah, right. Wouldn't that be a joke?"

I didn't know what else to say and Adam fell into a quiet slump. We were both like that, dazing off into our thoughts when Becky rushed outside. She had changed into khaki shorts and a loose top. Her hair was pulled into a high ponytail and she had a small amount of make-up on. Her eyelashes were black and long. I'd never seen her dressed how she was, even when we went to the party.

She looked nice and I cast a look at Adam underneath my eyelids. Did he think so? But he stood up and shot forward to his car. Her shoulders dropped an inch and the corners of her mouth turned down, but then she flashed me a bright smile.

"Do I look okay?" She touched the ends of her hair and patted them into place. They already were, but she kept pressing them down.

"You look good." And I meant it.

She cast me a furtive glance. "Not like you. You look great, like always."

I frowned.

"How was your date?" She put the chirpy note back in her voice and fell in line beside me as we followed where Adam had gone to his car. He waited for us, not within hearing distance.

I hesitated. Now I wasn't being the nice friend.

"Come on." She nudged me with her shoulder. "I really want to know."

"Becky." I grabbed her arm and held her back. "You like him."

Her mouth twisted, but she gave me a smile after. "It doesn't matter. He doesn't like me, not like that."

"He could."

"No, he couldn't. He practically drools any time you enter a room. He's always had a thing for you."

"What are you talking about?"

"Even before last year, he was interested. You were dating Jeff, though, so he asked Ashley out."

"Are you serious?"

"Yeah, duh." She rolled her eyes, but frowned when she saw that I was biting my lip. "You didn't know? Really?"

I shook my head. "I didn't know that Jess had been sleeping with Jeff for two years. How was I supposed to know this?"

"Oh. Well." Her shoulders lifted and dropped in a dramatic way. "You got your chance now."

Except I didn't and I didn't want it. Then I remembered last night when Mason touched me, how his fingers lingered on my thigh. I shivered as the same desire swept through me again.

Not good. None of this was good.

"Are you two coming or what?" Adam called us over.

"Yeah!" Becky shouted back and dragged me after with a forced excited look in her eyes. She tried to sit in the back, but I made her sit in the front.

As we went to the theatre I slumped in the back of the car and was quiet on the drive over. Both tried to pull me into the conversation, but admitted defeat when we got closer to the mall. I listened to them talking when we got our tickets and took our seats.

Their conversation wasn't forced. There was no taunting, strained silences, or fakeness. They sounded like two friends who'd known each other all their lives and then I realized that they *had* known each other all their lives. They were neighbors. Their parents were friends.

I made the decision then that I'd try to be the friend for Becky that she seemed to be for everyone else.

I sighed. If only I knew how.

CHAPTER ELEVEN

"We get out of practice early tonight. Your da—David's got something, I guess." Adam dropped a shoulder against the locker beside mine when I arrived the next morning to school. He folded his arms and his backpack's straps cut into the muscles on his arms and chest.

That annoyed me for some reason and I opened my locker to stuff the bag lunch Mousteff had shoved at me that morning. He had muttered, like he always did, but this time I was certain I'd heard a few curse words. And I was certain they were directed at me, well, me or my mother. Then I relaxed as I considered that. He was probably pissed about my mom again. That made more sense.

Adam had been watching me with an odd look. "Are you okay?"

"I'm fine," I bit out. I forced myself to relax. Sometimes being mean right off the bat wasn't good. And Adam had started to be one of the two people still there for me after my debacle with Jeff/Lydia/Jessica.

And speaking of, as I turned to Adam, I saw my two ex best friends at Jill Flatten's locker across the hall. All three of them were watching me with frowns on their faces. When they saw me, Jill giggled and leaned closer to the two. She whispered something and both of them started laughing.

Jeff stopped beside them, saw me, saw the exchange, and kept going.

Adam chuckled. "I think he's finally learning."

I rolled my eyes and started towards my first class. When Adam walked with me, I asked, "So what about you getting out of practice early?"

"I was thinking we could try that dinner again."

I saw Becky at her locker ahead. She dropped her bag. Books and papers fell out of it and she knelt beside and lurched to grab everything before people kicked her things away. A few laughed and did what she tried to prevent, but one other girl helped her gather her stuff.

I sighed. "I can't."

"Why not?" Then he saw where I'd been watching. He stopped me with a hand on my shoulder. "Becky and I are never going to date. We had a heart to heart last night after the movies."

"You did?"

"Yeah." He nodded. His eyes skirted over my face, scanning me constantly as if he were looking for something. "She's really okay with you and me..." He hesitated. "Getting to know one another?"

I smirked. "And do I get a say in this?"

"Well, yeah, of course." But his cheeks got red, just a bit, and he scratched the back of his head. "So do you want to have dinner tonight? I was thinking you could even eat the food this time."

I rolled my eyes. "Yeah, sure." I waited a beat. "Can I bring Becky?"

He froze and I moved ahead, laughing. Then he called after me, "You're not funny."

I shook my head and kept laughing. I was funny enough.

I had Lydia in my first two periods and she kept giving me weird looks. Jessica was in my third and fourth period. She refused to look at me. Then at lunch, when Becky dropped across from me and Adam went to sit with his football team, Jill joined their table along with Lydia and Jessica.

Becky looked over her shoulder and her eyes got wide. "I can't believe them."

"What?" I was cautious as I opened my bag lunch. Then I relaxed. Inside were an orange, a bag of chips, and a peanut butter sandwich. I gave her my chips, tossed the sandwich in the trash, and started to peel the orange.

"Jill Flatten. She's all over Jeff at the table. And I can't believe she's friends with *your* friends."

"They're not my friends."

"They were," she retorted and sent them a glare. Lydia had looked, but ducked her head down. "It's like Jill Flatten wants your life."

I sat back and fought off a yawn.

"Aren't you bothered at all by her?"

I shrugged. "Truthfully, no. It's sort of the last thing on my mind these days."

She gave me an incredulous look. "What else is going on in your life?"

If only she knew... I lifted a careless shoulder. "Jill Flatten does not bother me." Mason and Logan on the other hand... My mother... I shuddered. My whole life had fallen apart. Finding one good friend like Becky erased all the other friend drama.

"She bothers me." She peeked over her shoulder at them.

I looked this time too and saw all three of them had been staring at us. Lydia squeaked and looked at her food. Jessica's head whipped away and Jill only narrowed her eyes, but she held my gaze.

I narrowed mine back and stood.

Becky gasped, "What are you doing?"

I was tempted to shrug her off. I didn't know, but something propelled me across the lunch room. I stopped before their table and heard a lot of conversations hush. The football team sat at the 'popular' table, but most of the really popular girls sat at the other end where Adam was with the other varsity starters. Jill, Lydia, and Jessica sat at the far end where Jeff was, along with the other second string guys. Jeff was third string, actually.

Becky bumped into my elbow, and then apologized under her breath. She was panting from her hurry.

"Sam!" Adam called over and waved at us.

I ignored him.

Becky took my arm and hissed in my ear, "We can sit by him."

I shrugged her off and glanced up. I didn't know what made me look, but my fake father had entered the lunch room. He was dressed in his coach's apparel, a professional looking running suit with Fallen Crest Academy printed on his left shoulder underneath our school's crest.

"Yes?" Jill snapped at me. She tried to sound bored, like I was annoying her, but I heard the apprehension underneath it.

At the sight of David, everything hardened in me again. I was growing used to that feeling and I looked back at her. There was an added edge to me when I stepped close to their table and placed a hand right in front of her.

"Sam?" Jeff leaned forward and whispered. "What are you doing?"

Jessica still refused to look at me. Lydia had both her hands over her face, but her fingers were spread. She watched from behind them and I saw that she was holding her breath.

"You're wasting our lunch time," Jill snapped. "What do you want, Sam? You're pathetic."

Then Adam was beside me and his hand held my elbow. He pulled me back against him and spoke into my ear. As his lips moved, they brushed against me and I shivered from the teasing touch. "Sit with me. Let this go. Trust me, it won't be worth it."

"Fine." I released everything in me when I surrendered with that word.

He nodded and started to pull me away. I saw the looks of relief on Jessica, Lydia, and Jeff's faces. Jill looked disappointed, but David stepped in front of me. He gave Adam a polite nod. "Do you mind if I have a word with Samantha?"

I stiffened in Adam's hold and he cast a concerned look at me. Then he reluctantly nodded. "Sure."

David gestured towards the hall and I followed at a slower pace. I glanced back and saw that Adam had pulled Becky to sit beside him, but she watched me. Her eyes were small and she was biting her lip.

Then the door was pushed open and we stepped out into the empty hallway.

David gestured ahead. "My office?"

I rolled my eyes. "Is this about your car?"

"My office?"

I heard the forced politeness and followed. Everything in me was cement. I didn't care, not one iota, but I followed anyway. I was more curious to what he had to say and then when we were in his office and he shut the door, I knew he meant business. He indicated the couch across from his desk.

I perched on the end.

He took his seat and folded his hands on the desk. He looked at them.

I waited.

No one spoke.

Then he cursed under his breath and looked up. His eyes were bleak again.

I frowned. I didn't care why he looked like that. It made no difference to me now...

He started, "Do you know how much trouble you could've been?"

"If you had called the cops?"

"Yes," he snapped out. "Samantha, this is not a joke."

"I'm not laughing."

"If anyone else would've seen and had called the cops, I wouldn't have been able to protect you. The cops have the right to press charges, even if the offended party doesn't want them to."

"So you're saying you don't want me charged?"

He sighed and leaned back in his chair. "I didn't call the cops for a reason."

"Why's that?" I was in shock at my own voice. I sounded so bored.

He bit out a few curses. The hostility of them drew me upright again and something stirred in me. It was like I was coming awake again.

He glared at me. "Of course, I don't want you hurt. Why would you think that? I raised you, Samantha."

"Even though I'm not your daughter."

His chest heaved up and down and he looked like he was fighting for control. His voice was strained a second later. "I loved you, all your life, like you were my daughter. And what happened to you wasn't your fault—"

I shot to my feet, though I hugged myself. "According to Analise, it was both of your faults."

"I loved her." He laughed to himself. The sound sent chills down my back. "Because I don't make millions or because I'm not handsome like him doesn't mean that I didn't love your mother. I loved her very much."

I blinked. And everything was gone in the next moment. My anger vanished. My sarcasm, my self-loathing, my hatred for him—all was gone. And I collapsed down on the couch again. My face was buried in my hands.

He continued in a distant voice, "I loved how my marriage was." His chair squeaked and his voice was clearer now. "Stop hanging out with the Kade boys."

I looked up.

He watched me intently, his eyes never wavered away. "They are not good for you. They are dangerous to you."

It all shut down again and I stood. "I thought you said to make friends?"

"I was hoping for the best then. Now I'm preparing for the worst." His face was clouded. "Stay away from them, as much as possible. Please, Samantha."

I gave him a wry look. "If only it were that simple." And then I opened the door and went through the boys' locker room. The bell rang as I got to the hallway and I took refuge in my last three periods.

No Becky. No Adam. No one who cared was in those classes.

I was able to breathe easier knowing that.

After my last period, I escaped easily.

When I got to the mansion, I was surprised to find Logan in the dining room. He had books and papers spread out over the table and he glanced up idly. When he saw it was me, his focused snapped to attention. He gave me a lopsided grin, but my back straightened.

I wasn't fooled.

"We're doing a charity thing with your school this weekend."

I shrugged and went to the kitchen.

"It's another football game."

My hand paused when I reached for a water bottle.

"Your dad's going to be there." He'd gotten up and leaned against a counter close to me. "What are you going to do?"

I shut the door and watched him. "What do you mean?"

"Who are you going to cheer for? Your loser school or your new soon-to-be stepbrothers?"

"And why would you assume I'd be there?"

He shrugged, but I caught his cocky grin. "It's for charity. Your whole school will be there."

"When is it?"

"Saturday night."

"Why not Friday night?"

He rolled his eyes and pushed off from the counter. I tensed when he reached around me and opened the fridge. His arm brushed against my shoulder and he pulled out a container of juice. "Because we have our normal game that night. We play Collins. You should come, cheer us on."

"I think not." I pulled away and remained at a safe distance.

His eyes seemed to laugh at me. "Whatever. You've gotta come to the charity thing."

"And why's that?"

"Because we're going to win." He made it sound like it was the most obvious thing to do.

"Why do you think I care?"

"Because..." He chewed on his words. "Because Mason and I are the best. Why wouldn't you come?"

"Because I don't care about that?"

"Well, you should." He sounded miffed, like I had hurt his feelings.

I lifted a careless shoulder in the air.

He narrowed his eyes. "You're a bit odd in the head, aren't you?"

I couldn't hold back my grin. "What do you mean?"

"Most girls would blast it on the internet that we're your new stepbrothers. You act like we're your dirty secret."

"I like my privacy."

He shook his head. "We've got a couple parties this weekend too, if you want to go?"

"I'm good with my friends."

His eyes narrowed and he opened his mouth, but Mason came around the corner that instant. Logan clamped his mouth shut, but he continued to give me a puzzling stare.

"Let's go." Mason punched Logan in the shoulder as he bypassed us.

I looked over and held Mason's gaze before he went through the front door.

A different shiver went over my body at the sight of him and something left me when the door closed behind him. I refused to think it was anything more than hate...right?

CHAPTER TWELVE

That night I met Adam for burgers and he surprised me by bringing Becky. Everyone was happy until Jeff and Jill Flatten came in for their date night. They chose a booth across the restaurant so it was semi-easy to ignore them. When they left, Jeff gave me a once over and Jill gave me a glare.

Sigh.

I could've been a part of that.

Or not.

I shuddered at the thought of being with Jeff again, not to mention the deceit from Lydia and Jessica.

And since Becky must've been psychic, she shot forward and slammed a hand down on the table. "I heard Lydia telling Melissa Baker that Jeff asked about you."

Adam sat back.

"What are you talking about?"

She jerked her head up and down. "Uh huh. And Nancy Morrow overheard it too. He asked Lydia and Jessica about you, at Jessica's locker." She spoke like it was a hush-hush controversy.

"Come on, Becky. Jeff's not stupid."

"Yeah, he is."

"He knows that he's made his bed."

"My cousin is a jerk-one douche bag. I bet you fifty bucks that he's going to start talking to you again by the end of the month. And Jill knows it too." She pointed at the door with a French fry. "That's why she's upped her game against you."

"Since they got together, she's been like that."

"Yeah, but it's worse. I think she hates you." She glanced at Adam from underneath her eyelids. "And I think Ashley DeCortts is scared of you."

"Does she hate me too?" I hadn't done anything to anyone. Why did anyone care about me?

"No." Becky gave me a small smile. "It's not in Ashley to hate someone." She looked at Adam. "Right?"

He placed two hands against the table and pushed his chair back. When he stood, he plucked the bill from the table and went to the register.

"I think that's his answer for 'I don't care and let's get out of here.'"

Becky groaned. "I think he's mad at me."

"Why?"

"Because he brought me on your date, because he thought you wouldn't go without me, and now I'm bringing up Ashley." She leaned across the table and whispered behind her hands, "He still loves her, Sam."

When he started back to us, I stood. "Becky, you're just being you. Don't worry about it. You've got nothing to feel bad about."

She jumped to her feet and smoothed her hands down the front of her pants while she gave me an unsteady smile.

Adam stood behind me and asked in a low voice, "Sam, do you need a ride to school tomorrow?"

Becky's eyes got wide. She squeaked, but slapped both her hands over her mouth and jerked away.

As she hurried out the door, I couldn't stop a laugh. "Why are you like that to her?"

The corner of his mouth lifted. "Because she's so interested in everyone else's business. I don't think that's good for her."

"Let her be. That's just her being her."

"Yeah." His voice was wry. "I heard what you said to her."

I shrugged a shoulder. "That's how I feel."

As we both turned for the door, his hand cupped the back of my elbow. "You never answered about that ride."

I shook my head and pushed open the glass door. The evening had cooled and I knew I'd need a sweater soon.

Becky was already in his car, but I knew she could see us.

"Samantha?"

"My whole name?" I teased him before I gently twisted my elbow out of his hold. "I can give myself a ride. Thanks for the offer. That was sweet."

He tugged on the back of my pants when I was about to step down for the car and held me back. His voice was close to my ear. "I could give Becky and you a ride tomorrow."

I could imagine their reactions when they pulled up to the Kade mansion. And I chuckled dryly when I removed his hold from my pants. "That's okay, Don Juan, but I think Becky would appreciate a ride."

He laughed, huskily, and brushed against the back of my neck. "Maybe I'll do that then."

I gave him a curious look as I opened the front door and he rounded the car for his, but as he slid behind the steering wheel, his face was clouded. A wall had been put in place and from the little I knew Adam, I knew I wouldn't get that wall back down for a while.

When he drove us back to Becky's house where my car was parked, the ride was quiet. Even Becky was silent and I knew this was the right thing to do. He kept trying, but it wouldn't happen. It shouldn't happen. And he should give Becky rides. They were neighbors. A part of me felt he might start to like her, if only he'd get over whatever fascination he had for me.

I was broken. I didn't need to break anyone else with me.

When Adam pulled into his family's driveway, he didn't say goodbye. He got out of his side, shut the door, and strolled inside his family's house.

Becky gave me a sad smile as we were slower to get out. "He's mad. What'd you do?"

"Nothing." That was the truth. "He'll get over it."

"Yeah."

I sighed. How had I gotten into more drama? "I'll see you tomorrow."

"See you." She waved as I went to my car and drove off.

When I got home and after I had gone for a run, it was late. The place was empty, not a shocker. It always seemed empty except for the random sandwich wrapped in saran wrap that Mousteff would leave in the refrigerator for me. After I showered, I headed downstairs to the media room with a glass of water. I found Mason on the couch with the sports channel on the television and I hesitated in the doorway.

"Sit."

I jumped at his command, but I did.

He lounged back on the couch with a beer on the table beside it. The television lights played across his face. It gave him a dark look, a somber one that added to the alarm I always felt around him. His eyes were on the screen and then they were on me. I tensed at the sudden change, at the intensity in them, but steeled myself. I was starting to think this was what he'd always be like, primed and alert.

"Logan and Nate went to some party."

"Oh." I winced at how timid I sounded.

He yawned and looked away.

I was released from his gaze and my body sagged from the relief of it. "What party?"

He jerked a shoulder up. "Don't care."

"Oh."

Then he smirked. "Your mom wants to take Logan and me to dinner Sunday."

I narrowed my eyes. All the nerves I felt around him hardened at the mention of her. "Why?"

He looked back at me. The same caution was in his gaze as I felt in my body. "I was going to ask you the same question."

Then it clicked. "That's why you didn't go to the party. You wanted to question me about her."

He didn't blink. "You'd do the same."

He was right and I nodded. "If you want to know my mom's agenda, I'm guessing it's because she wants to get to know you guys."

"She told you on the patio that afternoon she knew us well enough."

So they *had* heard. I'd been wondering.

I sat up straighter in my chair. "She was lying."

He didn't say anything.

My voice grew bolder. "My mom wants everyone to do what she wants and she said those things so I'd do what she wanted. I think she wants to take you guys out for dinner to try and charm you."

"It won't work."

He said it so bluntly, but I knew it was the truth. A shiver went down my spine as I held his gaze in that darkened room with an empty mansion around us. Mason Kade was not stupid, far from it, and I wondered if I'd known it the whole time, if perhaps that's why I stayed away. He watched behaviors, he didn't listen to words. I wondered if Logan was the same and something in my gut told me he was.

"It worked on your father."

"My dad has a weakness for weak women."

Again, there was no judgment. It was a fact and he said it as such. The truth of it held more power because of the lack of emotion with him.

My throat had gone dry. "You called my mother weak."

"Isn't she?"

His gaze was searing into mine.

My chest tightened. My throat clamped up. "I—uh—"

He snorted in disgust. "You think so too, but you can't say the words, not to me. That's alright. I understand. She's your blood."

Then he looked away and again, my whole body almost fell from the chair. It was as if he had pinned me in place and I was free from the hold.

My hands curled in on themselves and I couldn't stop my fingers from trembling. I tucked them between my legs and took a breath. I needed to gain control of myself again.

In that moment, I realized that he always had that affect on me. The ice façade I reined over myself was plucked away whenever his attention was on me. He reached over and took it away like I was a baby with candy.

"Does my mom know you don't like her?" It was a weird question, but I wanted to know how he thought. I wanted to understand him.

He grinned at me. The power of that look with his piercing eyes, perfect teeth, and square jaw had me pinned against my chair again. I couldn't breathe for a moment.

Then I heard him laugh. "Your mom doesn't care. She cares if we're going to make a stink or not."

I snorted. That sounded just like her. "And are you?"

He shrugged and went back to the television. "As long as she doesn't screw with me and Logan or with our mom then I don't care who my dad pounds."

"And if they get married? My mom's not stupid."

"Your mom's a shark."

"Your father is wealthy."

Then he laughed again and the genuineness of it struck me. "My dad has money, but my mom is wealthy."

My eyes widened a fraction. I would put money down my mom had no idea about that tidbit. It made things a lot clearer, why the boys didn't seem to care too much about the marriage.

"Do you care?"

I was struck by how he seemed to really want to know. I shook my head. "Why would I?"

"Because your mom's going to look a fool when she learns how rich my mom is."

I hadn't considered it, but he was right. Analise was ambitious and she'd grown more ambitious since leaving my—David. It would burn her ego, in some way, and then I realized why he was telling me this. I was the one who'd pay for it. Analise would take her anger out on me and I sucked in my breath. I was grateful for his slight warning, because it was one that I'd need to keep tucked in the back of my mind.

We heard a door open upstairs and Logan's near-hysterical laughter followed a second later.

Mason grinned to himself before he stood up and left with his beer in hand.

"Mason! Dude, there was a girl with boobs out to here. I couldn't believe it." Logan's voice carried down the stairs. His laughter wouldn't stop. "Nate bagged her."

Mason's and Nate's voices joined in at a low murmur.

I tuned them out and turned the television to a different channel. When a bunch of rich women came on the screen, I settled back. My mom would've loved that show; she would've loved to have been on that show. When they started fighting with each other, I closed my eyes and fell asleep.

CHAPTER THIRTEEN

Becky gushed about her ride with Adam the next morning when she found me at my locker. She gushed about the charity football game at lunch. The next day was a similar chain of events except Adam sat with us at our table. It didn't faze Becky from raving about Saturday's game. On Thursday a few of his friends joined him at our table and one seemed amused by Becky's passionate monologue about the Kade brothers, who was better, who was better looking, etc. He teased and prodded her along until Becky seemed like she was going to shout from the rooftop how hot Mason and Logan Kade were. At one point I thought she'd been about to proclaim they could beat our entire football team, only the two of them.

She caught herself, blushed, and her head went down.

The guys didn't hold back their laughter and she turned to me. I patted her arm when she sighed, "I sounded like an idiot, didn't I?"

Even Adam couldn't hold back his grin.

And then things turned awkward when Jeff stopped at the end of our table. He had a tray of food in one hand and his backpack over the other shoulder. He hitched it higher and gave me a small wave. "Hey, Sam."

I leaned back.

Adam leaned forward. "What are you doing, Sallaway?"

Jeff looked around the guys and ended on Becky. "Hey, cousin. How's your mom doing?"

She glared. "She's fine."

"That's cool." He bobbed his head up and down.

"Jeff!"

Jill strode towards us with stiff legs. Her chin was clenched and her eyes glittered in anger.

One of the guys whistled under his breath. "Catfight."

Jeff shot him a look, but turned towards his girlfriend with a wide smile.

I saw it slip a little.

"Hey, babe. What's up?"

She latched onto his arm and her smile froze in place. "Nothing. What are you doing over here?"

He jerked his arm towards me. "I wanted to say hi."

"Why?" Her eyes seared at me.

Becky's hand rested on my arm under the table. I suppose she wanted to support me, but I was entertained. I grinned back at Jill and her mouth twitched a bit.

He shrugged again and tried to remain cool. "Because I think it's stupid that we're not talking. Lydia and Jess too. They were best friends." He stole a look underneath lidded eyes at Adam and the guys.

My back straightened. He was lying.

Jill's fingers curled into his arm and Jeff froze under her grip. Then he frowned and flung her hand off. "Ouch! Crap, woman. That hurt."

"So, Adam," Jill turned towards him. Fake warmth oozed from her pores. "How do you think the game will go on Saturday?"

One of the guys scoffed, "We have a real game on Friday."

Another added, "No one cares about that one."

Adam shot both a look and straightened in his chair. "I think we'll be fine."

"Why is that?" She leaned forward to give him a view of the upper curves of her boobs. Cleavage heaven was on display.

Jeff was eagerly lapping up his view.

Becky yipped out, "You don't think the team will win?"

Jill settled back on her heels and turned ice eyes towards her. "They did get creamed last week by them."

"Yeah, but that was a real game. It counted."

Adam shot Becky a dark look.

She didn't see it and plodded on, "This game doesn't really count. I heard the Kade brothers might not even play. They didn't come for the charity event last year."

"They have to come." Jill's eyes were sharp. "That's why we chose the football team, so they'd come."

Jeff moved back. "You want them to come?"

"What? I mean, you're going to do fine, honey."

"I don't play in a real game."

"Yeah, but it's for charity." She pressed herself against him and cooed again. "I bet their third string plays too. Charity for everyone."

Becky's mouth closed with an audible snap. The guys were silent for a second and then burst out laughing. Even Adam wiped at something in his eyes. Jill's eyebrows shot up and her smile froze in place.

Jeff tore himself away. "So I'm the charity? Is that what you're saying?"

"No, honey. Jeff! That's not what I meant." She hollered and went after as he stalked out of the cafeteria.

One of the guys whistled. "Man, Sam. You didn't even say a word. How'd you get out of that?"

I offered up a shoulder. "Talent?"

Both of Adam's friends laughed while Becky's eyes went wide. "You didn't, did you? I thought Jill was going to leap at you with her nails."

Adam shook his head. "I think that's why Sam kept quiet."

"Yeah, that pissed off Decimator even more. Good thinking."

"It hadn't been my plan, but I'll take it. Decimator?"

The guy struck a cocky pose. "She decimates her way through guys. The Decimator."

"I agree with that. She is a decimator." Becky went back to eating as she nodded her agreement.

Adam gave me a half grin. "You okay?" He lowered his voice and inched closer across the table.

I shrugged, but I didn't say anything because I didn't have anything to say. I didn't care about Jeff and I hadn't for a long time.

Adam kept giving me concerned looks through the rest of the day and the day after, but it didn't matter. I didn't care anymore and Jeff picked up on that too after I walked past him and Jill in the hallway. I hadn't known they were there until I almost bowled them over. They were with Lydia and Jessica. After I muttered a quick apology, one that I'd give to anybody, I hurried on my way. It wasn't until I was about to turn the corner that I looked back and realized who I had run into.

Jill seemed upset, but Jessica and Lydia stared at me. They watched me.

Jeff's shoulder slumped and he had a downcast expression on his face. When his eyes met mine for a brief second, I saw an apology flash through his.

It was over. Really over and he knew it as well.

My step had a lighter bounce to it for the rest of the day. That lasted until the end of the day when Lydia cornered me later. She'd been waiting at my car. I slowed when I saw her, but what could I do? I wasn't stupid enough or crazy enough to try running home again.

"Hey." She shot up from my car and twisted her hands together. "How are you?"

"What do you want?"

Hurt flashed in her eyes, but she looked down. "Nothing, I just—how are you?"

I let my bag drop to the ground before I unlocked my door. "I'm fine. You?"

She gave me a tentative smile. "I think Justin Beardsley might ask me out."

I nodded. "Cool."

"So you and Adam, huh?" A strand of her hair was wound in her hand and she began to twirl it around. "That's exciting, really exciting. I tried telling Jessica we should be happy for you, but—"

"Why would she?" My tone was flat. "She slept with my boyfriend for two years to get back at me."

Lydia fell silent.

"She doesn't care, now or then."

"Yes, she does. I know she does." But she sounded as if she wanted to convince herself.

"Jessica doesn't care. At least she has the decency not to fake it anymore."

Lydia's mouth opened, but nothing came out.

And Becky bounced up to us at that moment. "How's it going?" I knew she spoke to me, but her glare was directed at Lydia.

Lydia's hands started to twist together again. "Hi, Becky."

"Hi, Lydia. What are you doing?"

"I'm just saying hi to Sam." She sighed. "Is that okay?"

Becky jerked her shoulder up and frowned, but she looked away. "I guess. It's Sam's decision. I mean, you guys were friends before me after all."

I rolled my eyes. "Are you serious?"

Both girls jumped at my tone.

I tried to gentle it. "Are you two pissing on each other for my friendship? I don't deal with that. You both should know that."

Lydia seemed frozen in place as she watched me, but Becky hung her head. "I know. I'm sorry."

"I have to get home." I started to reach for my car door again.

"Are you coming to the game tonight?" Becky rushed forward.

"Probably not. Why would I?"

"Because they're playing Roussou. There might be a bunch of action tonight, with the guys being in town after what we heard the Kades had done to their coach's house and some of the other guys."

I frowned at that. "I haven't heard anything."

"Oh." She seemed confused. "I thought I told you about that."

"Well, you didn't."

"Anyway, are you coming tonight?"

"No." I didn't hesitate.

Lydia looked away. Her eyes had been glued to me, like I was a television show for her. Now her whole body seemed to retreat away.

I frowned at her, but was distracted when Becky asked in an excited breath, "And tomorrow? You have to come. It's for charity." Her voice turned into a whine.

I sighed, but I already knew I'd go. Logan had been harassing me over the past week with the same question. Mason never asked, but Nate told me once that he wanted me to come. I hadn't a clue why.

"I don't know. Probably, okay?"

Again, Lydia seemed struck by something. She fell back a couple of steps before she caught herself.

I snapped at her, "What's your problem?"

She blinked rapidly a few times before she rasped out, "Uh, nothing. You're, just, you've changed."

"Yeah. Life does that to you." Then I swung my door open and got inside. I couldn't explain it, but both annoyed me. And when I was able to get home and go on my run, my mind finally started to clear after a couple of hours. It took that long before I calmed myself down. When I returned home, the evening's darkness had started to creep in.

My mother waited for me at the dining room table. She had a large glass of wine before her and every room was lit up around us. Her fingers kept tapping the table in a nervous manner—or, as I got a better look at Analise—in an irritated manner.

I didn't even wait for her to say anything. I dropped to a chair at the table and waited.

My headache had come back.

"I am taking the boys out for dinner on Sunday after church. If you are able to refrain from physical violence, I'd like for you to join us."

Her tone felt like whiplash against me.

I jerked away, but readied myself again. She couldn't hurt me unless I allowed her. "Why do you want me there?"

She gave a dramatic long-drawn out sigh and whirled the wine around inside the glass. "Because you are my daughter. Mason and Logan are going to be my stepsons, your stepbrothers. You don't think I think about this? I'm concerned for you, Samantha. I really am."

"Really?" My tone was dry, I couldn't keep it out.

She winced against it, but swallowed it down. Then she forced out her bright sunshiney fake act. "How are things at school? Have you seen David at all?"

"Once."

"Oh." She seemed to pull away from me, though she didn't move in her chair. Then she threw the rest of her wine down the back of her throat. "That's good that you still have him in your life. Have you ever considered going to public schooling? Mason and Logan seem to do very well there."

I rolled my eyes. They would've been fine anywhere they went.

"So you want me at this dinner thing?"

"You are my daughter."

"And you can refrain from slapping me?"

She winced, but I knew the movement cost her. A slight curse slipped from her lips and she tried to hide it.

"Mother?"

"What?" She lifted glazed eyes to me. "I think the dinner will be great. I could cook something, maybe? No, that didn't end well the last time. You're right. Dinner out is the best idea. I'm so happy you think so."

Yeah. Me too.

CHAPTER FOURTEEN

Becky called me bright and early the next morning. "Bad news bears, Sam."

I rolled over and sat up with a yawn. "It's seven in the morning. On a Saturday morning."

"I know. I just got home."

"So you decided to call and say good morning? You suck."

"No." Her voice was bright and chirpy. "I'm still drunk so it's probably not sinking in yet, but I can't go to the game tonight."

I groaned. There went my one friend to sit with.

"There was a party on the beach by Lydia's house and I'm getting back. Mom caught me this morning so I'm grounded now."

"You went to Lydia's party?" I should've asked, 'Lydia had a party? And you went to it?'

"Oh no. The party was by her house, I think some other girl threw it, but I dunno. Anyways, we had to wait till Adam was sober enough to drive. I kept drinking all night. Lydia's actually kind of funny."

"You were with Lydia? You two were pissing on each other."

She giggled. "Not literally, but she explained a few things to me and I fell for her. Sort of. Not really. Oh well. So I'm not going to the game tonight so that means you don't have to go either. I know I was the only reason you were going anyway."

I picked at some lint on my bedcover. "I might've gone to cheer for Adam, too."

"Aw." Her voice melted. "That's so sweet. I'll make sure to tell him. It'll mean a lot to him. He doesn't think you care about him at all."

"Are you kidding me?" I grumbled into the phone. "You're the one that likes him."

"Yeah, but he doesn't like me."

"You're a bit not right in the head, Becky."

"I know!" she chirped again, followed by a giggle. "He held my hand to the car."

"Were you falling down drunk?"

"That and the sand was really tricky to walk through."

"I'm sure it was." I lay back down on the bed and closed my eyes. Something was telling me this phone call wasn't going to let me go back to sleep anytime soon.

"So, what'd you do last night?"

I grinned into the phone. "Well, I didn't get drunk and hold hands with my crush all night long."

She giggled again. "I wish it was all night long. Maybe I could get drunk more? You think he'd do that every time?"

"No."

"Yeah, you're right." She sighed. "It'd be nice, though. I wish I could hold his hand all the time."

"Why don't you just ask him out?"

"Because he doesn't like me. How many times do I have to tell you?"

"Whatever." I gripped the phone tighter. "I think there's something there. Maybe he'd have to man up and make a decision already."

Silence.

I sighed.

There was more silence on the phone.

Then I asked, "Did I say something wrong?"

Her voice was timid. "It's not that easy for some of us."

"What do you mean by that?"

"Sometimes all we have is our imagination."

I frowned and cursed under my breath. "Your imagination? Your fairytale that's holding you back?"

She sucked in her breath.

I bit back another curse. I'd forgotten Becky was one of those girls. "I'm sorry."

"For what?" She sounded like she had started to cry.

I cursed myself and hit my forehead with my hand. "For not being sensitive."

"It's okay," she hiccupped.

"No, I really am sorry."

"I know." She hiccupped again. "It's okay. I know you didn't mean it."

I gritted my teeth, but said nothing. The problem was that I did mean it; I meant every word of it and more.

"So, since we're not going to the game, my mom said you could come over tonight. You want to come over here? I think we'll do dinner and movies."

"Um." How could I lie myself out of this one? "My mom said something about dinner too."

"She did?"

"Yeah." I sat up and scooted to the edge of the bed. "But I don't know. I'm not sure what I should do. I might still go and cheer for Adam tonight."

"You're going to go alone?" She sounded so small.

"Maybe. I don't know."

"I don't want you to be alone."

"Oh no. I'll be fine."

My door opened at that moment and Logan stuck his head inside. When he saw I was on the phone, he lifted a hand in a half-wave and frowned at me. I motioned for him to go away, but he only grinned and pushed the door open to come inside.

"Uh," I said in a hurry. "I have to go, Becky. I'll call you later."

"You're really going to the game still? Alone?"

"Oh yeah. I'll be fine."

Logan stood right behind me. I turned around and he breathed on my neck now. I tried to shove him away.

TIJAN

"Okay…"

"See you. I'll call you tonight." And I hung up, breathless. Then I whirled around. "What are you doing?"

He smirked at me.

"This is my room. This is my privacy. Get out."

He laughed. "You're just pissed because one of your friends might've heard me."

"Do you blame me?"

"Nah, guess not." And he threw himself backwards on my bed before he scooted back to sit against the wall. "So you're coming tonight? You're going to cheer on your future brothers?"

My lip curled up in disgust. "Don't say that word again."

"Brothers?" Logan's hyena laugh came out and he twisted to chortle into my pillow. "I cnn't beliff ith."

I sighed and rolled my eyes before I took hold of his arm and started to pull him up. "Come on. Get out. I want to go for a run."

He dodged my hand and chuckled when he went to the door. "You should run with Mason sometime."

"What?"

"You should run with Mason sometime."

"What do you mean by that?"

He lifted a shoulder in the air. "He runs too, most of it's at practice, but I bet he'd smoke you."

I quirked an eyebrow up. "You think so?"

He puffed out his chest. "I know so."

"I can run for hours."

"So can he."

Then I shook my head and turned away. "I'm not going to get into this with you."

"What? That Mason's better than you at running?" Logan rushed around and blocked my way to the bathroom. His cocksure smirk was back in place and he folded his arms over his chest. "Why don't the two of you throw down? I'd like to see that."

264

I shoved him aside. "I'm not going to race, either of you."

He taunted behind me, "Scared?"

I froze. My shoulders went up, my chin hardened, and the hairs on the back of my neck stood straight up. I turned around slowly. "What did you say?"

He looked too sure of himself. "You heard me."

Both of my eyebrows went up.

"I think you're scared."

"Come again?" I laughed out with a pout.

He took a step close. "I think you're scared of losing."

"I wouldn't lose."

He took another step closer and he was against my chest. He peered down, through his thick eyelashes. His breath wafted over my skin. "I think you're scared of everything."

Something snapped and I shoved him back again, this time he slammed against my bed frame.

My arms were stiff against my side and I clipped out, "I'm not afraid of anything."

He laughed as he pushed himself up from the bed frame. "Whatever you say to yourself at night."

"I mean it."

"Yeah, yeah." He dismissed me with a wave. "See you, sister. Have a good one tonight."

When he left and the door had closed behind him, I let out a shaking breath and realized my fingers were pressed into the palm of my hands. I pulled them out and saw the blood start immediately. They'd been pressed so tight, so hard. I hadn't felt a thing.

My jaw trembled when I went back to the bathroom, but I turned on the shower.

I wasn't afraid. I wasn't afraid of anything.

The football stadium light's lit up the field, bleachers, and two of the parking lots around it. As I approached my school's field, a different sense filled me. I wasn't a fan of the game, but I had come at times to support David. Now I came to support the enemy, or who I had considered the enemy.

Lydia, Jessica, and Jeff at times had sat beside me.

After I got a soda and a football program, I sat alone this time. My two ex best friends were higher on the bleachers and I knew Lydia's mouth had fallen at the sight of me. Jessica refused to look, like always. Jill was on the track in front in her cheerleader outfit. She paused in her stretching to glare at me.

I sat back and drank some soda. Then I saluted her with the thing.

Her nose wrinkled up and she turned her back when Ashley DeCortts approached her. Both girls glanced over their shoulders at me after a moment. I gave them a wide smile this time.

It wasn't long before the teams ran out on the field. The Academy side gave Adam a big cheer when he was introduced in the line-up, but when Mason and Logan were introduced, I swore the ground shook.

I had no idea. It was as if they were gods. I shook at my head at how weird it seemed to me.

When the ball kicked off, I tried to pay attention to Adam, Mason, and Logan's numbers. The one that was most obvious was Jeff's, 33. It blared up at me as he stood right in front of where I sat. He didn't play the whole time, but that was fine by me.

During halftime there were a lot of announcements and drawings for the charity raffles. Ashley and Jill giggled into the microphone at one point for some sell-off. I had no idea what they were talking about. Their cheerleader-esque language kept creeping into the microphone. I grew tired of trying to figure out what 'pep' actually meant to them, but it seemed to go over well with the crowd. There was a big cheer and Jessica's name was announced after.

Lydia screamed the loudest. Jessica stood in surprise, but it was fake. She had a small smirk on her face and I knew whatever had been done was all a scam. She had known the whole time she was going to win. As she passed by me and didn't seem to realize I sat there, I sat up straighter. Whatever she had won must've been important for her to forget the chill-factor any time she was in my vicinity.

I nudged the girl next to me. "What'd she win?"

"A date with Logan Kade."

I grabbed her arm when she started to turn for her friends. "What?"

Her lip curled up and she gave me a look in disdain. "Like I said, a date with the ever-so-great Logan Kade. Get your hand off me."

I let go, but scooted closer. "Was that a drawing or something?"

She shrugged and rolled her eyes. "I have no idea. Can I talk to my friends now?"

"Oh yeah. Whatever."

The girl's bitchiness didn't bother me. She was a sophomore. She had two more years to get stepped on and I knew it'd happen. It always happened.

Then she surprised me when she looked back at me. "Aren't you Samantha Strattan?"

"Yeah. Why?"

"Shouldn't you know about your new brother being auctioned off?"

Everything stopped for me. The hairs on my neck stood up. My claws came out. My tongue fell thick, but I gave her the most polite look I would muster in all my years and asked in a voice so professional my mother would've been proud, "What do you mean by that?"

The sophomore narrowed her eyes, but rolled them after. "My twin sister goes to public. Logan Kade said that you were his new sister. Is that, like, not true?"

My heart started to pound and my chest got heavy. I felt a heart attack coming on, but I still asked in that painfully polite voice, "What do you mean?"

She made some sound and I felt snobbery written all over it. Then she tugged down her frayed mini skirt and wrapped her athletic jacket tighter around her. "Whatever. He probably made it all up."

"Yeah," I said faintly as she turned back away. "Probably."

Oh god. Logan had spilled the beans. People would know. My world was going to end.

Adam would know.

Jessica would know.

Lydia would know.

And, I gulped. Becky would know.

There'd be no anonymity any more. Everyone would know. Most would care. And I groaned as I lowered my head to my lap. People would either love me or they'd hate me. My guess is that they'd all hate me.

Round two of hell, here we come.

And, of course, Lydia dropped into the chair beside me at that moment. "Hi!"

I jumped from how cheery she sounded.

Then she scooted close and lowered her voice. "We only have a few minutes. Jessica's over the moon. I'm sure she'll be with Jill and Ashley for a while. How are you?" Her hand clamped onto mine and she gave it a squeeze.

"I'm...fine..."

Her smile stretched wide. "Good. That's good. I talked to Becky last night. She's so funny. Why didn't you tell me how funny she could be?"

"Because...." Had Lydia grown two heads? I swore one was sane, but this one—not so much. "I have no idea."

She doubled over with laughter.

I scooted an inch away.

She scooted with me and pressed her leg up against me. "Come on, Sam. How are you really?" She whispered behind a hand. "I heard that Adam likes you, like really likes you. That's great, although I knew that'd happen." Her hand squeezed again. "Are you excited?"

"Um."

She rushed in, "You'll make a great couple. I just know it."

The sophomore bitch turned back with eyebrows high. "You're dating Adam Quinn?" She gave me a once-over.

I returned the favor and spoke in her same bored, stuck-up tone, "Why's that your business?"

She clamped her mouth shut and turned away. A bunch of her friends behind us scooted forward and I knew the whispers were about me.

I was starting to get used to it.

"She's coming," Lydia hissed and shot from the chair.

A second later Jessica walked past my seat and back to her old one. When she saw me, her smile froze for a second, but then she murmured, "Hello."

I almost fell of my seat.

If Jessica gave me the time of day that meant she was happy, really happy, and that left me with a sense of dread. From the little time I'd had to get to know the real Jessica, I knew she wasn't happy unless she got whatever she had set her sights on.

Logan.

Maybe she thought she had him in her clutches after all?

I spent the rest of the game weighing my options. Jessica, ex best friend who'd been screwing my boyfriend for two years to get back at me and now she's best friends with his new girlfriend. Jessica wanted Logan. I happened to know the guy...what to do?

When the game ended and Fallen Crest Public had trounced my school, once again, I stood with the rest and started to make my way towards the parking lot. Lydia squealed my name as I was almost off the bleachers and gave me an excited wave with a thumbs-up sign.

I wasn't sure what she was thumbing-up, but I gave her a small wave back.

When I got to the parking lot, I had to stand back with a bunch of others as our team first ran through, followed by the next team.

And then two arms came from nowhere and lifted me off the ground. I was swung around before I was placed back on my feet.

I leaned back and saw Logan's smiling face. "We won! Did you have any doubt? Tell me you cheered for the winning team?"

Oh no... I looked around. Eyebrows were up. Hands were hiding mouths and heads were bent together. Then I saw Lydia and Jessica behind me. Both had frozen looks on them. Jessica was white as a ghost.

"Hey!" Logan embraced me again. "I scored three touch downs, of course Mason got all the blocks for me, but I scored. Aren't you going to congratulate me, sis?"

"What?" Jessica choked out.

Then a hand clamped on Logan's shoulder and he was pulled with the rest of his team. He turned back and yelled, "You're going out with us, Sammy. We're going to party tonight. No more loser parties for you!"

One of his teammate laughed and said something in his ear. Logan tipped his head back and his hyena laugh came out again.

Then I turned back around and felt the ground start to shake again.

Mason had stopped behind me. He had a quizzical look on his face and he reached a hand to scratch at the back of his head.

"Hi." I clutched a hand to my stomach and wondered why I was breathless all the sudden.

"Hey?" He looked where Lydia and Jessica stood. "Are they your friends?"

"No." I shook my head and moved closer to him.

He did too and we were almost touching, his pads to my shoulders. He bent his head so he could hear me. "They were my best friends."

"Got it." Then he gave me a small grimace. "Your mom mentioned that you were coming for dinner on Sunday?"

I jerked my head in a nod. I couldn't catch my breath.

"Good," he sighed.

I looked up in surprise.

He shrugged. "She's bearable when you're around." Then he frowned. "Did I hear Logan yell at you to party with us?"

"Yeah. He did."

"Good." He nodded. "We might have some actual fun." Then his hand touched my shoulder, lightly and briefly. "Wait for me after this. I'll give you a ride."

I was about to tell him that I had a car, but he had started to jog after his team. There was a line of girls who had been watching and all looked as he went past them.

Before their heads could snap back to me, I started to turn away. Lydia and Jessica were in front of me, both with fierce expressions on their faces.

I steered myself. This was not going to be good.

CHAPTER FIFTEEN

Lydia pushed herself forward and was an inch from my face. I felt her breath on me. "You know Mason Kade?" She had a sharp tone, but she was shoved aside as Jessica took her place.

Her eyes were narrowed, mouth tight, and I wondered if steam could come out of a person. She folded her arms over her chest and cooled her tone. "How do you know Logan?"

I glanced around. Jill and Ashley had stopped not far from us. Their cheerleading bags were both on the ground and I knew they heard every word. Each wore a different expression, one seemed wary and the other looked to share in Jessica's fury.

I sighed and stepped back. "I don't know what you're talking about."

Lydia sucked in her breath while Jessica's eye narrowed even more. "Logan hugged you and Mason talked to you. You can't lie about that."

I shrugged and grinned. "Guess they're playing some game with you, Jess, because I don't know them. Never have, never will, never want to."

"Are you serious?" Lydia frowned.

I rolled my eyes and tried to exude a bored attitude. "Not my problem."

"Samantha." Jessica planted herself in front of me when I tried to turn away. She put her hands on her hip. "You can't be lying about this."

"I don't know them." I paused. "And if I did, what business is it of yours?"

She seemed to hesitate now.

"Exactly." I shoved her aside and started for my car, but Nate intercepted me. He held out some keys and remarked, "Here are Mason's keys. Give me yours; I'll take your car home."

I didn't turn around, but I knew Jessica and Lydia had heard. I could feel their disbelief and anger rolling off of them. I sighed and held out my hand. "Whatever."

Nate grinned as he plucked my keys for Mason's. Then he glanced over my shoulder. "I take it those are the two who stabbed you in the back."

"Pretty much."

He frowned. "You haven't dealt with them yet?"

"Not yet."

I felt his eyes scanning my face when he asked, "Are you planning to?"

"Guess I have to now."

"Ah." He tipped his head back in understanding. "Cat's out of the bag, huh? Sorry about that."

"Logan's not. He shouted it to everyone."

He grinned at that. "Yeah, when he decides he likes someone he gets pretty excited about 'em." He folded his arms over his chest. "He doesn't like a lot of people."

I didn't look up when I asked, "And Mason?"

I heard his husky chuckle. "Logan wouldn't like you if Mason hadn't given the stamp of approval."

I looked up now, breathless again. "And when was that?"

He shrugged and looked past my shoulder again. "When he stopped you from hitting your mom. If he didn't give a damn about you, he would've watched you clobber her. Hell, I wanted to get snacks for the show. When Mason steps in, there's always a reason."

I nodded. "I'm starting to get that."

He clamped his hand on my shoulder. "Don't worry about this stuff, your friends and all. Logan's bound and determined to make you have fun tonight so I'd relax and let it happen."

I grinned. "Ah, what all rapists say to their intended victims."

Nate pulled back, narrowed his eyes, but barked out an abrupt laugh. "Yeah, I guess." Then he nodded in the direction of Jessica and Lydia. "You want me to play guard dog until you're in Mason's car?"

I spotted the black Escalade not far and shook my head. "Nah. I'm good." Then I chuckled to myself. "This is becoming a whole adventure."

"Guess you could look at it that way." He patted my shoulder again. "See you later."

"See you," I muttered under my breath as I watched him cut through Jessica and Lydia like a knife would go through butter. He didn't care who he rolled over and both jumped back, eyes wide in shock.

I shook my head and couldn't stop another chuckle as I swung towards Mason's car. "Samantha!" Jessica called after me, but I ignored her until I was close to his car. Then I turned back around, leaned against his hood, and crossed my legs. I wasn't about to hide inside.

They stood where I had left and watched me. Jill and Ashley joined them and all four didn't say a word as they stared.

I lifted my chin up.

We were at a stand-off, but it didn't last long. Adam came out of the locker room and started to walk to his car. He caught sight of the other girls, followed their gazes and saw me. He stopped in the middle of us before he shook his head and came over. When he drew near, he reached up and shook out some of his wet hair.

"Hey." He nodded across the parking lot. "What's with the brigade over there?"

I frowned. I hadn't considered Adam before. "It's nothing, just stupid stuff."

"This about Sallaway again?"

I barked out a laugh. "No, not this time."

"Oh." He gave me a small smile. "So you came without Becky, huh?"

"Yep. I sat with some snobby sophomore even. Good times."

He grinned. "I just got off the phone with her."

"The stuck-up sophomore?" I teased.

"Becky," he laughed. "She said something about a sleeping pill so now she can sneak out. Want to go with me? I was going to pick her up before some party the guys want to hit tonight."

"What party is that?"

He shrugged. "I'm not sure, but it's a Public one so I'm sure it'll be good. You want to come with?" Then his eyes widened a bit and a quick frown appeared. "Isn't this Mason Kade's car?"

I stood from the car. "About that, I should call Becky. There are some things I need to tell her first...before she hears it from the wrong people."

He stepped back and a wall came over him. "So you *do* know the Kades."

I hesitated and lifted my shoulders. There wasn't much I could say, not when I owed Becky an explanation first. She was the only one who really deserved one, if anyone even did.

"Got it." He nodded his head in an abrupt jerking movement. "Maybe I'll see you at the party, huh?"

"Adam." He turned and started for his car at a fast walk. I called after him again, "Adam."

"Are you dating your team's quarterback?"

I turned back around. Mason stood behind me and I searched for any inflection in his question. There was none. He didn't seem to care. His hair was wet from a shower and he wore a plain black tee shirt over jeans.

I shrugged now. "Not really."

He grinned and took his keys from my hand. "I would've sacked him harder if I knew that." As he unlocked the car and we both got in, he asked, "You hungry?"

Not after that, but I lifted a shoulder. "I guess."

"Good." He flashed me a smile. "I'm starving."

As he peeled out of the parking lot, we went past where Lydia and Jessica remained in place. Their mouths hung open, along with Jill's. Ashley seemed calm. She even lifted her hand in a small wave.

I ignored it, but a sense of unease settled deep in my stomach. It wasn't good. None of this was good. If only Logan hadn't announced it and if Mason had ignored me in the parking lot, or if I had gotten out of their way—this all could've been avoided. I could've prevented it by going straight to my car and not dawdling, but I had...had I done it for a reason? For this reason? Did I want my secret out?

"You want anything?"

I jerked my head up and saw we were in a burger joint's parking lot. "Uh, no. I'm good."

"You sure?" Mason jerked his head towards his door. "Come on. Come in with me. You'll need all the substance you can get once Logan finds you at the party."

I opened my door and rounded the car. My palms were sweaty so I wiped them down the front of my pants. My stomach's nerves kicked up a notch when Mason held the door for me. He let it go when I stepped inside and led the way through the next door until we got inside. The air conditioner was still on inside and it gave me goose bumps.

A girl stood behind the register and her eyes got wide when she saw Mason. I recognized her from my school and then I remembered who she was. Her father was the manager and he wasn't very nice from what Lydia had told me a year ago.

She gave me a timid smile. "Hi, Sam."

I waved, but didn't respond. I couldn't remember the girl's name.

Mason ordered for both of us and when he pulled out his wallet, her father came from the back. He shook his head and held out his hand. "Not from a Kade. I'm Walter Dubrois. I'm the manager of Burger Play."

Mason shook his hand. "Thanks, sir."

"Tell your father I said hello and you can eat free here anytime."

"Thanks again."

The food was quickly bagged up, by Walter himself, and I couldn't hold back a laugh in disbelief when we got into Mason's Escalade.

"What?"

I gestured to the building. "Does that happen often?"

He grimaced as he unwrapped his burger. "Sometimes, usually by some douche bag who wants to kiss my dad's ass."

I shook my head. "You get free food; you can basically sleep with any girl you want. You have a very different life than the rest of us."

"What do you mean by that?" There was an edge to his voice.

I looked over and held his gaze. The butterflies were long gone now. A storm had started to roll in. "I always knew you guys were like gods, but man, I didn't realize it was like this."

He lifted his burger. "Free fast food?"

"No." I sighed and sat back. "Never mind."

He grinned and turned the radio on. "Nah, I get it, but it's not all so great."

"Right."

"It's not." He gave me a hard look. "People are snakes, you just have to figure out their different colors, but they're all the same. Everybody wants something."

I put my food aside and hugged myself. "Like my mom."

"Yeah, like her." His tone hardened as well.

"I probably shouldn't say anything, but I'm sorry she bulldozed her way into your lives."

He watched me for a full minute before he put his burger away. "She's the same type of snake my dad is. I kind of think they belong together."

I grinned. "They'll screw each other up."

"I give it a year before he cheats on your mom."

I searched him for any indication of sarcasm or sorrow or even if he was laughing at my mom. Nothing. He was a blank slate. There was no emotion in him.

"I've started to wonder how much she cheated on David," I confessed.

"She was sniffing around my dad for almost two years."

His words stabbed me and my gut recoiled. "She told me a year."

"She lied."

I nodded. "I'm starting to get that."

"She met us a year ago, but she was around my dad for a year before that. Logan and I saw her go into one of his hotel conference rooms. He had just left our mom and she asked us to pick something up at the hotel—she's half owner. We were waiting for the general manager when we saw dad with some new sleaze." He gave me a wry look. "No offense."

"None taken." She was my mom and I should've defended her, but it was past the point where I could muster the energy. There was nothing left in me. Then I asked him something else. "Why are you and Logan being nice to me?"

Something sparked in his eyes. "Why wouldn't we?"

It was my turn to give him a wry look. "Come on. You guys are a-holes. You don't care and I doubt the fact that I might be your stepsister has anything to do with it."

He grinned and leaned back. "You didn't say anything about the cars before and you torched your coach's car for us."

"I didn't do that for you."

He shrugged. "Doesn't matter. You kept your mouth shut about a lot of stuff, most would've been trying to get close to us and use us. You didn't give us the time of day." He flashed his perfect white teeth at me. "It's refreshing. Then the day you were about to cream your mom, I realized you really don't care who we are. You hate your mom almost as much as we hate our dad." He shrugged again. "I don't know, makes me kind of like you." He chuckled. "Logan's told everyone about his new stepsister. He's proud of you."

My phone went off and I checked the text. It was from Becky: **At Kilbourn and 8th. Where r u? Adam said u wanted to talk?**

"Where's the party we're going to?"

"Fisher's house is on Kilbourn, by the parkway. Why?"

I sighed and sent a text: **Be there soon.** Then I looked up. "Just curious."

His eyes lingered on my phone. "Was that the quarterback?"

"Nope. She's the quarterback's friend. She's my only friend right now." Though, that could change after tonight.

He reached over and clipped my seat belt in, and then he dumped my food back in my lap. "You really should eat. Logan's got a list of shots he wants to pour down your throat. This is his way of hazing you into the family."

I'd gone numb, but I unwrapped my sandwich and ate every last bit. I had no taste, no sense of swallowing, but I did and when I was done, we were at the party. I looked up at a huge house on an even bigger hill. Lights and people streamed out of it and as I watched, a group of guys and girls slid down the hill and sailed through the air into a small lake. Their shrieks and laughs pierced the Escalade's wall, but the loud bass quickly covered them up.

"Fun," I bit out.

CHAPTER SIXTEEN

When we got inside, everyone knew Mason was there. Guys appeared from nowhere for a hand slap, a nod, or any greeting from him. Girls tried to curl on his arm, but he shook them off with an ease that was impressive. He left each behind and they all seemed not to realize what had happened before he was already gone. Then he stepped into the kitchen and a herald of cheers sounded out.

Logan was in the middle of the kitchen with his hand around the keg's nozzle. When he saw his brother, he lifted it up and let it go. Beer soaked everyone in the room, but no one was upset. The girls shrieked in laughter and the guys raised their drinks in salute.

So this was their life.

They were celebrities in Fallen Crest and I was starting to realize the magnitude of it all.

Then Logan was in front of me and bent forward. I was picked up in the air in the next moment and flung over his shoulder. He smacked my butt and turned me around. Then he lifted a cup in the air. The room quieted.

"This is my new stepsister. Help me and Mase welcome her to the family." He gave me a smirk when I twisted around. "By getting her drunk!"

Another round of cheers went through the room and I heard an echoing chorus throughout the house, though I doubt they knew what they had cheered for.

I hit him in the head. "Put me down."

When I was on my feet, I saw that Mason was in the far corner of the kitchen. He had a drink in hand and as I watched a blonde wrap herself around his arm. He didn't shake her off.

A glass was being nudged into my hand and I saw that Logan was trying to give me a shot. "What?"

"Take it. I'll do a shot with you."

I pulled him close and yelled in his ear, "I don't really drink, Logan."

His hand curved around my back. "Just let loose, for tonight only." Then he pressed his mouth to my ear and I heard the seriousness in his voice. "I want you to have fun and I won't let anything happen to you. Promise. Everyone will look out for you since I told 'em you're family."

He pulled away and clinked his glass with mine. "Drink up, sis."

"I'm not your sister."

"If your mom has anything to say about it, you will be."

A flash of anger went through me, but not at him. I gripped the shot glass and drained it. Logan whistled his approval and filled it again. And the night went on like that.

Mason disappeared and Logan wouldn't let me out of his eyesight. An hour later, after he'd been pulled downstairs for a game of pool, I looked up and saw Jessica. She was in a corner by herself. I didn't know anyone else in the room, but it was full of people and they all knew Logan. Most of the guys were tall and muscular with athletic builds so I assumed they were on the football team with him.

I searched for Lydia or Jill, but couldn't see them. Then I nudged someone beside me. When he turned with his pool stick in hand, I asked, "Anyone from Academy come tonight?"

He gestured outside. "They're all out by the lake. Why?" He narrowed his eyes. "You an Academy kid?"

"Ethan!" Logan barked from across the table. "Your shot."

Ethan gave me another suspicious scan and left. As he bent over and started to line up a shot, I felt someone beside me and looked up.

I sighed. Who else?

"Hi, Sam," Jessica spoke in a quiet voice. She inched closer when someone scooted past her.

I felt Logan's gaze, but he didn't join us. Thank goodness.

Her shoulders dropped an inch and I wondered if she had wanted the opposite, then I felt stupid. Of course, she did. Why else would my ex best friend talk to me?

"What do you want, Jess?"

"I need a reason to say hi to you? I thought we were friends."

Someone fell against the wall next to me and I didn't have to look. I held my breath for a moment and was thankful when Logan remained quiet.

"You screwed my boyfriend for two years. You haven't said a word to me since I found out."

Her smile seemed strained at the corners and she edged back a step. "What are you talking about? I talked to you at the game tonight."

I pushed off from the wall. "You said hi to me, after you had won a date with Logan."

"What?" Logan stood too.

"Yeah, Logan." She surged forward and gave him a sultry smile. "I won the date with you."

"What date?"

She faltered. "The one for charity. There was a raffle."

"You serious?"

Ethan leaned back from the table. "Dude, that pep girl asked you last week if you'd do it."

"Oh—I thought she was asking me out. She was hot." Logan flashed a smirk and whistled under his breath.

Ethan clapped him on the shoulder. "What'd you think when you never went out?"

"Nah, we did. Last night."

Jessica's shoulders dropped as each statement was spoken between the two. Her head hung almost to the floor now.

I had no sympathy for her, none at all.

Logan must've noticed my gaze because he spoke up, "Did you pay a lot for that date?"

Her head bounced back up. "Some."

A hard look entered his eyes. "Are you going to screw me afterwards?"

She gulped, but responded in a timid voice, "Is that what you want?"

"You think I take girls out for nothing?"

Ethan watched the exchange and I felt his gaze rest on me for a moment. Wisely, he kept quiet.

"Maybe if you liked her?"

Logan barked out a laugh. It sounded harsh. "You paid for me. You think you're a girl that I like? There's very few who'd fall in that category."

Jessica glanced at me. "You seem to like Samantha."

His arm came around my shoulders and he pulled me close. "Well, if she wasn't spoken for...and if her mom wasn't doing my dad then maybe..."

"Her mom?"

My face got hot. "None of your business. Logan, shut up about that."

His smirk vanished. "Sorry." I shoved his arm off and started to brush past him, but he caught my arm. "I am sorry. I didn't think about your situation."

There was a scathing comment on the tip of my tongue, but I twisted my arm free and shoved through the crowd that had appeared. I gritted my teeth as I had to push through the hallways. The house was huge, but it seemed the entire two schools had shown up. It was standing room only and that was an exaggeration.

I headed for the lake and took a deep breath when I was able to break free from the house. The crowds outside were widely dispersed over the backyard and down the hill by the lake. Bonfire smell filled the air, mixed with a moist feel that was from the lake and slip-n-slide.

Two girls dashed past me giggling and two more boys followed in pursuit. All of them were soaked head to toe. One almost bowled me over, but he caught me and rushed out, "Sorry, little Kade."

My blood boiled and I snapped, "I'm not a Kade!"

But he was gone.

Dammit, Logan.

As I made my way further down the hill, I spotted Mason and Nate. They were beside a bonfire in a far corner and each nodded in greeting, but they didn't come over and neither gestured for me to go to them.

Fine by me.

I relaxed a little and kept on. Finally I heard a voice I recognized.

Jeff.

"So you know the Kades?"

I turned around and braced myself, but there was no anger in his voice. After I searched his face, I didn't see any in his eyes either and relaxed again. "I guess."

He grinned. "You guess? You either know them or you don't. Man, Jessica crapped her pants tonight."

"Really?"

He nodded and twisted his fingers in his hair to pull it up. It was full of gel and stood straight up. It gave him a Mohawk look. Then he messed it up and flattened it again. "Jill's going crazy too. She doesn't know if she should kiss your rear or be a bigger bitch to you."

I glanced around. No one cared about our conversation. It was refreshing. "What do you think?"

He shrugged. "Whatever. Good for you."

I sighed. "Jeff, what are you doing?"

"What do you mean?" He stood straighter.

"Why are you talking to me now?"

He shrugged again and slid his hands into his back pockets. "I don't know. Guess it feels okay now, you know? I mean, I felt bad about what happened with us and then I was with Jill so quick. I didn't feel like I could apologize to you and then the other day...in the hallway..." He took a deep breath. "I know it's over."

I remembered and nodded. For some reason my throat felt closed off.

He gave me a bright smile. "And if you're going to be with Quinn, he's a nice guy usually, but you should know that he's not always."

I frowned. "What do you mean?"

He jerked an arm towards the docks and boats. "He's down there being an ass. I guess he's pissed about you and the Kades knowing each other."

Great. If Jeff was the one who warned me then it was bad, really bad. And as I got closer to a pontoon attached to the dock, I heard Adam's voice. He was drunk and when I stepped onto it and peered under the canopy I saw a girl in his lap and one of his hands between her legs. The other was stroking her knee.

I took a breath. Something told me to be prepared.

He murmured something in the girl's ear and she let out a throaty giggle. It grated against my ears, but when I heard another squeal, I looked closer. Becky was huddled in the seat behind them. Her knees were drawn against her chest and she was hugging them to her. When her eyes met mine for a second, she squealed again and ducked her head down.

"Well hey there, Sam!" Adam heralded. He threw an arm out. "Welcome to our lowly depths."

I rolled my eyes and sat stiff in a chair towards the front. I turned towards them. "I see you've been enjoying the party."

"Why shouldn't I?"

The girl in his lap squeaked and shifted under his hold.

He grinned and nipped at her shoulder.

I eyed the happy couple before I met Becky's gaze. The sadness in her was evident and when she wiped a tear away, I stood. "Can I talk to you, Becky?"

"Why talk to only her?" Adam stopped us. "You've been lying to me too. Or were you laughing at us behind our backs?"

"I wasn't laughing at anyone."

Becky stood, but hesitated behind him.

"Becky, please. I'd like to explain."

Her hands were clasped together and she looked down at them.

Adam deposited the girl to another chair and stood between us. He stepped closer to me and asked in a harsh tone, "You want to lie to her again? Hurt her some more?"

I frowned and looked up at him. "Are you trying to intimidate me? Are you really this hurt because I didn't tell you I knew the Kades?"

He bit out, "You played me for a fool."

Becky stepped around him and laid a hand on his arm. "He's just protecting me."

"From who?" I looked around. "Me? Because I didn't want people to know my parents are getting a divorce?"

Adam laughed and shook his head. "Yeah, right."

"You knew it was happening. You were there when I was in my dad's office. You helped tape my hands."

Becky looked at him. "Is that true?"

"Yeah, but I didn't know about the Kades."

My jaw hardened. "I know them, I'm not screwing them."

He didn't say anything.

And Becky looked at me. "You're not with Mason Kade? Lydia said you got in his car and..."

I rolled my eyes. "Oh, for god's sake. If Lydia said it, it must be true, right? I can't believe this. You're listening to my old best friend who knew my other best friend and boyfriend were sleeping together behind my back for two years. I'm sure she's the best source in the world to listen to."

She hesitated. "She said you seemed close."

"I saw you get in his car," Adam said in an accusing manner.

"I did, you're right. So, of course, that means I'm having sex with him. I've gotten in your car twice. Have I spread 'em for you too?"

He looked away. "It's not the same thing."

"Yes, it is. And, by the way, why do I have to explain anything to you? You've been my friend for what? Two weeks? You asked me out a couple times and I'm supposed to open my closet for you? How many dirty skeletons do you have that I don't know about?"

His mouth shut.

"Exactly." I swung towards Becky. "I'm sorry I didn't tell you I knew the Kades, but it's not something I want to talk about. It has to do with my parent's divorce, another thing I don't want spread around the school."

Both of them looked away.

I sighed. "Can I ask you both to keep this quiet?"

The girl who'd been on Adam's lap lifted her hand. "I won't say anything."

I snorted. "Thanks for that. Who are you?"

She gave me a bright smile and flicked her bleach blonde hair over her shoulder. "I'm Tanya. I know Logan so I definitely won't say anything."

I couldn't believe this girl. "You know Logan?"

"We went out last night."

Of all ironies. I glanced at Adam. "You got a keeper there."

He sighed and rolled his eyes. "I was pissed."

Then Becky reached out and squeezed my hand. "You know the Kades?" The excitement in her eyes made me pause. Then I grinned and shook my head. Becky never stayed down for long.

CHAPTER SEVENTEEN

It was five in the morning and I was drunk. Becky had passed out next to me on the pontoon while Adam took his pep girl home long ago. I lifted my red cup and tried to sip from it, but there wasn't anything in it. I tipped it over and not a drop fell out.

When had that happened?

"I was told Tanya was down here."

A leggy blonde stepped onto the pontoon and bent down to get a better look under the canopy. Becky snored and rolled over.

I squinted against the moonlight at this new stranger. She had long hair, slightly curled, that hung almost to her waist and she wore a classy v-neck sleeveless shirt over tight jeans. The high heels caught my attention. Their silver color matched her top perfectly.

I sighed. This girl was sober. I could tell. I was usually sober. Not tonight.

"So...is she here?" she asked further.

"Huh?"

"Tanya. Is she here? Was she here?" She rubbed at her arms as if she were cold.

I lifted my glass to her. "You could drink some beer and get warm."

"No thanks." She eyed my glass as her lip curled up. I was sure it was in disgust. "I don't drink."

"I don't either, but Logan didn't care about that tonight."

"Logan?" She tilted her head to the side. "Are you the new sister?"

"I'm not."

And I wasn't. I didn't think I'd ever consider myself in that role.

"Oh. Sorry. You said Logan before."

I narrowed my eyes at this girl again. She didn't say his name in the usual hopeful manner of most others. She said it as if she knew him, and knew him well. Still, I held my tongue. He'd already done enough damage for me to add more to it.

"A guy took her home."

She sighed and looked away. "I can't believe her. Another guy."

I frowned. "His name's Adam. He's a good guy."

"Doesn't matter at this point," she snapped and started to leave.

"You said Logan."

She stopped.

"Did you mean Logan Kade?"

"*You* said Logan's name before."

I nodded. "Do you know him?"

"Well enough." She yawned and glanced up at the house. "I should get going."

"How well?" I started to stand and climbed down from the pontoon.

She stopped a foot away on the dock and studied me. "Why?"

I shrugged.

"Look." She gave me a forced polite smile. "A lot of girls want to know Logan and a lot of girls have known Logan. If you're looking for a hookup, he's the guy for you, but if you're looking for a rich boyfriend—I'd look elsewhere. Logan's not that type, for anyone."

"You sound like you know him pretty well."

"I do." And she rolled her eyes. "I know him a little too well. We dated for two years, broke up a year ago."

"Really?" I surged forward a step, but held myself back. I didn't want to appear too eager. "What happened?"

"What else?" She laughed, but it sounded hollow. "He liked my friends and me. And I liked his brother."

My eyes went wide at that. Mason? "Did you date Mason too?"

She snorted and shook her head. "God, no. Like Mason Kade would ever be nice to any girl who wasn't his precious Marissa?"

Marissa?

"I can't believe I said any of this. I'm sorry. Thanks for telling me about Tanya and this Adam guy. You don't have his number, do you?"

I pulled out my phone and called him. She waited and hugged herself. When a breeze picked up and wafted over the lake to us, it swept her hair in the air and wrapped around her and I was glad I'd kept my hair pulled back in a low ponytail. Then I heard Adam's voicemail and ended the call.

"Sorry. It went to voice message and he would've picked up for me."

She studied me again. "You're good friends with this guy?"

"Not good like that." I grinned at her. Then I gestured towards the pontoon. "He's got a soft spot for Becky, she's his neighbor. He looks at her like a kid sister."

"Ah. I get it. Tanya likes those types."

"Tate?" Logan stood at the end of the dock. "What are you doing here?"

She gave him an exaggerated bright smile and said sarcastically, "I was hoping to see you, Logan."

He frowned and scratched at his head. "But you live in Forrest."

"Yes," she snapped at him. "I drove two hours on the slight hope you'd be at Ethan's house. In fact, I had no idea you'd be here. I got in my car and drove, just drove. My gut brought me here."

He looked at me. "You know Samantha?"

She snorted and gave me a withering look. "Yep, we're best friends. I gave her the whole scoop on you so if you haven't bagged her yet, she'll know how to make it good for you in bed."

He gave her a cocky grin.

She upped the withering glare to a hateful one at him before she looked back. "I thought you said you didn't know him."

I shrugged. "Who doesn't know Logan Kade?"

"Right." She shook her head. "Why did I come back here? That's right, my whorish cousin. That's why."

"I thought you said she was your best friend."

"One of and she's also a cousin." She swung her purse onto her arm and turned around with a hand poised on her hip. "Logan, do you know this Adam guy?"

He glanced over. "Quinn?"

I nodded.

"Sam knows him better."

"Logan!"

He rolled his eyes. "Fine. He's the quarterback for the Academy."

"Where does he live?"

I raised a hand. "He wouldn't take her to his house."

She kept her back turned to me. "Logan, where does he live? Tanya's not home."

Logan looked at me.

I sighed. "He lives on 8th and Saxton Ave. I don't know his house number, but it's got a red mailbox on it."

"Logan," she urged again.

"Oh my god," he groaned. "Sam, what does he drive?"

"A car. I don't know."

"Logan."

He spoke for her again. "You've been in his car, Sam. I've seen you. What kind of car is it?"

"Sam?" Becky stumbled out from under the canopy, rubbing at her eyes. "What's going on?"

"Hey." I rounded on her as a different thought occurred to me. "Adam drove you, didn't he?"

"Yeah." She yawned widely.

And that meant—I whirled back around. "He's still here. He wouldn't leave her so they're probably inside."

Tate stepped around me and folded her arms over her chest. She bent forward and peered into Becky's eyes. "He wouldn't leave you?"

She shook her head, confused. "Who are you?"

Her eyes flashed in annoyance. "Doesn't matter. I've heard what I need to. Thanks." And she brushed past all of us. As she swept past Logan, he stepped to the side so her shoulder wouldn't hit him and whistled under his breath as he watched her trudge up the hill. She flicked him off behind her back, but he only laughed.

"Hey." Becky stepped beside me and held onto my arm. She struggled to stay on her feet. "Could I get a ride home?"

"What about Adam?"

She grinned, but immediately covered her mouth with her hand and jerked to the side. After a couple minutes and after she had stopped vomiting, she stood back up. "He took off long ago."

"You said—"

"She was not being nice." Becky shrugged, but clasped onto my arm again.

I couldn't stop the smile from my face, but looked where Logan still stood. "Could we both get a ride home?"

He chuckled. "Yeah. Mason sent me down. He and Nate are waiting in the front, but we better hurry. If Tate finds out we lied, she'll be after our asses and I don't want to deal with that girl right now."

"You mean you're not up for an ex this morning?"

He groaned. "She told you that, huh?"

We both fell in step as I tried to help Becky stay upright. "And a bit more. Pretty sure she regrets it now."

"She could tell I like you and that threw her."

I looked at him sharply. "How do you know that?"

He shrugged. "I know her pretty well."

I wanted to know all about their relationship and what Mason had to do with it, but I held my tongue when we climbed into the back of his Escalade. Becky gave them both a sloppy grin and a slurred thank-you, but she crumbled into a heap on her chair as soon as she crawled up. I had to boost her butt over so Logan and I could get in too. When we pulled up to Becky's house, Nate came around the side and hoisted her over his shoulder. He followed me inside and we snuck her into her bedroom after I fumbled through her pockets for her keys.

When the four of us got to the mansion, it was nearing six in the morning. I wasn't tired at all. I was wide awake. The nagging questions of Tate/Logan's relationship and who Marissa was had me energized. I could've gone on a run.

And then I decided to do it.

As I went through the kitchen, a big black bag was in the foyer along with a hiking bag. Mason dumped a rolled up sleeping pad beside it a second later. He had changed into ratty green khaki shorts and a sleeveless black shirt. It was tattered along the edges and had two gaping holes in the back.

"Where are you going?"

It took me a second to realize he'd asked my question. I frowned at him. "I'm going on a run. Where are you going?"

He checked his watch. "It's after six. You were up all night."

I kicked at his bag and heard pots and pans rattle against each other. "Where are you going?"

Who's Marissa?

He grimaced for a moment and then flipped his black sunglasses over his eyes. I could no longer read him. "We're going camping."

"Camping?"

"Something we do." And he turned to leave again.

I was a bit miffed as I stood there. He'd been all buddy-buddy and now—nothing. Camping. That's it. No other explanation, but then again I had to remind myself—who was I kidding? These guys weren't my stepbrothers and I highly doubted their father would really marry my mother.

Everything hardened inside again.

The truth was that my mother and I'd be out within three months. That was my guess. When that happened, it'd be like none of this happened. No Logan. No Mason. No Nate. Nothing. And I'd have to deal with Lydia and Jessica once again.

With that thought, I felt another burst of adrenalin surge through me and I could barely hold it in as I jumped through the door and started running.

None of it matter. I mattered. I was the only one. I had to take care of myself.

Those thoughts kept flashing through my head as my feet pounded the pavement. I ran and then I ran some more. Sweat was dripping off of me and leaving trails wherever I went and I went everywhere. I soared past Adam and Becky's house once, and then ran past it again.

Then I found a park and sprinted over the bridge. Ducks and geese scattered for me and the water felt good as I darted through a small part of a pond.

When my legs started to hurt, I headed back. And as soon as I approached the front lawn, my body crumbled. I fell to a heap on the lawn and stayed there until my heart and chest slowed down.

I was barely aware of the sounds of a car pulling out of the garage until it slowed beside me.

"Samantha?"

A black Rolls Royce had stopped beside me and my mom peered over James who was in the driver's seat. She was dressed in a pink dress with a hat perched on top of her head.

I frowned as I sat up. Was I delusional? My mom looked like she was dressed for a role in a Southern movie. "Where are you guys going?"

"It's Sunday, honey. We're going to church." She frowned a little. "Would you like to come? We could go to the later service."

I couldn't hold back my full body grimace. "No. I'm okay."

"Did you go running this morning?"

I heard the strain in her voice, but ignored it when I tried to stand. My legs were still wobbly. "No. I just look like I did."

"Samantha."

I groaned. "What? Of course I did."

"Well. Okay. Go inside and drink lots of water. And please eat something, Samantha. You know how I worry."

James said something to her and my mom called out again, "Oh, honey. The boys went camping. They'll be gone most of the week so if you'd like to have any friends over, go ahead. Maybe Jessica and Lydia? Or even Jeff? Are you two still together?"

James said something else under his breath to her and my mom giggled. "Okay, honey. We have to go. Love you."

She waved as he pulled out of the driveway. And then it was just me. I had the mansion all to myself. I trudged through the place and into my shower. After that, I curled under my sheets and rolled over.

CHAPTER EIGHTEEN

The guys were gone for an entire week. I had no idea how they could do that, but they did. I shouldn't have been surprised. I avoided my mother during the week and only once spotted James. I'd been sitting in the study room, which looked like my school's library when he walked in.

The door shut behind him. I lifted my head from the book I'd been reading. We stared at each other.

He was dressed in a pinstripe black business suit and he had a black briefcase in hand. When I saw a small brown bag in his other hand, I hid a grin. Mousteff must've gotten to him too.

Then he took a deep breath. "I am aware your relationship with your mother is none of my business, but I would like to get to know you at some point. I love your mother very much and I do not plan on letting her go."

And then he left.

He came in as silently as he left and when I watched the door slide shut behind him, not a sound came from it.

Chills ran down my body and I pushed back from the table and went to where I'd once seen Mason pull some brandy from a counter. It was still there and I took a swig of it. Maybe daytime alcoholism would be my next venture?

I put the bottle away when my stomach started to churn. Then I heaved a deep breath. Nope, daytime alcoholism wouldn't mix with me and I went back to my room and for my running gear.

When I was running back, it had been dark for an hour and a set of headlights approached from behind. I was two blocks from the house and I veered to the side. Most cars swept past, some slowed for caution, but this one slowed so it followed behind me.

I kept going.

What else could I do?

I put on some more speed and soon I was sprinting. One block left.

The car's headlights engulfed me and my shadow sprang out in front of me. It seemed to be laughing at me, dancing vigorously. My heart was already pounding, but cold sweat formed on my forehead. It spread throughout my body and my teeth were soon chattering.

I stopped.

Half a block from my house.

I turned and stared at the car. It had stopped, now in front of me. Then I heard the window slide down and someone leaned out.

I yelled, "What do you want?"

There was laughter from inside.

My hands balled into fists and I started to jerk forward.

Mason's voice slid over me. "You're an idiot."

My breath spat from me before I could stop it. I grimaced when it landed on my leg, but I couldn't stop from laughing in relief. "I'm an idiot? You're the idiots."

Logan popped his head from the passenger side. "We could've been mass rapists, dude."

"Dude?" I shot him a look and walked to Mason's window on trembling legs. "I'm not your dude."

Logan eased back in and smirked at me. "Not yet."

Nate chuckled from the backseat as he watched the exchange.

"Hop in." Mason nodded to the back.

I gave him a silly grin, though I didn't care how silly it might've looked. "I'm a half block away. I think I can manage it."

He shrugged and flashed me a grin back. "Up to you." And then he sped off. My eyes widened as I spotted the puddle, but it was too late. He drove through it and I was drenched a second later.

"Ugh," I groaned and held my arms out.

Logan's hyena laugh sounded out until they turned into the driveway.

Then I gritted my teeth and sprang forward. When I sprinted around the corner, they had started to climb out and I spotted the hose their gardener left out by the house. Logan had set a few bags on the ground when he turned, but it was too late.

"Hey—" His shout was drowned out when I turned the hose on and aimed it at him. Before Nate could jump out of the way, I turned and got him too. As I looked for Mason, I was shoved to the ground and the hose was pulled out of my hands.

I looked up and he stood over me with the hose pointed towards the lawn. A wicked look was in his eyes and I opened my mouth to try and stop him, but the front door opened at that moment.

"Sam?"

I groaned and rolled to my feet.

Mason turned the water off and threw the hose back to the corner.

"Hi, guys..." She faltered as she frowned at me. "Sam, what are you doing on the ground?" Her eyes skirted from me to Mason.

I stood and brushed off my running shorts. "Nothing. I think I ran too much, tripped."

"Oh." Her eyes never left Mason.

He narrowed his and the same closed down look came over him.

I sighed on the inside. "Mom, I'm going inside."

"Wait, honey." She turned to Logan. "Since everyone's here, tomorrow is Saturday. I was wondering if we could have our dinner tomorrow night."

"What?" Logan dropped a bag from his fingers.

"The one we were supposed to have last Sunday was canceled since you guys wanted to go camping so I thought..." She threw her hands in the air with a bright smile. "How about tomorrow night?"

"I'm sure we'll be at a party tomorrow night."

"Oh." Her bright smile faded and she glanced at me.

I fought the urge to roll my eyes. I wanted so badly...

"How about you and me, Sam? What do you think? We can have a mother/daughter dinner like we used to."

I tried not to let her desperation get me, but I found myself crumbling.

Then Mason asked, "Doesn't your school's football team have their annual dinner tomorrow night?"

My head snapped up. My football team. My father. My not-father. And the old rage flared inside of me again.

My mom's eyes closed and she turned away.

I didn't care. I snapped, "I'm good without that, mom. I wouldn't want us to be fake and not talk about things."

"What?"

"Like how you hit me. Twice." My eyes were cold. Everything in me was cold again and I remembered the feeling of that first slap.

"Honey, I..." She stepped towards me with an extended hand.

Logan cleared his throat and gave us both a forced polite smile. "Don't mind us. We'll be showering and going back out. See you."

All three of them grabbed the rest of their bags and walked inside. When the door shut behind them, I flinched in reaction. But I hadn't started to calm my nerves before my mother stepped close.

"Samantha," she spoke in a soft voice. "We should talk about that night. We haven't really...did David ask you to go to their annual dinner?"

I wanted to snap so badly. She said it as if it were a personal attack to her, that the man who had raised me all my life might have the balls to invite me to a dinner? As if he had no right since he wasn't my biological father.

Anger was pumping through me.

"Sam?" She said it so quietly. She had turned into a timid mouse and my mother watched me with wide eyes, a begging question in her depths.

"What?" I growled.

"Are you going to that dinner with David? I know it's for the families too."

I sighed and turned away. "I don't know, mom. Maybe."

When I started to walk inside, she called after me, "It'd be okay, you know. I'd understand. I wouldn't want him to be alone."

And the door shut on her words when I stepped inside. I let it slam harder than normal. When I hurried upstairs and to my room, Mason's door was kicked open and he appeared. He was shirtless and in jeans. His hair was wet and he held a toothbrush in his mouth, but he watched me approach.

I whistled under my breath. "You shower quick."

He grinned over a mouthful of toothpaste and disappeared inside. A second later, he came back out and wiped his mouth with a towel. Then he grinned, sans his toothpaste, and leaned against his doorway. When he crossed his arms, his muscles bulged out, but it wasn't a show. That was him.

I fought the urge not to flinch under his steady gaze. "What?"

"Come out with us tonight."

"I don't think so."

Logan's door opened down the hall and he stepped out, but he didn't say a word. He waited.

"Why not? It'd be fun."

I wavered. "Where are you going?"

He lifted an easy shoulder. "Probably just some bonfire, nothing big."

And I hoped that meant there'd be no Lydia, Jessica, or even Adam. The week had been tolerable, but I felt the weight of all of them. Lydia wanted to be my best friend again and Jessica seemed torn. After Logan's humiliation, she had stayed away, but I still caught the few friendly grins she'd sent my way. Becky loved it. She was eating all the attention up, including how Adam still seemed pissed. She enjoyed being the go-between with him and me.

"Hey," Mason prompted me again.

I frowned as I tried to remember what Becky had said they were doing tonight. It was probably a party. It always seemed to be a party. "Don't you guys have a football game tonight?"

"Not for us."

"What do you mean?"

He shrugged again and scratched at his chin. "We skipped all week. No way can coach put us in."

"And that doesn't bother you?"

"He won't kick us off." He frowned. "Why do you care about that?"

His question threw me backwards a step. Why did I? I shrugged and slid my hands into the back pockets of my running shorts. I was trying to look cool. My sweat had dried, but my nose twitched at the smell of it as it hung in the air.

"Look," I started. "I'm not up for another party. Besides, I think that Tate girl is out for my head."

Mason shot up from the doorway and the wall slammed over his face again. "Tate?"

Logan's eyes clasped shut behind him and his head went down. His shoulders dropped.

I sucked in my breath and my eyes widened. "Uh...I mean..."

"You met Tate?"

I nodded.

"At the last party?"

I nodded again.

"Why'd she be pissed with you?"

I shrugged and looked away.

"Sam." He grasped my shoulder and I squeaked. I threw a look at Logan, but quickly glanced away. Too late. Mason followed my gaze and saw his brother. "Tate's in town?"

Logan's head lifted and a haunted look was in his eyes. "Yeah."

"When?" Mason's voice was biting.

"She came last Saturday. She was looking for a chick that Sam's quarterback was banging."

Mason looked back at me. His eyes were cold. "What does she want with you?"

"Becky and I lied to her. She seems like the type to hold a grudge."

"What the hell, man?"

It took me a second to realize Mason wasn't referring to me. I looked up with his hand still on my shoulder and saw something pass between the two brothers. Logan backed up and gave him a tight smile. "What do you want?"

"You're still covering for her."

Though Mason's statement came out quiet, there was a dangerous feel to it. The hairs on the back of my neck stood upright and I was frozen in place. His hands gripped my shoulder tighter. A bruise would appear there, but it didn't hurt. I didn't feel a thing at that moment.

"Sam, honey?" My mom's voice came up from the stairway.

Everyone reacted.

Mason shoved me away. When I caught my balance and looked up both of their doors had been shut. I hurried into mine and locked it when my mother turned the knob. "Sam, can you please talk to me? I'd really like to talk to you about David. And James told me he had a word with you. I'd like to talk to you about him as well." She waited a moment. "Please, honey?"

I stood on the other side and held my breath. My heart was pounding, but it wasn't from my mother, for once. And then when I heard her walk away, I let out that deep breath and sagged against the door. My hands and legs shook when I made my way to the shower so I slid down the wall and let the water slam over me.

It was an hour later before I went downstairs in sweats and a tank. My hair was pulled back by a headband and my body felt strong from the latest run. When I went into the kitchen, I expected everyone else to be gone, but drew up short. Logan sat at the table in the dark. A glass was in front of him and a bottle of Brandy beside that.

He looked up at me and his lip curved upwards in a snarl. "Hey, thanks."

"For what?" I eyed him, but relaxed when he didn't stand up.

"Tate."

"Where's Mason and Nate?"

"Where do you think?" he bit out and raised his glass for a drink. He set it down hard.

"What?" I couldn't believe this. "Are you being punished? Did they go out without you?"

He sighed and looked away.

"Are you twelve now?" Where had the cocky smooth-talker gone? Or the vindictive guy who had humiliated Jessica for me?

His voice came out low. "There's a lot of history that you don't know about."

"Why are you telling me that?"

His eyes found me and the seriousness in them held my breath. "So that you can tread carefully from now on." He pushed up from the table now. "My advice: shut up about what you don't know." He brushed past me as I stood still and finished the rest of his Brandy before he put the empty glass away. The bottle was left on the counter.

He left a second later and his yellow Escalade tore from the driveway.

It took me a moment to realize that my heart wasn't pounding. My legs were strong. And a sense of calm settled over me. What that meant, I had no idea.

CHAPTER NINETEEN

My phone woke me the next morning and I groaned when I saw that it was past eleven. "Hello?"

"Hi!" Becky chirped at me.

I swore under my breath and buried my head under my pillow. "Whatdoyouwand?"

"What?"

"Hold on." I sat up and wiped at my face. I needed to wake up. I couldn't handle how alert she sounded at that moment. "Hi..."

"Did you just wake up?"

When I tried to straighten my legs, they cramped up and I bit back more curses. Pain throbbed in them and I knew it was from the running. How long had I gone last night?

"Sam!"

"What?" I readjusted the phone when I felt myself waken more. "Tell me you're not going to bed now."

"I'm not." She giggled. "But my folks are going to the Fallen Crest Country Club with Adam's family. My mom wanted me to invite you. We'd pay for your entry and everything else is on Adam's dad. He has some account with the club, I think."

"Since when do you guys go to the Country Club?"

"My parents aren't members, but we go with Adam's parents sometimes. They're members."

That sounded right.

And then a different thought formed. "Is my mom a member there?"

She giggled again. "Do you mean is James Kade a member?"

I groaned. I'd forgotten she knew, hell—everyone knew. Maybe. I could spread a rumor that I paid the Kade brothers to act like they knew me. People would eat that up in an instant. Things would all go back to how they should've been, with me being alone.

"I have lots of gossip to tell you about last night too." She sounded breathless in her excitement and I perked up. Whatever it was would be good, or I hoped. I could use some gossip that had nothing to do with me.

"Okay. What time do you want me over there?" I swung my legs over and stood. They were a bit wobbly, but I pushed past it and hurried into my bathroom. "Should I meet you at the club?"

"We could pick you up?"

"Becky."

"Okay, okay. Yeah, meet us at the club. We're going to leave soon so call me when you get to the parking lot."

"Sounds good."

"Oh and I think Adam's bringing Tanya."

"Who's Tanya?" Then I remembered. "Is her cousin going to be there too?"

"I hope not." Becky kept giggling. "See you there!"

"See you," I mumbled into the phone before I ended the call and set it down. I frowned at it for a moment. She sounded very perky and very excited. Becky like that, with Adam bringing a girl, couldn't mean anything good...could it? Was I being paranoid?

I rolled my eyes at my reflection and went to work. My hair was a ratted mess, but by the time I had dressed in black skinny pants and a loose white long-sleeve shirt, my hair was back to its normal self. Straight and a little dull. It was how I liked it. I tucked it behind my ears when I slipped on some heeled sandals and grabbed my purse. This was the country club; I'd need to dress a little bit of the rich part.

No one was in the house when I breezed out except Mousteff. He poked his head out, saw my appearance and wolf whistled. I flicked him the middle finger, but he laughed as he went back to the kitchen.

When I pulled into the parking lot, it was full of brand new BMWs, Rolls Royces, and whatever other rich cars there were. I thought I spied a Lamborghini too. And then I straightened out my top as I started towards the door. With a text sent to Becky, I figured she'd meet me in the front foyer, but when I got there I drew up short.

Two guys in black suits stared at me with no welcoming smile.

Uh...

A different guy emerged from behind them with a headset attached to his ear. He was dressed in a white suit and he gave me a fake smile. "Your name, miss?"

"I'm here with friends." My hands itched to spread out my top again or readjust my pants. It was as if slugs had appeared over my body from how they were staring at me.

"Their names?" The guy was cold.

"Uh..." My mind blanked. "The Quinns. I'm friends with Adam Quinn."

"He already arrived with a guest." He gave me that same cold smile. "You'll have to leave."

"No, no, no." Becky rushed around them and linked elbows with mine. She was breathless when she hurried out, "My mom paid for her."

He didn't blink. "Her name, ma'am?"

Becky couldn't stop a giggle behind her hand. "Samantha Strattan."

"David Strattan?"

My head snapped up. "What?"

"Your name is listed underneath a member's name. He listed you as a guest." The polite chill from him emanated everywhere. His lips moved to form a smile, but it didn't fit with his features. "Your mother will be refunded her money."

He extended his hand for us to enter the club, but both of us were still surprised.

"You may go inside? Please."

We jumped forward at his slight bark. Then Becky bent over laughing when we rounded the corner. "Holy Hannah! I can't believe that happened. What is with that guy? I bet he'd never had an erection in his life."

I glanced over my shoulder and knew he could hear every word we said. "Nah. He bats for the other team."

Her laughter raised a notch and I pulled her away before he kicked us both out. I patted her on the arm. "I had no idea my dad was a member here."

Becky wiped at her mouth and I knew she was trying to stop laughing. "I know. Me neither."

When she seemed to have accepted my statement, I relaxed again. She might've known about the divorce, but she didn't know the other stuff. I hoped no one knew. Then we weaved our way through a fancy looking dining room with chandeliers and glass tables. I made sure not to bump into anything. If I broke even a fork, I was sure I couldn't afford to replace it. And Becky pulled me the last bit before I blinked back the sudden brightness. The sun was blinding when we went outside and I heard splashing, glasses clanking, and children's laughter. Conversation buzzed around us and when my vision grew clear again I saw the back patio was enormous. It was gorgeous with three waterfalls and two fountains.

She led me to a back patio where I recognized Laura and Becky's little brothers. Adam sat at a back table with the pep girl from last weekend's party. His smile slipped a little when he saw me, but by the time we got to the table it looked natural.

"Hey, Sam." He sounded normal when he welcomed me.

"Hi, Sam!" His friend beamed at me.

"Tanya." He nodded at her.

"I remembered. Hi, Tanya. Your cousin's not coming, is she?" I sat across from them in a similar wicker chair when Becky sat beside me and gestured for a waiter.

She laughed and pulled up her skinny legs in the chair. As she hugged them to her chest, she rested her head on them and smiled at Adam.

He shared the intimate look before he replied for her. "No, she's not."

Then Tanya lifted her head and looked over her knees. "Tate went home this morning after last night."

"Last night?" I stiffened and glanced sideways.

Becky gave me an excited look. "I have to tell you all about that."

Oh no.

A waiter appeared and placed a champagne flute of orange juice in front of me. A plate full of breakfast food was next with bacon, waffles, French toast, and sausage. A bowl of fruit was put to the side.

I caught the waiter's sleeve before he left. "Can I have coffee?"

"Of course, ma'am."

Ma'am. What's with the ma'am stuff?

"Sam!" Becky snapped her fingers in front of my face.

"What?" I jerked around.

Adam laughed and the sound of it calmed me a little. Somehow, somewhere I had started to care for him as a friend. Who would've thought? The idea of it made me grin, but I tuned into my other friend. She wanted center stage.

"...and then her cousin showed up last night."

"Wait. What are you talking about?" I glanced at Adam.

Becky rushed out, breathless, "Why aren't you listening to me? I just told you that Adam was with the Academy Elite last night."

"What are the Academy Elite?" I looked around. Was I the only one clueless?

Adam reached for his water. "It's her term for the top circle. Miranda Stewart had some people over last night."

Becky sneered at him. "It's not just my term. Everyone uses it." She turned to me and her eyes were beaming.

"Anyway, so Miranda had the Academy Elite over. You know, her, Emily, Amelia, and Cassandra. They're the top four girls in school, right?"

"Sure."

"Then Adam was invited—"

"I brought Tanya last night." He lifted their entwined hands.

They were an item now?

Becky poked me in the arm. "And Peter was there, so was Mark Decraw."

I nodded. They were the other two captains of the football team. This was the Academy Elite?

"And then—"

I interrupted her. "Were you there?"

She closed her mouth and flashed me a look. "No, but I heard all this from Adam."

He wiggled his eyebrows and kissed Tanya's hand.

I frowned at the display of affection.

Becky clapped her hands in front of me again. "Seriously, Sam! Pay attention."

"Okay, okay."

"So Jeff and Jill showed up. Miranda let them stay for an hour, since Jill's on the cheerleading squad and Jeff's third string. But then they kicked them out after an hour, only an hour. Can you believe that? And then Jessica and Lydia tried to get in too, but I guess they were turned away at the door. Peter Glasburg wouldn't even let them inside Miranda's house. Did you know those two were dating? I had no idea."

She didn't stop for a breath.

"And then, you won't believe it, but Logan Kade showed up!" She sat back in a dramatic break. Her chest heaved up and down and she held onto the table. "I couldn't believe it either, but he was drunk."

"I'm going to go to the bathroom." Tanya shot out of her chair and was gone in an instant.

I twisted around, but couldn't find her. I looked at Adam. "Is she okay?"

He indicated Becky and remained quiet.

She took another deep breath. "And then Logan started making fun of Tanya."

"Wait—what?"

"Yeah. I know." Her head bounced up and down. "He was really tearing into her, calling her loose and easy and all sorts of things. Tanya started to cry, but you know what happened?"

"Adam told him to shut up?"

Becky's lips clamped shut. After a beat, she looked at him.

I did too. "What?" Neither said a word. "You didn't?"

He looked away.

Becky opened her mouth. "So no one stopped him, no one. Not even Peter and we all know Peter rules the roost at these things."

"Do we?" I had no idea.

"He does, but then *she* shows up."

"Who?"

"Her cousin." Her eyes flashed in giddiness. "And she starts yelling at Logan instead. I think Tanya texted her, but you'll never guess what else happened?"

"Probably not," I deadpanned.

"So Logan was yelling at Tanya and then that girl started yelling at Logan, who took it. He completely shut up and just let her yell at him, but then his brother shows up a half hour later."

I sat up straight and narrowed my eyes. "Mason was there?"

Her head jumped up and down again and she was panting like a thirsty dog.

I felt Adam's quietness next to me and knew he was studying me.

"And then everybody got real quiet. She shut up."

"Who shut up?"

"Tanya's cousin."

Adam offered, "Tate. Her name is Tate."

"Tate completely shut up and she looked like she was going to faint or something."

"Her face got all green." He grinned and that was when I knew that Adam didn't like Tanya's cousin at all.

"I heard that Emily thought Tate had soiled her pants or something, it was that intense. And Mason hadn't even said anything at that time."

"But he's going to, right?" I was starting to see where this was going and a sense of dread was settling in.

"Yeah. He looked like a cat who'd found his favorite mouse wounded or something. It was eerie. And he started to make fun of her, like all cruel and stuff. The things he said to her were horrible and he was only playing with her. She didn't try to defend herself. I guess Mason Kade really hates that girl, and the way he ripped into her. It was something else."

"He enjoyed it." Adam's voice was quiet.

I looked over and held his gaze. Something dark was in their depths.

He spoke again, "It was like an animal that was playing with its kill before they fully killed it. That's what he was doing with her. I've never seen anything like it before."

I held his stare and the realization that he was scared of the Kades hit me hard. I could see he was terrified of them, but Adam broke the moment when he left the table.

Becky's eyes skirted between the two of us, but she leaned forward. "And then I guess Logan finally told him to leave."

"And did he?"

She jerked a shoulder up. "I don't know. Adam never told me that, but he said there was a strange comment Logan made to him."

"To Adam?"

"No, to Mason."

"What was it?"

"He said, 'you bruised her shoulder.'" She leaned back. I waited. Nothing. "And?"

"That was it. I guess Mason left after that."

"He bruised Tate's shoulder?"

She shook her head. "That's the thing. Adam said everyone looked at her shoulders, but there wasn't anything there. She had on some wrap-around shawl or something, but her shoulders were bare. No bruises. Nothing." And then her eyes fell to my shoulders.

I was glad for covering them up and I felt a small tingling sensation where a small bruise had formed from Mason's hand. I was tense, waiting for her to ask. But she didn't. I felt Becky's eagerness and knew she wanted to, but she held her tongue. I was grateful as I reached for my orange juice. I downed the whole thing. Champagne had been added to it and I sat back, surprised.

"What?" She held back a small grin.

"I just got served alcohol."

She giggled. "Your dad's the head coach for FC Academy and we're here with Adam's dad. Steven Quinn is powerful in this town too."

"Where did Adam go?"

She gestured to a back corner. Adam's father was close to another woman with his hand on her thigh. He leaned close to whisper something in her ear, but I looked further to the right where Adam stood and watched the exchange. When his jaw clenched, I knew he was angry, but then I sat up straight. My father had appeared out of my nowhere. Not my father. David.

And the heavily made-up woman whose hair was pulled up in a loose bun moved away from Adam's father and extended her red nails to my father. Her hand paused on his chest and she tilted her head to the side. Loose curls that fell from her bun slid over her shoulder and she seemed to be laughing when she swept them further back.

"Sam."

I ignored Becky's warning comment and stood.

CHAPTER TWENTY

"Sam." David moved back a step when I stopped near him. I felt Adam come up behind my elbow, but he remained quiet.

"Dad." And I waited. Would he correct me?

He gave me a tight smile and I knew he wouldn't. Instead he gestured towards the woman and Adam's father. "Have you met my daughter? This is Samantha."

The woman held out her arm and tried to melt me with her smile. "Hello, you're so precious, so beautiful. Penelope."

Adam's father moved away from the woman and nodded. "Steven. I think we've met once."

Adam spoke up, "No, dad. You didn't formally meet her. We left the house early that day."

"Oh yes, that's right." Then he turned to David. "David, what do you have planned for next week's game? You think we're going to pull out a win against Leers?"

David cleared his throat. "We're going to try, that's for certain."

"Dad, don't you guys have your annual football dinner tonight?"

He opened his mouth and stared at me. "Uh..."

"That's right." Penelope's laugh rang out. "I was just talking to your father about that. He said he's going to be alone tonight. Heavens, we can't have that, can we?"

"Certainly not." My jaw ached from how tight it was.

"Dad, you're going with me, right?" Adam brushed against my elbow when he moved forward. He stood close to me and I felt his tension.

"Well, this sounds perfect. Father and son." Penelope placed her hand on David's arm this time. "Father and daughter. It's almost romantic."

I tilted my head to the side and removed her hand. "And no sluts..."

There was a choked silence for a second.

And then David rasped out, "Samantha!"

Adam barked out a laugh.

His father jerked back a step.

"What?" I turned towards David with wide eyes, innocent eyes.

"Apologize."

"For what?" I eyed her up and down. "I call it how it is."

She bristled, but kept her mouth shut.

I narrowed my eyes and waited. The anger was mounting in her. Her hands clenched. Her shoulders grew tight. Her cheeks inflamed and her eyes closed till they were almost slits.

I counted down in my head. 3...2...1...and...

"What a little bitch you have, David." She leaned forward until her face was a few inches from mine.

I smirked and held steady. The Kades had taught me a few things.

She sucked in her breath and I knew her fury leapt higher. "I feel sorry for you, David, real sorry for you."

"Hey, now." He moved between us.

I sidestepped and never broke eye contact with her. "Are you bored with married men? Football coaches don't make that much money, you know."

She laughed harshly. "Private school coaches do."

"Penelope." Adam's father took hold of her elbow.

Adam's voice came out shrilly. "Hey dad, where's mom? Didn't you come with her?"

There was another brief moment of silence.

"Are you insinuating something, Adam?"

He laughed next to me and I found myself grinning along with it. "You're a smart man. What do you think?"

"Penelope."

Her head swiveled to me.

I gave her a cheeky grin. "When'd you pick up the trade?"

"The trade?"

"You know, having affairs, sleeping with married men, being a hooker?"

"That's enough, Samantha!" David clamped down on my arm and dragged me away. I twisted around and gave her a wave. "Stop it. Now."

I waited until he had taken me to the parking lot and then yanked my arm free. I rubbed where he had held onto. "That's the thanks I get from saving you from her?"

He drew upright and hissed out, "You did not save me from her. You made a fool of yourself."

"That's doubtful."

He started to pace in front of me with his hands on his hips. His tie flapped behind him as he turned and went the other way. I couldn't stop myself from smiling as I leaned against a car behind me.

He noticed and snapped, "What?"

"That's what you do when you're frustrated with the opposing team." I'd seen enough of those times when his football team wasn't playing as well as he wanted them to.

He stopped and then let out a small laugh as he reached behind his head to scratch. "I'd forgotten how smart you are."

"That woman was a filthy whore and you know it." I cooled my smile. "Just because you're lonely and had your heart broken by my mother doesn't mean you should get yourself mixed up with her."

"Samantha."

"She's bad news."

He held his arms out in surrender. "I wasn't going to get mixed up with her. I wasn't. I'm aware what kind of a woman she is, but you called her out for having an affair with Steven Quinn. He knows now that I know. She knows. His son knows. That spells trouble for a lot of people."

I shrugged. "Adam's known for a long time."

He stopped pacing. "Really?"

I nodded.

"Well, I guess that's a little better then."

"So can I still come for that dinner tonight? I know families are supposed to come."

He eyed me warily. "Does your mom know about this?"

I shrugged. "Like I care and yes, she does. She said I could go."

He opened his mouth.

I added, "And she said that in front of Mason and Logan Kade so she has to follow through with it."

His mouth closed, but I caught a flare of pride in his eyes. My chest swelled up and I looked away when a sudden burst of tears came to my eyes. I wiped them away quickly and glanced back. He'd been watching me with a sad smile. It vanished immediately.

"Are you okay?"

I was jolted at the sincerity of his voice. "What do you mean?"

"With all this, the changes, the truth coming out. Are you okay?"

"Why wouldn't I be?"

"Because you're a teenager." He said it so simply. "Because your mother can be one vicious and selfish woman. Because you got your life taken away from you." His voice gentled even more. "Remember that I know about Jeff and your friends. I know what they did to you. And because," his mouth twisted in a crooked smile, "you set my car on fire, remember?"

"Oh yeah!" I burst out in laughter and wiped more tears away. I didn't know why they were coming.

He took a small breath. "Are you okay, Samantha? Are you still running?"

I nodded.

"How long do you go for?"

I couldn't talk. My throat was so tight, it was blocked.

He sounded sad. "That long, huh?" And he took another deep breath. "I'm sorry, Sam. I really am."

I looked away. I couldn't see how haunted he sounded. Something would've broken inside of me and I was holding on tight. I was holding on so tight right now.

He continued, "If I had known what your mother wanted or what she needed, I would've tried to adopt you. I would've gone for something with the courts so that she couldn't have taken you away. I had no idea. I really didn't, but there was no way I could've been the man she wanted. I was the man she used to get her through her hard times."

"I'm sorry." My voice cracked. More tears flooded me. "I'm sorry for what she did to you."

He shook his head. "I can handle it. I have a good job. I'm still somewhat young and in shape. I'll be fine."

I took a deep breath.

"Are you going to be fine?"

I shook my head. I couldn't answer him, not then.

"I hear the gossip, you know. I heard the Kade brothers have taken you under their wing." He frowned. "I'm not sure if that's a good thing. Those boys can be cruel, but they do seem to back each other up. Are you okay with them?"

"They help...with her..."

Enough said. He nodded in understanding. "Well, I suppose I'll see you tonight then. Six o'clock. Back here."

"Okay."

He gave a small wave before he went back inside. I turned to my car, but Adam called my name and I paused and looked back. He grimaced as he approached. "Sorry about my dad and that woman."

I chuckled. "I thought I would've been the one apologizing to you."

"Nah. I liked it. You're tough."

"I didn't want her involved with David."

He nodded. "I can see that, but thanks. It's out now. My dad has to deal with it. He knows I know."

"I'm not apologizing to your dad."

He held his hands up. "Not asking you to."

I glanced back over my shoulder. "What about Becky and Tanya?"

"I'll take them both home." He gave me another tight smile and shoved his hands in his front pockets. It gave him a lean look, which emphasized his slender waist and broad shoulders.

"About Tanya..."

He shook his head. "Yes?"

"What are you doing?"

"I like her. I actually do."

"And it doesn't hurt Becky to see that...?"

"I don't know," he admitted. "I just know that I was playing a game with her before because of you. You liked Becky. I liked you. So I didn't do the right thing before, but I'm trying. I really am right now."

I nodded.

"What about you? Are you and Kade, you know?"

I shook my head. "It's about my parent's stuff and I don't want to talk about that."

"Really? No?"

"Nope."

"Oh." He ran a hand over his face. "I wouldn't have guessed that."

"Why not?" My voice cooled. "I told you that I know them, I'm not screwing them."

"No, no I know, but there was something there."

"What do you mean?"

He lifted both his shoulders up. "Does it matter?"

"Maybe. Maybe not."

He laughed again. "You're tough, Sam, tougher than I would've thought."

"Yeah..." I frowned. I was getting tired of hearing that from him. What did he think of me before? Then I rolled my eyes, like I really cared about that now. "Don't break Becky's heart, okay?"

He saluted me.

"Are you really going to start dating Tanya?"

"I think so."

I sighed. "Have fun with that, then."

He smirked. "I plan to."

And I laughed. This one was genuine, but then I waved goodbye and headed home. I had two hours before I needed to be back at the club for the football's annual dinner. I hurried through the house, but stopped short when I saw Mason in his room. Normally I would've taken the south stairs and I wouldn't have to go past his room, but I took the north stairs this time. When I breezed past, his door was open and he sat at his desk shirtless.

I braked and reversed.

He glanced up. "Hey."

"Hey." I went inside and sat on the edge of his bed.

He didn't turn around and kept his back to me as he looked at his computer's screen. "You seem in a rush?"

"I'm going to my dad's dinner tonight."

"Your dad?"

I cursed. I'd forgotten he knew, they all knew.

"My old dad's thing."

He grinned as he turned in his chair. "I understand. He's still your dad. Raised you, didn't he?"

I nodded and hugged myself. For some reason, a chill swept over me. I frowned. The windows weren't open in the room.

"Our folks are in the cities for the weekend. Again."

He didn't sound as if he cared. I frowned. "Are you pissed about that?"

Mason swung his hypnotic eyes back to me and narrowed them. I felt him searching inside of me, measuring whatever I had inside for what he might've needed. I always felt him probing me deep.

Then he said, "Does it matter? He's there. With her."

I frowned. "You say that like my mom's the other woman. Was she?" Wasn't he the other man for her?

319

He shrugged and stood to go in his bathroom. I waited a second, but took a deep breath and followed. As I stepped in the doorway, Mason let loose his shorts and turned on the shower.

I was struck by his nudity. He didn't care. Most guys might've done it for shock value, but he didn't care. This was Mason. Then he looked up and grinned. "Wanna join?"

I took a step inside.

His grin turned to something else.

I stepped closer and tilted my head up. He looked down and we stood close, close enough to touch. His hand brushed against my hipbone and I closed my eyes. His hand started to caress me there. A flooding filled me and a need started to throb between my legs. I held my breath and my head started to hang down. It rested against his chest.

Then I felt his lips against my forehead. He skimmed them lightly.

My hand reached up and curled onto his arm. It hung there.

When he bent forward and I felt his arm start to wrap around, I pulled back, breathless. My heart was pounding in my ears and I could only look at him, stricken. He gazed down at me and his lips moved. I knew he was saying something, but I couldn't hear over my heartbeat. I shook my head and tried to explain that to him, but I couldn't. My throat didn't work. My tongue didn't work. Nothing worked anymore except my feet. They pulled me away and I was soon hurrying to my room.

The door shut behind me, but it wasn't enough. I turned the lock and backed up three steps. I stared down and watched the handle. I waited for it to turn, but it never did. Nothing happened. He never came.

I kept backing up until I felt my bed behind my legs and sat abruptly. My arms were still wrapped around me. I sat there and waited for my heartbeat to settle, until I could hear things again. Everything was so deafening.

CHAPTER TWENTY-ONE

The football dinner was uneventful, at least for my latest standards of drama. Jill was there with Jeff and she sneered at me most of the time. Not surprising. Jessica had landed herself a date too, but I had no idea who he was. He was on the team, obviously. And while her newfound friend sneered at me, Jessica was void of emotion. She didn't ignore me like she had been till the Kade Coming Out news, but she didn't kiss my ass either. I caught her gaze a couple times and once thought she looked sad, but shrugged it off. She should be sad.

The only thing that bothered me at the dinner was the interest Malinda Decraw showed in David when she sat beside him after the second round of cocktails. She was the single mother of Mark Decraw; one of Becky's termed Academy Elite. He was co-captain and Amelia White's date that night. I knew Becky would be salivating at the gossip, but all I cared about was how many times Malinda did the hair flip.

She'd smile at David, lean close, and flip her hair. Then she would laugh, touch his arm or his shoulder (once), and flip the hair again.

When I left the dinner and spotted Mark and Amelia kissing by his car, I was tempted to corner them about Malinda's intentions. But I refrained. With my luck, that would bring more drama and as I let myself into the Kade mansion, I had enough on my hands.

Analise stood in the kitchen with a large glass of wine and two bottles beside her. Her eyes were glazed over and she swayed from side to side. Her hair was messed and looked haphazard while her white dress slipped off one shoulder. The top of her red bra was visible.

My mom was drunk.

Logan and Nate both sat on a counter with their legs dangling while Mason was propped against the doorway with his arms closed over his chest. As usual, he was unreadable while Logan had a look of delight on his face. Nate was fighting back his own laughter.

"Sam, you've been missing out!" Logan threw his arms wide. "Your mom's drunk like a sorority rush. Dad dropped her off an hour ago and she's getting drunker by the minute."

Analise rounded to me. Her body kept going, but Mason stopped her when his hand shot out and pushed her shoulder back upright.

"Thanks. You're bacb," she slurred, then took a big gulp of wine. She wiped her mouth with the back of her hand. "Housse your daddy?"

My eyes narrowed. "It was fine. Thanks."

She sniffled. "You always loved him more. Me, I'm the acdual parend. He neber wass."

"Thanks, mom. We all know that."

Her eyes got wide and her lips pursed into a sneer. "I swear, if you werend my daughter, I'd disown you."

"Really?" I arched an eyebrow.

"If you wanna him, you can hab him. Move in with him. I'm outta here." She swung her arm wide again. Her body kept going, but Nate was the one who caught her from the other side this time.

She tucked her head down. "Thanks."

He nodded.

Then she heaved a dramatic sigh and her arm dropped from her one hip. "You've god your wish, Samantha."

"What wish?"

"Me. And you. We're outta here. He kicked me out. I had a few doo many ad dinner and he kicked me out. Have to pack my stuff now. We're moving on, bucko!" Then she hung her head and a sniffle was heard. "David wond take me back now."

"Mom."

"Don't!" Her head snapped back up and her eyes were wild. "You always said it, we'd be gone. He wouldna marry me and you're righd. He won't. It's over. Finite. Finido. Finished."

I stepped around Mason, but he moved with me. When I started to get closer to her, he moved another inch. He was blocking me. He didn't want me close to her so I stayed put. I folded my arms. "Mom, you're drunk. Everything will be better in the morning. I promise."

"You don promise. You can't promise me anything. I'm the mother. I should be promiser one, but I'm not. I cand even do that for you. I've ruined it all, Sammy."

Her head was down again and another sniffle sounded.

"Mom, it'll be okay. We can get our own place."

Analise's shoulder jerked and her hand clenched around the wine glass. When she looked back, vehemence was in her eyes. The self-pity was gone and in its place was anger. I gulped; my mother was looking at me with fury now.

"It's your fault. All of this is your fault."

"How?" I challenged.

"David never loved you. Hell, I never loved you. I should've been with your father. I loved him, but he couldn't stay. He had to go. He always had to go. I had no one. Me and a baby." She threw her head back and an ugly sounding laugh came out. "Who's going want the package deal? Well, I found David. He loved me. Not you. He tolerated you, but me he loved. I should've been with your father, your real father. But he didn't have the time for me so fine. Screw him."

"Wait, what?" I surged forward, but Mason blocked me again. He didn't put a hand up, but he stepped in front an inch. It was enough of a barrier that held me back.

"David hates your father. He loathes him. He thinks he walked out on his daughter." A hysterical laugh came out, followed by a hysterical sob. She choked up for a moment and then shook her head clear of the emotions. "Jokes on him, isn't it. Your real daddy never knew about you. Like I'd stomach that. That he'd come back for his daughter, but not me. Oh no. If he wouldn't take both of us, he didn't get either of us. Your father has no idea about you." Her eyes found me, crystal clear.

A chill went down my back and I wondered if that was evil lurking in her depths. No. It couldn't be. She was drunk, just drunk...and sad.

She sneered at me. "And you'll never know. He'll never know about you, you'll never know about him. You can't leave me, Sam. I've all you got. David won't take you back. Are you kidding me? He's probably already got another woman, maybe even a kid too. He always liked to play the doting father type. Maybe he'll pick a son this time. The daughter he had ended up being a screw-up. You always picked the worst types, Sam. Jeff. Lydia. Jessica. They're your closest and they all screwed you. Even I knew it. You're the screw up."

When she was done, no one said a word. A fly would've sent echoes through the room, but then Analise choked out a simper. "Pack your stuff, Sam. We're leaving."

Mason chuckled.

She whirled to him. "What are you laughing about—?"

Logan and Nate jumped off the counter. Neither grinned now.

She stopped whatever she'd been about to say.

And Mason stepped away from her, but towards me. He ushered me further back, at a safer distance from my mother. When he stopped chuckling, he shook his head. His voice came out bored. "Are you this crazy?"

She gasped.

Logan smirked.

"I mean, you're effing crazy if you think you can talk to her like this. This is how you talk to the one person who's stayed by you?" He rolled his eyes. "Look, this is your daughter, but if you think she's going anywhere with you when you're like this, you're delusional too. She's not leaving. You are."

Analise went pale and her body stumbled back. It looked like a sudden violent wind had whipped against her. It came out of nowhere, but there was no wind.

"Just get lost, woman," Logan snickered. He circled around her while Nate stayed in place.

Mason stepped back again and this time was effectively in front of me. He completely blocked me, even from her vision. I tried to shift to the side, but he moved back again and had me trapped against the wall. So I snuck a hand on his side and peaked around him. He didn't stop me, but he tensed at my touch.

Logan moved again and all three had encircled her. She glanced around as panic started to set in her eyes.

Mason spoke, "We've been quiet, woman. We've taken your presence in this house like calm good little boys, but we're not good little boys."

"Not at all," Logan's hyena laugh came out. His eyes flashed hatred.

"What are you—what are you do..doing?" she stammered out.

Nate spoke in a calm voice, "We're not going to hurt you."

"No." Mason shook his head."But you are drunk. You're wacko in the head and you're being semi-abusive to your daughter." Logan's laugh gentled, but the sound still sent shivers down my body. "So we could say anything to you, do anything to you, and who'd believe you? Your own fiancé sent you packing tonight and went back to his dinner."

"You guys wouldn't." She was white as a ghost and her eyes jumped between the three of them. Then she found me and held a hand out. "Sam, he—"

Mason moved again so she couldn't see me. I heard a smacking sound and my mom cried out, "Ouch!"

I jerked behind him, but I didn't know what to do. Help her or help myself? I burrowed my head in the back of his shirt.

"How do you think this is going to end?" Mason was back in charge, so cold. It was like he'd asked about the weather.

"I..I—I—what?"

"Do you really think we're going to be bitches and let you talk to Sam like that?" Logan spoke now. "You're screwed up in the head if you think you've got the power to do that, especially in front of us."

"But—bu—you guys don't even like her!"

Nate laughed.

Mason sighed. It was a pitying sound. "Don't like her? We'd like anyone compared to you."

She gasped. "But—I didn't—your father—"

Logan snapped, "Stop choking like a little bitch. I thought you had bigger balls than that."

"Wha—huh? You guys can't talk to me like this..." But she didn't sound so certain.

Mason taunted her softly, "What he doesn't know, you're not going to tell."

"What?"

Logan came out strong, "Here's the way it's going to be. You're going to leave—"

Nate jumped in, "You're going to a hotel."

"And you're going to sleep off this drunk stupor," Mason ended.

My entire body shivered as I listened. All three of them spoke as one unit. They moved as one and they had their sights on my mother. I pressed even closer to Mason, not sure what to do, if I could at all. Did I even want to? It'd been so long since someone protected me...

"I'm not that drunk."

"You are." He said it so smooth, so soft, and so chilling. Now he left me. I fell forward a step, lost from his warmth, but contained myself. He moved as a stalker, silent as a ghost. Then he motioned to Nate.

A second later, my mom whimpered out in pain. I had my hands in front of my face, but when Logan started laughing again, the sound was so delightful and so dark, I couldn't hide anymore. I took a deep breath and looked up. He'd taken hold of the back of my mother's head and tilted her head back.

Mason watched. He didn't seem affected and then he motioned for Nate with his hand again.

"No-!" My mother screamed out.

"Come on," Logan chided her and then forcibly pulled her jaw down. Her mouth snapped opened and Nate poured something down her throat. She convulsed forward, choking as liquid spewed from between her lips. Her back spasmed backwards then, but Logan didn't let her go. He clamped her mouth shut again and ran a thumb down her throat. I watched as my mom fought, but in the end she swallowed.

They did it again.

And again.

After a fourth time, after Nate had almost emptied a bottle down her, he looked up. "I think that's enough."

Mason nodded and stepped back towards me again.

Logan swept my mother up in his arms. She'd grown weak during the ordeal and the fight had left her after the second time. Her eyes rolled back as she was cradled to his chest. When he turned for the door, Nate followed.

The door closed behind them and silence filled the room again. I couldn't stop from trembling. My teeth were chattering. My arms were jerking all over and then Mason swept me against him. He cradled my head to his chest and ran soothing hands down my arm.

My hands took hold of his shirt and hung on. I couldn't let go or I'd fall. I didn't want to fall. When I thought I could speak, I choked out, "What's going to happen to her?"

His lips skimmed my forehead, so soft. "She'll go to a hotel and sleep it off."

"But." I took a deep breath.

His lips pressed another kiss to my cheek.

I held on tighter. When his hand swept down and caught my leg, I climbed up him, grateful for the hold. I was going down otherwise. "What if she says something to your dad?" What would she do to me? I hadn't stopped it.

Mason lifted me so my legs were entwined around his waist. I hung onto him. My arms were wound around his neck. He ran a hand down my back as his other held me in place, splayed out on my bottom.

Then he kissed the side of my mouth and whispered against it, "She won't. She doesn't dare."

I sighed as he kissed the other side of my mouth. My lips moved against his. "What do you mean?"

"Your mom's a bitch and now she knows what we think of her."

She knew what they could do to her. My body couldn't stop shaking as I realized this and pressed my forehead into his shoulder. I held on tighter, but a thought nagged me. Why had he done that? Why had all three of them done that?

Mason chuckled against my hair. "Because she'll shut up now. That's why we did it. And because she needed to know we could."

I closed my eyes and felt him moving. I had no idea where he was taking me, but I wasn't going to ask. My body had stopped shaking and a different feeling had taken hold of me, one I didn't think I could fight off. I didn't want to. Need.

CHAPTER TWENTY-TWO

M ason sat me on the couch in my room and started rummaging through my closet. The need throbbed in me, it was slowly taking over when he started to lift my arms and pull my dress off. I blinked up at him. He seemed cold, hurried. This wasn't how I thought it would be.

My arms dropped back to my lap and I stared up. Desire was thick within me, blurring my vision. Why didn't he kiss me? I wanted him to and I reached up to palm the back of his head. Something was shoved down my arm instead. He slipped it over my head too. When he lifted my other arm and pushed it through a sleeve, I realized he was dressing me.

"What are you doing?" My voice was raspy.

Mason tugged me to my feet.

"Wha—?"

He pulled up some pants and I looked down at myself. I was fully dressed, even with socks and tennis shoes.

I blinked again. When had that happened?

"You couldn't go in that."

I spread my arms wide. "Like what?"

"We're taking off." He went back to going through my closet. More of my clothes were brought out and stuffed in a bag.

"We are?"

"When your mom wakes up sober, she's going to freak out. She'll call my dad hysterical."

"What?" I sat up further to clear my head. "They broke up..."

"No, they didn't." His head was in my closet again. "My dad called me and asked if we'd handle your mom. She got drunk at his business dinner and kept going on about you and your dad. He couldn't let her stay and he had to keep the meeting so we got babysitting duty."

I watched as he kept putting things in my bag and then disappeared inside the bathroom. "What are you going to say when he calls about tonight?"

"The truth." He came back with my toiletry bag. It was bulging at the zipper. "She kept drinking. You came home. She attacked you and then she started on us so we took her to a hotel."

"What are you going to tell him why we're leaving?" Where were we going?

"Nate's parents called to invite us up. We'll be back Monday or Tuesday we took you along so your mom wouldn't start in on you again. It's a long weekend anyway."

"What if she tells him what you guys did?"

He stopped and stared at me. His gaze was piercing. "She was drunk and crazy. We didn't do anything except to help." He narrowed his eyes. "It should be four to one."

Clarity slammed into me. I heard the veiled threat and surged to my feet. "You think I'm going to rat?"

He grinned and the tense moment was gone. "I didn't think so. Check to make sure I got everything. I need to get my own stuff."

"Where are we going? I don't know what to pack."

"Nate lives in the mountains, but he's got a Jacuzzi." And he left with those parting words.

My butt plopped down on the couch and I held my bag with numb fingers. It dangled from them to the floor. All I could do was sit there. What the hell had happened? And then I realized it didn't matter. He had everything covered for me, even my clothes. All I had to do was go downstairs and go for a ride. Did I go?

An hour later as I stood in the foyer, waiting, I knew that question was irrelevant. There'd never been a question not to go.

A bag crashed next to me and I jumped back. Then a second later, another bag followed with a third beside it. Logan and Nate peered down to me from the stairway and Logan waved. "Sorry!"

I frowned up at them, but they disappeared. It wasn't long before both were downstairs and in the foyer with me.

They looked happy, not happy—radiant. Logan was bouncing in place and Nate was bent over laughing at something. The two were full of adrenalin and excitement.

I shook my head. What was happening? It was all such a daze to me.

Then Logan threw his arm around my shoulder and jerked me against him. He breathed on me. "Are you ready to par-tay?"

"Party?" My eyes got big. "I thought we were going to the mountains."

"Uh, yeah...with thirty others." Logan sighed in exasperation and then frowned before he barked out, "Hey!"

I jumped again.

"What about your friends? You want to invite some of them?"

"My friends?"

"Yeah, that nerd girl and the quarterback who wants to bang you."

"He doesn't want to bang me."

Logan squeezed me against him and tipped his head back. His hyena laugh came out. Nate started to join in.

"He doesn't."

Both kept laughing and shook their heads.

"He doesn't."

Mason appeared with two bags in one hand and a black duffel bag on his back. He rolled his eyes and pulled out his keys. "You can't even lie to yourself. The douche bag has wanted to get in your pants for a long time."

I looked around. All three gave me knowing looks. Then I threw my arms in the air. "I don't even know why I was saying that."

Logan reached out and caught my shoulders when I started to leave. He pulled me back against his chest and enfolded his arms over my chest. "Ah, our little sister, trying to be all nice and saintly."

Mason snorted and opened the door. "Saints don't set cars on fire."

We all piled out behind him and Logan chuckled. "There's that, yeah."

When we got to Mason's Escalade, my bags were picked up and thrown inside. Logan nudged me with his shoulder. "If you want to invite your friends, you better call them now. We're picking up some others and heading out."

I pulled out my phone. "What do I say?"

He shrugged. "Tell them we're going to a kickass cabin for two days, but they have to be at Joe's Gas Station in thirty minutes. A minute late and they're dust."

"Give 'em forty. We have to swing by and pick up Marissa. She's in town at her aunt's." Mason brushed past me for the driver's seat. His hand swept against my thigh.

A small tingle shot threw me, but I frowned. Marissa again.

Logan gave me a knowing smirk, but headed to his own Escalade. After Nate and I got in Mason's, they tore out of there. When I called Becky, her response was to scream. She didn't say anything else, just started screaming and threw her phone aside. I could hear banging in the background, but disconnected the call soon after that. I could only imagine what she was doing. Adam's response was more reserved. He didn't respond for a moment, and then he said in a gruff voice, "I suppose I should make sure Becky gets there. We'll take my car."

After that was done and I'd put my phone away, the guys were quiet. Nate was looking at me and Mason kept glancing at me in the rear view mirror.

"What?"

Mason snorted again and looked away.

Nate gave me a polite smile. "Nothing."

"What?" I asked again, but I knew they wouldn't respond. And they didn't. Neither said a word as we drove around town. At each house they stopped at, people would come out with bags already packed. A few got in Logan's car, but soon two others drove their cars and filled them up. No one else got in Mason's and then Logan's Escalade pulled up next to ours. Each rolled down their windows.

"Go to the gas station and deal with all that stuff. I'll pick up Marissa."

Logan nodded and craned his head to meet my gaze. "Hop on over here, little sister."

"What? Why?"

The two brothers shared a look, but Logan responded, "We need you there to meet your friends. You're going to ride with them."

"Oh. Okay." And since that made perfect sense, I climbed out and got into his backseat. Two of his friends scooted over while another two jumped in the back with the bags. We took off one way and Mason went the other way.

When we got to the gas station, the sight was almost unbelievable. Twenty different cars were parked in the back lot and people were milling around. Bags were on the ground, some were being strapped on top of other cars, and then I caught sight of Adam's car. He had parked in the far corner, away from the frenzy. When Logan parked, I hopped out, but he hollered at me, "Don't go too far."

I turned around and kept walking backwards. "You aren't actually my big brother, you know."

He flashed me blinding smile. "Not my intent, Sam, not my intent."

I frowned and opened my mouth to ask what he meant, but he was pulled away by two of his friends. The smell of booze was ripe in the air and I knew the festivities had already started. As I got to Adam's car, Becky yelled my name and I turned around. She had two plastic bags in her hands and she ran the rest of the way from the station.

When she got to me, she started to jump up and down. Her hair bounced with her. "I'm so excited for this! You can't even believe me."

I grinned at the sight.

"My giddy radar exploded at the top. I had to beg my mom to let me come. She almost didn't, but I told her I'd do dishes for the rest of the year. I'm not sure if that was a good idea, but I don't care right now." She dropped both bags on the floor and grabbed my shoulders as she started to bounce around me. "I don't care if I look stupid. I'm so excited, so excited."

Adam's car door opened and he stood up. He was watching her with wary eyes and ran a hand through his hair. "You wouldn't be able to believe the sight I found when I went to her house. I swear the entire place had been thrown around. It looked like a hundred raccoons stormed through it."

She kept giggling and her eyes got bigger. "I don't know what I'm more excited about, the cabin, that it's a Kade party, or that we got invited and not Lydia and Jessica!"

"Yeah," I had to admit. "There is that." I glanced at Adam. "Your parents let you come?"

The small smile he'd had was wiped clean. His shoulders stiffened and I saw how his jaw clenched together. "They don't have much say in me anymore."

I was about to ask what had happened, when Becky gasped and stopped bouncing.

I closed my eyes. Oh no. It'd been too good to be true. A sense of doom filled me. I turned, opening my eyes.

Becky's mouth dropped and she pointed over my shoulder. "Look!"

I couldn't believe what I was seeing. Jessica, Lydia, Jill...and Ashley Decortts piled out of a car. Each of them had different expressions on their face, but none could hide their own excitement.

The ground fell out from beneath me. If they went, I wasn't. Bottom line.

At that moment, Mason's Escalade breezed to a halt. He parked beside Adam's car and when he got out beside me, he saw my face. "What is it?"

I nodded at them. "If they go, I'm not."

He followed my gaze and shrugged. "Consider it done." Then he nodded at Nate, whose grin couldn't be wiped off his face as he went in search for Logan. Mason stood next to me, but I couldn't look away from what was happening. Nate found Logan and the two bent their heads together for a second. Logan's head snapped up and he found me instantly. An evil grin came to his face and he snapped his fingers before he gestured to their car.

"Get 'em out," he hollered.

"No, no, no." Jessica, Lydia, Jill and Ashley all started to shake their heads and hold their hands up in surrender. It didn't matter. They were ushered out of there in record time. One of the guys pounded on top of the car. Jill poked her head out and snarled at them, but the guys started laughing and chucking bottles at them. Garbage was thrown next. They hurried to raise their windows, but it didn't matter. Someone threw paint inside. Jessica was drenched and Lydia screamed from the back.

"Get out of here!" Jessica screeched at the top of her lungs.

Their car was soon out of there, but I couldn't look away. A tension had taken hold of me. Its grip was so tight, so powerful. I couldn't believe what had almost happened, what *had* just happened...because of me.

"Happy?" Mason asked in a quiet voice.

I jerked my head up and realized he had remained close the whole time. The rest of his car had vacated.

"Yeah." I nodded my head abruptly.

"You sure?"

He was so close. I felt his breath on me and it teased me. That same tingle started back, nagging me. It wouldn't go away... I shook my head. It had to go away. There was no other way.

"Sam?"

I choked out, "I'm fine." And I swung away. I needed to get away from him, from how he could pull me in, how I wanted him to pull me in.

Hell, I wanted to pull *him* in.

I closed my eyes, but Mason stepped back then. I took a deep breath and tried to calm my nerves. Goodness. I wanted to jump him right there and when I opened my eyes, under heavy eyelids, I saw he wanted the same thing. His eyes were dark with desire, but then he closed his eyes. As he opened them, he wore a mask once again. He was in control and he gave me a half grin. "I want your car behind mine or Logan's, okay?"

I nodded.

He nodded at Adam. "You got that?"

Adam gave him a nod from across the top of his car, with an unreadable gaze.

Mason narrowed his eyes and held his stare for a second. Neither said a word, but I knew there was some form of message shared between the two. The heated look was broken when a small girl with brown curly hair approached from around the side of Mason's car. She had bright almond eyes, a timid smile, and a white sweater that engulfed her.

"You're Sam?" Warmth oozed from her.

"Not now." Mason touched her shoulder and urged her in front of him as they walked to Logan's side of the lot.

She looked back and gave me another smile before Mason blocked her view of me.

I frowned as I realized what he was doing. He'd done the same thing with my mother. At that time, he'd been protecting me, but who was he protecting now?

"Oh." Becky panted. "My." She heaved an exaggerated breath. "Gawd."

Adam shook his head. "Can you chill the dramatics a bit?"

She looked over, still panting like a dog. "Did you see what I did? I don't even know which thing to talk about first? I can't prioritize them. This is drama overload." Her shoulders sagged heavily and she dropped her arms to her side. "It's all weighing me down. I have to get it off my chest, I just have to."

Then Adam grinned and pointed at an incoming car. "You're going to have to add a bit more to your list."

As a Bentley stopped on the other side of Adam's car, my radar went on high alert. A brand new, straight from the dealership, Porsche Cayenne wheeled in on the other side and the doors were thrown open.

The Academy Elite had arrived. And judging from their packed vehicles, they were coming on the trip.

I watched in horror as Mark Decraw went over and pumped fists with Logan.

Becky groaned next to me. "I think I'm about to collapse."

CHAPTER TWENTY-THREE

It was a three hour drive and by the time we got there, I had one thing in mind. Could I go running and if I could, how long did I have to wait before I went? The itch to get away and run free was so strong; I had to force my legs down to the floor a few times. I wanted to hurl myself out of the car each time we stopped at a stoplight in some small town.

Becky had stopped questioning me about the Kades when I went mute two minutes into the trip. Adam hadn't filled my silence either and so Becky sat back and chatted away to herself. She talked about everything: the Kades, the Academy Elite, how liberating it was to watch Jessica and Lydia get pushed out. She went on and on.

Then, after Adam got a text message, she squealed again when she snatched it from him. She twisted around in the seat and exclaimed, "Tanya's coming with her cousin!" She sang out, "So much drama!"

Adam grunted, "You need to get a life."

"I have a life." She was breathless. "Both of yours."

And then Logan's car, who'd been in the lead, slowed beside a gated driveway. We were in the middle of nowhere with trees thick on either side of the road. The last town seemed forever ago, but when the gate slowly swung open and Logan led the way through it, it was the same; a long narrow road with thick forest around it. Finally, he rounded another curve and a gigantic log mansion stood in a clearing.

It could've been on MTV cribs.

"Whoa," Adam laughed under his breath. "That's a freaking hotel. I wondered how they were going to house everyone."

Becky had fallen silent with wide eyes. Her mouth formed a silent oval and she pressed closed fists to it.

I jumped out of the car and hurried to Logan. "Where's my stuff?"

He frowned at me. "What's up with you?"

"I need to run."

"Gotcha." He glanced at my shoes. "Can you run in those? It's going to take a while to get to your bags."

I jerked my head in a nod. It'd have to do.

He gestured to a trail that started behind a garage. "It's still dark out, but it should be light soon. I'll make sure you get a good room. That trail goes up and around a lake. It'll be pretty by the time you get there. And it should be safe. Nate's parents have an electric fence that runs the perimeter so no big animals should be out there. Take your phone."

When I didn't start right away, he tapped my shoulder. "Go. It's fine."

Then I started. I walked to the back of the garage. When Becky called out and asked where I was going, Logan said something to her. I knew I was covered and as soon as I was hidden from view, I took off.

The path was covered in woodchips and it went uphill.

I pumped my knees and arms high, and even more the higher I went. When the trail veered to the right, my body leaned with it. I wasn't running. I was sprinting. I knew I should slow down. I didn't want to burn out too soon, but I couldn't. Something in me was making me go faster and faster. Sweat was soon dripping off me, but I didn't care. I barely felt it.

The mountain morning air felt cool and it fueled me for more.

The path flattened out after a steep incline. There were a few dips, all of them welcomed, but I loved the climb. My heart beat faster and it wasn't from the exertion.

It might've been an hour, I wasn't sure, but the forest opened around me and I was given a breathtaking view of a lake below. It was in a valley between two mountains. Waves rippled over it. I couldn't see through it, not from how high I was, but the water seemed to give me another burst of adrenalin.

I kicked off at a higher speed and soared past it.

The trees were a blur as I raced past them and I kept going. When my chest felt like it couldn't expand anymore and my arms had started to feel like cement, I slowed my pace. I lifted my head and breathed in the air.

I could feel the elevation in my lungs, but it only made me slow a bit more.

After what seemed like another hour, I turned and started back. When I returned to the lake, I stopped and bent over. I caught my breath, but I couldn't stop looking at the lake. Something calmed and excited me at the same time. I wanted to be a part of it and I felt crazy admitting that to myself, but I did.

And then, as I turned and headed to the mansion, I realized I wasn't scared. Maybe I ran it out of me; maybe I ran away from it enough. I wasn't sure, but a contented feeling settled over me. And then I slowed to a walk the closer I got to the mansion. I could hear bass music blaring through the woods. It might've been a mile away when I started to hear laughter.

There was a slight clearing from the hill where I was and I stopped. My feet were rooted in place.

I could see a large pool behind the mansion. It was filled with people with others streaming around it. There looked to be a hot tub and sauna as well. A few tables were kept separate behind a barrier of plants with a steel grill beside a large bar structure. I heard laughter as a few guys shoved some girls into the pool. They squealed as they were soaked.

A breeze swept around me and goose bumps covered me. I was completely drenched in sweat, but I didn't care. That had been the best run of my life. I was already anticipating my next one.

When I got back to the house and walked through the garage, there were people everywhere. I walked through, drenched in sweat, and a few girls gave me the snub. They looked me over, their lips curled up, and they turned away. I couldn't hold back a grin as this happened. I might not have wanted to buy into being protected by Mason or Logan, but I knew these girls didn't know who I was. And I sighed as I realized that. These girls were being real. They weren't being fake towards me. They weren't kissing my ass because who might've been my new stepbrothers.

More than a few guys didn't look away. My shirt and pants stuck to me like a second skin. It wasn't until I ducked into the kitchen and heard Nate's laugh when he saw me that I realized how foolish I might've looked. He saw me, his mouth opened, and he bent over in laughter.

"Shut up." I frowned at him.

He shook his head, still laughing. "Not at you, not at you..." More laughter and he clapped a hand to his knee a few times. "Look at you." He held a hand up. "You look like you went swimming and I know it's because you went running. Most girls want to look their hottest and you're...I'm sorry to say, but you go the opposite way. I like it. I really do. I admire it."

"Shut up." I frowned at him. "Where's my room?"

He pointed upstairs, still laughing, and choked out, "Fourth floor, second door on your right."

Fourth floor. I couldn't believe there was a fourth floor. And then I remembered the Kade mansion, which wasn't that small compared to this beast of a home, and decided to keep my mouth closed. When I was rounding the first set of stairs, I ran into Adam. He was going downstairs dressed in his swimming trunks and a glass of something in his hand.

He drew back and grinned. "Hey."

"Hey." I eyed the plastic cup. "What are we drinking?"

He grimaced and rolled his eyes. "Something to get me in the party mood. Where'd you go? You took off right away and Logan said you had something to do. No one questioned him, we didn't feel we could, but...where'd you go?"

I shrugged. "I went running."

He frowned. "You run?"

"Yeah."

"Oh." He skimmed me up and down.

I fidgeted under the weight of his gaze, now self-conscious. "So, anyway...you and Becky are on this floor?"

"Yeah." He drew upright. "We're in a back corner."

"And Tanya? Becky said she was coming?"

He looked away and scratched the back of his head. "Yeah...I think her and Tate will share a room in the basement. I think those are the only rooms left."

I nodded. "Does Logan know Tate is coming?"

He met my gaze for a second and just for a second the real Adam was there, the one who meant it when he promised me the world. He spoke in regret, "No..."

I shook my head. "Do you know what you're doing? Logan is going to flip when he knows she's here."

"From what I hear Logan isn't the problem." His jaw clenched and he looked away.

There it was. The unspeakable name, one of the many reasons Adam and I no longer trusted each other and as I confessed that, I wondered when that had happened—when I lost my trust in him and when he did with me? Well, I could guess when he'd lost his with me.

I took a breath and braved the front. I named the name that was between us. "Mason will know you invited her. Mason hates her."

He swung his gaze to me and I saw the pained look in them.

I fought myself from cringing in sympathy.

He wrung out, "Do you even know why he hates her so much? And what does that have to do with you?"

"Do you?"

"No." He shook his head. "But I don't have to deal with it. I care less who he likes or who he doesn't—"

"Are you kidding me?" I folded my arms over my chest and cut in. My chest was starting to rise, up and down, up and down. My heart was starting to race again. "You don't care? About me? You don't care about me? Because you know I'm connected to them. I'm connected to them in a way that few are. They're going to be my family, Adam. I can't ignore that. And I think you want me to do that, but I can't."

"Sam, she isn't your issue. She has nothing to do with you!"

"She already has!" I yelled back at him and pushed him away.

He fell back, surprised, but he quieted.

I closed my eyes and turned away. What had I said? I couldn't believe I'd let that slip.

"Don't torture yourself. You were honest just now. You were honest with me, maybe the first time." He took a breath and touched the back of my elbow. His voice was soft. "You were saying that Tate's already had something to do with you? What did you mean by that? I'd like to know. I care about you."

And then movement appeared from a back corner. I swung my gaze up, stricken. I hadn't even known a back corner existed.

Mason gave me an unreadable look, but he spoke to Adam, "What do you want here?"

Adam's head jerked up and I knew he was surprised.

I turned away. I wasn't. I'd witnessed when Mason went in for the kill. I knew it was happening now.

"What are you talking about?"

Mason laughed to himself and gestured to me. "What do you think, dickhead? What do you want? Her?"

Adam's eyes went wide.

Mason's eyes went to disdain. "Be honest. Right now, right here. You and me. Her. You want her, right? I know you do. Just say it. Put it out there, it might work."

I glanced at him. What was he doing? Mason refused to meet my gaze. His jaw was hard. Everything about him was hard in that moment. And no matter what Adam said, I knew he'd already dealt his hand.

No one won against Mason.

Then Adam broke and threw his arms out wide. "What do you want? Yes, I want her." His chest heaved up and down. "I want her, okay? I've known her all my life."

Mason grinned. "How long have you wanted her?"

"For half of that," Adam spat back at him. "Are you happy? I've wanted her since seventh grade, since the first time Sallaway noticed her."

"That's a long time."

"Stop," I snarled at Mason. He was encouraging him.

He ignored me and narrowed his eyes. Slowly, his hand reached out and grasped my elbow. He pulled me behind him and moved himself forward. It was done so slowly and so smoothly that Adam didn't notice.

I held my breath and waited for his reaction. It never came.

"You've wanted her a long time?"

"Yes," Adam cried out. "Can you blame me? You want her too. I can tell."

Mason shrugged. It was another moment like my mother's. He went in for the kill and I was pressed against his back. I pressed against him, not to hide myself, but to keep myself from saying something I'd regret. And what would I even say? I pressed the back of my hand against my mouth. I had no idea. My heart was beating so fast. It was like I was running still.

"You're right." Mason's voice was so soft, almost delicate. "I do. I'm not denying that."

"Oh god."

I flinched when I heard the disgust in Adam's voice.

Mason pressed on, almost tender still, "But I'm not going to screw another girl wishing she were Sam in my head. I'm not going to do that because you know why?"

There he was. He was going in for the kill. Adam cowered now.

It was enough. I swung away and shoved him back.

Mason glanced over.

I pushed him some more. "Go away."

"Sam."

"Now!" I pointed downstairs. "You don't have the right."

His jaw clenched. "Are you kidding me?"

"I'm not your whore. I'm not your stepsister. I'm not your anything. I thought I was your friend, but maybe not even that. You don't have a right, Mason. You'd never do this for Lo—"

He shoved his face in mine and I gasped as I fell back against the wall. "This is exactly what I did for him. You want to know what that whore did?"

I couldn't look away. My eyes were wide. My back was against the wall.

Adam ceased to exist.

I couldn't breathe. He was so close.

He pressed into me and placed both hands against the wall beside me. He trapped me, but I didn't want to go anywhere. When his knee nudged between my legs and moved up, I closed my eyes and fought back a sigh. The need throbbed inside of me again.

I was starting to think that need for him would never leave. It was so powerful, so consuming.

He nuzzled against my cheek and asked quietly, his breath a caress to me, "You want to know what she did to hurt Logan and me?"

I fell against him. I couldn't hold my head up.

I felt him smile against me, but he held me upright. He took my weight. "She screwed him. She got him to love her. For two years, Sam, she had him thinking he loved her and then she decided she wanted me."

I felt the coldness in him, even as he rested against me, and I reached out to it. I slid my hands up his arms, over his shoulders, around them, and kneaded the back of his neck. I wanted the tension gone. I was blind in it. And I was blind how he now held me in place. His hands moved to cup my bottom and my legs wrapped him. I wanted him. The need throbbed in me and I pressed against him.

I felt his reaction and grinned against his cheek.

"She came to me at home one day. I was in my room. She'd been in his and Logan was asleep. They'd screwed and she came to my room." Mason lifted me away from the wall.

I held onto him as I had the previous night. He had protected me then. He was protecting me again? Lust had confused all rational thought within me. I didn't know where we were anymore, but it didn't matter.

I slid a hand to his cheek and cupped it. I wanted him. I moved my lips so they brushed against his as he spoke.

"She wanted me. She had him and she thought I'd want her. I don't know why. I'd never given her any reason to think that, but she thought she could have two brothers instead of one. I called him. I let her try and seduce me and I let him hear the whole thing. It didn't take as long as it seemed. I saw when the call ended. Three minutes, that was all it took. Logan came around the corner with his phone to his ear. She saw it and looked at me. I held mine up and told her he'd heard the whole thing."

A tremor wracked through me.

He kissed my ear, my cheek, my neck. He whispered to me, "She tried to come between me and my brother. That's why I hate the bitch, but he still loves her. That's why he has a soft spot for her."

"Mason," I breathed out, holding on tight. I grabbed his face and held him still. I pulled back and met his gaze.

They were cloudy with desire, much like my own. Satisfaction surged through me. I affected him the same as how he affected me. It went both ways.

And then he killed the moment when he turned to the side. A ruthless emotion came through, thick and heavy, when he clipped out, "Have you been watching? This is why I'll never do what you have to do. I have her. I won't have to dream about her."

Everything stopped in me. A cold shower went over me and I was sputtering in the harsh reality.

CHAPTER TWENTY-FOUR

Adam stormed off.

We were alone.

Mason slowly lowered me so I could stand on my own and he stepped back. He watched me as if I were an animal, waiting to attack. He was ready.

He'd been hot and heavy, or so I thought, but he'd really been cold and calculating the whole time. That same unreadable mask was over him now.

"You're an asshole," I said softly.

He nodded.

"Why'd you do that?"

He didn't respond. It took another beat before he looked away and ran a hand over his head. "Don't get all girly and shit on me. That was a show. You performed well and he bought it."

My eyes bulged out of my head. I couldn't believe this was where he was taking it. "Are you kidding me?"

Something flashed in his eyes. It was gone in that next instant. He shook his head and lifted his shoulders. "What do you want from me?"

"You played me; you pulled all the right strings."

A cocksure smirk came out. "Like you said, I'm an asshole. That's what we do."

I took a deep breath. Something cold started in the pit of my stomach. It grew with each word he said and each second I was away from his touch. I hated how he affected me, the power he had and he knew it as well. He was fully aware of the power he had over me.

Chills broke out over me. I had to get away from him. I just had to. "I have to shower."

He jerked his head in a nod and started to leave.

My feet wouldn't go. My mind was yelling at me to leave, but my body wouldn't go. It didn't want to go. He had power over me...but I was pretty sure I had power over him too.

He stopped as he was about to go down the stairs. "What's wrong?"

I turned and locked eyes with him. I didn't know what he saw, but it worked. His hand clenched on the banister, his shoulders jerked upright. He sucked in a breath. I watched as his chest rose higher and higher.

I choked out, "Was that all a show?"

Desire was thick in his eyes. He narrowed them, licked his lips, and jerked his head in refusal.

Something flared throughout me and my legs moved now. I caught his hand and pulled him with me.

"This way." He pulled me a different way.

My heart was pounding as I held onto his hand. I was blind in my need. I could only focus on him. He led me through a myriad of stairs, through some doors, and finally he pulled me through the last one. I had no idea where we were, I hadn't cared to pay attention, but I knew we were far away from the party.

Mason dropped my hand and gazed at me. His room was dark. The shades were pulled so the morning light filtered through, but we were still in shadow.

He was watching me with an intensity that made my heart skip a beat. Fear froze me. I stumbled out, "I need to shower. I reek."

And then he reached forward and wrapped two arms around my waist and raised me off my feet as he walked to a bathroom. The shower was turned on and he stepped underneath. The cold water splashed down on me and I gasped. I surged forward in reaction and pressed my chest against him, but his mouth landed down on mine.

Oh god.

My hands curled into his shirt and I could only hold on.

His lips were hard on mine, a flame exploded inside of me, and I wanted more of him. I needed more. Then he started to move against me. His lips coaxed, nibbled, slid, and whispered against mine. His tongue touched the tip of my mouth and I let him in. I wasn't allowed not to. My body answered whatever demand he made. The thought of denial wasn't in me.

When my tongue touched his and his body trembled under my arms, I realized the power I had. It was addicting. It burst within me and I climbed up him. It was as before, but this time I didn't wait for him. I slipped my hand under his shirt and lifted it over his head.

Mason let it slip over and he hungrily already had mine off. My bra was stripped away in the next second and he cupped my breasts.

I gasped into his mouth when his thumb touched the tip of my nipple. He teased it and laughed against me. I nibbled at the corner of his mouth and then moved back. He caught me with a hand to my back and met my gaze.

We held each other's gaze. I couldn't look away. His eyes were dark, hungry, and they grew darker the longer we stared at the other. Then I lifted a hand and touched the side of his face. I traced the edge of him, his forehead, the corner of his eye, the side of his cheek, his lips.

He was beautiful.

His muscles shifted under me and I felt him lower me back to my feet.

I groaned in protest. I didn't want to leave him, but he bent forward and caught my lips in a hungry kiss, a long kiss. I couldn't tear away from him if I had to. Mewling, I pressed against him again and then his hands were under my bare legs. He lifted them again and as I wrapped them around his waist, he came in full contact against me.

I gasped at the feel of him. He was hard and ready.

He bent and kissed my neck, on my shoulder bone, and moved around to the other side as he walked backward and pressed me against the wall. When his hands no longer needed to hold me, he started to caress me. One slid over my stomach, up to my breasts, and he stroked them. They were hard and full. I ached for his touch. I wanted him in me, between my legs.

And then his hand moved down there. He caressed the insides of my thigh and then over my stomach, back down the other thigh. He encircled the area that throbbed for him. And then, as I gasped against his mouth, his finger slipped inside of me. His tongue swept against mine at the same time.

His other held the back of my head as his mouth consumed me, while his finger started to slip in and out. He went deeper with each thrust. I clung to him, pleading with him for more as my hips moved in rhythm. Then my hand slid down his arm, circled his slim waist, and wrapped around him.

He gasped against me this time and held still.

I grinned, intoxicated with power and need. I wanted more. I wanted him and I kissed his ear to whisper that to him.

With a guttural groan ripped from him, he pulled me from the wall and walked to the bedroom. A second finger slipped in and he curved them deep in me, deeper than before. As he lowered me to the bed, I gasped and arched my back. His fingers pushed further. He didn't need to move them anymore.

I felt it building. Spasms of pleasure joined into one long momentous ride and I rode it out. Wave after wave crashed into me. My body trembled from the climax and I lay weak in his arms. When I had settled, he grinned down at me.

I brushed back a lock of his black hair the fell forward and rasped out, "What?"

"You ready for round two?" He pulled out a condom.

I groaned and soon he joined with me.

I watched him as he bent over me. He thrust in me and when he saw me watching, he thrust harder. He pinned my arms above my head and stretched me. My breasts lifted for him and he took one in his mouth. His tongue swept around the nipple, it flicked over it, teasing it. Then his thrusts got harder, rougher. He went as far as possible. When I wanted him to go faster, he held back. He kept a slow pace. It built within me, driving me crazy. I wanted more. I screamed at him, but he only grinned back. Then his tongue dipped to my neck. He licked me and I screamed again.

My legs clamped around him and rose higher. I wanted him further inside, but then he cupped the bottom of my legs and he held them at the right spot. His penis touched the back of me and another climax ripped from me. I would've yelled, but his mouth drowned me out. He trembled along with me as we both went over the edge together.

When I was able to move again, I shivered as I remembered what we'd done.

I grew wet again and Mason lifted his head from my chest. He gave me a lazy and slow smile. "Already?"

I laughed huskily and shoved him out of me. His penis slid out. I missed it as soon as it was gone. Something was missing.

I shook my head at that yearning. "I have a feeling we'll be going again if we don't get some distance." Then I fell back again and laughed. He rose above me and cupped the side of my face. When he turned me towards him, my eyes met his.

They were narrowed and somber.

I was breathless again. My chest wanted to rise and fall, but it was frozen in place.

Then he leaned down and touched his lips to mine. It was a soft kiss, tender. As he pulled away, he pressed another to my forehead before he stood up. I sat up and watched as he strolled to the bathroom. His body was made of contour and muscles. He was sculpted as a statue. The added comfort he had with his body, which he didn't give a damn if he were naked or wore clothes, took my breath away.

I climbed out of the bed and followed him to the shower.

He opened the door, but I shook my head and climbed onto the counter. I leaned back against the mirror and watched him shower. When he realized what I was going to do, his eyes darkened and the corner of his mouth curved up, but he finished washing himself. He left the door open and as he was done, he leaned over me to reach for a towel.

His chest rubbed against my breasts.

He held himself across me. I looked over, he must've had a towel by then, but his lips caught mine. He'd been waiting for me. After a long and hungry kiss, he pulled back and strolled to the bedroom.

I tipped my head back and groaned. Everything in me was mush. My legs were jelly, but I managed to push off the counter and went into the shower. The water cooled me down. When I went back to the room, Mason was on the edge of the bed. He had pulled on a pair of jeans that rode low on his hips. As he reached for a shirt in the closet, he glanced over. "Do you have any clothes?"

"In my room." I fell back on his bed with a towel wrapped around me.

My whole body tingled with awareness. I felt alive. It was like I'd gone for another three hour run. And then his question penetrated and I jerked upright. "I don't have any clothes!"

He chuckled and sat beside me. His thigh brushed against my bare one. "That's why I asked. You want me to go and get you some?"

"How far away is my room?"

He grimaced. "Logan assigned the rooms and he put you on the opposite side of the house."

I glared at him.

He grinned. "Logan's way of a joke."

I groaned. "I can't believe this."

Mason flicked me on the shoulder and stood. As he lifted his arms above his head and stretched, he remarked, "Chill. I'll go get you some clothes."

"And if someone sees you?"

His arms dropped to his sides and he chuckled. The genuine sound of it sent another burst of tingles through me. He shrugged. "Who cares? I can always pull the sister card if I have to."

I groaned again.

He went to the door and glanced back to wink. "Not that I gave a shit about that before. I'll be back." He tapped the door twice and sent me a farewell grin before he disappeared behind it.

And I was left alone.

Alarm shot through me. What had we just done?

And then I remembered. The images of us flashed in my mind. A shiver from desire came over me and I melted into his sheets.

I wanted him again.

As more images flared through me, I rolled over and let loose a yell into his pillows. I knew that I'd want him for a long time.

What the hell was I going to do?

It wasn't long before the door opened again and he threw some clothes at me. They landed beside me and he held my gaze. My body reacted, my chest started to heave, my pulse picked up, my hands got clammy, and the need throbbed between my legs.

His eyes darkened and then he cursed as he slammed the door behind him.

I met him halfway, but he carried us back to the bed.

CHAPTER TWENTY-FIVE

When I woke later, I rolled over and looked down. Two more condoms had joined the first one on the floor and then I heard his chuckle behind me. His hand rubbed at the bottom of my back and massaged its way up to my shoulders. He sat forward, landed a kiss on my shoulder bone and scooted to the backboard. "You think I'd forget those puppies?"

I glanced back. "I did."

He grinned and stretched with a big yawn. "Those things are like putting on pants. I'd have to be drugged to forget 'em."

My shoulders sagged forward when I heard his sentiment. Some guys wouldn't agree, but I was relieved to hear his viewpoint. Then I yawned as well. "What time is it?"

He shrugged. "I could sleep the rest of the day. Good sex does that for me."

A different tingle shot through me at his words, but I frowned. I didn't want to dissect any of it and then I glanced at the clock. My eyebrows shot up. "It's six o'clock. Oh my god. I have to get out of here." I started to throw back the covers to scramble out.

"Why?" His hand caught me around the waist and pulled me backwards. His body curled behind me and he wrapped both arms around me.

Warmth and a frenzy of desire were starting to build again, but I clamped my legs shut and turned over. When he gave me a lazy grin, I smoothed a thumb over his forehead. Then I leaned close and kissed both of his closed eyelids before I whispered, "We have to get up or everyone's going to know."

He chuckled. The sound of it teased against my collarbone. "Everyone probably does."

I groaned and pushed him away. Then I did scramble out of his bed. "I hope not."

"What are you doing?" He patted the empty spot next to him. "Come back to bed."

I grimaced, though I wanted. I wanted badly, but I shook my head and threw my top over my head. "For my sake, I can't."

"Your sake?" He sat up again and frowned as he ran a hand through his hair. "What are you talking about?"

"I'm your stepsister. I'm sleeping with you. Do you realize what kind of a reputation I'm going to get?"

He crossed his arms over his chest and I averted my eyes when his chest muscles protruded out. Heavens, that boy...

"I didn't even think about that."

"Yeah, well, think about it." I gave him a short wave. "I have to go."

When I shut the door, his laughter followed behind and as I soon realized I had no idea where I was, he had reason to laugh at me. Three doors later, four hallways, and another two sets of stairs I pushed my way through a last door to find myself beside an indoor pool. Who had an indoor pool? My goodness. And then I looked up and the incredulity of the situation died down.

Logan sat on the other side with some of his friends and Mark Decraw.

My inner claws came out.

"Hey! How did you get there?" Logan waved me over.

Everyone else looked up. Most of the guys were friendly. Most of the girls' weren't, but it didn't matter. As I drew closer, I ignored the knowing smirk on Logan's face and studied Mark's reserved one instead.

"Where have you been all day?"

"Huh?" I looked down.

Logan rolled his eyes. "You've been missing in action since this morning. Most people took naps, but they didn't sleep the whole day away."

I shrugged. I couldn't peel my eyes off of Mark, whose eyes were directed anywhere but at me. "I don't even know where I slept. I never found my room."

He whistled. "Are you serious? I was sure I saw Mason showing you."

My hand clamped down on his shoulder and he winced, howling under his breath. "Remove the claws, Sam. Seriously."

I forced a laugh from me. "Ha ha...ha, Logan."

He rolled his eyes again. "Your friends are on the bottom patio outside. I know that's where you'll be the rest of the night."

I gave him a thankful grin and started forward, only to stop and look back. "How do I get there?"

Mark stood and pointed through a doorway. "You go through there, up the left stairs and the door will take you to the kitchen. The patios are out from there."

I narrowed my eyes at him. Why was he being helpful? Did he not know of his mother's intentions? I knew I should've thanked him, but I clipped out, "How's your mom?"

He frowned. "She's fine...Why?" His eyes seemed wary.

I shrugged. "No reason."

Logan's gaze had been skirting between us with a frown on his face. A look of frustration passed over him. "Where's Mason, Sam?"

I jumped. "Why would I know?"

"You saw him last?"

I looked away and cursed when my face went in flames. "I have no idea. I've been asleep the whole afternoon."

"Uh huh. Right."

When I glanced back, I was grateful to see that only Logan studied me. He gave me a tight smile and I knew that he knew. Guilt and anger coursed through me, but I frowned back at him. Then I stuck my tongue out at him before I pushed through a set of doors that led where Mark had told me to go.

When I pushed into the kitchen, so many people poured everywhere. No one looked at me and I got an extra bounce in my step from that. No one cared. That was good, very good. And I meandered through to the patios. From the top, I looked down and my eyes went wide again. When Logan said my friends were on the bottom patio, he'd declined to tell me there were six different patios. There were walkways that connected them and each patio was set beneath the other one.

When I got to the bottom, that patio was settled between a tennis court and a sand volleyball court.

Who were Nate's parents and what did they do for a living?

"Sam!" Becky saw me first and pumped her hand in the air. The fierceness of her movements sent most of her drink over the glass' edge that she held in her other hand. Amelia White scrambled up next to her and brushed frantically at her lap.

As I approached, she had snapped something at Becky, who didn't seem to care as her grin was etched from ear to ear. She pulled over an empty seat next to her and shoved it out to me. "Here. Sit here."

I sat.

Amelia scoffed and rolled her eyes as she moved a seat away on the other side of Becky. Her two other friends, Miranda and Cassandra both gave me polite smiles before they sipped their drinks. Adam was surrounded by Peter and a second guy that I didn't know. He looked like the Academy Elite, preppy and stuck-up.

"Where did you go?" Becky gushed. "I didn't know you ran. Adam said you went running. How far did you?"

I shrugged. "Far enough."

"That's so cool. You should go out for cross country. I bet you'd be awesome at it."

Adam gave me a biting smile. "Did you rest up this afternoon?"

I wanted to glare at him, but I held back and took a breath instead. "I did. You?"

Cassandra laughed shrilly and placed a hand over his. She gave me a forced smile. "Oh, you wouldn't believe how long he napped."

I frowned. "I wouldn't?"

"No." She heartedly shook her head. "Not at all, not one bit." Then she wiggled two fingers at me. "You're so secretive, Samantha. We had no idea you liked to run."

My eyebrow shot up. "Well, how could you? We've been such great friends since..." I waited a beat and gave my own forced laugh. "Oh, that's right. We're not friends."

Her smile clamped up and she glared instead. "You don't have to be mean."

I smiled back. "Why not? It's so much fun."

Becky gasped and patted her chest in an exaggerated fashion. "Could this be? Has Cassandra Uppity met her match?"

She turned her glare on her and an added coldness sparked in her depths. "Watch it, Sallaway. You're two steps from being ousted at school."

Becky seemed to purr in her smile. "Adam's been my neighbor all my life. We're good friends too."

Cassandra's eyes were sharp. "I don't see him defending you right now. Two steps, outcast, two steps and your humiliation is all mine. I like to serve my dishes best cold."

Becky lifted her hand and pretended to claw her. "Retract 'em, beeotch. We all know what they say about felines."

"What?"

She seemed to search for words. "That...they're the female version of the human species: catty, moody, and sneaky."

"You're a girl."

Becky shrugged. "I'm more a dog."

The smile on Cassandra's face was the crème of the crème and she leaned back. "You're right. You like to bound around looking like a fool most of the time when everyone knows you're just panting for any scraps from your master. You're low class, Rebecca. You used to accept it."

Becky turned green and looked away. I leaned forward, not sure what to do, but Adam remarked as he continued to lounge back in his chair, "Sullivan, chill."

She glared at him. "Why?"

He stared her down. "She's my friend."

She rolled her eyes and harrumphed before she shot from the table and stormed away.

Becky looked back up from her lap. A small smile started on her face. "Did she just leave?"

The other two Academy Elite females didn't say a word, but shared a look.

I frowned at that. What did that mean? And then we were all distracted when two new arrivals showed up. They were by the beach and paused in clear view from the mansion's top decks.

I sighed.

Tate and Tanya had arrived.

Both looked stylish, dressed in tight khakis and tank tops. Tanya's blonde hair was in curls as it lay past her shoulders and Tate's hair was swept up in some French-twist thing. I didn't know what it was, but it looked sophisticated.

Adam shot forward, but he didn't stand from the table. He raised his hand.

Tanya spotted him and gave him a bright smile and a wave in return. She started for him until Logan stepped in the middle and swept a hand around her waist. He pulled her close and seemed to whisper something in her ear. Tanya laid a hand on his shoulder and frowned, torn at some decision. When he continued to whisper and his hand started to massage her waist, she melted into him. Her head rested on his shoulder and Logan met my gaze with a brief flash of triumph before he took her hand.

Tate stood behind them with her mouth on the floor. One hand was poised on her hip.

As Logan whisked her away, no one said a word until Cassandra choked on a laugh. "Did that *just* happen?"

I did a double take. When had she come back?

Becky was quiet as she cast nervous glances at Adam. Her hands were in her lap and I watched as she kept twisting them together. When I laid a hand over them to calm her, she gave me a nervous look but pulled free. Her eyes never left Adam.

I sat back with a frown on my face.

Adam shrugged and looked away. His jaw clenched. "It doesn't matter. She was his before anyway."

"Yeah, but..." Cassandra bit out another laugh. She wiped at her mouth. "I can't believe I saw that. I love the Kade brothers. Man!"

Adam frowned at her.

She raised her hands in the air. "Did you not see that?"

"Thanks for your support." Adam shoved from the table and stalked away.

Becky went with and Cassandra snorted in disgust as she folded her arms over her chest. She stuck her chin out to glower. "Whatever. It's not my fault he's stupid enough to go after some tramp the Kades had first. You'd think he'd learn, wouldn't you? I mean, first Ashley and now Tanya... who else?"

My chest was tight. My hands were in fists, pressed on my lap. I didn't know what I was going to do, but I knew I was angry about it.

Miranda said in a soft voice, "Shut it, Cass. You're not helping."

Cass lifted a rebellious chin. "Not helping who? Or what?"

"Anyone." Her leader gave her a pointed look before she seemed to melt back in her chair.

"Look." Amelia pointed and we all turned.

Tate stood in the middle with her arms crossed over her chest. Her two bags were beside her. She stood alone, but she raised her chin and looked around. When her gaze met mine, I felt seared by it. Her eyes narrowed and I felt that she wanted to come over and say something. And then Mason stepped out from some corner.

All eyes went to him.

Tate turned towards him.

She seemed to be waiting, but he didn't do anything. He looked at her, then looked at me, and left.

His gaze scorched me as well, but Tate turned back to me. There was a question in her depths and I gulped. I knew I wouldn't be able to hide from her for long.

CHAPTER TWENTY-SIX

Becky wrinkled up her nose and peered over her glass. "Look at them." I ducked closer and bumped heads with her. Both of us giggled, but Becky waved a hand over her face. "I'm serious. Look!"

"Oh." She was serious so I did. "Who am I looking at? There's so many."

"Adam!" She pointed again. "I can't believe him. I thought he was in love with Tanya, but look at him."

I scanned all of the packed decks and finally spotted him. He was squished at a table with the Academy Elite. When he ran his hands down the legs of...I peered across... Cassandra, I sat up straight. "When did that happen?"

She slumped next to me and crossed her arms in a huff. "They've been like that for the past hour. I can't take it anymore."

Then it clicked. "You're jealous!"

She clamped her hand over my mouth. "You don't have to screech it, but yes. Duh. You know I like him."

I waved a hand over my face. "I'm a bit drunk."

"I know. Me too."

And after we looked at each other, we convulsed together in another gigglefest. We'd been doing that a lot in the past hour. Then she pulled away and sounded out a dramatic sigh. "I'm serious, Sam. He bounced right from Tanya to her. I can't believe it. I hate that girl."

When I glanced back over there, I caught the glower Adam was sending our way and I patted Becky's hand. "I wouldn't worry too much about it. His ego's bruised. She's his band aid so he doesn't feel so wounded."

"Why couldn't I be his band aid?"

I shot her a grin. "Could you be anymore whiney about that? And besides, he values you. He couldn't use you in that way."

She sniffled. "He does?"

I rolled my eyes. "You know he does. Stop the pity party. We're supposed to be having fun."

"So says you. You don't have the Academy Snub Team breathing down their noses on you. They'd love if I curled in a ball and vanished into thin air. And Cassandra keeps throwing those snooty looks over here."

I sighed and rested against the couch we'd both procured long ago. It was set in a back corner of a side deck and gave us privacy where no one could hear us or see us, but we had a grand view of all the action around us. When the couch had emptied, Becky and I made a mad dash for it and had been drinking ever since.

She'd been sore over Adam, but as I reached for my drink, I couldn't stop from glancing at the deck above ours. Mason sat in a back corner with Marissa on one side, Nate on her other side, and Logan with Tanya over his lap across from them. There were a few others, but everyone knew that was the top tier of the social scene. When Mason grazed the top of Marissa's knees, my hand clenched around my drink and I threw it all back. It should've burned my throat, but I had ceased feeling a while ago.

It had seemed like a good idea then.

"Sam." Becky waved a hand in front of my face.

"What?" I snapped to attention.

She looked annoyed. "What are we going to do about Adam?"

What was I going to do about Mason?

"Huh?"

I caught myself. Had I said those words out loud? But I shook my head. "Why is Cassandra so mean to you?"

"I know!" She lifted her arms up and down. She pushed out her bottom lip in a pout. "I haven't done anything to her.

I've always been nice to her and who am I to them anyway? Besides being good friends with Adam...and now you...and you're close with the Kades..." Her face brightened. "Do you think I'm a threat to her? Because of you and Adam, you know. No, that doesn't make sense. I'm the same boring Becky like always."

I patted her leg. I'd been doing that for the last hour. "It'll all work out. I know it. I think you and Adam will get together."

"You think so?"

I swung my arm wide in a grand gesture. Some of my drink spilled over, but neither of us cared. "Yes, I do. It might not be in high school."

Her face fell.

"But I think it'll happen. Adam's too caught up in social stuff. He can't appreciate you now because he's not mature enough."

Becky nodded. "For being drunk, we're very clear headed right now."

I nodded too. "I know and I'm talking very articulate."

"More than you usually do. You don't usually talk at all; well you do, but not really."

My face clouded. "Maybe I should shut up?"

"No." Her hand grabbed onto mine. "You need to talk more. You have very good points for me to hear. I never thought of Adam as being immature, but I can see why you think that."

She hiccupped, so did I, and we both fell back giggling again.

Then we became aware of someone who had come onto our deck. I gasped and Becky cooed.

Mason frowned down at us for a moment before he spoke. Then he tossed his phone on my lap. "Call your mom. She's going crazy. She thinks we kidnapped you."

Becky peeled her head back in laughter and I struggled to keep from joining her.

He shook his head at us. "Are you drunk?"

More laughter peeled from beside me and I nodded as I bit my lip.

"Hell, you're probably having more fun than most of us." He sank down next to me and ran a hand through his hair.

I watched the movement and wanted to do the same. A wave of need rushed over me, but I breathed out and remembered we were in public. I tried fanning myself.

When Becky had stopped giggling so much, she sat up with glazed eyes and squinted at him. "Who's your girlfriend?"

I jumped next to him.

She frowned at me.

Mason sat stiffly beside me. He didn't look at her.

"Hello!" She reached over me and waved a hand in front of his face.

He looked away and took a breath. I felt the movement when his arm brushed against mine.

She fell back and heaved a sigh. "I can't believe it. I'm your best friend, he's going to be your brother, and he ignores me too. Everyone ignores me. I'm more beneath people than I realized."

I looked at her. "You're not beneath me."

She gave me a tight smile, but spoke to Mason, "I know you can hear me and I know you're not being cruel to me because of Sam, but who's the girlfriend? I've never seen her before. She seems nice."

Mason jerked his gaze to mine. "Can you call your mom? Find me later to give me my phone."

He tore out of there and Becky shook her head as she watched him leave. "I must be really drunk because I know I shouldn't have talked to him like that, but I don't really care right now."

I shrugged and dialed my mom's number. "He's a jerk. You can talk to him however you want to."

Becky gave me a blinding smile. "Thanks, Sam."

I gave her one back. "Anytime." And then my mom's hysterical voice sounded in my ear and I cursed when I pulled it away. That was going to hurt. As I rubbed my ear, I moved away. Music, laughter, and the general shrieking sounds of a party were going to make this phone call last longer than I wanted.

When I found a semi-quiet corner, I lifted the phone again. "Hi, mom."

"Samantha!" She heaved out. "You're okay. I've been so worried. You have no idea. I thought about calling the cops."

"Why would you do that?"

"Because of what they did to me. I can't believe you didn't help me, but then I thought maybe you couldn't. Maybe you were too scared of them."

Alarms went off in my head and I sat back on my heels. "Are you kidding me right now?"

She got quiet. "Samantha, you were there. You saw what they did to me."

I sighed into the phone. "Mom, are you drunk again?"

A shadow moved over me and I spun around, my heart stopped for a second, but my shoulders dropped when I recognized Mason. He grinned and moved forward to curve a hand around my waist. As he bent close to listen in, he brushed against me and his breath caressed my cheek.

"Sam, are you there?"

I choked out, my throat full with desire, "I can't deal with this, mom. I'm fine. We went away to Nate's cabin. I told you about it last night, but you were so crazy and drunk. I suppose I'm not surprised you didn't remember." I waited a beat.

Mason's hand started to rub circles on my hip.

I bit out, my voice rushed, "You haven't been saying any of this crazy stuff to anybody else?"

There was silence on the other end.

"I can't believe you, mom. What have you done this time?"

"Sam, stop lying to me."

"Okay." I remembered when I had walked into my old house and saw her with tears in her eyes and two empty bottles of wine beside her. It was when she had told me we were leaving. "That's what I'm doing. I'm lying. I'm always lying to you. I'm the crazy one in this family. I'm the one who was married to David and left him for James. Yes, I'm the one lying right now."

"You don't have to be so mean to me."

"Oh, mom. Stop drinking. I don't want to hear what else you've cooked up. I'm fine. We're all fine. Stop saying crazy stories like that, unless you're trying to do something. Are you trying to do something?"

"Why would I make that up?"

"I don't know. Why do you ever do anything? For more money? I have no idea." And I ended the call.

Mason stood still next to me and then he swept me up in his arms. "That was great."

I tried to stop myself from smiling against his neck. "Why?"

"You knew my dad was listening?"

When he set me back on my feet, I gave him a small grin. "I didn't, but it'd be something she would've done."

He laughed again and slid his phone in his pocket.

I took a deep breath. "Why'd you ignore my friend before?"

His jaw tightened and he pressed his lips together before he looked away.

I added in a quiet voice, "And who is the girlfriend with you?"

He swung his gaze back and gave me a hard look. "Are you kidding me? You know that's Marissa."

"I don't. You've never introduced her."

"What are you doing right now?"

"Nothing." I started to move away, but he caught my arm and pulled me back.

"Come on, Sam. Don't be all jealous and insecure. Marissa is a good friend of mine. I'm protective of her."

He used to be protective of me too. I swallowed back that pain. "You're right. I'm sorry about that."

"Sorry about what?" He studied me intently. "What are we talking about?"

"We had a good time. It's not anything more than that. Just, please don't admit anything to Logan. I think he already knows and if he knows for sure, can you imagine all the teasing I'm going to get from him?"

Mason gave me a disgusted look. "Are you serious? I'm protective of Marissa because I'm the reason she had to switch schools a couple years ago."

I fell silent, but I didn't pull my arm away.

"She's a nice person, she's genuine. Some girls didn't like that we were friends and they tore her to pieces. Catty stuff always happens to her whenever she's around me. She doesn't have any female friends. That's why I didn't want to introduce her to you or anyone else. You have friends, Sam. She doesn't. If she met you, you would've introduced her to your friends, and that's when that crap usually happens. I nipped it from the beginning."

I remembered Tate's words. "Was it Tate that tore her to pieces?"

"She was the ring leader, yeah. And she'd do it again. If Marissa isn't with me, she's with Nate. It's that bad. Tate blames her for why I hate *her* so much."

I nodded. "Okay."

"Okay. What?" He seemed to be measuring me. I felt him trying to get inside me. "Are you okay now? I'm not going to apologize for your friend. She freaks me out. I'm not going to lie. I don't like her, but I'll tolerate her for you."

A chuckle escaped me. He felt the tension leave me and pulled me against him. "Yeah, I can see that."

He pressed a kiss to my forehead. "Are you going to get wasted tonight?"

"Seems like." I gave him a sloppy grin and he pressed a kiss to it. I sighed as his lips left mine. "It seems like it's my night with Becky tonight, she's down in the dumps because of Adam."

"The quarterback who wants to bang you?"

I shook my head. He knew exactly who Adam was. "Yes, she likes him."

He grimaced. "She could have better taste in men."

"You want her to go after you instead?"

His eyes got wide. "You should encourage those two to date."

I laughed and pressed against him some more. His hands dropped down and started to caress the inside of my thigh. He cupped the side of my face and started to bend down when someone burst through the foliage that had granted us our privacy.

We whirled around and froze.

Logan stared at us with his mouth hanging open. Then he snapped his fingers and threw his arms around in the air. "I knew it! I knew it! Oh hell yeah! I knew it!"

Mason tackled him and hissed, "Shut up about it!"

Logan pushed him off, laughing. "I won't say anything, but man—I knew it."

Mason shoved him back. "What are you doing here?"

He gestured to me. "The mom thing. I knew she was going to call her. Did you?"

I nodded.

"She covered us and made it seem like her mom made the whole thing up."

"Really?" Logan glanced at me with wide eyes.

I shrugged. "If your dad really loves her, he'll forgive her."

He choked out a laugh. "And if he doesn't and you guys are sent packing?"

I knew my eyes had a chill in them when both moved back a step. "I'm pretty sure I can move back in with David until college."

"And your mom?"

Ice went down my veins. "And I'm sure she'll find some other guy to mooch from."

"Man, you really loathe your mom, huh?" Logan whistled under his breath. "I'm just happy that we got dad off our backs."

Mason gave him a sharp look. "He send you something?"

"Yeah, an apology text."

He rolled his eyes and took Logan's phone. "Guess that's supposed to make up for the other ones, huh?"

"Whatever. We're covered. And I've got my own piece to pound tonight." Logan gave us a salute. "See you later, siblings. Have fun with your incest relations."

Mason punched him, but Logan dodged it and ducked from our hidden spot.

I grinned at him when Mason turned back. "Becky's going to come looking for me."

He grinned back and touched my shoulder. "Have fun getting drunk again. Don't screw the quarterback."

"Ha ha!" I flipped him the middle finger as he left, but couldn't wipe the grin off my face when I heard his laughter.

CHAPTER TWENTY-SEVEN

When I woke up, I rolled over and found myself in a large bed with Becky half scrawled on me. As I pushed up, pain flared through me and I touched the side of my face. "Ouch!" I hissed and hurried to a mirror. A large bruise had formed on the side of my jaw. It was swollen and had already started to turn color. I groaned and rested my forehead against the mirror.

How had that happened? It was fresh so I'd have the bruise for a few weeks. Great.

"Hh...whassis?" Becky blinked at me rapidly as she struggled to keep her mouth from hanging open. She wiped at her eyes and sat further up. "What happened? Where am I?"

I chuckled, surprised at the hoarseness of my voice. "My guess is that we're hungover." I grimaced as I sat down on a couch. My rear was sore so I moved even slower because of it. "What happened to my face?"

Becky choked out a gasp and covered her face as she fell back against the bed.

I winced against the pain. My whole face was now throbbing. "Tell me I didn't make a fool out of myself."

She groaned as she stopped whimpering. "It hurts to laugh."

"Tell me about it. It hurts to breathe."

She raised her hand to brush back some of her hair, but it dropped to her lap with a thump. "Everything's so hard right now. This sucks."

"Becky." I cleared my throat. "My face. What happened?"

"Oh, that."

"Yes, that."

She tried to hide a yawn, but it won in the end. After she finished, she started to yawn again. "I don't really know what happened, but you had to go to the bathroom so we snuck off somewhere. You kept saying you knew about a private bathroom. I don't know."

I groaned on the inside. I'd probably been trying to find Mason's room.

She added with a sour look on her face, "Anyway, we finally found a room and we snuck in. We didn't know whose it was, but then that girl who was attached to Mason's hip was in there and that girl, Tanya's cousin, was in there too."

I sat up straighter, or I would've. Pain seemed to slice through me with each movement I made.

"What was her name again?"

"Tate," I rasped out.

"Oh yeah!" She started to smile, but it died right away. "Tate was in there and she was being really mean to that girl, who for being Mason's girlfriend, doesn't have any fight at all. The girl just took it and she was standing there crying. She kept saying something about where Nate was, but I couldn't make it out. We were both so wasted."

I closed my eyes. I couldn't imagine what I had done.

"And then you clobbered Tate."

"I did what?"

"Yeah." She nodded with her eyes wide, semi wide for being hung-over. "You just swung your hand out and punched her. Then you started to say something about being a bully and she was the disloyal bitch and that was it. She went back at you. That girl kept crying so I started screaming for help. You got way more wallops in than she did. You're pretty spry. I had no idea." She started to laugh, but hissed from the movement. "She kept trying to hit you and you'd just run around her. Then you'd hit her from behind or something. You're hilarious when you're drunk."

"Oh no." I groaned into my hands. Had I really gotten into a fight? "Anyway, some guys ran in and separated you two. I didn't see you for a while because they carried you to where Mason was. He took you into some back room and then Logan rushed in there from somewhere else. He was only wearing jeans, which weren't buttoned or zipped up so everyone knew what he'd been doing." She wiggled her eyebrows. "If you know what I'm saying."

So I'd interrupted one of his many romps with the pep girl. Something in me didn't care at all.

"And then they kicked Tate out."

"What?" I looked back up.

"Yeah." She gave me a lazy grin. "Mason came out and shoved her outside. Someone had her bags packed and they threw them out. She must've had her keys in them because I heard that she drove away in the middle of the night. Nobody really cared, but I guess she had a few friends here. They were saying that wasn't fair to her, but then Mason and Logan's friend, that one that's always around said they could go as well. Everybody shut up after that."

"Mason and Logan didn't say anything?"

"Nah." She shook her head as another yawn came over it. "They'd already gone back to you by then. Oh, and we could hear that girl crying through the door. She should've shut up by then, I mean, you punched someone out for her. She could've been more appreciative."

I shook my head. I had no recollection of any of it. "So how'd we get here?"

"This is your room. You were in there for about thirty minutes and then somehow you snuck out."

"I said that?" I grinned slightly.

She nodded her head with a wide smile as well. "You said something about not needing their protection and you snuck out. I guess Mason and Logan got into some tiff. That's what you told me."

"I said that too?"

"Uh huh." She chuckled. "And then you and I went to the indoor pool. I had no idea it was even there, but you did.

No one else was in there. We stayed down there the rest of the night until...that's where my black out starts. I have no idea. I remember drinking and swimming and you lecturing me how we weren't being smart, but we were being fun."

I groaned with my head in my hands. "I don't want to deal with anyone today. What time is it?"

Becky shrugged, still curled up among the bedcovers. "I'm sure it's time to start packing. Everyone was going to leave after breakfast today."

I swung my heavy head to the side and saw both my bags in the corner. I grunted. "Looks like I'm packed."

Becky snorted before she rolled off the bed. "I gotta find my room. See you in a bit."

"See you." I waved as she stumbled out the door.

She hadn't been gone long before someone else knocked. I tried to yell for them to come in, but it sounded like a frog's croak so I heaved myself up and opened the door wide. I expected Mason or even Logan, but instead I was in for a surprise.

Miranda Stewart, Fallen Academy's elite queen bee stood at my door.

She gave me a timid smile and brushed a strand of her auburn hair back. I didn't know why, it looked perfect pulled high in a clip with small braids decorating her head. A few wisps were allowed out and it gave her a softer look. Maybe that's what she was going for.

Her emerald eyes sparked in warmth and she folded her hands in front of her. "Hi, Samantha."

The sound of my full name kicked me in gear. It sounded so formal and it should've. We weren't friends.

"Miranda."

She glanced over my shoulder. "Can I come in or do you have company?"

I chuckled. "Becky just left."

"Oh." She glanced down at her hands. Then she laughed softly. "I realized how that sounded. I didn't mean to imply anything."

I narrowed my eyes. The Miranda Stewart I knew wasn't this self-conscious shy girl. She was tough and smart enough to control the rest of the Academy Elite. She was the brains behind so many operations. I didn't know what I'd done to warrant her attention.

"Well." She took a deep breath. "I'm sure you're wondering why I'm here."

My mouth stayed closed, but I gestured for her to come in. As she perched on the coach, I leaned against my dresser. The bed looked tempting, but I didn't trust myself to stay out of it the rest of the day.

"I came to apologize for Cassandra. She tends to react before she thinks sometimes."

"Why are you saying this to me?" I was surprised at my blunt tone. Maybe it was Mason's boldness or how the truth seemed to always fall off Becky's tongue, but one of them had rubbed off on me.

From the slight widening of her eyes, Miranda must've shared in my sentiments. She sighed. "Because I don't want an enemy from you."

"Why?"

"The truth?"

I lifted a shoulder. "What else?"

She took another deep breath and smoothed her hands down her jeans. "Because you're really powerful right now and I don't want a war at school."

I was stunned once again. "Why would there be a war?"

"Because Cassandra is jealous of you." Her eyes darkened and she looked at her lap.

Ah ha. I nodded in understanding. "So you're saying that she's not going to stop with her jabs?"

There seemed to be genuine regret in her eyes. "Yes, but you have to understand where it's coming from. Adam's always liked you and he's always championed for you. He wanted you to come into the group, and not as his girlfriend. When you turned him down, it seemed to hurt him even more and he'd already been hurt by Ashley too. Cassandra is very protective of him."

"And she wants to date him."

"I can't say anything about that, but I know she wasn't nice to you or Rebecca last night."

"So what do you want from me?"

She stood and gave me that same sad smile. "Cassandra is one of my best friends and I love her to death, but know that she doesn't have our support if she's mean to you. She doesn't have my support. I like you, Samantha. I always agreed with Adam. I thought you would've been a great addition to the group."

When she glanced at her watch and then the door, I knew her visit had ended. She said what she wanted so I followed her to the door and held it open for her. "I guess I should say thanks for your warning then?"

She laughed again, the sound was so delicate. No wonder she'd been made the Queen. I wanted to give her a crown myself and stand guard before her.

"I guess. Thanks for being... understanding?" She gave me a small wave before she left. "See you at school today."

After I closed the door, I stood in the middle of my room for a while. The whole thing was odd to me. She thought I would've been a great addition to the group; that meant I was out. Then I shrugged. That sounded like too much drama anyway.

As another yawn came over me, I tried to hurry into the bathroom and not think about Miranda's odd visit. What would've taken me twenty minutes took an hour. I wasn't moving at a fast pace, nor was I thinking at a fast one. When I heaved my two bags to the bottom of the stairs, my arms felt like lead and Logan's hyena laugh scraped against my ears.

I covered them and groaned when I saw him come around a corner. "Stop, please."

He laughed even louder and scooped me up in the air. I was bundled against his chest and he twirled me around.

"What's wrong, sister? Too much activity for you last night? You aren't sore or anything, are you?"

I burrowed into his chest. "Stop. Please. I beg you."

"Your new nickname is Slugger. One wallop and that's how you handle business." He was gleeful in his amusement.

It was sickening.

He started to bounce me in his arms. "My Slugger Sister. I'm going to make you a tee shirt with that slogan. Slugger Sister. Everyone will call you that!"

Tanya came around the corner in a tight white tee shirt, low cut v neck, and slinky jeans. She wrapped her arms around his waist and pressed against his back. "She's not my sister. I can't call her that."

Logan held still as she continued to press against him, then he smirked at me. "Sorry, sis. Someone else is needing my attention."

After he deposited me back on my feet, I smoothed out my clothes. "Somehow I think I'll get over it. Thank you, Tanya."

She gave me a blinding smile as Logan swept her up instead. "No problem, Sam. See you." She started giggling as he skipped out the door with her.

"Hey." Mason came around the corner with a duffel bag over his shoulder. He bent and picked up my two. "You're riding with me. Your quarterback took off this morning."

"You have room?"

He flashed me a grin as he held open the door with his shoulder. I ducked around him and tried to ignore the flare of warmth that sizzled through me. "Nate's headed back home today and he's taking Marissa with him."

"Really?"

I wasn't sure if I was disappointed.

"Yeah." He threw all of the bags in the back of his Escalade and slammed it shut again. I wasn't surprised to see it was full with other bags. "And your buddy can come too, but I don't want her talking to me. She can talk to you, that's fine, but no questions to me."

I gave him a salute.

"Very funny."

"I thought so." I couldn't hold back a small grin before I went and told Becky the news. And as I expected, when I found her with a plate full of pancakes and muffins, she dropped all of it and started screaming.

"Three hours in the same car as Mason Kade!" She grabbed my arms and started jumping up and down.

"Ugh. Stop." Pain seared through me. I backed away and tried to hold down whatever last meal I'd had. "I am never ever going to get in another fight again."

"You better not drink like that then."

"That too."

Becky giggled behind her hands. "I'm sorry, Sam. It's so exciting."

I shook my head. "You can't talk to him, you know."

She nodded. Her smile couldn't be wiped off.

"You're a bit strange in the head."

"You already told me that once," Becky informed me as she followed me out to the car. It was as if she'd never been hung-over. The Becky I woke up beside had transformed at the news of our car ride. Energy flowed out of her and I sighed. It was going to be a long drive.

I needed coffee.

CHAPTER TWENTY-EIGHT

Mason dropped us off at school. My bag stayed in his backseat, but Becky tugged hers out. When he asked what time to pick me up, she started giggling. We glanced over and she saluted us with her hand. "I'll find my own ride home. Thanks." Then she pivoted on her feet, clapped her heels together, and marched off.

He gave me an unreadable look and I sighed. "She's tired and...snarky..."

He shook his head. "I don't care. What time do you want me here?"

I scratched the back of my head. "Uh...quarter after three?"

"Done. See you." And he zoomed away.

As I turned and headed after Becky, I caught a lot of stares from those who lingered in the parking lot. Then when I entered the hallway, I got even more. I groaned as I glanced at my phone. It was a little after noon—lunch hour. No wonder there'd been so many around their cars.

Becky was nowhere in sight so I targeted my locker instead. As I got there, Miranda Stewart greeted me. She seemed to appear from nowhere. She gave me one of those serene smiles that hovered on her lips. Her hair hung loose in shining curls this time and she readjusted the books in her hands. Warmth oozed from her. "You got here!"

I frowned as I opened my locker. "You seem happy about that?"

She glanced over her shoulders and then gave me another smile, this one seemed secretive. "Everyone knows about the Kade Trip."

I fought the urge to hang my head. Of course everyone would know.

She stepped closer and lowered her voice. "I spoke to the rest of the group on the way back and they want to return the favor to Mason and Logan."

"What are you talking about?"

Her eyes seemed to dance. They were sparkling. "Come on, like you don't know."

"I don't. What are you talking about?"

"Logan's friends with Mark, but they're not that great of friends. I assumed we were invited because of you."

"You weren't."

"Oh." Her back straightened and her shoulders stiffened. Then she let out a soft laugh. "Regardless, I'm throwing an intimate dinner. I've extended invitations to Mason and Logan, but I wanted to invite you in person."

"An intimate dinner?"

"I throw them all the time, but it's usually only for our close friends."

"The Academy Elite," I mused and tried to remember what book I needed for the next class. It was fifth period... My hung-over brain was still going slow.

She laughed again. "That's right. I'd forgotten you knew about that name. That's what your friend calls us, right?"

"And Adam's."

"Hmmm?"

I looked up and held her gaze. "She's Adam's friend too. He's got a soft spot for her."

"Oh, I know. I know." The corners of her mouth turned downwards, but they flipped up a second later. "So I would love if all three of you guys would come to my dinner tonight."

I sighed and turned to her. "Look, don't do this."

"Do what?"

"Mason and Logan won't come to your dinner."

"But you haven't even talked to them about it yet."

"Have they ever come before?"

"I've never invited them..." A small frown had come back to her as she started to look around. A small audience had appeared around us. They weren't close, but they were within hearing distance.

Here we go again...

"They won't come. I know them. They don't care about anyone except themselves. Trust me."

She looked down at her feet. "They seem to care about you..."

I lifted a shoulder. "If they do, they do, but don't invite them. They won't come and it'll make you look bad. You told me this morning you didn't want a war, but that's what you're starting. It won't work with Mason and Logan. Everyone knows they're jerks because they don't care about anything or anyone."

When she looked back up, she was transformed. A fierce determination shone through her emerald eyes and pinned me down, but she edged closer and lowered her voice to a whisper, "You're right. You're completely right. Thank you. I know this came from a good spot with you so I'm not going to invite them. I never was."

"I thought you said—"

She gave me a tight smile. "I didn't. I was testing you. I wanted to know what you would do and you proved me right. You proved some others wrong."

"What are you talking about?" I shook my head. Was she mad? "There's no dinner?"

"There's a dinner, but do you really think I'm crazy enough to invite the Kade brothers? Everyone knows they don't care and we all know that we weren't really invited on that trip. You invited Adam, he invited us, and no one else cared if we went or not. That's how we went on the trip. You're completely right. Mason and Logan don't care about us, though I think they should. Everyone knows they should've gone to this school. They should be our friends, but they're not. They made their choice."

I eyed her up and down and noted how her hands were in small fists, how her jaw was stiff, and how her shoulders were bunched together. A massive knot was going to form between them.

I spoke softly, "You're a bit pissed with them, huh?"

"What?" She looked taken aback.

"Nothing." I grabbed my fifth period book. "So no dinner tonight?"

"Oh no. I'm having a dinner and you're invited. You don't have to come; no offense will be taken if you don't. We all know you're probably tired." She lingered on my bruise. "But if you do, Adam will pick you up."

I grinned now. "He's not picking up Cassandra?"

Miranda grimaced. "Between you and me, I hope those two don't do more than their flirting. He doesn't care enough about her, and she deserves someone who's going to be there for her. Adam cares like that about you."

Oh no…

She laughed and waved at me. "Don't worry. I'm not going to play matchmaker. Everyone can tell that Sallaway did a number on you, but I do hope you'll come to dinner tonight."

"Can Becky come?"

Her eyes held mine steady. She didn't blink. "No."

So that's how it was going to be. I should've known.

Miranda looked over my shoulder and she chuckled to herself. "Look at that, I did you another favor."

Another one? I looked over and saw Jessica, Jill, Lydia, and Ashley at some lockers. All four of them stared at us with different emotions. Jessica was livid, as was Jill. Lydia was trying to fight off a smile at me and Ashley surprised me when she grinned.

Miranda added, "They wanted to confront you about why you wouldn't let them come on the trip, but now that I've deemed you one of my friends," she laid a hand on my shoulder. "They wouldn't dare." Her laugh was confident, it bordered on the verge of being cocky. "Welcome to the Elite, Samantha. I hope to see you at dinner tonight."

As she strolled down the hallway and linked elbows with Emily Connsway, the only female in their group who hadn't gone on the trip, Miranda stopped and lifted her head for a kiss from Peter Glasburg. He hadn't gone on the trip either. When both of them looked over and gave me a grin, I was jolted enough to jerk my hand up in a wave.

"What'd she want?"

I turned around. Becky was frowning at them with something else in her eyes. I narrowed mine, was she hurt that I had talked to her?

"She was giving me a heads up that Jessica and Jill wanted to confront me about the trip."

Becky's eyes narrowed and I knew there was suspicion in them, but then she yawned suddenly and her shoulders sagged down. "I'm so tired. I can't handle any more fights."

"You can't?" I touched the side of my face. It was still tender and the pain started to throb again. "I don't remember you helping out from your version of the story."

She grinned and linked her hands together in front of her. It was a self-conscious movement. "I would've, but you were so funny to watch. And you kept telling me she could handle it. You were taunting her, actually."

"Was I?" An old comfort settled between my shoulders. That sounded like something I'd do. "Did it piss her off?"

"Oh yeah. She started to swing at you more and more. She got sloppier after that and you kept dodging her, then you'd give her an uppercut from nowhere."

I gave her a sloppy grin. That had made me happy. "Want to go for burgers tonight? I think I need some protein."

"Can we do pizza instead? There's an air hockey table at Gino's." As we passed a group of football players, she looked up, but quickly looked back down.

Adam was in the center of the group. He leaned against the lockers with his feet crossed beneath him. Cassandra

Sullivan was pressed against him, as close as she could be without his arm around her. She had a hand splayed over his chest and was smiling up at him. When he met my gaze, his grew cold and he straightened.

A few of the guys looked over and said hello to me.

My feet tripped over themselves, but I stumbled down the hallway with a frown. When did football players say hello to me? Even when I had dated Jeff, and some of them were his friends, they'd never spoken to me.

Then I looked up as Becky and I were about to head into the classroom. Miranda met my gaze down the hallway. Her eyes seemed to be laughing at me, but I had an odd sense that she knew exactly what happened and she knew why it happened. Then she pretended to tip an imaginary hat to me.

Was that her first favor?

Welcome to the Elite, Samantha.

Her words came back to haunt me. Had I joined their ranks without realizing it? And if I had, what did that mean?

And then something else happened that took my breath away.

Jessica and Jill sat at a table behind Becky and me. I was tense, ready for whatever they were going to say to me, but they each gave me a bright smile. "Hi, Sam! How was the party?"

My mouth dropped.

Hell froze over.

Becky's head dropped to her lap and she couldn't silence her giggles. Her shoulders shook.

"What?" I said to them.

Jill's smile widened and Jessica's stayed, but the ends of her mouth seemed strained. Lydia plopped between them and clasped my hands. She nearly smacked her forehead against mine. "I didn't know you were friends with Miranda Stewart! That's awesome, Sam. Why didn't you tell me?"

The teacher started roll call, but I couldn't shake a chill when I turned back around. That had been the favor

Miranda had referenced. She cast me as her friend, no one would touch me now…except the Academy Elite.

I clasped my eyes shut.

I didn't want to deal with them. They were on a whole other league.

The rest of the day followed the same pattern. Amelia White asked me to sit with her in sixth period. She offered her notes from the morning classes I missed and Emily Connsway saved a seat beside her in our last period. Mark Decraw gave me a few wary looks, but he extended his fingers in a wave once. And then Miranda passed me in the hallway after school. She called out, "See you later, Samantha!" before she bent her head and laughed at something Emily said to her.

I shook my head as I pulled out the two books I would need for homework and turned around. I bumped back against my locker when I saw Jeff behind me. His dark hair was gelled up in a haphazard nest and his eyes were fierce. He frowned at me. "What are you doing?"

My hung-over cloud of confusion cleared suddenly and I snapped back to reality. I shoved him back. "What are you doing? Whatever you have to say, you have no right to say it. Get out of my face, Jeff."

He rolled his eyes and stepped closer. He lowered his voice to a grumble. "Jess is crapping her pants. Now you're suddenly all powerful and popular. What'd you do? How'd that happen? And what are you going to do to her?"

I reared back and took a long look at him. I thought he was angry, but I saw concern in his eyes now and something akin to fear?

I lowered my voice as well. "Why are you worried about Jessica? Shouldn't you be concerned about Jill, your girlfriend?"

"You weren't betrayed by Jill. You weren't friends with her. Jessica's the one that stabbed you in the back."

"Exactly!" I said in a sharp tone.

Heads turned our way.

I rolled my eyes, but quieted my voice. "I was the one stabbed in the back. Jessica could probably stop worrying if she'd apologize to me."

"What are you talking about? She has—"

"She hasn't said a thing to me."

He held my gaze for a minute and then edged back. "Are you serious? I thought she apologized a long time ago. I thought you were being stuck up and not accepting it."

I was amazed at his stupidity. "For one, I don't automatically have to accept an apology and two; you're the only one who's seemed sorry for what you did. Lydia's a beach ball. She keeps blowing from one side to the other. She's never apologized either and Jessica hasn't said a thing. She ignored me and then said hi once to me. I'm not going to sweep it under the rug."

He ran his hands through his hair, pulled his hair into a spiky Mohawk, and messed it up again. "I know they're both real sorry. It's got Jill paranoid. She thinks they're going to dump her for you and now all this crap." He swept his hand up and down the hallway. "You're in with the popular clique. How did that happen? You've never cared about any of that crap."

"Jeff," I sighed. "You and me are okay. I think you should leave it alone. Don't try to protect or apologize for Jessica and Lydia. That's for them to do, not you."

"Yeah, I know." He let out a ragged breath. "I'm just so pissed for messing our group up. I tore us apart. I should've said no to Jessica, but she kept asking. She made it seem so exciting..."

When my phone vibrated, I saw it was Mason. He sent a text: **Here**.

"Look, I have to go. My ride's waiting."

He nodded his head and pulled the ends of his shirt together. The movement emphasized how thin his frame was. I'd forgotten how skinny Jeff had always been, but he pulled the look off. Trendy baggy jeans and a polo that was supposed to look vintage gave him a preppy look with an edge.

I chuckled and punched his shoulder lightly. "You look good, Sallaway. Jill must be good for you."

The side of his mouth curved up. "Hey, thanks, Strattan. That means a lot coming from you."

I shook my head, still chuckling, and headed to the parking lot. I figured Mason would have football practice to get back to so I didn't want to make him late. When I cleared the school and saw him parked front and center, I was aware of the attention he was warranting.

His window was rolled down and he flashed me a grin. He tapped the side of his car twice. "Come on. Coach is making us do two practices tonight."

I picked up my pace and got inside. As Mason wheeled his Escalade through the parking lot, he drove past Adam. He held my gaze as we passed him and I watched as his mouth tightened. Cassandra was beside him. Her expression mirrored his.

Mason chuckled, "Your quarterback's pissed."

I took a deep breath and tried to relax in his seat. "Yeah, well, I have a feeling a lot of people are going to be pissed at me."

He glanced at me. "What are you talking about?"

I shook my head. "I'm going to make some people very angry in the next week."

CHAPTER TWENTY-NINE

Mason dropped me at home and took off for his practice right away. As I lugged my bags through the mansion and up to my room, I found a note on the kitchen table.

Hi, honey! James and I are in the cities, gone to the Bangor for dinner. We'll be back tonight! Love you! XOXO

I dropped it back on the table and fought the urge to tear it up.

Since I knew I'd do my homework later, I pulled out my running shoes and laced them up. Then I hit the pavement hard. I ran for two hours, three would've winded me too much, my body was wheezing too much when I rounded the last curve to the mansion. Panting, with sweat streaking down my body, I went back to my room and as I got into my shower, I was tempted to lock my door.

No one was home yet, but I didn't want to deal with Analise when they did return.

An hour later my phone vibrated and I answered, "Hey, Becky."

She groaned on the other side. "I can't go out for dinner."

"Really?" I tried to hold back the disappointment.

"Yeah, my mom is all furious at me. She said I could go as long as I didn't miss school, but she found out that I missed half the day today. I didn't do it on purpose and she found out that it'd been a Kade party we went to. I had no idea how she found that out. I told her I was going with you and your family to a cabin. She likes you, but now she knows all about your parents' divorce and everything. I could murder whoever told her that stuff."

I crawled onto my bed and rolled on my back. "Gossip's pretty rampant. I'm sure it got out somehow about the party."

"Not to mention that your mom's hooked up with James Kade. My mom seemed pretty bent about that one for some reason."

I frowned into the phone. "Does your mom know mine?"

"Your mom used to be in some committee at the country club with her, but I think my mom's more mad because of your dad. You know everyone loves Coach Strattan."

"Yeah, there is that..."

"Anyways, so I was just calling because she won't let me go out to Gino's with you."

From the way her voice quieted, I felt a kick in my gut. I knew something else was going on and I sat up. "She won't let you go to Gino's or she doesn't want you to go with me?"

"Both."

I could imagine the glower on her face.

Becky added, "Oh gawd, I'm so sorry. My mom doesn't want me to be friends with you anymore. I guess she called a bunch of other moms and they were told by their kids that you're tight with the Kade brothers. My mom's scared of them, everyone's moms are. My dad was ecstatic. He wants to meet them; he wants to talk football with Mason. Yeah right, like that's going to happen."

I drew my knees against my chest and hugged them tight. "So we can't talk at school?"

She snorted. "Forget that. I'm still going to be friends with you. My mom can't tell me what to do with that, but she won't let me go to Gino's tonight. I'm sorry, Sam. I know you wanted to go so you didn't have to go to that Elite dinner thing."

"You knew about that?" I grinned into the phone. Of course, she knew

"Of course I knew. Who do you think I am? It's not my first day on the gossip pages. Everyone knows that Miranda invited you to the Elite dinner tonight. Only I knew that you weren't going to go." She paused for a beat. "Are you going to go now?"

"Uh…"

I was about to say that I wasn't sure, but Mason threw open my door. "Logan's going crazy on your mom." And he was gone in a flash.

I said in a rush, "I have to go."

"What? What's going on—"

I pressed the disconnect button and threw it on the bed as I hurried down to the kitchen.

"Are you kidding me?!" Logan cursed as he stood in the foyer. His chest was rising up and down at a rapid pace and his hands were balled into fists, pressed tight against his legs. His eyes were wild in anger and his jaw kept clenching and unclenching.

Analise looked annoyed dressed in a white lace dress. She still held onto her white clutch. A string of white pearls were nestled between in her cleavage. James stood between them, dressed in a black formal suit. Whatever Bangor was, it must've been for the formal and expensive.

I snorted to myself. Of course it would've been.

Mason stopped in the doorframe and held onto the post above his head. He was quiet and my mother glanced back at him every now and then.

Logan spat out, "Are you seriously trying to tell me what I can't do?" His eyes were narrowed at an alarming level.

My mom patted her chest in a dainty fashion. "I am voicing my opinion. It's eight at night. I don't think it's appropriate for you to go out this late. You should be studying, staying in."

Logan snorted out a laugh as he shook his head. His hands were still in fists. He opened them and closed them back up. He kept doing it. "I can't believe you. Who the hell are you, woman?"

Analise glanced back at Mason and then she saw me behind him. Her shoulders lifted a bit and she stood a tiny bit straighter on her feet. "Since everyone is here, I'd like to make an announcement."

"Not another one," Logan muttered under his breath, still glaring at my mother.

She cleared her throat and took James' hand in hers. "I have gone room to room and emptied out all of the liquor that was in this household."

Mason didn't react, but a nerve in his shoulder jumped. Other than that, not a muscle moved. Logan shook his head and cursed some more. Both of his hands rose in the air like he wanted to put them around her neck. "Dad, control your whore."

James was in his face in the next second. "You will watch your mouth, son."

Logan's mouth clamped shut, but he heaved a deep breath and continued to shake his head. "I can't believe you. You're going to let her tell us what we can drink or not drink?"

His father's voice was quiet. "All three children in this home are underage. And since all three of you claimed Analise was in a drunken fit the other night, both of us deemed it a responsible choice to be rid of all alcohol."

Logan's smile was dangerous. "You think we're the problem?"

His father stepped back once. "No, I don't. I saw her that evening as well. She *had* been drinking too much." He glanced at me. "She was under a lot of emotional anxiety that night, but this is an answer that can help multiple levels for a problem I'm sure that's yet to be unearthed."

Mason bit out a laugh. His hands clenched around the post above and his muscles grew tighter at the movement.

Everyone looked at him and quieted.

"She doesn't want you to go out?" he spoke to Logan.

He gave a short nod. "She thinks I'm being irresponsible."

Mason turned his gaze towards his father, but spoke to Analise, "You might be her mother." He gestured towards me, over his shoulder. "But you're not ours. We have a mother." Then his eyes met his father's again for a brief second. It was a meaningful one.

James turned on his heel and left the room.

My mother's mouth dropped open and her hand jerked after him. "Wha—uh? What are you doing? James!"

Logan grinned in victory and shared a meaningful look with his brother.

Mason dropped his arms abruptly. "Our mom's got custody of us. We can go back to her anytime we want. You might want to remember that."

Tight fists flung against her legs and she stomped her feet. "I cannot believe you two! You are the two most horrible children I have ever met—"

"We're not children." Logan got in her face. "And we're not yours. If you dare try to tell us what to do, you'll regret it. I promise that."

She looked around and I saw how frantic she was. When she found me in the corner, she spewed out, "I don't know what you have done to her, but I will make it my mission to destroy you two."

I jerked forward in surprise.

Logan's hyena laugh sounded out, but Mason tilted his head to the side, just a slight movement.

Analise sputtered to a halt. Her hands were forcibly pressed against her as her knees trembled.

"You really need to stop threatening us. It makes it worse." Mason turned with a hard smirk on his face. He touched my shoulder and glanced back at her. "You should think about that."

She gasped and choked on it. Her cheeks filled up and her hands fluttered around her in a helpless pace. Tears filled her face and she brushed furiously at them. "You don't—you don't—you don't threaten me, *boy*!"

His chuckle was a soft one, but it hit her hard. My mother started waving her fists around in the air.

Logan rolled his eyes and pulled out his keys. When he turned for the door, she screeched at him, "Where are you going?!"

He ignored her and the door shut on his heels.

Mason had already disappeared back upstairs when my mother turned back around. She bent over and took deep breaths, all while she was patting her chest at the same time. Then she looked up with fresh tears in her eyes. She tried to wipe them away.

"How do you do it?"

I frowned. "What do you mean?"

"They like you. How did you do it?"

I shrugged. "They're never going to respect you."

She looked away. I watched as she wiped more tears away. Then she turned back. "What do I do?"

I gave her a sad smile. It was almost heartbreaking to see her like this, almost. "You'll never win against them. All you can do is exist beside them. That's it."

"That's it?"

"Like he said, you're not their mother." When she opened her mouth, I cut her off. "And you're not mine anymore, not really."

She was jolted back.

I narrowed my eyes. "I don't like you. I don't know if I ever did. I love you, but I don't respect you either. And I doubt I ever will again. You're lucky to still have me here. You haven't done anything to help me, nothing at all. You only hurt me, mom."

She pressed the back of her hand to her mouth. More tears streaked down her face. "I'm sorry, Samantha. I really am."

My eyes held hers. I didn't know what I was looking for, maybe a weakening within her or something I could grasp onto. I had no idea. I saw emptiness instead. And I felt it within me. It rose up as I watched my mother break before my eyes.

I took a deep breath and spoke in a quiet voice, "Look at you. This is what they've done to you already and they haven't even tried. They could destroy you, mom. It's not the other way around. You could never touch them. You're an annoying gnat to them. They've put up with your presence because James loves you. I can see that too. He does." It hurt to say what I was going to say next. "Focus on him. Focus on your relationship with him. Ours is gone, but maybe it could come back someday. Not today. Or next year, but sometime in the future. Just...focus on your future husband, mom. That's all you can do right now."

I turned away and started for my room, but I paused when I heard her whisper. "I'm sorry, honey. I'm so sorry."

Then I gripped the rail and went back to my room.

It was 8:30 when I checked my phone again and I had three text messages from Miranda, along with a voice message from her. Dinner had come and gone. They wanted to know where I was, if I was going. I had finished listening to her message when Mason knocked on my door.

I frowned and motioned for him to come in.

He studied my face. "What's wrong?"

I shook my head. "Nothing I can't handle."

My phone vibrated again. It was another text from Miranda—they'd all gone to some bar. I glanced up at Mason and asked, "You don't want to go somewhere with me, do you?"

He grinned back at me. "What? This late? What would your mother say?"

I couldn't stop my laugh. "I don't think she'll be saying much after what I said to her."

He stopped grinning. "What did you say?"

"Nothing, that she was lucky I was still here and we didn't really have a relationship anymore."

His eyes studied me. I felt his intensity and wanted to curl up against it. He asked me, "Did you mean that?"

I jerked my head in a nod. "I did." My eyes found his. "I'm close to asking David if I can live with him. He raised me all my life. If my mom knows who my real dad is or not doesn't matter to me. David raised me. He's my dad and she knows I'll push that if we'd ever go to court. The fact that I'm here, it's by a hairs' width."

He came inside and perched on the arm of one of my couches. "So where did you want to go?"

"Some bar. Some people at school invited me to their dinner. I didn't go and now they're out. I feel a little bad that I ditched on them."

Mason shook his head. "Let me guess, these aren't the people that are used to being ditched?"

I shook my head too.

"Do you know what you're doing?"

I wrapped my arms around my knees. "No."

His eyes held mine.

And I grinned. "But I don't really care either."

He mirrored my grin. "What bar are they at?"

I texted Miranda the question and she gave me an answer a second later. I held the phone up. "The Ryder."

Mason bit back a laugh and pulled out his phone. "I'm sure Logan's had his piece by now. Maybe he'd meet us there."

I stood and ran sweaty hands down my pants. I frowned at them. Why were they so sweaty? Then Mason looked back up when he was done. He grabbed my hand and pulled me between his legs. I held my breath as he leaned in close and pressed a kiss to the crook of my neck. He inhaled and held me close. I felt him fit between my legs and almost closed my eyes. I wanted to tell him to forget it and pull him to my bed.

When his phone vibrated, he lifted it for me to see.

We're there!

He chuckled against my neck and kissed it lightly. His hand curved around my waist and held me tighter. "Looks like its game on. Your quarterback's going to be there?"

I wrapped my arms around him and tilted my neck at an angle. His mouth started to explore it. Then I sighed against him. I didn't know if I'd ever get enough of him.

Mason moved back and whispered as his lips teased my skin, "You're going to ride me long and hard tonight."

I grinned against his neck. It was what every girl wanted to hear.

CHAPTER THIRTY

When we got to The Ryder, I saw it was a bar attached to a hotel. As soon as we entered, I remembered that Amelia's dad owned the place. It explained why they could drink at the bar and when we got there, they had congregated in a back corner, away from the other customers. It was a ritzy hotel and the neon red and black lighting set an intimate tone to the bar.

Miranda saw me first and waved us over by a pool table. She stood in a tight black dress with a red belt around her midriff. The rest of the girls were dressed in similar dresses, all tight and in different colors. I wondered if they planned it. They looked cliquey and expensive. Each of them wore dangling diamond earrings that matched their dress color.

"Hi, guys!" Miranda gave me a big hug. "I'm so glad you could come. The rest were disappointed you didn't come to the dinner."

Mason gave her one of his unreadable looks and she shifted on her feet. Her hand twitched for a second. It was the only movement I caught that made me wonder if she was uncomfortable. I would be.

"Mason, thanks for coming." She was so formal and gracious.

He shoved his hands in his pockets and went to the bar.

As he did, she laughed and touched the base of her neck. "I'm not going to take that personal. I shouldn't, right?"

I shrugged. "I told you. They're assholes."

"He certainly must like you. Mason Kade has never come to one of my get-togethers."

"I thought he showed up at the one last weekend?"

She peeled out another burst of laughter. It was high pitched enough to make me pause. Was she being fake or was she drunk? Something wasn't fitting with her. She giggled into her hand. "That wasn't him coming as a guest. We all thought he had come for his brother, but instead he came to lay into that girl." Her eyes lingered on my bruise again. "You remember—the one I heard you got into a fight with."

Miranda seemed to be waiting for me to say something, but I wasn't sure what it was. When I started to ask something stupid, I was picked up and thrown over someone's shoulders. Logan's hyena laugh sounded as he twirled me around, bent over with my rear on display. I felt him patting it and he whistled under his breath. "You've got a tight ass, Sam. No wonder your quarterback wants to bang you so hard."

Someone gasped and someone else choked on their drink.

"Put me down, Logan." I tried to be fierce.

He laughed some more, but lowered me down. As he sat me on my feet, he lifted back up, but was close enough to brush against my body. When his eyes met mine, I saw a dark humor in them. I tensed and got ready.

I didn't want to be friends with these guys, but I wasn't sure what to do about it. Mason asked in the ride over if I wanted to piss them off now or wait for the perfect moment. I didn't have an answer and I still didn't. Still, whatever Logan was doing I knew he wanted to piss someone off.

As I caught a jerking movement from the corner of my eye, I wondered if he'd come for Adam. I watched as my former friend had a scowl on his face and he downed the rest of his drink in a savage motion. Cassandra was beside him with his arm around her waist. She wore a frown as she watched him. I thought I saw some concern in her depths as well.

Miranda gutted out a laugh and stepped forward again. "Logan, you've come as well."

He curved an arm around my waist and raised an eyebrow. "Weren't we invited?" His tone was too confident, too smooth.

She visibly swallowed and looked around. "Uh, of course you guys were invited. I assumed Samantha told you. You're both here."

Logan shot Adam a look. "I thought about bringing Tanya, but she thought it would be awkward. Plus, she needed an hour to get ready..."

Adam's scowl grew darker, but he didn't respond. Peter Glasburg and Mark Decraw stood between the two. They tried to look casual as they stood with their pool-sticks, but each couldn't contain their frowns. They threw Mason looks as he remained at the bar. He had a drink in hand and looked relaxed.

"Uh...she could've come if you liked?" Miranda's nervous laugh rang out high pitched. She cleared her throat and sounded more normal as she said, "All of you could've brought dates with you. That option is always open to the group."

Emily snorted out, "Of course, most of us are already paired up."

Miranda stared hard at her. "What are you talking about, Emily?"

The brunette smirked at her and sipped from her martini glass. "Come on, Miranda. You're with Peter. Cass is with Adam now. Amelia and Mark suck face most of the time."

Logan's grin grew as she continued.

"You should've brought in a guy next, not Samantha Strattan." She lifted her martini glass to me. "No offense, Sam, but everyone can tell you don't care about social things. Everyone knew Jessica Larsen slept with your boyfriend for two years. That would humiliate most people, but you acted like you didn't care and I don't think that was an act. I think you really *didn't* care." She scoffed at Miranda again. "You just wanted to bring her in because you hoped Mason and Logan would come with her. You never cared about her until you heard she was close to them."

"You're drunk, Emily." Miranda glared at her. "You should go sleep this off. You don't want to be rude."

She snorted again and tipped her head back to finish the rest of her martini. Her thin legs wavered underneath her, but she kept her balance when she raised her empty glass. "Another, bartender!"

Logan chuckled as she went to the bar. "I like her."

"You do?" Miranda had grown pale.

"She tells the truth." He sent her a smirk. "That's all we can ask for...right?"

"The truth?" Adam barked out as he straightened from the wall in a sudden movement. Peter and Mark jumped back in reaction. "What's the truth, Logan? Huh?" He started to stalk forward, but Cassandra tried to slow him down. She was in front with a hand on his chest.

Logan slipped his arm from my waist and maneuvered me behind him. In the blink of an eye, Mason was in front of me too. Miranda gasped and looked around wide eyed. She kept glancing from the Kades to Adam.

Everyone watched him.

His angry scowl intensified and he bit out, "Why'd you take Tanya? You didn't care about her before."

Logan's shoulders jostled in silent laughter. "Are you kidding me?"

"No!"

His shoulders stopped and stretched out instead. "Are you pissed because you never got there?"

"I think...um...I think..." Miranda stepped between them. Her arms were shaking.

Peter moved her aside and puffed out his chest. "Guys, let's be civil here."

"No!" Adam tried to shove him aside, but Mark shot between them instead. Cassandra was pulled out of the way by Miranda.

Logan sounded calm, too calm, as he chuckled. "Let him through. He's got something on his chest. Let's help him get it off. This is the trust tree, right? Here we go, therapy group for everyone."

"You think you're so awesome, don't you?" Adam growled. He had a glass of beer in his hand now. He waved it back and forth in the air now.

"I prefer badass."

The growl grew. "'You're so rich', 'you're so hot', 'everybody wants you.' I am so sick of you two—"

"Both of us?" Mason's voice was low, eerily low.

Everyone snapped their attention to him.

Logan laughed. "Wait your turn, Mase. My fun first."

Mason shot him a dry look, but Logan ignored it. His grin grew wider and he beamed at Adam. "Come on, tell me more. I'd love to hear what else you hate about me." He tsked him with a finger in the air. "Just me, though. You hear that? We'll move onto my big brother in the next session."

Rage leapt to Adam's eyes. I stepped back from instinct. I'd never seen so much rage within him before. My heart started to pound. It grew in speed as Adam bent his head. His mouth had curved in a hateful scowl.

"You laugh at me? Are you kidding me right now? Do you know who you're messing with?"

Logan's laugh sounded genuine. "Do you think I care? You're the guy who gets the leftovers. That's what I know about you."

Adam grew silent. My heart was pounding so loudly. It was deafening to my ears.

"I had Ashley before you, and during you." Logan's smirk grew. "I had Tanya before you and *again* before you. Who else is there?" He made a show as he turned around. He tapped his finger to his chin and he paused when his gaze rested on me. "Who else is there?"

"Logan." It was a quiet warning from Mason.

Logan twisted back around; the delight on his face was unsettling. "There's got to be others. Tina Schnieder? She told me you wanted to date her too, but no one knows about that one. She goes to public. She's beneath you, right? Isn't that you thought about Tanya? You thought for sure you had her in the bag, she goes to public. All those girls are beneath you, isn't that what you think?"

Adam's face was set in stone. The hand that clenched his glass was white around the knuckles. A quiet crack was heard. The group had grown silent and everyone heard it. Another crack sounded.

Logan's voice was so quiet now, going in for the kill. He bent his head forward and his eyes were narrowed. "What about your friend Casssandra there?"

She whipped her head around. Fear was evident as she started to shake. "What are you talking about..." She stammered out, "I..id...Idnever..." She bent forward and took some shuddering breaths. Miranda scurried away from her with a look of terror on her own face. Peter held her hand in his now and he lifted it to his chest.

Adam was white around the corner of his mouth. He turned his head slowly, so slowly. My heart pounded in my ears. My hands started to tremble and I knew my knees were quaking against each other.

He asked in a soft voice, "Is it true?"

Cassandra's mouth hung open. Her eyes bulged out as she looked from Logan's confident smirk to Adam's tightly controlled face. "I...I..."

"Is it true?" Adam asked again.

The tenderness in his voice sent chills down my back. I hugged myself and tried to ward off the promise of violence in the air.

"I can't believe you." He seemed so calm, but his eyes were too dark. "You know how much I hate them."

Logan and Mason glanced at each other and both wore a small grin.

Cassandra's voice was hoarse. "I didn't—it was stupid of me, but... Oh gawd. I'm so sorry, Adam."

Emily started laughing by the bar. She saluted her martini glass in the air. "Way to go, Cassie. Way to start the New Year by being honest."

Cassandra hissed at her, "Shut up, Emily. Like you haven't done the same thing. Logan's probably slept with all of us, Miranda included."

Miranda's eyes got wide and Peter jolted away from her like he'd been burned. She turned to him and pressed her hands to her mouth. "I haven't, baby. I haven't. I swear."

He studied her with narrowed eyes. "You've always wanted Logan to be in the group. You've talked about it for years."

Her hand shot out and she pointed at them. Her foot stomped down. "Only because they should've been in our group. They were supposed to pick our school. We have the better school. Just because they have a better football team, that's the only reason they picked public. They were supposed to be in our group, but instead everyone wants to go to the public parties. Everyone thinks Fallen Crest Public High is so great, all because of them! They were supposed to be at our school. Fallen Crest Academy is the better school. That other school is beneath us, it should be beneath us. They should be kissing our feet. That's the only reason why I've talked about them. I swear, baby!"

Logan bent over laughing. He slapped a hand on his leg. "Man, you guys are so easy. It's been, what? Ten minutes?" He continued laughing as he shook his head. "My job here is done. Have a great night, ya'll."

Adam frowned. "What are you saying? You didn't sleep with Cassandra?"

"Oh no. I did, at the party actually. I was just with Tanya later. Emily was one time and I think," He frowned at Amelia who stood beside Mark. "...Halloween last year?"

She gaped at him, but jerked her head in a nod.

"He's joking," Mark burst out, but he turned sharply on her.

She closed her mouth and slowly turned her head from side to side.

"Amelia!"

Her shoulders lifted up and she held her palms outward. "You didn't want exclusivity, Mark. What do you expect? He's hot."

"You're a slut."

Everyone turned to Miranda who was glaring at Logan. Her hands held her glass tightly. Her arms were still shaking, but not from fear this time. She repeated, "You're a slut."

Logan smirked and glanced at Peter. "I don't hide it."

Her eyes went wide again and she whirled to her boyfriend, who looked away at the same time.

Emily exclaimed, "This was a great idea, Miranda. We should invite Strattan every time."

At this, all eyes went to me. I realized that it looked like I was cowering behind Mason and Logan so I shouldered past them and straightened my back. My chin rose and I stared Miranda down. "You sent me text after text tonight and you called me. You were begging me to come. So I came. If you want to blame me for this, fine. I told you to stay away from Mason and Logan, but you didn't."

"I didn't invite them."

I rolled my eyes. "We all know you wanted them here so here they are. You got what you wanted. I bet you don't want it anymore. You can't control them and you can't control me."

Her eyes narrowed. "Who said I wanted to control you?"

"You've been trying since you warned me Cassandra was jealous of me."

Cassandra gasped. "Miranda!"

Miranda moved back against Peter, who raised a hand to her shoulder. He started to rub up and down her arm in a soothing motion. She sent me a withering look. "You can leave, Samantha. Good luck at school tomorrow."

"Sam," Adam spoke up.

I met his gaze and saw the loathing there. "Don't bother, Adam." I tugged on Logan's arm. "Let's go." And both of us started for the door, but when we realized Mason wasn't following, we turned back.

He watched us with lidded eyes.

Logan frowned. "What are you doing?"

Mason gave him a tight grin. It didn't reach to his eyes. "We have a problem now." He turned towards the group. "She's one of ours and you declared open season on her."

"I didn't." Miranda seemed to melt back into Peter's arms.

He gave her a hard look. "You did."

Logan went to his side. His mouth curved upwards, mocking them. "I did this for sport tonight. You really want me to go after you, pissed if you've done something to Sam?"

Mason shot him a look. "Because it's all you, right?"

Logan grinned at him. "I told you. My fun first."

He rolled his eyes and walked to me. As he drew abreast, he took my arm, and tugged me behind him. "Logan, they got the message."

"I hope they do." Logan's eyes held a much deeper message as he scanned the group.

My legs were shaking so much. As we drew closer to Mason's Escalade, he swept me in his arms and I hung on. I wouldn't have made it otherwise. He deposited me in the seat and went to his own. Logan paused in his open door. He frowned over at me. "Are you okay?"

"I'll be fine, just shaken up."

All amusement had vanished. Both of them watched me with grave eyes. Then Logan sighed. "What do we do?"

Mason continued to watch me as he spoke to him, "We wait and see what happens."

"And if they do something to her? We can't be there during school hours. This is why we didn't go to their school. We didn't want to deal with them."

"I know."

I swallowed as my eyes held Mason's. A promise passed through him to me and my body warmed to it. I wanted it, even now, I wanted him.

"Mason, hell. I think I opened a bigger can of worms than I thought." Logan slapped his hand on the Escalade's door. "I'm sorry, Samantha."

I tried to shrug against the seat. My shoulder lifted halfway. "I've dealt with worse."

"They're vengeful bitches. And they don't forget."

My eyes held onto Mason's. "I told you I was going to piss off some people this week."

He grinned back at me. His hand touched my knee and I clasped onto it.

CHAPTER THIRTY-ONE

I rolled out from underneath Mason's arm that he had thrown over me. One of his hands cupped my breast and I fought back a snort. Of course he'd fallen asleep cupping a feel. After I snuck to my room and got ready for school, I headed downstairs. Moustefff always had a lunch bag ready for me, but I was surprised to see my mom behind the table. The lunch bag was plopped in front of her and she had a steaming cup of coffee beside it.

"You're drinking coffee again?"

She snorted and picked it up. "I hate tea. I tried it, but I hate it." She took a big whiff of the coffee. "And this stuff, it's so addicting."

I eyed her up and down. "Are you feeling okay?"

She gave me a polite look and pulled the ends of her robe tight. "I went to your room earlier, but you weren't there. I guess you went for a run, huh? Anyway, I owe you an apology. Hell, I owe you a lot of apologies."

"Mom?" I glanced around. "What's going on?"

"I was completely wrong about everything." And she brought out a manila folder.

"What's that?"

"It's a tentative deal with David." She took a deep breath. "It says that he has rights to you as a father and you can live with him, if you'd like...or you can visit him...whatever's your choice. I can't keep you from him anymore."

"Anymore?" I picked up the folder, but hesitated to open it. "What are you talking about?"

"He got a lawyer, honey, and that lawyer said he had rights to you. Plus, with everything you've said to me and how I seem to be the worst mother in the world, I didn't fight it. It's the right thing to do. He raised you. He's your father, not some hotshot lawyer out in Boston."

"My real dad's a hotshot lawyer in Boston?"

She shrugged. "It doesn't matter now. I contacted him last night and told him about you. So you might be having two fathers to deal with."

"And the change of heart came because...?"

"Because I was wrong." She looked up. My heart skipped a beat. She seemed so earnest. "I do love you and I haven't been the best mother to you. I've put myself first. I've continued to do so, but you were right last night. I saw that I lost you. Losing your respect, when it's spoken to you from a seventeen year old who's looking at you like they're thirty-that said a lot to me." Her laugh sounded hollow. "It said a whole hell of a lot."

I fingered the edge of the packet and glanced up. "You told my dad about me?" I was breathless, though I didn't know why I should've been.

She took a big sip of coffee. "I wouldn't get your hopes up, hon. He's a big arse."

"No, I know, but...um..." I looked at the manila folder in my hands. "So I could live with David if I really wanted to?"

She took another deep breath and nodded. Her head moved so slowly. "You sure could. You could be there tonight even."

"Really?"

"He's been fighting for you since day one."

"He has?"

"Yep, he has." She looked away and wiped something away from her eyes. When she looked back, she gave me another bright smile. Her lip trembled. "I wanted to keep you all to myself. I didn't want to share you or lose you, but I can't control that. I see that now. You told me that last night. But, honey, I love you so much." She lurched forward and grabbed my arm. "You know that, right?"

"I know, mom."

It felt right to call her that. She'd been Analise so much, but she was my mom at that moment. I gave her another smile. "I'm not going to leave, mom. I'd like to see David, but you're my mom. This has become my home."

I glanced up and saw Mason. He hesitated on the stairwell.

When I gave him a small smile, he came into the kitchen. His eyes fell on the folder in my hands. "You want a ride to school?"

"Sure." I tried to say it brightly, but my life had just been spun around. Two dads. I couldn't get that through my head. What did that mean?

Mason grabbed something from the kitchen and started for the door. I turned to follow and my mom shot up from the table. "Honey, are you okay with this?"

"Yeah." I beamed back at her, or I tried to. "I'll be fine, mom."

"Are you sure? I could call in for you. You don't have to go to school today. I'm sure it's a lot to take in." She seemed timid as she stood beside the table. Her steaming coffee cup was forgotten behind her.

I waved as I went through the front door. I heard Mason get into his Escalade. "I'll be fine, mom. Promise. Have a good day."

"You too, honey."

He pulled out of the driveway and waited until we'd gone a block. "So what was that about?"

I still held the manila folder in my lap. "She gave rights to David. I can see him if I want to and she called my real dad last night. I guess he's some hotshot lawyer in Boston."

After a few blocks, Mason wheeled into a fast food drive-through. "You want anything?"

I shook my head. I couldn't believe this was happening. He ordered me a coffee anyway.

He handed it over. "So are you going to stay with him now? That's what you wanted, right?"

I shot him a look and sipped my coffee. I hissed when I felt how scalding it was. "Yeah, but there's..." I glanced at him warily. "That's not in the cards."

He grinned from the side of his mouth and eased his Escalade into my school's parking lot. "You snuck out of bed this morning. I was hoping for a morning ride."

I grinned as memories from last night sent a surge of heat through my body. Need started to throb between my legs again and I clamped them together. I couldn't go to school hot and bothered, and aching all over...again. Last night had passed from one sensual moment to another. Mason had taken me on an insatiable journey and every time I thought I was done, he slid back in and started it all over again.

We'd slept for two hours, tops.

As he parked front and center, I spotted Adam at his car. He was with Mark Decraw and Peter Glasburg. Everything sexual left me and I tightened my hold on my coffee. "Yeah, well, we'll have to do it another time."

He nodded in their direction. "You want me to stay for a while?"

"No." I did. "You have to get to your own school."

"Alright. I can't run you home after school."

"Why not?"

He grimaced as he stretched back in his seat. "I'll have enough time to come get you and head back for my practice. Can you hang out there for a while? I think Logan would love it. He can show off his throwing arm for you."

"Sure. See you." As I reached for the door, the first warning bell went off and everyone started to head inside. Our eyes met and held as I walked around the front to the door. As I neared it, I expected to hear him zoom off. It never happened and I turned around.

A blast of cold air hit me. It drenched me.

Mason was out of his car and he was face to face with Adam. Peter and Mark were behind him. All three of them had fierce expressions on their faces and firm jaws, but Mason looked relaxed as he eyed each of them up and down.

My stomach dropped. This was not good.

"Hey, hey, hey!" I ran back and shoved between them. Not good. Not good. That kept going through my head.

"Where's your little bitch boy now?" Adam tried to reach around me.

Mason smirked. He looked calm. The other three were shifting on their feet, but he never moved, not an inch. He drawled out, "Bitch boy? That was a bitch move. You waited until a girl stepped between us?"

Adam flushed, but snarled. "One swing, Kade. One swing. Isn't that what they say about you?" His lip curled up. "It only takes one punch for Mason Kade."

"Stop!"

"Usually." He shrugged and as he lifted a hand to scratch his chin, all three jerked in reaction. Mason's smirk grew wider at that.

"I mean it!" I turned around and around.

"Is that right?" Adam tried to push at him again. Mark and Peter both grabbed him as they got in front.

I surged forward and tried to help, but I was bumped backwards. I skidded from the movement, but Mason caught me. He slid an arm around my waist and lifted me to the side. "Trying to hurt a girl?"

Adam growled and lunged again. "Let me go. I can take him."

"Come on, man. Think about this."

"Adam, please. Don't do this." I started forward again. Mason caught me and held me in place. His hand stayed on my hip. "Just stop, Adam. This won't do anything."

Adam choked out a hoarse laugh. "Are you kidding me, Sam? Someone needs to knock 'em down a step, him and his bitch boy. They think they're gods around here. I don't think so. I don't think so!" He spat on the ground. "He's got nerve to show up on my territory. This is mine, Kade!"

Mason lifted an eyebrow. "She yours too?"

"Mason!"

His eyes went wider and he choked back his retort to lunge forward again. His friends grunted and strained to hold him back. Peter snapped at him, "This is what he wants. You're playing into his hands."

Mark was whispering something to Adam while Peter kept a wary eye on Mason.

"I don't care," Adam ripped out. "I don't care one bit. I want this done. This has to be done. Someone's gotta do it. Everyone else is too scared so I'll do it. Let me do it!"

Mason's soft chuckle enraged him further.

A knot of dread and fear expanded from my stomach. It was crawling all over me. My legs started to shake, but then I caught movement around us. People were starting to congregate towards us. I cringed when I heard someone yell 'fight' and then a bevy of lockers slammed shut from inside.

"Your sidekick's not here. What are you going to do, man?" Both of Adam's arms were lifted up and pushed backwards by Peter and Mark. They continued to hold him back as they leaned all of their weight on him.

"I don't fight with words." The corner of Mason's lip was curled up. "I'm quite capable of handling Quinn all on my own. Let him go. Come on. That's what he wants."

"Shut up!" Mark glared at him.

The last bell rang and I glanced around. No one was in class. The crowd doubled in size and a loose circle had started to form around us. Becky dodged around a group of guys and started to come to my side. I shot my hand out and shook my head so she braked a few yards from me, but edged in closer. When she mouthed if I was okay, I shook my head.

No, I wasn't okay. Mason was severely outnumbered.

Suddenly, Adam shoved Mark aside and his elbow caught me in the face.

"Hey!" Mason barked as he caught me and pulled me behind him. "If you want to fight, fight me, not your buddies. Sam just got clipped."

Mark cried out as he caught one of Adam's arms, "I'm sorry, man. Sorry, Sam—" He was about to say more, but

Adam cursed and lunged once again. "You're a piece of crap, Kade!" He continued to bite out curses.

Mason sighed and motioned for him to come forward. "Just let him go. This will get done a lot faster. I have school too."

Peter lifted his head and yelled, "If you'd shut up, man. You're not helping."

I felt Mason's impatience. The one hand he kept on me was tense, so tense I wondered if he realized he was going to leave a bruise. Then I stopped wondering. He looked like he was amused by the whole thing, but a nerve jerked under his shirt. I saw it through the opening of his shirt. It was his only tell; everything else about him was silent. He was completely still.

I knew he was ready for an opening.

And then something happened. He jerked forward, hooked an arm around Peter's neck and threw him to the aside. Adam swung, but Mason dodged and instead tackled Mark to the left. They both fell to the ground, but he scrambled back up in the blink of an eye. He turned around and it was now him and Adam, no one else.

Adam took a step forward and opened his mouth—

Crack!

Mason punched him between the cheek and mouth, one time, and then he stepped back.

It looked like it happened in slow motion.

Adam's eyes rolled to the back of his head and he fell with a loud thud to the ground. His head smacked against the cement twice and his limbs bounced back up before they settled down.

There was silence in the crowd.

"Oh my god!" a girl screamed. Another started to sob.

I rushed to Adam's side and patted his cheek. "Adam? Adam..."

"What's going on here?" a teacher cried out.

"Holy, man..." "Did you see that?" "Shiite." Another guy whooped in laughter and others started to yell back and forth. People were starting to push and shove against each other.

Becky's mouth had dropped open. She was frozen in place.

More teachers were starting to push their way in and then I heard my dad's voice in the background. "What's going on? Let us through."

"Oh no—" I hurried up and started to push Mason into the crowd. "You have to go."

When we got to his Escalade, he smirked down at me. "Why? They'll say it was me. I knocked him out cold, Sam."

"You can leave. You might not get in trouble."

He rolled his eyes. "Are you serious? I'm not going anywhere. I'll face the firing squad here."

I sighed. "Do you know what you did?"

He turned back to the crowd, but shrugged. "I don't care."

"You attacked a student on school grounds. They could get you expelled from your school."

"Maybe." His jaw stiffened.

"Samantha!" my dad hollered.

I jerked around, but he hadn't spotted us yet. "Go, Mason. I mean it."

He shook his head. "I'm not going anywhere."

"Samantha!" David's voice was closer now. And then he broke through the crowd to us.

I turned to face my father, but I hissed behind me, "He could have you arrested."

David stopped in front of us and he placed both hands on his hips. He stared at me for a moment and then Mason before he took off his coach's hat and rubbed at his head. "Do you know what you've done, son?"

"Yes, sir."

My eyebrows went up when I didn't see a smirk on his face and heard respect in his tone.

"Basey," David hollered behind him.

One of his assistant coaches popped up. "He'll be fine, sir. He'll come around. We just gotta get him inside."

My dad took a deep breath. "Alright, well, you heard him. Let's all head inside." He pointed at Mason. "You, go to the principal's office."

He nodded. "Sure. Where's that at?"

"Sam?"

"Yeah, dad?"

"Take him to the principal's office."

"Sure thing."

"And do me another favor?"

I halted at the frustration in my dad's voice. "Yeah?"

"Call your mother and his father." He turned around, but I heard him mutter, "This should be fun."

CHAPTER
THIRTY-TWO

Mason and I were in an empty classroom. His head was bent down, cushioned by his arms and I was starting to wonder if he'd fallen asleep. He couldn't have. And then someone sped past the door, screeched to a halt, and backtracked to stand in the doorway. Logan greeted us with his arms spread wide and a bright smile on his face.

"One punch, Mase?" Logan laughed and launched himself on our table. "Next time I think you should get him to knock himself out."

"Logan, dude." Another guy followed him in, looking irritable. I recognized him from one of their parties. "You just took off. This place is bitch heaven, at least grace me with some bread crumbs."

"Ethan, chill. They're easy."

He grimaced. "I'm not talking about those; I'm talking about the dudes. They're all over. Their pants are pressed so tight I keep expecting to smell aromatherapy or whatever my mom sells with her scentsy stuff. They fart daisies. I know it."

Logan laughed and hit him in the backside of his head. Ethan shot away and glared again. His eyebrows rose at an alarming height.

Mason sighed and leaned back in his chair. "We've been cooped up here for four hours. Dad showed up after an hour and we were hauled back here."

Logan smirked. "Was he dressed to impress?"

"You know it. Remind 'em who brings the money in." He glanced at me. "Her mom had some lacey bridal dress on."

I glanced down and folded my arms. A stab of pain went through my gut when I remembered how Analise had pranced through my school's doorway. It'd been her second time to visit. The first time had been an event for David.

Both brothers shared a grin. "You're totally going to get off for this."

Ethan shared in their dark humor and grinned. "Isn't one punch considered assault or something? My cousin knocked a guy out cold. That dude had been harassing him and his girlfriend and my cousin got the rap for it."

Mason shrugged and stood. He started to pace. Even with his muscular physique, the gracefulness of his walk reminded me of a lean panther trapped in a cage. He kept glancing at the open door. The bell had rung again and students passed by. I had stopped watching after a while. Not one person went by that didn't look in. They all wanted to get a glimpse. We were on display at a human zoo.

I asked Logan, "Aren't you guys supposed to be in school? It's one in the afternoon."

"Yeah, right. I'm not going to be there when my brother's over here. Besides, coach sent me over." He nodded at Mason. "We have twofers for the rest of the week. He said you have to make them all, tonight too, if you're going to play."

Irritation flared over his face and he scowled. "Against Roussou? Of course I'm going to play. It's our second chance to beat them. I hate their quarterback."

"More than the Academy's?" Ethan joked.

Logan tipped his head back to cackle while Mason flexed his knuckles. "Whatever. I'm sick of this. I'm starting to wish I hadn't finished him."

Logan looked taken aback and thrust his hand out towards me. "Whatever. The guy's going to back down. He knows you can beat his—"

Ethan interjected, "One punch, mofo."

"—and now he might calm down. His panties are all twisted because of Sam anyway—"

"Hey!"

Ethan frowned at me.

"—but now he'll go away and lick his balls a bit. I think we should do it again to make sure he's down for the count and knows who is boss. What do you say? Hunt him down after we kill Roussou Friday night?"

Mason stopped and glared at him. He looked ready to bark something, but changed his mind and pointed to the door. "Ethan, leave."

He jerked his head up. "What?"

"Leave. Five minutes." Mason gestured to the door again.

Logan tossed his car keys at him. "Go get some sandwiches, I'm hungry."

"Are you kidding me?"

I lifted a hand. "Can you get me a latte?"

His mouth fell.

"See you. Thanks." Logan chuckled and waved his fingers at him. "Family meeting, mofo."

He growled and then stomped out the door. As soon as he was gone, Logan folded his arms and stuck his chin out. "You've got the floor, Mason. Go ahead."

Mason threw him a dark look before he swiftly pivoted on his heel and pulled the door shut. As soon as it clicked in place, he was in Logan's face. "Are you kidding me? You want another go at this kid?"

"Yeah. I want to be there this time."

"Logan, this kid isn't some public student. He's Academy. His dad does business with ours. We can't keep fighting these pricks."

"Why not? He's a loser?"

"Because dad could suffer for what we're doing."

Logan rolled his eyes. "Oh, come on. Dad owns this town. He's running half the state. He's got businesses all over the world. I don't think we need to worry about this kid." He gestured to me again. "Besides, you really like how he keeps sniffing around Sam? You know he's rallying to come back around with her again. I bet you anything he was going to try last night, but she shot him down."

"This isn't about Sam."

"Yeah, it is."

Mason stood in front of him and faced him squarely. "You're going to be selling that crap?"

Logan lifted his chest up. "Why wouldn't I? It's the truth."

"Then you're on his level. You want to see who has the biggest balls. Congratulations, Logan. I do. I punched him out."

Logan narrowed his eyes. "You're putting me on his level?"

Mason shoved his face against his. "I'll punch you out too."

Logan shoved him back and jumped off the desk. I braced myself, ready for round two, but Mason shook his head and backed away. "Grow up, Logan. It's fun and all, but dad's involved. You think this is good for him where he has to throw his weight around so I don't go to jail and you want to do it again? Pricks like this guy don't get bullied down."

The corner of Logan's mouth twitched. And then he exuded a deep breath and jumped to the floor. He shook his hands in front of him and seemed to be shaking something off. "Whatever. Fine. You're right."

Mason growled and crossed his arms over his chest. "Damn right I am. *If* I get out of this, we stay away from these guys for a while, alright?" He tapped Logan's chest with a finger. "Okay?"

Logan shoved his finger away, but the corner of his mouth curved up. "Fine. You're usually right about these things, but man—I wanted to punch that kid. You don't know how hard it was to get that text that you knocked him out and I wasn't there."

"Take it out on Roussou Friday. Those guys are a better fight."

"Yeah, maybe."

They both fell into a shared silence and I held my breath. I was unsure what to say or if I wanted to break whatever camaraderie they'd fallen into. My hands were shaking and I tucked them under my legs, but I tried to quell my voice. "I don't really understand what just happened with you guys, but am I the only one worried about Mason here?"

Logan cracked a grin and he was back to his usual cocksure way. "He'll be fine. Dad will get him off. We need to worry more about your situation."

I shivered as I remembered the few times I had glimpsed when Miranda or any member of the Elite had walked past our doorway. If looks could kill...

"We can't do much about that." Mason shot me a brief look and I saw the apology in his eyes. "Mom's coming."

Logan shot up straight. "How do you know?"

"I texted her."

"Why? Dad can handle this."

"Yeah, but what if he can't. She's got better connections."

Logan expelled another breath and shook his head. "Oh man, you're playing with fire. Dad, Analise, and mom in the same room."

I lifted a hand. "And David...with my real dad maybe coming someday?"

"What are you talking about?" Logan shot Mason a look. "What is she talking about?"

He lifted a shoulder. "Her mom called her real dad. He might be coming."

"What? No. She's with us." Logan looked at me. "You're with us. You can't leave."

One of my eyebrows went up. "Uh...I wasn't planning on leaving. I don't even know who he is."

His shoulders relaxed. "Oh, good. I like having a sister that's banging my brother."

"And shut it with those references." Mason reached out and pushed him back a step. "I'm getting sick of it."

Logan's smile slipped and he shoved his hands in his pockets. "Yeah, sure. No problem."

No sooner had he uttered those words when the door opened again. We expected Ethan, but I sat up straight when David walked in. James and Analise came in behind him, but they rounded to the other side of the room while my dad stopped inside of the door.

James shared a look with Mason, but Analise kept fidgeting with her hands in front of her. She'd glance up every now and then and I followed her gaze the last time and my own widened as I sat up. Malinda Decraw had come inside and stood beside David. She touched his hand for a brief moment before he took a breath and stepped towards us. She remained behind him, but I couldn't get that touch out of my head. It was a sensual caress, one for comfort? Why was it so sensual? Why was she here?

David cleared his throat and tugged his shirt out an inch. "I—uh—a decision's been made." His eyes found Mason's and they hardened.

Mason lifted his chin, but that was his only reaction.

David narrowed his. "When Adam woke up, he wouldn't tell us what the fight was about." His eyes skirted to me with a dark question in them. "But he admitted that he was the initial aggressor. He said you were trying to leave, but he wouldn't let you. Then when you got out of your vehicle, he harassed you and threatened you. Fallen Crest Academy does not take Adam's actions lightly, but since you charged him and knocked him out, we've decided on a punishment. Adam's parents do not wish to pursue criminal charges against you. Instead, they have agreed with the following discipline in three parts."

Mason's mouth hardened, but he was stone face otherwise.

David glanced at me again. An unreadable emotion flashed in them, but he slipped back into his professional mode. "Since you are not a student at Fallen Crest Academy, they are unable to seek expulsion or suspension in any form. However, we've already sent word to your school's officials and we highly recommend that you be suspended from them—"

Logan surged forward. "No way, he'd be out of the game on Friday. We need him against Roussou."

"Son." James clasped a hand on his shoulder. "Let Coach Strattan finish."

Logan quieted, but glared at my dad.

David continued, "As I was saying, we are seeking a suspension for you, but it will be up to your school if they follow through with that recommendation. Now, after four hours of deliberations we've decided that you will volunteer at our school's alumni festival this Saturday."

"What does that mean?" Mason had leaned back against the table where I sat, but he stood now. His arm brushed against my leg.

I glanced down at the contact. A shiver went through me, but my heart pounded. He had said three parts, those were only two.

"You will help with the set up, you will do whatever I tell you to do throughout the day to help out, and you will help with the clean up. There is a dinner that night for the volunteer and staff. I will determine if you will be invited to that or not."

"Oh." Mason leaned back beside me again. His arm was loose again. "That's fair."

David frowned at him.

"You said three parts," I spoke up. David turned towards me and pinned me with his gaze. He was trying to search inside of me. His eyes narrowed and they glanced back and forth from Mason and me.

"Sam," my mom hissed.

David held a hand up. "No, that's fine, Analise. I did say three parts and the third part's already been taken care of. Your father has made a generous donation to the school."

Logan snorted. "Dad, you bought his way out—"

James turned on him. "You will keep your mouth shut, Logan."

His eyes widened and his mouth jerked in reaction, but Logan shrunk against the counter he sat on. His eyes took on an angry leer.

James' eyes were lidded, but he turned towards my father and jerked his head down in a nod. "As you were saying, David..."

My dad cleared his throat once more.

Malinda moved forward a step and touched the small of his back.

My heart snapped and I jumped to my feet. "What are you doing in here?"

"Samantha!"

I ignored my dad and walked to her. "You're Mark's mother. You have no connection to anyone in here. Why are you here?"

Her mouth formed a small oval, but she looked to David.

He stepped between us and spoke in a quiet voice, "She is here for me. She's become a good friend to me, Samantha."

I fell back, reeling, and looked at my mother. She had grown pale with a hand pressed against her chest. Her other hand clung to one of James'. It was hidden from eyesight, but I still saw it. When she realized that I saw it, she gasped and retracted her hand to her side.

Why was she pale? And why did she need comfort from James...then I understood. My heart sank and my stomach had dropped to the floor. It was really over with them. My mom had moved on with James, David was starting to move on as well... My head fell forward and I hugged myself.

A hand touched my side gently. Mason tugged me back by the belt loop on my jeans. He tucked me behind him and moved forward a step. "I heard that festival is for two days?"

David was still looking between us. "Uh—yes—yes, it is." He frowned. "Why?"

"I could volunteer both days."

"You could?"

"Man," Logan hissed softly.

Mason nodded. He held his gaze steadily. "It's the least I could do."

David gave him a sad smile. "Your school won't suspend you. We both know that, they need you for their football game."

The corner of Mason's mouth twitched. "What time should I be here on Saturday?"

"Seven sharp. Come to my office."

Mason's head jerked in a nod. "Will do."

David looked at me. "Would you come to my office later today?"

I stared at Malinda behind him. "No."

"Sam."

He waved a hand in the air. "It's fine, Analise. I can talk to her next week."

My mom trembled, but she nodded at him and tried to muster a smile.

For a moment, David looked around the room and then he gave out a soft sigh. "I guess I'll be in touch then…"

James strode forward and held out a hand. "Thank you, David."

They clasped their hands in a firm handshake and studied each other for a beat. Then David nodded again and turned for the door. He held it open as Malinda swept out before him. Pain sliced through me when I saw his hand touch the small of her back and remain there, even after they went in the hallway.

When the door closed, I was barely aware of Mason. He stood and I heard his voice at a distance, "Mom's coming to town. We'd like to stay with her at the hotel."

"I think that'd be for the best this week…"

"Fine."

"Fine."

And then there was silence. David and Analise were actually done... The realization settled on my chest and a wave of tears threatened me. I rushed from the room and shoved through the hallway. When I found an empty backroom, I locked the door, kept the lights off, and slid to the ground. My forehead touched my knees and I sobbed.

CHAPTER THIRTY-THREE

I went to my last two classes, though I didn't learn a thing. My body had gone numb again. I missed that feeling and I was itching for another three hour run. My body ached for it.

Becky chatted to me after school. I had no idea what she said, but I nodded my head at random moments and she kept chatting away. When I looked for my keys in my bag, I cursed and hit my head against my locker.

"What?"

I mumbled, "Mason drove me today."

"He did?" She straightened from a locker. "Oh, right. That makes sense, why he was here...wait...is he coming back to give you a ride home?"

Then my phone beeped and I pulled it out. He had sent me four text messages and the last one read: **Two practices tonight, then with mom and Logan. Can you get a ride home? Need me to send someone?**

I cursed again. "Can I get a ride home with you?"

Becky's eyes got wide and her lips clamped together. A strange gurgle escaped her lips.

"What does that mean?"

She whispered, "Adam gave me a ride." She jumped back and pressed a hand to her mouth. "I'm sorry."

"No, that's fine. I'll think of something."

She edged closer a step. "He can't come and get you?"

I shook my head. My throat was so closed up, had been all day. "No, they have two practices tonight and their mom's in town." And that meant I wouldn't see either of them all week...probably... I swallowed over a lump.

"Hey, I bet Adam would give you a ride!" Her head bounced up and down. "Yeah, yeah. I bet he would. I think

427

he feels real bad. He called me last night and said that he wanted to make things better with you. He wanted all three of us to be friends again."

"He did?"

"Uh, yeah. I mean, why would he make that up if he didn't mean it?" Her grin turned sloppy and a glaze drifted over her eyes.

Oh boy. I recognized that look.

She sighed dreamily, "Wouldn't it be wonderful if all three of us hung out again? And then maybe he'd realize he needed me in his life?"

I gave her a blank stare. "What do you mean? You are in his life; he gave you a ride to school."

"Yeah, I know." Her eyes drifted downwards and she bit the corner of her lip. "I was just meaning that if us three were better friends. It felt like we were going to be before, but then he got all weird and mad at you. It changed when he found out about the Kades, now that I think about it."

"Becky."

She turned to me. Her eyes clicked into focus. "Uh?"

"What's going on with you?"

Her eyeballs went from side to side. "What do you mean?"

"You're weird, weirder than normal." Then it clicked in place. "What have people been saying about me?"

As soon as I said that, she sucked in her breath dramatically and scooted away from me.

"Becky." I clamped onto her arm so she couldn't go any further. "What's going on?"

She patted her chest and it rose higher and higher. It looked like she was hyperventilating or having a panic attack. I hoped not, I needed answers.

"Becky!"

"Okay, okay." She dragged me down the hallway and into the empty theatre. It was dark where we were, but the lights were bright on the stage where a group of people stood in a small circle. I didn't care what they were doing up there.

"Spill. Now."

She looked in pain as she rushed out, "MirandaStewarthatesyouandnow everyoneelsedoestoo." She took a deep breath. "And everyone thinks Adam and Mason fought over you. Everybody knows something happened at the Elite dinner Miranda had and that you guys went there, but no one will say what happened...so...people are figuring out their own guesses."

"People think Mason and Adam fought over me?" A blast of cold air rocked me again. My stomach dropped out again and a surreal feeling of terror started to settle in. Was I ready for this? The knot had doubled in size. I forcibly swallowed one more time. I knew what would happen if people found out...

"No, yes, I mean—I don't know. We don't really know. Some people think it's about Logan. I'm not sure why, because of Tanya or something. I have no idea. Everyone knows Logan took Tanya away from Adam and we all saw that Cassandra and Adam were flirting. Now they don't even talk to each other. Something happened."

"Oh." Relief washed over me. Adam's fight with Logan over Tanya made more sense, didn't it? "Yeah, I mean, Logan wasn't nice at the dinner. He rubbed it in Adam's face."

"Rubbed it in?" A hollow laugh came from behind me. Jessica gripped her books tight and glared at me. "We heard he was practically having sex with Tanya at the dinner. No wonder Adam popped his cherry and went after Mason today." She eyed me up and down and curled her lip in a sneer. "We also heard that Emily Connsway laughed in your face. Way to go, Sam."

The theatre door was open and a small group had congregated behind us.

"Give it a rest, Jess." Lydia sidled up beside her and leveled her with a piercing look. "Stop making up lies, stop being a bitch, and apologize to Sam for what you did."

Jessica's back straightened. "Me? Apologize? What did *I* do to her? She stood there and let Logan Kade humiliate me.

He used to like me and she ruined that. You ruined my life, Sam. Thanks a lot."

Jill pushed forward to stand beside them and chewed on her lip. Then she burst out, "I'm sorry for being a bitch, Sam. I was threatened because of Jeff." She waved towards Jessica and Lydia. "And I didn't want them to do to me what they did to you so I tried to be friends with them. You know, get closer with your enemies and all...that..." She hung her head and trailed off.

Jessica whirled towards her. "You're such a whore, Jill. Sam's not going to be your friend. She hates you and me. She hates Lydia too."

Lydia gasped. "I don't think she hates me. I'm trying to be her friend." She looked at me with pleading eyes. "I'm really sorry. I really am. And I don't care if Jessica hates me after this. I should never have covered for her and Jeff and lied to you. I should've apologized to you right away too." She edged closer and shoved Jessica back a few steps in the process. "I really miss you and I'll do anything to be your friend again."

"Lydia!"

She ignored Jessica and gave me a shaky smile. "I don't care if the Elite don't like you. I'll support you and stand by you the whole time. They don't scare me."

Jill sighed. "Yes, they do. They scare everybody...well, except for maybe Sam, but still."

"Hey...?" Jeff stood at the back of the crowd, and they opened for him. His face was twisted in confusion. "What's... what's going on here...? Do I even want to know?"

Jessica turned her glare off and went to his side. She gave him a seductive smile as her hand traveled up his arm. "Hi, Jeff."

"Hey!" Jill removed her hand from his arm. "I'm not going to let you sleep with him."

Jessica's eyes didn't blink. "Can you give me a ride home, Jeff? My car's in the shop for an oil change."

He blinked at her. "Uh...sure...yeah, okay."

"Jeff!" Jill seethed.

He met my gaze for a second, but shrugged at his girlfriend. "It's just a ride home. I'm not going to sleep with her or anything." Then he motioned for Jessica to follow and the two left.

Becky's mouth hung open. "I—" She blinked. "I can't believe that happened."

"Lydia, do you think they're going to...?" Jill blinked back some tears. Her voice hitched on a sob.

"Yes." Lydia didn't waste a second. "They are. I'd dump him in a heartbeat if I were you."

My eyebrow rose. This was a different side to Lydia that I'd never seen before. When she gave me a small smile, I almost gave her one back. Almost.

Jill's mouth fell open and tears started to fall down her cheeks. She wiped them away, but turned and darted down the hallway.

Lydia shook her head. "I don't feel bad for her. She knew what they did to you."

I shrugged. "I don't care anymore." I never had. "So you and Jessica aren't friends anymore? She's going to think you betrayed her for me."

"I know."

"She's not going to let that go."

"I know." Lydia gave me a sad look. "I miss being your friend. I'd like to earn that back and that's what I'm going to do from now on."

"Hey!" Becky grabbed my arm. A smile spread from ear to ear. "She can give you a ride home."

"You need a ride home?"

"Uh, no. I'm okay." Nightmares flashed in my head. I wasn't sure who knew that I was staying at the Kade mansion and I wasn't going to let Lydia be the first one to know for certain. "I'll find—or call—someone else."

"Are you sure? I can give you a ride home. It's on my way, you know."

"I'm okay. Really." Every cell inside of me relaxed. She still thought I was at David's.

"Wait. Are you still at your dad's house or...?"

I gave her a bright smile. "Speaking of my dad, he wanted me to talk to him so I'll see you guys later." I pushed through the crowd and hurried away before either of them formed more questions. People would figure it out, if they hadn't already, but I wasn't going to help it.

As I got to my locker, I grabbed my bag and phone. When I went to the parking lot, I started to call my mom, and I couldn't believe she was my last resort, but stopped abruptly. I blinked a few times, but then I put my phone away. My mom was already there. She was waiting in her convertible.

"Hi, honey." She waved her fingers at me. "I got you a coffee."

"Mom," I started as I got inside. "I really can't handle much right now so if you've got any more bombs to lay on me, can you leave them for another day?"

Her smile slipped a bit. "Are you okay, honey?"

I stared at her. Had she not been there when I stormed out of the classroom? "I'm perfect."

She laughed. "Well, I don't know about that, but you're pretty good."

My mouth wanted to fall to the ground. Where had the mom from this morning gone? She professed she wanted to change and now I got the Barbie fake mom again.

At a stoplight, she let out a deep breath. Her voice dropped to a normal tone. "Well, I'm sorry about those bombs, but I do have one to drop on you." She paused for a beat. "Your father's in town."

I closed my eyes.

"And he wants to meet you."

"Oh no."

"Tonight."

I wanted that run. I needed that run right now.

I looked at her. "How long is he in town?" My voice came out breathless.

"It depends on you." She held my gaze until the light turned green. As we started forward again, she gripped the steering wheel with clenched knuckles. "I don't like that he's here, but he is. David's going to flip about this."

My heart was pounding again. It was a horse track. "Mom, I can't."

Her hand clasped onto mine and she squeezed it. "I'm sorry, honey. I really am, but your father's a jerk. If I tell him you don't want to see him, he won't believe me. He'll show up anyway and I'd like to avoid that, if possible."

"Mom." My voice was a whisper now. "I can't. I really can't."

She kept driving and we were almost home when she murmured, "Okay, honey. I'll tell him you're not ready."

Everything sagged forward at that. As soon as we got home, I unbuckled and bolted for the door. I was back on the pavement within ten minutes with my running shoes on and my headphones in my ears.

Three hours later when I turned into the driveway, my stomach had stopped rumbling. Everything was numb in me, it was the way I liked it, and I was blind to the three cars I passed as I let myself inside. I trailed through the house and eyed the droplets of sweat that slipped from me. I doubted my mom would care, not that I ever did, but the small grin that formed on my face was wiped away when I went past the dining room.

A man sat at the table with my mother and James. He had striking blue eyes and broad shoulders. He looked in his forties with a strong jaw and a lean physique. Confidence and authority exhumed from him. As he turned towards me, he never blinked. I felt pinned under his gaze and steeled myself. He was trying to read into me, as only Mason tended to do sometimes.

"Sam, honey." Analise jumped up. "You're back from your run."

I couldn't answer her. I couldn't look away from this man.

She laughed nervously. "This is your father. Garrett Brickshire."

"You're the hotshot lawyer from Boston?"

The corner of his lip twitched. "You're the pain in the ass daughter I never knew about?"

"My mom said you were a jerk." I paused. "That was an understatement."

"She said the same thing to me." He stood and my eyes widened. He kept standing up. And he towered above my mom and James.

"How tall are you?"

"I'm six four. How far did you run?"

I would've shrugged, but my body couldn't respond to me anymore. "I have no idea."

"You're not training for a marathon?"

"I run to run."

We were locked in some form of battle. Neither of us could look away, neither of us could back down.

His mouth twitched now to a mocking grin. "You should keep track of what you do. Your achievements define you."

My lip curled upwards. "Then I'm not worth your time. I don't have any achievements. You can go back to Boston and your hotshot lawyer life."

He blinked.

He broke. I won.

Then he laughed in a smooth baritone voice. "Yeah, you're my kid alright." He turned to Analise. "I still want the test done, but I'm 99% sure she's mine."

She huffed out, "Like I'd lie to you after seventeen years, Garrett."

He chuckled. "I think you lie so much you don't know when you're not." His eyes met James. "No offense to your future bride. I'm sure she loves you well enough."

A look twitched in James' eyes. "You've seen her for

yourself. Now you can return to your hotel to wait until Samantha is ready. I believe she should determine when and if she's ready to meet with you again."

The cockiness vanished in Garrett's eyes and he drew himself to an impressive height. He reached for James' hand. As they shook, he said, "I've heard of a James Kade. Though the circumstances are strained, I'm glad to have met you."

"You as well, Mr. Brickshire."

They studied each other for a moment. It reminded me of the exchange between David and James earlier, but this one was different. There was an edge to it that I hadn't felt in the classroom with David.

Then the moment was broken as Garrett passed by me. "I'll see you later, kid!" He thumped me on the shoulder before the door shut behind him.

I needed another run.

CHAPTER THIRTY-FOUR

The rest of the week was quiet. I knew Garrett was at some ritzy hotel. Analise told me he offered to pay for my own suite so we could get to know one another, but that was the one and only time she mentioned him. I was content to let him sit and wait.

School was also quiet. Lydia never left my side, which was refreshing. Becky was right beside her and the two seemed like long-lost kindred souls. She insisted that Adam wanted to make things right again, but he never approached me. I caught a few looks from him, but that was the extent of it. The Elite had fallen quiet as well. Miranda and Amelia glared every now and then, but as the week progressed their glares faded. Cassandra rolled her eyes whenever she saw me and she would whisper to whatever friend was nearby, but I never let it bother me. It hadn't before, why would I start now?

Of the four Elite girls, Emily was the one who hadn't changed with me. She never talked to me before and she didn't now. There were no glares or eye rolls either. One time she bumped into me, but kept going. From the distracted look on her face, I was inclined she didn't know who she had bumped into. And judging from how she hurried away, I didn't think she cared.

The only Elite member who did talk to me was Mark, and both of us felt awkward about the exchange.

He stopped at my locker one day and looked above my head.

I turned around to see who was behind me, but there was no one. "Can I help you?"

He cleared his throat and looked in pain as he did it. "Mark? Hello?"

I spotted Lydia and Becky down the hallway. They were giggling about something, but both stopped in their tracks when they saw who was in front of me. Hands flew over their mouths and their heads bumped together. They scurried into a nearby bathroom and I knew they wouldn't save me either.

He continued to stare over my head and his mouth kept twitching. I grew tired of waiting and snapped my fingers in front of him. "Hey, I'm down here. Look at me if you're going to talk to me."

His eyes widened a fraction. "Oh yeah..."

Oh goodness. Here we go again.

"Um...okay, this is really *weird* to say, but...uh... My mom wanted me to invite you to our house tomorrow night."

"Why?"

"For dinner." He looked down now and almost jumped back a foot. He frowned, twisted at his shirt's collar, and looked away. "This is so uncomfortable."

"And perplexing." I grabbed his shirt and hauled his face down so he was eye level with me. "Why does your mom want me over for dinner?"

"Because of Coach."

"Explain."

"Oh, uh, they're dating." He reared back. "You didn't know?"

My heart shrunk. "I had hoped to forget it. Thanks for reminding me."

His mouth twitched up now. "Hey, no problem. Okay, so she wants you to come over around six. Can you bring a bottle of wine?"

"I'm underage."

He shrugged. "Get one from your mom; tell her it's for the dinner."

"And is it?"

He grinned again. "Nah, man. We can drink it later. I figure you can come to dinner and then we can take off for the party afterwards. It'd look cool to show up with a bottle of wine, you know. It's like we're mature and grown up."

"What the hell are you talking about?"

"The Kade party." He frowned at me. "You didn't know?"

I glared at him. "Well I do now, don't I?"

"Yeah, it's going to be awesome. They're throwing it in some huge suite at a hotel. My dad's stayed there a few times. It's supposed to be out of this world."

So they had time to spread the word about a party, but not invite me? I folded my arms over my chest and leaned back against my locker when Mark bounced away. He slapped hands with another guy as he did so and they started laughing. I watched his lips and knew he was talking about the Kade party, the one I hadn't been informed about. Then again, I shouldn't have been surprised. Mason and Logan disappeared after Tuesday. They were with their mother the whole week. James went to their hotel one night, but Analise and I hadn't been asked to go along.

I never heard from them the rest of the week. A part of me tried to be reasonable. They were busy. They had lots of practices and I knew both were intent on demolishing Roussou, tonight's game.

It made sense why I had slipped their minds.

I groaned and let my head fall back with a thump against my locker. It made no sense. They should've called me, or texted.

"Hey." A soft voice spoke and I opened my eyes. Adam stood in front of me with a grim look on his face.

"Hey."

He looked around. "Do you think we could talk somewhere?"

I gestured for him to lead. I had no idea where to go.

He gave me a small grin before he started off and looked back every now and then to make sure I was following behind. As we passed the bathroom, Lydia and Becky popped back out. Their eyes went wide again and there was a repeat performance from before. They scurried back in with hands over their mouths and heads together.

I rolled my eyes and saw a mirrored reaction on Adam's face.

When he pushed open a door, I saw we were in some room with televisions, keyboards, and computer screens loitering around. Cords were everywhere. "What is this?"

"It's where the media geeks hang out."

"Won't they need this room?"

"I don't care. They won't come in until we're done."

And with those words, an awkward silence fell over us. I looked at him, he looked at me. Neither of us spoke. So I slumped down on some couch. When did the media geeks get a couch for their room? Then I stopped caring as Adam cleared his throat and fiddled with his thumbs.

"Just say what you need to say, Adam. We can leave as soon as you're done."

He expelled a deep breath. "That's the thing; it's harder to do this than I thought it would be."

"To do what?"

His eyes found mine and pierced me. "To apologize. I've been trying to do it all week, since Tuesday, but I couldn't muster the courage."

"You need courage to be nice to me?"

He laughed. "I need courage to humiliate myself for you again."

I frowned. Humiliate?

He ran a hand through his hair and rubbed at his jaw. "Look, I'm real sorry about everything that's happened. I've been a huge ass and I know that doesn't even cover how I've been towards you."

I looked away. Did I want to hear this? Then I sighed. It didn't matter. Here it went...

He continued, "You know that I liked you, I still do if I'm being honest. When I found out that you were tight with the Kade brothers, I went crazy. I was jealous and I was a prick and you have every right to never talk to me again. I was acting like a spoiled douche bag that didn't get his prize."

I looked down. "I think that's putting it mildly."

He chuckled. "Yeah, probably. Look, Mason had every right to knock me out. I said something horrible about you to him."

My head jerked up. "What'd you say?"

He choked on his next words. "What? He didn't tell you?"

"No, he didn't so you tell me. What'd you say?"

He grimaced. "I'd rather not."

"Adam."

"You're going to hate me even more now. I thought you knew."

I couldn't ignore how he kept looking at the door. "Adam. Speak now."

He groaned and messed up his hair. "Oh—fine. I might've mentioned something about if he was dropping off his whore...or something like that. I'm not sure what word exactly I used, but it wasn't a nice one."

I swallowed a lump of coal down my throat. "And what'd he say in return?"

"Besides the punch? He might've said something like I looked pathetic, I'm not sure. That whole day was jumbled up to me. I was stupid that day, real stupid. I deserved what happened to me."

"You deserve to get hit again, if you ask me."

He grimaced. "I know and I'm sorry. I'm really sorry. My dad asked me what I said to piss off Mason Kade. When I told him, he said the same thing. He said I was being stupid and then my mom told me I was acting like a spoiled brat."

"Why were you? I never told you I was going to date you."

"See, that's the thing." He sat on another couch and cursed when a bunch of cords obstructed his way. He shoved them aside. "I thought maybe you didn't want to date me because you weren't over Sallaway. I thought you needed time and I was going to try and give that to you. I wanted to give that to you, but then I saw how Kade handled you. Literally handled you at their party and I went crazy. I couldn't believe that ass—" He stopped as he saw my face. "I'm just real sorry. I am, Sam. And I'd really like for you and me to be okay. I know Becky's been hammering at my ass since day one with you. She won't let it go."

"So are you here for me or for her?"

"Both," he groaned. A grin slipped past his lips. "Miranda is livid with me. She wanted to upstage you, but the whole thing between me and Mason made it impossible for her to do what she wanted. I kept telling her it wouldn't work. You wouldn't care."

"What was she going to do?"

"I'm not sure what it was, but she was sure you were going to get mad."

"How would you know I wouldn't care?"

He threw me a look. "Because you don't care about anything. It's your M.O. You don't give a damn and no one can touch you because of it."

I folded my arms over my chest. "Really?"

"Yeah. I think that's why you go on those long runs, so you don't feel anything."

My foot twitched as he said that. Since Mark told me about the party, I was planning on going for a run as soon as I got home after school. Being numb got me through every day. Why mess up a good thing?

"So...are you still pissed at me?"

I started laughing and once I started, I found that I couldn't stop. I bent over and continued to laugh into my knees. My shoulders were shaking so much. Then sobs started to come and I couldn't stop them either.

"Sam?"

I couldn't respond. Tears flowed freely down my face, but I kept laughing. They started to blend in a form of hiccups that my body kept bursting out with.

"I'm really confused. Are you okay?" He sat beside me and I felt his hand touch my back. He jerked it up right away, and then touched between my shoulder blades again. "Are you okay?"

I wasn't. My word, I wasn't.

The laughter subsided and I kept crying. I couldn't stop the tears. Each sob wracked its way through my body and then Adam turned me into him. I couldn't help it. I knew I shouldn't have, but I burrowed into him and more and more sobs kept wreaking havoc over me. He patted my shoulder and then held me against him. He lowered his head so his chin rested on my shoulder and he murmured against my neck, "Let it all go. Let it out. It's the only way. Let it all out, Sam." His hand started to rub circles on my back.

"Oh my god. I'm sorry." I pulled away and wiped at my cheeks. I couldn't believe I'd done this. "I've been a mess lately."

He frowned and his lip twitched. I knew he had something to say, but he held it back. Whatever it was, I didn't want to hear it. I couldn't handle it so I stood and backed away.

"Sam, you can cry, you know. I'm here for you. Anytime. Call me and I'll come get you. I promise."

He seemed so sincere. Something dark filled me and I shook my head. "And when you see me with Mason again? What are you going to do then?"

His hands pressed against his side and his shoulders straightened. He kept his voice neutral. "Nothing. I promise. I won't do a thing anymore." Each word seemed to bring him pain. "If you want to be with him, then so be it. I wish you happiness."

He looked away and his jaw clenched.

It wasn't over. "You might mean your apology now, but nothing's really changed. You hate that I'm with him—"

"If you're with him then why are you crying on my shoulder?" he bit out. "He's not here for you. Have you ever cried on his shoulder?"

"This was good timing for you."

"Like hell it was! You broke down in front of me. I rather doubt there are a lot of people that you've broken down in front of. You're always so in control of your emotions, but not now. You let me in. That's what happened here. You trust me, even if you don't know it, you trust me. I know you do."

"Stop." The word slipped from me. My voice was shaky.

"Sam, think about that." He held a hand out to me and I couldn't bear the sight of his pleading.

I shouldered away his hand and slipped from the room. As soon as I had collected my bag, I bolted from school. The week had started with a bang and it ended with one. As soon as I got home, I went on a run and three and a half hours later I limped my way home.

I'd been running too much. It was starting to become unhealthy, but it did its job. I collapsed in my bed as soon as I left the shower. When I woke it was dark out and I grimaced in confusion. My phone peeled through the cool night air and it lit up my desk.

I groaned, but pulled myself up and stumbled to it.

Logan's name flashed across the screen.

I snapped it open, not sure if I was ready for this. I mumbled out, "Ello?"

"You didn't come to the game?"

"Huh?" I squinted at the clock. It was after nine? I should still be in bed. "Logan," I groaned. "I was sleeping."

"Our biggest game this season and you weren't here!"

"Oh god." I pressed a hand to my head. "You're not going away, are you?"

"No, look, I'm pissed. You should've been here tonight."

My insides started to stir awake. "Are you kidding me? How was I supposed to know? I haven't talked to either of you all week."

There was silence for a second. "You haven't?"

"No," I snapped out. "I had to hear from Mark Decraw that you guys are having a party tomorrow night."

"Oh...I'm sorry, Sam. I really am. I thought we told you about that."

"How would you? You'd have to communicate with me to do that."

"No, I thought, oh man, I thought Mason must've been talking to you since the two of you are..."

"Stop right there. We're not dating. We're not anything. For me to know what we are there'd have to be a conversation about it and I haven't heard a word from him so there's definitely been no conversation about that." My chest was heaving up and down. I patted at it. I needed to calm down.

My phone beeped in my ear and I cursed as I pulled it away. Mason had sent me a text: **Want to eat? I'm hungry.**

I groaned into the phone. "Is he there with you?"

"Who?"

"You know who."

"No," he sighed. "I was calling to chew you out, but that didn't turn out how I thought it would—"

"Where's Mason?"

"I don't know. I'm being honest. Some of the guys are headed out for pizza and then there's a party. I was going to see if you wanted to come with, but now I'm scared to ask you. Why? Did he call you now?"

"Yeah."

"Call him back. I'll see you tonight." His voice got cheery and the dial tone blared in my ear next.

I cursed as I glared at the phone. It beeped again and it was another text from Mason: **Are you home?**

Then I heard his voice in the hallway. "Sam?"

It wasn't long before my door was pushed open and he flicked my light on. I was blinded for a moment.

"Hey, did you get my texts?"

I snapped my phone shut and drew my robe tighter around me. "Yes."

He grinned and ran a hand through his wet hair. He looked like he'd showered. "You pissed at me because I haven't called all week?"

"Nope. Not at all. I cried on Adam's shoulder today."

His eyes narrowed and lingered on my face. "Did you?"

"Yep. I did."

"Okay. I don't know what to do with that. You want to get some food with me? There's a party tonight."

"Is there?" I cringed at the jealousy in my voice. It wasn't like me. "I'm sorry. I'm acting stupid."

His eyes took on a darker look and he shut the door behind him. He turned the light off and it wasn't long before his hand was on my knee. He murmured against my skin as he tenderly nudged me back down on the bed. "I'm sorry I haven't called this week. I am."

My neck arched when his lips found it. His hand swept from my cheek, down my arm, to my waist, and swept back up to cup my breast. I groaned when I felt his hand work its way past my robe and his thumb grazed over my nipple. His mouth replaced his thumb and I felt his tongue sweeping around it next.

He whispered against my breast, "It won't mean much, but I thought about you. All week. I wanted to do this and I knew if I called you, I'd come over and do this."

I braided my hands through his hair and pulled his head up. "Shut up."

He chuckled before his mouth slammed onto mine.

CHAPTER THIRTY-FIVE

He thrust in me a last time. My legs were wrapped around his waist and one of his hands held them up as the other braced himself on the bed above my head. My entire body lifted off the bed as my climax ripped through me. Waves of pleasure rode through me and I trembled as he held me in his arms. He trembled with me and then tucked me in front of him to curl around me. He tucked his chin into the crook of my neck.

When he yawned, his whole body yawned with him.

Something fluttered in my stomach at the feel of that and I laced my fingers through his. "No party for us tonight?"

He chuckled and his breath caressed my skin. "It's three in the morning. It's a bit late for that."

As he tightened his hold on my waist, my eyelids started to close, but my whole body felt renewed and invigorated. "Are you going to stay the night?"

He cursed and reached over me. "I need to set the alarm."

When he was done, I turned and slid one of my legs through his, the other was on top of his and I snuggled against him. He pressed a kiss to my forehead and my body tingled as he brushed back some of my hair.

"Your mom's not expecting you?"

"Nah. She knows we're out. She's not stupid. Logan probably won't go to the hotel either." He chuckled and skimmed a hand down my side. "He dropped that girl. Did you hear about that?"

"Tanya, the one Adam liked?"

He smirked. "The *other* one he liked, yeah. He dropped her after the game and went off with some other girl."

"He called me after your game. He was pissed I wasn't there."

He smoothed back some of my hair and ran a thumb over my cheek to my lips. "I wasn't sure if you'd come. I figured if you came, I'd want to bend you over." He grinned. "No offense, but you get in my head."

"Do I?" I grinned as I caressed up his arms. His muscles twitched under my touch.

He groaned and wrapped his arms around me to hold me tighter. He rolled to his back and pulled me on top. I laughed huskily as he ran his hands over my body. When he hardened between my legs, I closed my eyes to enjoy it. The heat was gathering again. As he smoothed circles on my back, I laid my head on his chest.

I was intoxicated with him and I murmured against his skin, "When do you have to get up?"

"In three hours."

His hands started to explore some more and when he dipped a finger inside of me, I was helpless. Desire coursed through me and I was soon throbbing again. It wasn't long before I had enough and sunk onto him. He responded quickly, but after he had thrust deep, he gasped and shoved me off.

"What?" The need for him was making me blind. I only wanted him.

"Condom," he rasped out. He rolled over and reached for one. As soon as I heard that wrapper, I reached for him again. When it was slid on, I raised my hips and sunk down again. I pushed him deep and he fell back with a groan. Then I rolled my hips and started a rhythm. His hands grasped onto my thighs and he pushed and pulled me until we were both gasping for breath. As my climax was nearing, I dipped my head and touched his lips with mine. His tongue swept against mine and took control of the kiss. A primal emotion took root. I was helpless against it. Our hips slammed against each other and we hurdled over the edge together. Waves exploded in me and I trembled as each rushed through me.

"Sam." It was a whispered caress from his lips before he placed a gentle kiss on my lips again. Then he held me against him as his own body trembled with mine. After our breathing had steadied, he murmured, "I only need two hours of sleep anyway."

I bit back a laugh and raised my head. "So now we sleep?"

His eyes were on my lips as his hand cupped the side of my face. And then he cursed. "I can't get enough of you."

"You *have* been gone all week."

"Yeah." His hand started to trace up and down my back now. "I think my mom's going to stick around for the month. She's got some friends that she wanted to visit. Dad's going to love that."

"I met my dad." I flushed as I said it. I hadn't meant to, but as soon the words left me, something lifted off my chest.

He met my gaze through the darkness. "You did?"

I nodded before I pressed my forehead to his chest. "He was here Tuesday night when I got back from a run. We didn't talk much."

"What'd you talk about?"

"He asked if I kept track of my achievements and I told him he could go home, I wasn't worth his time."

He chuckled, but then his hands skimmed down to my waist and he lifted me higher on him. He started to nuzzle underneath my chin and as the same need started to stir inside of me, I closed my eyes and surrendered. We both knew he wouldn't get any sleep.

And when his alarm went off, neither of us slept a wink. With a huge yawn, he rolled over and shut the alarm off before he slowly turned and sat on the edge of the bed.

I sat up and scooted against my headboard with the sheet gathered around me. "Are you going to be okay today?"

He shook his head and then shrugged. "Shower. Then I'll tell you."

When he stood from the bed, he checked his phone, cursed, and yawned again. I watched as he tried to shake the yawn away, but it didn't go anywhere. Then I realized I had one also. I was still yawning when he came back from the shower.

He came to the bed and bent down to press a kiss to my forehead. "I'm going to get some clothes from my room and take off." He swept a hand down the side of my face and lifted my chin. I gazed at him through sleep deprived eyeballs. They should've been sucking the moisture out of the air, but I didn't feel an inch of my exhaustion.

"Okay."

"I'll see you tonight?"

I nodded and my eyelids were already starting to droop as I nestled under the covers. I was faintly aware of my door opening, but my bed was so comfortable. I was asleep before it closed.

***

When I walked into the festival, I wasn't sure what to expect. I had never been one for school events so the sight of streamers, balloons, blown-up slides and fun houses wasn't what I had in mind. Booths were spread out everywhere within the school. They started in the parking lot with one for coffee and cappuccino and one was even snuggled in a back janitor's closet for Fallen Crest Academy flags.

Little kids darted around my feet. I saw more than enough of my classmates and our teachers positioned everywhere. When I passed the football booth that had footballs with Fallen Crest Academy's name on it and made with our colors, I saw David chatting with some parents. Then I realized they had old varsity jackets on and knew these were the alumni.

I wandered through the entire school, even up to the third floor, before I found Mason. He had been tucked near the art room behind a table of white lacey doilies. He was lounging back in his chair, his arms crossed over his chest, his legs crossed underneath the table, and his cap pulled low enough to cover his eyes. As his chest rose up and down at a steady rhythm, I enjoyed the sight for a moment before I kicked his feet.

He jerked back, startled, and threw back his cap. A snarl lit over his face, but he relaxed when he saw me. "I didn't know you were coming today."

"What if I'd been my dad?" I shrugged. "Why not come, it's my school."

He grunted. "What does he expect? He stuck me up here selling some church ladies' handkerchief things. No one wants these." He eyed the coffee in my hand. "You got another one of those?"

I grinned and pulled out an energy drink.

"Thanks." Then he nudged the other chair out. "Want a seat? Keep me company?"

"So you can sleep and I'll sell the doilies?" I was aware of his hungry gaze as I sat beside him. Every nerve in my body was awake and kicking because of it. Who needed coffee when I had him?

"No one wants to buy from me. I look angry when I'm tired."

As he yawned again and tried to cover it with his hand, I thought he looked adorable. His eyes were softer from the fatigue and his eyelids drooped a bit. His lips were a little swollen from our kisses and his skin looked bright with color. When I caught sight of the hickey I'd left under his shirt's collar, I reached over to tug his shirt to the side.

He grinned when he realized what I was doing. "Yeah, I keep moving my shirt too, but it always goes back. I'm sure people have already seen it."

"I hope not." What if David had seen it?

"Who cares if they do?" He studied me as he said that.

"What? I'm supposed to say something or...what?" Was he testing me?

He cracked a grin and squeezed my knee. "I'm messing with you, but I don't care if they see it or not."

I'm not sure how to react so I grew quiet and sat back. After a few minutes, I knew he'd fallen back asleep, but it was a relief. His presence affected me so much. I had a hard time making clear decisions, especially when it came to him or us. After an hour and after I had sold three doilies, I nudged his foot. His eyes opened and he was awake, just like that. There was no sudden movement, no snort. Sometimes he reminded me of a machine.

"I'm going to wander around."

He groaned. "Please stay. You make this somewhat bearable."

I grinned at him. "Could you be more dramatic?"

"Yes."

Something bolted inside of me when I saw he spoke the truth. He was unreadable again and my finger itched to reach out and touch his lips. Those delicious and earth-shattering lips that could do wonders on me... I shook my head to clear the lustful thoughts.

His eyes had darkened as he watched me. "You want to go to my car? I have a lunch break coming up."

"Your car? Now that's romantic."

"It's the best I can do. I don't know this place and I'm pretty sure every hidden nook and cranny is being used."

I arched an eyebrow, but I saw the teasing light in his eyes. Oh how those eyes could unravel my wardrobe in a heartbeat. "I'm going to get some more coffee."

"Get me some?"

I nodded and moved past him. He leaned forward and his hand grazed the back of my thighs as I went.

A jolt of lust coursed through me, but I readied against it. It was a feeling that I was starting to grow accustomed to, but as I pushed into the bathroom, I wasn't ready for the sight I saw in the mirror. The girl who looked back had sex-crazed written all over her. Her lips curved up in a seductive tease with a blush to her cheeks. And the lust in her eyes had darkened them so they wore an unrecognizable gleam. My skin glowed and I touched it in wonder.

Who was this stranger?

The door shoved open behind me and I turned away, but I was too late.

Cassandra laughed abruptly as she stood beside me and washed her hands. She eyed me in the mirror. "Who've you been banging, Strattan? You look good."

I flushed under her gaze and watched with helpless horror as my skin seemed to glow even more. "Maybe I should be asking you that. How are things with Adam?"

She snorted and reached for a paper towel. "I think you'd know more about that than me. He told me you two made up yesterday."

I looked down at my hands. Had we? Maybe...

She continued as she patted her hair, "I'm not stupid. I know he wants you, he's always wanted you, but you don't want him." She snorted again. "And he doesn't have a chance against the Kades. I'm just waiting until he realizes that and gives up."

I looked back up. She was so cold.

She shrugged and smiled brightly. "What do I care? It's not like I really need a serious boyfriend now anyway." She laughed to herself. "And I heard Logan's back on the market. He was at Fischer's again with some other chick."

Every cell in my body had snapped to attention when she came in. I spoke through stiff lips now. "Maybe Adam will want Tanya back?"

She tossed her hair over her shoulder and her laugh seemed genuine. "Yeah, right. Adam didn't even like her that much. No way he'll take her back after Logan had her twice over him. Hell, he did it to rub it in Adam's face that he could get any girl he wanted." She eyed me up and down in the mirror. "You haven't been with Logan, have you? That'd be surprising."

My eyes grew wide at her suggestion and my chest was suddenly so heavy. There was no way she could guess the truth; she was so close to it... My heart started to pound in my ears again.

"Have you?" She blinked at me. She seemed more earnest now.

"No." The disgust was evident in my voice as I spat out that word.

She relaxed and laughed again. "Oh, for a minute I thought...Nah. You don't have the stones to do that. I mean, your dad would freak for one."

My heart continued to pound.

Then she finished with a taunt, "And you'd never live down your new rap as a whore. Everyone would call you a whore." She smirked to herself in the mirror and finished patting her hair. "On second thought, get to it. Maybe Adam will finally let you go. I could use the break."

As she swooshed from the bathroom, I was barely aware of her departure. I kept hearing her words. *Everyone would call you a whore.*

I gulped and looked down. My hands had started to tremble again. My knees quaked against each other and I clung to the sink to steady myself.

Everyone would call you a whore.

What was I doing?

CHAPTER THIRTY-SIX

When I left the bathroom and headed for the coffee cart, I wasn't sure what I was feeling. Was I worried about everyone finding out about Mason and me—yes. Was it enough to paralyze me with fear—no. With that decision made, I was more annoyed than normal when I snapped my order to the girl behind the coffee counter.

"Whoa, what's wrong?"

I stopped in my tracks at the sight of Adam. And then I tried to force myself to relax. "Hey, how are you?"

"You okay?" His eyebrows were arched high with his own cup of coffee in hand.

I rolled my shoulders back. "Yeah, I'm fine or I will be."

"Huh?"

"Nothing, just an annoying run-in with Cassandra in the bathroom."

"Ah." He nodded his head. "Gotcha. She does that to me too."

"I think she's decided to try her luck with Logan again."

"Yeah, she told me the same thing." Something sad flashed in his eyes. "It won't work, will it?"

I shook my head. "Nope and if it does, I'll tie him down and do a drug test on him."

He grinned. "Yeah, you seem pretty tight with both of them."

"I guess..." I eyed him warily. We were treading into forbidden land, could he handle that reality? He couldn't before.

He spread his hand wide. "Hey, I'm okay with this. Really. I've given up on that, but I won't for your friendship. I'm going to do whatever it takes to keep your friendship."

An arm was thrown around my shoulders and Logan's body fell hard against my side. He smirked. "Really?"

Adam drew to his fullest height and the gentleness in his eyes vanished. A hard look entered instead when he clipped out, "Really."

Logan's body shook in silent laughter. "You just want to keep her friendship, huh?"

"You got a problem with that?"

"Yeah, I do. She's going to be my sister, man. You think I want a parasite hanging around her because that's what you are. You're one of those guys who sit back and wait for the guy to screw up. When she's hurting or lonely, you guys swoop in. Hell, I should tip my hat to you guys. I couldn't do it. I couldn't wait around and watch the woman I wanted be with another guy, waiting until there's a break with them, until she's vulnerable." He mocked him. "Yeah, it must take a special kind of guy to do that."

Adam's eyes had narrowed to a dangerous level. His hand was clenched into a fist, but he kept it down and pressed against his side.

Logan continued, "Or maybe that's what makes creepers. I've got a different viewpoint on stalkers now."

Adam's lip curled up as he tried to mask a sneer. "You're calling me the creeper? What are you doing?" His eyes pointedly slid to me and it took Logan a second before he launched himself forward. His arm was thrown back, his fist ready, and look of hatred came to his eyes.

Adam's eyes went wide as he saw it in slow motion, but before Logan's fist connected, Mason tucked an arm around his chest and threw him backwards.

He cursed as he tried to twist away from his hold. "Let me at him, Mase. Come on."

Shaken, Adam puffed out his chest and smoothed his hands down the front of his pants. "Hey, man. If it weren't true..."

Mason glanced over his shoulder. The look of warning made Adam shut his lips. "Shut up or we'll do round two, somewhere private."

Logan threw over his brother's shoulders, "Where there won't be teachers or some girl to save you."

Mason glanced at me and I narrowed my eyes. There was a searching look in him. I lifted my chin. What was he looking for? Then I tried to search inside of him. What was he thinking?

He blinked and the look was gone. The normal unreadable wall was back in place. He threw Logan in front of him and neither seemed to care about the crowd that had formed or who Logan ran into.

Adam seemed frozen in place.

Cassandra's voice came from behind me. I gritted my teeth as I heard her coo, "Logan, are you okay? Did he hurt you?"

Logan barked out an ugly-sounding laugh and shoved her to the side. "Back off. You've got no chance."

I tried to suppress a smile at that, but couldn't so I looked down.

"Oh shut up," she cried out in anger. "You do not laugh at me, whore."

My head came up and my eyes widened. Her fury was directed at me. She approached with two steps and a hand in the air. "You dare to laugh at me? Do you know who I am? Or what I could do to you? I would demolish you, slut. I would run your name through the mud so much you'd beg me to let you out of your misery. You'd be—"

Something snapped inside of me and I marched up to her. I knew my eyes were dead when they met hers and she shrunk away, a little bit. "You think you scare me? Nothing scares me. Nothing, Sullivan."

"Whatever." She tried to laugh it off and turn away.

My hand clasped onto her arm and I whirled her back around. I was in her face and all the hatred I had boiled to the top. "You want all the dirt on me. Here you go. I hope you take notes. My mom's a cheater. She left my dad for another guy and took me with. I was living with two guys who hated me because of that. Then I found out my boyfriend was screwing my best friend and my other best friend knew about it, for two years. Next bombshell—my dad's not my dad. Think it could get worse? It did. I had no one. No friends, no nothing. The guy who raised me all my life couldn't talk to me because of stupid legalities. Now my real dad's in town, my mom's hit me a couple times, and I'm screwing my future stepbrother. You think I'm scared of you?" A hollow laugh broke out of me. "I can handle anything you've got up your sleeve."

There was silence around me and then she belted out a hysterical laugh. "I knew you were sleeping with Logan. Of all—"

I slapped her.

Then I stood there and waited for her reaction. She gasped and reeled back with a hand pressed to her cheek. Her eyes bulged out and she was seething. "You just—"

My face was calm, devoid of emotion. I didn't feel a thing. "I did. What are you going to do about it?"

She watched me, torn for some reason.

My eyebrow lifted. "Are you going to hit back or are you going to tattle on me?"

The tension was thick in the air. I felt it swirl around inside of me and knew she could see the storm inside of me. I wanted her to hit me. I wanted to hit her again. I wanted a reason to unleash my hell on someone.

Her shoulders slumped forward and she looked down as she stepped back.

I clipped out, "Are you backing away from me?"

She looked up. I caught the scared look in them. Then she turned and was swallowed up in the crowd.

I stared after her and started to look around. Miranda Stewart stood there, so did the rest of the Elite. I met all of their gazes unflinching. One by one they looked away. When

I got to the last one, I was surprised to see pity in Adam's gaze.

"What are you looking at?"

His chest lifted up and down. "I told you. We're friends. I may hate your stepbrothers, but not you. Never you."

Logan bit out a curse. "Is he serious?"

Mason turned on him. "Shut up." He strode forward until he blocked me from Adam's gaze. His back was to me, like so many other times. "Message received, Quinn. You're not going anywhere, but neither are we."

Adam flinched, but a resolved look came over him.

Then Mason reached behind him and grasped my arm. He turned and led through the crowd, dragging me behind. Logan followed, but threw a few dirty looks behind him. He muttered under his breath, "Gonna bust your face open."

We hadn't gotten to Mason's car before David's voice hollered through the parking lot, "You can't leave, Mason. You agreed for the whole day and tomorrow."

Mason let go of my arm and cursed as he turned back around. Empty cars were parked all around us and a slight chill breezed around us after a soft rain. The cars were wet and small puddles had formed on the pavement. David approached us with a forceful stride. His jaw was clenched tight and his shoulders were thrown back.

He raked his gaze over me, but spoke to Mason, "You can't leave. That's part of your discipline."

Mason cursed at him. "Forget your little agreement. I'm not staying in there where my brother and your daughter get attacked. You've got a bunch of angry pussies on your team. They don't know when to shut up and leave things alone."

David's mouth turned into a frown. I felt his gaze over me again as he asked softly, "You were attacked, Samantha?"

I jerked away.

Mason stepped in front of me again. "Quinn's obsessed with her. That doesn't bode well with the rest of the girls in your school. She should switch to public school. We could protect her there."

458

David stepped around him and reached for my arm. "Sam, is this true?"

I hissed as I swung my arm away, but I sent Mason a searching look. What was he doing?

"Sam."

"What?" I wheeled to the only father I knew. "What do you want? The guys in there hate Mason and Logan. You were stupid to think this would work out and Mason could last the whole weekend."

David looked down. "I tried to steer him clear from them."

"It didn't work. Think of another plan, but surrounding him with those guys won't work, especially if he's alone. Logan and I were there to support him."

David's jaw clenched. "Who were they, Sam? Who targeted him?"

I wanted to throw my hands up in frustration. He wasn't hearing me. He didn't get it. "No one, but they don't mix. Mason, Logan, and me—we don't mix with this school."

"You've gone here all your life."

"I don't mix anymore."

"You don't want to go to school here anymore?"

Logan stepped forward and brushed me back with his arm. "She's not saying that, sir. Fallen Academy is a good school. Sam will be fine, but she's saying that you can't ask us to get along with your football team. It won't work, sir."

David looked between the three of us. He breathed in and out and then murmured, "So it's like that, huh?"

I closed my eyes. His hurt was evident.

He added in a quiet voice, "You're one of them, aren't you? I tried to tell you—"

My eyelids came back up. "Are you kidding me? Is this really about Mason and Logan or is this about you and mom? Why'd you want Mason to volunteer at the festival? Was it really because you needed the help or is it because you wanted one of James Kade's sons under your thumb, for even a little bit?"

"Sam." Mason touched my arm.

I whirled to him. "Back off."

He moved a step away, but there was no judgment in his eyes, only understanding. My heart jerked at the sight of that. I didn't want him to understand me. No one could. They'd only pity me instead.

He blinked and it was gone. His hand moved away from my arm.

David looked between the two us, but sighed. "Samantha, your mother said I could have joint custody of you—"

"My real dad's in town."

He had his mouth open and a sound choked out of him before he shut his mouth.

I glanced down. "She's lying to you, whatever's going on between you two about me, it's all a lie. She called my dad a week ago and he's in town. He wants to get to know me." I looked back up and tears had formed at the corners. "I'm eighteen in four months, David. None of this will matter anyway. I don't know why you're even going along with it."

"Because I care about you." He touched my arm instead. "You're my daughter, Sam. I raised you. It's never going to matter who your real dad is or what your mom says. I've been there since you were born. You're my family too."

The dam broke in me and I turned as I covered my face. David hugged me to him and I cried into his chest.

We stood like that for a while until Logan cleared his throat. "This is touching and all, but I'm uncomfortable right now."

I could sense the disapproval from David as I lifted my gaze. A smile touched the corner of my lips instead. "Get in touch with your emotions, Kade. It might do you some good."

He looked in pain. "Yeah."

Mason cleared his throat. "Can we go? The touchy-feeling scene is done."

David shook his head. "What my daughter sees in the two of you—"

"She's not really your daughter." Mason didn't blink as he leveled him with a look. "She comes from someone else and you were the one who swooped in to raise her, but like she said—she's going to be eighteen and it's not going to make a difference. It'll be her choice." He stepped forward and his chest touched my back. An arm curved around my waist and he pulled me against him before he kissed my shoulder where my shirt had been pulled to the side. His breath fanned against my skin. "And she's made her choice, a couple times now...with me."

David's face had turned to stone.

My stomach twisted into a knot and I felt it drop to my feet. I didn't know how to undo what he'd done.

Logan covered up a laugh behind us, but I knew he wasn't hiding back his smirk.

Then David bit out, "Why did you want me to know that?"

Mason fell silent.

My dad jerked forward a step. His eyes gleamed with some emotion I couldn't place. His jaw was so rigid. "You made a grand show here, Mason, and you wanted me to know that my daughter is sleeping with you. Congratulations. I figured it out long ago, but your delivery was in poor sportsmanship. Why'd you do it?"

"Do what?"

"Deliver your triumph how you did." David's eyes were unyielding. "You wanted to hurt me. You wanted me to know that she's sleeping with you. Why? Are you threatened by me? Do you think she'll listen to me if I tell her to dump you?"

Mason's arm stiffened around my waist, but he remained quiet.

David went on, "I don't like you. I don't like either of you, but I respect you as football players. I don't think you've ever been coached by someone that you respect and I don't think you've ever respected another man, even your father.

I've watched the two of you on the field. Everyone has in this state and you are both ruthless. You're the best and you make damn sure everyone knows it on the field, but the one thing that always strikes me isn't how good you both are, it's your level of respect. You don't respect anyone else on the field, but you respect the game. Every time I watch you, I think to myself what kind of men are you two? What motivates you?"

"You think you're the coach that we're going to respect? Did you raise Samantha with Disney movies too?" Mason's tone was mocking and it sent chills down my back. His arm wasn't moving around my waist.

David moved back a step and he sounded sorry when he spoke. "I think of the men you could've been under my watch. You would've been twice the men you are now."

Logan had grown quiet, but Mason let go of my waist and moved me behind him. He was face to face with my father now and his tone had gentled. "You think we're two kids who grew up with bad parenting, but you're wrong. I might not respect my dad, but I love him and I respect my mother. You've never met her. You don't know a damn thing about Logan and me, but you're reaching for straws. I don't like you, but you're a great coach. I've watched you too and I know you're a great coach, but your players don't respect you, sir. They listen to you because you motivate them, but don't misunderstand that. They don't respect you. If they did, Quinn would never treat Samantha how he does. She's a prize to him. You want to paint us as the bastards that grew up with no competition. You want to paint our dad as someone less than you, but you couldn't be farther from the truth. We grew up knowing who we're going to have to deal with during our lives and guys like you, guys like Quinn are a dime a dozen. They're around every bend in the road. Logan and I aren't stupid enough to buy the crap most adults try to sell."

He turned and met my gaze. I flinched under his stare, but held it. He was looking for something inside of me and I knew I couldn't look away. I couldn't quake or tremble so I settled my nerves, stood upright, and lifted my jaw. My eyes were hard as I stared back at him.

Mason turned back to my father. "I respect you as a coach, but I don't respect you as a man. You should've never let Sam go."

The fallen look on my dad would haunt me forever. That knowledge trembled inside of me and I turned away to press into Mason's arms. He swept me up and pressed a kiss against my forehead. As he deposited me in his vehicle, I didn't hear anything. Logan should've been laughing. My dad should've been yelling. I should've been crying, but there was nothing. Just silence.

It echoed throughout my body.

CHAPTER THIRTY-SEVEN

We went to their hotel. It was some ritzy place. I didn't care and I trudged behind them as we rode the elevator to their top floor. Of course they'd be staying in the top suite, it only made sense, but as we got there Mason pressed a different button. Logan got off and gave us a salute with a cocky smirk. "See you later." The elevators slid to a close on his words and we rode the elevator down two floors. It stopped on the one between and as it opened, I stepped back into Mason's side.

Garrett stood there, waiting for the elevator. His shocked gaze swept over me and then Mason. He murmured in a fake Southern drawl, "A bee's bit my asscheeks to be seeing you here. How are you?"

I pressed my forehead into Mason's side and his hand swept around me. He answered for me. "Who are you?"

"Her dad."

I flinched at his tone.

I heard the smile in Mason's voice. "Really?"

"Aren't you Helen's kid?"

"What about her?"

I jumped at the sudden intensity in Mason's voice, but his hand swept up and down my back. He held me against him.

"Nothing. I like your mother. She's quite a woman."

"I think so."

"So how do you know my daughter?"

Mason chuckled. "That's something you can ask her when she's ready for questions."

There was a heavy silence after that. I knew both of them were waiting for me, but

I shuddered and melted against Mason. His hand held me close and I felt a soft kiss on my shoulder.

I needed it. I needed all the support I could get at that point. Everything was out. It wouldn't take a genius to figure out that I never meant Logan, but Mason. I knew my whole school would be buzzing about my relationship and my father—David—what could I say about him? He was gone. I felt it in my bones. And now we saw my other dad...what did I even think about him?

He knew Mason and Logan's mom.

That was weird.

Garrett chuckled as the elevator opened on our floor. "You and your men, little girl. They're all waiting for when you're ready."

Mason hit the emergency stop and turned to face him. I had started to step off, but waited with a pounding headache and a tight chest. What was going to happen now? I wasn't sure how much more I could handle.

"What are you talking about?"

Garrett wiggled his eyebrows up and down and skimmed a hand over his face. "I figured it out, took me a second, but I forgot Helen was married to James Kade. It all makes sense now. So what are the two of you doing here? I'm guessing Analise doesn't know about this relationship... *is* it a relationship or you two kids bumping uglies to piss the folks off?"

Mason's smile was a veiled threat. "And it's your business because...?"

Garrett narrowed his eyes and studied Mason for a moment. My heart pounded in my ears as I waited. It seemed to stretch out into strained silence as the two stared at each other and then Garrett broke with a curve of his lips. He shook his head and stepped forward to unlock the emergency brake. "You got balls, kid. Helen would be proud."

As the doors started to slide close, Mason's hand stopped them. They retreated back and he narrowed his eyes this time. "You're the guy bumping uglies with my mom?"

Garrett's eyes widened a fraction. "How do you figure that?"

"She came to town for me, but she's staying because a friend of hers showed up. The timeline makes sense. You've got the floor below us."

"That's a leap, kid."

"Not a kid and it's not a leap if it's true." Mason's face was chiseled in stone. His eyes didn't twitch. "You're the guy, aren't you?"

The amused smirk vanished from Garrett and he pushed up from his leaning stance. He stretched to his highest height and moved a step closer. As he looked down his nose at Mason, a warning look came over him. "You could be breaking a few hearts if you start spreading that around."

Mason smirked and stepped back. His hand fell to his side. "She told me he was married."

My mouth fell down, but no sound came out. My heart was deafening now.

Garrett's eyes slid to mine. As the doors started to close again, he drawled, "Ya gotta keeper there, girlie."

When the doors had closed and the elevator moved down, Mason swept a hand around my back and propelled me towards one of the two doors on the floor. He slid his card in and opened it as I entered first.

I didn't look around before I whirled back to him. "My biological dad is cheating on his wife with your mom?"

Mason grinned as he started to shred his clothes, but it didn't reach his eyes. "I guess."

"Your mom is a cheater."

He toed off his shoes and grabbed my hand before he pulled me towards a king size bed in a corner of the room. As he sat down, he tugged me between his legs and looked up. "My mom's a bit hard when it comes to men, especially after what my dad did to her."

"She's the other woman." I slid my fingers through his hair and took hold. As he started to rest his forehead against my stomach, I raised his face to look up.

His eyes were bleak. "She wasn't before and it's complicated."

"It's always complicated."

"Your mom was the other woman too. My dad was the other man."

My heart started to pound again. When I heard a slight condemnation in his tone, I was breathless as I asked, "Is that what you think is normal?"

Would he cheat like they all did?

"Cheating?" A dark loathing flared over his face and I stepped back in reaction. It was intense. It rattled me for a second. "Cheaters are weak. They're selfish and they're cowards. No, I'm not a cheater and I never intend to be." He focused on me. "Why? Are you?"

A laugh ripped out of me. My hand reached for him again and I closed a fist over his hair. "After my mother, now my biological dad, and what Jeff did to me? Are you kidding me?"

His eyes softened and he slid a hand underneath my shirt. "People don't know what they're made of until they're tested. You need to pull yourself out of a situation and think of the collateral damages, if it's worth it."

"You speak from experience?"

He grinned and leaned forward to kiss my stomach. My shirt was lifted higher and he started to tug me down onto him. Both of his hands went around my back and up to my shoulders as he pressed me down. I sunk down and felt him harden between my legs. He kissed his way around my neck to my lips and whispered against them, "I had a girlfriend once."

I wound both arms around him and held him against me, tighter than I knew I could. "Oh yeah?"

"She cheated on me." He leaned back and waited for my reaction.

"What?"

He laughed and nipped at the corner of my mouth. His lips nibbled their way around my lips before he opened against them. His tongue touched the corner of my lips and I opened for him. He swept inside and his hand gripped the back of my head to hold me still. The ache started to throb inside of me and I squirmed against his lap. I needed to get closer, I had to.

Then he pulled back and fell against the bed. He gazed at me with lust in his eyes. They darkened as he nudged me higher on his waist. "My friend, Marissa. She cheated on me."

"Are you joking?" I frowned at him.

He laughed and lifted my shirt over my head. "Yeah, I am about her. I didn't date Marissa. I had a few other girlfriends and most of them cheated, but I wasn't surprised. I wasn't dating them for their caliber, if you know what I mean?"

"You didn't cheat on them?" His hand slid to my back and he tipped me down to him. I was breathless as my head landed on his shoulder where I turned and licked. My body stretched as his hands slid to my bottom. He cupped my cheeks and grinded me against him.

"I've never cheated. Being faithful was one thing I valued as I grew up. I made my mind long ago that I'd never be like my dad. I'd never do that to a woman I respected, even to someone I didn't respect. I won't lower myself to those standards."

I whispered against the side of his mouth, "Logan cheats."

He caught my mouth with his and whispered back, his lips brushed against mine, "Not if he loves the girl and I don't give a damn what he does." Then his mouth took command of mine and I was lost after that.

I tipped my head back, but I was blind with lust. As his hand slid to my pants and he slipped two fingers inside of me, my throat was full. I couldn't talk anymore and I groaned when he rolled me underneath him.

Thirty minutes later, after Mason arched over me for his last thrust, my body collapsed onto the bed and I waited as the waves rode over me. He groaned and fell onto me. I welcomed his weight. He entrapped me, but I felt sheltered. Safe. My legs felt heavy with exhaustion and slid down the length of his to fall onto the bed.

It wasn't long after that when he propped himself on an elbow beside me. My throat was still thick with desire and I gazed at him. My fingers twitched to touch the side of his face, to feel how soft his eyelashes were, the slight stubble on his chin, the dip in his shoulders where his muscles attached together...I wanted to touch all of him again.

I struggled to clear my throat and asked in a hoarse voice, "Is it always like this?"

He shook his head in a slow motion. "No. It's not." His eyes darkened again and he bent down to me.

I tipped my head back and met his lips with mine. It was a soft kiss, but it didn't deepen into more because a soft beep sounded before the door swung open. Mason cursed and jumped to block me from whoever entered.

"You better put some clothes on because if you think that sheet's going to keep me from having a word with your new girlfriend, then you're not the son I thought you were."

Mason cringed. "Mother, leave."

"I want to talk to her—"

He spoke over her, "We will come upstairs to have this conversation."

She laughed and the sound gave me chills. There was an intelligent shrewd tone in her voice, but the anger sat me up in attention. "With Logan to interject with his snide comments, I think not. This conversation will happen without your brother's snarky attitude. You think I'm a fool so the three of you can team up against me? I'm no fool, Mason James. Logan likes your litty bitty. He's told me that he supports the two of you." She drew in an angry breath. "I'm not having it."

"Fine, mom." Mason had been holding a sheet in front of him and let it drop. "We'll have it out like this."

"Put something on," she hissed. "I'm not some high school cheerleader you can intimidate or make me squirm by showing your penis. I've seen it before. I was the one who changed your diapers."

He bit out a laugh and sat down instead. He gathered the sheet around his lap again, but kept his back to me.

"Oh for the love of your grandfather, she's going to have to face me at some point. Get some clothes, Mason. I've been waiting all week to meet Analise's daughter. It might as well be now," her tone gentled.

Mason's shoulders stiffened. "It's not going to happen like this, mom. Go upstairs. We'll be up in a few minutes."

There was a silence that filled the air with more tension. Then she sighed. "You're not going to budge, are you?"

"And you're not going to come over and move me."

"You're as stubborn as me." She bit out a laugh that resembled Mason's. "I don't know if I should curse your genetics or mine. Fine. Be upstairs in five minutes, not a minute late or I'm coming back down."

When the door shut, he looked back and grimaced. "She's been after us all week to call you. She's the real reason we didn't call."

I drew my knees against my chest and hugged them tight. "Why does she want to meet me so much?"

"Now it's because of this, but it was about revenge against your mom before."

"Revenge?"

He ran a hand over his face and looked exhausted. His shoulders slumped and he let out a deep sigh. "My mom's not dumb. She's known about Analise since she was poking around dad. And knowing that the guy she's been seeing is your biological dad, I'm not too surprised. My mom can be calculating, Sam."

I swallowed over a painful knot. "Why did she want to see me before so much?"

He stood and started to pull some clothes on. As he poked his head inside of his shirt and tugged it down, he remarked, "I think she wanted you to like her more than your mom. Logan and I haven't been quiet. She knew you weren't happy with Analise any more than we were. But now…" He trailed off as he looked towards the door.

"But now," I prompted.

He shook his head and bent to grab my clothes. He handed them over as he sat beside me again. "I have no idea."

As I fitted my bra on and reached back to clasp it, I muttered, "I bet she thinks I'm like my mom now."

He didn't respond.

I looked up and saw the pity in his eyes.

"Don't," I hissed at him. "You don't feel sorry for me, not now after all the crap that's happened to me."

The corner of his mouth curved up. "You don't know my mom."

"I know you respect her." I held his gaze for a long drawn out moment. "I know you love her and you want to protect her."

"I did." He leaned forward and kissed me. "But that was before I realized something."

"What's that?"

He stood and waited until I pulled on my underwear and jeans to tug me beside him. Then he drew me in his arms for a tight hug and spoke against my shoulder, "I'm pretty sure my mom went after your bio dad to get back at your mom."

I lifted my arms and hugged him back. "Why do you think that?"

"Because in my mom's thinking, Garrett's the only guy your mom couldn't get."

"Why do you think that?" I leaned back and looked up.

He ran a finger down the side of my face in a gentle caress. "It's something I might do, if I was pissed off enough."

"If that's true, then…" A stone dropped to the pit of my stomach and a cold feeling started to sweep through my body. "Then you're right. I should be scared of your mom."

He grinned down and lifted me so I wrapped my legs around his waist. Our eyes met and held as his hand spread out over the bottom of my back. He leaned forward and nipped at my lips. I grinned and caught him in a deep kiss when he did it again.

When he started to walk out of the room and to the elevator, he sighed against my lips, "I won't let her do anything, Logan too." He breathed against me again. "I think that's why she's so mad. We won't let her hurt you."

When the elevator rose to their floor, he set me on my feet. The door opened and he took my hand in his. "You ready for this?"

I gave his hand a squeeze.

CHAPTER THIRTY-EIGHT

When we entered the top suite, I drew in a deep breath and let go of Mason's hand. He glanced back, but I shook my head. I needed to do this on my own, somewhat. Logan sat on a couch in the corner. He had two bags of chips on the table in front of him, a small television in his corner, and a cooler beside him. His smile couldn't be wider on his face and when he saw our entrance, his hand slid into the cooler. It came back up with a beer and he started to chug half of it down.

"Are they here?"

I flinched at the tone of their mother. When no one answered, she came around the corner. Her hand was raised to fix an earring in place. When her eyes lit on me, her hand fell down in slow motion. She straightened and crossed her arms over her chest as she lifted her head high and her shoulders were squared.

For a moment, I was speechless. She was beautiful. She had a model's body, tall and lean with long legs. She wore a white business skirt with a pale pink cashmere sweater over it. A necklace of white diamonds rested above her cleavage. They matched the diamonds in her ears and I caught a flash from her wrist. My eyes couldn't get any bigger at the sight of the diamond bracelet there. Even her pale pink high heels shimmered from the diamonds on their straps.

She had golden blonde hair, which looked streaked from sunlight and that rested high in a loose bun. Tendrils fell to the nape of her neck and with her clear blue eyes; she looked the image of a goddess. But her lips had formed into a sneer as she took her time to study me in turn.

Her wrist flicked at me with irritation. "This is Analise's daughter?"

Logan choked out a laugh, but guzzled some more of his beer.

Mason and their mother threw him a glare. He sank back against the couch and raised a hand across his lips. They were zipped.

Mason frowned at him, but sighed. "Yes, mother. This is Samantha."

Someone buzzed on the door and Logan jumped to his feet. He scurried around the room to open the door. Garrett Brickshire straightened as he viewed the room dressed in a navy blue suit. He'd been leaning with an arm near the top of the door.

"What's he doing here?" Mason rounded to his mother.

Logan's eyes widened. His smile grew and he hurried back to his seat. He picked up a bag of chips this time and started to munch on them.

Their mother grimaced, but swept past us. She rested a hand to Garrett's chest as his lips skimmed a kiss to her cheek. She gave Mason a small smile. "I figured it's appropriate. He is her real father after all, and you know about the two of us. We can deal with two birds with one stone tonight. Mmmm? Don't you agree?"

Mason glanced at Logan. "You okay with this?"

He made a show of showing his zipped lips again and shrugged.

"Thanks." Mason didn't hold back a wry tone to his voice.

Logan bobbed his head up and down as he reached for another beer.

And then there was another buzz at the door. Helen frowned as she walked to it and peered through the peephole. "Who could that be—oh my god." She turned back with a panicked look on her face. Her chest started to rise and fall at a rapid pace and she seethed at Mason, "Were you behind this?"

"What—no..."

Garrett rubbed a hand over his jaw and shook his head. A low baritone chuckle escaped him. "Now, darling, it only seemed appropriate for me to call her. She is my daughter's real mother after all."

"Garrett," she snapped and cursed at him. "Now's not the time to be charming."

He lifted a shoulder and arched an eyebrow before he perched on a couch's end. "Answer it, darling. They're going to find out anyway and it might as well be now. They can't be angry at us later for withholding information. I know Analise would throw that at me."

"Mom, what's going on..." The words died in Mason's throat as she opened the door and his father walked in, followed by my mother. Both of them wore reserved expressions, but when Analise saw Garrett, she sucked in her breath. Her face stretched at every angle over her skull. She looked in pain and then her eyes swung towards Helen. A confused look replaced the horrified one.

Logan groaned behind us. Something that sounded like a mix of laughter and curses slipped out. He snorted next and pressed his head into a couch cushion as his shoulders shook.

"Honey, what are you doing here?" Analise asked me. She was cold and formal.

"Helen? Why are we here?"

All eyes turned towards James, who was frowning at Mason.

Garrett stood from his perch and stretched to his fullest height. "She didn't call you. I did."

Analise jerked forward with fists clenched to her sides. "Why?"

He swung his head towards us. "Ask them. I was doing my fatherly duty." His lip curled up in a mocking manner.

"Sam?"

"Mason?"

"Garrett, what are you doing here? Sam, did you call him?"

I choked on my own vomit. "Are you kidding me?"

He drawled out again, "Nah, the girl doesn't want anything to do with me, Lise. You did a good job. She hates the sight of me."

I ducked my head and wished I could disappear. This was not somewhere I wanted to be.

"Why? What did you do to her?"

"Honey," James tone was soothing. "We were called here for a reason. Helen, you weren't behind this?"

She choked out an angry snort. "Are you kidding me? I'd like to handle our sons without your interference."

"And why would you have to handle them?" His tone cooled. "Mason? What is your mother referring to?"

Analise's look was filled with loathing as she glared towards Garrett. "Why in the world are you here?"

Helen's laughter peeled out this time. "I can take credit for that one, Analise." Her lip curled up in disdain. "You're going to find out anyway. Everything's going to come out now."

"What are you talking about, Helen?"

"Helen, let's spare some of the sordid details."

She threw a seductive grin towards Garrett. "I think I'm going to have to. Your ex doesn't look like she can handle all the details, not just yet anyway."

My mother paled and she jerked forward a step. "What are you talking about? Garrett, what is she talking about?"

He threw his head back and rolled back his shoulders. A cocky smirk came out. "I'm leaving my wife, Lise. I fell in love with someone else." And he threw a pointed look towards the middle of the room.

Analise seared everyone with a glare. "And why do I get the feeling you're not talking about your daughter?"

Helen smirked and poised with a hand to her hip. "He's talking about me, *Lise*. We were going to wait until his divorce was final, but we're engaged." And with that, she flipped a ring around on her finger. The diamond was double the size of my mother's. It sparkled as she wiggled her fingers around. "You like it? It matches the rest of my accessories. Only another woman can appreciate my outfit."

Mason groaned next to me and sat on the couch beside Logan. He passed the chips and the two munched away.

Analise gasped as the information sunk in and James cursed under his breath. He pulled his fiancé back with a hand tucked around her arm. "Are you kidding me, Helen? And how did the two of you meet? I'm supposed to believe it was by chance?"

"Oh no." Helen oozed with arrogance. "You see, when you started to run around behind my back with her, I hired a private investigator. And I learned all sorts of things, including the biological father of Samantha Jacquelyn Strattan. From there, all the pieces fell into place. It wasn't even hard to get the man Analise never could. Garrett and I had instant chemistry—"

He grunted. "We did. Screwed on the first date." He shrugged then. "Of course, it helped that my wife had already cheated on me and I learned about it that day."

"Oh my goodness." Analise bent over as she started to pant. "Honey, I can't breathe."

There was a look of enjoyment in Helen's eyes that had me snarling. I shot to my feet. "They called you here because of me. I'm screwing Mason."

And then someone else buzzed at the door.

James bit out a curse as he wrenched it open. He stopped in shock as David stood there, with Malinda behind him.

David scanned the inside and turned back. It wasn't long before Malinda left and he stepped inside.

"Great." Analise was livid. "This is great. Where'd your girlfriend go this time? She's not here to support you?"

David frowned, but his eyes rested on me. A tinge of concern had seeped into them. "I can see this is a family-only matter. Malinda came with me for support if I should need it. Her son came as well. I believe he's attending a party in this suite later on."

Logan choked on some beer and struggled to keep it in. Mason belted him on the back.

"Who called you?"

David glanced around, but Garrett lifted another finger in the air. The look of amusement was evident as he couldn't hold back a grin. "I did. Again, I thought it was only appropriate."

"Garrett," Helen hissed. "Stop interfering."

He extended a hand towards me. "She's my daughter. I called her mother and the man who's her real father. He raised her all her life." Then he strode forward and shook hands with David. "I'm the sperm donor. Nice to meet you."

"You too." The two sized each other up and after a moment stepped back.

Analise rolled her eyes. "You two are okay with each other?"

Garrett gave her a polite smile. "We've both had to deal with you."

David added, "It's a bonding experience."

Logan choked back another laugh. When everyone turned to glare, he displayed his zipped lips again and stuffed a handful of chips in his mouth.

"You let them drink in the open?"

Helen turned, at a loss. "Excuse me?"

"They're underage, Helen. They aren't allowed to drink." He gestured towards his sons, who both had a beer in hand. "And they're throwing a party here tonight?"

"Well," she glanced towards Garrett. "I had no idea. I had dinner plans for the evening."

My mother cleared her throat. "Can we get back to the part where my daughter said she was screwing her future stepbrother?" She glared at me. "I'd love to hear how this came about and why no one else seemed surprised."

No one spoke a word.

Her head started to swivel around. As her eyes found James, he gave her an apologetic look. "I had my suspicions."

She gasped.

Garrett lifted another finger. "I knew too. I caught 'em in the elevator."

"You did not." My hands found my hips. "We were standing in there and you got on. End of story."

"He had his arm around you and he kissed your shoulder. It was pretty evident, sweetie."

I snarled at him, "I'm not your sweetie."

David cleared his throat. "I knew as well, Analise. I was going to tell you, but I had hoped for a family dinner of my own this evening first." His eyes held mine. I felt my stomach drop at the sorrow in them. "That didn't occur as I had planned."

I looked away, burning. What did it matter? What did he matter anymore? He let me go... A small voice in my head told me that he didn't, though. He had fought for me since the beginning. I swung back to him and he gave me a small smile for encouragement.

"Who else knew about them?"

Helen gave her a polite, but lethal. "I walked in on them. They'd just had sex."

"You're screwed, brother," Logan whispered out of the corner of his mouth. Mason shot him a look, but stood beside me. He regarded the group with a grave look on his face. "What do you all care about? I screw girls. You know this."

"Not your stepsister!" my mother cried out.

He bore her down with a look that silenced her. Shivers went down my back, but I didn't dare glance up. I didn't want to remember that from him. Then he taunted her in a soft voice. "You should be happy, Analise. My father isn't a mechanic and my mother's not a cashier at the local grocery store. Your daughter did well for finding a bedmate."

Logan hooted out in laughter now.

She flushed as she remembered her own words. "This is not right. The two of you should not be—"

Garrett rolled to his feet again. "You can't do a thing to stop her, Lise."

She whirled to him. "Shut up, Garrett. You've had nothing to do with her all your life. You have no right to start now—"

With two steps he was in her face. "I have every right. I had a daughter that I didn't know about. You kept her from me! You had no right to do that. Maybe it's my turn now. Maybe I should be her parent now."

She paled even further. "No!"

David stepped forward. "I wouldn't be averse to that. I've been in talks with Analise about sharing responsibility of Samantha. I've offered to pay for her college already."

"You have?"

"I have." His eyes gentled as he turned to me. "I wanted to talk with you about some of those plans I've made with your mother at dinner tonight."

"You did?"

"Well, that's just dandy! You all knew my daughter was boning her stepbrother and no one had the decency to call me?"

"Watch it, Analise. Your age is showing." Garrett smirked at her. "And I did call you."

David stiffened as he turned. "Why would I call you when you haven't had the decency to consult me in any matter? You wanted to take her from me completely. You wanted to wipe her from my life."

"She's a bitch, isn't she?" Garrett threw an arm around David's shoulder.

"She is." Then his lip turned downwards. "Samantha, as the man who has raised you all your life..." He glanced upwards.

Garrett gave him an approving nod and patted his shoulder.

David continued, "I have to ask if this is a cry for help? Are you with Mason because you wanted all of our attention?"

Helen snorted and crossed her arms again. "Well, she got it."

I glared at her, but gentled as I looked at my father. "It's not a cry for help, David. It's—"

"They're hot as hell for each other!" Logan shot to his feet. "I can't keep quiet anymore. You all are stupid idiots if you think that. Don't you know her? Don't you know Mason? My god, I'm embarrassed to call you *ass*-dults!"

"Logan," his mother hissed. "Shut up. You promised."

He flipped up his middle finger. "I don't care. I can't handle this. My game is talk. You tried to take that away." He shot an arm towards Mason. "He fights. I talk. That's the magic of our twosome fearsome. Sam's one of us, man. She's got the guts to do the dirty deeds if we don't. She watches out for us too. Ya'll are stupid if you didn't see this coming." He thrust his arms out wide. "The three of us are a magical team. No way are you screwing this up."

James asked him with a dry voice, "Really?"

Logan puffed up his chest before he downed the rest of his beer. "You don't know what it's like being a Kade. Sam does. She's conquered and proved her loyalty runs deep." He flinched. "Real deep if I'm guessing at how far Mason goes in her—"

"Logan, shut the hell up!" Mason smacked him in the back of his head.

He came back up with a brighter smile. "And I'm proven right, again! You guys should hire me for this talent I have. Mom, I bet you have a better sex life with that Garrett dude than you did with dad."

"Logan!"

He turned towards James. "And dad, I bet your sex life is pretty good with Analise. She strikes me as the slutty type."

"Logan!"

He grinned broadly. "And David, I don't know you that well, but you strike me as conservative. You're only going to be with a conservative woman, maybe one that looks exotic though. I can tell you have control issues. You don't like anyone who is wilder than you, probably why you had problems with your ex, huh? As for the current one, she's hot under the covers, but I don't know if you want her to be." He shook his head in sympathy. "You might want to take care of that."

David frowned as he looked away.

"And Garrett," Logan tsked tsked him in approval. "You're a wild one, I can tell. That's why I know Mason's got a good one. You and Analise both are hot ones in bed. I can tell. It's why my mom and dad like the both of you. Both of them are vanilla in bed, I bet. I'm sorry about that. I bet the two of you had wild sex together." He shook his head in wonderment. "Two of the same types rarely work out, too much drama. A wild one and a vanilla one always go the distance. They balance each other out."

Garrett chewed the inside of his cheek for a moment as he regarded the sudden outburst. Then he nodded in approval. "I like you. You speak the truth. Inappropriate, but the truth."

Logan puffed out his chest. Then the smirk dropped from his face and he clipped out, "Good. Then leave Sam and Mason the fuck alone. You've screwed up our lives enough."

Mason slid him a look. "I was going to get to that. I was waiting for the right time."

Logan looked annoyed. "Whatever. I had enough being quiet."

I slid my eyes towards him and he saluted me before he dropped back on the couch. "Continue on as you were..." He pretended to bow to them as he opened another beer, and passed one to Mason.

I caught mine as I sat on the couch with him.

Mason slid down beside me and Logan curled an arm around my shoulder. He drawled against my cheek, "It'll throw them off. Their visionary senses will tell them we're screwing and they'll get confused." His hand slid down towards my breast.

Mason warned, "Don't even try it, Logan. I'm the fighter, remember?"

His hand slid back up to my shoulder. He gave me a pat. "Threesome fearsome. No one stands a chance."

I grinned at him. "What about Nate?"

He tapped his beer with mine. "When he's around, it's the foursome fearsome. You can add any 'some to that name. Thank goodness, huh?" Then he groaned. "I really need to get laid tonight."

Mason tipped his head back. I felt the tension in his body and reached for his hand.

Logan leaned forward. "We might be having that party in your suite." Then we looked at the room as their voices were raised at each other. "Something's telling me the adults aren't going anywhere tonight."

My mom chose that moment to lift her hands in the air. "I don't care what you think I've done wrong in my parenting. I've been the one there for her all her life."

I closed my eyes. It was going to be a long night. I already knew it.

CHAPTER
THIRTY-NINE

The adults remained in the top suite so the party was moved down two floors when Logan paid for the other suite on Mason's floor. Text messages were sent out and soon the elevator had started to ring its arrival. The two doors were left open and it wasn't long before a swarm of people filled the floor. I had been with Mason and Logan for a while until their public friends started to show. After Ethan sent me a few frowns and narrowed glances, I took my exit and it wasn't long before I heard Becky's excited voice.

She squealed somewhere, "I can't believe this! This is awesome!"

When I stepped on a chair, I saw them inside the doorway and sent a text that I was near the kitchen. It wasn't long before Becky and Lydia pushed their way to me and landed with flushed faces.

"Hey, guys." I narrowed my eyes.

Lydia let out a silent burp and tugged her skirt down to flaunt her hipbones.

"You guys are drunk."

Becky flung herself at me for a hug. As she fell against me, she gurgled out, "Am not. Spoilshoret."

"We're not drunk." Lydia pulled her back and linked their elbows together. She puffed up her chest and flipped her hair over her shoulder.

"You are. I know what you look like when you're drunk and I can smell the booze on Becky's breath."

"So what if we're drunk?! It's Friday night. We're allowed." Becky seemed sure of herself. "And besides we're celebrating your awesomeness. Oh yeah. You're awesome.

You're the queen of being awesome. You are a god-dess, you are." Her head bounced up and down with each word and her smile grew at each nod. "And you're my friend. I'm so glad you're my friend."

"Mine too." Lydia beamed.

"Oh boy." I sipped the beer Logan made me take. "How are you getting home?"

Becky pointed a finger at me. "How are you getting home, missy? Or are you sleeping here...with your boyfriend?!"

"Yeah. Your boyfriend." Lydia giggled at Becky, who bumped heads with her.

"Don't worry," Adam's voice came from behind me. "I promised Becky's parents that I'd watch out for her. They weren't keen on letting her attend a Kade party, but I persuaded them. Plus, I think Lydia's staying at Becky's tonight anyway." He gave me a small smile, but I caught the apprehension in his depths.

"Thanks," I said lightly.

Lydia had been watching us and cooed, "You guys will make a great couple."

Becky nudged her.

"I mean, someday...maybe...not." She hung her head, but snapped back up with a bright smile. "I forgot to tell you. Jessica's hating you right now. She's so jealous of you. You got Logan Kade. Can you believe it? Well...I guess you can, but still—you're dating Logan Kade."

An arm was thrown around my shoulder and I closed my eyes. *Speak of the devil...*

I didn't need to look to know a very smug smirk was on Logan's face as he drew me against him. "When did this phenomenon happen?"

Becky's eyes went wide, but Lydia edged closer with a secretive smile. "Maybe about the time you realized you couldn't ignore her phone calls. I mean, she lives with you, right?"

Logan drew back with a frown. His arm tightened around my shoulders. "You're saying that I'm stuck with her?" He threw me a look. "Your friends suck."

Lydia flushed and moved back again.

Becky's mouth dropped open before she got red in the face. "Hey, I'm sick of people saying that Sam doesn't have good friends. I'm her friend. I'm her best friend, even if she doesn't know it, but I know I am."

Adam added, "She is. I've seen her in action."

Her finger jerked back up. "And you better treat her right, not like her last boyfriend. He sucks." She pounded her chest with a beer in hand. "I know. I'm his cousin. I can say that. And he cheated on her. He was a fool. You better not cheat on her, Logan Kade."

A look of admiration took root in his eyes, but he deadpanned, "And if I do?"

"I'm going to come for you."

He chuckled. "Really?"

She stepped forward and bumped her chest to his. The movement wasn't smooth and she would've tripped if Adam hadn't caught her elbow.

"You're right. You have ninja moves," he encouraged her.

"Stop," I said under my breath to him.

Then, with a different sounding laugh, he squeezed me against him again and kissed the side of my head. "No worries. I'll be your boyfriend for as long as you want me to be." He glanced at Becky. "I hope I won't meet you in a dark alley, little girl."

Her eyes rounded. "Really?"

"I've got moves too, little red." Logan shook his head and laughed under his breath before he tapped my arm once and left.

Lydia swooned, swaying on her feet. "I need dry panties."

"Lydia!"

Becky frowned at her.

Adam cringed behind them, but gave me a wry look. "Are you going to tell them?"

I shrugged.

"Tell us what?"

"Yeah, what?" They looked back and forth.

"Hey, dude!" Mark Decraw pushed his way through the crowd and slapped a hand on Adam's shoulder. "I've been waiting for you for an hour, man."

Adam grimaced. "Yeah, it took longer than I thought it would. Sorry about the wait."

"No worries. I scored some free drinks at the pool downstairs." Then his gaze swung wide and he took the rest of us in. His eyes widened a fraction when he saw me. "Hey, Sam. I heard upstairs got intense."

My eyes cooled. "Yeah..."

"You think everything's going to work out? You know, with you and M—"

"I don't want to talk about it." I folded my arms over my chest and waited. My heart started to pound. What right did he have to talk about my family struggles? He wasn't family. He didn't know a thing about it.

"Oh. Okay." He looked towards Adam and shifted to the back of his heels.

Adam looked around the room.

So did Lydia while Becky's eyes were glued to me as she mouthed, *What upstairs?*

Then someone laughed as they passed by. "Awkward!"

Lydia and Becky made eye contact and bent over giggling. Adam frowned more and he started to scratch his head.

I wasn't sure what I was supposed to do. Did I join in? Did I pretend I didn't know what Mark was talking about? Did I pretend I was friends with Adam again? I had no idea, but I did know that I was separate from the group now. My relationship with the Kades had shifted me higher than my friends, but if they were like this with the assumption that

I was sleeping with Logan, what'd they be like when they learned it was Mason?

I closed my eyes as I felt the urge to find the treadmill in the hotel's gym. It was already closed, but I was sure the Kade name had some pull.

"Oh hey," Mark tried to sound normal. He failed. "There's Pete and the crew. I'll see you guys later. Sam…"

I jerked my head in a stiff nod, but I couldn't keep the scowl from my face. Who did he think he was now because he was privy to information about my family?

Becky and Lydia's heads squashed together, but Adam tugged me backwards, away from them. He spoke in my ear, "Calm down. Mark didn't mean anything by it."

I hissed out, "He doesn't know me. He doesn't know anything and now he's talking to me about my life? Who the hell does he think he is?"

He gave me a pained smile. "He's my friend and he wants to get to know you."

"What?" I stared up at him. "Why?"

"Because he wants to break the news that he thinks his mom and Coach are going to get hitched, but he doesn't know how to."

"What?!" Everything in me sunk at that moment.

"Yeah." Adam raised a hand down the backside of his head and rubbed at his neck. "He thinks you should know, but I guess it's supposed to be a spontaneous thing. He's going to be family, Sam. And he's stepping out from Miranda's wrath."

I closed my eyes. I couldn't do anything else. And I stood there.

Adam reached for my shoulders to pull me close. I shrugged him off. And I could hear the bitterness in his voice. "Look, Stewart doesn't want any of us to be friends with you, much less talk to you. I told her to go to hell and so did Mark. He's doing this for his mom and for Coach and, in some weird way, for you too. He feels bad about your situation."

I spoke through gritted teeth, "I don't care about being in the Elite."

"I know. We all know that and I think that pisses Miranda off the most, but it doesn't change the fact. You've got another year at the Academy, much less the rest of this year. Look, the girls won't go against Miranda. They might not all agree with her, but they won't go against her. If you—"

A hand wrapped my waist and pulled me backwards. I closed my eyes because I didn't need to look. Heat and lust washed over me when Mason urged me to turn around with a hand on my hip. I met his gaze once and when I saw the smoldering depths there, I knew the game was up. I was swept against his chest and burrowed there as he started to rub my back while the other one cradled my head to him. He spoke over me, "You're starting to piss me off, Quinn."

Adam's hostility was evident. "I'm friends with her friends. What do you expect of me, Kade?"

Mason's arm tightened on my back. He swept down and started to massage the side of my hip, grinding me against him in the same motion. My heart pounded and the need started to throb again. I gasped against his chest and started to move with him.

"Isn't that convenient." Acid dripped from Mason's voice.

"What's going on?"

Some of the tension left Mason at the sound of his brother's voice.

"Mase, why you holding my girlfriend?" He sounded bright, cheery. Then he turned serious. "Ah, got it. Truth time, huh? Quinn, why are you always around Sam? You must have a boner every time you talk to her, or think about her, smell her... Do you use your mom's lotion? The pretty smelling stuff when you jerk it?"

"Um..." Becky was hushed immediately. "No, I won't shut up. What's going on? Sam?"

My eyes snapped open, but I knew I couldn't turn around. It was all over my face. I'd been in his arms for a minute and I wanted to drag him to a bedroom. My face was heated and I could imagine what the rest of me looked like. They'd call me a whore after this and it would stick. I knew it.

When I started to turn, Mason kept me in place. His voice was rough as he clipped out, "Stay away from her Quinn. If you keep trying to get in her pants, we're going to have a problem."

Logan sidled up next to us. I felt his presence beside Mason. "And stop playing the dumbass game. You know what we're talking about."

There was silence for a heartbeat and then Adam's laugh grated out. "Are you two serious? You don't think I know what you're doing with her? You're just having fun with her. You're using her to piss off your parents. Mark's told me a little bit. I thought Sam had daddy issues, but the two of you—"

I was transferred to Logan's arms in a flash, but I whirled in time to see Mason lunge for Adam. He knocked him backwards and then took hold of his shirt and slammed him against the wall. Adam didn't fight back, but the two glared at each other as Mason bent close. His mouth moved and Adam's face went white. He lost more and more coloring as Mason continued to speak in his ear. Then, after Mason stopped and held his gaze for a long tension-filled second, he stepped back and delivered one last punch to the side of Adam's face.

He went down, but he wasn't knocked unconscious. As he lay on the ground, he stared at Mason with fear starting to take root in his eyes. No one went to his side, but Becky broke through the crowd and dropped to her knees beside him. She touched the side of his face, but glared at Mason. "What's your problem? He's a good guy."

Mason's eyes cooled, but he glanced at me before he turned back.

My gut twitched as I realized he was in control. He'd been in control the whole time. He hadn't lost it when he went for Adam. Then Logan murmured in my ear, "Quinn's not the hero your friend thinks he is. It's time it came out."

But I was riveted by the scene unfolding before me when Mason placed his hands on his hips and gave my friend a look of regret. I shoved out of Logan's hold and scrambled to his side as he spoke to her, "You think he's a good guy? He used you to get to her."

Becky's eyes were scorching. "Did he tell you this?"

Mason shook his head. "I'm a guy. He didn't have to say a goddamn word. He's been sniffing around Sam since she was done with that other guy."

I touched his arm and was surprised. He wasn't tense. As he looked at me, he swept me against his side and pressed a kiss to my forehead.

"Sam? None of this makes sense."

My heart broke. She was a little girl in that moment. I closed my eyes as a sense of déjà vu hurled through me. She sounded how I felt when I walked into my home and was told we were leaving my dad.

Shattered.

"Sam." Adam spoke this time. He sat up with a hand still cradling the side of his face. "Just tell her. Tell her everything."

My tongue was thick as I struggled out, "Adam told me that he was using you to get to me. He admitted it to me, Becky. You were the only one I talked with after I found out about Jeff's cheating. And he's known about me and Mason—"

"You and Mason?" Lydia's were narrowed as she stood behind them. "I thought, but then..."

Logan whooped out, "You guys are so stupid! The two are together. They're hitched at the hip, literally right now. I'm starting to get pissed. Why's it so easy to think she's with me, but not my brother?"

"Because you're you..." Miranda spoke up. The Elite had joined the crowd around us. "And he's..."

"What?" Logan puffed out his chest and narrowed his eyes at her. "I'm what?"

"Nothing." She clamped her mouth shut and her cheeks grew pink. She didn't look away when he stepped closer to her.

"I'm what?" he asked again, softer this time.

"You're...no one can get Mason. No one's gotten him before."

Mason growled next to me. "This is starting to get stupid. That's enough." He stepped in front of Logan and pushed him back. "What are you doing? You're making this worse."

"Am I?" The corner of his lip curled up, but his tone was hostile. "You can't handle hearing how everyone thinks you're better than me?"

Mason yanked him close and whispered in his ear. As he spoke, Logan's chest started to heave up and down. His mouth tightened and his eyes went flat, and then he shoved him back in a violent push.

"Logan."

"Stop," he snarled at him and pushed through the crowd. As he was swallowed up, Mason stood there and stared after him. Something changed then. He turned towards Miranda and a deadly aura came over him.

But then someone else stepped towards him. "Mason."

I gasped in relief at the sight of Nate. He flashed me a small grin, but urged his best friend away from the crowd. I hurried to follow and found them in a private corner to hear the last words, "I'll take care of him."

Mason shook his head. "You sure? That bitch—"

Nate stopped him. "I'll take care of it, okay?" As I stepped closer, he smiled and pulled me in for a hug. "It's good to see you. I'm happy to hear about you and Mason. He'll treat you good. I promise."

Mason tugged me back and lifted me so I wrapped my legs around him. He held me in place, but spoke over my shoulder, "You'll make sure he's okay? This is important, Nate."

"I know. Chill. I'm not an idiot. I know what I'm doing."

"I don't want problems between me and my brother—"

"Would you stop acting like this is my first job? We've been doing this crap for years. It's not like I don't know how to handle Logan, you know. I *am* friends with him."

Mason's hand started to rub against my bottom and he kissed my shoulder. Then he added, "I know. I'm worried because of—"

"He's over Tate. He knew you were being a good brother." Nate shook his head. "For my sake, take her in the back and get happy. Both of you. Everything will be sorted out. Logan will be his normal self tomorrow."

I twisted around. "How are you going to do that?"

Nate gave me a smug look and a chill went over me. A flash of memories washed over me then.

"When Nate and Mason team up, they always do something."

"He's bad news, like really bad news. I heard him and Kade are not a good team together."

My own mother's voice on the phone, *'I'm sure he's not that bad of a boy. Mason seems very sure of himself.'*

I never asked, but I was sure she'd been talking about Nate and now I started to wonder what they meant. Nate had been kind to me, but I saw a different side of him as he answered me. "I'll get him to bang the queen of your school. He already started the groundwork and she bit, she bit hard."

"Miranda Stewart?" A sick feeling started in my stomach. "She's dating Peter Glasburg."

Nate's eyebrows furrowed together. "Because that always means she won't cheat, huh?"

I flushed and buried my head in Mason's neck. His hand rubbed up and down my back. "Fix it, Nate."

"I will."

I felt Mason nodding. "Thanks. And thanks for coming."

Nate laughed on a carefree note. "Yeah, it took me longer than I thought. Never knew I'd be thankful for some pirate movie they're shooting in Brazil."

"Your parents are strict."

"Yeah, well, we gave them reason to be."

Mason's body shook in laughter. "Yeah, we did." He nodded once again and then took me to a back bedroom.

As he sat me down, he flipped the lights on and locked the door. A king size bed was in a corner with a couch and kitchen area on the other side. A small bathroom was attached and I spotted a Jacuzzi inside. A fleeting thought passed through me, I would've thought people would've found this room before now.

"I had a key card to it. No one could get in here."

"Oh." I hadn't realized I'd spoken out loud.

Mason regarded me for a heartbeat before he sat on the edge of the bed. He bent forward and raked his hands through his hair. His elbows rested on his knees and he stayed like that as I crossed the room to sit beside him. I took one of his hands in mine and he looked up. There was a haunted look in him and I gasped. I knew it'd haunt me now as well. I lifted a hand to smooth out the lines in his forehead and asked, quietly, "Why am I a little scared of you right now?"

He closed his eyes and rested his forehead against mine. He breathed out, "Because I'm a jerk."

I swallowed painfully as my heart was pounding. My breathing picked up and it became erratic. "Why do I feel sorry for Logan right now?"

"Because I'm hurting him."

A piece of bark formed in my throat. "How are you doing that?"

He whispered against my lips, "Because you're the second girl that he's wanted and I got."

My heart picked up its pace. A herd of elephants were stampeding in my ear, but I asked the question I never considered it until now, but I had to ask it. "Does he love me?"

With our foreheads against each other, he looked up and met my gaze. His eyelashes touched mine and I felt his breath against my lips. "I don't think he does, not in that way."

My heart was beating so fast now. It was a continuous beat. I was breathless as I opened my mouth. "Do you love me?"

His hand encircled the back of my neck and he lifted my face as he adjusted on the bed. He peered into my depths. And then he moved so he was below me and I straddled him. His hands slid to my back and he ground me against him. I gasped as I pressed down harder. I couldn't get closer. I needed to get closer. I was starting to become blind with the need.

As he touched his lips to mine, I heard him whisper, "Yes." And then he rolled me underneath him and I was lost. Again.

CHAPTER FORTY

I wasn't sure what time it was the next morning when I woke. I had knocked the clock off the nightstand at some point and a jolt of warmth rushed through me at the memory of it. Mason was sprawled out on the other side of the bed. I blinked at the sight of his tight butt. The sheets had slipped down to his thigh and I was tempted to run a finger up the backside of his leg and over his cheeks. They were tanned, muscular, and itching for my touch.

"Don't even think it," he mumbled out of the corner of his mouth. One of his eyes opened enough to see me with his face pressed into his pillow. A half smile spread over him and then he tugged the sheet across my lap. It was wrapped around my legs and I was soon pulled into his arms.

He nuzzled my neck and pulled me over so I was across his chest.

When he started tickling under my arm, I pulled away, breathless. "Stop it!"

He chuckled and gave me a quick kiss. "You have morning breath."

"So do you." I kissed him back and soon he rolled us to our side. Our legs and arms were wrapped around each other and it wasn't long before I felt him harden against my stomach. "How long do you have the suite?"

He ran a finger down my arm and grinned as goose bumps poked up. "For as long my mom's around. Logan and I didn't want to stay with her so we got this one. He'll probably keep that other suite for the day until everybody's been kicked out."

I shivered when he started to plant soft kisses under my jaw. "Will he be okay? You know...about me and stuff?"

His mouth lingered at the corner of my mouth before he pulled back and settled on his side. He propped himself up on his elbow. "Yeah, he'll be fine. Logan's not an idiot. He doesn't really want you, but that bitch pushed his button."

"And that is?"

He groaned and fell to his back. "Ever since Tate, Logan's never forgotten that she wanted me. He loved her, but she wanted me and worked her way through him to get to me."

"They were together for two years."

"Yeah." He gave me a rueful look. "I'm not exactly welcoming to girls."

"But I saw you with that girl at the house when I caught Jeff."

He shrugged. "She'd been on me for a while and I never pushed her away. I had an itch to scratch, but she was too drunk. We didn't do anything."

"You said that you had some girlfriends before?"

"A while ago, when I was young and stupid. I haven't had to work at getting sex for a long time. If I want it, I can pick the girl. Basically."

"And me?" I grinned down at him and he gave me a knowing smirk.

"What do you think?"

"Am I just for sex? I *am* convenient."

He tugged me down so I was sprawled over him again and lifted his hips against mine. "Does that feel convenient to you?" His voice was breathless as he cupped my head and turned my lips to his. He brushed against them. "You've been on my mind ever since that damn gas station. I couldn't shake you and then when you moved in, it's been torture. I get hard the second you walk in a room."

"So you're saying..." I opened my mouth and his tongue swept in. He took control of the kiss and I tasted his desperation. I pulled back as I realized it was for me. The hunger in him was insatiable.

"What?" He reached for me again.

I scrambled up as a different emotion raced through me. My teeth started to rattle against each other and my arms started to shake. My knees buckled when I tried to get up so I scooted to the farthest side of the bed.

"Sam? What's wrong?" Concern was thick in his voice.

"I..." I closed my mouth and stared in horror. He held my gaze, but there was no fear. There was no self-consciousness or doubt. That's when I realized that he never questioned himself. He was so strong, on the inside and out. For the first time I was intimidated by Mason Kade and I had no idea what to do about it. So I stumbled out the truth, "I love you."

"I know."

"You know?" I didn't even know.

"Sam, I'm not stupid. You've been on lockdown since you moved in. That's why you go running. Any time you start to feel something, you numb yourself. I get it. Trust me, I do. But I know you wouldn't be with me or done half the stuff with me that you have if you didn't love me."

"But..." I hadn't known. Why hadn't I? A cold feeling took root in my gut.

"Hey," he said in a soft voice and moved so he was close again. He moved on his side and tugged me so I faced him. His forehead rested against mine again. "Everything will be okay. I promise."

I sucked in a tortured breath. And then I surrendered. "I'm scared."

"I know."

"After everything's that happened..." I didn't know I was trembling until he wrapped an arm around me and pulled me tight. The shaking stopped and a sense of safety started to seep in. This time it wasn't a temporary feeling, it wasn't going to leave after he left the bed.

"I'm tired, Mason."

"I know."

We both knew I wasn't referring to sleep.

And then nothing mattered. His lips touched mine and it was tender. He didn't roll me underneath him this time, but lifted so I was on top and then he let me set the pace. After I climaxed and collapsed on top of him, I blinked back tears. It was different. The tears were different. Our love making had been different and the way he held me was different. Or maybe I was the different one?

"Stop thinking." Mason brushed a kiss against my shoulder and laughed. "We'll have plenty of time for that later. Right now, we need to shower. I'm hungry too." And he picked me up, bed sheets and all, and started for the bathroom.

I shrieked, laughing, as I hit his shoulder. "Put me down." I was gasping as he did and danced out of his reach when he pretended to lunge for me again. I felt drunk. I wanted to giggle and smile, and never stop doing both of them. As we showered together, a delicious tingle raced up and down my spine. My heart never stopped pounding and I was lightheaded by the end. Afterwards, he slid on some jeans and started to tug me towards the door. I laughed and dug my feet in. "Let me put some clothes on first."

The corner of his mouth curved up, but his eyes darkened as he watched me.

I sighed. "You should too."

He smirked at me and dropped his jeans to pull some boxers on. He left the shirt and socks behind as he caught my hand. I dressed in a hurry and finished tugging my shirt down when he dragged me behind him and out the door.

As soon as we stepped outside, his demeanor dropped. The standoffish Mason was back in place, but his hand continued to hold mine. A buzzing sensation spread through me when I realized I was grateful for the touch. I missed the feel of his body against mine and knew I was addicted. Then I admitted to myself that I didn't want to kick this addiction. It was threatening to take control of my life and I was okay with that.

Nate smirked at us as we approached the kitchenette and gestured from the coffee maker. "I called in the works. Bagels, omelets, bacon, pancakes." He held out a cup for me. "And coffee."

I inhaled the aroma and groaned. "I just cheated on Mason."

There was a moment of silence before Nate burst out laughing. "Sorry, bud. I think I'm going for your girl."

Mason flashed him a cocky smile and popped some bacon in his mouth. "No worries. I had her primed before we came out."

I shot them both a look and sank down in a chair with my coffee. And then I started to take in the scene around us. A few girls sat at the table with their hair pulled up in haphazard ponytails. They were sprawled in chairs with bags under their eyes. One of the girls narrowed her eyes at me, but stopped halfway. She lifted a hand and let it drop down with a loud smack. "Hi. I'm too tired right now. I'm Natalie."

I nodded and sipped my coffee.

She jerked a thumb beside her. "This is Kate and Parker. We go to school with these dickwads."

Nate laughed as he lifted one of the girls and took the seat beneath her. He held her on his lap, but she never resisted. The movement had been done with an ease that spoke of its history. He'd done this many times with that girl. She nestled back in his chest and gave me a droopy smile. Her eyes shot over my shoulder. "Logan's missing in action, Mason. We're not sure where he is."

He had taken a cup of coffee for himself and lounged against the farthest counter. He lowered it from his mouth now. A scowl took form. "Nate?"

"Relax," Nate hissed at him and pointedly looked at the girls. "It's done."

Mason visibly relaxed. His coffee was lifted again.

And then the door to the suite was thrown open. Logan entered with his arms spread wide and an arrogant smirk on his face. "The deal has been done."

Natalie lifted haughty eyes. "What's done, Logan?"

He winked at her, but crossed the room and pressed a kiss to my forehead. He whispered to me, "Last night was a show. Did Mason fill you in?"

"A show?" I turned hard eyes towards the kitchenette. "Mason."

He held my gaze for a minute and looked past my shoulders in a pointed fashion. A sick feeling took root before I turned. Everything seemed in slow motion and I froze at the sight of Miranda Stewart in the doorway. She wore nothing except for a long white buttoned-down shirt that grazed beneath her bottom. Black lacy panties could be seen and she looked back with wide eyes. I gulped as I saw fear in them. That look doubled when she surveyed the room and I turned as well. All three girls had disdain on their faces and each of them didn't contain a smug look.

Miranda's throat jerked up and down as she met my gaze.

A normal girl would've had sympathy for her. Everything went flat inside of me and I stood to stand beside Mason. He lifted his arms over my chest and leaned forward to rest his head on my shoulder. We watched together as Logan motioned for her to come in. As she did, her throat moved up and down again and she dashed for his lap. As soon as she was there, she curled in his arms and turned her back to the table.

Natalie spoke, "Oh. My. Gawd."

Another started laughing. "Are you serious, Logan?"

The third girl in Nate's arms laughed with her friends, but pressed her face against his arm.

I asked underneath my breath, "What is going on?"

"Logan's got a new girlfriend. That's what's going on." Mason sounded amused.

I twisted my pinkie to curl around his and leaned all my weight back on him. "Was that his idea or yours?"

"Mine."

"Does Logan know that?"

His chest moved up and down. There was no response.

"Mason," I prompted. My heart was pounding again. I wasn't sure if I wanted to hear his response.

"No."

I sighed, "At least you don't sound proud for that fact. You manipulated him and you got Nate to do the dirty work. He thinks he's dating Miranda to protect me, doesn't he. And he's not. He's doing it because you got mad at her because she pushed the one button you're worried about. That Logan will go away someday because Tate wanted you and you got me too."

"Don't tell him. Please."

I turned around in his arms and looked up. He gazed down and the wall fell aside. It was the guy who was with me in the bedroom, the one who told me he loved me. And my heart broke. I couldn't look away. I couldn't move away. I couldn't tell his secret and when I turned back around to the group I knew everything changed in that moment.

My fingers slid through his and clasped on. Hard.

Mason and I were linked together with that one plea. And as a shiver of dark excitement wound through my body, I didn't want to be anywhere else except at his side, no matter where it would take us.

FALLEN CREST FAMILY

Book 2

TIJAN

CHAPTER ONE

When I arrived at the party, it was the largest I had ever seen. The mansion was filled with people. The doors had been left open and the overflow spilled out to the front lawn. The driveway went around a large fountain, which a few girls had gotten into. Their shirts were soaked to their skin and their hair was messily rumpled, giving them the wet sexy look. I knew the guys, who stood with their drinks at the side, enjoyed the view. More than a few had that dark promise in their eyes. They wanted sex and they wanted it now. One of the girls squealed as a guy swept her in the air.

I rolled my eyes and pushed past.

Public parties were always considered the best, but this was in a whole new league.

When I stepped onto the front steps, a blast of heat came at me from inside. There were people everywhere. I pushed through the crowd until I was on a back patio. The backyard stretched out with another pool, a basketball court, and a tennis court. There was too much to even look at with all the people, but I could tell the place was phenomenal.

Some girls dashed past me, giggling, while guys chased after them.

Then someone bumped into me from behind. I heard, "Oh, I'm sorry," before I turned around and saw who it was. I found myself staring in the crystal blue eyes of Adam Quinn, someone whom I had considered a friend until two months ago.

"Oh." His voice dropped, and he stood there without saying anything else. After a moment passed, he glanced to the side and slid his hands into the front pockets of his jeans.

I smirked. He was dressed appropriately with custom-tailored jeans and a loose-flowing shirt that was left unbuttoned. A white tank was underneath. It fitted like a second skin to his abdominal muscles and chest. I saw that he had been working out more, but whatever. What did I care? He had dropped our friendship two months ago, and since Adam was the Golden Boy for our school, Fallen Crest Academy, everybody else had followed suit. No one talked to me anymore, even his neighbor, the one person I had come to consider as a real friend.

I asked, though maybe I shouldn't have, "How's Becky?"

He flinched.

A small sense of triumph flared through me, but it was so small, and it was gone instantly.

"Uh," he looked away before his jaw hardened, and he met my gaze again. This time he didn't blink. "She's good. I think she's dating someone from your school."

"My school?"

"FCP. You know what I mean. Their school, you're one of them now, so...your school."

"I still go to Fallen Crest Academy."

He clenched his jaw. "I heard something else."

All senses went on alert. I knew what he was talking about, but I hadn't known it was already on the gossip mill. This wasn't good. "What'd you hear?"

He shrugged and looked away. There it was. I knew it was only a matter of time. Adam could never be honest with me for too long.

"What'd you hear?"

"Come on, Sam."

"Come on, what?" I knew he was going to leave. I sensed it and grabbed his arm as he started to inch away. "What did you hear?"

"Let go of me." His eyes hardened as he looked over my shoulder. "I don't think I'm supposed to be talking to you."

"What are you talking about..." But the words left me as

an arm snaked around my waist and pulled me back against a hard chest, a very hard chest.

Mason's chin came to rest on my shoulder and he breathed out. The air caressed my neck, and I felt the possession in his demeanor. A tingle raced through me, especially when his hand slid down my waist to rest on my hip. He pressed me back against him again. I felt every inch of him now and fought against closing my eyes when my desire started to overtake me.

"I should be going," Adam mumbled before he turned. But then he stopped. His face was twisted in an unnamed emotion. "Thanks for inviting everyone to the party."

"Not my party." Mason straightened against my back. His hands held me firmly in place, but I could feel the coldness from him now.

Adam didn't squirm; he straightened and never looked away. He had learned. Then his eyes caught mine for a second before he looked away again. A shiver went over me. I saw his anger in that second, but he only replied, "Your best friend's place. Your party."

"This is Nate's party?" I twisted around, but Mason didn't let go of me. His hands had a firm grasp on my hips. When he didn't look down, his gaze still fixed over my shoulder, I slid a hand around his neck and tilted him downwards. He met my gaze then and I tried to stop myself from melting. His green eyes softened and a small grin came over him. When he lifted a hand to rub against the top of my lip, I closed my eyes. A groan escaped me before I realized what I was doing. Then I grabbed his hand. "Stop."

"Stop what?" His amusement was evident.

"This is Nate's party?" That meant one thing. This was his place, but did that mean..."Is Nate moving back?"

And then someone threw his arms around us and we were pulled in for an even tighter hug. "Hello, my peeps!" Logan's breath smelled of booze and as he hugged us again. "I love you guys and you know what else I love?"

Mason grimaced, but I still caught the small grin at the corners of his lips. He deadpanned, "Nate's pussy?"

Logan threw his head back and let loose a hoot. Then, even as he died down, he couldn't wipe the silly grin off his face. And he wasn't trying, not even the slightest. "Yeah, maybe." His eyes turned to me and I was caught by the intensity in them. An abnormal look of earnestness was in them, albeit slightly blurred from booze, but it was there. It was the most sincere expression Logan had allowed me to see in a long while. He reminded me of a five-year-old little boy in that moment, one with shaggy brown curls and dark chocolate eyes that made so many girls' hearts melt. "Did Mason tell you? Nate's moving back for the last half of the year. How fucking fantastic is that?"

Very. Nate was the fourth member in our group, but it hurt. He hadn't said a word, but Mason couldn't stop from grinning at Logan so I forced myself to put it away. Nate was back. That was all that mattered, and then realization hit me as I looked around. This enormous place was his.

"This is Nate's place?"

Yet, even as I asked, I knew it was. Both of them didn't answer, silent as I looked around again. There were so many people at the party. I recognized a few from my school, obviously with Adam there, and I knew there were students from Fallen Crest Public as well. I saw a few of Mason and Logan's friends and figured more from their school were there as well, but two schools couldn't have been everyone? Who else was there?

"Dude, tell her."

Mason admitted with a smirk, "Nate's got some high placed friends."

Just then a well-known actor strolled past us with his arm around two girls.

My mouth dropped open. I couldn't believe it, but I should've. Nate's parents were movie directors. When he wasn't getting in trouble with Mason and Logan, they tried to keep him with them as often as possible. Of course he would've met more than a few from the Hollywood scene. But, still, I couldn't believe it.

I grasped Mason's hand and squeezed tight. "My mom has a huge crush on him."

He wrenched his hand away as he stepped back. Logan held up both arms. "Hey, whoa. Too much information, girly."

"What?"

Mason grimaced. "We don't want to know who your mom jerks off to."

"What?" Oh my word. They thought—I sputtered out, "No, I didn't mean, I mean, NO!"

Then both started to laugh. Soon their shoulders shook as more laughter slipped from their clasped lips.

A wave of embarrassment came over me. I was pissed and mortified. When I lifted a hand to slap Mason's arm, he caught it instead and twirled me so I was in his arms again. My back was to his chest and his arms came around in front of me. He turned so we faced Logan before his hands slid down to hold my hips still as he started to rub against me.

Logan cringed. "Oh please, guys. I live with you."

Mason bent forward so his lips were next to my ear. I felt them curve into a grin. His breath tickled my skin. "Feel free to go away now, brother."

"Correction." Logan flashed us a dark look. "I have to live with you. I need to rectify that soon." Then he saluted us both with two fingers in the air as he turned and walked away. He hadn't gone more than a few steps before his stroll turned into a saunter. His hands slid into his front pockets, his shoulders leaned forward a bit, and a different vibe came over him. It wasn't a surprise when a group of girls clambered over to him. With his shoulders hunched forward, it gave him a vulnerable appeal that was almost irresistible to girls when it was mixed with an already dangerous reputation.

Mason chuckled against my ear. Then he caught it with his teeth and bit down gently.

Tingles raced through me and I lifted to my toes as his teeth scraped against the bottom of my earlobe. He drew it out, gently and lovingly. Sensually. A burst of heat flared between my legs. The same throb started deep. As his hips moved forward, I felt him behind me and closed my eyes from the pleasure. The throbbing was almost too much now. The same desire I always felt for him started to take over. I felt my control slipping.

"Mason," I gasped as I arched my back against him. My arm lifted to behind his neck. When I held him in place, his lips started to nibble downwards and I was barely conscious of being turned in his arms. My breasts were pushed against his chest and he lifted one of my legs so he could fit further between them. I arched against him. I gasped for breath, but his mouth covered mine instantly.

He took control.

He commanded his entrance, and I was helpless against him. His tongue slipped inside my mouth. Mine brushed against his. A growl emanated from him. It sent a rush of power through me that was intoxicating. I wanted more and my tongue met his again, this time to brush slowly against his. Then I pulled away, but not before I flicked the tip of my tongue against his top lip. As my eyelids lifted, heavy and saturated from lust, I saw the answering yearning in his. Then his eyes flashed in determination, and I knew it wouldn't be long before Mason would be in me, deep and hard.

An elated shiver ran through me. I wanted nothing more than that.

"I know the two of you are horny rabbits and in love and all that, but I don't think you want to make an amateur sex tape right here."

We broke apart, panting, and took in the grinning sight of Nate's face. He gestured to where a group had congregated. I saw more than a few cameras in the air with fingers to the record buttons.

"Hi, Nate," I croaked out. A heated rush of embarrassment flooded me. I couldn't believe I had almost lost control or that Mason had as well. He set the tone most of the times. I trusted him, but a tingle of addictive power went through me as I remembered the sound of his own groan. I held him as captivated as he held me.

Mason cursed under his breath but swept us around so his back was to the group and I was shielded from the audience.

"Hi, Sam."

I flinched at how cheery Nate sounded. Mason's hand swept down before he held my face to his shoulder. I felt his tension as his voice reverberated through his chest. "Thanks, man."

"Any time." His tone was amused. Then I felt Nate's lips on my forehead. He whispered before he darted off, "It's good to see you too, Sam. Take care of my boy."

Mason groaned as he brushed my hair from my face and looked down into my eyes. I tilted backwards and saw the warmth in his gaze. My heart skipped a beat. I couldn't believe it. We'd been official for two months, but it never got old. He never got old. He never tired of me. I wasn't sure what I would do if that happened, if any of those nightmares occurred.

All I knew, as Mason continued to hold me to his chest, was that I couldn't lose him. Who the hell was I trying to kid? I couldn't lose any of them, Mason, Logan, or even Nate. They were the only friends I had in my life now.

I felt panic start to rise, but I forced it down. I had to. I couldn't lose it, not in his arms. Never in his arms.

CHAPTER TWO

The rest of the night had been free of drama, and I was relieved. Mason stuck close to me as he always did when I would attend parties, but I knew there were a ton of his friends who wanted his attention. For the most part, the friends from their school stuck close to each other. I wasn't part of that group. Even though I was dating Mason, they still considered me as an Academite, their term for the snotty rich kids. That was fine. I was far from the normal economic status of my classmates, but I knew that wasn't the real reason I hadn't been welcomed into the group. Mason and Logan's father was one of the wealthiest men in town, but they were accepted into any circle.

I wasn't stupid.

The girls didn't like me because I got Mason, who had been deemed unavailable except for the few times he chose someone for sex. Now he has a girlfriend, and they're pissed. The girls in their tight circle cursed at me, insulted me, even pushed me against a wall a few times, but it was always done when Mason or Logan weren't around. As for the guys, a few of them would glare at me while the others stayed away. Nate told me during one of his visits that some of the guys worried if I would change Mason.

I made a point not to.

I never argued when Mason said he was going to a party. After the third time of getting tripped or elbowed by the girls, I stopped going with him. He'd been confused, but I shrugged when he questioned me about it. I told him that I'd rather go for a long run and he dropped the conversation. It hadn't even been a lie. I loved running, and I had never enjoyed parties. I had gone before because my two best friends and boyfriend wanted me to go. But they weren't my friends anymore. I had no friends at my own school; no one would invite me to the parties, even the ones that weren't Public Parties, the name coined for those thrown by anyone who went to Fallen Crest Public School. They were the best ones.

And Nate's party exceeded everyone's expectations.

When I had stood in line for the bathroom, a girl said she saw people from four different schools. I hadn't been surprised. Mason and Logan ruled their school. Those at Fallen Crest Academy clamored for their attention as well, and with Nate's contribution, I was surprised more schools hadn't shown up. Even after Nate had been forced to move away after getting into too much trouble with Mason, he came back for visits often enough to feel as if he lived there. He came back for his and Mason's last semester in high school. They would end it together, and then they would start again. Mason didn't talk about college much, but I knew that he had already committed to a university where he would play football for them. Nate was going as well. They were going to be roommates, and if anyone were to ask my opinion, I had a feeling that Logan felt out of the loop. He and I had one more year in high school, but this was the point in my thoughts when I stopped thinking.

I didn't like to think of that time when Mason would go away. Hell, I didn't even like to think of my dilemma for next semester.

"You're thinking," Mason mumbled next to me as he rolled over and wrapped his arms around me. He reached over my waist and tugged me back against him. One of his legs shifted over mine, and I was securely enveloped by him.

I grinned when the tingle started. It didn't take much anymore, just a touch and the memory of what was to come rushed through me. When I turned to face him, his eyes were sparkling down at me. A small grin curved up and his green eyes searched mine. They darkened with lust when I lifted a hand to cup the side of his cheek. I licked my lips as my throat went dry and moved even closer to him.

I couldn't get enough of him.

"Sam," he murmured.

"Hmmm?" I started to explore his chest. My hand slipped down and rounded his slender waist. I rubbed over his muscles—they were structured and photo-shopped to perfection. When one of my fingers slipped underneath his boxer's waistband, he sucked in his breath. I grinned from the anticipation and addiction I had to him. I loved touching him. I loved making him groan in pleasure, and, as I pushed him to his back and settled over him, I loved looking down and seeing him helpless to my touch. It made two of us.

"Fuck, woman," he growled in a husky voice. His hands settled on my thighs as I straddled him. His fingers dug in when I dipped down and licked his neck. Then I moved farther down, and his hands dug in even farther. He had a cement hold on me when I teased the edge of his boxers, but then his phone went off and we both froze.

It rang again.

Our eyes met because we both knew who that was. We had discussed it the night before when I made the decision to turn my phone off. Since the party was at Nate's home, or his parent's home as Mason explained, he wanted to stay the night. It was an easy decision. The Kade mansion, where my mother had started to boycott any nights Mason slept in my bed, or his best friend's place? There'd been no need for a discussion. We did, however, have to discuss what we were going to do when my mother would start calling. I wasn't a fan of turning off my phone. Not many called or texted, but there'd been times when Mason or Logan had been hurt. I missed a phone call one time after Mason had been in a bad fight. I vowed never to experience that panic again. However, Mason promised that if I turned my phone off, he would deal with my mother and his father in the morning.

The phone rang for the third time.

He growled and cursed at the same time as he rolled out from underneath me. He picked his phone up in one swift movement as he stood from the bed and went into the bathroom. "What?"

The shower turned on, and when I crossed to the doorway, he had put the phone on the counter and was ignoring it as he stepped underneath the spray. When he shut the water off, his father's voice was still going strong over the phone. He sounded furious, but I knew it was more from my mother. Analise was like a starving dog going after a bone when she got something in her head. And she had decided that I would not be fornicating with my stepbrother.

That didn't go over well with Mason, who told them both to fuck off. More fights ensued, raised voices, threats, even blackmail had been mentioned once. None of it fazed Mason. He withstood all of it and I started running longer and longer each day. Then one day, after I returned from a five hour run, my mother surprised us both as she told me that we could see each other, but we were not to sleep together. Ever.

That rule wasn't followed, but she was still trying to enforce it. God bless her determination.

"...and you will tell Samantha to return her mother's phone call. Analise is beside herself. We had to go to the hospital for her to calm down. She couldn't sleep last night."

Mason rolled his eyes after he finished drying himself off with a towel. He stepped close, pressed a kiss to my forehead, and shooed me into the shower. With a quick wink and a slap on my ass, he strolled back to the room with his phone in hand.

When I was done showering, the bedroom was empty so I dressed and headed for the kitchen. Our room was in a small hallway, but I stepped out onto the second level that was in a circle. There were more bedrooms on the side as I passed them towards the stairs at the end of the circle. The entire house was set up in a large circle, with the fountain centered below. As I went down the stairs, the water was flowing freely, but I heard noises from a back corner so I veered to the left. I went through a living room and cut across the top corner to the kitchen.

A large group had congregated around the counters and the island in the middle. Nate was at the stove. One of their female friends was plastered against his side. She wore a skimpy piece of white cloth that barely covered her breasts, sans bra, and ripped jean shorts that hardly covered her cheeks. As she gazed up at Nate, seduction written all over her face, I couldn't stop the gag from my mouth.

The sound echoed over the room, and all conversation stopped.

I didn't see Mason or Logan. It was the group of friends who barely held back their loathing. One of the guys straightened from the counter, beer in hand, and glared at me. "You got a problem?"

Nate was in front of him within seconds. "Ethan, man, don't start this."

"Start what? Did you hear her?"

"Yeah." Nate's seductress positioned her hand to her hip. She struck a defiant pose. "Did you hear her? It was rude, Nate. It was directed at me. She thinks I'm a joke."

"And you haven't been rude to her?"

A shiver went down my back as I remembered the look in Nate's eyes when I first approached. He'd been easygoing, laid-back. Then he went to a neutral stance, but now his eyes glittered with rage. An aura of authority emanated from him. The girl stepped back and everyone fell silent. It was my first glimpse of this side of Mason's best friend. If I had ever doubted their bond before, I didn't anymore. Change the body, the looks, and he could've been Mason. They held the same authority. Nate was just showing his in front of me for the first time.

His lip curved up in an ugly sneer as he stepped closer to Ethan, who had straightened from the counter. The beer spilled as his hand jerked around it, squashing the can in a crinkled ball of metal.

Nate's voice was cold, eerily cold. "You've all been rude to her, and they don't know a thing." He waited a beat as his gaze swept the group. "Why don't you ponder on that, huh? You think they'd stand for your attitude towards her?" Then he whipped his gaze back to Ethan, whose jaw clenched from the scrutiny. "You want your ass kicked? Keep being a bitch to her." He stopped abruptly. His chest heaved up and down before he bit out, "She hasn't said a word. Ponder that too, you asswipes."

"Baby," the girl whimpered. She held a hand out.

Nate ignored her and brushed past me. His jaw was still clenching and before he disappeared around a corner, his hand turned into a fist. But then he was gone, and I was left alone with a group that hated me.

All of them turned their hostile gazes to me.

I gulped. Oh my.

I held my breath, waiting. Did I attack? Hell no. But should I wait to be attacked? I knew they would and then heard a whispered snarl, "You bitch!"

There it was.

It was Nate's seductress. She stood in front of me, brazen with nearly nothing on, and tossed her long brown hair over her shoulder. Something shifted in me. I had come to remember a few of their names. Kate was the ring leader. I was pretty certain she had a 'benefits' relationship with Mason before he went steady with me, and this girl was her best friend forever...Parker, if I remembered correctly?

I opened my mouth, ready for some retort. I wasn't sure what I was about to say, but it was coming. I only hoped it made sense, or that it didn't get me in more trouble. I'd grown tired of the female catty showdowns, and this was certainly one of them.

But then Ethan flung his beer can into the sink and grunted. "Leave her alone, Parks."

Her mouth fell open on a gasp and she rounded to him. Her boobs flopped side to side from the motion. "Are you kidding me?!"

He sighed as he ran a hand over his tired face. "Come on. Nate's right, man. Leave her alone. Kade likes her, leave her be. She ain't going anywhere, and I'm getting tired of this. I don't want to get my ass handed to me by them, and you know it's gonna happen. You're going to say something in front of them and everything will go to hell for us."

"But—"

He stepped away from the counter as he crossed his arms over his chest. The sleeveless, ripped shirt exposed the biceps that now bulged from the motion. His chest grew in size as well. "It ain't happening, not on my watch. Get going. Go tell all the little girlies. I know they'll have a hay day with this one."

Her mouth hung open, no sound came from it. Then one of the guys let loose a snicker and she exploded, "Shut the hell up, Strauss! This ain't got a goddamn thing to do with you."

His snicker doubled in volume. A slap to his thigh was heard as he chuckled, "It sure fun to watch you getting your rear end handed to you."

If she could've killed me, she would've in that moment. The blood drained from her face, and she crossed her arms over her chest. Her lips were stiff as she promised, "I will make you pay for this. The guys might be okay with you, but the girls won't be and we're no picnic, honey. You better watch out from now on."

As she stormed away, I knew her shoulder was going to slam into mine. With gritted teeth, I reacted before I thought about the consequences and I shoulder-checked her instead. She bounced back into a counter, and gasped again. The loathing had always been there, but now white-hot hatred came at me. A low growl emitted from her throat before she rushed from the room.

Again, there was silence in the room.

My heart dropped to my gut as I waited for the next showdown. There were a handful of girls spread out among the other guys.

I wasn't stupid. I had learned that Mason and Logan's friends from Fallen Crest Public were the rough and tumble sort of kids. They weren't from money. They didn't give a damn about whose daddy paid for their trip overseas or the secret trysts of which daddy was with which mommy, or even who was cheating with whose secretary. These were the kids that partied hard, played harder, and turned into a single unit against an outsider. They were tight-knit. They were closed-mouthed. And they weren't stupid, even though I knew those from my school would mislabel them as that. They were far from stupid and I knew something pivotal had just happened.

Ethan, the fourth in command after Mason, Logan, and Nate, had turned against one of the girls. I also knew that meant there would be a divide. The girls would hate me, while the guys were now okay. And judging by the relieved shoulders and carefree laughter in the room, the guys might've been hoping for this for awhile. Then again, who would willingly want to go against Mason and Logan?

But I still had a fight on my hands. The girls were going to be the toughest, and since they had divorced from the guys' support, I figured they would be worse than normal. This was going to be hell.

Kate was the leader. Parker was her sidekick, but there was another twosome that made up the core group of their four. Natalie and Jasmine. They weren't in the kitchen that morning, but I knew they were somewhere. They were going to be coming for me, somehow, someplace.

Ethan went to the refrigerator and grabbed another beer. As he leaned against a counter, crossed one faded jean-clad leg over the other, and folded his arms across his chest again, he smirked at me. "You need to learn how to kick some ass because you're going to need it. Those girls don't care two hoots if Mason and Logan don't like it. Those girls are vicious. They stick together like a pack of jacked-up wolves. You best get some bite to you."

Oh great. I didn't think running long distances was going to help me with that, but I couldn't be surprised. I had known this would come. This was a group that you had to fight your way in to prove you deserved your spot amongst them.

There was a reason why Mason and Logan were friends with them.

CHAPTER THREE

Mason wasn't in our room when I went back, so I went in search for him. As I was going past some stairs that led to the basement, or one of the basement areas, a whistle stopped me.

"Sam, what's going on?"

Logan came up with no shirt and his jeans unbuttoned. His hair was messily rumpled, as if he'd just woken up or just had sex. With him, I never knew. And then I got my answer.

My eyes went wide. Jessica was behind him. Her shirt was twisted to the side and she was zipping up her own jeans when she saw me. A thick bunch of her hair slipped over her face and covered her eyes, but she brushed it back before she stopped behind Logan.

A smug smirk came over her as she leaned against the wall. "Hiya, Sam. How's it going?"

I rounded on Logan. "Are you kidding me?"

Regret flashed over his face, but then he reached for my hand. "You okay? You seem upset."

"You screwed her?"

"You seemed upset before you saw us. What's going on?"

"Oh." I bit my lip. He didn't want to talk about Jessica, I got the message. I hated it. I hated the idea of him and her together. It was one of my worst nightmares. "If you date her, I'm gone."

His eyes widened a fraction, but that was the only reaction I got from him. A cocky glimmer came over him and he rolled his shoulders back. "Oh, come on, Sam. It's not like that. I promise."

"Jerk," Jessica hissed.

"But something else is going on. What is it?"

"Logan." I pressed my hands against my forehead. A headache was coming on. I already knew that I couldn't stop it. It'd be full blown within an hour and I'd be on the bathroom floor very soon. "I can't deal with this right now. Do you know where Mason is?"

A snort came from the sideline.

I whirled on her. "Do not make one more sound. This morning hasn't been the greatest, and I'd love to take it out on you. I really would."

Her haughty eyes met mine, but there was no retort. I was shocked. Jessica wasn't one to not have a hateful comment ready on the tip of her tongue. That was who she was, spiteful and mean. But then I realized she was keeping quiet because of Logan. I wanted to throw my hands in the air and pull my hair out. She was back to him. I couldn't believe it. I didn't know what she had said to him or done to him to do whatever they did together, but I knew it was sneaky. Then I remembered something else.

"Aren't you dating Jeff?"

She shrugged. "Yeah, but it's not like we're based on good relationship morals. You should know that more than anyone." A smug look came over her.

I wanted that look gone, and I reacted before I thought about it. I raised my hand and slapped her.

She gasped. When her face snapped back to mine, the old Jessica was back in place. The hatred I always saw from her was there. She sucked in her breath. Her chest rose up and down in dramatic breaths, and I knew she was trying to keep herself under control.

I said, heated, "You were my best friend for years. I dated Jeff for three years. If you think I was more hurt because you screwed my boyfriend for two years, then you really are a shallow person. I lost a friend, you idiot. I lost *both* of my best friends at the same time."

A different look came to her then. Her hand fell from her cheek slowly.

"Hey. Okay." Logan stepped between us. His hand touched my elbow, and he urged me up the stairs. "What's going on? What happened this morning?"

I let him lead me down a hallway and away from her. When I glanced back, Jessica slipped further down the hallway. I hoped she was leaving. I couldn't handle her being there, not in my world. I wouldn't let her destroy my life again.

"Hey."

I snapped back to him. I was still shaking from the anger inside of me. "Did you sleep with her?"

He grimaced again and ran a hand through his hair. As he rubbed at his jaw, he let loose a deep breath. "Man, I wasn't thinking that through last night."

"So you did."

It stung, it stung a lot.

"Yeah," he whispered. "I am sorry, Sam. I didn't think about you. That seemed so long ago, and I was drunk. I was alone. I was on the couch downstairs, and she was there. She was whispering all these great promises to me. Her hands were all over me. I liked her touch last night. I liked it a lot. That girl is good in bed, but damn, I should've thought more clearly. I really am sorry."

"She took my friends away." It hurt to admit that, but it was the truth. Jeff hadn't been a stand-up guy, but I was certain that she had seduced him. And she had gotten Lydia to cover for them. She took them both away. When it had come out, she tried to turn more against me. Whatever I had done to her, it must've been horrible, but I had no idea. That was the worst part of it. I had no idea why someone who I had loved since we were kids hated me so much. Had we ever really been friends?

A strong arm wrapped around my shoulders, and I was pulled against Logan's hard chest. He dipped his head and pressed a kiss to my forehead. "I'm really sorry, Sam. But I promise last night was the one and only time. I won't have anything to do with her again. I'm sorry."

I nodded. It took some of the pain away, but until Jessica had sprung up in my life again, I had no idea how much I'd been hurt by her. The door was open now, and more pain came through. Then I blocked it. I repressed it all back down again, and tuned into what Logan was saying, "...pool house maybe."

"Huh?"

"If you're looking for Mason, he's probably in the pool house. It's where he and Nate hang out. They think no one knows about it, but we all do. It's their alone time together." He winked at me as he squeezed me close for one more hug. "You okay?"

I nodded. "Yeah, I'll be fine. She brings bad memories. That's all."

"Okay." Then he yawned and ran a hand over his face again. "I've got to wake up. Man. You eat yet?"

"I was in there, yeah."

"Okay, go check the pool house. I'm sure he's in there. I'm going to get some grub." He pressed one more kiss to my forehead before he let me go. As he left, I watched him saunter away. I rolled my eyes. I didn't think Logan knew how to walk without a cocky strut.

When I slipped out through one of the patio doors, there were more people in the pool. A group had congregated at some of the tables near it. I didn't recognize any of them so I continued to the pool house. When I stepped inside, Mason was at the bar. He sat on a stool with a cup of coffee in front of him. It looked like it hadn't been touched, but the steam still rose in the air. He was hunched over with his phone stuck to his ear.

"Hey."

I jumped and whirled around. Nate sat on a couch with a grin from ear to ear. His shoulders shook in amusement, but he gestured towards Mason. "He's been on the phone the whole time."

"He was talking to his dad." I glanced over, but he hadn't looked up or acknowledged me. Then I heard his next words,

"Fuck off, dad. I mean it!" The hostility in them blasted me. I jumped in reaction but was dumbfounded when I heard Nate's soft laughter. I whirled back around. "You think that's funny?"

"Yeah." The laughter died away, but a small grin was still in place. He lounged back on the couch and threw one arm to rest on the top. "When Mason gets pissed, it's never good for the other person. And since it's his dad, I'm excited for what we're going to be doing."

"If that's what you want, fine." Mason's loud exclamation was followed with a curse as he dropped his phone on the bar. He shoved back from the stool but stopped when he saw me. All the rage drained from him, and he sighed before his head slowly hung down. "I'm sorry, Sam. I am."

"What are you talking about?" My throat was suddenly so dry. It was painful for me to speak. "What did your dad say?"

"Your mom's being a bitch. We're supposed to head home right now."

"What else did he say?" I knew there was more. I could see it on his face, but he shook his head. "Mason."

"We should go home."

This wasn't good. Mason didn't stand down to anyone and that was what he was doing. Dread turned to a sick feeling. I didn't want to go into that house. I didn't want to deal with my mother, not when she had affected him like this.

Nate stood with us. He had a small grin on his face, like he was anticipating some fireworks. But Mason held a hand out. "No, man. Just me and Sam."

The grin vanished. Nate straightened to his fullest height of six feet and one inch. His shoulders squared back. "You sure?"

"Yeah."

"Logan?"

"Don't tell him what's going on." Mason touched the small of my back and urged me ahead of him. He paused at the door. "Keep him here. Keep him happy. He can't rush into this, he'd make it worse."

Nate nodded. Mission received and accepted.

As I watched the exchange, a different perverse feeling came over me. This was the dynamic between the two that I didn't like, where they cut everyone else out. If they did it with Logan, I knew they could do it with me. That didn't sit well with me. I didn't like the idea of Mason having someone 'handle' me as he had Nate handle Logan at times.

But I didn't say anything. I was too scared to, not because of how Mason would react, but because I couldn't handle any more deep stuff. The hurt that I was blasted with when I saw Jessica still felt raw. It made me realize how much I had suppressed at the beginning of the year, and that was just the tip of the iceberg. There was so much more pain where that came from, and right now, as Mason and I slipped around the side of the house and went to his car, I knew we weren't headed to an afternoon of kissing and cuddling. We were headed to meet with my mom and his dad. Not good.

Once we had left the driveway and headed back towards town, I reached over and turned the radio off. Then I leaned back and took a breath. I readied myself. "Okay, so what did your dad say?"

Mason kept driving. He didn't visibly react, but I knew he tensed. I felt it from him. Then he clipped out, "Your mom wants one of us out of the house."

"What?"

He jerked his head in a nod. "And I don't want to go. I don't want you sleeping somewhere else or me somewhere else. I don't want to have to sneak in to see my girlfriend or even having your mom breathing down our backs when one of us is in the house. I've dealt with so much more than her. It's pissing me off. And you, where was she when she dumped you in our house with no friends and no father? She took off with my dad. Now she suddenly wants to come and act like your mother?" He cursed again and shook his head.

The anger in his eyes made them glimmer. "I can't believe her and I can't believe my dad. He's always known the deal. We raised ourselves. I raised Logan. He was never around. He was either cheating on our mom or away on business trips. I raised Logan. He didn't. I swear to god, he wants to start laying the law down as my father? I'm eighteen. I'm gone the end of the summer and he's doing this now?"

I'm gone the end of the summer. Those words hit me hard. I fell back against my seat. I knew Mason would be leaving, but I hadn't really thought about it. He was going. He was really going.

He would be gone.

I didn't want to go back to the mansion. "Stop the car."

"What?"

"Stop the car." Something fierce came over me. "Stop the car now."

"Why?" But he slowed it down and turned into a parking lot. "What's going on?"

I shook my head and rasped out, "I'm not doing this with them. You're right. I know my mom wants us to stop sleeping together, but we can't." I wouldn't stop. I couldn't.

"Hey, hey." His voice was low and smooth. He cupped the end of my elbow and turned me towards him. "We won't. I promise. I just don't know what to do with your mom. My dad said that she's going nuts. She's making all these threats—" He stopped abruptly.

Oh god.

I asked, with my heart pounding, "What is she saying?"

"She's threatening to leave him if I won't stop seeing you."

"Are you kidding me?"

He shook his head. There was a deep pain in his eyes. It stabbed me in the chest. "What else?" I knew there was more. I needed to know all of it now.

"She said that if he can't control his kid, then she'll control hers. She's saying that she'll leave him and take you away."

I waited a beat.

I let his words sink in. And then I went with my gut. "She's lying."

She had to be lying. That was all there was to it.

Mason didn't say a word.

I knew my mother, and I knew she wouldn't leave James Kade. There was no way. He was her bread and butter. He was her soulmate, or so she thought, and he loved her. I knew David loved her, but he didn't love her as much as James Kade did.

I squeezed Mason's hand. I squeezed until I feared it might come off, but I couldn't stop. "She's lying. Analise knows that James won't want to lose her. He loves her that much, so she's bluffing. She won't leave him. She knows he'll step in and stop her before she does."

He fell back against his seat and said quietly, "I know, but it's going to work. He's going to kick me out to keep her."

My eyes closed. My mom really was a bastard. So much other emotions came up within me, but I pushed them back down. I rasped out, "What do we do?"

"We can't call her bluff. Then he'll really do it."

And that was the crux of it. My mother was sending an ultimatum. Her or his son. James had to choose and we knew who that would be.

CHAPTER FOUR

We didn't go back to the Kade mansion. We had another two weeks of break before we had to make any decisions so we went to Los Angeles. Just him and me. It was needed.

He called Nate after we turned the car around. He told him that we were going to be staying at one of his mother's places. Then he called Logan and told him the same, except he said that it was because we wanted some alone time. Neither had been happy, particularly when he said it might be for awhile, but neither argued.

I knew both wanted their partner in crime for whatever adventures they thought would happen, but the truth was that I wanted to get away. The tension had become unbearable at home between Analise and Mason. Neither would back down, and I was scared of what could happen. Logan stayed out of it, mostly, but there were times he would stir the pot. A smartass comment would come out or he would insinuate how the sex must've been good between Mason and me. And he loved to share his own sexual stories. Analise looked ready to explode when she was reminded how sexually experienced they were.

My stomach twisted in knots again as I remembered a few of those times. James and I were the quiet ones, but I could tell he was affected as well. I didn't understand the dynamic between him and his sons, but I knew it was a strange one.

"Here we are." Mason slowed his Escalade and turned into a cobblestone driveway that led to a large door. A doorman was in front of the sliding glass doors. As a black limousine paused in front of us, a woman in a nude-colored dress stepped out. She wore sunglasses and her blonde hair was swept up in a fancy bun. As we watched, she waited for the driver to pull a piece of luggage out of the back for her. Instead of handing it to her, it was handed to the doorman, who swept his hand out so the doors slid open. Then he followed her inside. It wasn't long before the driver returned to his seat and the limousine pulled away from the doors.

"Your mom has a place in this building?"

"Yep, she's got one of the top floors."

My mouth dropped.

He flashed a grin. "I told you my mom was wealthy. My dad's money can't touch hers. This is only *one* of her places, and trust me, this is the one she rarely uses. You saw that lady just now?"

I nodded.

"My mom hates her." He shrugged. "No idea why."

"That's why your mom doesn't come here that often?"

He nodded as the doorman appeared again. Then he pulled his Escalade up to the door. When we both got out, the doorman broke out into a friendly grin. He wore a navy blue suit with a yellow tie. He looked older, possibly in his fifties, with graying hair. His smile lit up his face. The blue in his eyes turned warm, and the affection he felt for Mason was evident. He drew him in for a hug and clasped him on the shoulder with his black leather gloves. "It's good to see you, Master Kade! It's been so long."

Mason's own smile was ear to ear when he stepped back. "It has been."

The man still held onto his arms. He didn't drop them when his smile slipped a little bit. "And your mother? Is she here with you?"

"Nah, Stuart. I hope she won't find out that I'm here." Then he extended a hand towards me. "This is my girlfriend, Sam. We're on break from school so we're hiding out."

The warm eyes turned towards me, and they sparkled as he took me in. "I see." His hands fell away from Mason's arms. "She is a beauty, Mason. You have done well."

"I think so."

With both of their attention on me, I flushed and looked away. Beauty? What was he smoking?

"And Logan?"

"Nope. It's just me and Sam."

"Ah, I see. One of those vacations."

"Yeah and mum's the word, Stu."

"Of course, Master Kade."

A curse slipped out. "Come on, Stu. Mason. You're supposed to call me Mason."

"Of course, Master Kade." Then I looked back and he held out a hand to me. "And what shall I call this exquisite beautiful creature? I cannot call you by your personal name, Sam. Samantha? Mistress, hmmm? What is your last name?"

"You can call her Samantha."

I took his hand, and my eyes went wide when he lifted it for a kiss. His cool lips pressed a chaste kiss to the back of my hand, but the friendliness in his eyes overwhelmed me. He wasn't inappropriately friendly. I knew it was from the respect he held for Mason. It took my breath away for a moment.

"I cannot," he murmured as he let go of my hand. "I have not earned the right to use her first name. What is your last name?"

"Strattan."

"Mistress Strattan it is." His smile deepened an inch.

I wanted to groan as I realized that I would be called that from now on. Awkward. And if any of my friends heard him—no. I didn't have any friends. It didn't matter.

The front lobby wasn't big. There was a front desk, an elevator, and a small sitting area. As we went to the elevator and reached the 24th floor, I found myself staring at something I would've seen on a television show. The floor was modern and chic with white couches in front of a fireplace and a red table beside the kitchen. When Mason took my hand and led me to our bedroom, there was a plush white comforter on the bed with gold trim. The far wall was a floor to ceiling window, with a view that overlooked Los Angeles. It was spectacular.

"As promised," Mason drew my attention towards the closet. He toed it open for me. "You won't need clothes. My mom keeps clothes here for everyone. We have a few cousins your size and she loves to dote on them. When they come here, they know they don't have to pack."

"And you?"

He grinned and gestured towards the dresser that was painted white. It matched the comforter. "I keep clothes here, so does Logan. This is the place we use when we come to see her."

"You have cousins?" He'd never told me about them before.

"Yeah." A fond grin appeared. "They're crazy and spoiled, but I think you'd like them."

"From your mother's side?" Obviously.

"She has two brothers and a little sister. They all have kids. Logan and I stay with dad, but we try to see them every now and then. It's been awhile."

"How long?"

"Since the summer. We went on a cruise with our cousins. My mom was in heaven. She loved having us with her side of the family."

"Mason." My chest hurt. The question I was about to ask was one that I'd had for awhile. "Why do you live with your dad? Why is it so important for you to stay?"

He seemed taken aback as he sat on the bed. Then, with a somber expression, he lifted his hand for me. My heart pounded with each step I took until I touched his hand with mine. His fingers were cool at first. He wrapped his hand around mine and warmth from him enveloped me soon after. Then he tugged me between his legs. As he fell down, he lifted me with him to straddle his waist. Then he gazed at me. The somber expression darkened to something else, something that stirred my heart.

He spoke in a soft voice, "Before this year, it was because of football. We stayed with our mom after they got divorced, but the school we were going to didn't have a good football team. Then dad told us about *your* dad. He wanted us to go to Fallen Crest Academy, but when we actually moved there and toured the school, I knew the team wasn't going to be good enough to get recruits. So we went to Public. They got a new coach, someone I had heard about. It seemed more promising. The team was better. The guys were bigger, tougher. They were more serious about football, so we went there. It was the right move for me. I don't know about Logan. He's not as serious about football as me. I think he just played because I did."

"And now?"

His grin softened as he reached up and traced the side of my face with his finger. He brought it down before he cupped the side of my face. His lips touched my cheek, softly and tenderly. My eyes closed as he moved to my lips. Heat started low within me but rose at a rapid pace. My heart picked up, and I was panting before his lips touched mine fully. Then he opened them, demanding more, commanding more from me, and I answered. My mouth opened. As his tongue swept inside, mine rubbed against his. It was one of my favorite things to do. We were connected, inside and out. Then I wanted more. It was always the same. I'd always want more with him.

As he pulled away, I groaned, but grinned as I heard his soft chuckle. I rested my forehead on his when he panted out, "What do you think?"

I grinned, feeling silly from how happy I was. "Because of me?"

His hand cupped under my head and tilted me back. My eyes opened and widened when I saw the fierceness in his. "I won't get run off from you. I love you, Sam. I said it before and I mean it. I won't let your mom control my life."

When a thread of hostility slipped into his tone, my heart raced. I knew he didn't like my mother, but I was starting to wonder if he hated her.

He continued, "I was okay with her moving in. I had one year left. I didn't figure she could do much damage in that one year."

"What about Logan?" My hands lifted to his shoulders. I took hold there.

He shrugged as he bent and placed a soft kiss on my shoulder. Then he sat further up and slid a hand underneath me. He lifted me even closer so I wrapped my legs around his back. We were fully aligned together. Remove his jeans, mine and he could've slipped inside of me. I felt him harden against me. The feeling of him was intoxicating.

"Before you, I think he would've moved back with our mom. He liked our old school. He liked going to school with our cousins. Two of them, James and Will, are just like Logan. They're the three musketeers."

I shuddered at that thought. "Three Logans?"

"Yeah." Mason chuckled again as he gazed up at me. "But that was awhile ago. Why are you asking?"

"You think he'll stay another year?"

"He will since you'll be there. You know both of us want you to transfer to Public. We have a better track team. I've talked to you about that before."

I sighed as I remembered those conversations. Mason brought it up once when we had been in bed. Then it was raised again at the kitchen table. Logan brought up the topic, Mason jumped in, and I was double-teamed. I never told them what I had decided, but the truth was that I wasn't sure.

Fallen Crest Academy was a better school, but they were right. Fallen Crest Public had a better track team. Mason went to their track coach. He agreed to meet with me and he watched me run every day over the last week. He timed how long I would go on their inside track, but he hadn't said anything during our last session. I wanted to wait until I knew that it would be worth the transfer.

"I don't get it, Sam. Why do you want to stay there? Douchebag turned everyone against you."

I grinned down at him, at the frustration in his voice. "You look cute when you're pissed with me."

"Then I must be cute whenever we talk about this. I'm always pissed with you about this. Why won't you transfer? It makes no sense to me. You could get a scholarship, Sam. Let's be real here. Do you really want to depend on your mom's help to go to college? Or your dads'? Neither of them has contacted you recently. Have they? And what's up with that?"

A different headache was coming on. It was low and probing. I shook my head. I didn't want to discuss either of them. "I understand why you want me to transfer. I get it. I do. But I don't know if it'll be worth it. I haven't even heard back from Coach Grath. I might not make the team, so why would I transfer schools?"

"Besides not going to school with Douchebag and all his little followers?" He grumbled, "You have no friends over there. They're weak as hell."

"Maybe." They were. "But it's a good school. I've always gone there and my dad—"

I looked away, but his fingers were quick as lightning. He grabbed my chin and kept me from turning away. I started to struggle, but his hold tightened. It was useless. He'd already heard.

His eyes narrowed to slits. "That's why you don't want to transfer, isn't it? Because of your dad. You think it's one way to still see him, don't you?"

I fell quiet. It wasn't because I didn't want to talk about that. It was because I couldn't. My throat swelled and it felt like an elephant was on my chest. It hurt to push past both of those emotions, or ignore how my heart rate skyrocketed.

"Sam."

I shook my head. I tried to look away, but a tear slipped out.

He cursed under his breath and then bundled me in his arms once more. I curled up in his lap as he folded me against his chest so we were both settled against the bed's headboard. Then he brushed some of my hair away from my forehead. His fingers slid down and brushed away more of my tears. I couldn't stop them. I never could when I really thought about my dad. So instead, I tried to never think about him.

Another soft curse slipped past his lips. He pressed a kiss to my forehead. "I'm sorry. I am."

My hands curled into his shirt. I held on with a desperation I never would've shown four months ago. Now I couldn't help myself with him. I needed him. Hell, I starved for him at times.

He continued to brush more of my hair from my eyes. "How long has it been?"

I shook my head. It still hurt to talk.

"If they won't reach out to you, you should reach out to them."

I looked up now. Panic coursed through me. He couldn't be suggesting...

He nodded. "You heard me. You go to them and find out what the hell is going on."

A ragged chuckle ripped from me. It was so easy for him. If people stood in his way, Mason went through them. It wasn't a question if they would stop him. It was a question of how he would go through them, if he would stomp them down, barrel through them, or just throw them out of his way.

Things were different with me.

"Why are you laughing?" He tilted my head back again.

536

I shook my head. God, it hurt sometimes.

"Talk to me, Sam," he groaned.

I closed my eyes. "It's not why we're here."

"What?"

"We're here to get away from all that stuff. I don't want to talk about them right now. We're here to spend time together, just you and me."

His hand fell away from my hip. "Are you serious?"

I lifted a shoulder, but I looked away. Then I bit my lip. My heart started to pound again. And I waited...

There was a heavy silence between us.

I continued to wait.

"Fine."

Relief flared through me. My shoulders relaxed as the sudden tension lifted from them. I didn't realize how important it was for him not to press the point. I would handle my fathers, the biological one and the one that raised me, one day. I just couldn't handle them this day, but one day... I would have to one day.

CHAPTER FIVE

It was early when his phone lit up. Logan was the first to call at six in the morning. When Mason checked the time, he cursed and sat upright as he took the call. I listened from beside him, even though I turned my own phone on and saw twelve voice messages from my mother.

"Wait, slow down."

I could hear Logan's excited voice still going strong on the other side. After another minute, a savage curse came from Mason. His shoulders tightened and his jaw clenched.

My heart sank. It wasn't good.

Then I sighed and got up from the bed. It was time for me to handle my mother. Mason and Logan were great buffers, but I was the only one who had the voice to quiet her. As I dressed, I felt his eyes on me. After I emerged from the bathroom, showered and fully dressed, he stood and held his hand over the phone. "What are you doing?"

"We're going back."

His eyebrows went high. "We just got here."

"I know." My heart was in the pit of my stomach. I was tired of feeling it there. I needed to stop hiding from my mother and from the situation. I'd been hiding since our parents found out about us. This had to stop.

"You're sure?"

I nodded. I knew I had the resolved face on and Mason removed his hand from the phone. "Hang on, Logan. We're coming back."

It didn't take long to pack our stuff. We hadn't packed anything to begin with. As for the break from reality, this one had been a short one. A part of me was pissed that we had even come. Enough was enough. I wasn't going to be harassed through phone calls by my mother. And I wasn't going to hear her threats through other people anymore.

Stuart held the door for us as we left. The Escalade had been pulled up, waiting for us. The smile on Stuart's face slipped a bit when he caught my eye, but he gave Mason a hug before he drove off. After a quick stop for breakfast and coffee, we were on our way back. The ride was passed in silence, tense silence for me. I glanced at Mason, but he seemed relaxed. Then again, this was his lifestyle. He didn't relish confrontations, but he didn't fear them either.

I wished I had that same quality. Sparring off against a catty girl was different from going against my mother, a mother that I knew I should've respected. I should've followed her rules from day one, but to be truthful, if my relationship with her had been better than my relationship with Mason, things might've been different. I bit my lip as I admitted to myself that I might not have slept with him. I loved him. I needed him, but I had been alone. I had been hurting. And I had been wasting away. He came at the perfect time, but things changed because of him. I was stronger now.

I had to be.

It was a few hours later when Mason took my hand in his. "You ready for this?"

The words couldn't come. I watched as he turned into the driveway. My mom's car was there. Logan's Escalade was beside hers and there was an SUV that I didn't recognize.

"I can turn around again. You don't have to go in there."

"I do." The words ripped from me and came out a hoarse whisper. I was terrified of my mother in that moment. This wasn't going to go well.

"Sam."

His voice stopped me when I was going to reach for the door. I looked back and melted. A soft plea was in his eyes.

His hand took mine again. He held on tight. "Don't let her ruin this."

I nodded, but there was a ball in my throat. The tears were about to spill.

"I can't promise what I'll do if your mom fucks with our relationship anymore. If she ruins this..." Raw desperation slipped from him, but it was mixed with a deadly warning as well.

I rushed across the car and pressed against him. My lips found his, and I tried to give him everything in that kiss. I wanted to give him my soul so I didn't let the kiss end. When he was about to pull away, I held on tighter.

"I won't let her change anything." I couldn't.

As we headed inside, the raised voices carried over us. I was sure the neighbors could hear when my mother shrieked before something shattered in the next room. My feet froze in place. My heart lurched into a stampede and a wave of dizziness swept over me. Good god. I was transported back to another time when my mother threw a fit. She screamed bloody murder that night, so long ago, as she tore pictures to pieces. She threw plates across the room. A bat was taken to the China cabinet. All the dishes had been destroyed. At the end of her fit, four hours later, there had been nothing left intact.

"*You did this!*" she raged as she pointed her finger at me.

But that'd been six years ago. I was a month away from turning into an adult. I swallowed those emotions and pushed them down. I hadn't been haunted by them for so long; I wasn't going to start now. She wouldn't have that power over me.

"You okay?" Mason tugged on my hand with a frown.

Sweat broke out on my forehead. Heat flared inside of me. He couldn't see me like this. I had kept it together for so long; I didn't want him to see how that night had left me broken. So I swallowed all of it and nodded.

I tried to remember that I was seventeen. We were in a different home. We had a different life now.

"Sam."

"Yes?" The word ripped from my throat. I winced as I heard how hoarse my voice was. But then I was taken aback when he lifted his hand and brushed away some tears. His hand was cool against my skin. I breathed his touch in. It was soft, tender. I needed it at that moment. Hell. I needed his strength. My mother had taken all of mine in that one second.

"Hey, hey." He stepped close to me and framed my face in his hands. He peered down with concern. "What's wrong?"

I shook my head and pulled away.

"Stop."

I brushed his hands away.

"She did this to me!"

I jumped back from the ferocity in her scream. There was a rage there that I thought she had lost so long ago, but I was wrong. I wondered if she'd kept it hidden from James? Had it been there the whole time?

I swallowed a breath. My shoulders lifted up and rolled back. I knew what I would face in the next room, and then I stepped forward. I was ready for it.

Logan laughed before he ended it with a snort. "Are you fucking with me? No wonder she ran away from you."

"Logan!"

Analise screamed again before something shattered once more.

Logan cheered, "Do it again! Do it again, Psycho Woman!"

"Logan, shut up!"

"Oh, come on, dad. Look at her. She's crazy—"

I stepped around the corner, with Mason right behind me. The amusement fled from Logan as he took in the sight of us, or me. I couldn't have looked normal as my heart was pounding. My gut was telling me to run away from her. But I didn't. Mason brushed his hand against mine as he stepped around to shield me.

James swallowed when he looked up, but I couldn't take my eyes from my mother.

Analise was in her bathrobe with her hair done up. She looked like they had gone to a formal event the night before and she had gone to bed with her hair and make-up still done up. But there were black splotches on her face from where her mascara bled and her eyes were wild. Some of her hair stuck up, and she never calmed the strands. A plate was in her hand, but she lowered it as she raked me over with her eyes. They were cold, so cold. A chill went down my back.

This was the mother I feared from so long ago. She was back.

"You," she seethed.

I scrambled back a step before I realized what I was doing, but it was too late. Triumph flared in her depths. She still had that power over me, and her chest swelled up. As I watched her, I could see the power swelter inside of her. She thrived on it, but then Logan jumped to his feet. He had been sitting on a chair in the back. He cursed now.

She sucked in her breath and turned. I knew she was ready to blast him.

"And you want to know why we took off?" Mason's icy tone stopped everything. He gestured towards his dad and then swept a hand towards Analise. "Look at her. She's off her rails, dad. I don't want Sam near her."

Analise's eyes widened. Her hand clenched around the plate again.

I was frozen in place. Mason's hand reached behind him, and he pulled me close so I was pressed against his back. Then I closed my eyes. I was supposed to be the one fighting. I knew it had to be me, but I rested my forehead against his back. She had taken all the strength from me that I had accumulated over the last five months. She sucked me dry, and I was left trembling like I had when I was eleven years old.

"Samantha," she said in a sharp tone. "Look at me."

I trembled.

Mason laughed at her. "Fuck that."

"Screw you." This time it was Logan. His voice rose, as did his anger. "Who are you to talk to her like that?"

Analise sucked in her breath. "She is my daughter. I am her mother. That's who I am."

"Then act like it," Mason's tone was savage. He had stiffened to stone before me. "I don't know who raised you, but my mom and dad would never talk to me like that."

"Maybe they should've," she proclaimed.

My eyes clasped tighter, but I could see her in my mind. I knew her chin was in the air, her eyes were brazen, and she was open to a fight. My mother was a beautiful woman with dark black hair that was straight and sleek. She had a slim build and when she was dressed in form-fitting dresses, she looked elegant. A classic sophisticated look clung to her and made her seem angelic to men. I always knew when she wanted something because she would put on her soft-pink dress and cozy up to David with an endearing smile. She would use caresses over dinner to get what she wanted, and it always worked. He folded every time and from what I had witnessed, James Kade wasn't any different. She could've beaten me up and she would only need a trembling lip, a few tears, and remorseful eyes to pull him back in.

Analise might've been crazy, but she had power over the opposite sex. She used it as a weapon.

"Analise!" James scolded her this time.

I sucked in my breath. My hands were now fisted into the back of Mason's shirt.

"What—James?"

Gone was the rage. Her voice softened. She had stepped wrong. I started the countdown in my head. 3...

"You can't say things like that, not about my own children."

2...

Logan snickered.

1…

"Oh, honey," her voice melted. "I didn't mean it like that. I'm so sorry. I am. It's just—I've been worried about my baby. He took her away from me, and I'm losing her, James. I can't lose my daughter."

Cue the sniffles.

She whimpered, "I just love her so much, James. You can understand that, can't you?"

"Oh my god." Logan's disgust was evident.

"Logan," his dad barked, but he had already softened. "It might be best if you leave the room. All of you."

"Are you kidding me?" Mason gutted out. His hands rose in the air, in fists. "She's working you, dad. You're falling for this?"

James sucked in his breath. Then he delivered with cold disdain, "Your mother called today. She would like for you and Logan to spend your break with her at the Malibu Estate. I think it would be best for everyone to leave as soon as possible."

He cursed. "I'm not leaving Sam here. If I go, she goes."

"What—"Analise started.

"Honey." James' sharp rebuke quieted her. Then he turned again. "Mason, I think it's best if there was some distance between you and Samantha. You have proven that neither of you can act responsibly. I had hoped you would've when we first learned of your relationship, but your disappearing trick did not help your credibility at all." He sounded tired all of the sudden. "I have asked you on many occasions to cease from being intimate, at least under this roof, but you have discarded my wishes on every matter. You have given me no other choice. I will not allow you to disappear with Samantha one more time. Her mother was beside herself and you put both of us through hell as we worried where you might've gone or even if you were going to come back."

When he finished, the room was silent for a moment. And then Logan threw his hands in the air, cursing as Mason bit out, "Are you fucking with me now?"

"No way." Logan shook his head. "We're not going. We go, she goes."

"I'm sorry, boys. I am. But neither of you are welcome in this home for the duration of your winter break." James seemed beaten down as he gestured to the side.

A large man came forward. He was dressed in a three-piece suit that stretched over his muscular shoulders and trim waist. His eyes lacked emotion as he nodded to Mason and then Logan. "Gentlemen."

"Are you serious, dad?" More curses came from Logan. "I can't believe this. What have *I* done?"

"Logan, we all know you support their relationship and have a soft spot for Samantha as well."

"She's like my sister."

"Regardless, you both protect her, which I find admirable, but you have become destructive to her relationship with her mother. You both need to go. You remember Howard?"

"And what if I refuse to go?" Mason stepped forward. His tone was hard.

"Mr. Mason." Howard stepped forward. "Your bags have already been packed and your mother is waiting for our arrival—"

"I'm not going," Mason cut him off. "Sorry, Howard, but I'm not twelve this time. You can't force me to go anywhere. I'm eighteen, dad. You can't bus me off anymore, and I won't play along this time."

"Fine, but you will not be allowed to see Samantha while she lives under this house."

"And what if she doesn't?" Mason folded his arms over his chest.

Everyone stood still at the stand-off between father and son.

I held my breath as my feet were still rooted where I clung to Mason's back. I yearned for his warmth, but my head hung down. I couldn't bear the idea of making eye contact with my mother. I knew she would've won then. She would've known that she had reduced me to that eleven-year-old so long ago again. I cringed as I remembered that time. I couldn't go back to that pain, not anymore.

"Howard," James spoke. "You will accompany Logan to the car. If Mason refuses to go with you, you are instructed to leave within ten minutes."

"But—"

"Yes, sir." Howard turned. "Mr. Logan? The car, please."

"What—no way." Logan's mouth hung open. He was speechless, but then he rebooted. "Dad, come on. This is insane. You're kicking me out? Are you kidding me?"

James turned to him. He was so stiff. "I have been forced to play my hand and this is it, Logan. If you wish to remain in my household and spend the rest of your high school years here, with Samantha, you will do as I have told. You will vacation with your mother for the break. When you return, you will respect my rules. If you do not, you will have two choices. You can live with your mother or I will have you arrested as a runaway. You are not eighteen, Logan." Then he turned on his heel and addressed his oldest son. "And Mason, those rules pertain to you as well. I cannot make you go to your mother's, but what we *can* do is enforce those rules to Samantha. She is still a minor. If she leaves her mother's household, she will be arrested as a runaway."

My eyes closed again as I heard my worst nightmare come true. She had trapped me. New panic came over me and I gulped for breath, but then I heard Mason's shrewd laughter. His voice was soft, so soft it sent chills down my spine. "You've forgotten one fact, dad."

"And what's that?"

"You've got one month. She turns eighteen in one month."

Analise sucked in her breath and James seemed visibly shaken, but he sighed. "Fine, then. I have one month to undo the damage you've unleashed on their relationship."

"What?" Logan cried out again. "You seriously think—"

"Logan, LEAVE!" his father roared.

Logan's mouth snapped shut as Howard cleared his throat. Then his shoulders dropped in surrender. "Yeah, yeah. Whatever. I'm going."

When he shuffled past me, he folded me in his arms and whispered, "Don't worry, Sammy. The game's just begun. Take care." He pressed a kiss to my forehead before he headed outside. The big stiff followed behind, and then the door closed behind both of them.

Mason shook his head. "This is ridiculous. She's brainwashed you, dad. You don't see that?"

James closed his eyes before he rubbed a weary hand over his jaw. His hair seemed to have grayed over the last ten minutes. His voice was exhausted as he spoke, "I'm sorry that you feel that way, Mason. I truly am, but I have to stand with my future wife. Things have been run by you and your brother for too long. It's time I made things right again."

I glanced up at Mason. The dark promises in his depths made my stomach fall to the ground. I knew without asking that this was only the beginning. And for a second, I worried what he was going to do.

CHAPTER SIX

An hour later and I still couldn't wrap my head around how things had changed. Logan was gone, like gone gone. I wouldn't see him for two more weeks, when school would start again. And Mason was at Nate's.

I drew in a shuddering breath as I sat at my desk. My computer was on, but my hands hadn't touched the keyboard.

Mason was gone.

Mason couldn't see me.

Analise forbade me to see him and if I did, then what? I gulped. She made it clear that she would follow through with James' threat. The first moment that I would go to him, she would call the cops and have me arrested as a runaway. Could she even do that? I had no idea. Could she really force all of this? But Mason was right. I had one more month before I was legally on my own.

As I sat there, I saw a blinking light on my phone and pressed to hear the message.

A deep voice came over the phone, "This is Edward Grath, Coach Grath. I apologize for not getting back to you after last Friday, but I wanted to run your times by a few other coaches in the area." He drew in an excited breath. "Not only can I guarantee you a spot on our track team, but I will guarantee that you will get a scholarship after this year. I've already put feelers out for recruiters and one called me. They're very interested in you. If you keep running at these times, you will have no problem receiving a full scholarship to a college. Congratulations, Samantha. Give me a call this week. I'd like to start a training regime with you as soon as possible."

I sat there. I'd gotten on the team? He guaranteed a scholarship? I blinked as his words registered with me, then I scrambled for the phone again. This time I hit the button for Mason, but the line went flat. The operator informed me the line had been disconnected.

What the hell?

I pulled the phone away and stared at it. Had I hit the right button? He was on my speed dial. It should've been right, but after I did it again and then located his number in my contacts I was left speechless. Mason's phone was no more. I tried Logan, but it was the same results. They both disconnected their lines? Was it something against their dad? Why hadn't they given me their new numbers? I knew they would've.

Holy. I sat there, even more dejected than before. I had this great news and I couldn't tell the two people who cared about me.

Nate.

Even as the idea popped in my head, I knew I didn't have his number so I pushed away from my desk and grabbed my purse. I stepped into the hallway, but stopped short. Analise was there in a silk robe and a frown. She crossed her arms. "Where are you going?"

"I'm going to see Mason."

"No, you're not."

"Yes, I am."

Her eyes narrowed and my old fear flickered in me again. Since I had remembered that night so long ago, I couldn't undo the effects. I thought I had been rid of that power over me, but she had me in the grip of her hand. If she squeezed, I didn't know how I would react.

"No," she said slowly and softly. It was menacing. "You're not."

I swallowed a ball of emotion and rubbed my hands against my pants. Then I rasped out, "What are you going to do, Analise? What are you going to do if I don't listen to you?"

"Analise," she hissed. "You call me by my first name now?"

"I'm seventeen. I'll be an adult in one month. Your attempt to control me is pathetic." My words were so brave, but I struggled to keep my knees from knocking against each other. She'd hear and she couldn't know.

To my surprise, when I expected the old rage to return, she shook her head and stepped back. Her head bent down, and she swallowed back a tear. I heard the hitch in her voice, and I sucked in my own breath. I couldn't believe what I had just heard. But she spoke so softly, I strained to hear her. "Do you realize that having sexual intercourse with a minor is against the law?"

Silence. Complete silence.

Her words hit me like a ton of bricks. I felt blown over and kicked while I was still down. She wouldn't—she couldn't—but, wait...she could. "You wouldn't."

She lifted her head. A challenge was there. "Not yet, I haven't."

"No way." I shook my head. She wouldn't do that. She could ruin his life...

Then she cleared her throat and sighed. "I don't want to, Samantha, but I have been losing you since we moved in. I won't stand for it anymore. No one is going to come in here and take my daughter away from me. No one. Not your father, not your boyfriend, not your friends, no one." Her chest rose with each statement. She was bristling with anger again. "I won't even let you get in the way of our relationship."

She started down the hallway, but stopped and twisted back around. "And we're monitoring your internet if you decide to reach out to them. I don't want you anywhere near Mason *or* Logan."

"You can't keep me caged up like an animal. I'm an adult in one month."

"Then I have one month to get my daughter back. And I will do it." Her eyes narrowed. "If you go anywhere near

Mason, I will have him arrested for statutory rape. I believe there are enough people who can testify that you've had intercourse with him."

No one would. People suspected. I wasn't a fool. Mason was a Kade, of course he was having sex with his girlfriend, but there was no proof. However, did I call her bluff? Then my heart sank. I couldn't risk it. It was Mason's life on the line now, and it was one month.

I took a deep breath. One month. I couldn't see him for one month.

Oh god.

I went back to my room, but it wasn't long before it hit me, really hit me. I couldn't see Mason. I couldn't see Logan. Panic settled over me and I went to the shower. With my clothes on, I turned the spray on full blast and sunk to the floor. When the water warmed, I hugged my knees to my chest and rested my forehead between them. Then I took in one gulping breath after another.

I could do this. I knew I could do this.

Hell.

I've done it before, when I had two best friends who weren't friends at all. That was when the names of Mason and Logan had seemed surreal. I considered them assholes then. I took care of myself then. I could do it again.

The hallway was dark and narrow. The walls stretched higher than I could see and as I walked to the bathroom, I couldn't catch my breath. There was something thundering in my ear. It wouldn't stop. I frowned against the pain, but I had to go to the bathroom. I knew my mom wouldn't be happy if I disturbed anything so I trekked down the hallway as silent as I could. My bare feet were so cold. The carpet didn't warm them up. I should've worn the socks my mom insisted I wear to bed, but I always pulled them off when she left my room. I hated sleeping in them. They would get caught on my blankets, and I would wake up with my blankets tangled all around me. As I stubbed my toe against something, I whimpered and fell to the ground. I opened and closed my mouth as I tried not to let any sound out. If my mom was sleeping, I dared not wake her. She would get so mad.

When the pain subsided and I knew I wouldn't cry out, I stood back up and limped forward. I really had to pee now, but I went slower. I didn't want to hurt my toes again so I felt along the wall as I went. When I got to the corner, I turned and paused. The light was on in the bathroom. The crack underneath was lit.

Oh no.

I pressed my hands between my legs. I had to pee so bad. I couldn't go there. My mom would be really mad then.

I started to shake back and forth. It was too dark out to use the bathroom downstairs. And too cold. I was shivering already as I waited for what I should do, but then I wondered if anyone was really in there. Maybe my mom had left it on by accident—no, not possible. She double-checked everything before she went to bed. Every light was turned off. Every door was locked. All the windows were checked three times.

If anyone left it on, then it was dad. Relief went through me. If he had done it, then I could use it. Or if he was in there, he wouldn't be mad at me. He never was.

Oh my god. I had to pee!

I inched closer to the door, but I didn't hear anything. Then I knelt and tried to see underneath the door. I couldn't see anyone either. Then, with a deep breath (I was so nervous) I started to turn the doorknob.

When it wasn't locked, a big smile came over me. It would've been locked if someone had been in there so I pushed it open.

Then I froze.

My eyes went wide as I saw the blood first.

"AHHHHH!" I jerked awake and bolted upright in bed. My scream stopped abruptly and my chest heaved up and down. I couldn't get enough breath. I pounded on my chest. My heart was racing.

I tumbled out of bed. My legs weren't steady so I fell to the ground. The sheets were tangled around my legs and I sat there shivering. I wasn't cold. I was hot. I felt my forehead and wondered if the burning was in my mind or not? But no, I wiped my hand over my forehead and felt the sweat from it.

Oh my god.

I took more breaths. I needed to calm down.

It was awhile before I could move. The sheer terror was still there. I felt it in my chest and I wanted to pound on it so it would go away, but it didn't. It lingered. Oh god. I wanted Mason. He should've been beside me. He would've caught me and I would've been in his arms by now, but I remembered what happened the day before.

I closed my eyes. Everything would be fine. It was only a month, but as I said that to myself, it didn't matter. I needed him then. So I did the next best thing I could think of—I grabbed my blanket and went to his room.

I stood in the middle of his room, and I breathed it in. It smelled of him, of men's cologne and his aftershave. I calmed a little bit because of that, but then I crawled underneath his covers. I had used his body to warm me up before, but I wouldn't have that now. I spread my blanket on top and curled underneath. I hugged his pillow to me and tried to go back to sleep again.

Two hours later, I was still awake. I rolled over and glanced at his clock. It was now three in the morning.

Screw it.

I hurried from his bed and flipped on his bathroom light. I pulled on a pair of his black warm-up pants with one of his school sweatshirts. Then I went to my room, slipped on my shoes, and grabbed my purse. On the way downstairs, I grabbed my keys and went out the door. When it locked behind me, I got into my car and headed to Nate's house.

It was a risk. A big one, but I needed to see Mason. It was 3:23 in the morning when I pulled into his driveway. All the lights were off and I didn't have a phone number to wake him up so I had one option. I pounded on his door and rang the doorbell until someone woke up. When some lights were turned on inside and I heard cursing, I stepped back and waited.

Nate threw the door open. His face was in a scowl, but he took one look at me and turned back. "Mason!" Then he threw the door open and I swept inside.

"Where is he?"

He gestured upstairs. "The room you guys used before."

I ran upstairs and met him halfway. Mason's eyes went wide as he saw me, but he didn't say a word. He caught me on the stairs, lifted me in the air, and turned right around. I couldn't take my eyes off of him. I drank in the sight of him.

My hand touched the side of his face, where it was rough with stubble, and I breathed out, "You look so damn good."

He groaned and looked down with a soft smile. "You too." Then we were inside the room. He kicked the door shut behind him and sank onto the bed with me. His lips fused onto mine, and I gasped. I arched up against him as I clung to him, and my legs wrapped around his waist.

I was starving for him. I was ready to explode before he even touched me, but when he did, I shoved him back and scrambled on top of him. It wasn't long after that when he flipped me back over and we both groaned as he slid inside of me.

When he moved to thrust in and out, my head fell back on the pillow. I was intoxicated with the feel of him. I would never get enough of him, but for now, for the next two hours, I would try.

CHAPTER SEVEN

After we made love a second time, I got up from the bed and started to pick up my clothes.

Mason shifted on the bed. "What are you doing?"

"I have to go back."

"Come on. They're not going to arrest you for running away. I called someone I know in law school. He doesn't even think they can do that."

"No, but they can have you arrested for statutory rape," I snapped at him but stopped and gulped as I saw his eyes widen. He jumped out of the bed and came towards me. I shook my head as I held up my hands. "Don't. I have to go back. I shouldn't have even come over."

"Hey, hey."

"Stop, Mason." I shrugged off his hand. But then my head jerked back up. "Did you get a new phone number?"

"What?"

"Your number's been disconnected."

"Are you serious?" He crossed to his jeans and pulled out his phone, and then he scrolled through and tried to call me. Nothing.

"Logan's too."

He tried calling a few others and cursed. "What the hell? My phone's dead." Then he groaned. "I can't believe this. He killed our phones. Shit." But there was another emotion there. Mason chuckled a second later as he shook his head. "That was a good move."

My mouth dropped. "Good move?" I took two steps, grabbed his phone and threw it against the wall. My chest was heaving as the fury churned deep in me. "This isn't chess, Mason. I couldn't call you. I freaked out tonight—I had a nightmare and I—" I couldn't talk about it. I didn't want to.

"Hey." His voice dropped to a soothing note. Then his hands were next. They touched my shoulders gently.

I stiffened and twisted away from him. He didn't get it. He didn't get it at all. "This isn't a vacation, Mason. My mom's not normal anymore—"

He snorted. "Was she ever?"

He didn't understand. He wouldn't. He hadn't lived with her when she—I closed my eyes. No. I wouldn't think of it. But the nightmare came back to me. All that blood. I shivered as I felt transported back to that time, in that hallway, as I pushed the door open and saw her.

"Sam!"

"What?" I was jerked back as Mason shook my shoulders. When I clicked back to our reality, I had to blink a few times to clear my eyes. He'd gone pale and he looked shaken. "What?" I missed something. I could tell.

He cursed. "Don't ever do that again."

"Do what?"

"You checked out, like you went somewhere else. You scared the crap out of me." His hand shook as he pulled me close to him and cradled my head to his chest. His head tucked down against mine as he tried to soothe me, or maybe himself.

I pulled away to collect my purse. "I have to go. I have to be back before she finds me gone."

He snorted again, but followed me downstairs and to my car. When I slipped inside, he knelt beside the window.

"Mason, I *have* to go."

Panic was starting to seep in. He just didn't get it.

"I know." Irritation flashed over his face. "Look, how do I see you? I'm not following these stupid rules. Forget it."

"She'll have you arrested—"

He rolled his eyes. "No, she won't. I know my dad. He won't allow that."

I shook my head. "Mason, you didn't hear my mom. She really meant it. She'll do it without his approval. He might not even know about it, but I know she'll do it. Something's happened to my mom. She's not the same anymore. She's how she used to be—" I bit off my words. Again. It was best if no one knew how she had been. They wouldn't know how to handle her. They didn't know how to handle her now.

Then I felt his eyes on me. They were seeing through me like they always had. Everything was going to be ruined. I felt it in my bones. She was going to ruin everything.

"Look, I love you. I won't let her do anything, okay? How do I see you?"

I shrugged, but I needed to go. It was five in the morning. James would be up soon. He was the early riser in the family. I had thirty minutes and it took me over twenty to drive there. "I have to go!"

"Okay, okay."

He jerked away from the car and I pushed down the accelerator. My car shot out of there. On the drive there, I gripped onto the steering wheel with white knuckles. I could barely breathe. Every light seemed to turn red when I got there. Curses slipped from me as I fought myself from tearing through the lights. It wasn't the worry of safety since traffic wasn't too bad, but I couldn't risk the chance of getting a ticket. Then they'd know. My mom would know.

As soon as I pulled into the driveway, I sprinted to the basement area and slid in through the bottom door. Then I let loose a huge breath. My hands were trembling, but I tried to be as silent as I could as I made my way up the back steps to my room.

When I got to my room, I couldn't calm down. Panic rose within me. My arms still shook. I tried crawling into Mason's bed. That didn't help either. There was a ball at the bottom of my stomach. It was twisting and churning, rolling over and over. The unease in me was burning up and all my emotions were fuel to its fire. It was lit and as I tried to ignore it, the flame built and built. Finally, I threw back the covers and went to my room for my running clothes. As soon as my sneakers were on and my earbuds were in, I bolted from the house. Everything inside of me was ablaze so I pushed hard in my run.

After an hour, the panic was still in me. It was slick and slimy. It crawled all over my body and I couldn't get rid of it. So I pushed harder. Another hour went by, but I was still feverish. My heart was pounding as the fear acted as a poison. It sent everything into hyperdrive. I was soaked in a cold sweat an hour after that. Then my hands started to tingle, but I continued to go faster. I felt something at my heels. I could hear Analise's voice. She chased me as I was now sprinting down the street. No matter how far I went, how fast I went, I couldn't outrun her. And then I collapsed.

I fell to the ground on someone's front lawn. My arms and legs were spread out and my chest heaved up and down. My pulse pounded throughout my body. It was one solid *thumpthumpthump*. I felt it all the way through my toes.

I couldn't move so I remained there and stared at the sky. The sun had risen a few hours ago, but the sounds of the morning were just starting. I should've moved. I looked like a crazy woman, but I couldn't. My limbs had turned off and refused to listen to my brain. I knew to get up, but my heart said to stay still.

I kept breathing. My chest rose up and down. The sick panic in my gut never went away, but I gulped breath after breath and I tried to numb it down.

"Sam?"

Oh god.

My eyes closed as I recognized that voice. I couldn't face him, not like this.

The sound of his car hit me like a cold wave. His tires moved slowly over the gravel on the road as he pulled to the side. Then his engine turned off and I gulped. I knew what was happening. When his door opened and closed, I needed to face facts. He was coming over. He was going to see the near-hysteria on me and he was going to ask questions.

Everything clenched inside of me. Then, as my body lifted up by its own accord, I looked at him with grave eyes. At the sight of him, freshly showered, with a pair of jeans and a tight tee shirt, everything went dead inside of me.

He was everything I was not.

He was the golden boy of a rich private school. He was gorgeous. He had talent. He was the football quarterback, most popular and most wanted guy in our school. He had it all. I had none of it.

I took a gaping breath and tried to remember who I had become, but it didn't matter. In that moment there was no Mason, there was no Logan. Not even Nate. They'd been stripped from me, and I was the same as I always wanted to deny before. I was the unwanted child to a hustler. My mother. I never wanted to admit it, but it was the truth. She had loved someone else, became pregnant with me, and hustled a stand-up guy to marry her. Enter David Strattan. He raised me, loved me—or so I thought—and loved my mother. Then came the time when she found another con, another one that fell in love with her, a better one—wealthier one—than David Strattan.

It was hard to swallow.

Adam crossed the street now, but I couldn't stop the thoughts racing in my head.

I was nothing. I had always been nothing. My mother tolerated me because I came from her. I felt like her. I felt like I had conned Mason into loving me. I had conned Logan into protecting me, but it was all a lie. If they saw inside of me—how I was the dirty spawn from my mother—would they still stand by me?

Adam's foot stepped onto the lawn where I sat.

I swallowed everything down. All the gravity, all the deadness, all the truth. Down it went, and I blinked at him, back to the shell I projected to everyone.

"It is you." He blinked in confusion. "Are you okay?"

I pushed it down so fast that I could almost pretend it was never there. I grinned up at him and grimaced at the same time. "I'm a mess, but yeah. I'm fine."

He shared my grin. The corner of his lip curved up to his cheek and a dimple showed. "I'm not going to disagree with you. One of those mornings, huh?"

My stomach dropped. My smile stayed the same. "Where are you headed?"

"Uh." He scanned up and down the street, but then shrugged before he dropped down to sit next to me. He drew up his knees in the same way I sat. His arms hung from them as he looked casual and relaxed. "To tell you the truth, I was going on a date."

"A date?" On a Tuesday morning?

"Yeah." His head ducked down in a sheepish manner. "It's my mom's idea to help fix her marriage."

I blinked at him. "Come again?"

He grimaced and rolled his eyes. "I know. It's stupid." Then he groaned as his head fell between his knees. "I can't believe I'm even doing this."

"How is your date going to fix her marriage?"

"Gawd, I have no idea. I really have no idea, but it's my mom's latest project. She likes to focus on everybody else's life rather than her own."

His head shot up and bitterness flashed over him. I expected it to go away the next second, but it stayed. Then I sat farther up. This wasn't the Adam who was angry at me because I was dating Mason. This was the friend I once thought I had.

He added, "He didn't come home last night so, of course, when I got up for basketball practice this morning she had already called a friend of hers whose daughter just moved here. I'm supposed to meet this Felicia girl at the Country Club." A hollow laugh escaped him. "And she timed it as the perfect excuse so I could 'teach' the girl how to play tennis at the exact same time my dad always has a match. I bet we're even on the next court from him." He shook his head, raking a hand through his hair. "I'm supposed to spy for her."

"She said that?"

"No, but she'll want to know everything about the 'date' and by date, I mean my dad's match." He glanced over and quirked an eyebrow up. "Did I tell you that my dad's been playing one of his executive assistants at matches? And she's got the boobs, the ass, the tan—everything for her to be a younger version of my mom?"

"You think he's trying to replace her?"

His arms dropped off his knees and he stood. His jaw clenched as he looked away from me. "I have no idea, but that's what my mom thinks. From the screaming she was doing on the phone earlier, I don't think she even cares who hears her anymore. Hell. She might already be playing the custody card. I wouldn't put it past her."

"What do you mean?" But I knew. This was something my mother would've done as well, but I had to admit that my mom was better. She would've been two steps ahead of Adam's dad.

"Playing the sympathy card so my little sis will take her side. I know my little brother already thinks my dad's an asshole."

"Isn't he?"

His shoulders slumped suddenly. A defeated breath left him. "Yeah, but I keep hoping he'll prove me wrong." He glanced down. "I'll never be like him, Sam."

"Why are you telling me this?"

"Because I have to say it out loud. I have to say it to someone so that it's real to me. My dad won't ever change. I know he's having an affair, but it isn't with his tennis partner."

"Who then?"

He looked away. His mouth flattened. "Does it matter? He's going to leave her and she knows it. Do you know what that does to our family? What it's like to live in that? It's like living in a war zone, but no one wants to admit that they could get shot any second. I hate it." The same bitterness came out again. "I hate him. I hate her. Who would put up with that?"

I shot to my feet. Unnerved at the honesty from him and how exposed he revealed himself to me, I burst out, "Why are you telling me this? You dropped our friendship two months ago."

His mouth curved into a frown. His voice grew soft. "Because I was the asshole to you that I see my dad being to my mom every day. I'm sorry. I know you wanted my friendship. Hell, you needed my friendship. I knew that and I hurt you because you hurt me."

"You knew about Mason—"

He shot back, "That didn't mean I wanted to. I waited so long for you, Sam, and then you got scooped up by him." An ugly laugh wrung out from him. "That was a hard thing to swallow. I hate that guy." I opened my mouth, but his hand shot up. "Let me finish."

I closed it.

"I always thought the Kades were assholes. I still do, but I can't deny what I've seen with my own two eyes. They're good to you. They care about you, and he loves you. I see it in his eyes. He watches you when you have no idea he's even in the room. It's sickening to watch at times, but it's there and I have to deal with it. I hurt you, and I'm sorry for that."

I closed my eyes. Mason watched me when I didn't know it? That same familiar flutter came back in my stomach but tripled. I tried to hold back the smile that wanted to come out. Mason did love me, despite who my mother was.

"And I'm sorry about Becky. I lied to her so she wouldn't be your friend again. I already told her the truth and she's pissed with me, but she's scared of reaching out to you. She's embarrassed."

"What did you lie about?"

"I told her that you were using her because you had no other friends. I told her that you laughed at her behind her back a few times and that you looked down on her."

I gaped at him. Outrage was starting to boil inside of me.

He held up a hand in surrender. "I know. I know. I'm sorry. I really am and I'm going to make everything right. I will." His eyes held his promise. "I saw a counselor two weeks ago, and she said a few things that resonated. For me not to become like my dad, I actually have to *not* do the same things that he does. So I'm done lying. I won't lie to you anymore. I promise."

Why was he saying all these things? Not now, not when Mason had been taken from me and I was alone. But Becky— my heart sank at the lies he told her. If I was in her place, I might've done the same thing and gone away. Who wanted a friend who thought they were better than them?

"Can we be friends again, Sam?"

I expelled a ragged breath. A sense of doom started to settle, but I found myself nodding.

"You won't regret this."

I already did.

Adam visited with me a little bit more, but I had a hard time hearing his words. My mind was reeling as so much had changed in the last twenty-four hours. Mason and Logan had been ripped away. Adam and maybe Becky had come back in. And where was I?

When he left for his date, he was late but had a bright grin on his face. I finished my run back home. I felt raw. I felt exposed and vulnerable to anyone at that moment, but then I stopped in my tracks when I came to the house.

A security van was parked in our driveway. A man was kneeling at the door as I walked past him to the kitchen. There were two more focused on something on the wall. Analise stood with another who must've been their boss. He held the clipboard and was nodding as she gestured around the room.

Then she saw me. A dark smile came to her face. "Good morning, honey. I saw your sneakers were gone so I guessed you had gone on a run."

I gulped against the gloating in her eye. "What are they doing?"

She lifted a shoulder. "Oh, nothing much, honey. Nothing for you to worry about." Then her smile turned into a triumphant smirk. "They're installing a new security system."

My heart dropped. The cold sweat was back.

"We'll have security cameras in the house now."

CHAPTER EIGHT

I couldn't email Mason.

I couldn't call Mason.

I definitely couldn't see Mason.

By the afternoon, I was a caged animal: prowling my room, pacing back and forth, walking in circles, and snarling to myself.

So I did what I always did, I went running for the second time that day. Except this time my body was sluggish, my legs felt like lead, and I had a hard time pushing my demons at bay. After an hour of forcing myself to move faster than a crawl, I gave up and walked. And then I walked some more. After the second hour of walking, I realized that I was in a part of Fallen Crest that I was not familiar. It wasn't the 'bad' section, but it was definitely further than any of the hangouts I frequented.

"Screw you, Brandon! If you sleep with one more girl, there won't be anyone left to help out." A screen door banged shut and a rail-thin girl stood in front of it. She flung her arms back, one with a cigarette, and screamed inside, "I can't do it all alone, you know!"

Her response was a low curse, but she threw her head back in disgust before extending him the middle finger. Then she threw herself onto a metal chair behind the door. Another sat beside it with a bowl of cigarette butts between them. When the girl lit up, she exhaled dramatically and leaned back in the chair. A long pale leg braced on the wire rim that looked like a mini-bonfire container, and she pushed up so her chair rested on the back legs. As she sent out another puff, her eyes opened and then locked on me.

Shit.

I'd been staring the whole time, but I couldn't look away. That would be ridiculous now, like she'd caught me doing a bad thing.

Her hair was a dirty blonde mess. It was greasy, but for some reason it worked on her. It gave her a just-had-the-best-sex look. Her eyes were heavily made up to give her a smoky image, and her lips pursed together as she blew out some more smoke. "Hey, you."

"Yeah?"

"Come here." She waved her little fingers to me, beckoning me over. As I did, she gestured to the chair beside her. "Pop a squat." Then she leaned back again and studied me. After another drag, she narrowed her eyes. "Do I know you? You look familiar."

Everything was tense inside of me. I should've been exhausted. I ran for four hours earlier, followed by a two hour walk. Albeit that it was a slow as molasses walk, but it was still walking. It was movement, anything to keep me from doing something I couldn't do. When I had started out, I almost took my car, but I didn't trust myself in any vehicle. I would turn it around and go to Mason, I'd do it without a thought, and it wouldn't be until after both of us climaxed that I would realize the consequences. He didn't take my mother seriously, but I did. I had to for him or I would lose him.

A stabbing sensation seared through me. No one knew the lengths my mother would go to if she was pushed into a corner. Something had happened to make her feel boxed in. I had no idea what it was, but her true craziness was about to be unleashed.

"Hey!" The girl snapped her fingers in front of my face.

"Oh." I blinked rapidly. "Sorry."

She leaned back again on her chair after she flicked the butt onto the bowl between us. A second one was lit immediately, and she took another drag. "I know I know you. How do I know you?"

I swallowed a knot in my throat. "Do you go to Fallen Crest Academy?"

She snorted before a full-hearted laugh came from her throat. It was a low and raspy laugh. "God no. Thank god. Why? Do you?"

I nodded. "My dad's the football coach."

"No way." Her eyes snapped to attention. "My brother used to play football against them, that was three years ago. He ain't done nothing since—"

"I own this bar, Heather!" A roar came from inside. "I do *too* do crap."

She rolled her eyes. "Like I said, he hasn't done anything except screw my friends and run off ALL MY HELP." Her voice rose so he would hear inside.

She was awarded with another curse, but she chuckled softly as she took another drag from her cigarette. "Anyways, what's your name? Mine's Heather Jax. Idiot inside is Brandon, and my pops owns the diner side of our humble abode inside."

"Humble abode?" It was a run-down dive, and the customers gave me the feeling most had come straight from being incarcerated. The sign out front had the name Manny's scrawled over it in big white lettering on a black background with a green arrow pointed downwards. I'd never seen the place before, but what caught my attention had been Heather's screaming. The longer I sat there, the more a possible scenario played in my head.

She blew out the rest of her second cigarette. As she ground it into the bowl, I expected her to light up a third, but she merely folded back in her chair. Then she frowned and shot forward. "Hold on. Be right back." She was inside in the blink of an eye but back just as quickly with two Coronas. As she sat down and handed one over, she laughed. It was such a deep-throated sound that I knew Logan would've been all about her within seconds of meeting.

"Yeah, I guess you could call this place our humble abode." She shook her head as a wry grin curved a corner of her lip upwards. She tilted the bottle back and took a long drag. "It's ours and ours alone, no goddamn corporation owns it. We run it. Hell, we breathe this place. My mom bought it when I was three, but she took off when I was six. My dad raised us, the three of us, and we help out as much as we can. Brad's off playing football now. He got scouted to play for some big college across the country, but Brandon stayed. He does school online and runs the bar side of things. Dad does the books and I run the diner."

I had yet to take a sip from my beer.

She eyed me, half done with her own. "You sure I don't know you?"

Of course, she knew me. It didn't take a genius for me to realize this girl went to Fallen Crest Public. If she went there, she knew Mason and Logan, and chances were high that she had seen me at a party with them. Everyone went to those parties.

But a sixth sense nagged me. This girl didn't seem to give two cents about who Mason and Logan were. I wondered, no—I worried that she would hold it against me, and I didn't want that. I really didn't want that because as soon as I heard her yelling at her brother I already knew I wanted a job there. I wanted a place to hide from my mother as I tried to stay away from Mason for the month and this would be perfect.

"Are your customers dangerous?" The question slipped out before I realized how stupid that sounded, and offensive. God, what was my problem? "I'm sorry—"

Another deep-throated laugh sounded from her as she threw her head back. Then she finished the rest of her beer and tossed it into the bonfire. "Nah. No, they'd like you to think that, but they're all harmless. The most dangerous is Gus, but it's only because his farts are lethal. He lets them rip all the time."

"Really?"

"Yeah." Fondness lit up her eyes, but they grew serious after a moment. She focused back on me. "Come on, tell me straight. How do I know you?"

I hesitated. But then I went with my gut. She would be more pissed when she found out later, and I knew she would. It was inevitable. "I'm dating Mason Kade." Then I waited. The reaction would vary. She might want to use me, she might kick me out, or...I wasn't sure.

"Well damn then." She shot inside for another beer and clinked it against mine. "You got balls dating that one."

My mouth almost fell down. There was nothing, just... nothing. "I had a feeling you'd for sure send me off after I told you that."

Heather grinned and chuckled as she shook her head. She brushed back a bunch of her hair and yawned a full body yawn as she stretched. Her arms went wide, her chest went out, and her back arched against the metal chair. That's when I knew for sure Logan would've been salivating for the girl. She wore a tight red shirt, ripped at her waist to show off her midriff with a tight pair of washed-out jeans, torn at her knees and the ends. The girl looked like sex on a stick, or that's what Logan would've said.

"Nah." She gave me lopsided grin. "Something tells me you're a smart one and you picked me for a reason, just like I called you over. You want a job here, don't you?"

I did. I really did, but I bit my lip. I didn't know if Mason would approve, but it didn't matter. I needed something, anything to keep me from running to him. And this was the perfect hideout. It would make my mother furious.

"Yes." My confession left me in a rush.

"I saw that right away. It's why I called you over, plus, I've got a feeling that you've got spine if you know what I mean."

I snorted and, for the first time, relaxed into my chair. My hands folded into my lap as I settled more comfortably. "So do I have the job?"

"You ever waitressed before?"

No. "Yes."

"Liar." But she didn't hide the grin on her face. "You're hired. You start tonight?"

So much tension left me in that moment. I couldn't believe it. And I nodded, suddenly choked up for some reason. "Yeah. What time?"

She chewed on her lip as she scanned me up and down again. "The night shift starts in an hour. If you're dating Mason Kade, then that makes you their future stepsister. It's all that some of those wishy-washies talk about so I know that you live at the big fancy mansion of theirs and if you came walking all this way, there's no way you can make it there and back, can you?"

I shook my head and bit my own lip. Would I lose the job?

She jerked a thumb over her shoulder. "That crappy looking house is ours. If you want, you can shower in there. I could spot you some clothes for the shift, and then your fancy boyfriend can give you a ride home tonight? How's that sound?"

Wonderful, but I grimaced. I had no idea how I'd get home. I couldn't call Mason—even if I could reach him, I would end up in his bed tonight. Then it didn't matter. I'd figure something out so I jerked my head in a nod. "Sounds good."

She grunted in an approving sound as she stood. Then she hollered inside, "She's got a boyfriend, Brandon. Hands off."

"Yeah, yeah!" he grumbled back before he shouted a curse to follow.

She flipped him her middle finger, but it was only met with a smattering of laughter from inside. As we headed to their two-story home, she stuffed her hands into her back pocket. Her legs stretched out in a walk that I knew would've had Logan groaning from behind her. Sex on a stick. I tried to hold back my anticipation of introducing the two.

But then I was distracted as she showed me through the front door. The screen door banged open, and she strutted past a living room with two worn-out couches and a television positioned on a stand in the corner. The kitchen was small and sparse. A bare table sat in the dining room with boxes of liquor placed all over. When she noticed my gaze, she shrugged. "Sometimes my dad uses this place for storage. He thinks it's safer than in the bar where a few of our old employees weren't so trustworthy, if you know what I mean."

When I met her gaze, she nodded towards the rickety stairs. "Shower's upstairs. I won't scare you off by making you use Brandon and dad's shower. That whole area of the house is disgusting. Come on. I'll grab you some clothes too."

After she showed me the shower, which was in a bathroom that was clean and decorated in lace and pink, I relaxed a bit. It'd been awhile since I had been at a place that wasn't the lap of luxury. For some reason, this grounded me. I felt more settled, like no one was going to swipe me off my feet and run away laughing. Then I stepped inside the shower and breathed in the smell of lilies. When I used some of her body wash, I held back a grin at the image of Mason's hands on my body. He would've loved the smell on me. He would've loved to lather me with it before he would pull my body back against his. Then his hands would slide to my waist and slip down—

"We don't really have a uniform policy."

My elbow jerked up as Heather tore me from my thoughts. As it banged against the shower, a stabbing pain flooded me, but I bit back a curse.

She fell silent for a second before she cleared her throat. "You okay?" Her voice grew as she must've opened the door and stepped inside. Then she snorted at herself. "I don't even know your name. What is it?"

"Samantha," I called over the water. I hurried to finish rinsing my hair and everything else.

"Oh. Hello again. Mine's Heather. Again." She chuckled again. "I sound like a virgin on her first date with the Hulk. Stupid as shit." But she laughed again. "Anyways, what I was saying before is that we don't really have a uniform policy, but the girls all started wearing jeans and a tee shirt. They liked to show the girls and usually tore off the bottom to show off their stomachs, more tips. We have a lot of regulars, but on the weekends we'll get some rich pricks too. They're usually trying to hide from the wives or girlfriends, but they come around enough. The tips are good."

Rich pricks. I frowned as I wondered if Mason knew of the place.

Heather interrupted my thoughts again. "I put some jeans and shirts on the bed. Take your time washing up; just come down whenever you're done. You were sweating a bunch so I'll make some food too. You're going to need some good sustenance in you to get through the night. There are a few of the other servers that'll be bitches to you, especially if you tell 'em who you're dating." She paused a beat. "Not that I'll say a word. I won't. That's for you to share if you want. Something tells me that you're a bit on the secret side, but to each her own. My brother will go crazy. He loves the Kade boys. He reminisces about when Mason first showed up on their team all the time. You woulda thought that the Lord himself came to save their team from damnation from the way Brandon puts it. Okay, I'll be downstairs. See you in a few."

Brandon knew Mason? The other girls knew them? Then I cursed at myself. Of course they knew them. What the hell had I been thinking? But as I got out of the shower and finished dressing, I headed downstairs to find out because I wasn't going anywhere. This wasn't about Mason and me; this was about my mother and me. My chin locked with determination as I turned the corner and saw Heather in the kitchen. She handed me a plate with a sandwich on it.

Analise might not know it yet, but I was going to make her regret forcing Mason away from me. And getting a job at Manny's was the perfect start to enact some revenge.

CHAPTER NINE

Training that night was easy. The most difficult thing was staying friendly when a few of the customers got *too* friendly, but Heather stepped in and handled those situations. I figured out how to take orders, how to write it down on the pad, and to time when the food would be done for customers. Filling drink orders was easier, but I got frustrated a few times I would get one drink only to have the other customer at the same table decide on something else. Heather chuckled as she watched me get flustered, but she linked elbows at one point and gave the table a polite smile as she took their orders. I would've headed straight to the bar to fill 'em, but she completed another task on her way to the bar.

Multi-tasking was going to be a skill I'd need to learn, but by the end of the night I felt more confident. It helped that Brandon was nice every time I came to him with a question. He took the time to explain the different drinks and always told me not to worry; I would catch on soon enough. By the fourth time he issued that same support, I caught a frown from Heather across the diner. Something told me he hadn't really heard her warning that I was dating someone, but it didn't matter. I wasn't going to date him.

There were two other servers that showed up, both of them were nice, so nice that I wondered about Heather's warning from before. That was until the nine o'clock girl showed up. Her name was Gia and she would've been elated to reign with the Elite at my school. She had platinum blonde hair, manufactured boobs, and an outfit that barely covered her. A swimsuit might've covered more, but she was the shot girl as Heather explained. It was to be expected.

By the end of the night, I felt ready to do an entire shift on my own. Heather had cut me down to handling a few tables on my own. My feet killed, but I hoped it had more to do with my four hour run and the two of walking. And with that thought, I should've called Coach Grath back that day, but when I saw Heather earlier, I put it off. I would call him the next day and my training would start in the mornings since Heather told me that she needed me every night during break. I would get every other Thursday off, along with the opposite Tuesdays when school would start again. When I asked about the weekends, she assured me that I would want them.

After cleaning up, when everyone left, I was faced with a dilemma.

I had no way home.

I had my phone, but no number to call Mason even if I wanted to. I never got Nate's number and Logan's line had been disconnected as well. They would have no clue to come get me so I was left with one choice.

I called Adam.

He pulled into the parking lot within ten minutes, dressed in a green polo and khaki cargo pants. As I got a whiff of his pine cologne, I asked if he'd been on a date. Even his hair looked styled to perfection. He gave me an odd look, but shook his head. He had been at a party.

No surprise there.

When he asked if I wanted to go, I declined. Then he said the magic words. "It's at Nate Monson's house."

Oh god.

My stomach flipped over and my eyes closed. A girl could only have so much self-discipline. I already knew my decision when I braced myself. "Would you do me a favor?"

"Sure."

Then I asked for the impossible. "Come to my house with me and tell my mom that I'm hanging out with you and your friends only."

He flashed me a grin. "Your mom's not handling your relationship very well?"

"Try not at all." I held my tongue on the threats, the ultimatums, and what was actually at stake. I shouldn't be going, but I couldn't stop myself. One day. Only one day and I was already folding under the need to see him.

But, as it turned out, my mother was ecstatic to see Adam. She gushed about his father, and then asked how his mother was. The two had lunch plans the next day at the country club. When I expressed my concern that his mom might tell Analise where he'd actually been the night before, Adam assured me not to worry.

He rolled his eyes at me. "My mom has no idea what I do. We're not close, remember?"

I relaxed. I did remember, and I noticed how his hands tightened around the steering wheel. His knuckles were white by the time he pulled into Nate's massive driveway. But then I stopped paying attention to Adam when I saw how many cars were lined up and down the driveway. I couldn't count them, they covered his entire yard and they had still parked down the street. This party was massive. Hell, forget massive—this party was gigantic. My eyes were just as huge as I gazed over the crowd. They were everywhere, by the cars, roaming the driveway, on the road even. Adam had to slow down as he waited for a group to get out of the way. When they didn't, he touched his horn lightly and they moved to the side.

"I thought the last party was huge, but this one..." Oh my god.

"Yeah, Peter texted me that he saw people from seven different schools here." Adam shrugged. "Its winter break and it's the Kades, with Monson." He glanced over. "But you'd know all about that."

Yeah, I would. A small tingle sparked from the anticipation. Then I frowned. Peter—I cringed. That mean the Elite would be there, but of course they'd be there. Everyone was there. "Peter's here?"

He nodded.

That meant that Miranda was too. She had been dating Peter before she fell hook, line, and sinker for Logan. I tensed as I remembered the past few months. The Elite crowd at my school tried to use me to pull Mason and Logan into their group. More than a few times Logan had laughed in their faces. Miranda had referred to him as a manwhore and any girl who fell for him was a slut. So she looked like the fool when he turned his charms on her. It took one party, only one party, and she was walking around with his shirt on the next morning.

Logan dated her for a month. He had been persuaded to date her to protect me since she was the Queen Bee at my school and she made a few threats of making my life hell. If she was connected to Logan, she'd be happy and she wouldn't continue to go after me. But that hadn't been the real reason. That had only been the spin put on it so he would follow through with Mason's plan.

The real reason that Mason wanted Logan to date Miranda was to humiliate her. He knew if she started dating Logan, she would look like a hypocritical bitch. And she had. The rest of the Elite group revoked her role as their leader. She had condemned all the other girls for sleeping with Logan, only to dump her boyfriend of three years for him in one night?

The whole situation left me feeling uneasy. Logan had been used and he still didn't know it.

Mason wanted to hurt Miranda, but only Nate and I knew the real motivation behind it. Miranda pushed a button that Mason knew could've threatened his relationship with his brother. Me. There'd been another girl Logan had loved, really loved, who used him to get closer to Mason. Then I came into their lives. I fell in love with Mason, but he worried that Logan had feelings for me as well. When Miranda taunted him that he got the girl Logan really wanted, Mason nipped that threat in the bud. That was the real reason he had Nate convince Logan to screw her for a month.

Everything went off without a hitch.

Miranda's friends lost respect for her. Logan thought he was protecting me and Mason knew he wouldn't have to worry about Miranda anymore.

It left a sour taste in my mouth.

And then Adam dropped the last bomb. "Yeah, and I guess some of the Kades' cousins are here too. They brought half of the party with them when they showed with Logan."

"Logan's here?" I jerked forward in my seat. My heart started racing. Logan was here. Mason was here. This party was too big for any parent not to know about. I had to get out of there. "Stop. Stop the car."

"What—wait!"

It was too late.

He slowed for another group of people that crossed the driveway and I shot out of there. I had no idea what I was doing or where I was going, but I started to run towards the road. My heart was pounding; it was a solid thump in my ears. The same panic started again, it threatened to choke me, but I kept going.

I was distantly aware of Adam calling my name, but I kept going.

"Hey, whoa!" A husky chuckle sounded next to me as I tore through a group. An arm snaked in front of my chest. As I ran into it, I started to fall, but a strong arm curled into my waist and I was lifted before I fell to the ground. I was held against a massive chest, but I gulped as I saw Heather through a haze in my eyes.

She'd been laughing before. I saw the small lines still around the corners of her lips, but she grew serious as she saw my fear. My chest kept heaving up and down and I clawed at the arm that held me in place. He grunted behind me. "Damn, Heather. She's going to make me bleed."

"Hold her still, Norm!" Heather snapped at him. She softened her voice and brushed some of my hair out of my eyes. "Hey, hey. What's going on? What's wrong? What happened between here and Manny's?"

"You know this chick, Heather?" A different voice chimed in.

She gave him a dirty look over her shoulder. "Yeah, so shut your pie-hole. She's my friend."

"She's Kade's bitch. Drop her, Norm."

"Shut up, Channing!" She gave Norm a look over my shoulder. "You drop her and I will rip your balls off tonight after you've passed out. She's my friend."

The arm tightened around me. A deep voice rumbled through the chest that held me. "I don't know, Heather. I don't want to mess with the Kades. They might be rich pricks, but they don't mess around."

"They're not preps, Heather." That same voice argued from the side. It was low and full of warning. "You might like the girl, but she's theirs. We shouldn't even be here. I knew it was a stupid idea to come."

Heather's eyes snapped in irritation before she twisted back around. "There are no other parties. This one is it. Besides, we're not doing anything wrong. I know this girl and she's scared. I want to know what happened—"

"And if it's because the Kades did something to her? What then?" the guy mused. He didn't sound threatened, just reasonable. "She's not our problem. You're not sticking your neck out for her."

Her mouth dropped, ready to fight back—

He spoke over her, "I don't care. You're not pulling us into a fight against them and I won't let them hurt you. If it comes to it, we're walking away. All of us. You too."

"Channing," she seethed.

As she turned back, the haze had dissipated enough so I could think a bit clearer. I could also see clearer, and the guy who had been speaking was tall and lean. He had a model's face, but his body was covered in tattoos. The simple black tee shirt that he wore didn't hide the muscular build he had despite his lean physique. And I'd been right. There was no fear in his dark eyes, but he was wary. As he gazed down at Heather in front of him, there was also concern.

The plan I had to introduce her to Logan was gone now. I didn't know the story between those two, but she wasn't single. As I thought about it, I never asked if she had a boyfriend or not. I'd been so focused on keeping my own love life to myself.

"Norm." The guy sent him a pointed look. "Drop her."

"Don't—" Heather gasped.

But the arm abruptly released me and down I went. I caught myself before I fell all the way and choked from the sudden oxygen I could now breathe. When I looked up, with tears in my eyes, I saw that the guy who'd been holding me could've been a bodybuilder. He was a giant, but he gave me a timid smile. "Sorry about that. He said drop so I dropped."

I nodded as I still coughed from all the air. "No problem."

Heather glared at him before she touched my arm. "Hey, you okay, hon? What had you so spooked before?"

I shook my head. I couldn't tell anyone about it.

"Sam?"

It didn't matter now.

I turned and stared at Mason, who stood a few feet from the group. His hands were clenched in fists. There was no one behind him. He had come alone. His eyes never left mine, but I felt the sudden question in his depths.

I didn't think. I couldn't.

I ran toward him and he caught me as I threw myself at him. His arms felt like home as he held me against his chest and I breathed him in. My legs wrapped around his waist. When his hand brushed my hair back and he kissed my forehead, I burrowed into him. I couldn't have been anywhere else.

We were both going to hell.

CHAPTER TEN

Still enveloped in Mason's arms, I felt him look over his shoulder. "It's fine. I'll take care of her."

"You sure? She freaked." Adam's voice sounded far away.

I sucked in my breath as his hand ran down my face and arm. I didn't want the moment to end. I wanted to make it last as long as it could because when the real world came back, I knew there would be consequences, serious consequences, and I couldn't think about them now. The damage was done. I was already in his arms. My mom said not to see him and I had already broken that rule once.

"Yeah, she's fine." Mason's voice had a rough edge to it.

"Who's she scared of?"

I held my breath again as Heather joined the conversation.

Mason stiffened beneath me. He hated explaining himself. I lifted my head this time and looked at her. Slowly, but too fast for my liking, I moved so I could slide back to my feet. Mason kept his arms around me. He anchored me against his chest.

I met Heather's gaze and saw the concern in them. Something flickered in my gut. "My mom."

"Sam—"

I ignored him. "She's made threats if—"

Mason's arms swung me back up. He started walking back to the house immediately.

"Hey! Wait!"

He threw over his shoulder, "It's none of your damn business, Jax. Leave her alone."

"It is my business! She's my friend."

"Since when?"

I looked over his shoulder and shook my head. I didn't want her to tell him about my job. That was for me to do. As she saw the plea on my face, the words died in her throat. Mason kept going. When he went a few more steps, I saw the other guy grab Heather's arm. He pulled her back to their group, but then Mason carried me past Adam and as he fell into step behind us, he blocked her from me.

When we went into the mansion, the music tripled in volume. I felt the bass through the floors, through Mason as he swept up the stairs and towards our room. Our room. An excited shudder left me as I thought about the sanctuary of that room. It'd just be me and him...and Adam as he followed us inside.

Mason turned back, still holding me. "Dude."

"I just want to know that she's alright. I picked her up outside some bar tonight."

"You what?" He whipped his head to me and lowered me to the ground. "You were at a bar?"

Adam added, "Alone."

"You were *alone* at a bar tonight?"

I opened my mouth, ready to explain everything when the door was thrown open. Logan strolled in with a charming smile on his face and his arms spread wide. He snapped his fingers on both hands and bowed to us. "I've got it all fixed, Sam. You don't have to do anything your mother says."

I closed my mouth.

Mason groaned.

Adam spoke up, "Huh?"

Logan twisted around, frowning. "Dude, what the hell are you doing here?"

Adam had drawn to his fullest height, but his frown turned into a glower. His eyes took on a mean glint as he clipped his head towards me in a nod. "I'm the one who brought her here. I'm the one who lied to her mother for you.

So I'm thinking I have some goddamn right to hear what the hell is going on."

Logan's brows furrowed together as his lips puckered. "You what?" He twisted around to me. "He what?"

I sighed, moving away from Mason's shelter, and crossed my arms over my chest. My stomach was in knots, but maybe Adam had a point? I had a feeling I would need more of him before this month was over. "Maybe he should hear all of this?"

"No—" Logan started.

Mason finished, "NO!"

I drew in a deep breath. Both of them already looked infuriated, but then the door opened again. Nate strolled in with a case of beer. He started to shut the door, but a hand shot through and slapped it back. Two heads popped in, grinning with red cheeks and glazed eyes. They had the same hair, brown and wavy like Logan's, and each of them had similar dimples in both cheeks. Wait—they were mirror images of each other.

Mason groaned, "Not now, you guys."

One of them ignored him and strode inside. His hand was stretched out as he marched towards me. His mouth was set in place with determination and he stopped before me. "Will Leighton." He slapped a hand on his brother's shoulder, who had followed close behind. Both had wide smiles on their faces. "This here's my brother James."

"James?"

He giggled as Will's smile became blinding. "It's a family name. Don't hold it against him."

"The ladies call me Jamison. Works better on their panties. Gets 'em a lot wetter, don't know why. Only the cousins call me James still." The other brother stuck his hand out as well.

I looked at both of their hands, held steady and waiting.

"Well?" the first prompted. "Mason's being grouchy and I know he's two seconds away from punching me, but I'd rather shake your hand first. We've heard a lot about you—"

Jamison giggled again. "Not anything good. Our moms are sisters."

Will nudged him in the chest with his shoulder. He moved him back a step. "Don't mind, James. He takes up for our mom. Not me. I've got Logan's back. And he's got yours so if you need anything from me or idiot here, you don't hesitate a second."

"Okay." Mason started to step forward, but Jamison shot a hand out to stop him.

"No, no, cousin dear. We're going. We know this is family meeting time, though you know Logan will spill it all to us later."

Will barked out a laugh, following his brother to the door. "Yeah, over a case of Guinness and soggy trousers by the pool."

Logan frowned. "That was one time. You assholes pushed me in. I couldn't take both of you."

Jamison threw an arm around his brother's shoulders. They turned so they were facing us and backed out of the room. "You were sniveling like a brokenhearted girl. And we have to take advantage every time Mase isn't with you."

Will shot his fist in the air. "And we'd do it again!"

"Out!" Mason strode to them, pushing them through the doorway before he slammed it shut.

There was a moment of silence before they knocked on the door and shouted, "Sniveling like a girl, Logan." The other howled in laughter. "Soggy trousers! Can't forget the soggy trousers."

Mason pounded on the door. "Leave!" Then he waited until the giggling faded.

Adam shook his head, perplexed. "Who the hell were those guys?"

"Idiots," Mason and Logan said at the same time.

Nate tossed a beer to both of them and popped open his own as he studied Adam with narrowed eyes. "They're cousins. What are you doing here?"

Adam drew in a deep breath. His shoulders lifted, his chest rose, and the tendons in his neck stretched. He was ready to explode, but I stepped forward. I held my hand out to stop any more interrogation. "He helped me out, okay? That's why he's here."

"Sam." Mason stepped closer to me. "Remember what he did to you."

Reality sunk in.

Adam snarled, "You're such a jerk. I'm trying to be her friend. I'm trying to—"

Mason had him against the wall in the next second. He growled at him, "I already told you what I'd do to you if you wouldn't stay away from her. Now you're trying this angle? Friendship?"

He struggled against his hold, but it didn't matter. With a cold mask over him, Mason looked lethal. He clipped out, "You turned her friends against her. I don't know what you've done to get her to forgive you, but it's not going to work. I won't let you screw her over again."

Nate and Logan wore similar expressions and as Adam looked around the room, the fight left him. He swallowed before his shoulders slumped down in defeat. Then he turned to me, but the damage was done.

I remembered. He had lied and pushed a friend away. He wanted to punish me because I wouldn't date him, and now after one afternoon where he apologized, I was ready to take him back into my world of friendship? I was nuts.

But he lied to my mom for me. He had the power to take back his words and my night would be blown. I swallowed painfully. He had the power to send Mason to jail. He couldn't do that. I couldn't let him do that. When I looked up and caught Mason's gaze, I knew he saw the fear on my face. I couldn't mask it. My hands started to tremble. I couldn't lose him.

Mason made the decision for all of us. "You're going to leave, Quinn. You're not going to say a word about any of this to anyone. If you want to try the friendship angle, fine. Help out. Be a pal to her. But if I get wind that you're working a different angle, I *will* follow through. Now, this is family only. We appreciate that you brought her here, but you're not welcome any further."

Logan grunted in agreement.

Adam gazed around the room with a soft plea. "Look, I care about her too. I won't do anything to hurt her."

Nate decided to speak up, "Yeah, well, you've hurt her enough. We all know it."

Shocked, I whipped my gaze to him. He had a serious look in his eye, threatening even as he stared Adam down. Then Adam stuffed his hands in his front pockets. His demeanor was submissive, but his next words lashed out in a snarl. "Family only? You got a screwed up family."

I sucked in my breath. Closing my eyes, I wanted to bang my head against a wall. Why had he gone there?

Logan flared up, but Mason grabbed Adam's arm and yanked it behind him. As he fell to the ground with a panicked scream, Mason twisted his arm and started to clench his fist around one of Adam's. His screams grew and he began to tremble on the ground.

"I told you what I would do," Mason warned, looking calm and cold.

Adam's screams cut off and a sob started deep from his throat. He began weeping instead as he pounded the floor with his free hand. He cried out, "I'll sue you. I'll sue all of you—"

Nate stepped forward. He was the closest to me and drew me behind him. Then he spoke in a quiet voice, "You already took her friend from her."

His sobs grew and an inhumane shriek came next. I could hear him struggling underneath Mason's hold.

Logan pulled me into his chest. He wrapped his arms around me and blanketed my head into his chest. He held his other hand over my ear.

Nate continued and I could still hear him. The softness of his voice sent chills down my back. "You keep saying that you want to be her friend, but you're hurting her. You're not hurting us. We don't care if you like us or if you sue us, but she does. Be the man you keep thinking you are." He stopped as he let his words settle for a second. "Taking her friend from her, that's what a coward does. It makes you look pitiful."

I didn't know how they knew about Becky, but I wasn't surprised they did. And Nate was right. I never would have done that to him.

There was silence for awhile. Everyone was eerily still. The room was already thick with tension, but now a different danger filled it. I closed my eyes. They could hurt him. If they really wanted to, they could do it. I didn't want them to hurt him. Adam could hurt Mason back. And then I heard Adam choke out, "Sam. Please. I'm sorry. I am. I—"

Relief flooded me.

"That's enough," Mason remarked, so calm while the anger simmered within him. It gave him a brutal edge that would've terrified me if I didn't know him from the inside out. I closed my eyes as I heard him saying something in a softer tone to Adam. I couldn't make out the words, but a sudden need to be in his arms surged over me. I needed his shelter.

"Leave."

My head jerked up. Logan's eyes glimmered in fury as his hand had dropped from my ear. It was curled into a fist now. His jaw was clenched tight. "Leave, man. Forget whatever the hell my brother's saying to you. Leave her alone. I mean it. If you don't, I'll pound your ass and send you to the hospital."

"Logan." Mason stepped away from Adam, but he kept a hand to one of his shoulders to hold him in place.

"What?" Logan jerked his gaze to his brother's. "You're going to let him go with that? Are you kidding me? He hurt

Samantha, we all know it. Whatever the hell he said to that girl did the deed. We all know she stopped being friends with her. She doesn't have any friends anymore and it's because of this piece of crap. We pissed him off so he hurt Sam instead. You're damn straight that I want to beat the shit out of him. Let me at him. If he tries to sue us, he's gonna have to sue all of us. Four against one. If he's smart, he'll take the beating and keep his mouth shut."

Mason was torn. His one hand jerked in reaction and I knew he wanted to do what Logan was threatening, but then he caught my gaze. We both remembered the other bomb my mom could drop on us and Adam held a part of his life in his hands. If my mom knew I was here, she'd go to the police. She would file for statutory rape and Mason would be found guilty. Everyone knew he had sex, everyone knew that he had sex with me. If Mason was found guilty, who knew how long the damages could last for him, for us.

I jerked away from Logan. Adam had apologized. Why couldn't he have let it alone?

Then Logan continued to add to my nightmare.

He turned to me, his eyes pleading. "I talked to some people, Sam. Nothing will happen to you. So what if you get arrested as a runaway? Nothing happens the first time and the second time," he rolled his eyes. "You might get house arrest. That'd be drawn out in court, longer than a month. You can do whatever you want and your mom can't do a thing to you. You don't need to be indebted to this trash."

But the statutory rape charges would hold.

I drew in a shuddering breath. I hadn't talked to a lawyer, but I had a good feeling those charges could hold for a long time, longer than the month before I was an adult.

"Runaway?" Adam asked.

Mason turned to him. "Shut up."

Then Nate moved forward. A look of disgust twisted his features as he grabbed Adam and dragged him to the door. When he opened it, he clipped out, "You say a goddamn thing, and you'll regret it. By the time we're done with you, you'd be getting off easy with a pounding. Trust me. We've done worse to people for less."

Adam opened his mouth, but Nate shoved him out and slammed the door in his face. When he surveyed the room again, he slumped against the door. His head leaned back and he heaved a deep sigh.

I looked at Mason and found his eyes on mine. A look of vulnerability flashed over him. I shot forward and pulled him against me. His head dropped to my shoulder. Swallowing a knot, this was my fault. If he went to jail, it would be because of me. I couldn't let that happen. No matter what, no matter what I had to do, I was going to make this right. My eyes closed and despair swept over me. I'd have to go to my mom. I'd have to do what she wanted, anything, but she couldn't hurt Mason that way. No way.

"Why do I get the feeling something else is going on?" Logan pulled me back to the room. He raked a hand over his face and shook his head. "What the hell is going on?"

Nate and I both looked at Mason. It was his decision. He was the leader and it was his life, but when his head fell down my gut flared. He was going to lie. I knew it and I held my breath as I heard him mutter, "Nothing's going on, but it'll go on her record, Logan."

"What? Come on—"

Mason's head snapped back up and his eyes were inflamed. "Leave. It. I mean it. She could get arrested and that'll be on her record, for life, Logan. Drop it."

"But—"

"I mean it!" His voice raised an octave.

Then Logan threw his arms up. A litany of curses spewed from his mouth as he shook his head. "This is bullshit. We don't have to play by their rules. So what if it'll go on her record. She can fight it. She's not running away. This is such a load of crap—"

Then Nate spoke up, "It's not your call, Logan."

"What?" He swung around. A snarl was fixed on his features and his chest heaved up and down.

Nate faced him squarely. His gaze never faltered, he never blinked. "It's not your call. This has nothing to do with you."

"I got shipped off because of it. This is my brother. She's my—"

"It's their relationship. It's her life, it's her mother. They eliminated you from the equation because you support them, but right now you might be hurting them more than helping."

"But—"

"Stop!" A whisper escaped my lips. I couldn't hear any more of it. I couldn't bear it. I clapped my hands over my ears and turned away from everyone. "Stop, please."

I could only hear myself breathing. I was panting, not breathing. I couldn't get enough oxygen and everything suddenly hurt in my body. All my limbs, everything hurt and I collapsed onto the chair by the desk. I had no idea what was going on behind me. I couldn't hear it. I couldn't sense it, but it didn't matter.

I had torn them apart.

My mother had torn them apart, like she tore my own family apart.

I clasped my eyes closed and bent over. With my head buried in my lap, I hugged my arms around my legs and started to rock back and forth. I kept going. The movement kept me from breaking down.

CHAPTER ELEVEN

At some point, two strong arms slid underneath me and lifted me from the chair. I curled into Mason's shoulder. I didn't need to look; I would know those arms anywhere. He carried me to the bed and set me down gently. As he pulled away, I reached for his shoulder in protest. I didn't want him to go. I couldn't be without him anymore.

"Ssh." He pressed a soft kiss to my forehead. "I'm just going to lock the door."

It wasn't long before he was back. The light was switched off and I heard him undressing before he lifted me back up and slid both of us under the sheets. Then I rolled over to him, my eyes were wide, and there was a gaping hole in my chest. Only he could fill it. It was cheesy, but it was true. As his eyes caught mine, he held still for a moment. His chest rose in the air and I pressed my palm over it. His heart picked up its pace at the touch as I kept my hand there, and Mason closed his eyes. Then he caught my hand with his, bent his head to kiss my palm, and gently placed his other at my hip. He moved me over some more before turning to tug me into his arms. Our legs intertwined together and I rested my head on his chest.

This was it, this was home.

Analise might try to take this away from me, but I knew that somehow we would stop her.

"What's wrong?" He felt my tension.

I shook my head. I didn't want to talk about it, but found myself mumbling, "My mom..."

He drew in another deep breath as he tightened his arms around me. I felt his head rest on top of mine; his breath tickled my hair. He brushed back some of my hair from my forehead and shifted so he could press a kiss to it. His cheek rested there again. "I called my uncle. He's a lawyer."

I sucked in my breath and pulled away to look up. When he didn't meet my gaze, I grabbed his chin and made him. I saw the torn look in his depths and I froze.

No, she couldn't win...

"Mason," I whispered.

He clasped his eyes closed, his mouth twisted, but then he opened them again. Pain flared in them, bright and clear, before he sighed. "Your mom's right. I could be charged with statutory rape. And if I was found guilty, I'd be labeled a sex offender all my life. He said there's a seven year limit on pressing charges from when the act was committed."

I felt punched in the gut. "Are you serious?"

He nodded before his head dropped to my shoulder.

My hand went to his shoulder, I don't know what for. To soothe him? Reassure him with a massage? My touch felt insignificant compared to the burden that'd been placed on him, but then I shook my head. My mom was not going to get away with this. I pushed him back. She would not do this to him.

"Sam?" He cupped the side of my face.

He looked so sad, and that broke my heart. But it made me even angrier. She had done this, and why? Why was she doing this to me? To him? Mason didn't fold to anyone—that was one of the reasons I had fallen in love with him. But my mom had gotten to him, and she held something over his head that he couldn't ignore, evade, or scare away from her.

I sat up and cupped both sides of his face.

"Sam?" he asked again.

I shook my head and ignored the tear that fell. "I won't let her do that. I will make this go away, I have to, Mason."

A myriad of emotions flashed over his face, wariness, sadness, anger, darkness. He sat up and scooted against the headboard, and then he took both my arms. He'd been scared before, but now he let me see his fury.

My stomach wrapped in knots. Oh yes. There was the guy that I'd fallen in love with. I saw the danger lurking in his gaze. I had a sudden thought to rush from the bed and hurry to my mom, to get to her before he did, because as I continued to hold his gaze I knew he was capable of things worse than what I was going to dish out.

"Your mom is becoming crazy—" He stopped suddenly and looked away. As his chest rose and fell at a rapid pace, he was trying to keep control. When he looked back, the fire had diminished, but only slightly. "Your mom's going nuts because she's lost you. She knows it and she's blaming me. What happens when you're eighteen, Sam?"

"I'm gone." The words ripped from me, from my vehemence. She couldn't do a thing to me then.

He nodded. "Exactly. You're gone." Then he waited for me to figure it out...

When I did, my eyes went wide and surged forward. "She doesn't want to lose me—" Like the last time she had lost something and the last time I saw that look of madness in her eyes. I shivered at the memory.

The blood was everywhere as I pushed open the door. My mother was slouched on the floor. She sat with her back to the tub and her nightgown was soaked in sweat and something red. As I pushed the door wider, the pool of blood sat beneath her. It grew slowly. The red on her gown was blood. She was covered in it.

"Mom," I whimpered. I was frozen in the doorway. My legs trembled, I couldn't move. Then something trickled down my leg. It was warm on my skin, but I barely felt it.

I no longer had to go to the bathroom.

"Mom..." I tried not to cry. Her eyes were closed and she was so white, as white as her nightgown—but no. It was red now. All of it was covered in blood.

My cheeks were wet and I raised a hand there. I couldn't have—oh—I was crying. Those were tears, I wiped them off roughly. She couldn't see me cry. She'd get mad.

Oh god.

"Mom." I couldn't leave her, but she wasn't answering. Then I looked back to the hallway. Was dad awake? I should go to him, but my knees were knocking against each other. Because I couldn't stand, I fell to the ground. My knees touched the blood now... oh god...I couldn't stop crying. She wouldn't want me to make any sound. She never wanted me to make a sound, but this...I tried crawling to her.

"Mom..."

"Hey!"

Mason was crouched on the bed, on top of me. His legs straddled me as his head was bent low, eye level to me. He'd grown pale, but when I gasped, he visibly relaxed. He didn't move from my lap, his head fell low to my chest and his hands clasped my waist. His thumbs rubbed back and forth, a fresh set of tingles went through me. As he pressed a kiss to the dip between my breasts, his shoulders shook.

I lifted my hands there. Was he laughing?

No. As I bit my lip, confused at what had happened, he lifted his head again. His concern was evident as he lifted a hand to run his finger over my lip and cheek. Then he cupped my face again and breathed out, "Where did you go? I almost crapped my pants, Sam."

I let go of a long breath. As it rushed past my lips, my insides clenched together. The horror from that night was back. I couldn't get it out of me. I had forgotten it, pushed it down, and numbed myself, but it was back.

"Hey, hey," Mason soothed in a quiet tone. He pressed his soft lips to my forehead. "What's wrong? What's happening?"

I couldn't tell him. I hadn't told anyone, not even David. He should've been told long ago.

"Sam!"

I cried out, still held prisoner by those memories, but then I shook my head. My hands were trembling.

"What's wrong? Tell me. Please."

Everything was quaking in me, my legs jerked against his; I couldn't lift my arms because they were shaking so much. I knew my voice was going to break so I kept quiet and laid my head against his chest. I couldn't do anything. I waited, hoping he would let it go. I couldn't tell him, and after awhile his arms swept around me again. He lifted me above the sheets and curled me into his lap.

It was going to be okay. He was going to push that nightmare aside, he always did.

He murmured, "I have no idea what just happened, but you scared the shit out of me. You're going to have to tell me, Sam. Sometime, you're going to have to tell me."

But not today, not yet.

I closed my eyes and I burrowed even further against his chest. I wanted to curl into a ball and disappear.

"Sam, do you hear me?"

I nodded as I clung to him.

Then he relaxed, slowly, as he sank down into the bed. The memory was still with me, I felt its dirtiness on me as if I were actually back in that bathroom again so I tried to concentrate as I told myself I wasn't there. Her blood wasn't all over me and I was with Mason, I was safe. After a while, a long while, my heart slowed to a regular pace, and then exhaustion kicked in. Mason pulled the blankets back over us.

The sounds of the party were still loud, but in his arms, as his warmth sheltered me, I didn't really hear anyone else. It was just him and me.

It was early in the morning when I woke, but it didn't matter. The security cameras were up, the code had been keyed in. I was screwed. Analise would know where I'd been since she knew I would never spend the night with Adam Quinn.

Adam.

I sighed. Crap. What was I going to do about him?

Mason shifted in the bed. His arm lifted as he reached for me, but instead of letting him pull me back down, I sat up on the edge of the bed. Everything seemed harsh as I slipped away from the warmth of the blankets. The morning seemed brighter than normal, and it was damn cold.

I didn't slide back under the covers. I couldn't close my eyes and burrow into him anymore. When he rolled back over and continued sleeping, I decided that this was the day everything either went to shit or everything went fine.

With my mother, everything was probably going to go to shit.

I ducked inside the shower before I dressed and headed out. I hoped to find someone still awake downstairs that could give me a ride back home, but if not, then I would wake Mason. I just didn't want to. If he took me home, he would come inside and the confrontation would be worse.

My hair was wet and I had Heather's clothes in a bag, grateful that Mason took some of my clothes with him to Nate's earlier. I thought his foresight had been ludicrous, but he hadn't. He was convinced I would be there sooner rather than later—he'd been right on two occasions already.

When I slipped from the room, I didn't look at Mason. I couldn't or I would've crawled back with him.

People were everywhere. Some had fallen asleep near the stairs, a few at the bottom of the stairs. As I circled around the set of couches on one side of the house, I saw a lot of people I didn't recognize. When I crossed over the center area and bypassed the square set of couches there, there were a few from my school. Then I smelled the coffee and a big smile came over me.

That smell would pull me anywhere, but then I turned around. "Oh."

Adam gave me a sheepish wave. "Hey."

My stomach dropped. "Morning."

He gestured to the coffee pot and slid his hands into his front pockets. The green polo and pants were wrinkled.

When I glanced around to see who else was awake, Adam misunderstood. "It's six in the morning."

"You stayed here last night?"

Of course, he had. I flushed at the stupid question.

He hesitated before he surged forward a step. Uncertainty was all over him as he cleared his throat, "Hey, uh, they're wrong, you know. I don't like them. I almost hate them, but not you. I don't want to hurt you. And I really meant it when I said I want to be friends. I...I told you about my dad, Sam."

I didn't move. I didn't say a thing, but I waited. He had something to say so I would listen...I also needed a ride home...

"I apologized for what I did and I came clean to Becky long ago." He jerked a tight shoulder up in a shrug. "She hasn't come to you, even though I told her that I came clean to you. That's on her; I'm more worried about my friendship with you. I do care about you and yeah, it might not be in the strictly platonic way, but I'm above that...or I'm trying to be above that. I'd never hurt you and I know hurting him would be hurting you too. I'd never sue. I don't want Mason and Logan to get between our friendship. I really do want to be your friend."

He sounded sincere. He looked sincere, and I sighed. I hoped he was sincere because I needed a favor. "Can you give me a ride home?"

He paused. Then he rapidly blinked in surprise. "That's it?"

I shrugged. "What do you want? We already had our heart to heart."

"Oh." He fell back against the counter. He seemed dumbstruck.

I waited. I wasn't going to pour my heart to Adam. I had cared about him before and he'd been a friend at times, but I was desperate. Mason would be pissed that I snuck out, but I really needed to get home before he got there. Everything could be destroyed if I didn't get there first.

"Look," I cleared my throat. This was going to sound awkward, but here went my best shot. "I—uh—as far as you and me, I figure we're good." As his shock deepened, I expanded, "I mean, I get it. You don't like Mason and Logan. You don't have to, but I knew that you wouldn't sue."

Well, he might've, but that wasn't the situation at that time. My situation was at my house, where I needed to get. Now.

My hands lifted in the air in a rolling motion. I needed this to hurry along. "So can you do me a favor?"

"Ugh." A beat passed as he struggled to comprehend the sudden turn of events, but then he shot up from the counter. "Yeah, I uh, yeah." He raked a hand through his hair and looked around, then felt his pockets. "My keys..."

He lost his keys in this house? With this amount of people? Panic started to rise up again...

"Oh, wait!" He patted his back pockets and pulled them out. He gestured to the door. "Lead the way."

CHAPTER TWELVE

When he pulled into the driveway, I couldn't move. I had convinced myself that Adam could lie for me again. He would say that I fell asleep at his friend's house, where there were only Academy students at. But I couldn't bring myself to ask him to do that. I couldn't owe him any more, not after Mason almost beat him up.

But the problem would still exist.

Mason said there was a seven year limit. She could file charges within the next seven years and have that over our heads long into our adulthood. Then I remembered his other words—she didn't want to lose me. When an image of the blood flashed in my head, I pushed it away. I couldn't keep going forward if I remained in the past. This wasn't then. This was now. Things were different.

And, not really feeling the bravery that I was trying to convince myself I was, I thanked Adam for the ride.

I felt like I was going to throw up.

He frowned. "You okay?"

No. "Yes."

His frown deepened. "Are you sure?"

No. "Yes."

"Oookay. Uh." He was at a loss for words. "Well, I guess I'll see you later? What are you doing tonight?"

I jerked back in my seat as I saw the front door open. My mom poked her head out as she lifted a hand to shade her eyes. I knew the exact second she saw me in the car and when she saw who was with me. Her shoulders visibly dropped two inches, and then she gave me a small wave before she went back inside.

I let out the breath I'd been holding.

"Sam." Adam touched my arm. He had turned to face me completely. "Are you sure everything's alright? You said things weren't good with your mom and your relationship with Mason. Is there more to it? Things seemed heated in the room last night. I don't think I'm overstepping my role as your friend by being worried here." He stopped, then slumped back in his seat. "I'd really just like to help."

"No, I'm sorry." I tried to give him a reassuring smile. "I've gotta take care of something right now, but hey, I'm working at Manny's now if you ever want to come for food or something."

"That bar I picked you up from last night? You work there?"

I nodded, but shrunk back. I hadn't explained that to Mason yet either. He still thought I'd been alone at a bar before. Ugh. A headache was threatening to come, but I pressed my hands to my temples. It couldn't, not now.

"I'll see you later, Adam." As I shut the door, I gave him a small wave.

I didn't wait for him to leave; I turned around and regarded the mansion. It was as intimidating as it had been the first day we moved in, but this time it was from my family inside, not the Kades. When I went inside, I saw the green light on the security system and figured Analise had turned it off for the day. It'd been red when I headed out for the second run/two hour walk.

"Hi, honey."

I stiffened in the doorway, but went further towards the kitchen. Her tone was cheery, too cheery. When I rounded the corner there was a pile of mail in front of her. She was sorting through it as the coffee was brewing behind her.

What the hell?

My mom was the epitome of the perfect housewife, make-up all done, hair sprayed into place, and a sexy white robe that showed off the lacy nightgown underneath. There was a good hello peek at her cleavage.

I narrowed my eyes. Then I realized that she thought I had been with Adam all night. Anger rushed through me. Adam was okay, but Mason wasn't? Why was that? But I kept it from boiling out as I asked, in a controlled voice, "What are you doing?"

"Oh, nothing. You want some coffee?" She turned for the cups.

"No."

Nothing. She didn't pause. She only grabbed one for herself and then added some creamer to it.

I waited as she rested on one of the stools, and then went back to looking through the mail. A big fat envelope was plopped on the table. She pushed it towards me.

"What's that?"

She shrugged. Drops of the sun could've dripped from her voice. "Oh, nothing. I think that's a college application."

"What?"

It said Columbia University, with a New York address in the top corner. What the hell? "I never requested an application from them."

"Maybe I did."

Her head came up now and there was an underlying message there. Our gazes caught and held. I found myself unable to breathe as I tried to sort through what she was doing. Then it clicked. And I couldn't believe it.

My voice was soft, so soft, "You're going to pay for my college tuition there?"

She picked up the coffee mug, smooth and smug now. "Maybe." Then she took a sip. Her eyes never wavered.

Bitch.

I drew in another breath. I couldn't believe this was happening. "You're bribing me?"

Her eyes narrowed to slits. Her hand tightened on the handle, but she didn't stutter. "Yes."

"Because?"

My heart started to pound now. The thumping sounded closer together, harder against my chest.

"I know where you were last night, Samantha. Do you think I'm an idiot?"

A choked laugh ripped from me. "Things would be a lot easier if you were."

She drew in a soft breath. Her knuckles were now white as she gripped the mug. It started to shake from her hold. "Are you fucking with me?"

Something shifted in her gaze and the wall fell down. Malice and meanness shone through and that was the mom I remembered six years ago. She was the one I heard as she destroyed our entire house. My gut shifted at the reminder.

"It's your fault!" she screeched with wild eyes before she lunged at me. Her finger had pointed at me, but then it turned into a fist. I closed my eyes as I braced for the impact—

I spat out now, "You heard me."

The mug shattered on the floor. She never moved, not an inch, as her eyes were glued to mine. Outrage poured in them, but then the fury gurgled up. A strangled scream started from the base of her throat—

"Honey?" James appeared from around the corner.

The scream stopped short and she blanched. She fell back two steps as everything was stuffed back into place. The warm and sunny façade she had when I got home was back in full force. She was sugary sweet again. "Honey! Good morning."

I felt punched in the stomach. I stumbled backwards.

"Sam?" James sent me a frown. "Are you okay?"

With a hand over me, as if she really had kicked me, I couldn't look away. I was disgusted. This was my mother. This was the woman that gave birth to me, tried to use me to keep Garrett, and then found another man to raise me as his own. Had she ever loved David?

I saw her now with James and I thought she really loved him. I thought that was why she left David for him, but now

I wondered. Did she even love James? She couldn't have, not if she was going to turn Mason in for statutory rape. She had to know that he would be irate with her. She would've ruined Mason's life. That was his son. I didn't know James that well, but I knew he loved Mason and Logan. I knew he would do what was right, what he thought was right. That was why he supported her and sent his sons away. He thought he was doing the right thing for her relationship with her daughter, because he understood from his own point of view of being a father.

My mouth fell open as I studied her.

She frowned at me, behind James.

Oh god.

I gasped and I knew what she'd been planning on doing. It couldn't wait, not when he was there. I had to do what I could to foil her plan. I blurted out, "She's going to press charges against Mason!"

A fierce frown flared over James. He turned, slightly to Analise, who paled at my words.

I pointed a finger at her. My voice rose because I was so sure of it now. "You were going to press charges against him and then you were going to try and take it back, weren't you? When he found out, you knew he would've been furious so you would pretend that you hadn't thought." I could hear it now. She would cry, acting desperate and so despondent. My voice hardened, "You would've told him that you hadn't thought it through, that you were so desperate to keep me from him. You were, weren't you? That was your plan. And you were going to go and try to drop the charges, but you know they can't do that. I bet that once you make a claim like that, they can't drop it. They have to pursue it and you wouldn't be blamed for it at all."

I felt sick.

From the rage in her eyes, I knew that had been her plan. My mother was sick, she was not right. Oh god. How could she have done that?

James whirled around to her. His back was to me now, but I staggered to the table behind me and sat down. I couldn't move; I could only sit as he drew to his fullest height. But he didn't say anything, not a thing. The room was so tense, my heart continued to race.

"Honey—" She tried, but she stopped.

Slowly, so slowly, he turned and left the room. And that was enough.

I'd just broken what love he had for her.

"Get. Out."

I fell off the chair. Her tone was ferocious, and as I saw the enraged eyes, the fisted hands, I knew she was close again. The robe fell open, and she was braced in front of me. The nightgown was white, like the one from that night, except this one wasn't drenched in blood. A part of me fell away and slipped back to the memory. She'd been so quiet, almost dead, in the bathroom with the pool of blood beneath her. Her eyes had been murderous days later.

My mother took a step towards me. She drew in her breath, as the veins on her neck stood out. One of her hands started to shake back and forth, but it wasn't from fear. I stood now, numb suddenly, and looked at my mother.

"OUT!"

I flinched, but I couldn't move. She wanted me to leave? But—

"GET OUT! NOOOOW!"

"Analise!" James rushed back into the room. "Do not speak to her like that!"

My heart picked up again, I couldn't breathe once more, and I fell against the wall behind me. It was all closing in around me. This wasn't how I thought it was going to be. She wanted me gone, actually gone... I cared. I hadn't known that I cared.

When I heard a thump, she was on the floor. A hand was to her chest and she was out cold.

"Oh my god." James dropped to his knees beside her. He skimmed his hands over her body, checking for anything wrong with her. When there was nothing, he pressed his fingers to her neck and felt her pulse.

She was breathing. I watched as her chest moved up and down, but I saw it from the distance. I had detached from myself. I was floating away, to somewhere safer than in that room.

"...911 now!..."

"Huh?" I looked at him through a fog now.

"911, Samantha!"

I frowned. 911? She was faking, didn't he know that? But I couldn't speak. The words never came as he rushed past me for the phone. It was attached to the wall behind me, and as he grabbed and lifted it to his ear, he accidentally pushed me backwards.

I reached out for something to hold onto, but there wasn't anything. It was just wall and then I fell to the floor. I scooted up against the wall and sat there as he spoke on the phone.

Everything happened in slow motion. It was surreal. I was watching a movie played out in front of me. The ambulance hadn't taken long. Two EMTs checked her vitals and interrogated James with questions. When they couldn't find anything wrong, they loaded her onto a stretcher and left.

James went with them. He glanced back at me once and asked me a question, but I couldn't make sense of it. I saw his mouth moving, but I couldn't hear him. There was a buzzing sound in my head, it drowned out everything else. When I only looked at him, he gave me a small frown, but grabbed a set of keys from a drawer. He left after that.

I was like that when I heard pounding on the door.

I couldn't move. I knew I should get up to see who that was, but I couldn't. But then—no. I had to get up. She'd been faking it. Why was I in shock about that? So, slowly, I pushed myself up and then went to the door.

I turned the lock the whole way and the door was shoved open. My hands braced against it, and I was thrown against the wall. Before I could fall or steady myself, Mason grabbed me. He hauled me close.

I gasped, everything came flooding back.

God, the buzzing sound was still there. It felt like someone was stomping their foot on my head.

"Where'd they go?"

Logan rushed past Mason into the kitchen. He came back a second later and lifted his hands. "They're gone." He looked at me. "Did they go to the hospital already?"

I shook my head. "She was faking it." She had to have been.

Mason clutched me tighter against him before he pressed a rough kiss against my forehead. "Are you okay?"

Logan stepped closer, concerned as well.

What were they so scared about? She was faking.

"Sam." Mason cupped both sides of my face. "Your mom collapsed. Dad called us. He said you were in shock. Are you okay?"

"She didn't," my voice cracked. I shook my head. Why did everyone believe her? "She's faking." I knew it, she had to have been. The convenient timing, how dramatic it had been. All of this was nuts. It was over the top, how Analise liked to live. I shook my head clear of the shock and my voice became clearer. "I told your dad what she was going to do, that she was going to press charges against you and then pretend she hadn't been thinking straight. She saw it, she saw his face." I hadn't. His back had been turned to me, but how he'd grown quiet, how he had left the room. I'd been so sure that it was done, that they were done. How could he have stayed with her after knowing that?

"Huh?" Logan scratched his head.

Mason cursed under his breath. "Nothing."

"Wait, that's not nothing." Logan stepped closer. "What aren't you telling me?"

Mason stiffened, but when I knew he was going to feed him another lie, I spilled the beans. "My mom was going to press charges of statutory rape against Mason. It's illegal to have sex with a minor. He's eighteen. It would've stuck."

Logan's eyes went wide. He sucked in his breath and gaped at us. Curses spewed from him as he shook his head. "And you weren't going to tell me? What the hell, Mason?! What the fucking hell?" He stopped abruptly, but then his gaze shot back to us. "Nate knew, didn't he? When did you know about this?"

Mason cursed under his breath.

My hand found his and I held tight to it. "She told me the same day you guys left. I was coming to see Mason and she was waiting for me. She knew I would." I swallowed over a knot. "That was the ace up her sleeve. It would've ruined his life."

"Fuck."

Mason let out a soft breath behind me. His hand wrapped around my waist, and he tugged me back against him. As he held me, I watched Logan from his shelter. I waited for his response, whatever it was going to be. It wouldn't be good. I knew that much. He'd been lied to.

"Fuck you!"

I closed my eyes. There it was.

"Fuck you! Seriously." He scooted away from us, all the way to the back wall.

I started for him, but Mason went instead. He stood close to him as he lifted his hands up, as if to his shoulder. Then he dropped them. "What would you have done?"

Logan glanced up, his gaze stormy. "I would've done something."

"Exactly." Mason sighed. His hands found his waist and his head hung down. His voice came out soft, "You would've come over here and threatened her, or you would've done something worse. You've been asking every day to tie her up and scare the crap out of her."

Logan gave a weak laugh. "I wouldn't have really done that."

"I don't care. This needed to be handled the right way and I had no idea what to do, not until last night..." He lifted his gaze to me.

I realized that he wanted me to confront her. He knew that I was the only one that could've. Shame flared through me. I should've done this sooner. Now it was all a mess.

I sighed, "She kicked me out."

"What?" The surprise was clear with both of them. Then Mason turned back to me. He asked again, "Does she really want you gone?"

I shrugged. "It seemed like it."

"Are we sure she was faking?" Logan frowned. "Are we completely sure that there wasn't something wrong with her?"

Mason started to reach for his phone, but I stopped him. I put my hand on his arm. "She's done this before."

"What?"

Logan poked his head around Mason. "What?"

"She lost a baby...before..." But as I said it I realized the truth, I realized why I had spoken up in the first place. "No, she killed her baby."

CHAPTER THIRTEEN

"*D*ad!" *I ran down the hallway and shoved open their bedroom door, but there wasn't anyone inside. The television was on so I circled around the bed and threw open the bathroom door. Still no one.* "Dad?"

"Sam!"

I jerked and my bag went flying across the room. I cursed.

Logan laughed from the doorway, a bag slung over his own shoulder. "You ready?"

Was I ready? I looked around my room, it'd been my home for the last five months and now I would move into another one. No, I wasn't ready, but I was at the same time. A sigh left me. "Yeah..."

"Oh, come on." He sauntered in the room and threw an arm around my shoulder. As he pulled me tight against his side, his hand spanned the rest of the room. "Think of it this way, your next room's going to be orgasm-friendly. That's good feng shui, right? Heh? Heh?" He wiggled his eyebrows at me, chuckling. "That's all about natural bliss and stuff like that, isn't it?"

I shrugged off his arm and grabbed my two bags. "Come on, let's get out of here." I went to the door. He didn't. I looked back. "What?"

Logan had an odd look on his face. He glanced to me and then back to the room. Then he took a breath. "Did you want to go to the hospital?"

"Why?"

I knew why. I wasn't stupid, but god, I wasn't going to give her the satisfaction.

"You know," he hesitated. "I know Mason went there to make sure that she really was faking, but did you want to go too? To make sure that what she was said was legit? That she's actually kicking you out? I mean, I don't know, Sam. Your mom's crazy, certifiable, but she's nuts about you. Since we all got close, your mom's gone off the deep end because she's scared of losing you."

My stomach clenched as I remembered the murderous look in her eye, the one I saw before she collapsed today.

"Being kicked out is a big deal. You might act like you don't care now, but you will. I'm sure of it."

The sincerity in his voice had me blinking back tears. My throat swelled with emotion and I clasped my eyes shut.

"Hey."

I shrugged out of his hold. He had no idea. His dad had cheated, but he wasn't crazy. James had always and would always love his sons, and while their mom was intimidating, I knew she loved them as well. He had no idea.

"Look," his voice grew gruff. "I didn't say that to make you cry. I only meant that it sucks to be on the outs. You know? I've gotten kicked out of the house a few times and I always acted like I didn't care, but I did. I cared a lot. I think the only person who might not care would be Mason."

I chuckled, but it sounded more of a whimpered sob.

"So...did you want to go to the hospital and make sure this is the real thing? That you're actually being kicked out?"

I needed to pick up the pieces and move forward. I shook my head.

Logan put his arm around my shoulders and flashed me a grin. Pulling me into his side, he dipped his head down. He breathed out against my forehead. "Think of it this way. You no longer have to go to the party. The party will come to you, so that makes you the party...in a way. I guess." Frowning, he murmured, "No, that doesn't make sense either."

Another soft chuckle escaped me. Relieved by the brief respite, I thumped him on the chest. "Thanks for distracting me, but you know that I'll never be considered the party."

"You might, if you got really really drunk and started stripping." His eyes narrowed. "No, because then my big brother would sweep you up and take you for your own private party. You only would've been considered the party if you never knew us and still got really really drunk and then stripped. Then you would definitely be the party."

I rolled my eyes. "So I'm only fun if I had never met you guys?"

"Yep, sounds about right." He wiggled his eyebrows at me and flashed some charm. "So what do you think? Break up with Mason and go get wasted?"

"Are you serious?"

"No." His smile remained, but the laughter faded from his voice. "Not really. Kind of. Do you want to?"

"What kind of brother are you? You're encouraging me to break up with Mason."

"Not really."

My eyebrow arched high. "Really?"

"No, no. In this world we're all friends, no romance at all. That stuff's just too much drama anyways. In this world, you can go off and forget about your mom. Forget everything. Get drunk, or not since you don't really drink, but do whatever you do to take the edge off."

"I run."

"Not that," he said. "I want to be a part of this fun that I'm envisioning for you and that means that I'd have to run. I don't like to run, not unless I'm chasing someone or someone's trying to kick my ass. Then I'd run with you, but not in this world."

"This world? Your world, the one where you're not considered delusional?"

"Yeah." Logan's smile doubled. His eyes sparkled from anticipation. "I might be delusional, but what about Vegas? That sounds like a perfect world to go to. We can do all sorts of forgetting." Tugging my hand, he led the way out of my room, out of the house, and then he drove us towards my new home. My next home.

We were almost to Nate's when I frowned at him. "Were you serious about Vegas?" I didn't dare ask him about the other part, I did not want to know if he'd been joking or not.

At my words, his shoulders dropped and he let loose a deep breath. "Damn."

"What?"

"Ten minutes."

"Huh?"

"You forgot about your mom for ten minutes. That wasn't very long at all, Sam." He winked at me. "You're going to have to do better than ten minutes. Maybe Paris? Let's dream about going to Paris, you and me. What would we do there?"

Laughing now, I joined in. What the hell? "Not Paris. We wouldn't go to Paris if it were only you and me. That's too romantic."

"Ouch."

Ignoring him, I mused, "We'd go..."

"Yes?..."

"Germany." I nodded to myself. That sounded right. "You could drink all the beer you wanted."

"Damn good beer."

There was a silly grin on my face, but I didn't want to think about it. Then it'd go away and it'd been so long. But I couldn't help to ask, "Why only you and me? Why not Mason too?"

He rolled his eyes as he turned the car onto Nate's Road. "Because he's the real deal for you. You and me, all fantasies. Only fun, no drama."

"No drama?" I teased, "What about the twins?"

He grimaced. "Too much drama. We can't have any of that. None whatsoever."

It sounded like heaven, but then we pulled into the driveway and heaven fell back to earth. There were six other cars beside Logan's Escalade. I never would've been concerned if it had been Mason with me—I knew he would've smiled in greeting at their friends, taken my hand, and gone upstairs with me. But it wasn't Mason with me. It was Logan, and Logan was the social butterfly. I knew it wouldn't be long before I'd be upstairs and alone while more and more people joined the party. This was Nate's home and now Mason's home. Of course, the party would be there.

"We don't have to stay long."

"What?" I looked over and found that Logan had been watching me. There was no humor or spark. He was only serious.

He repeated, "If you're worried about Will and James, they left this morning. My aunt called and wanted them back home, but we don't have to stay long. We can put our stuff away and head to the hospital right away, if you want."

Did I want that? No, that was why Mason went. He would get to the bottom of everything for me. It was why I asked him to go. Logan and I stayed back to finish packing whatever we needed since now all of us had been kicked out of the house.

Faintly, I murmured, "I think I'm going to go for a run."

He frowned. "You sure? You don't have to, you know."

I did. Oh my god, I really did. I gave him a fleeting smile. "It's okay. I need to get out and stretch my legs."

"Okay," but his frown lingered. I felt it follow me as I headed inside and veered up the stairs. When I got to the bedroom, I closed the door, heaving a deep breath as I rested against it for a moment. This day might've been the hardest in my life. Then I thought about it, nope. I had a lot of days that sucked.

I put my two bags beside the closet and started to search for my running clothes when I felt my phone vibrate in my pocket. A thrill went through me when I saw it was Mason calling. "Hey!"

"Hey," he was tired and tense.

I straightened abruptly. "What happened?"

He hesitated.

"Mason."

Then he gave in, "Your mom's a class act, Sam. And my dad's a clueless bastard. I can't believe it, but he's buying everything she said."

"Are you serious?" He couldn't be, but my heart sank. I had already known that James was going to believe her. He loved her, he had to.

"Yeah, but listen, she's faking. Even some of the doctors think it too. I heard one of the nurses talking about it in some office. They didn't know I could hear, but they were laughing at some diagnosis the doctor gave her. I guess it's given to headcases when they can't find anything wrong. They all recognized her from the ER trips she took during our road trip."

"Did you talk to my mom?"

Again, another strained silence before he admitted, "No."

So many emotions flared in me—disappointment, hurt, relief, and so many more.

He added, "I'm sorry, I really am. She banned me from the room. What I got from talking to my dad was that she's sticking to her story that she collapsed. She's saying it's because of all the anxiety we're giving her."

Of course.

I looked down. When would I learn? She was never going to change.

"I told my dad that you and Logan are going to move into Nate's. He agreed that it was for the best." I heard noises from his phone and knew that he had stepped outside. There was a rustling sound. Then there was a ding, a slam, and complete silence again. It wasn't long before his engine started and the rustling stopped. His voice came from far away, "Sorry about that, I'm on my way home now."

Home. Despite all the stress, a tingle of excitement flared in my stomach. My heart picked up its pace. He was coming home to me, with no parents, no hiding. We were living together, like a normal couple.

"I'll see you in a bit. Do you want me to pick you up something to eat? I was thinking of grabbing some food."

I was already shaking my head when I responded, "No. I'm going to go for a run. I've got enough time before I have to get back and head out again."

"Head out? Head out where—"

But I didn't hear him and hurried out, "Bye. See you later." Tossing the phone on the counter, I rushed to get dressed. I felt the old itch start up and knew that I wouldn't be able to quell it until I was sweating, panting, and sprinting on the road for an hour. Before I started out the door with my earbuds already in, I spied the phone and nabbed it quick. When I went down the stairs, I stashed it in a pocket, but I didn't worry about keys.

A large group had congregated to the back patio. As I went outside, more cars had accumulated so I knew I'd have no problem getting inside the house after my run. I had a feeling everyone would be there long until the next morning.

But then I stopped thinking and I started to salivate at the idea of a new running route. There'd be new roads, new parks, maybe even a running trail that would turn into a wooded maze. I couldn't help myself. I was sprinting by the time I got to the end of the driveway. After an hour I slowed down to a fast jog and kept that going for another hour. I figure two hours was good enough since Heather had already told me she needed me from five till close for my second day of training. As I started back, it didn't take me as long as I thought it would, or I ran faster than I realized, so my adrenaline was still pumping through me when I turned into the driveway.

The cars had multiplied. I wasn't surprised.

When I went inside, they were still on the back patio. The sounds of splashing and cheers told me they were in the pool. A few girls were in the kitchen and looked up as I came inside, panting and sweating. They were covered in string bikinis with long tanned bodies, holding frilly drinks.

I stopped, grabbed the end of my shirt and used it to mop the sweat from my face. Their noses wrinkled up and were giggling as they went through the open door to the patio.

"Hey!"

I had turned for the stairs, but stopped. My knees buckled as Mason strode away from the group. God. My mouth watered, my drool mixed with my perspiration, and I was one wet girlfriend. As he walked towards me, I noticed that he had lost a little bit of weight. When had that happened? He'd been muscular before, but the slight leanness made the muscles on his arms even more striking. His shirt clung to his chest. It molded over the muscles that looked like an intricate map, one that only I got to explore. At the thought of tracing each and every dip with my finger, I grew wet between my legs.

Goodness.

"You okay?" He stopped before me, but the slight smirk that flashed at the corner of his mouth told me that he knew exactly what was going on with me. "I know how running can spur you on. I never knew it could turn you on too."

"Smartass."

The smirk doubled and his eyes darkened with desire as he stepped even closer. His chest brushed against my front, he was intimately close, and his lips lingered on my lips. "Goddamn Sam, you looking wet makes me hard."

My throat jerked in reaction and his eyes were glued to mine. Then his hand curled around my waist, and he tugged me closer. One of his legs slid between mine, hoisting me off the ground so I was straddling him as we both stood there.

"Mason," I whispered.

He bent forward, going slow to draw it out. My eyes widened, I hungered for him. At the thought of his lips on mine, my mouth parted. Eager. Then his hand slid around my neck and cupped the back of my head. He anchored me in place as he slowly, so slowly, leaned down until I felt the soft tip of his lips against mine. A deep groan left me, I heard it from a distance, and then I opened my mouth further for him. His tongue swept in and everything flared inside of me. I gasped at the feel of him and surged upwards against him. When my legs tried to climb higher, he grabbed under my thighs and lifted me. I wrapped my legs all the way around his waist. As my arms held onto his shoulders, I clasped my legs tighter around him and then sunk down.

Mason grunted from the contact between us but deepened the kiss even more. His touch was commanding and I didn't want to stop it. In the far distance of my consciousness, I felt us moving and then a door closing behind us, and a moment later, I felt the hot torrents of water spray down as he stepped inside the shower. He pressed me against the wall and slid a hand under my shirt to cup my breast. When his finger caressed the tip, I fell back against the wall gasping.

"God, Sam, I love you," he whispered as his touch grew more demanding.

I loved him. I needed him.

I needed *more*.

"Wait." He pulled away, panting, and rested his forehead to mine.

I felt him trembling under my hands and reveled in the power of it. Sliding my hand under his shirt and over his chest, he drew in a deep breath. I leaned forward and pressed my mouth there, he quivered under my kiss. Then I flicked my tongue and he gasped, surging into motion at the same time. I was pulled from the wall, and after he kicked open the shower door, he plopped me on the counter before his fingers hooked inside of my shorts. They were whisked off the next second. Heated, I reached for him. My fingers couldn't undo his zipper. I cursed, but Mason helped me. As soon as he sprang free, he clamped a hand under my thigh, arching me back and slid inside with one smooth movement.

A gasped scream ripped from my throat at the sudden contact. It was intoxicating, but not enough. I pushed up from the counter and moved in motion with him as he thrust in and out. The speed picked up, he went deeper and rougher with each thrust until I couldn't think. I could only feel as I rode with him in every movement, every back and forth, climbing closer to climax. When we were nearly there, he didn't linger. He thrust in one last time, the deepest yet. I exploded as I went over the edge with him, my body arched into the air. His penis touched the back of me and another burst of spasms coursed through me.

Before I fell back down, Mason scooped an arm around and held me to his chest. My body trembled and a second orgasm ripped through me. Crying out, I clamped onto his shoulders, still shaking in his arms.

He held me there, cradled in his arms, as he brushed a hand down my back until I stopped quivering. Weak from the climaxes, the adrenaline I had from running melted into exhaustion and I didn't protest when Mason carried me to the bed. When he slid us both under the covers, my head hit the pillow and I let out a contented sigh. Then his arms slid around my waist, he pulled me back against him, and I was home.

CHAPTER FOURTEEN

I woke up and lunged for the nearest thing that told time. 4:45—holy shit. I rolled out of bed to my feet and was in the shower faster than I could've imagined. I impressed myself, but when the door opened, I met Mason's lust-filled gaze and dropped the shampoo. I was going to be late for my second day of work.

My back hit the wall again as music started blaring below us. When he slid inside, he kept rhythm with the bass underneath. We were both climaxing during the bridge of the second song. As he let me back down, he braced an arm above me and gasped a few shuddering breaths. I grinned at the feeling of intoxication. Being with Mason was something I would never tire of, no matter the drama, no matter the obstacles. He made me alive. When I slid a hand up his chest and around his neck to draw him down, I pressed my lips to his and felt the same power over him that he had with me.

It was liberating.

"Hell, woman," he grunted as he braced a hand against the wall behind me so he could lean over me. "You're going to kill me."

A grin teased the corners of my mouth, but I held my breath as he moved down, closer and closer, until he was a hair's width away from me. His breath fanned over me while I waited for his touch with my heart pounding. Just like that, even after we had been together, I still felt the intoxication sweep through me again. It was powerful and heady. When he didn't press his lips to mine, my eyes flicked up. His had darkened with desire, and he slammed his mouth on mine, melting the world away.

Once more, I was swept off my feet as he picked me up and carried me to the bed. When he slid me back down, I caught sight of his clock—6:00. Panic overtook me like a bucket of ice thrown on us, and I shoved him away.

"Wha—what are you doing?" His first question fell away as I scrambled off the bed and hurried to my bag.

I grabbed the first thing my hand touched and threw it on. As I hopped around, trying to get my shoe on, Mason moved to sit on the edge of the bed. "What are you doing?"

"I'm late." *Where the hell was that other shoe?*

"You're late?"

I glanced up, distracted, but crashed into the couch as I saw the blood drain from his face. His eyes were wide with horror. It clicked with me. "No, no, no. I'm not pregnant."

"OH!" His shoulders slumped with relief. "Thank god."

Ah ha! I spied my other shoe and pulled it on right away. "I'm late for work. Gotta go." I grabbed my purse, my keys, and flew out the door. The crowd had moved to the center area around the fountain. I raced down the stairs and jumped over a girl who sat on the bottom step.

Mason followed, standing in the bedroom's doorway, shirtless with a pair of unzipped jeans. He hollered after me, "You have a job?"

"Yeah!" Ignoring the stares and sudden lull in conversation, I yelled back, "Manny's. Started yesterday. See you!"

I was out the door and in my car within seconds but had to slam on the brakes when I looked in the rearview mirror. There were cars in front of me, on the side of me, and behind me. I was boxed in.

"AH!" My forehead hit the steering wheel from frustration. I was never going to get there. Heather was going to fire me on my second day.

What was I going to do? But I didn't have the time to consider my choices—she needed to know what was going on so I looked through my purse for my phone when I heard a tapping on my window. Glancing up, a heady rush went through me when Mason bent down and had his set of keys dangling from his hand. He was still shirtless. I wasn't going to complain.

He said through the closed window, "Come on. I'm not blocked in. I'll give you a ride."

When I got out, he led the way and I had a good view of his backside. Goodness. I forgot how he was just as well sculpted in the back as the front. The only times I looked at his back was when I pressed against him. It was his front side that always held my attention. I blushed as I remembered the reason why I was late for work and at how wanton my behavior had been. I should've been used to it, but when he sauntered to his Escalade with a natural grace that only the best athletes seemed to possess, I knew I never wanted to get used to our times together. I wanted every time to feel like the first.

"What's the hold up? You coming?"

Oh god. I had paused beside his door and was staring at him, lust in my thoughts. My head ducked down as I hurried around to the passenger side. I rolled my eyes. I was like a schoolgirl crushing on the local god. But I was, and he was, and we were together. My shoulders came back up at that thought. When I slipped inside, he gave me a questioning glance but pulled out and veered around the cars in the driveway.

"You good?"

I nodded, biting my lip. His jeans were still not zipped up, but he was only dropping me off. "I won't be done until the bar closes."

"You help out in the bar too?"

"Yeah." I gave him a sheepish look. "I'm sorry I didn't tell you, a lot of stuff happened today, but I meant to."

"It's no problem. I'm just surprised."

"Really?" For some reason, I had thought he would've been upset that I got a job. But now as I saw that he didn't care,

I relaxed. A small flutter started in the pit of my stomach, but it was a good flutter. I wanted a job; it hadn't been all about avoiding my mother. Correction, I wanted this job. I liked working at Manny's. I liked working with Heather.

He grinned as he glanced at me from the corner of his eye. "Yeah, why? You think I'd be pissed or something?"

I shifted in my seat. "Well...yeah..." But why? That'd been a ludicrous thought, but then I understood. My mom would've been mad. She would've hated the idea, she always did. I slumped even further in my seat. Mason wasn't my mother. He wouldn't want to keep me only to the house or out with the only friends he approved. Lydia and Jessica had gotten Analise's stamp of approval. That ended with disaster. Then a sick feeling came to me, and I looked back over at Mason.

"What's wrong?" His voice was so quiet. He glanced from me to the road, but he could tell.

I took another breath. Could I even say this out loud? "My mom liked Lydia and Jessica. Do you think—" I hesitated. I couldn't say it.

"Do I think...what?"

But I knew I would always wonder. "Do you think she liked them because they were like her? I mean, they were mean and didn't really care about me."

His eyes widened a fraction of an inch, but that was his only reaction. The air seemed tense, though, and my gut twisted. I knew why it had changed as soon as I said those words. It was true, and Mason knew it but didn't know how to say those words to me. I shook my head and looked away. "It doesn't matter. I know what you're going to say."

"No, you don't."

I nodded. Drawing in a painful breath, I leaned my forehead against the window. I'd been so blind. She had made comments. She always knew that Jeff was a cheater—could she recognize it in him because she was one too? Was that why she liked Jessica most of all? Because she was like her? She hadn't liked Lydia as much—was that because Lydia cared the most for me out of all three of them?

It was sick. I didn't want to think about it anymore.

"Hey," Mason spoke. He was cautious.

My shoulders tightened and bunched around me. "I don't want to talk about that. I really don't."

"Well, you need to. You sure you have to work tonight?"

I swung around at his gruff voice. What was he mad about? Even though his eyes weren't on me but on the road, I saw the glimmer of fury there. His jaw clenched and his grip tightened on the steering wheel. I asked, "Are you mad at me?"

"What?" He whipped his gaze to me. Then spat out, "No! I'm mad at that bitch you call your mother. Did she pick your friends for you?"

My stomach dropped. She had.

He saw my answer, and a disgusted sound came from him. "I can't believe her—no, I can. She's controlling and possessive. That's why she never liked the idea of you and me, because she couldn't control me and because she knew I cared about you. You want to know my guess as to why she liked those two for you?"

Did I? No, but I knew I needed to.

He continued as his voice grew savage. "Because she wanted people around you that would hurt you. She wanted them to hurt you because then you'd stay with her. You would never know what else was out there, that there are good people out there. I'm not a saint, I know that, but when I love someone, I love them with everything." A curse ripped from him, and he pulled into Manny's parking lot in a rush of gravel before he braked to a stop. Then he was on my side of the car. His eyes were fierce, but his hands were gentle as they turned me to him. He pressed his forehead against mine. I felt how he was keeping himself in control. He expelled a deep breath. "I want the best for you. I don't want to keep you imprisoned to me. I want you to reach your fullest, find friends who really care about you, get a job that you like. I want you to go to my school and get a track scholarship. I want you to do all of that in spite of your mother, because if she had her way, you'd never go anywhere. She would ruin it."

I closed my eyes. She would. The truth stabbed me in the gut.

His hand cupped the side of my face and lifted me up. He whispered, "Look at me."

A whimper escaped me. His eyes burned with love. The emotion was there, an extra layer to the windows of what he felt. It hurt, but it was the good hurt. Something unlocked inside of me, that was him. I had everything boxed inside, kept away so I wouldn't feel, but with Mason, all I could do was feel. That was because of him, because he loved me. I whispered back, "Thank you."

"For what?"

"For loving me." For giving me what my mother should have—unconditional love. That hurt to admit. Another whimper slipped out, but I was lifted into his arms and held against his chest. He rocked me back and forth with his head tucked down. I didn't want to be anywhere else.

When I walked into Manny's, much later, Heather was behind the bar counter. She wore a similar red shirt from yesterday with ripped jeans that stuck to her like a second skin. With a towel and glass in hand, she dried and placed it back behind the counter. She picked up another as I went over. One of her eyebrows lifted in the air. "I hope this isn't a pattern because, girl, if it is we have to rethink this job for you."

"I'm sorry, I am. My mom collapsed this morning. She was rushed to the hospital."

Her mouth dropped. When an apology flashed over her face, I looked away. Mason told me the lie would work and it had, but there was a ball of guilt on the bottom of my stomach. I only hoped to work it away. That meant showing up on time and no more afternoon quickies. Mason never let them last as quickies. They grew into full-blown afternooners.

"I'm sorry, Sam. I figured something happened from last night, but I didn't think it was your mom." She nodded towards the door. "I saw Kade drop you off, it looked intense in there."

I flushed. She had seen that?

"Uh, yeah." A sudden rush overtook me. I wanted to tell her all about it, but I couldn't. Well, I could, but she wasn't my friend. I had never trusted any of my friends, but after only knowing her a day, I wanted to confide in her. Confused by that, I pushed it away. I was here for a job. "Where do you want me today?"

She gestured to the back of the bar. "You can stay here with me today. It shouldn't be too busy until later, but Brandon will take over by then."

As I settled beside her, there were some customers I recognized from last night's party. A few older couples were there as well, along with a young family.

"Jason!" a mother hollered as her two-year-old darted down the hallway, giggling. He pumped his chubby legs harder and his giggles increased.

Heather and I shared a look of amusement as the mother raced past us. "They come here every morning, and little Jason loves going to the back office to see my dad."

"They come here every morning?" I grabbed a towel and glass to dry.

She nodded as she picked up another. "Yep. Coral and Jeff, her husband, have opposite schedules. He's on the road with his job at night, so they meet here for some time together. It'd probably be easier if they did it at home, but I think Coral enjoys the break from watching all three of their little ones. My dad dotes on Jason." She nodded to the table where a girl and another boy looked the same age. Food was plastered over their faces and hands. Their dad wore deep bags underneath his eyes as he tried to feed the baby. Heather chuckled, "Jake and Jenna too."

"Triplets?"

"Yep. They're almost a part of the family now. Coral keeps trying to set up Brandon with her co-workers. She's a nurse, she'll go in for a twelve hour shift."

Watching that table and hearing the fondness in Heather's voice, I felt slapped in the face. That was what a family was. They cared for each other. Her dad came out of his office with the two year old in his arms. His mother followed behind, cooing and smiling as Jason flailed his arms over Manny's shoulders at her. Another chuckle came from Heather as her dad sat at their table. The other two flocked to his lap, and soon all three of them were crawling all over him.

They weren't blood, but they were family.

"You okay?"

I jerked from my thoughts, but caught the glass before it went flying from my hands. A full face flush was coming. I ducked down and grabbed another glass to dry. "I'm good. Do you need me to grab some more glasses to shine?"

I was aware of the skeptical look she gave me but ignored it. When she remarked, "I suppose you could polish some of the silverware—" I had that tray in my hands before she could finish her sentence and scurried to a far table. It hurt to watch that loving family.

CHAPTER FIFTEEN

Brandon arrived and went behind the bar so Heather and I could help Lily and Anne, the other two servers from the diner. After the third hour of full tables with more people still streaming in, I asked Heather if it was always like this and she nodded with a rueful grin on her face. "Why do you think I get so pissed at Brandon for banging my friends? They quit after he breaks up with them. I can't keep losing anymore girls."

"Watch out!" Lily called as she hurried towards us and collapsed a bin full of dishes on the counter. "Whoa. I almost dropped that. Manny would have my hide."

Heather snorted, "Yeah, right. My dad? He can't even bring himself to squash a ladybug. Your job's safe if you break a few dishes." When the door opened and a bunch of guys walked in, she groaned but started towards them.

Lily grinned as she turned to watch her beside me. "She's right, you know."

"About?"

"About her dad. He's a softie, that's why so much of the other stuff falls on Heather and Brandon's shoulders. They do the firing and hiring. If anyone would fire me, it'd be Heather."

When the guys folded around a table in the back corner, Heather stood with pad in hand. All of them stopped and scanned her up and down. She shifted her weight to one side so her hip stuck out and lifted her chin up. They looked up with cocky smirks already starting, but those fell away as soon as they caught whatever expression she wore. A few cleared their throats before snatching up the menus she plopped on the table.

I chuckled. She had stopped their flirting in its tracks. Heather was not someone I wanted to mess with.

"So what's your deal?"

"Huh?" I looked over. I had expected Lily to leave the dishes and hurry away again, but she had been watching me as I watched Heather. "What do you mean?"

She shrugged. "Heather likes you, a lot. If another girl had shown up two hours late on her second day, she would've been sent away at the door."

"Oh." I shifted around and reached for the bin of dishes. I could wash them, anything to get away from this line of questioning. I liked Lily and Anne from the night before. Both were on the heavy side with friendly smiles, but I grew uneasy at the keenness in her eyes now. It hadn't been there the night before. "It's nothing. My mom went to the hospital today. I was late because of that—"

"Oh my gosh!" Her hand clamped on my arm.

Startled, I let go of the bin, and it landed with a thump back on the counter. "No, it's okay. I mean, it was a shock, but my mom will be fine. I think it was—"

"Logan Kade just walked in here," she hissed. Her hand tightened on my arm. I gritted my teeth against the pain from her hold but processed her words. Sure enough. Logan waltzed through the front door as if he owned the place. His eyes were narrowed, but the same cocksure smirk was there as he scanned the room. When he saw me, he paused in question, but I shook my head so he nodded and turned to the bar. He lifted a hand in the air. "Yo."

"Kade!" Brandon boomed from the bar. "Get your ass over here, man!"

The two bumped fists together when Logan claimed a stool at the bar. The two acted like long-lost best friends. It wasn't long before they were having shots. After an hour, the enjoyment of each other's presence wasn't fading. I was mystified. Logan never sought me out. He seemed content to swap stories with Brandon, who I was reminded had played football with Logan and Mason a year ago. That startled me as well. Heather's brother owned and ran the bar, but he had only graduated high school a year ago. That was a lot of responsibility, but he seemed to handle it fine, like Heather did with running the diner.

Just then, she slapped a hand on the counter beside me. "I need a smoke break. You game?"

"Game?"

She jerked her head through the back door. "Come with? You're up for a break soon, aren't you? Lily and Anne can handle our tables for awhile."

"Tables? You mean my two and your ten?"

She flashed a grin as she reached for her purse under the counter. "Come on. This'll be interesting."

"What will?"

But I didn't have to wait long. The second we went through the door, Logan popped out behind us and shut both doors so no one could see or hear us. He claimed a chair on the other side of Heather since I was next to the door.

She lit her cigarette, took a drag, and leaned back to watch us.

"You don't want to talk to me in there?" Logan leaned forward on his elbows. He'd been happy inside, he was intense now.

I ignored that question. "Mason told you?"

"You yelled it across the room."

"Oh." I flushed as I remembered. With Mason shirtless, I hadn't noticed anyone else. But he wasn't there to question me about my job. "What's going on?"

He expelled a breath and glanced at Heather.

She blew out a long puff of white smoke before she lifted the cigarette again. "I ain't going anywhere, pretty boy. This is my place. This is my break. She's my friend now. You got something to say, share it here or keep it till later, but I ain't going anywhere."

He frowned and then shot her a dark look. "Whatever."

She rolled her eyes and took another long drag from her cigarette.

"Logan."

His eyes jerked back to mine. "Right. So." His eyebrows furrowed together.

"So?"

He chewed his lip for a second before bursting out, "Why didn't you say anything about what your mom was going to do? You told Mason, he told Nate, but no one told me. What's up with that?"

My stomach clenched in knots. I leaned forward and lowered my voice, "Why didn't you bring this up in the car, when it was just you and me?"

He shot me an incredulous look. "Because your mom *just* went to the hospital. You were doing your numb shit."

"My numb shit?"

"Yeah." He jerked his head in a quick nod. "When you don't want to feel all your crap or your mom's crap so you shut down—but it wasn't working then. You were feeling it and you were freaking. I could see it. Remember? I distracted you."

I rolled my eyes. "That would've distracted me too, and it would've been a lot more private."

Heather snorted but turned her head and blew out her smoke again.

"Or tonight too. You could've waited until tonight."

Logan snorted this time. "Yeah, right. Like I could tear you away from my brother. If you're home and he's home, you two are always with each other." His voice went low, almost threatening. "It sucked being a third wheel before, but I don't appreciate being a fourth wheel now."

I sucked in my breath. What was he saying?

"If Mason doesn't tell me, you should. Don't kid yourself, Sam. Nate's not here for you or me. He's here for Mason. If my brother wasn't so straight with you, I'd think those two were a happy gay couple. They're so giddy living together and making their plans for college." Logan kicked up a leg to rest on the edge of my chair. He pushed his chair in the air so it rested on the back two legs as he grumbled, "I forgot what those two were like when Nate actually lived here."

I sighed. What the hell did I do here? Logan was hurt, that was obvious. Mason had been shutting him out lately, but why? Was it my place to intervene? As I considered that, I remembered the party two months ago when Mason and Nate worked together like a slick team and manipulated Logan. He meant to protect me while Mason wanted to protect his relationship with his brother as well as with me. It worked. The threat had been silenced, and Miranda never even knew she had hit the one button that could've unraveled the brothers' relationship.

I was seeing another button now, the tight bond between Nate and Mason. Logan was hurting because of it, and he was right. If Mason wasn't going to look out for him, I would. He'd done it for me too many times to count.

I leaned over and touched his arm. "I'm sorry, Logan."

"For what?" He had tensed under my touch but didn't take his eyes away from me.

"For not telling you. I don't care what Mason says, I'll tell you from now on."

Some tension left him, and his shoulders relaxed. "Thanks, Sam. I know he does it to protect me, but it pisses me off."

I bit my lip. What would happen if Logan ever found out how they had manipulated him? A knot formed in my throat at the idea of that day. I knew it was coming. All secrets came out, no matter how long or deep they were buried.

Then Logan switched his gaze to Heather. The cocky smirk slid back into place. "So, how's Channing?"

Heather froze, but then threw him a seductive look and blew a puff of smoke into his face. "Oh, you know. He's probably still sleeping from all the sex we had last night."

Logan's eyes lit up. "Yeah?"

"Oh yeah." She nodded. Her voice lowered to a husky tone, full of promises. "I tired him out, especially when I brought out the handcuffs. I hope I remembered to uncuff him this morning." She feigned concern before her lips curved into a sultry smile. "I'm sure I did and if I didn't, I'll have to make it up to him tonight."

"You're into handcuffs?"

"Oh, I'm into a lot of stuff, Logan. A whole lot of painful dominatrix sort of things, only the good kink that every couple wishes they could do. You know what I mean."

I caught the wink she sent at me behind her hand.

Logan licked his lips. "Oh yeah. I love it when a girl lifts her legs like a pretzel. Do you do that for Channing?"

"Of course." Her voice lowered even more as her finger slid from her throat to the front of her shirt. She paused in the valley between her breasts, above where she had knotted the ends of her shirt together. "He loves it. He really does."

Logan sucked in a breath; his eyes enraptured where her finger paused.

Then she snapped them together in front of his face. He jerked back, startled from the sudden movement, but Heather calmly grounded out her cigarette. "Anyways. Break time is over for me. Enlightening, Kade, every time you come here. It's always so enlightening." She caught my gaze. "You can stay for awhile if you'd like. You never took your half hour for supper."

When she went inside, I was surprised to see Logan grinning.

"She was joking."

He lifted a shoulder. "I don't care. Jax can be hella hot. I forgot how much fun it is to mess with her."

"You were friends with her?"

"Somewhat. She was best friends with Tate."

My gaze shot to his. "What?"

He nodded as his grin thinned.

"Tate as in the Tate that you dated for two years, that you loved, that tried to cheat on you with Mason?"

He nodded before yawning, "Yeah, that Tate. She wasn't always the prissy bitch you met a few months ago, Sam. Tate was cool. I wouldn't have dated anyone who wasn't cool. Her and Heather had been friends for years."

My eyes widened. "Did she used to work here?"

His lips pressed together, but he didn't say anything.

"Oh god. She did, didn't she?"

Then laughter boiled out of him. He slid further in his chair with a wicked smile. "Yeah, she worked here. She quit after she'd been with me for a year, that was when she became the bitch you met a few months ago."

"She wasn't before?"

"Nah, not until she became obsessed with Mason, then she became one." The wicked glint in his eye depleted as memories rolled over him. His voice grew softer. "Tate was really laidback at first, but she wouldn't stand for any bullshit. She never let the guys mess with her, not even me. I think that's why I liked her. She knew what she wanted and she went after it."

"You?"

The humor was gone now. "No, Mason. She wanted him. I was the means to get to him. I should've recognized the signs earlier than I did, but I don't think I wanted to see them. She talked about how Mason was the alpha male at school. She'd say things about how every person needed their other half, that they were supposed to be equals. That's about the time that she started to become more of a bitch to everyone. She tried to become the female alpha that was his equal, I guess. When she became friends with Kate and Parker, that crew, her and Heather parted ways. Tate was awesome in bed. I was getting great sex so I didn't put two and two together until Mason called me from his room." His jaw clenched.

I could see the anger and hurt still there.

"She used me. That girl used me, straight out. She was a cold bitch the first time we slept together. But to give her some credit," he winced, "I don't think she counted on me actually falling for her. But that first night lasted to two, then three. I was taking her on dates, coming here to hang out with her."

"That's why you and Brandon acted like long-lost friends."

He nodded. "I guess. I don't know. I always liked Brandon. He was cool to hang out with." He flashed me a dimple. "He got us free alcohol, you know. Even when we were sophomores. I think his older brother was running the bar then, but Brandon still snuck a keg for us." He paused. "Or two."

The door opened then and Brandon popped his head out. "Hey, Sam. My sis needs your help."

"Okay." With a small smile at Logan, I headed inside. I wasn't sure how I felt about everything he had revealed, but I couldn't dwell on it. As I stepped through the door, my eyes got big. The crowd had doubled. Then I saw Mason and Nate come in through the door. Great, they brought the entire party from the house here.

Brandon was still in the doorway, but I looked around him to Logan. "Everyone from the house is here."

He sat up straight in his chair. "Everyone?"

I nodded. "Yep, Mason and Nate brought everyone."

Oh joy.

CHAPTER SIXTEEN

When the dishwasher had to go home for a family emergency, I offered to take his place. I wanted to avoid the extra attention. Time flew after that. Bins of dishes were pushed through the window. I hurried to wash them, get them dried, and back into place for the cook. After two more hours, it didn't look to be lessening, and I heard Heather sigh as she picked up the phone. She was calling in reinforcements. Another girl came in to be a server, and there was another cook in the kitchen. At one point, Heather stuck her head through the window to where I stood and asked if it was okay if I did dishes for the rest of the night.

I nodded. Hell, I was relieved.

At one point, the new server that I hadn't met snapped at me. I'd been stacking the dishes and didn't get out of her way fast enough. I ducked back into the kitchen, but heard Lily hiss, "Watch it, that's Mason Kade's girlfriend."

"What?" the new server exclaimed. "Are you kidding me?"

Lily whispered to her, "Don't worry. She seems really nice."

"Oh." The girl mumbled something else to her, but I couldn't hear anymore. They moved away from my window.

"I thought you were a waitress?"

Mason stood in the back doorway with an odd grin. As he came closer, he reached for an apron and tied it around his waist. His eyes were glazed over.

I snorted, reaching for more plates to pile on the crate. "You're drunk."

He settled beside me and sighed. "Yeah, a bit." Then he bent down and placed a soft kiss on my shoulder.

I wanted to melt into him, and I did, for a second. Then I pulled away and began lining up the plates in their slots again. "Frank had to go home so I volunteered to take his place. What are you doing back here?"

He narrowed his eyes at me. "You like it back here, don't you?"

"Yeah," I confessed. "I kind of do."

He reached out and brushed some hair back from my forehead. When he leaned close again, I felt his lips there and snuggled against him.

"Employees only, Kade!" Heather rapped on the window. "Out."

He wrapped an arm around my waist. "Make me, Jax."

"Are you serious?" She shifted and one hand went to her hip.

I hid a grin at the movement. After watching her yesterday and today, that was what she did when she was all business. She'd shift back on her left heel, her hand went to her hip, and she narrowed her eyes at whoever was giving her trouble. Her elbow stuck out when she really meant business. She did it all now, but then threw both hands in the air. "Fine. Fine. Just actually help your girl. If you distract her and we get behind because we have no dishes, I'm throwing you out."

"Whatever."

"Don't think I won't call a few of Brad's buddies. They're bigger than you, Kade."

He chuckled but sighed when she narrowed her eyes again in a warning. "Fine. Yes, I'll help her. Why do you think I'm here?"

"You're here to see your girl. When your posse came in, she went back there so then you had to go back there to see her. I'm not a moron, Kade. I know why you're back there, and I don't want any sex going on in my diner. You hear me?"

"Yeah, yeah."

"My diner, Kade!"

"I get it," he barked back now. "Your diner, your job. My girlfriend."

She stuck out her chin at him. "She's my worker and she's my friend."

Mason grew stiff beside me. I wasn't surprised when his next words came out as a threat, "I already told you I'll help her back here. If you keep talking to me like that, you and I are going to have a real problem."

I knew neither of these two would back down so I moved Mason to the back end of the dishwasher. Ignoring Heather's hawk-like scrutiny, I lifted the door and pulled out the crate that'd been washed. "You need to wait until they're all dry and then stack them in those places over there."

He glanced to where I pointed and nodded. All the other dishes were easy to see. As he started to dry, I went back to loading more dishes onto the crates to put through the washer. Heather hadn't moved.

"Sam," she started.

My hand shot in the air. "Don't. If I was dating Logan and he were back here, you wouldn't care. I know you don't like Mason, but I love him. He's being a good guy right now. If you think that I would let my relationship interfere with my job, then I need to show you that's not who I am. I am sorry about being late today, but you have my word it will never happen again."

Her hand fell from her hip again and her shoulders dropped. "I'm sorry. I was being a bitch." She chewed on her lip for a second before she gave me a sheepish grin. "I kind of think I'm in love with you myself. I get it now. I see why those two care so much about you." Her eyes twinkled in humor. "If I were a lesbian, I'd want you as my girlfriend. I have a straight boner for you, Sam. Hot damn."

Mason cursed behind me.

Her smile widened even more before she left.

When I heard a groan behind me, I turned. "What?"

Mason had a towel in one hand and a bowl in the other. He glared at me now. "She's going to be your new best friend, isn't she?"

I straightened at his words. Was she? Then I shrugged. "I have no idea. Would that bother you?"

He rolled his eyes. "Your friends are either scared of me, want to screw me, or think I'm an asshole. Can't you find some girl who is *just* a good friend to you? Who doesn't care that I'm your boyfriend?"

A snort came out of me. "Please. Do you realize how ridiculous that sounds? One, you are an asshole. Two, a lot of girls want to screw you. And three, if they don't fall into those two slots then they're going to be scared of you, like Becky was."

He grimaced as he reached for another mixing bowl to dry. "I just don't like feeling that I can't be around my girlfriend. I'm sick of having to jump through hoops and sneak around to be with you."

My voice softened. "If what you say is true and Heather and I become good friends, she might turn into that girl who doesn't care about you. She's looking at you through the same lens as everyone else right now. She hasn't seen you with me enough to know how good you treat me. And she's not my mom."

His shoulders relaxed. "Yeah, I know." Then his eyes shot back to me again. "Things aren't done with your mom, you know. We're just in the waiting stage while she regroups." He moved to put the dishes away. When he came back, I pushed another load out of the washer for him. He picked up a plate and leaned back against the wall as he dried it. "My dad's suspicious of her now so she'll focus on him and play nice for awhile. Once she's got him brain-dumb again, she'll start back on you."

I felt stabbed in the gut. I'd always be her second priority. The man was number one.

"Hey," Mason called over, his voice soft again. "You okay?"

I nodded, but I couldn't speak. The emotions were choking me again.

"I said something wrong?"

I shook my head, turning to load more dishes onto the crates. When the washer beeped another cycle, I avoided his gaze and pushed another crate through. He didn't push me, and slowly the emotions started to settle down again. We worked in silence for awhile, maybe an hour, before I noticed that the dishes had stopped piling up so much.

"What the hell, man?" Logan's voice made us both jump as he boomed through the window. "You're both back there? I want to go back there."

Mason came up behind me. I felt his heat as he pressed against me, but he didn't slide his arms around me how I expected. Disappointment flared in me. Then he spoke over my shoulder, "Where's Nate?"

Logan bristled, "Who cares? I don't know. He's with Parker, I think."

Tension replaced my disappointment. Those girls were here too? Did everyone go where Mason and Logan went?

Mason's hand splayed out on the small of my back. I knew he felt how stiff I became at the mention of those girls, but he didn't say anything. For that, I was relieved. Instead, he asked, "When's everyone heading out?"

Logan rolled his eyes and threw an irritated glance over his shoulder. "I think they're all waiting to see what we do. What are you thinking?"

His arms slid around my waist, and I was finally pulled back into him. I breathed a little easier. As he spoke, I felt the rumbling through his chest. "Tell Ethan to have the party at his place."

Logan's eyebrow arched.

Mason's voice had an edge to it. "Why do they always have to be at Nate's? That's our home too. We only had people over to the house when we wanted them."

"Nate initiated the open-door policy."

Mason bit back a growl, but his hand clamped tighter on my waist. "He only did that for us. He'll do whatever we say—"

"Whatever you say, you mean."

"Whatever!" He growled now at his brother. "What's your problem? You've been pissy all day."

My eyes went wide. I knew Logan was just waiting for an opening to start something and Mason had given it to him, but now was not the time or the place. "Okay." I turned and shoved Mason back, then gave Logan a meaningful look. "Get everybody out of here. We'll come to the party when I'm done with work, but I would enjoy a quiet house tonight."

"Yeah. Okay," he grumbled before he glowered at me. Then he sighed and left to do my bidding.

"What was that about?"

I glared at Mason. "Not now, and you know what that was about. Don't play stupid with me."

His head reared back, but a slow smile grew across his face. His eyes darkened, and he licked his lips when he took a step towards me. "I forgot how hot you can get when you're mad at me. You sure about the no sex at work?"

"Mason!"

He laughed but moved back to finish the dishes.

When everyone left and the kitchen closed, Heather assigned me two tables in the bar section. That was fine with me. The other server and Anne were released to leave for the night, leaving Heather, Lily, and me for staff alongside Brandon, who was still behind the bar. As the night drew to a close, I grinned as Mason, Brandon, and Gus watched a game on the television. A few girls remained, all whom were captivated by the guys at the bar. When they wandered over and perched on seats, I knew why Mason chose to sit near one end. The girls were on the other side of Gus, who choked on his drink when the first smiled at him. The other two craned their necks around to see Mason, but he was the good boyfriend. His gaze remained trained on the game, even when two of the girls started a conversation about the game. Brandon was the first to join. He poured their drinks and answered each giggling question they sent his way. Gus piped up too, and when my last customers left, I couldn't stop from watching the show.

"Ah." Heather jumped on the stool next to me as her last table left. "Gus loves when we close. He comes in late sometimes and hangs out with Brandon because he knows that's his best time to get a girl. They're so drunk by then, and he thinks that Brandon makes him look better for his chances. He's in heaven tonight, sitting beside the god-like Mason Kade."

I heard the cynicism and frowned. "You really don't like Mason, do you?"

She hesitated, but then shrugged. "I...I'll be honest, I can't be objective with him. He's the reason Tate isn't around and why she and I stopped being friends. But I like you and you like him and he likes you, so I'm woman enough to say that maybe there's more to him than the asshole everyone says he is."

"With a referral like that, who wouldn't want to get to know him," I teased, but sat up straighter when one of the girls took a deep breath and walked around Gus. She approached Mason, who still hadn't taken his eyes off the television. As she slid onto the one open stool beside him, he still didn't look over. He yawned, instead.

Heather choked on a laugh. She hit her chest and bent over, her shoulders shaking. "Man, if that's not a burn then I don't know what is. The girl is stupid."

Lily stopped on the other side of the counter with a washcloth in hand. "I think she's being brave." Her eyes met mine, and she gave me a timid smile. "I know he's your boyfriend, but a lot of girls don't believe it. She's being brave. She's going for it."

Heather snorted, "She's going to crash and burn. Mason has never been open to cold approaches. Logan, on the other hand, doesn't give a damn, but not that Kade. That Kade has whipped out some doozies for rejections. You know how many girls I've found crying in the bathroom?"

We all grew silent when the girl touched his arm and opened her mouth. There it was. The pick-up line was coming, but then her mouth dropped in shock. Mason stood and threw some money on the counter. He tapped the counter and said something to Brandon before he looked for me. When he saw the small audience, he smirked as he came over.

The girl watched him. When he pulled me into his arms, her mouth snapped shut. I saw the glimmer of anger in her eyes, but then her other friend tugged on her arm and they hurried out of the diner. The door had just about shut when it swung back open and the girl stomped inside. Her hands were on her tiny hips and her mouth was twisted with disgust, but Heather stepped forward. She folded her arms over her chest and lowered her head. As she stood in front of Mason and me, her stance told everyone not to mess with her. It worked. The girl faltered, then wrinkled her nose at us, and glared back at Heather before she turned on her heel. She stormed out once more and slammed the door.

The diner was quiet for a moment before Brandon tipped his head back in laughter. "My sister, the bulldog! Don't mess with a Jax!"

Heather's arms fell to her side and her shoulders came back up. She shook her head, but I heard a soft chuckle escape her mouth. Then she hollered, "Brandon, get Gus out of here and finish cleaning."

"Yeah, yeah."

Lily chuckled behind us as she wiped the counter off. I picked up the other washcloth and it was a half hour later, after the money had been locked away and the last floors were mopped, when everyone filed out to the parking lot. Lily and Brandon sat down on the patio chairs, so Mason and I did the same as everyone waited for Heather. She was the last one.

When she came out, she locked the doors. "We had triple the business tonight than a regular night."

Brandon gestured to Mason. "Because of him and their friends."

I felt my hand squeezed, and Mason whispered in my ear, "I'll wait for you in the car."

I nodded. As he left, Brandon stood up. "I'm tuckered out. See you ladies tomorrow."

Lily called out goodnight to him, and I gave him a small wave as he disappeared around the side of the bar towards their house. As he went, Lily gave us a small smile and wave of her own before she went over to her car.

Heather pulled out a cigarette. When it was lit, she gestured to Mason's Escalade. "He didn't want to stick around and hear our thanks for the business?"

I shrugged. I had no idea. "Ethan Fischer is having a party tonight. We said we'd go. You want to come?"

As she took a drag, she paused for a second. "Are you kidding me?"

I frowned. "No, why would I be? You went to the one last night."

"Yeah, but we shouldn't have gone there. Channing had been opposed the whole time."

"So why did you?"

She took another drag off her cigarette. "Can I be honest?"

Her eyes found mine and fixed there. I felt her studying me in the same way Mason would when he wanted to read my mind. "Sure." But I didn't know why she wouldn't have been honest?

"I saw you last night, after we closed. I waited around because I wasn't sure if you had a ride or not. I know you told me Kade was your boyfriend, but I had my doubts. Then I saw that other guy pick you up and I don't know." She inhaled, and then exhaled. Her head fell down. "I went to the party to see if you were there and if you were okay. I figured any girlfriend of Mason Kade's would be at his party so..."

"You went there to see if I actually was his girlfriend?" Disbelief slammed into my chest. I wasn't used to that reaction. Most girls hated me when they learned the truth, but Heather's reaction was almost refreshing.

"I went there to make sure you were okay."

"Oh."

"Look," she stood from the wall and took another drag. "They haven't told you so I guess I have to. I'm good friends with Channing."

"Okay." I nodded. "Why's that such a big deal?"

She didn't answer again, not right away. But when she did, it all made sense. "He goes to school in Roussou."

CHAPTER SEVENTEEN

Coach Grath met me at a park near my old home where David lived, if he still lived there. I didn't ask why my new coach picked that park, but it was fine with me. This was one of my normal running routes. When I got there, he pointed to the grass, "Stretch out."

He was all business.

Coach Grath had a gruff face. His square jaw gave a no-nonsense vibe and there were no wrinkles around his mouth, like he never smiled or laughed. He was dressed in a crisp-looking track suit with the Fallen Crest Public school colors, red and black. A whistle hung around his neck, and he held a clipboard in his meaty hand. As soon as I was done stretching, he grunted, checked his watch, wrote something down on his clipboard, and gestured to the walking trail. "Keep to the right, circle the park, and come back here. It's one mile. I'm recording your time." He paused before his eyes went flat. "Go."

The abrupt command startled me, but I started off. I wasn't sure what he wanted, but I wasn't going to go my fastest, not until my muscles were looser. When I came back around, he checked his watch again, wrote the time, and told me to go again. As I hauled off, he yelled after me, "Go faster this time."

So I did.

That was my training routine—each mile was timed, and with each lap, he told me to go faster. After I had been running for 90 minutes, he asked how much longer I could go.

"My longest run has been four hours." All at one time with no breaks, but I didn't share that bit with him.

He nodded, wrote something more on his clipboard and pointed at the trail again. "I want you to go your fastest now and don't stop until you're out of gas."

My eyes widened. Did he know what he was getting into? But then he said, "When you're done, remember the time and distance. Report back to me tomorrow, same time, same place. No late nights. Start buying almonds, whole-grains, oranges, and vegetables. Don't carbo-load the night before your long runs."

"I never have."

He had started to leave, but turned back. He didn't blink. "What'd you say?"

"I've never loaded up on carbs the night before. I don't want to change my eating habits, sir."

"Coach."

"Coach."

Then he frowned. "What do you usually eat?"

I shrugged. "Chicken, a bagel every now and then."

He nodded. "Chicken's good. Salmon's better, but don't stretch your bank account. Do what you're already doing for this month. Next month we'll try it my way and see which one has the better results."

I stepped back. "Excuse me, sir?"

"Coach!"

I winced. "Coach. Are you challenging me?"

He folded his clipboard against his chest and tucked his chin down as he gave me a long searching stare. Then he sighed. "Strattan, you came to me. If you want a scholarship, you'll play by my rules. I'm not challenging you, I'm pushing you. You're going to be the best damn runner you can be and if you stick with my rules through the track season and cross country season next fall, you'll be going to a school with a full ride."

"Cross country?"

"Running's a solitary thing for you. It's like that for the best runners, but you better start getting used to not doing everything your way or no way. You're joining both teams whether you like it or not. Make sure to stop at the school sometime this week and fill out all your paperwork. We run at 6 in the morning, every morning."

He didn't wait for my response. As he got inside his car, he hollered back to me, "Run, Strattan! Time and distance, Strattan. Time and distance."

I stood there, not sure what to think so when he tapped his horn once, I got to running. Even though I knew I would be dead for the rest of the day, I did what he ordered. I ran until I had no gas left, and then I ran some more. By the time I was done, I collapsed on the grass and waited until my heart would stop pounding. Then I remembered he said to mark the time and distance. The numbers didn't make sense to me, not much did at that moment, but I knew that I had to stretch and I needed to call for a ride.

Stretching was torture, and by the time Mason arrived, I had fallen asleep.

"Sam." He touched my arm.

I opened my eyes, frowned as he was bent over me. Then I let out a deep groan, "Oh my god."

I couldn't sit up. I tried. I failed.

Mason caught my arm and pulled me to my feet. When I would've fallen back down, he scooped me up and carried me to his car. It wasn't long before he had me buckled in and was in his own seat. Then he pointed to my car. "You want me and Logan to come back and get that?"

I nodded, feeling weak. Why had I run so much? I croaked out, "What time is it?" But my eyes were already closing. I needed sleep, just sleep.

"You have two hours before your shift."

I cursed under my breath. Why the hell had I run so much? But I remembered Coach Grath's barking orders and knew the look on his face would be worth it. His gruff exterior pissed me off. I felt like I had to prove myself to him. No matter what he said, I still felt that he didn't believe in me. I wondered if he was meeting with me as a favor to...I looked sideways. Mason seemed clueless to my thoughts as he drove to Manny's.

Wait, to Manny's? I sat up. "What are you doing?"

He wheeled into the parking lot and turned the engine off. "You're eating. What else would I be doing?"

My mouth fell open. "Mason, I stink! I can't go in there. Everybody will leave because I smell so bad."

He grinned but shook his head. "With Gus as close competition? I doubt it. Come on, Sam. You need to eat and we don't have anything good at the house."

My head fell back with a thump. He went inside. My ass did not. He was nuts if he thought I was going in there. But I did, after he came out and carried me inside. Lily grinned when she saw the state I was in. And after our food orders were taken, I glanced around. I hadn't before, I didn't want to see the reactions to my messy appearance when Mason walked through the diner, but couldn't stop myself now.

The place was full, but Mason chose a corner table for me. There was a fan beside me, so I dried off quickly, and it was pointed out the side door. All my sweaty fumes went that way. Still, while I wanted to be invisible, I knew whom I was with. Mason attracted attention, and with him beside me and how I looked, we were getting a lot of attention. It was unavoidable.

Heather came over with our water, but instead of leaving, she dropped into the chair beside me. "You want to tell me why you look like you ran a marathon?"

Mason grunted but reached for his glass.

I slunk further down my chair. "That bad, huh?"

"Sammy, don't tell me you ran a marathon? You're on shift in two hours."

"I know, I know." I opened my mouth, ready to start explaining how my new coach was a potential ass, when the door opened and more people strolled inside. "Where did all these people come from?"

"Oh." She jerked a thumb towards Mason. "You can thank your boy here."

"Huh?"

He narrowed his eyes, but didn't say a word.

"Mason?"

"Or maybe it's because of you." Heather studied me again.

Mason gave me a strained smile before he stood up. "I'll be back in a few."

I watched him walk over to a table in the back section, close to the bar, before Heather pulled my attention back by saying, "My dad's over the moon."

"Huh?"

She nodded in Mason's direction. "Word got out that Mason and Logan Kade were both here last night, then word got out that their stepsister works here, and everybody put two and two together. Judging from the crowd we had this morning and how it hasn't let up since, I'm figuring my baby is the new hang-out."

Dread formed in my gut. I liked this place because it was small and private. That was gone now. Then my eyes widened again as I saw the section by the front door. "Academy students are here too?"

"Yeah." She turned to look too. "Those some friends of yours?"

Definitely not.

Jessica shot daggers at me while Lydia sat beside her. Across from them were Becky and another guy who was bouncing in his chair. Jeff sat on his other side, laughing at something he said, but it was the table next to them that had me surging to my feet. Adam was the closest to Becky. He had a hand out to her chair and the two were conversing while the Academy Elite sat around the rest of his table. Miranda's lips thinned as she scanned the diner. The other three girls had spotted me and converged together. When their hands came up to block their mouths I knew the whispering gossip had started. Again. The only two who seemed semi normal were Peter and Mark, but when I caught Mark's gaze for a second, I flinched and turned away.

"...he wants to break the news that he thinks his mom and Coach are going to get hitched, but he doesn't know how to."

I couldn't deal with that. I couldn't think about David and his mother together. Was that the reason my dad had stopped calling me? Adam said that to me two months ago, which now feels like ages ago. Mark was going to be family to me. I felt a burning in my chest. It was tightening, suffocating me. I jerked away from my table, but ran into someone.

"Okay." A strong hand took hold of my elbow and pulled me through the crowd. I couldn't see anyone. I had no idea where Mason was, he had left me. The door was kicked open and we were outside. Barely registering the fresh air, I was pushed down in a chair and my head was shoved between my legs. "Breathe, Sam. Jeez, just breathe."

I took gasping breaths and my eyes closed against the visions that assaulted me.

I pushed open the bathroom door, but he wasn't in there either. "Dad?" Where had he gone? Mom needed him. Mom was bleeding. I hurried back around the bed, but tripped over something. There was a bag on the floor—no, it was a suitcase. Mom was going somewhere? A sob came up in my throat and I whimpered, "Daddy."

His clothes were in the suitcase. Some of his other clothes were spread all over the room. They'd been thrown like that. Why would he do that? He wasn't like that.

Mom was bleeding. I had to go to her.

I pushed myself up, stepped over the suitcase, and hurried down the hallway again. As I neared it, I slowed down. I didn't want to go in there. She was so still and so white. I had only seen another person that white before, when my dad picked me up after I fell off our patio. He took me to the hospital—mom needed the hospital. I turned and went for the phone.

"Hey." Mason's calming voice brought me back as he picked me up and held me in his arms. Then I felt him turning away.

"Where are you taking her, Kade?"

His voice was rough as he threw over his shoulder, "She just needs a minute. She'll be fine. Don't worry."

"Come on, Kade—"

He twisted back around. "I said, she'll be fine. Leave it, Jax."

The edge left her tone. "Take her to my house. It's not the Grand Ritz you guys live in, but it's private. She can shower there. I have a pile of clothes next to my bed. I lent some to her before; she can pick what she wants to wear."

He stiffened underneath me. I knew he wanted to take me home, but enough reason had filtered back to me that I lifted my head from his shoulder. My voice was still weak, "That's fine, Mason. I have to work. I can't miss my shift."

"You sure?" His eyes searched mine.

I nodded but started to tremble at the look of concern in his depths. There was so much love. I lifted my hands to his face and cupped it. His eyes closed and he drew in a ragged breath. My thumb caressed over his cheek. He was so handsome. Perfect. And he was mine. I pressed a kiss to his lips. He hesitated, but I whispered, "I'm fine. I'm fine." Then his mouth opened underneath mine, and he took over the kiss.

I pressed closer, but he had already gentled the kiss by the time he stepped around the back of Manny's. As he put me back down on my feet, he indicated the house. "This is the place?"

"Uh..." I could only focus on how much I wanted to feel him, only him. "Yeah, I guess."

He stepped onto the squeaky patio and opened the screen door. I followed when he went inside, and he stopped to peruse their small living room and kitchen. The stairs were straight ahead with an open door beside them. I saw now that it led to a bedroom. The same boxes of liquor were inside, along with clothes, and dirty dishes.

I gestured upstairs. "Her room's up there. I'm going to shower and change. You'll be okay down here?"

He hadn't stopped looking at the living room. A ratted couch was covered with a bed sheet. The table in front of was covered with magazines, dirtied plates, and cans of beer and soda. Against the wall, their large screen television was the only thing that looked expensive. Mason took a step around the couch and lifted one of the remotes. When he saw that I was waiting, he nodded, "I'll be fine. You're okay up there?"

I nodded. I knew he was really asking if I'd have any more panic attacks, but it hadn't been a full-fledged one. Or maybe I was becoming used to them. "I'll be fine. I'll hurry down."

"No, no." He waved a hand at me. "Take your time."

"You sure?"

"Yeah. I'll be fine."

"Okay." I grinned as he stood in the middle of the living room, searching where to sit. There was a loveseat next to the couch, but it was covered with a similar bedsheet. He bent down and removed a pile of magazines from one corner and perched on the edge. When the television turned on, I headed upstairs.

CHAPTER EIGHTEEN

I heard raised voices when I got out of the shower and ran downstairs. My body was tired. Actually, my heart was tired. But when I heard Mason, a jolt of adrenaline burst through me. I grabbed a towel on the way and had it wrapped around me when I skidded to a halt at the bottom of the stairs. Mason had his back to me. His shoulders were tense and bunched forward. His hands were in fists at his side, and I knew he was a heartbeat away from a fight. When I took another step down, my eyes widened. Heather stood in front of that guy, the model with tattoos. He was in the doorway and had a similar stance as Mason's, but her hands were braced to his chest. A snarl was on her face until she threw a look over her shoulder and saw me. Her eyes bulged out.

"Chill, Chan. Seriously. There's the evidence, smack dab in a towel. You see her?" She shoved her friend back a step. Then she swung an arm and pointed at me. "He was here for her, not me."

Mason glanced back and bit out a curse. "Sam." He stepped up to block me from view. "Go get some clothes on."

"But," I searched around him.

The guy had visibly relaxed, but Heather was still in front of him. Her arms were crossed, and I knew from the tension in her shoulders that she was glaring at him.

"Go." Mason's hands gripped my hips as he urged me up a step.

"Go with her," Heather spoke over her shoulder.

"Better idea. Let's go."

"What was going on?"

But he wasn't listening. When I didn't move, he scooped me up in his arms and carried me up the stairs. His arm wrapped around the back of my legs and my body kept straight so I watched over his shoulder. Heather glanced at us and shook her head. She rolled her eyes, but the guy said something to her. As she looked back at him, she swatted at his shoulder. And then I couldn't see anymore as Mason stopped at the top of the stairs.

"What happened down there?"

"I'll tell you when you've got some clothes on."

"Oh."

"Exactly."

I'd forgotten about my state of undress. I giggled. And then I really thought about the situation. I had a mini-panic attack, Mason brought me here to regroup and shower, and then I walked in on him about to get into a fight with only a towel on. Goodness. The swift change of events had me feeling light-headed as I sat on Heather's bed.

"What's wrong?"

I shook my head, still dazed. "I take it that guy didn't like that you were here?"

He grimaced and then sighed. "Where are those clothes? I'll feel better when you're dressed."

"Okay." But I didn't move.

"Seriously?" He raked a hand through his hair, the little he had with his crew cut. His eyes widened and irritation flashed over them. His shirt lifted from the movement. I caught a glimpse of his abdominal muscles, sculpted with perfection. The oblique muscles had been hardened and stuck out as they disappeared under jeans that hung low on his hips.

I licked my lips. God, those muscles. I wanted to touch them. I wanted to—his hand caught mine and he hauled me off the bed and into his arms. I found myself staring into heated eyes, lined with suppressed anger and more. A groan escaped me, and I started to close my eyes as my head bent down. I needed him. His kiss before had sparked the flame, but now it raged inside of me. I couldn't bank it down now.

"Are you two kidding me?"

Heather's voice was like a bucket of cold water being thrown over us. I shoved back from Mason. I would've pulled him down to the bed. Even if he had protested, I knew that I would've made him forget where we were. Goodness. I drew in a gaping breath as I clutched my towel, the only thing covering me still.

I croaked out, "Heather."

She was in the doorway with a fierce frown on her face. Her arms were crossed, but she jerked a thumb over her shoulder. "I brought your food over here, figured you'd need some grub in you." Then she looked at Mason. "I'm sorry about Channing. He's a bit protective of me, and you're... you..."

He clipped his head in a nod but didn't say a word. As he turned to look out the window, he stuffed his hands into his pockets.

"So..." Heather watched me now.

I flushed and grabbed some of her clothes. "I'll put these on and head downstairs."

She waved at me. "Take your time. I wanted to check on you, didn't realize what I'd be walking in on. But whatever. Logan showed up and filled me in on some things. Your friends are all still there so you're going to be dishwasher again tonight. I hope that's okay."

Relief washed over me. I nodded, unable to speak for a moment.

"Frank went home. His wife is coming in. I was going to have you cover a full section tonight, but I get what's going on. Rosa will fill in for you. When things get crazy busy like this, you can go to the back. We'll figure it out as we go. Sound good?"

I nodded again. It sounded perfect.

Her eyes lingered on Mason before she looked back to me. Her concern was evident. "You'll be okay for the night?"

"Yes. I mean it." I did. Determination spread through me. I wasn't going to disrupt anyone else's life because of my issues. "I can sit if I need to in the back."

Mason turned around, now more in control. He said in a soft tone, "I'll help her too."

Heather nodded. "I figured you might want to."

His jaw clenched. His eyes touched on me for a split second, but he turned back for the window. When his tension didn't leave him, I nodded to Heather's unspoken question if he would be alright. She frowned, but left a second later. As soon as she went down the stairs, I shut the door. "What's going on with you?"

"Nothing."

"Mason," I sighed. His answer had been short, too short. "I'm sorry that I freaked out before—"

He swung around. This time he didn't hold back his anger and I was startled from the fierceness of it. "You're sorry? What the hell happened? I never have any idea when you're going to flip out or sprint off for one of those long-ass runs you do. They're not healthy, Sam. I've been quiet for a long time, but you need to start telling me what going on with you."

"Mason," I started.

"I mean it." His jaw was clenched tight, and his eyes glittered with emotion. He'd had enough.

I saw it then and knew that my hiding was done. I slumped down on the bed and hung my head. This was going to be painful.

I took a deep breath. I was going to need it. "I've been having flashbacks to that night with my mom."

"Your mom? What night?"

"The night she lost the baby—"

His shoulders loosened a fraction, but he remained by the window. "You said she killed her baby."

I nodded. A storm of emotions swirled inside of me, but I couldn't deal with them, not now. "Yeah, I know. She did, but I didn't know then and I keep remembering it in bits and pieces."

"Oh."

I needed to tell him more. I needed to explain it all to him. So I rasped out, "I saw Mark Decraw in the diner and it sent me into a tailspin. I'm sorry. I really am, just the sight of him reminded me of his mom, who might be married to my dad now and..." I drew in a shuddering breath. The pain ripped through me, stabbing me in the gut. "I have no idea if he married her or not. He hasn't reached out to me at all."

Mason sat beside me on the bed and picked up one of my hands. He held it in his lap. "David's not married to that woman. The divorce isn't even finalized with your mom."

"Oh."

I blinked in surprise. I should've known that.

"Logan told me about that before, but I didn't realize you bought into it. Decraw has no idea about your parent's divorce. He's a dumbass. Don't listen to anything he says."

"Oh."

"Was that it?" He frowned at me.

I couldn't get over how stupid I'd been.

"Sam."

"What?"

He narrowed his eyes and studied me again. One of his fingers tipped my chin up so I was looking him straight into the eyes. I couldn't look away. While his eyes held mine captive, he asked further, "What else happened before? Your dad being a neglectful asshole didn't push you over the edge. You had a flashback again?"

I nodded. My throat was full as I remembered it all again. I couldn't explain how the reminder of David took me back to the night he had left me again—no, when he left me the first time. I shook my head as tears leaked out. I didn't want to tell him that I called for an ambulance, all on my own, or how I sat beside my mother. I sat in her blood.

He should've been there.

That thought raced through me, along with a bolt of anger. My jaw hardened. He should've been there. I shouldn't have had to do that on my own. I'd only been eleven. A goddamn eleven-year-old and I had to call 911 for my mother.

"What are you thinking right now?"

The words slipped from me, "It was the first time he left, Mason." My chest lifted. A dull ache started in my gut. "She tried to kill the baby on her own and I found her. I went and looked for him, but he wasn't there. I think," I drew in a deep breath. "I think they had a fight or something. His suitcase was on the floor and his clothes were everywhere. I don't know what happened, but I remembered hearing them before. They'd been fighting. He was going to leave her..." I couldn't finish. I didn't want to remember anymore.

"You okay?"

I couldn't tell him anymore. It was too painful. But then I didn't have to. Mason slid an arm underneath my legs and he lifted me again. He folded me onto his lap, and I curled into him. His hand smoothed up and down my back. It was a comforting motion, one that I needed so much, but after we sat in silence for awhile, I needed to pull away. I had to work soon and he couldn't keep holding my hand every time I felt like I was going to break.

My eyes shot to his, bleak and exhausted. He mirrored what I was feeling. "What was going on downstairs? That guy thought you were here with Heather?'

He jerked his head in a nod. His body stiffened underneath me.

"Mason."

With gentle hands, he deposited me back onto the bed but didn't move away. I was relieved. Instead, he held my hand and rested his arms on his legs. "Heather brought the food over. She'd been here two seconds before he showed up. He went berserk when he saw her and me together. We weren't even on the same couch or anything. She was in the kitchen and I was in the living room, but he saw me in her home and connected the wrong dots together."

"She told me that he goes to Roussou. It's because of that, isn't it? I know you guys hate that school."

"There's more to it than that, but yeah, he's from Roussou. He doesn't run with the same crew as the Broudou brothers, but he knows my history with them. I'm sure that's part of it."

"The Broudou brothers?"

Mason nodded. His shoulders had filled again with tension. "Yeah, there are three of them. Two are seniors this year, twins, and they have a third little brother in your grade. But all of them hate me."

"Why you?" Other than the normal high school football rivalry, I meant. I remembered the first night I saw them and knew I'd be moving in with them. Two cars had pulled up and an instant fight exploded, then they lit their cars on fire.

"Those three hate me because of their sister."

Blank.

Uh, what?

"Huh?"

He chuckled at my reaction. "Don't worry. Nothing happened with me and her, but that's not what she's told them."

"So what do they think?"

"That I met her at a party, slept with her, and never called her back. They think I treated her like trash."

I blinked again, startled. Mason wasn't always the nicest to girls, but he wasn't known to sleep around. But I knew he hadn't been a monk. "Did you?"

"No!"

I held up my hands in surrender at his glare. "I'm sorry. I had to know for sure."

His eyes narrowed. Instead of the tension leaving him, it increased. "I would never touch a girl like that. She tried to seduce Nate first, but he threw her aside. Then she tried

Logan. Even he didn't want anything to do with her. We all knew who she was."

"When did this happen?"

"Two years ago. Logan had broken up with Tate, and because that had just happened, I swore off girls. I didn't have a great view of her gender already and then Broudou started saying that I slept with her and dropped her. Her brothers demanded that I do right and date her, but like hell I was going to do that. I wasn't going to do a goddamn thing anyone told me to do. I was sick and tired of people trying to manipulate me."

Oh god. My forehead fell against his arm. I already knew how he must've handled that. "You didn't kill anyone, did you?"

He chuckled. The sound of it sounded foreign from the tension in his body. "No, but I wanted to. I wanted to kill her. I'll be honest. After Tate, then her, I had a piss poor opinion of girls."

I sighed. "What happened after that?"

"Nothing. She still claims the same story. Her brothers hate me, have hated me ever since. And you know the rest. Things aren't exactly friendly whenever we have any interaction with someone from Roussou."

And that was the reason for Channing's reaction downstairs.

"I'm sorry."

"For what?" He looked down at me. The anger was still brimming within him, but it had softened. "You had nothing to do with that."

"Yeah, but I always thought you guys were jerks before. I didn't know the history with Roussou, but I judged you before I even knew you."

A grin curved up from the corners of his mouth. Then he shifted so he could pull me back into his lap. He smiled at me. "Well, you said it before. I am an asshole."

"But not that time, not with her."

He shrugged. "I'm not going to let some shady bitch affect me."

I could've pointed out that she had, but I held my tongue. Mason didn't think of it that way, and I knew if he did, I would have reason to fear what he would do because that girl, whatever her name was, had changed things for him and Logan. I didn't know all of the ramifications, but I had a feeling they went deeper than even he realized.

"What's her name?"

"Why?" He shot me a look.

I smiled at him, to show that I didn't have an agenda. "No reason, but if I run into her, I'll know to go the other way."

"Oh." He frowned, but then replied, "Shannon Broudou."

I didn't need to commit that name to memory. It was already seared in, permanently, but I had lied to him. I very much had an agenda, and if I ever met her, there was no way I was going to go the other way. For the first time in a long time, I knew that was a confrontation that I didn't want to avoid. That was one that I wanted. She had hurt my family.

CHAPTER NINETEEN

That night set a pattern for the rest of my break. I ran in the mornings for Coach Grath and worked at Manny's in the evenings. I didn't run as much as I had that first time, but when I reported my time and distance the next day, he blinked. It wasn't much of a reaction, but as I started to get to know my coach over the next week, I realized that had been a huge reaction for him. He pushed me to beat my times each day until I told him that I was on my feet the rest of the day at my job. So, then he told me to beat my times on the days I didn't work, which I planned to do anyways. I was already salivating for my next day off.

"Hey, baby girl."

Heather broke my reverie, and I jerked the dishwasher head so it sprayed all over me. "Ah!" I dropped it and jumped back. As it twisted from the cord, it sprayed her in the window and she yelped. "Turn it off, turn it off!"

I scrambled for the faucet and rotated it to the side. The water stopped, but the damage was done. Both of us were wet from head to toe. Great. I had to work in these clothes for the rest of the night, seven hours left to go.

Laughing, Heather jerked a thumb over her shoulder. "I'll grab you some clothes. This will suck when the rush comes."

"Thanks."

Lily glanced in, and she grinned from ear to ear. "It's a good look. Those Roussou guys will enjoy it."

My eyes went wide. Roussou?

Heather froze for a moment. "Oh, uh..." Then she turned to me. There was a warning there.

Oh no. A deep knot formed in my gut. This couldn't be good.

Lily cocked her head to the side. Her long black hair had been pulled high into a ponytail, and she caught the end over one shoulder. She twirled it in one hand as her smile dimmed an inch. "Joke, guys. That was a joke."

Heather twisted around. Her shoulders stiffened before she whipped back to me and her wet hair slapped Lily in the face. With white knuckles, she gripped the window's edge and leaned close. "Brett and Budd are here. You don't leave this room, not one foot out there, you hear?"

Everything had gone numb at her reaction. If Heather was this scared...I gulped. I didn't want to finish that thought.

"Text your boy. Make up some lie. He cannot come here tonight."

"I—"

"They'll jump him, Sam," she hissed. "They'll do worse to you if they find out who you are." The warning heated up in her eyes. "I won't let them hurt you, but they must know you're here. They wouldn't have come if they didn't."

"Okay." Lily forced out a laugh. "You guys are making me nervous. I was just joking before. I know you didn't get wet on purpose. What's going on?"

Heather's hand shot to her arm. She latched on with a death grip. "You stay with those guys all night. You smile, you serve, you make them happy, but you don't say a word to them about Sam, the Kades, or anything that has anything to do with them."

Lily's eyes went wide and she took a step back. "You guys are really starting to freak me out. Wait; is this because of the school pranks and stuff? I didn't think it was that bad."

"Just do what I say." Then she paused, frowning. "Where'd they sit?"

"In the back section. Anne already got their drinks."

"Take over her section."

"What about Gia? She's supposed to come in at 5:00 today."

A spew of curses came from Heather as she glared out at the diner. "I'll call her. I know she'll say something. I'll have Rosa come in for her instead." She turned and fixed us with a steely gaze. She meant business. "We good on the plan?"

Both of us nodded. My hand itched to salute her.

"Good. I'm going to run home quick. Be back in five."

When she dashed out, Lily looked back at me. "Is it really that bad?"

I took a deep breath as I gripped the rinse head in my hands. "Let's just say those guys hate Mason and if they hate him..." My eyebrows went up as she finished the sentence in her head.

She gasped. "You think they'd hurt you?"

I deadpanned, "Heather doesn't freak out for no reason."

She paled. "Oh, dear."

Oh dear, indeed.

I grimaced. Tonight was not going to be fun.

And it wasn't.

I had my suspicions, but I found out for sure that Brett and Budd's last name was Broudou. I figured, judging from Heather's reaction, but I wanted to know for certain. One time, I snuck a peek and saw two mammoth size linebackers at a back table. There were other guys with them and a few girls too. A short stocky girl with blonde hair had a similar face as theirs, square and tough, had me wondering if that was their sister. She glanced at me and I stepped back inside, but a part of me didn't want to.

I didn't want to hide from this girl, not when I knew how she had lied and caused so many problems for Mason and Logan. It wasn't the right time, though the need to say something to her was burning the back of my heels.

More and more customers poured into the diner and I eventually forgot about the Broudou siblings. I rushed to catch up with the dishes and even stepped out to load the glassware behind the bar. When my bladder was screaming for release, I shot past the table and hurried into the bathroom. It wasn't until I was returning that I remembered Heather's warning. Too late. I tried to slip past their table, but a muscular guy stumbled backwards, straight into my pathway. He would've knocked me over if I hadn't sidestepped him.

"Hey, whoa." Two meaty hands wrapped around my arms from behind. "Steady there, girl."

I wrenched my arms away and shot the guy a dark glare.

"Whoa," he said again as his eyes went wide. He stepped back.

It was one of the brothers.

A shrill feminine laugh peeled out, "She don't want your help, Brett. You're not good enough for her."

His eyes had seemed startled before, but now they darkened. A tinge of anger seeped in, and his jaw locked in place. Another chair scraped against the floor and the other mammoth stepped next to him. His eyes were already filled with dark intent. A cruel smile spread over his face before he cleared his throat. "Is that true, girly? My brother's not good enough for you?"

"Hey!"

Heather's shout jolted us. She stood behind their friend, the one who had stumbled in front of me, and wielded a long towel in one hand. A butcher knife was in the other. Her legs were planted apart. She looked ready to fight. My eyes trailed past her shoulder. Brandon was behind her. He folded his arms over his chest. Even Gus was watching the exchange with a somber expression.

Both of the brothers' heads shot up, but it was Budd who gave her a fierce frown. "What do you want, Jax?"

"Get away from her!" She pointed at me.

His eyes narrowed, and he sent me a long sidelong look before his chest puffed up. "Oh yeah? Why's that?"

"Budd." She growled in warning.

"Brett was only talking to her. That's it. What's all the fuss about?" But his narrowed eyes wouldn't stop flitting back to me. I could see the wheels turning. It was then that

I knew he didn't know who I was. Relief washed over me. My knees almost buckled, but I caught myself and folded my arms over my own chest. I tried to quench the sudden trembling.

"I mean it, Budd. Let her pass."

His hand started to lift. I sucked in my breath. I knew he was reaching for me...

At the same time, he asked, "Why? What's she to you?"

In slow motion, I watched as Heather's stormy eyes filled with even more anger. She opened her mouth. I knew she was going to let it slip, she thought they already knew, but I had to stop her.

I grabbed Budd's hand and twisted it. In a flash, I wrapped his arm behind his back and yanked at his wrist.

A scream came from him. He buckled under the force I was putting on his wrist. I was a tenth of his weight, but in that moment I could've snapped his wrist in two. A strangled cry came from him as he cursed, but then I was pulled away from him. When I expected rough hands, I was surprised to feel a gentle touch as Brett lifted me in the air and took three steps from his brother and around their friend. He placed me on my feet in front of Heather. As he frowned at me, he said to her, "We didn't mean any harm, Heather."

Her glower slipped a notch, but she still glared. "She's my friend." She stressed the last word.

His frown deepened. "We figured. We didn't mean any harm."

A sudden light clicked on in her depths, and I stepped in front of her. I said to the hulk, "We're friends and she's protective because I work here too."

He nodded, his eyebrows bunched together. "I figured that too. Look, we didn't come to hurt no girl."

"Then why are you here?" Heather scoffed behind me. She was more composed now. "This diner's in Fallen Crest. This ain't your town, and it ain't your crowd. What are you doing here?"

"Truth?" He scratched the back of his head.

Her eyes narrowed to slits. "You'd lie to me now?"

"No, no. I didn't mean that. But," he twisted around and took in the varying emotions from his family and friends. "We came for a brawl. We heard the Kades hang here a bunch. We were hoping to see them."

Heather nudged me with her elbow. I gulped—I hadn't had time to text Mason yet. He didn't know to not come tonight. Again, oh dear.

Brandon stepped closer to our group. "Hey, uh, Brett, I think maybe it's best if you guys take off."

"Why?"

Heather snorted. Her hand found her hip and her chin jutted out. "Are you serious? You admitted that you came here for a fight? At my establishment."

Brandon coughed.

She amended, "At my family's establishment."

"That's better."

She rolled her eyes. "I'm not as nice as my brother. Get out. I want your whole brood out. No one's fighting here. You're not going to destroy my family's livelihood, and you're definitely not going to scare away our *regular* customers."

"Oh, um." He turned back to his group. "They want us to go."

The blonde gasped. She shot forward from the table and was in Heather's face within two steps. "Are you effing kidding me?"

"Hey, whoa, Shannon. She's—"

"Back off, Shannon!"

Heather sucked in her breath, but tattooed-model Channing stepped around Brandon and got in the Broudou's little sister's face.

It was confirmed.

This was Shannon. This was the girl that had caused so many problems for Mason and Logan. My eyes narrowed to slits and my head went low. I wanted to hurt her. I wanted to do more than that. I wanted to hurt her like she hurt Mason. The need for violence was starting to sizzle deep inside of me. It was on a low burn, but the notch was turning up. It was going to be going full blast in a minute.

I was distantly aware that one of the mammoth brothers said something to Heather's model, who said something back. The Shannon bitch had melted once she realized who snapped at her. A seductive smile was on her face now. I felt Heather's tension beside me and touched her arm. When she looked at me, she gasped and then shuffled so she blocked me from their view. Her hands went to my shoulders and she whispered to Brandon, "Get her out of here. Now."

His hand grasped the top of my arm, and he dragged me out the side door. As soon as the screen door slammed shut, he closed the second door as well. Then he started towards the house and I went. Wait, no. What was I doing? I dug my heels in and pulled away.

"Stop."

"No." His hand adjusted his hold and he yanked me even further after him.

"I have to go back. That girl," I gasped. That girl had been the start of all of it. If I said something, if I told them what happened—

"Hey!" someone yelled from the parking lot.

Brandon cursed but kept going.

I twisted around and frowned as I saw dark silhouettes. Someone was running towards us, there were more behind him. As he drew closer, he yelled again, "Let her go!"

Adam.

Brandon stopped and turned to face him. "Look, man. You don't know what's going on."

Adam's face twisted in a scowl. As he caught up to us, he ripped Brandon's hand from my arm and pulled me away. "No, man. You don't know what's going on. You okay, Sam? What were you doing?"

But I wasn't listening. I had turned back. It was that girl. I had to get to her. I didn't care about the consequences.

They'd know about me, but they were going to find out anyway. It was on my time, this way. I chose it. I chose how. I chose when. I decided what they would be told. I started back. I heard Adam and Brandon's voices behind me, but I kept going.

"Stop her!" Brandon barked behind me.

"Hey, whoa." Adam moved to block him. "Back off, buddy. I mean it."

"Adam?"

I was focused on the side door, but the soft voice made me pause. I turned, everything was in slow motion now, and I couldn't believe what I saw. Becky was there, in person, with frightened eyes. Her red hair was pulled back in some fancy braided hairstyle. She held hands with a scruffy-looking guy beside her. His eyes were glazed over and his hair stuck up in all directions. He wore a ratty tee shirt over baggy and torn jeans. When he noticed my attention, he gave me a blinding smile. It was soft at the corners, and the focus in his eyes dimmed. Then he lifted his free hand. "Heya there."

Becky was dating someone. I remembered Adam telling me that. She was dating someone from Fallen Crest Public. I sucked in my breath. This was him, had to be. A different kind of pain sliced through me. She hadn't stuck up for me when Adam lied to her. She hadn't stuck beside me, and when he told her the truth, she still hadn't come to me to apologize. This was the one friend I thought would've stuck with me through everything. She hadn't. Now she had a boyfriend, and she never told me.

It was trivial to be hurt by that, but it stung.

I didn't notice her pale features until her voice trembled, "Sam?"

I stopped thinking. I forgot about what was going on behind me and what was happening in the diner. Someone that I had considered a friend was in front of me. So I opened my mouth and said the first thing that came to mind, "I have a new friend."

She reared back as if I had slapped her.

I kept going. My voice sounded distant. "She's tough. She's in there right now." I gestured towards the side door. "She's covering my back and you know what else?" I waited. Becky was looking everywhere but me. Then her jaw stopped shaking, and she made eye contact. Finally. "Mason and Logan respect her."

She flinched again.

Adam cursed behind me. "Sam! Seriously." He grabbed my arm and jerked me behind him. "Becky, go back to the car."

Her feet didn't move. Her head went down and her shoulders started to shake as if she were crying. The guy next to her stepped closer. A half frown was on his face, and he lifted a hand to her back.

Then Brandon moved forward. "You guys are friends with her?"

Becky's crying grew louder. She hiccupped now.

Adam grimaced. "Yeah. We are."

"Then get her out of here. Otherwise a massive fight's going to erupt."

I whipped my gaze from Becky as Brandon strode past us and yanked open the door. He went through and it slammed behind him. Then I heard a click and physically cringed from the sound of it. He locked the door. If I wanted in, I'd have to go through the front door, and I already knew Heather would shoo me out immediately.

"What just happened?" Adam frowned at the locked door.

My shoulders lifted in a deep breath. "I got the night off."

CHAPTER TWENTY

I didn't know where else to go, and I needed to find Mason so we went to Nate's house. In Adam's car was Becky with her boyfriend, Adam and me. I found out the boyfriend's name was Raz and he thought Logan was "neat-o." When we drove up to the mansion, Adam frowned and parked around the fountain. "No lights are on. No one's home?"

It didn't matter. I got out and pressed the code to the garage. As we went in, I flipped on the lights.

"Oh, wow." Becky spun in a tight circle as the mansion was flooded with light. "I didn't expect that."

Raz held onto her hand and blasted me a bright smile.

I frowned. The kid seemed off, but she seemed happy with him. He had comforted her in the alley and then made her giggle in the backseat. Everyone knew she'd been tense because of me. I wondered how long they'd been dating or how they got together, but then she glanced at me and I stopped wondering.

Her eyes were full of questions, along with something dark. She couldn't be sorry. She chose her fate. She had nothing to feel sad about.

I felt a swift kick to my gut again. She'd been the friend I thought would stay no matter what and she bailed.

The corner of her lip started to tremble. But I moved away. Becky wasn't my problem anymore. She stopped being my problem the moment she believed Adam's lie.

"Where's Kade?" Adam frowned at me.

I shook my head. "Hold on." I hurried up the stairs and to our bedroom, but no one was in there. No note, nothing. I wasn't sure what I was looking for, but I hadn't expected the empty house. Reaching for my back pocket, I cursed. I left my purse and phone at the diner.

"Adam," I called out as I went out to the banister.

"Yeah?"

"My stuff's at the diner. I left it all there."

He held a finger up. "Hold on." Then pulled out his phone and pressed a number. It wasn't long before we heard him ask, "Can I speak to Heather Jax? Oh, hey! This is Adam Quinn....Yeah, I'm a friend of Sam's...Yeah, we brought her home, but listen....yeah, her stuff's still there." He nodded a few more times, murmured 'yeah' again, and then said, "That sounds great. Thanks."

He looked up. "She's going to bring it over after closing, but she said there was a text from Mason. She read one and it said something about a family meeting with his mom?" He frowned. "You know what that meant?"

Relief rushed through me. They were in L.A. They were not headed to the diner. I nodded. "Yeah, I know. They won't be home till tomorrow."

Raz let out a whoop. "Hellsayeaha! Party in the Monson's bisnatch!"

Becky glared and slapped her hand to his chest.

He grunted and doubled over but peeked at her from the corner of his eye. When she rolled her eyes, he wrapped his arms around her and twirled her in the air. More giggles came from her with his laughter intermixed. The two disappeared down the hallway.

As I came down the stairs, Adam followed me into the kitchen area and sat on a bar stool. I started looking through the cupboards when he asked, "It's weird with her?"

I spied the rum and snatched it up. When I put it on the counter between us, I ignored his shock and looked for two shot glasses. I didn't like the hard stuff, but this rum was citrus flavored. This stuff I could drink just fine. Logan would be so proud of me right now.

"So it is weird." He nodded as he answered himself.

I pursed my lips from annoyance. I didn't want to talk about Becky. I didn't want to think about Becky, and I certainly didn't want to acknowledge that she was even in my home now. I put the two shot glasses between us and filled both to the rim. I slid one towards him and gripped the other. "Here's to not thinking about how we should go back to Manny's so I can beat that girl's ass."

Adam choked on his drink. "What?!"

I took my shot in one gulp. It was there. It was gone. I filled it again. As I tossed that one back, I started for a third, but Adam grabbed the bottle away from me.

His eyes were searching me. "What are you talking about? What girl?"

I wanted that bottle back. I needed it to help me forget. She had hurt Mason. I wanted to hurt her. I was starting to forget the consequences of going back and doing just that. What could her brothers do to me anyway? Heather could've been overreacting.

"Nothing," I clipped out.

"Sam."

I eyed the bottle in his hand, and when his hand relaxed, I grabbed it from him. I had my third shot poured within a second. He sat back with a defeated sigh so I filled a second one for him. Then I put the bottle between us as we both took our glasses and lifted them in the air. As he drank his, I leaned against the counter. Then I found myself saying, "There's a girl back there that did something to Mason. She caused a lot of problems for him and I really want to hurt her."

"Sam."

I grimaced against the sympathy in his voice and downed that third shot. It didn't burn. None of the three drinks had, but I didn't taste the sweetness anymore.

I pressed my hands against my eyes. What was I doing? I didn't drink my problems away. I wasn't that girl. I drew in a shuddering breath. What was going on? So much had happened and in such a short amount of time.

"Sam." Adam's voice was soft this time. He had moved around the counter and stood close as he pulled my hands away. "What's going on?"

"Nothing."

I pulled away from him, but he didn't release my hands. He kept them in his grip and he bent down so he could see me eye to eye. "Sam, talk to me. What is going on with you? I'm lying to your mom. Logan said about you running away and how they can't press charges against you? Then you took this job at Manny's, which I kind of understand, but now you're living here? What happened with your mom?"

"Sam?"

A whimper came from the doorway. I knew Becky had heard everything. Oh god. The secrets were out, but were they even secrets?

"Sam." Adam pulled me into him and wrapped his arms around me. He rested his chin on top of my head and smoothed a hand down my back. "You can talk to us. Becky messed up—"

She scooted closer. "I did. I really did. I'm sorry, Sam. I really am."

He continued after a deep breath, "—but she still cares about you. So do I, and I'm trying to embrace this platonic stuff here. I don't know what boundary is where and what line says only friendship, but you need to start helping out. I think if you talked to us, that'd be okay. Right?" He looked over his shoulder to Becky. "You'd ask this, right?"

She bobbed her head up and down. Her hands were folded in front of her as she scooted closer two steps. "Yes. I would. I'd want to know—"

I pushed away from Adam and rounded on her. "You don't get to do this."

Her eyes went wide. "Do what?"

"Come in here and try to get around your apology."

"My apology?" She gulped. Raz sidled up next to her, but he only took one of her hands in his.

All the anger, all the turmoil inside of me wrapped together as I lashed out, "You knew Adam was hurt by me. You knew he was angry, and you still believed him. What'd he even say, Becky? That I laughed at you behind your back? Does that sound like me? When have I ever laughed at someone? Ever! And you thought I was laughing at you, the only person who was my friend after what Jeff did to me, after what Jessica and Lydia did to me? Did you really think that I would laugh at you?"

Her head hung down again. Her soft, "No," was almost inaudible, but I heard.

It stung.

I reared back a step. I couldn't believe what I had heard. "You didn't believe him?"

"No." Her head came back up, and all the blood was gone. She was pale and trembling. Raz tried to stop both of her hands, but her legs were shaking too. "I knew you wouldn't have done that to me, but it hurt when he said it. I did believe him at first, kind of, but I didn't at the same time. It made sense to me. You were dating Mason Kade. You were friends with his brother. I mean, why would you be friends with me? I'm nothing." She stopped as her voice started to quiver.

I wanted to curse at her. She hurt me, and I was supposed to feel sorry for her? "Give me a break."

She gasped. Her eyes were wide once again. She visibly swallowed, clinging to her boyfriend's hand.

I shook my head. All the hurt and anger, I needed it out of me. I already had so much for Analise. I didn't need any more. It needed to be gone. But I couldn't deny what I felt. "You're not nothing. You've never been nothing. You were the only friend I had, even before I started dating Mason."

"You had me," Adam spoke up.

I snorted at him. "Really?"

He flashed me a tight grin. "Shutting up. This isn't about me."

"Thank you."

More tears had fallen over Becky's face, but she ignored them. "I'm really sorry, Sam. I really am. I was so stupid, and I was hurt."

"Why?" That made no sense.

"Because I felt left out. I knew you were close to the Kades, but it wasn't until that last party when I realized how tight you were with them. I mean, hello. Mason Kade is fighting for you, and then Logan snubs Lydia for you. She came onto him and he smacked her back and for what? For you. Those two care so much about you and when you're with them, it's like no one else matters except you three. You never even invited me to your home before, like I wasn't good enough or something."

"The four of them."

"What?" She looked at Adam.

He stiffened. "The four of them. Nate Monson's in there too."

"Oh yeah. I know, but he wasn't always around then. But that too. Look at this place. You're living at his house. He moved back, and now you're here with them. It's the four of you guys again."

I didn't know what to say. A part of me didn't care anymore. Her feelings were hurt? Well, she'd gotten me back. Good for her.

Becky hadn't stopped crying. Her boyfriend raised his skinny hand and wiped a few tears away. His thumb caressed her cheek and skimmed under her eye. The touch was gentle and loving. She was with someone who loved her. I could tell, just from watching him. I drew in an anguished breath. Becky was dating someone. She had someone who loved her. It started to really dawn on me. She had met a boy, dated a boy, had more dates with him, and hadn't told me. That was my job as her friend—I felt robbed of that.

I closed my eyes and turned away. I knew what I needed to do and it hurt. But it needed to be done.

"Sam?" Her voice dropped to a hoarse whisper. "Can you please forgive me? I'm sorry. I'm really sorry for believing Adam's lies."

I shook my head. I needed to forgive her and I knew I would, but she needed to realize something. I looked up with a tear in my own eye. "You wanted to believe him."

She flinched, like I had slapped her.

I pressed, "I didn't leave you behind. I didn't laugh at you behind your back. I wasn't using you. And you knew all of that, but you wanted to believe Adam's lie even when you knew it wasn't true. I think you did it because you were mad at me."

"But—" Her mouth hung open.

Adam frowned. "Why would she be mad at you?"

I shrugged, though my eyes never left hers. Then I saw it. Guilt. When her head went back down, I knew I'd been right. "She was mad at me because I had what she wanted. You were jealous, weren't you?"

Her head nodded up and down, but she didn't say a word.

"I had what you wanted, didn't I?"

As she looked back up, the anguish was all over her. More tears flooded her, her mouth was turned down in a frown, and she shook her head. "I'm so stupid, right? You went to the top, Sam. You got the guys that no one could get. I mean, you got both of them. Logan Kade worships the ground you walk on. You got what everyone wanted, not just me. Can you blame me for being jealous? Isn't that a human thing for me to do? To be jealous?" A sickened laugh bubbled out of her. "Yeah, I was mad at you. Yeah, I was jealous of you, but I was your friend. I'm sorry that I let myself believe Adam's lie. It was horrible of me. I know that and I really regret it. I really do, Sam. I really really do."

My heart sank with each word she said, but I couldn't argue with them. I knew there were more girls, a lot more, that felt the same as she did. Who was I to be taken in by the Kades? What was so special about me? I knew Becky wouldn't voice those questions to me. I knew she might never want to admit to those thoughts, but they were there. I had them too.

"This is bullshit," Adam cursed behind me. He moved next to me with disgust. "This is about the Kades? Again? Are you serious?"

Becky covered her mouth with her hand. More whimpers escaped her, and then she turned to her boyfriend. His arms came around her, and he patted the back of her head as he shot Adam a dark look. "Man. Respect it."

Adam rolled his eyes. "I'm so sick of this. Can we not have one night without talking about them?"

I hissed at him, "You're not helping."

He threw up his hands. "I'm not trying anymore. I didn't know all this boiled down to those guys again. What's so damn special about them? Their looks? I'm good looking. That they're athletic? I'm the freaking quarterback for FCA. I *was* the quarterback. Whatever! What's so damn special about them?"

Raz spoke up, "Dude, they're legends. Legit and smack dab. Legends, dude. That's all. Legends."

Adam snorted. "This is ridiculous." He turned to me, frustrated. "Are you okay?"

I nodded. Strangely, I was. When Becky sniffled and wiped her nose, all the hurt and anger was gone. She had admitted it, and that was what I needed. I guess...

"I'm going. I'm not sticking around to hear about how godly these douches are. See you, Sam. Becky, you two want a ride home?"

She looked at me, a deep question in her, but I slunk back against the counter. She could stay if she wanted. She could go if she wanted. This was her time to choose if she was going to be there for me or not. I wasn't going to tell her what to do.

"I..." She opened her mouth, then closed it.

Raz spoke up again, "She's staying. I'm coming. Let's go to the Hop-It. All this crying made me hungry."

He pressed a kiss to Becky's forehead and whispered something in her ear, which had her grinning. She relaxed in his arms, but then he skipped around her, swatted Adam on the butt, and led the way out of the room.

Adam followed behind him, "It's the IHOP, Raz. It's not the Hop-It."

Raz called to him, "It's always the Hop-It. That's what you do. You hop it, you get it?"

A long frustrated sigh came from Adam before the door closed behind them.

Both of us looked at each other, now alone in Nate's fortress. It never seemed larger than in that moment. A clock should've been ticking behind us. The awkwardness of the moment would've fit well with that idea. As I grinned to myself, she took the leap first. "Why are you living here, Sam?"

There was the old Becky, she was my friend again.

CHAPTER TWENTY-ONE

"So…"

She gave me a timid smile. There was a twinge of hope in there, but I didn't know what to do about it. I wasn't mad anymore, but I didn't trust her either. I gave her a small grin back and said the same, "So…"

Her smile fell flat. "Oh."

I sighed. "What do you want, Becky? Thank you for being honest and thank you for apologizing, but we can't bounce back to what we were before. I don't trust you anymore."

"You don't?"

I shook my head. "Nope."

"Oh." Her shoulders lifted up in a small shrug. "Well, I guess I understand. I wouldn't either, if I was in your place. I mean, well, I might've. I don't know. I've never had anyone be jealous of me before. I don't know what I would do."

"It's not about you being jealous. You believed a lie about me, even though you knew it wasn't true, to get back at me. You knew it'd hurt me if you stopped talking to me. Congratulations. You hurt me."

"I really am sorry," she whispered.

Then we heard the door open and someone yelled out, "Hey! Yo! I took off early, figured you'd want your phone asap. It keeps flashing that you've got texts, didn't know if they were important or not."

Becky froze, but I relaxed. It wasn't long before Heather strolled around the corner. She saw Becky and stopped in her tracks. "Oh. Hi?"

I sighed. Heather's eyes narrowed as she raked her up and down with a sneer while the other looked ready to piss her pants. "Uh..." I swept a hand between the two. "Becky, this is Heather. Heather, Becky."

Becky took a small breath. "You're the new friend."

Heather's eyebrows shot up. "That means you're the old one?"

I laughed.

Becky threw me a dark look.

"Sorry. I—sorry." I waved for them to forget me.

Heather snorted as she fished something from her pocket and tossed it to me. I caught it, my phone. When I glanced at it, my eyes went wide. She'd been right. There were a few from Mason.

Our mom called. She's pissed. Found out we got kicked out.

Family meeting called. Have to head with Logan. I won't be at Manny's tonight. You'll be alright? That one was followed with: **love u**.

I checked the rest: **Things got interesting, can't text for awhile**.

The last text was sent an hour ago: **Hoping you're ok and work is just busy. Not good here**.

"Things okay?" Heather was frowning as she lounged against the wall. Becky was against the opposite wall with her arms folded across her chest.

A raging headache was coming. I felt it at my temples and pressed my hands there for a moment.

"Sam?" It sounded like a whimper from Becky.

"What?" I tried to hold back my own glare. This wasn't about her and she was making it like that.

The pout twisted into a confused scowl, then a grimace. "Are you okay?"

"No."

"Where's he at?" Heather gestured to my phone.

I shook my head. "Family meeting. It doesn't matter."

"Aren't you in the family?"

"Not that one. It's with his mom."

Heather grinned. "I heard about the Wicked Witch of L.A. She's a pretentious socialite, isn't she?"

I shrugged. Helen was more than that in my opinion. "She's...confident."

"Confident?" The amusement on Heather's face didn't deplete. It doubled. She threw her head back as a smooth chuckle slid out. "I've never heard that one used to describe her, but then again," she eyed me up and down, "you are in that family so I hear ya. I gotcha."

Becky had been scowling as she looked back and forth between us. "What is going on? Your mom is confident? Your mom is mean, Sam."

"No," I sighed, but stopped. Maybe it was for the best if she thought we were talking about my mother.

Just then we heard the garage door slam shut. I held my breath; my heart racing when Nate turned the corner. Then a small hand appeared around his chest from behind, and a pair of tan legs slid between his as the hand groped farther south. A low moan sounded next. It ended in a feminine sigh as a pair of lips started to press against his arm and move upwards.

He stopped as he saw the three of us, but his eyes zeroed in on me. "What are you doing here?"

I jumped at the intensity from him. "What?"

All amusement fled from Heather as she turned to him, a scowl locked in place. "What's with the attitude, Monson? I thought she lived here."

His gaze went to hers, but the intensity was gone. He locked it behind a wall, and now he regarded her with a blank expression. I sighed. It was the same look Mason used on people when he wanted them to feel unwelcomed. It was a master tactic to make the other feel like scum beneath their shoes.

I gritted my teeth. He would not use that on her. "Stop, Nate. And what are you talking about, what am I doing here? I got off work early and Mason said he's at a family meeting."

The mask slipped a bit, and there was wariness instead. "Yeah, *your* family. Helen's out for Analise's blood."

The blood drained from my body. "What?"

He gave me a smirk now. It sent a shiver down my back, and not a good one like I felt with Mason. I was rattled to the bone when he said further, "They're at your house, Sam, with your mom. You're the odd-man out."

Shock started to form in my gut, but I heard myself mutter from a distance, "Why are you being a dick to me?"

His eyes went wide and his eyebrows shot up. "I'm not."

"You are," Heather retorted.

He frowned at her, but the girl behind him moaned in his ear, "Baby, can they go away?"

I narrowed my eyes. I recognized that voice. Everything slammed back into focus with me. Parker pressed against the front of him now. Her shirt had been tied around her neck, but it was undone. It fell around her waist, still on her as the knot hadn't been untied around her waist, but her breasts were against him. She wore no bra, and the jean shorts on her were loose in the back so they must've been unzipped from the front.

That's why he'd been a dick. He was with her, one of the four that still hated me. When I shared a look with Heather, I remembered her warning about the Tommy P's. It was her nickname for those four, Parker, her best friend Kate, and the other two whose names I couldn't remember. Jasmine and Natalie? Maybe. I preferred Heather's reference to them, the Tomboy Princesses. The name fit them perfectly, and the one trying to lure Nate away from the kitchen had been the worst so far.

"Parker." Annoyance dripped from his voice as he gripped her arm and held her away. Her breasts sagged, but she didn't cover them. She seemed shocked as she looked up. Disdain now filtered in as he finished, "Go to my room."

"But—"

"Go!"

She snapped to attention, but not before she sent me a loathing glare.

I lifted my chin in a challenge. The time would come when I'd need to deal with her and her friends, but it wasn't now. I thought about my new school and my gut dropped. It was her school; it was their territory. I was grateful for my job at Manny's. Heather would support me when I went there, as much as she could, as much as anyone could.

"Your girlfriend's a bitch," she informed Nate as soon as we heard an upstairs door slam shut.

"She's not my girlfriend." He shot her a dark look but then shrugged a second later and looked at me. "I'm sorry, Sam, if I was being a dick. I didn't mean to be."

It was who he'd been with. Her derision must've rubbed off on him, but I held my tongue. Heather bit her lip as she frowned at me, but then my phone beeped again. I read the text from Mason: **Can you come as soon as you're done with work? At the house. Your mom threw a bowl at my mom.**

"I have to go."

But I had no car—I looked at Heather. She grinned. "I'll give you a ride." She winked at Becky. "You too, oldie but goodie?"

"Huh?"

"Yeah." I latched a hand onto Becky's arm and dragged her behind me. "Her too."

Nate gave me a nod with a small grin as we swept out of the house. I knew it was his way of sending me another apology, but as I got into Heather's car, I wondered if that was the side of him that most people saw. He seemed nice and respectful, reserved even, whenever he was with Mason and Logan, but this Nate was different. Again, I remembered the comments about the trouble he and Mason would get into, the reason why his parents had him move away in the first place. But he was back...and I knew Logan already regretted it.

"Sam."

Becky was trying to hold back a smile.

My eyebrows shot up. "What?"

Then she handed me her phone.

"What is this?"

"Just look."

And I did, gasping when I saw the picture she had taken. It was a full frontal of Parker, when Nate had pushed her back. Her breasts were on display. "You snuck this picture?"

She nodded, biting her lip from excitement.

"Let me see." Heather held her hand out and took a quick peak. She busted out laughing and handed it back. "Your oldie but goodie is a sneaky one, Sam. Good one, back there."

Becky leaned back, pleased with herself. "I couldn't help it. She was so mean. They weren't paying me any attention so..."

"Don't do anything with that picture but don't delete it either."

"Yeah." Heather looked into the rearview mirror. "We might need that someday, but I agree with Sam. Don't post that anywhere or even show anyone else."

"Don't show your boyfriend, Becky."

Her grin was gone. "What?"

"Who's her boyfriend?"

"Someone named Raz?"

I looked at Becky for confirmation when I said his name. She nodded, but then Heather burst into laughter once again. "Are you kidding me? Raz has a girlfriend? That's great." Her eyes met Becky's once again. "Raz is a good guy, but I agree with Sam. Don't show that picture to him. He'd put that on a tee shirt and wear it to school. He doesn't get it sometimes."

"Yeah," Becky sighed. "You're right. But the picture was good, wasn't it?"

I nodded. "You did good, Becky."

"Thanks."

When Heather kept driving and she turned at all the right turns, I realized she knew where I used to live. I wanted to smack my forehead. Everyone knew where Mason and Logan lived. They had enough parties on the beach, even Becky had been there a few times, but never to the first floor of the house or the other two floors above. A few had been invited to the basement, but not to the top levels. That was reserved for a select few and when Heather parked in the driveway, her hand went to her seatbelt and I knew she had every intention of joining that small group who had seen the inside of the Kade museum.

"Uh," Becky watched as Heather got out of the car.

"Let's go." Heather slammed her door shut.

I was torn. Did I let them inside? I knew they wouldn't be welcomed, but Heather was already at the front door. She pushed it open and my decision was made for me.

I gestured at Becky. "Come on. Might as well see what's going on."

She grinned, and her cheeks flamed as she scrambled behind me. But then we were inside, and it was dead silent. Heather waited for us in the foyer. Her mouth had fallen open as she gazed around. Oh yes. I'd forgotten what the Kade mansion looked like to the virgin eyes.

"This place is an effing museum." She couldn't tear her eyes from the life-sized statue of a Greek goddess. "Is that real?"

I shrugged. My mom had bought it a month ago. She gushed over it when it was delivered so I figured it was real. My mom didn't know that Logan had taken a black marker to the backside of the statue and drawn a tramp stamp with an arrow pointing downwards that said, 'insert here.' The statue hadn't been moved since its arrival, but I knew when it was and Analise saw the added artwork, she'd go ballistic. I only hoped Logan would be here to see her reaction.

"Oh wow," Becky breathed out behind me. "This place is beautiful."

Heather snorted. "And we're not even past the foyer. You must think I live in a hole compared to this place and Monson's mansion."

"I liked your home."

It was the truth. When she searched me, Heather saw that I meant it. Her shoulders relaxed. "You're a good person, Sam."

I frowned. I was?

"I second that." Becky gave me a timid grin.

I was uncomfortable with the praise, but we heard a shriek from the kitchen, followed with the sounds of breaking dishes, and I chuckled. The uncomfortable feeling went away, and I was grounded again. I'd grown used to the chaos that surrounded Analise. "You guys should go. This could get ugly."

"Sam!"

Logan saw me and jogged down the hallway towards us. He grabbed my arm. "You need to come quick. Your mom's unhinged and my mom's making her fold. Helen's standing there, all cold as ice, and your mom can't shake her. It's awesome. Mason's stuck in the back corner. He couldn't get out, but we heard the door so I figured it was you."

"Sam," Heather called out.

Logan stopped and looked back. He was startled for a moment before a lewd grin covered his face. "Didn't see you there, Jax. Looking good." His eyes raked her up and down. "Real good."

Becky flushed beside her, but Heather rolled her eyes. "Eyes up here, Kade."

They stayed on her front, where her tight red shirt strained against her breasts. The black bra could be seen through the shirt and the longer his gaze stayed on her, the tighter her shirt became. I knew she was getting annoyed, but then I saw some redness that started on her neck and traveled upwards.

Shock settled inside of me. Was there more than friendly annoyance between those two? But no, Heather was with that model tattoo guy...wasn't she?

She folded her arms over her chest. "Stop it, Logan!"

He grinned, cocky and so self-assured. "Heard a rumor about you today, Jax."

"Oh yeah?" She struck a defiant pose with her hand on her hip. "What was that?"

"That you and Channing aren't really an item, not yet anyway."

Her hand fell away from her hip, and she took a step back.

Was that true? Maybe there really was something going on between Heather and Logan, but I remembered Channing coming to my defense in the diner. He stopped the Broudou siblings from—from hurting Heather. In the moment, I thought he had come to my defense, but it had been for her. He always seemed to be there for her. I studied her and Logan for another second and then sighed. I hoped he knew what he was doing because I didn't want him to get hurt.

As Heather tossed her hair back and Logan's eyes lit up, something fell to the bottom of my gut. He liked her. I could see it, plain as day to me now, but I wouldn't let him get hurt. There was no way I would let Logan get hurt, not again, not like with Tate.

"Logan!"

I jumped at the shrill sound that came around the corner. Helen was calling.

He chuckled and grabbed my arm. "Come on, little Kade. Prepare to be entertained." Then he saluted Heather. "Off you go, Jax. You're always welcome in my bed, but not here. No fornicating allowed, her mom's rule. See you later."

Heather rolled her eyes and grabbed Becky's arm. "See you, Sam. Call me."

687

I nodded as she dragged Becky behind her. The door shut with a heavy thud behind them, but then Logan curved an arm around my waist. He didn't immediately take me to the kitchen. Instead, he held me in a hug for a moment and let out a deep sigh. His shoulders dropped and his head rested on my shoulder.

He'd been acting. The entire jovial side of him had been a facade. I hugged him back. "How bad is it?"

He flinched from the question but drew back. His wall fell and I reeled as I saw the torment in them. "It's not good, Sam. It's not going to get better either."

Oh no.

CHAPTER TWENTY-TWO

When I walked into the room, everything was wrong. I knew it. I felt it. I could see it. Helen was impeccable. She was dressed in a white business suit with a skirt and matching high heels, a lethal tip at the end. Her hair was swept up in some fancy bun to the side, but it was the pressed red lips and the cold ice in her blue eyes that sent the first reverberations through me. The second wave was sent from James as he stood between the kitchen and dining room. He leaned against a counter with his tie undone and his shirt pulled from his pants. The suit looked like it could've come from a GQ magazine, but it was wrinkled and wrung into knots as he lifted his hands to ring out his collar. From how it was already loosened, I knew he'd been doing that more than a few times. Then the third repercussion hit me from my mother herself. She stopped her pacing when she saw me, but it wasn't warmth that came to her, it was the lack of it. Even Helen noted it with a snort. She extended her hand to me. "And the root of the problem has made her appearance."

All jokes were gone.

Mason shoved his chair back and rounded the table. He took my arm and moved in front as Logan went and hopped onto the table. He flashed me a grin, more to reassure me than anything else, as he propped his feet on a chair in front of him. Then he leaned back on the table with his arms outstretched behind him, his eyes alert as he scanned the rest of the room.

That was the fourth.

Logan was alarmed. Logan was never alarmed.

The last reverberation was Mason as I touched his arm. It was cement. I felt his back and the rest of him was the same. He was rigid as stone. But he hadn't let me see it when I came around the corner. There'd been a look of amusement. I hadn't seen it when it fell away to the real emotion underneath. I'd been distracted by the tension in the room. Now I closed my eyes as the shock still rocked inside of me. Logan and Mason were both on edge.

I sucked in a breath. This wasn't going to end well. Then I opened my eyes and focused once more.

Here we go.

"Where were you, Samantha?" my mother clipped out. Her hands rested on her hips and her eyes bugged out. She looked ready to shriek again.

It clicked in me. I wouldn't fear her. The rightful anger was back again. She wouldn't scare me away no matter how intimidating she might've been. I wasn't eleven anymore. I shrugged as I moved to stand beside Mason. His hand curled around my waist. He anchored me against him.

She sucked in her breath. "Answer me."

"Why?" Logan sat forward on the table. His elbows rested on his knees now and his shoulders hunched down. He was getting ready for a fight.

"What do you mean why? She's my daughter."

He rolled his eyes. "Are you sure about that? You don't treat her like any family I've known."

"Logan," his father murmured, shaking his head. "Stop."

"Why?" Same question, same reaction. He wanted instant irritation.

A low growl came from Analise.

He was getting it.

"It's not your place." James sent him a pointed look and then transferred his gaze to Mason, who gripped my waist tighter.

I sunk into his side, grateful for the rock he had become for me.

Helen cleared her throat and refolded her arms over her chest. "This is not entertaining anymore." She fixed her ex-husband with a sneer. "Now that the prodigal daughter has returned, I'd like to continue our discussion as to why my sons got kicked out of your home and not *her* daughter."

Analise showed her teeth, it was so unlike the socialite she wanted to become since we moved into the Kade mansion. She resembled a caged animal, and it was the truth. My mom had been backed into a corner by Helen. We were all staring at her, waiting for her.

"Because." James hung his head.

"Because?" Helen tightened her mouth and lifted her chin another centimeter. "Just because? Are you toying with me, James? Our sons chose to stay here because of school. They didn't want to live in Los Angeles, and you agreed it was the better arrangement. A small town had a better environment for them. Then I hear from my sister that you've kicked them out? Mason is living with that Monson child—"

Logan grinned.

Mason bristled. "Don't start, mom."

"—and I hope to God that Logan's been with him the whole time because he hasn't been with me."

James looked back up. "I sent him to you."

She threw her arms in the air. "For one day! I got him for one day and then he took off with James and Will. They said they were going to Nate Monson's home. I thought they meant Calabasas. I had no idea they were coming here. I should've been informed when Nate moved back here." She turned towards Mason. "You should've told me."

He narrowed his eyes but remained silent. His hand on my hip turned into a fist, but his reactions stopped there. He had become a statue, or, as I shivered, he was biding his time and waiting for the right moment. I wasn't sure, but this felt like it was only the beginning.

James cleared his throat this time and wrung out his collar again. "Well, regardless, things have changed a bit in this house. I told Mason and Logan that if they didn't agree with my wishes, they would need to live with their mother. Logan was supposed to have been with you this whole time, but Mason is an adult. I cannot force him to do anything."

"You never could." Disdain dripped from her tone.

"You tell him, mom!"

"Shut it, Logan."

He hunched down. "Just saying."

Another deep sigh came from James as he stuffed his hands deep in his pockets. His shoulders hunched forward, "I understand that you're upset. I should've cleared everything with you—"

Analise gasped.

He froze for a nanosecond and then continued, "—but Analise and I made a decision together."

Helen's glare doubled with derision. She transferred it to my mother now. "I'm sure you did, by doing what she wanted for her reasons and not your own."

"You don't start," Analise rasped out. "This is not your family anymore—"

"This is my family! These are my sons and you threw them out like garbage." Helen's hands fell to her side and she jerked forward a step. Fury had replaced the cold condemnation and her eyes sparked with every bit the emotion that my mother was showing.

James glanced between them and swallowed.

"Garbage?" Analise started forward with a hand in the air. "Your son has treated my daughter like garbage. He had an itch and he used Samantha to scratch it. She was vulnerable. She'd just been dumped by her boyfriend and her friends turned their backs on her—"

"That is not true!" Logan shouted first as he hopped off the table. He started towards her, but Mason transferred me behind him and blocked his brother. As Logan bounced off him, Mason threw an arm out and shuffled him backwards. As they both moved to the farthest wall, I felt for the table. I couldn't see it anymore. Everything was rushing around me, my heart was racing, but when my hand touched it, I almost cried from relief. I folded into one of the chairs and pressed my palms against my temples. The raging headache had arrived.

My mom finished, "Samantha was convenient for him and he's made it worse. They've let her think that she matters to them, like they're going to protect her. She's my daughter. She's my family—"

"Okay, Lise. Stop." James held her with a firm hand. "Mason did not use Samantha like that and you know it. He cares for her."

My mother hit his arm down. She seethed at him, "You're blind when it comes to your sons. They're evil. You don't know the things they've done to me and now they've taken my daughter away from me. It was the last straw, James. I won't lose my daughter, not to anyone."

Helen laughed. The sound was shrill and harsh, and it shut my mother up. Her lip curled up higher. "This is so ridiculous, it's a comedy. You've lost your daughter to my sons? Is that why you banned Garrett from seeing her? Were you worried about an inappropriate relationship there as well?"

I went cold at her words. My heart slowed...

She continued, sounding like she was enjoying herself, "It's laughable! You're so nuts. Way to pick 'em, James. I thought you had a doozy on your hands with the fourth mistress. She was your secretary? No, that's not right. She was your assistant. And she hated me. I could always tell, but this one." She shook her head. "This one takes the cake."

Garrett had been banned? I started to stand up...

"Shut up, you bitch!" my mom shrieked.

Helen snapped her mouth shut, but her eyes glittered from suppressed anger. She shook her head again. "I'm the bitch? Look at what you've done to my family. You kicked my sons out. How dare you! And how dare you, James! When it involves my children, you bring me into the discussion.

This relationship between our children makes it a family situation. I should've been brought in and brought up to date. I wasn't aware of the intimacy that they've reached—"

James barked out a laugh. "Are you joking with me?" He turned to face her squarely but kept Analise behind him with a hand on her wrist. His gaze settled on his ex-wife. "No, Helen. How dare you. You didn't know the level of intimacy between them?" His shoulders shook as more laughter poured out from him. "You walked in on them. And that was on your watch. He was at the hotel with you."

She sputtered out, "Not in my room. He had his own room."

"That you allowed." He pointed a hand at Mason, who was very still and very silent. "You know what our sons do. They have sex. They drink. They've both been in physical altercations. How many times have you bribed officials for them? I've done it a handful of times. I know you've dirtied your hands a few times, more than a few times. You can't stand there and spout that you thought Mason was this innocent son of ours."

"I didn't." Her jaw clamped shut, so tight. As she gritted her teeth together, the movement was visible. "I've never said that Mason and Logan are innocent little boys, but they're my little boys. You had no right to throw them out of the house."

"I didn't. I said they couldn't live here if they didn't comply with my wishes, and it's within reason to wish that my own son would not have sexual intercourse with his future stepsister, not under my roof."

Helen snorted. "Your roof? This was my father's home. Don't you forget that."

James raised his voice, "I got this house in the divorce settlement. It is my home. Let's not have you forget that!"

She threw her arms over her chest again and folded them. "It doesn't change the fact that you kicked our sons out, for any short amount of time or for any reason. You kicked both our sons out. Only one of them is sleeping with the girl."

"You didn't want Logan with you?"

"Of course, I did, but I wasn't given the chance to make sure that he came to me. He showed up one day, stayed a day, and took off with his cousins. I thought my son wanted to see me and I relished that time with him. I had no idea he was supposed to be there the entire break."

"He couldn't stay, not when he supports their relationship."

"Then kick the girl out!" Helen yelled.

She wasn't ladylike anymore, nor did she remain cold. The fury had taken over, and she was heated in anger. Her chest rose up and down at a rapid rate.

"She's my daughter," Analise yelled back. She started forward, but James crowded her back to the sink. "This is my home now. This will be my husband. My daughter will stay in my home. She has no other home to go to."

Helen reared her head back. "Are you kidding me?"

James closed his eyes.

Analise's eyes bulged out, even more enraged. She tried to launch herself forward, but he blocked her with his body. As she started to crawl over him, he turned to face her. He tugged her back down. She twisted around his side and snarled, "Get out of this house. Get out right now!"

"No," Helen clipped out. "Garrett told me about your quick little divorce, but as far as my private investigator knows, you haven't married my ex-husband yet. So, no, this isn't your home. You have no legal right to throw me out either, although I shouldn't be surprised. Isn't that what you do? Throw people out when they don't fall in line and pretend you're not crazy? Isn't that why you really kicked my sons out or why your own daughter isn't living here anymore?"

The room fell silent.

David and Analise were divorced. It was final.

I shook my head. I'd process that later.

Then Helen's cruel snicker filled the room. "I can't believe your nerve. You don't think I didn't come here with the facts? Do you not have any idea of who I am? You're going to be my sons' stepmother. You better get your act together, honey, because if you harm one hair on my sons, I'll slap you with a lawsuit. And you won't have any chance at winning because your insanity, Analise, has been well-documented."

"Shut. Up." But Analise paled, and the words said were whispered from clenched lips.

"Oh, yes, honey." Helen's control was back in place. She drew upright. Her chin lifted, her jaw squared into place, and her shoulders smoothed so her suit was impeccable once again. There were no wrinkles. She was a glossy version of an ice queen. "You don't think I'm aware of how you threatened Garrett from seeing his daughter? That if he even tried to make contact with her, you would take your daughter and disappear so he'd never find her again." Her eyes shifted to James. "I don't think there was much merit in that threat, but it scared the hell out of him. Or maybe," the cruel smirk on her face appeared again, "there was another reason Garrett would be scared for his daughter. Tell me, *Lise*, have you ever hurt anyone before?"

A cold sick feeling was spreading inside. I looked up in slow motion...Helen continued, but her voice sounded far away. I heard a whooshing sound, and it grew louder and louder. I shook my head. It was only me. It was only in my head. I needed to clear it away. I needed to hear what else she had to say.

"It's not like you've tried to kill yourself? It's not like a week later your daughter was hospitalized with evidence that she'd been beat up? You didn't do that, did you? My PI certainly thinks you did, but there was no condemning evidence and your own daughter was too scared to say anything." She continued, in a nightmare, "Where was your husband at that time?"

"Stop, Helen."

She ignored James. She was only getting started. "He had left you, but he came back, didn't he? She wasn't his real daughter. He had no way to protect her so he took you back. And the way you screwed him over later, cheating on him and getting James to fall for you. I should take lessons from you. No, I shouldn't because you're crazy. Your own daughter can't even be in the same room with you anymore. I know that you've hit her again. You slapped her twice four months ago. Have you done it since?"

All the blood was gone from my mother's face. She clutched onto James with white knuckles. Her knees buckled, but he held her up and looked over his shoulder. "Stop, Helen." He said it with more authority this time.

It worked.

Helen stopped, but she cast a wary look at me as I stepped up next to her. Then she added in a soft voice, "I'm sorry that you have such a bitch for a mother, but you might want to look into her divorce settlement. I think there'd be a few things that might interest you."

"That's enough, mom."

She turned around. "What, Mason? If you care for her as much as you say you do, you'd want her to know that the man who raised her isn't allowed to speak to her, not until she turns 18." She lifted an easy shoulder. "I would've gone for it too. He's being paid to stay away from his daughter, but she's not even his real daughter. He bides his time, waits around, and then he can talk to her all he wants. He's only got to wait another week and a half. And Garrett, who knows what she really threatened him with before he went back to Boston."

Garrett was in Boston?

Analise burst out laughing. "He left you, didn't he?"

Helen wheeled around. Her eyes narrowed to slits. "You don't know anything about that—"

"But I do." Analise's voice rose again. She felt in control once again. "He left you the week after we saw you last. And

I know why." She giggled now. The sound was twisted and unnatural.

My stomach dropped as the sickened sensation spread through me.

"He went back to his wife. I know he did. He told me he was going back to her. Too bad for you, Helen. You couldn't hold onto him, and that was your only way of getting back at me. But I've got the life you wanted. I've got the man that you loved. I've got the home with your husband and your sons. And I've got a hold on Garrett that you'll never have. I have his daughter and as long as I have her, he'll never leave me, not like he left you."

Helen crossed the room in three steps. She lifted her hand and slapped my mother. It happened before anyone could comprehend what was going on, but the sound of it echoed in the air.

I jumped from the shock of it.

"Whore!"

"Mom!" Mason rushed around me and lifted Helen away as she raised her hand for a second slap.

James grunted, but held onto Analise as she shrunk back. She stayed there for a second and then launched forward. She raked her nails over his back, trying to find a foothold so she could get free from him. He yelled in her ear, "Stop, Lise!" Logan rushed and took hold of my mother's arms. He lifted them in the air and James wrapped his arms around her waist again. My mother was in the air as they tried to wrestle her down. Her entire body was convulsing back and forth, desperate to get free.

CHAPTER TWENTY-THREE

"How long does mom have to be in the hospital?" It must've been the third time I asked dad. It'd been so long, and she was still in there. He always said the same thing, another day, but it seemed longer than that. Two whole days had passed since he picked me up from Jessica's.

"She's coming home this weekend, honey."

"Really?"

"Really." He gave me a smile and hunched down for me. Then he cleared his throat. "Honey, I want to talk to you about that night you found your mom in the bathroom."

"Yeah?" I could tell he wanted to talk about it. Dad's voice always changed when there was something important he wanted to say, but I looked away. I didn't want to talk about that night. Mom was fine. Dad was back. Everything was fine. I knew it. I was fine.

"Yeah, honey." He cleared his throat again and folded up his sleeves over his arms. "Listen, Jolene called me from the hospital when she picked you up. That was nice of her, wasn't it? I'm glad the social workers found someone to watch you so quickly. Were you a good girl for her? She didn't have to go down to the hospital to pick you up. Wasn't that nice of her?"

I shrugged. "I guess."

His smile relaxed, and he expelled a deep breath. "Good. Um, do you have any questions about your mother?"

"She's coming home this weekend?"

He nodded. He didn't say anything.

Things weren't okay. When he stood and walked to his back office, I knew things weren't okay. I was eleven, I wasn't four. But mom was coming home. She'd make everything okay. She had to; I didn't want to stay at Jessica's house again. Her mom wasn't nice.

"Sam!"

I blinked suddenly when Mason touched my arm. "You okay?" He still had an arm around Helen, but she had calmed down and leaned against the wall. Her eyes closed as exhaustion settled over her face. Her hair had been yanked free from the bun. It spilled down, but she didn't smooth any of it back. It stayed how it fell.

"Uh." I blinked again, clearing the memories.

"Logan!" My mom shrieked. She tried to bat him away as he kept a restraining hand on one of her arms. James ducked his head into her side. A scratch was on his cheek, some blood already spilled from it. "Get away from me!"

He hissed when she swung down again, but jumped back. She sagged forward, crumbling to the floor before she slapped a hand to the ground and pushed herself back up. Her eyes were wild, her hair was a mess, and the front of her dress was ripped. A tan bustier covered her up, but the dress was in ruins. She started to grab it and rip it off, but I stepped towards her.

She stopped. Her eyes jumped to mine, widened, and her mouth opened.

"Stop."

She did.

As I took another step closer, Mason murmured behind me, "Sam."

I shook my head. He didn't move away, but he didn't stop me. Logan straightened as well. The adults grew still, but James spoke, "I don't think this is the best—"

"Shut up, dad!" Logan barked at him.

There was movement behind me. I sensed it, but I could only stare at my mother. She was alone now, and her hand started to tremble. "Samantha—"

"I said, stop."

She clamped her mouth shut, but stood to her tallest height. Her chin lifted. Her shoulders squared back and the wildness in her eyes calmed down a notch. But she was still mad. I could see it.

I no longer cared. "You took them away from me."

She winced as if I had slapped her. "Honey—"

I held a hand up and she quieted. Then I shook my head. My stomach twisted into knots and the need to throw up was climbing in my throat. I felt it coming, but I couldn't deal with any of that. She made me sick. I'd never get that feeling out of me. My throat felt raw. "You took David away from me."

She grimaced again. Her head turned to the side as if I really had slapped her.

"You threatened Garrett from me?"

She didn't respond.

"Did you?"

She bit her lip. A sob convulsed from her, but she nodded once.

I gripped my stomach. The betrayal was there. I wished that she would've stabbed me. It would've been less painful than what I felt now. When would she stop hurting me?

I pressed on, whispering, "You kept him from me all my life."

"Sam," she choked out.

"Shut up, woman!" Logan surged next to me. "Let her talk."

Mason stepped closer to me. He didn't touch me, though I expected him to, but he was there. I knew he was there, in case I fell.

"You took my little sister from me?" Helen said Analise tried to kill herself, but that wasn't true. That had been the lie concocted to cover it up. She had committed murder.

"Oh god," she whimpered now. Her face crumbled, and she slipped to the floor. A hand held onto the counter, but it didn't help her. She held on, helplessly, as she curled into a ball on top of the tiles.

"Or did I have a little brother?" The question was ripped from me.

Her shoulders shook now and a sob sounded out. It was low and feral. It came from her core, but I didn't care. Not anymore. I knelt at her head, but she had it pressed into her knees. Tears and blood slipped over her skin. I didn't care where the blood had come from. I didn't even care that she was crying.

I whispered to her, "Did I have a little sister or a little brother?" It meant something to me. I needed to know. I had never asked. I had been too scared for too long, and then I had forgotten. "Mom!"

"Both!" she screamed. Her voice was muffled, pressed against her knees.

I stumbled back and fell. I could only stare at her in shock. Both? She was going to have twins?

She sobbed out, "Both! I was going to have twins. That's why there was so much blood loss. That's why I almost died. I wanted to die. I wanted to die..." Her shoulders shook with renewed frenzy as more sobs came from her.

Disgust flared within me.

Then I was being lifted back onto my feet. Mason had reached down and picked me up. He held me in front of him, but I shook my head. I wasn't ready to go so he waited. His hands never left my hips.

"You bitch."

Analise's entire body jerked from a tremor, but she didn't look up. She stayed in her ball and she kept crying.

No one went to help her.

I couldn't look away from her now. The great and almighty Analise was at my feet, literally. I'd been so scared of her for so long, then I had been angry at how selfish she was, but now I remembered so much more. She would never change. She had never been a mother to me. She never would.

There'd been so many questions swirling in me. How much had she paid David to stay away from me? No, how much had James paid. My mother had no money. She had nothing except for James and me, but she didn't have me anymore. I was done with her. But my little brother and sister. She had taken them from me. I gasped as the vomit almost came up. It was at the top of my throat. It wanted to spew out, but I pushed it down. I wouldn't let her see that reaction from me.

"Come on," Mason whispered in my ear. His hand curled around my arm, and he tugged me back.

I didn't move. I couldn't.

He bent and picked me up. I curled into his chest as he took me out to his car. As he placed me in the seat and clipped the seat belt for me, I couldn't move. I should've, but my insides had been gutted empty. She had done that— she had taken everything inside of me and ripped it all out. There was so much damage inside of me. I was damaged. How could anyone want to be around me? I was my mother's child.

As Mason shut my door and rounded to his side, I watched him through the glass. He was tense. His jaw was hard from repressed fury. The Mason I knew would've gone inside and wreaked havoc, but this one didn't. He was with me. He was taking care of me and being the stronghold that I needed.

He would wreak havoc another day.

He saw the small grin on my face as he got inside and started the car. "What's that for?"

A peace settled inside. His question was simple, but genuine. I heard his concern. I heard his love, and because there were no conditions to his love, it healed something inside of me. I knew it wasn't all of it, it wasn't even a sixteenth of it, but it was enough for now.

I reached over for his hand. At the touch, another little piece in me settled. I drew in a deep breath and held onto his hand tighter. The tears spilled now. I couldn't see anything as he pulled out from the driveway and started down the road. My throat was full of emotion. I couldn't say anything either. I just held onto him.

He drove for awhile, stopping for food a few times and even buying a coffee for me at one point. I took it, gratefully. As I sipped, the warm flavor settled my stomach a bit. That was when I noticed that he had turned his phone off. It sat in the console between us with no blinking lights. This was Mason. If it had been on, there would've been flashing lights. His phone never stayed silent for long. Someone was always calling or texting. Then I thought about my own and checked it. It was nearing midnight.

I sucked in my breath. What had happened to the night? Then I asked, my voice was raspy, "Where are we going?"

He shrugged. "Just driving. Where do you want to go?"

I settled back into my seat. It felt right—being with him, alone, in the middle of the night. It had started to rain outside, but we were protected inside the car. We could've driven all night and I wouldn't have cared. I murmured as much, "I don't care."

He nodded. "Do you work tomorrow?"

I shook my head. "First and last night off till school starts. I have to train in the morning with Coach Grath."

"Call him. Tell him you'll do the running on your own."

"Why?"

"We'll go back to L.A., to that apartment again. My mom won't think to even check the place."

"How would she do that?"

He shrugged again. "Call the front desk? Ask if we're there? I don't know. She seems to always find out what she wants to know." He grinned. "If she knows to look for something, she finds it. If she doesn't, she doesn't know about it."

"Someone told her about you guys?"

He nodded. "My aunt. I'm guessing one of my cousins spilled the beans. James was always an idiot. He probably said something without even thinking."

"And your mom came up here right away?"

He grimaced and tightened his hold on the steering wheel. Lights from the street flashed over him, illuminating the shadows on his face, before they slid away until the next light. My heart fluttered with each highlight. He looked like a dark angel, with beautiful features but a rough edge. He opened his mouth, "Yeah. She came up as soon as she heard. She'd been going after my dad for a long time before we came over. She called us, not him. I think my dad didn't want us involved."

"Or my mom?"

"Her too." A small smile graced his features. He glanced over with warmth in his eyes. "I don't think my mom realized how much of a hellcat your mom is." A low smooth chuckle sounded from him. "Helen likes to be cool, calm, and collected. Your mom put a stop to that today."

I remembered the harried expression on Helen's face. Her hair was a mess and she had sunk back against the wall, as if in surrender. "I don't think she realized how crazy my mom is."

"Yeah." Mason flashed me a grin. "Your mom is crazy, but mine's ruthless and cunning."

"So is Analise."

"In a different way."

I cocked my head to the side. "How so?"

He jerked a shoulder up as he turned back to the road. "Your mom is violent. She's tried to keep it together, but she can't. She's a loose cannon. My mom's not violent. She'd never do the things your mom has. I'm not stupid, Sam. I heard my mom and if a PI thinks you were beat up by your own mother, I believe him. You've never said it, but you're scared of her. You weren't as scared of her before, but something happened and now you almost pee your pants when you're around her."

Pee my pants? I folded my arms over my chest. I didn't do that...

He let loose another string of curses. "I don't know what happened back then. I know something happened and I know it was bad. I was keeping it together because your mom was already going off, so was mine, and you needed me to support you, but I wanted to..." His knuckled wrapped around the steering wheel. They turned white as he fought to control himself. His jaw was rigid as he clipped out, "If I get the opportunity to hurt your mom and never have it bounce back to you, I'm taking it. I'm not going to lay a hand on her, but she hurt you. No one hurts you, Sam. I'm not okay with that."

I drew in a shuddering breath. A black hole had opened inside of me, and as I started to form the words, it grew and grew. But I had to say it. I had to say it to someone else. I had to get it out of me.

Mason had grown silent. He kept driving, and the silence of the car made me feel safe. This was the right place to talk about it. So I opened my mouth and the rest spilled free, "I was eleven and I had to go to the bathroom, but I was scared. I didn't want to wake her up, but I didn't want to go in my pants. She'd be so mad if I did that. I had, once. She slapped me so hard that time." My voice faltered. My head had hit a table on that occasion. Analise told David I'd been roller skating in the house again. The pain should've been overwhelming again, but it wasn't. As I remembered, I grew numb. "When I got to the bathroom, she was inside."

I drew in another breath.

"I didn't know what was wrong with her." I looked out the window, but I didn't see the lights. I didn't see my reflection. I saw my mom. "There was so much blood. She had on a nightgown and blood was coming from between her legs. I could tell. Her nightgown was soaked with it, and it was all over the floor around her legs."

I closed my eyes, but it didn't go away. The image became more vivid.

"I tried to say something to her, but she didn't answer so I went to find David." A tear slipped down. "I think that was the first time he left her. I didn't know it, but I figured it out now. There'd been a suitcase on the floor and his clothes were thrown all over. I think...I think they had a fight. Maybe he tried to pack a bag, but she didn't let him. I don't know, but he wasn't there. They couldn't locate him for three days."

I had stayed at Jessica's house for two of those days. The first night was spent at the hospital.

"I called 911, and the paramedics showed up right away. I was with her and they kept ringing the doorbell, but I didn't hear it. The 911 operator called me back and told me to open the door for them. I felt so bad that I made them wait outside. It was cold that night, or maybe it wasn't. I don't know. I was cold. But they bundled her onto the cot thing and took her out. It happened so quickly. I think they took her blood pressure and stuff. I don't know."

I stopped. I couldn't explain how it had been in the ambulance. Cold and alone. I was terrified. She never made a sound the whole ride. Her eyes never opened. Her hand didn't even twitch. The paramedic lifted it to feel her pulse. When he let it go, it fell with a thump back down. It was like she was dead.

"What then, Sam?"

I gasped from his voice. More tears came. I ignored them now. They slid down. I couldn't stop. But I continued, "They asked me where my dad was, but I couldn't tell them. I had no idea. I don't know how they found him. Jessica's mom came down. I think my mom had put her name on the medical forms so I stayed with Jessica until David came to get me. When he did, he didn't want to talk about it."

I stopped again. This was the worst part of it.

"They told David she tried to commit suicide or maybe that was a lie he told me. But there was a wire hanger next to her. I saw it when I went in the bathroom. One of the paramedic guys kicked it underneath a dresser in the bathroom. When David took me back to the house, I got it and cleaned it up. Then I threw it in the trash. I don't know why I did that. I don't think I wanted anyone to know what she really did. I realized now maybe he knew, maybe they all knew, but I wanted to protect her. I don't know why anymore."

I was eleven. I shouldn't have had thoughts like that at that age.

"I didn't want David to find out because if he did, I was scared that he was going to leave again. I couldn't handle being alone with my mom. She would've gone nuts, but she did anyway. Later..."

"Sam?"

I shook my head. I couldn't tell him what happened later. It was too painful, too much. I whispered, "I can't."

"It's okay." He reached for my hand and squeezed it. He pressed a kiss to it before he rested our hands in his lap.

That was good. He was warm. He was safe. He was strong. I breathed a little easier. I needed his touch. I needed to remember that it was okay now. I was okay now.

Then I said something that I never remembered before. "Mason."

"Hmmm?"

I remembered their voices one night. My mom's and David's. I had crouched outside of their door and stuck my ear against it. I'd been so scared he was always going to leave, but he never did. This was another fight. I hoped he wouldn't go, but I heard her scream. And I heard his response.

"Sam?"

"I don't think they were David's."

"What?"

I opened my eyes and turned to him. Another repulsive feeling started to grow. "They had a fight that night; she wanted kids, but he couldn't give her any. He told her he couldn't have kids. I remember it now." I stopped as I realized the extent of what my mother had done. "She had cheated on him. She got pregnant. Then she killed the babies."

"Because they weren't his?" His voice broke at the end.

I nodded. "That fight was before." Then I sucked in my breath. "That fight was *that* night."

CHAPTER TWENTY-FOUR

We didn't talk about our families after that. The only thing that we discussed was what would happen, but Mason just shrugged. Things were left unsettled. I couldn't be around my mother. I knew that much. I also knew that Mason and Logan wouldn't be moving back without me. So all the questions and decisions regarding my mother and his father were left unsaid, Mason said things would get settled one day so I left it alone. When we got to that extravagant apartment, the normal doorman wasn't there. Mason said he didn't work nights, but a young college kid was instead. After a substantial amount of money, he agreed that if anyone called, we weren't there.

When we got upstairs, Mason texted Nate and Logan to let them know that we went away for a night. He didn't tell them where, but I knew how close all of them were. I'm sure the other two could figure it out. When I asked what they were doing, Mason gave me a crooked grin and picked me up. He didn't say anything more and neither did I. The rest of the night was spent with moans, kisses, caresses, and the need to get as close as our bodies would allow.

I started to fall asleep when the sun began to peek through the blinds. Mason rolled over and pressed a kiss to my shoulder. A jolt of pleasure coursed through me, and I grinned into the pillow. I snuggled deeper into the blankets and drifted off with his hand on my back.

When I woke, the room was masked in darkness. After a shower, I left the shelter of the bedroom, and the sunlight blinded me. I'd forgotten the apartment had windows for its walls. No one could see inside so I wasn't worried about that, but the light that shone through was staggering.

"You'll get used to it." Mason's voice trailed from the kitchen. He grinned as he stirred something in a pan on the stove. With only a pair of sweats that rested low on his hips, my mouth watered as I took in the sight of him shirtless. His oblique muscles curved underneath his pants' drawstring, but his stomach and back ones rippled as he continued to stir.

Everything about him was perfect.

"I bought juice." He gestured to their refrigerator.

"Coffee?"

Grinning, he nodded to a cup on the counter. Steam rose from the small opening in the lid. "Figured you'd want that too."

"Did you?" As I went to grab it, I trailed the tips of my fingers across the bottom of his back.

He whirled in a flash. Before my hands could touch the coffee cup, I was lifted onto the counter beside him. He was between my legs in the next heartbeat, and his mouth was slammed on top of mine before anything else registered with me.

Hunger, deep and primitive, rushed through me, and I gasped. I needed more. Wrapping my arms around him, I clamped my legs around his waist. I held him tightly against me, urging his hips closer and closer.

His tongue swept in before he gasped, "I never get enough, never enough."

My tongue swished against his and he groaned. His hands pushed underneath my hips and he pulled me out for better access. I was throbbing between my legs. I tried to get him even closer, but his hand slid between us.

A groan ripped from the bottom of my throat. I needed him. I was blind with desire for him. Then his finger stroked me at the top. I shuddered in his arms. Two of his fingers slipped inside. I couldn't help it. I fell back, but he caught and lowered me to the counter until I was stretched out before him. As he readjusted my hold around his waist, his fingers continued to slide in and out.

I groaned. Pleasure spiked through me. I needed him inside of me. That was all I needed.

As I closed my eyes, he smoothed his hand from my shoulder to my neck. He lingered on my breast and ran a thumb over the tip before he cupped it. Then he leaned down and I gasped as his mouth replaced his hand. He sucked on the nipple and ran his tongue around the edge. My hands slid through his hair to anchor him to me. He knew exactly what I liked. Teasing my nipple with his teeth, he murmured, "Open your eyes."

I did.

His fingers kept going in and out. I started to feel it building.

"Mason," I gasped. I couldn't close my mouth. He grinned at me while his tongue swirled around my breast again. His fingers picked up their pace. He pushed them deeper and deeper. Then his eyes changed color. They darkened as he watched me getting closer and closer. When I exploded on his hand, he withdrew, tugged me down even farther, and slid inside of me before I could catch my breath. I gasped as I fell back again.

He was hard and thick as he filled me. With the first thrust, he went all the way into me before he paused and slid back out, only to repeat the same motion. My hips moved in rhythm and a curse fell from his lips. He braced himself slightly over me while his other hand moved to my hip to hold me stationery. He continued to thrust into me, but his eyes never left mine. I closed my eyes once, but his hand left my hip to cup the back of my head.

"Hey," he murmured. His voice was low and hoarse.

My eyelids flew up. I gulped at the naked need in his depths. He didn't bank the emotion. Instead, it intensified as our eyes held and he continued thrusting into me.

I couldn't look away.

His hand fell back to my hip, and he thrust harder into me. My legs wound tighter around him, my ankles locking together as I urged him to keep going. When my climax started to build, I started to tremble. As it grew and grew, I could barely hold on. Then his thumb touched me again and I went over the edge. My body convulsed around him and he soon joined me as I felt him shoot inside of me before collapsing on top.

Our heartbeats raced and then settled into the same beat together.

When we were able to catch our breath, I swept a hand down his sweat-soaked back. He groaned against my skin. His lips reached out and brushed a kiss to the side of my breast before he lifted his hand and cupped it again.

I closed my eyes as he started to kiss me all over.

We didn't talk for the rest of the day or that night except for when I left Coach Grath a message. He sent me a text later and reminded me that I needed to register for classes before Monday. After another night in the apartment, our sanctuary, Mason and I headed back the following morning. It was the Friday before classes started again. I had three days until I would be in a new school.

When we drove back, I couldn't shake thoughts about David. I wouldn't see him again. He didn't coach at the public school, and I wasn't sure if I was relieved or disappointed. He'd been paid to stay away from me. What father would do that? But that was the problem.

He wasn't my father.

Pain sliced through me at the reminder.

"You okay?" Mason squeezed my hand.

I looked down at our joined hands. We hadn't stopped touching since we arrived at the apartment. There was always some contact between us. Even when I used the bathroom, he stood next to me brushing his teeth with our feet touching.

"Yeah," I sighed. I would be, because of him.

He wheeled into a gas station and turned off the engine. "You want food? We can get some here or stop somewhere. We'll be back in time to get to the school."

"We can stop somewhere." My voice was hoarse.

He grinned at me, pressed a kiss to my forehead, and hopped out. I stared at my hand. It felt so natural to always hold onto his. It wasn't long before he got back inside and turned the car onto the highway. Without a word, he reached for my hand again.

I closed my eyes at the natural fit and rested my head against my seat. I felt at peace.

When we got to the school, Mason went in search for his basketball coach. He left me alone in the office with the beady-eyed secretary. Her hair was swept into a salt and pepper bun with a pink cardigan tied over her shoulders like she was an Ivy Leaguer. The lady must've been 86, but she was thorough. It took me an hour to fill out all the papers. I didn't even know there were that many papers needed to switch schools, but when I told her that Coach Grath was the one mentoring me, everything got a lot simpler. The papers disappeared after that, and when she found out that I'd be 18 in a week, she waved me off and told me that I was done. I was registered for all my classes.

When I went back to the hallway, I had no idea where to go.

The school was huge, like a cathedral, and it was a foreign land to me. The only times I had been at their school were for football games. Those occurred outside, not inside. Fallen Crest Academy didn't play Fallen Crest Public in any other sports. FCP was in a higher competitive league and only played the football teams because of some local agreement. I knew their football coach respected my da—David a lot. They were all good friends, but I wasn't sure about the basketball coaches or the rest of the sports. I think it had more to do with David than anything else. He tended to have friendships with a lot of schools. I knew he was friendly with the Roussou coach as well.

I waited for Mason in the athletic hallway. Glass cases were mounted on the wall with trophies and team pictures inside.

"Samantha?"

Everything stopped.

A surreal emotion came over me and I looked up. Then my eyes bugged out. I clamped onto my other arm with a death grip and I stopped breathing. I saw his reflection in the trophy glass first before I turned. It was a struggle. My knees locked, and I almost fell into the glass.

David caught my other arm and pulled me upright.

"Thanks." A weak squeak came from me.

He was dressed in a tracksuit with the letters FCA above the Academy's emblem. A whistle hung from his neck, and he held a bunch of papers in his hand.

"What are you doing here?" My voice sounded strangled.

"Oh. Uh." He gave me a tired look and rubbed a hand over his jaw. "Coaches meeting. It was held here today instead of the normal place."

"Normal place?"

"Yeah, we usually grab lunch somewhere. Lenny asked if he could cater in for us. He had something else going on and needed to be back right away." Then he frowned. "What are you doing here?"

"I'm..." Could I tell him? Then I remembered that he'd been paid off. Did he deserve to know? I hadn't processed anything from that night. I didn't know if I wanted to process anything, but I heard myself saying, "I'm going to school here next semester."

"Oh." He took a step back, blinking in surprise. "O—you are?"

I nodded.

He glanced up and down the hallway as he took a deep breath. His shoulders lifted up and descended. It wasn't meant to be dramatic, but it seemed like it. David was 45. He looked in his fifties at that moment. There was no graying in his hair. It was the same dark brown, combed to the side like always, but he looked old. He looked defeated.

Then he sighed, "I see."

"What do you see?"

There was disappointment in his depths as he gave me a sad look. "Does your mother know about your plans?"

I didn't hold back the bitterness. "I don't think my mother has any say in my life. She's made it clear to me that she only cares about herself, and maybe James. She needs to keep one guy in her life. He has to bankroll her whenever she needs it." I scanned him up and down. "But then again, she might not even have him anymore."

He narrowed his eyes. "What are you talking about, Samantha?"

My chest tightened and I jerked a shoulder up. "What do you care? You got paid to not care."

He took another step back, as if blown back by a sudden gust of wind. He blinked rapidly as he rubbed his jaw again. "I'm not following you. Wha—what are you talking about?"

"She. Paid. You. To. Stay. Away. From. Me."

"Honey—"

He reached for my arm, but I yanked it away. "Don't call me that," I seethed. My teeth were clenched together. "Don't ever call me that again."

"Samantha." His arm fell, as did his voice.

"Did she pay you to stay away?"

I needed to know this answer; I needed to know it so much. If she had, I didn't know how I would handle it.

"No."

I jerked back.

His eyes were steady on me. He was imploring me to hear him. "I was not paid to stay away from you. I stayed away from you because I feared for you. Your mother's not healthy. She's not been in a right frame of mind lately. She paid me to sign the divorce papers and not fight anything. I didn't fight any of it. I didn't even read them because I don't want anything from your mother. The only thing I ever cared about was you, but I worried what she would do." *If she would harm you.*

716

I stumbled as I heard those unspoken words. They flashed in my mind. I saw the same stricken look on him. He thought the same thing. A memory flared through me.

I was in the hospital room, in a nightgown. Analise had left, and I was crying. It hurt so much. Everything hurt. I couldn't breathe, but then David came in. He brushed my hair back and whispered as he kissed my forehead, "I will never leave you. I promise."

"You did leave me," I whispered.

He winced as if he'd been slapped. He nodded. Then he choked on a breath. "I'm sorry, Samantha. I really am. Your mother left me, and she took you with. I had no legal leg to stand on. I consulted with a lawyer, but I never adopted you. She was your mother, you were her daughter. I couldn't fight her, and then Garrett came into the picture. I didn't know what to think of him, if he was going to fight for you too. But you're seventeen."

"So?" I hissed at him.

"So." His shoulders drooped. "Any legal fight for you would've lasted a long time, possibly years. I didn't have years to fight. I didn't want to anger your mother. I didn't know what she would've done. I had no way of knowing what she could've said to you. She might've brainwashed you against me. I had no idea. All I could do was wait and hope that she wouldn't take you away from here."

"And if she had?"

His head jerked up. A fierce determination came over him. "Then I would've searched for you, and I would've fought for you. I wouldn't have given a damn what she had done or said, or how far she would've gone. I would've fought. But you are still here. You're still in town. You were still going to my school—not anymore, but you're here in town. You're still here. I can still see you, and you'll be 18 in a week."

"I moved out."

Surprise flared in his eyes. "You did?"

I nodded. "She threatened to leave James if Mason didn't stop seeing me; then she threatened to report him to the police because I'm still a minor. It was too much, all of it. And..." I shrugged and looked away. "It doesn't matter now. I moved out. I'm not moving back in." But even as I said it, I thought about Mason and Logan. They should live with their father. I was even thinking about James. He shouldn't lose his last few months with Mason before he went to college. And Logan, what about him? Where would we live in the next year? Nate would be gone. I wouldn't be able to live in his home, and Helen wouldn't approve of Logan being my only roommate if we rented an apartment.

The more I considered it, the more I realized that she would demand that Logan move in with her. That meant that he'd go to Los Angeles, or she would move back. But again, where would I go? She wouldn't let me live with them.

I glanced at David, but I knew I couldn't live with him. Too much had happened. There was too much distance between us.

My heart sank with that thought.

I would never get back the father that I had before.

He let out a breath of relief. "Well, that's good then. That's really good, Samantha. Would you—I mean—would you consider—where are you—" He struggled for words, but settled on, "What are you doing for your birthday?"

I waited, but when he finished with that question, I was dumbfounded. "What?"

"Your birthday is next weekend. I can imagine that Mason and Logan have a big party planned, but would you consider having dinner with me? We could go out? Or stay in? You could come back to the house." He nodded, so eager now. "We could make a homemade pizza, or no. I could order in. Chinese. You used to like Chinese. We could go to that restaurant you always liked when you were little."

"I..." I closed my mouth. I never considered my birthday plans. I'd been too consumed with the thought of being free from her, but that was done. And I was free now. So maybe dinner with David sounded like a good thing. That's what I'd been wanting, wasn't it? "Sure."

My phone buzzed at that moment. It was a text from Mason. **In the car.**

"I'm, um, I'm going to go."

He nodded, a bright smile on his face. "Okay. That sounds good. I'm excited for your birthday, Samantha. I really am. I'm glad that there are boundaries with your relationship with Analise too. I've worried about you so much. You have no idea."

"I..." Again, I closed my mouth. I didn't know what to say to him anymore. Too much had happened. He wasn't my father anymore. Pain seared inside me. And what about Garrett? He was gone too. Both of them had abandoned me, maybe for good reasons, maybe not, but they were gone. I had survived my mother without them.

As I left, I didn't hear what else he said. I didn't care anymore. When I got into the car and shut the door, the shock was reeling inside of me. I didn't care anymore. I didn't care about David or Garrett. I had always cared, but not anymore.

"What's wrong?"

"I saw my dad."

"Garrett?" His eyebrows shot up.

"No." I shook my head. I was in a daze. "David. I saw him and...I don't care anymore."

He frowned. "What do you mean?"

I swallowed over a ball in my throat and turned to him. Everything seemed clearer now. "I thought that all I cared about was why he left me, why he wasn't trying to see me, and now I know that he was waiting. He was scared of what my mom would do."

He snorted. "Bat shit crazy."

"He wants to have dinner with me next weekend for my birthday."

"He does?"

I nodded, tearing up. Why was I crying now? "I can see my dad again, but I don't want to anymore."

Mason sighed and reached for my hand. He enveloped it in his strong hold and squeezed. "Things have changed, Sam. You're not living under your mom's thumb anymore. You don't have to be so scared anymore. You might care tomorrow."

"If I don't?"

He shrugged. "Then you don't. It's your life. You live it how you want. No matter the reasons, your dad screwed up. He stayed away. He shouldn't have. He didn't protect you."

"He didn't, did he?"

"No." His voice had a rough edge.

"Thank you."

"For what?" He narrowed his eyes as he frowned.

"For protecting me."

Mason smirked. "I didn't protect you."

"You didn't?"

He shook his head and leaned close. Then he whispered, his breath caressing my skin, "You protected me."

"I did, didn't I? I'm always protecting you." A smile came over me. As I looked up into his eyes, my heart constricted with love.

His grin widened. "Yeah, you do. That's what family does." Then his lips were on mine and nothing mattered besides that.

CHAPTER
TWENTY-FIVE

It was the last Friday before school started again. When Mason and I got to the mansion, Logan and Nate were there with a few of their friends. I relaxed when I saw it was the guys from their school. I had only ever really interacted with Ethan before, but I was starting to recognize a few of the others. Strauss was one of them. He wore tight cowboy jeans with a big belt buckle and cowboy boots. I wasn't sure if his name was a nickname or his real name. I never asked.

They all gave us friendly nods, but Logan was the first one to reach us. He wrapped his arms around me and lifted me off the ground. "I did you a favor. Ask me what the favor was. Ask me! Come on!"

When he set me back down, I grinned. "What favor did you do for me?"

"I got your shift covered at Manny's!" He was so pleased with himself.

"What?"

"Yeah." He gestured to Nate, who came over and clapped a hand on Mason's shoulder in greeting. "We went to Manny's and asked who could cover for you tonight."

"Why?" My heart skipped a few beats. What had Heather said?

"Because we're having a huge party tonight. And I want you to be a part of it." He threw an arm around my shoulder and pressed me to his side. He bent close; the booze on his breath was strong. "So that Rosa chick said she'd fill in. And I invited all your friends to the party. They're coming after their shifts."

"Heather's coming?" She was the only one I wanted, but I doubted she would. She was too close to the Roussou side—

721

and I remembered my brush with the Broudou siblings. I still hadn't told Mason about it. That was a conversation I wasn't eager to start. I didn't know how he would react, him or Logan.

Logan's grin slipped a bit. "Not sure about Jax. You know she runs with Channing."

Oh yeah. He knew.

Mason touched my hand and gestured upstairs. "I'm going to go shower." His eyes held the rest of his question if I was coming.

I nodded and followed.

It was after we had showered and were getting dressed that he brought Heather back up. He was in the closet with only a pair of jeans on, and as he was choosing which shirt he wanted, he said over his shoulder, "You like that girl, huh?"

I paused in my own dressing. I was wearing skintight black jeans that looked more like leggings and had finished pulling a sleeveless black shirt on. I tugged it around my waist and drew a deep breath. Here it was, the moment. "Yeah. I do."

He turned with a shirt in hand, but he made no move to put it on. He stared at me, long and hard. "She's Roussou territory, Sam. She's with Channing. He's a big player over there."

"But he's not the only one."

He narrowed his eyes. "No, he's not, but Jax has always been friends with that group. She's not going to change."

I sighed, "I like her." I needed a friend when I went to their school. Mason and Logan could only help me so far.

"She likes you. I know that. I've seen it, but I'm just preparing you. She's not going to start coming to our parties. Jax is fine by herself, but not the group she runs with."

What was this? A Jax intervention? I grumbled, "Why's she friends with them anyway? Why isn't she friends with you guys like all the normal girls at your school?"

"Do you know Jax? She's not a normal girl." Mason snorted before he pulled his shirt on in two movements. It fit perfectly over his chest, highlighting his muscular shoulders and trim waist. I couldn't stop myself from watching how his stomach muscles rippled and clenched. Even now, after we'd been together a record number of times over the last twenty-four hours, I still wanted him. The throbbing started between my legs again.

His eyes darkened, I knew he had caught my reaction. He stalked towards me, his desire strong. He bent and lifted me with one arm so I entwined my legs around his waist. His other hand rubbed up my back, holding me in place while his eyes held my gaze. Intense. Then he leaned forward, ever so slowly. His lips touched mine, gently at first.

I groaned. I'd never get enough of him.

That was all he needed. His mouth opened over mine commandingly. He wanted inside. I gasped against him, and his tongue swept in, claiming me.

"You guys are too horny. I don't think it's normal." Logan was propped against the doorway. He rolled his eyes and came inside as Mason shot him a dark look, helping me back down to the floor. "I feel like I should give you two the birds and the bees speech. You know, before she gets pregnant or something."

I laughed, but Mason froze beside me so I whacked him on the chest. "You know I'm covered."

He gave me a pointed look, reminding both of us about the apartment. It had been the first time he hadn't used a condom, but I was on birth control. We were both clean. I hoped the one time wouldn't produce a baby. I was sure it wouldn't, but he stopped for more condoms anyways. Mason liked to make sure everything was covered.

"We're celebrating, Sam."

"We are?"

"Yep." Logan nodded his head with a look of intent on his face. "Come on. You signed up for our school. It's all official and shit. I've got shots ready downstairs." Then he caught a look from his brother and held up his hands. "Just all in good fun, Mase. She'll be fine. Promise."

Mason rolled his eyes. His hand touched the small of my back as we followed Logan downstairs. "She'll be fine because I'm here, not because of you. You'll be hooking up with someone before the night is half over."

Logan flashed him a grin. "Yeah, maybe."

"Maybe?" I scoffed.

"Okay. Probably." A group of girls walked into the center area from underneath us. "Definitely."

"Shots," Mason reminded him.

"Right. This way." Logan weaved through the crowd that had already formed. He slapped a hand on the counter. "Six shots, Strauss. Give it to me, Cowboy man!"

Six shot glasses were turned over and filled with something pink. Logan pushed two to each of us and lifted his first. "To Sam coming to our school and to Mason always fucking her!"

"Logan!"

Mason laughed as he tapped his shot with his brother's. Both swallowed theirs at the same time before looking at me. Oh, fine. I threw mine back. We heard the same toast again with the second round. I couldn't help but shake my head as the alcohol went down my throat. Still, it didn't taste too bad. I turned for Mason and tugged on his belt loop. "One more."

His arms came around me to rest on the counter. He nodded to his friend. "Strauss, another round."

"Really?"

"I'm off. See you two lovebirds later."

Before we could look, Logan had already disappeared into the crowd.

Mason swung a finger from me to him. "Make that just for us two."

Strauss flipped over three shot glasses. As the pink stuff went into them again, he lifted one for himself. "I wouldn't dare make that same toast, but here's to your girl joining the gang."

"Nice." Mason grinned before he took his shot.

Mine was held suspended. Join their group? The girls hated me.

"Sam?"

I shook my head. "Nothing." And down the alcohol went. It burned this time, for some reason. "Where's Nate?"

Strauss gestured towards the back patio. "He's out there with the guys. I think he's resting before Parker gets her claws on him tonight."

"Parker's been here every night?"

His friend lifted an easygoing shoulder. "I think so. According to her."

"What does Nate say?"

Strauss gave him a pointed look. "You know Nate won't say anything to us. He would to you, not the rest of us."

Mason frowned. "I haven't thought to ask. I thought he didn't want to make that exclusive?"

I frowned at the tension I felt from him. His hands moved to my hips in a strong grip. His fingers tightened into my skin, and he pulled me against him. As he pressed his hips into me, I didn't feel the usual bulge that Mason always had when we stood like this. Instead, I felt his anger.

Strauss frowned a bit but shrugged again. "I don't know. You don't want that exclusive?"

"It don't matter to me—not my relationship." But the bite that came from his tone said otherwise.

"Or is it a Parker thing? You don't want her having too much say with him?"

I became aware of Strauss's scrutiny as his gaze skirted back and forth from Mason to me. After the fourth stare, I straightened and rolled back my shoulders. I knew he was wondering if I had told them about the girls' vendetta against me, if that was his problem with Nate being so close with Parker. I shook my head. It was the tiniest of movements, but he caught it and his eyes widened even more. I couldn't tell if he was relieved or worried.

Mason's hands gripped me tighter and he pressed all of his body against mine. This time I felt the bulge and my eyes closed. The need for him started to rise in me, and the throbbing began again. As he brushed back and forth against me, I started not to care where we were.

Mason lowered his head to my neck. He breathed out, his nostrils flared, and I felt his possessiveness over me. His hand lifted one of my arms so it was entwined around his neck. My hand splayed out over the back of his neck as his other hand slid around to the front of me. Every inch of us molded together as his hand slid inside of my pants.

He never answered his friend's question, but it didn't matter. Before my eyelids dropped, heavy and laden with lust, I saw that Strauss had left. Then I was only aware of Mason lifting me and turning me around. I was placed on the counter and he was between my legs. His mouth was on mine, urgent and demanding.

"Don't you two breathe?"

We jerked apart, but Mason groaned and rolled his eyes as he saw who interrupted us. "What are you doing here, Tate?"

The tall leggy blonde looked fresh and healthy. She was dressed in similar jeans as mine, brown instead of black, and wore an off-the shoulder cream sweater that draped to give a glimpse of her lacy tan-colored bra. Her hair was swept to the side, and with a glow on her cheeks, she looked like she had stepped off the cover of a fashion magazine. Grinning like a Cheshire, she lifted her shoulders and flashed her dimples at him. "I heard about the happy couple. I wanted to congratulate you two."

Mason rested his forehead against the side of me as he glared at her. "Leave." His hand twitched on my hip. I knew he was holding back.

"Or what?" She widened her eyes in a dramatic fashion. "Or you'll make me leave?" She rolled her eyes. "You're going to have to get used to me. I'm moving back, Kade."

His eyes narrowed, and he sucked in his breath—just a little, but enough so that I felt it. My hand rested against his chest. I felt his heartbeat pick up as his muscles clenched underneath my touch. "Like hell, you are."

"I am." The smiling façade fell away. She stared back at him long and hard. "Get used to me. I'm not going anywhere." Then her grin picked back up, a slow malicious glint appeared. "I heard that you've been ignoring your precious Marissa's phone calls. Tsk, tsk, Mason. How noble is that? Was she your charitable donation at the time, an attempt to persuade yourself that you're not that bad of a guy?" Her eyes slid to mine. "But now that you've got the good girl you can screw, you don't care about the Saintly Marissa anymore? I saw her, you know. Her parents moved to my town, and she even cried to me one time at a coffee shop. You're heartless, Kade, but then again—I never forgot that about you." She gave him a withering look. "Now your little friend knows that side of you exists and she's all the more humiliated because of it."

Mason was a cement slab of stone. As he grilled her with his eyes, I touched the side of his face. Nothing. There was no reaction. It was as if he had forgotten I was there. It made me wonder if there was more to his loathing than just the Logan situation. Had something else happened between the two? Or maybe he had wanted her as she had him? But no. I sucked in my breath. That couldn't have been the case. Mason hated this girl because she hurt Logan. She had been the one person who had managed that feat.

It was enough for me. "You might want to leave before you're thrown out."

Her eyes snapped to mine. She seemed energized by the new target. "Oh really?"

"Really."

"I heard this isn't their house."

"No, but it is Nate's."

Her smile fell flat.

My own doubled. "You don't think he'll kick you out because Mason told him to?"

She straightened away from us and backed up a few steps. Her eyes went flat as she skimmed me up and down. "Look, I came here as a sign of respect."

Mason snorted in disbelief.

"I did." She glared at him. "I'm moving back. I don't want any trouble from you guys."

"Off on the wrong foot, don't you think?" I snapped at her.

She ignored me and transferred her gaze to Mason. Her tone softened. "I still love Logan—"

He released me in a flash and gripped her arm. "You never loved Logan."

Her eyes widened in fear, but she shot back, "Yes, I did. I made a horrible mistake. I was stupid and an egomaniac, but I loved him. I really did—"

His hand tightened around her arm. "Get out of here, Tate. Now. And stay away from my brother." He pushed her back. There would be an imprint from where his hand had been. It was already reddening on her skin.

She stumbled back a few more steps. Her eyes seemed in a daze as she took in the sight of Mason, but then she found her footing and straightened again. A wistful smile came over her. "Man, I forgot what you look like when you're threatened."

"I'm not threatened. I'm pissed." He stalked closer to her until he was in her face again. "I can make your life hell."

"Yeah." She nodded with a thoughtful look in her eye. "You can, but I can do the same to you." She glanced over his shoulder to me. "I think I'm the one of two people who could do that to you. You might not want to piss me off, Kade. I can take your brother away from you and you know it."

"Get. Out."

She looked ready to say something more, but at that moment, Nate entered the kitchen. He took everything in and wrapped an arm around her waist. Picking her up, he grunted when she started to struggle. "You're not welcome, Tate. Ever." Then he gave Mason a reassuring nod before disappearing with her. The crowd that had formed to watch was silent now.

Mason barked at them. "Get lost!"

They jumped back into action. The conversations doubled in volume.

Sighing as he came back to me, he raked a hand through his hair and growled. "I hate that bitch."

My hand touched the side of his jaw, but it was still rigid. Then I sighed. "Looks like the next semester won't be as much fun as you thought."

He grimaced and his jaw flexed against my hand. Then, because it had been bugging me, I had to ask, "Is she right?"

"About what?"

"Does Logan still love her?"

A wall slammed over him, and he turned away. That's when I knew it was true, and that's when I realized how threatening this girl really was to their relationship. Maybe it was karmic coincidence, but it was at that moment when I looked up and saw members of the Elite in the kitchen. They had stayed away from me since Logan dumped Miranda so long ago, but she was there. In Peter's arms, dressed all in white, laughing at something one of the others had said and looking radiant in her happiness. But she hadn't been, not after Logan screwed with her. She'd been humiliated.

Miranda had been a blip on Mason's radar from the one time she taunted him that Logan might've had feelings for me. If he had reacted like that to her, I had no idea how he would handle Tate. She was the real threat.

Chills went down my spine.

When Nate returned, he gave Mason a look. An understanding transmitted between them, just the two of them. My teeth gritted together. For some reason, I didn't like the closeness those two had, not anymore.

CHAPTER TWENTY-SIX

Later in the evening, I was on the back patio. Mason lounged next to me with an arm around my waist and his head next to my shoulder. He lay there as if he were a lion, resting for his next battle. Since Tate had left, he kept a hand on me at all times. It was a possessive touch, not the loving touch from the apartment, but I couldn't deny the reaction it was having with me. A primal thrill had been burning deep in me. It mixed with a sick excitement.

Everyone else seemed to react to this side of Mason too. They were more alert, a bit more silent than at other parties. Nate hadn't left Mason's side since Tate's arrival either and sat on the other side of him. One of his legs was kicked up to rest on the table in front of us while a few of their guy friends sat in the remaining seats across from us.

Logan emerged from wherever he'd been and joined us on the patio.

As if it had been practiced and scripted, Ethan, Strauss and another guy stood up and left. When a few girls started up the stairs, they blocked them at the bottom. Then all three of them got comfortable. They were the guard dogs.

Logan watched them too before he slunk into one of the empty chairs and stuffed his hands into his pockets. "What's going on?" His voice was guarded.

I sighed. He had closed off. This wasn't going to go well.

Mason leaned forward. Nate remained silent.

"Maybe I should go." I started to stand up.

Mason clamped a hand on my arm. He kept me in place while Logan rolled his eyes. "Stay, Sam. You're family."

So I stayed, but my chest swelled with a smidgen of fear. I couldn't deny it. As I watched Mason turn hawk-like eyes on his brother, I wondered why he seemed so upset. Logan hadn't done anything.

Then it started, "Your ex was here."

Logan's eyes flashed. The hands came out of his pockets and he straightened in his chair. "Are you kidding me?"

Mason jerked his head to the side. "She says she's moving back."

"Are you messing with me?" Logan's nostrils flared now. Anger started to swirl in his depths, it mixed with something else, something that sent chills down my back again. Danger.

He shook his head. "No. I wish." He gestured to his side. "Nate kicked her out."

"But she'll come back," Logan clipped out.

Nate swiveled his head over to look at him, but there was no reaction. Mason's best friend was like a Greek god statue, made of stone. He showed no emotion. He was there for Mason. Logan was right when he said that Nate was only there for Mason. He wasn't there for Logan and me. He struck me as another silent guard dog, but I sensed ruthlessness in him that I have never experienced before. It wasn't the first time that I'd been struck off-balance by him, but it was the first time that I was starting to fear him a little bit.

He spoke now, "She won't be allowed to any of my parties."

Mason frowned at him. "That's not the point." He turned back to his brother. "She says she loves you. She wants you back."

Too many emotions crossed over Logan before he shut it off. He collapsed against the back of his seat. His hands gripped the sides of it. "Whatever. The bitch took enough skin from me, she won't get any more."

Mason leaned back. His chest never relaxed; instead, it tightened even more. "You sure?"

He didn't believe him.

Logan shot back a dark look. "Back off. She hurt me, not you."

"She hurt my brother, that means she hurt me too," Mason whipped out, bristling from his anger.

The air was thick now, filled with tension.

The only one who didn't seem affected was Nate as he stood. "I'll be back."

Logan snorted and kicked his feet up on the table. He scooted down in his chair, restless and on edge. He reminded me a coiled cobra, ready to strike but without a target in sight. "What's with him?"

"Parker." Mason watched his best friend weave through the crowd with lidded eyes. As Nate grabbed the girl by her arm, he led her away from her friends and further inside. The frown on Mason's face showed his disapproval.

Logan grunted. "Not to be a dick to Nate, but he's always preaching against pussy. Look at him now. She's the most regular vagina he tastes. He's getting domesticated."

I frowned.

Logan flashed me a grin. "No offense, Sam. You're family. You're not normal."

"None taken?"

Mason jerked his head in a nod and the three guys from the bottom of the stairs filed back up. Each took a seat and it was back to being me with the guys. Mason lounged back and wrapped a hand around my shoulder this time. He pulled me tight against him.

Tingles reared inside of me. I didn't think they'd ever stop. He was claiming me. He always had before, but there were new threats tonight so he was showing it again. Adrenaline rushed through me when his hand started to brush against the back of my neck. His thumb rubbed back and forth. He would apply pressure under my ear so I would tilt my head, then he would press his lips there. He continued his soft kisses, and I could barely breathe an hour later. The need for him was pumping through my blood, strong and urgent. I squirmed under his hand and I felt him grin against my skin. He knew what he was doing.

The guys ignored us. They chatted together while someone kept bringing drinks to the patio. Mason gave me a few more shots and I'd take them, but we never broke eye contact. His had darkened so much they looked black, full of promises for the rest of the night. I wanted that now. My body was demanding it and I started to raise myself so I was in his lap when Nate joined the group again. He was alone, thankfully.

"The girl happy now? Did you satisfy her?" Logan threw an empty shot glass at him as he took the old seat on the other side of Mason. His tone was jovial, but there was a dark underlining edge to him. As he glanced at me, I knew I wasn't alone with my concern about Mason's best friend.

Nate frowned as he caught the glass. He chucked it back. "What's your problem with her?"

"Nothing." Logan caught it with a quick grab.

The rest of the guys grew quiet.

He continued, "But for the guy who doesn't like girlfriends, you seem to have one."

"Parker's not my girlfriend."

"She know that?" Logan goaded.

"It's none of your business, Logan. Stay out of it."

A few of the guys shared looks, but Mason seemed unaffected. His hand rubbed up and down my back as he scooped me into his lap. He nuzzled my neck and I closed my eyes. My bones melted into him. I couldn't leave, no way. But he didn't seem to mind. His arms wrapped around me and his hand rested low on my stomach. His thumb caressed me there, back and forth in a normally soothing motion.

Now, however, it was anything but soothing. I squirmed in his lap from the desire pulsating through me. The flames of lust had been lit before, but now they were a fire. I'd be a bonfire if he kept up his ministrations.

"*You* stay out of it," Logan retorted. "I'm getting sick of Parker's attitude. She prances around here and brings her friends over like they own the place."

"No, they don't." Irritation was evident on Nate's face. His eyes flared in anger. "Why don't you say what you're really pissed about? I doubt it's anything to do with Parker." He paused a beat. "Maybe you got a girl on your mind, one who actually was your girl. Is she what this is about? Your panties all twisted because Tate made an appearance tonight?"

Mason's lips left my shoulder and he looked up. His hand continued to rub my stomach. It shifted further down and slipped underneath my pants, but stayed there. I was burning up.

"Shut up about Tate."

Nate leaned forward. "Shut up about Parker then."

"I'm not fucking Tate."

"And I'm not fucking Parker." He paused again with a wicked grin. "Right now. I'm sitting here. Right now."

Logan rolled his eyes. "So funny, Nate. You're a riot."

"You think you're the only funny one here?"

I frowned; the burning from Mason's caresses had started to ebb. Nate and Logan were scowling at each other from across the table. The other guys were silent, their eyes darting back and forth as they listened to the argument. Everyone waited to see what Mason would do. He could speak up, end it, or he could let it keep going. For now, he had stilled underneath me. He was listening, but he wasn't tense yet. I knew he wasn't going to step in yet.

"You're saying that you can be funny with that stick up your ass?"

I sucked in my breath, so did the others.

Mason tensed beneath me now and I tensed with him.

Nate grilled him with a warning. "Back off, Logan, about this. I'm the only one containing the girls. They haven't done shit to Sam because I won't let Parker do a thing—"

Logan's eyes flared. "What?"

One of the guys moaned, "Fuckkk mee."

Nate clamped his mouth shut when he realized what he let slip.

Mason was like stone beneath me now. He turned to me, a mask over his face, before he looked back at his best friend. "You want to explain that comment?"

Nate closed his eyes, cursing himself, but when he opened them again, they were strained. "I'm sorry, Mase. I should've said something earlier—"

"—Yeah," Mason interrupted him. "You should've, but you better explain it now." His hand kept me on his lap with an iron hold. I couldn't even squirm. His other hand formed into a fist.

Nate's eyes were on that fist as he started, "The girls haven't been too welcoming to Sam."

"Since when?"

"Since," his eyes shot to mine. He flashed an apology in them. "Since you started dating and bringing her around. They don't like her at all."

"Why not?"

"Why not?" Nate laughed softly. "You're kidding, right? You know those four. No one gets in unless they put the girl through hell and misery. You think they're going to let Sam into the group without the same conditions? It don't matter if she's with you. Probably makes it worse, you know, since Kate's the ring leader."

"Kate was nothing to me." A dark scowl had formed on Mason. It grew with each word Nate added.

"She knows that *now*. You threw her aside." He hesitated, choosing his words with caution. "She's boiling because you dropped her. They're all boiling mad because you don't give them the time of day anymore."

Mason leaned back. He kept me on his lap. "They're not my friends. They're yours. They're the guys' friends, they aren't mine."

Logan cursed.

Ethan spoke up, "The girls don't look at it like that. They think they're friends with you."

Mason narrowed his eyes. "I could give a shit about them. I'm not friends with girls anyway, much less now when I'm with Sam. The only female friend I had was Marissa."

Nate spoke up, "Yeah and look at what happened to her. She had to leave school because of those girls."

"That was because of Tate."

"And who was she friends with? The four of them. You know what they're like with new girls. You didn't think about how'd they be with Samantha?"

"She's with me." Mason scowled at him.

Logan added, "And she's family. She's my family."

Nate shrugged. "That's why no one's spoke about this to you guys. They knew how you'd react."

Logan's eyes switched to mine. They were dark and angry. I stiffened as he asked me, "Why didn't you say anything?"

"Because it's my problem, not yours."

Mason exploded now. He lifted me in the air so I was straddling him. Grabbing my chin, he peered into my eyes. "Are you kidding me?"

I gulped at the rage from him, but I tightened my resolve. "It's my problem, not yours. I'm the girl coming into their group. I'm the one who's going to have to deal with them in the locker rooms or the bathrooms. You can't protect me everywhere, Mason."

"They won't touch you. I won't allow it."

I stuck my chin out and folded my arms. "I can't earn their respect if you're the one that's demanding it. I have to demand it. I have to earn it from them." I waited a heartbeat. I was too scared to breathe. "You know I'm right."

Mason was locked in a stand-off against me. He knew I was right. I knew I was right. His intimidation could only go so far, especially with these girls. These four girls were at the top of their school. They were tough. They weren't afraid of getting dirty, and they were loyal to each other. If I didn't want to go to school with fear every day, I would have to stand on my own against them. Mason would be gone after a semester; then it'd just be me and Logan. I needed to do this now.

He sighed and leaned back. He grumbled, "This is bullshit, Sam."

Relief burst inside of me. It was overwhelming, and I almost slumped against him, but I kept myself sitting up. My thighs tightened around him and I sucked in a ragged breath. I couldn't believe it had been that easy.

But it wasn't.

He lifted his head and met the gazes of his friends, one by one. "But the girls are exiled." He turned to Nate. "Is that going to be a problem with you?"

Logan let loose a whoop, but covered it up with a cough. The wicked grin couldn't be hidden.

Nate groaned, "Fine. That's not a problem."

"You sure?" Mason asked, heated.

"I'm sure. Like I said, Parker's not an exclusive thing. Might be good if she starts to realize that sooner rather than later."

Mason looked across the table. "Is that a problem, Fischer? I know you and Jasmine hook up."

He lifted his hands in surrender. "No problem at all. I knew it'd come to this anyway." He gave him a crooked grin.

The two other guys nodded their agreement, and it was done. Just like that. Whatever Mason meant by exiled, the rest of the guys would follow through.

After another hour on the patio, I grew restless and needed a bathroom break. Mason looked up, silently asking if I needed him with me, but I shook my head. I needed to start handling the girls on my own; besides, I had spotted a few of my friends below us. Adam was there, and I knew Becky and her boyfriend wouldn't be far. I spotted Lily and Anne from the diner as well, so I wanted to say hello.

As I weaved through the crowd, I caught sight of Heather. She looked out of place. Her eyebrows were bunched together in confusion. Two guys stepped into her but she swung to the side and evaded their drunken steps. That was when she saw me and her face cleared of all anxiety.

"There you are."

As she drew close, I frowned. "Hi. What are you doing here?"

She was shoved forward from someone, but she rounded with a growl emanating deep from her throat. They were already gone. Her shoulders dropped and she turned back. "I wanted to make sure you were okay."

I continued to frown at her.

"I didn't know if you had told Mason and Logan about the Broudou siblings?"

"Oh yeah." It all flooded back to me, but I shrugged. "A lot happened that night. I haven't even gotten around to telling Mason about those guys."

"You haven't?" Her eyes went wide.

"Yeah." I grinned, ruefully, and led the way for the bathroom. "Like I said, a lot has happened."

"Like what?" Interest sparked in her.

"I'll tell you later, much later. It's a long story." We grew closer to the bathroom. I didn't want to use mine since Mason kept the doors locked during parties so I picked one in the basement. The downstairs was less crowded, and there wasn't a line. But the door opened and Parker led her group out of the room. They were headed upstairs, we were headed behind them.

It was a stale-mate as Parker careened to a halt. The rest of her group stopped with varying stages of hostility.

I gulped.

Parker stood and sneered at me, and her best friend Kate stepped to the side. The other two went to her other side, Jasmine and Natalie...I think?

Heather bristled next to me. "What are you looking at?"

Kate, who had a wiry body and snapping hazel eyes, skimmed her up and down. She had a similar sneer to her thin lips and brushed some of her dark brown hair back. While Parker was dressed in tight blue jeans, ripped at the knees, and a tight white top, her best friend was dressed in black. Her pants were a second skin and the top molded to her body. The other two had similar outfits, all tight, all slutty. Their bra straps were visible, except for Kate. She didn't seem to be wearing a bra. All of them had athletic bodies, with tight muscles, but I knew Heather could hold her own.

Kate advised against it. "Don't get involved, Jax."

She folded her arms. "You think that's ever stopped me before."

Natalie spoke up, flicking her long black hair over her shoulder at the same time, "Tate's back. Did you know that?"

Heather froze, her eyes went wide. Something that looked close to panic started to appear, but then she shook her head. Her own hostility showed now. "You're pissing me off. So what? Tate and I stopped being friends long ago, around the time she got friendly with you, Tommy P's."

"Tommy P's." Kate rolled her eyes. She folded her arms and stepped forward. She was the leader. "You seriously still call us that? We're not princesses anymore." Then her eyes slid to mine and hardened. "We're more like bullies now."

"Oh, jeez." Heather threw her hands up as curses spilled from her lips. "It's going to be like that?"

"Yeah," Kate snapped. Her eyes were heated. "So stay out of it."

Then an elbow was linked with mine, and she tugged me close. "No. I'm sick and tired of watching you guys do the same crap to other girls." Her chin hardened and she raised it a notch. "You've never gone after me so maybe it's my turn. Maybe if you're going after my friend, you're going to have to go after me too. And you might be surprised at how many friends I have at our school, friends that you don't even know about. How's that for fighting words?"

"Your funeral." Kate was cold as she raised an eyebrow, but then she stepped back. She commented under her breath as her friends circled around us, "Duly noted, Jax." Her eyes snapped to mine. "And thanks for the exile, bitch. You just made it worse."

Heather sucked in her breath as the four filed in a single line and went up the stairs. Once they were out of earshot, she whirled to me. "They were exiled?"

I nodded. That couldn't be good, I knew that much.

"Do you know what that means?"

I shook my head.

"They're out, Sam." Her hands gripped both of my arms and squeezed tight. "They're fully on the outs with the guys."

"What does that mean?"

"That means that they're not included with anything anymore. The guys are closing ranks and those girls," she jerked a thumb over her shoulder, "were the only girls they included in their group, but now they're on the outs. That means no talking to them, no sleeping with them, not even hanging out. The guys won't acknowledge them in the hallways or anywhere. Being exiled means that they're strangers to the guys. Oh. My. God. Mason did that?"

I gulped. That seemed harsh, excessively harsh. *But that's who Mason is...*

Heather started to jump up and down.

I'd never seen her so excited.

"You have no idea what this means, do you?"

I shook my head. "This was my life about five months ago."

"Yeah, but not for those four. This is awesome, Sam. Get excited. Your boy delivered a huge blow to them, and it's going to sting for a *long* time." A smile stretched from ear to ear over her face. "And you have no idea how many other girls hate those four in school. Those four just got a lot of enemies that can finally push back. You have no idea!"

"You said that you have friends at school?"

Heather stopped bouncing. Her smile fell flat. "Yeah, I lied about that. I've got a few, but most of my friends go to Roussou."

"What's wrong?"

She glanced over her shoulder and bit her lip. "I'm still getting comfortable with this crowd. I'm used to being considered the enemy."

"You came here for me?"

She gave me a fleeting smile. "Yep, so you're stuck with me now. Let's go."

I gestured to the bathroom. "I really do need to go."

"Okay." But she kept looking around.

"What are you doing, Heather?"

"Looking for new friends." Her eyes snapped with a warning. "We're going to need them if we're going against the Tommy P's."

"I thought you said there were a lot of girls who could push back now?"

"Doesn't mean they're going to help us." She gestured towards the pool table. "I'm going to be over there. I know a few of those girls from the short time I was on the tennis team. Kate hates tennis, if I'm remembering right, and I know a few of those girls hated her back." She shooed me away. "Hurry up with the bathroom. There are a lot of people you need to meet."

She sauntered towards a group that looked perfect with smooth golden hair, tanned bodies, and faces that could've been in magazines. Each of them seemed cautious as Heather approached them, but it wasn't long until the group had circled her; listening intently.

Heather would have no problem making friends. I remembered Mason's words when he said Heather Jax wasn't a normal girl. I was glad she had befriended me. My gut was telling me I'd need all the friends I could get, and making friends was not a skill I had.

I turned around, and found myself face to face with someone else. I scowled. "What are you doing here?"

Jeff rolled his shoulders back and stuck his fingers in his hair. The ends were sticking up, but he spiked it higher. He flashed me a grin. "What do you think? Too high?"

I crossed my arms over my chest. "Jeff."

"Alright, alright." He stuck his hands in his pockets and his shoulders hunched together. He looked even smaller, and he was skinny enough. "So what's up with you and Jax?"

My eyes narrowed. "You know Heather?"

"Been to her place a few times."

There it was again, his same vague answers that I heard for three years. "Jeff," I warned. I didn't have time for his games. I needed to be making friends. No, I had to pee first.

"Okay, okay." He chuckled, "I come to you as a friend."

"You aren't anything else."

He frowned. "I know. You don't have to sound so happy about that."

"You cheated on me. For two years."

He lifted a shoulder in an easygoing shrug. "Bygones. I thought we made peace."

"I thought so too."

He studied me for a moment and then smirked, laughing some more. "Okay. I got it. No games, but seriously, how do you know Jax?"

"I work at Manny's." I frowned. "I thought you knew that."

"I didn't. Things make sense now."

I was growing tired of the conversation, but I knew something was wrong. He was stalling. "Are you going to tell me what you want or not? I just got served papers from the Tommy Princesses. Heather and I have to scramble so I don't get my ass handed to me at school."

"You?" His grin turned into a leer and he looked me up and down. "You can take 'em."

"There are four of them."

He shrugged again. "You could still take 'em. I heard about your rumble with Tate at that cabin party. You're tougher than you look. I think its cause you've got runners' legs. Might look stringy, but damn there are muscles there. If anything, you could just run in circles or run away. They won't catch you."

"Not helping," I growled before I started to move past him. He had wasted enough of my time.

"Okay, hey, hey. Stop. Please." He backtracked in front of me with his hands held in the air. I started another way, but he blocked me. "Please, Sam. I'm embarrassed about this and I don't know who else to talk to. You and me are different."

"I know. There is no 'you and me.'"

He scratched at his head. "No, I mean you're different than all the other girls. I know you and me weren't a good thing—"

My eyebrow arched.

He amended, "—and by that I mean to say that I wasn't good in a relationship. I'm still not good in a relationship."

"Wait." Wariness came over me now. "Are you still dating Jessica?"

His hand fell to his side with a thump. "Are you kidding? She's dating some wrestler from community college."

And from how he looked away, I knew there was more to it. I guessed, "And she's cheating on him with you?"

He looked down at the floor.

"Do you not learn, Jeff? My god." I wanted to wring his neck, but I needed to make myself clear. "Whatever you're going to ask of me, there will be no Jessica or Lydia attached at your hip. I mean it. You go back and forth with Jessica. I have no idea why, but I won't have her in my life again. I am done with both of them."

"I'm done with them too. I mean it. And that isn't what this is about. I promise."

I heard the insistency in his tone. I wanted to walk away from him, the guy deserved it after what he had done to me, but my feet didn't move. Then I realized what I heard, there was also desperation in him. And something that sounded close to...agony? When I looked again, I was seeing a different Jeff. He'd been a sarcastic badboy, but there was something new now. Vulnerability.

"What do you want?" I folded, but I was cursing at myself in my head.

A grin flared before he nodded, somber again. "Okay. So, we both know our history. I cheat on every girl I date. But I've met someone new."

I already knew where he was going with this. "And you don't want to do that to her?"

He nodded.

"You don't want to cheat on her?"

He nodded again, more eager.

"And you want to be the good guy she thinks you are?"

"Yeah! See you're perfect for this. It's like you know me."

I smacked him in the back of his head. "Because I do and you're not that guy. You cheat, that's what you do. Stop cheating and your problem is solved. Stop wasting my time. I have a mission."

"What mission?"

"I need friends. I have to make friends."

"I'm your friend."

"No, you're not. You're my ex boyfriend. We're not friends."

I started to leave again, but he darted in front. "Hear me out, please."

I growled at him.

"I will help you with your mission."

"You will?" Suspicion slammed against my chest. "How?"

"I know a lot of these girls. I cheated on you, a lot."

I growled at him again.

"You help me learn how to be a good boyfriend and I'll rally some girls to look out for you at your new school."

The suspicion lessened a little. "You heard about that, huh?"

"Everybody did. It's big news when Kade's girl won't be going to our school anymore. The Elite are crestfallen. They can't use you to get to them."

I frowned. "I thought they gave up on that long ago."

He shrugged. "I heard they were regrouping. Miranda's the leader again. She's preaching against any girl who sleeps with Logan Kade again."

I shook my head. "Will she never learn?"

"Who cares. Their funerals if they want to mess with the Kades again. Being burned by being a hypocritical bitch didn't teach her a lesson. Who's to stop her from getting burned again?" He winked at me with a devilish smirk.

"I didn't know you weren't such a fan of Miranda Stewart's?"

He glanced away as his shoulders tensed. "A lot's been going on you don't know about."

"Like what?"

"Look, will you help me learn how to not cheat? I'll get those girls to help you, promise. I'm good for that. I mean it."

"There will be no 'us' anymore. We're clear on that?"

Horror flared in his eyes before he shook his head, grimacing. "You think I want to get killed? No way in hell do I want to mess with either of those Kades." Then his face transformed. The same devilish look came back and he turned into the smooth Casanova I knew he could become. "I wouldn't mind meeting Logan Kade, though. I like to think of myself as an apprentice of his. We're cut from the same cloth."

"The same cloth?"

"Yeah." At my disbelief, he nodded again. "With the ladies. They love us."

"Logan had a serious girlfriend one time."

"He did?"

"You want to know how he handled that and his 'ladies'?"

He leaned forward. "I'm eager to learn. Yeah, how'd he handle having a relationship?"

"He didn't cheat on her." I grabbed his shirt and yanked him out of the way. Then I smacked him on the back of his head again. "Problem solved. Now go away."

As I pushed through the crowd, he called after me, "That doesn't help me, but fine. I'll hold up my side of the bargain, Sam. You'll see and then you'll help me! I know you will."

"Idiot," I mumbled under my breath.

CHAPTER TWENTY-SEVEN

"You did this!" she screamed at me. Her hands were raised, and she didn't look right. I gulped for breath. I couldn't breathe. My chest hurt, why did it hurt so much? But I couldn't tear my eyes away from her.

I whimpered, "Mom?"

She shook her head from side to side. She kept going, faster and faster, until she slid down the wall stopping in a huddle on the floor. She curled into a ball and rocked herself as her head kept shaking.

Oh god. I fell to my knees beside her. "Mom?" This wasn't right. I knew this wasn't right, but I didn't know what to do. "Please say something, mom."

Her hand twitched on her leg. Her head whipped up, and she hissed before she launched herself at me.

I jerked awake. My heart was pounding.

It was hot, too hot. I kicked at the covers so I could feel some cool air, and then I took deep breaths. I needed to calm down. My heart kept racing. It wouldn't stop. Easing to the edge of the bed, I pressed my forehead between my legs and gulped for more oxygen. My hands were clammy. My forehead was wet from sweat, the same sweat that I felt over the rest of my body.

Mason moaned next to me and I held still. I didn't want to wake him up. Slowly, inch by inch, I eased out of the bed but tripped as I reached for a robe on the couch. Catching myself before I fell all the way to the floor, I gritted my teeth and waited until my legs felt sturdier. I put on one of his

TIJAN

sweatshirts and his sweatpants. Safe. I took another breath and felt my pulse slowing down. I felt better.

But I shook my head. I couldn't get her out of there. Flashes of my mother kept coming at me and I wanted to stop remembering that night. Even thinking about it made my heart start pounding again. I pressed a finger against my neck and felt my vein pulsating.

I was in a nightmare. She was always there now. Every time I closed my eyes, that night was there and I remembered the attack. I clenched my teeth together and clasped my eyes shut. I couldn't—I wouldn't. Not again.

Mason rolled over in bed. His hand started to reach for me, but he tucked it under his pillow. The sheet slipped down to his waist. His shoulders bulged as both of his arms were curled under his pillow. The movement set his shoulder blades out and his back tapered down to where the sheet had fallen, over his narrow waist.

I'd never get enough of him. I knew that, then and there, and a pang of guilt speared me.

He wasn't living with his dad because of me. I had come between them, and Mason would be gone after a semester. My stomach shook at that reminder so I focused on the year after. It'd be me and Logan, all alone.

It wasn't a viable option for Logan and me to live at Nate's for the next year. Mason wouldn't want that. I wouldn't even want that, so what then? And Helen? I knew she wouldn't accept this situation. I would bet money that she already had some plan concocted. She would want Logan to move back with her in L.A. or she would come here and he would live in her house.

Not me. I was alone. Every scenario ended with me being alone.

No mother. No father, neither of them. Something wet fell on my cheek and I brushed it away. I was so stupid. Why was I crying? But I was. I huddled back in the chair and lifted my legs. Pressing them against my chest, I wrapped my arms around them and drew in a shuddering breath.

748

I had to make the situation better.

I had to fix things.

My stomach dropped. I knew what I had to do.

I grabbed my phone and texted her. Then I waited with my heart pounding, but it wasn't long. I got the response within a minute and it was settled.

With lead in my gut, I got up and slipped on some shoes, and then I turned and headed out the door.

When I stepped into the Kade foyer, everything was dark and my heart skipped a beat. Maybe she wasn't there? A part of me didn't want her to be there, but I heard her move and my heart skipped over another beat.

There she was. She was in a chair at the table. The moonlight filtered in through the large windows behind her.

She spoke first, as if nothing happened. "Hello, Samantha."

I scowled, but hid it in the next breath. "Hello."

"No mother? No Analise? What have we come to?"

I readied myself. "So bright and cheery, it's like you've never done a thing to hurt me or my family."

She sucked in her breath. "It was my family too."

"No, mom. Your family is yourself, maybe James since he hasn't left you. But I doubt that'll last. You'll do something to push him away. You'll cheat on him, kill his baby, attack him even."

"You watch your words." Her tone was stone cold. "Right now."

"Fine."

"Fine."

A moment of silence passed between us, but there was so much I wanted to say.

"So you called me for this meeting," she prompted me.

My heart went flat. I couldn't say what I wanted to say, not to her. She wouldn't listen. She would defend. She would attack. She'd never listen so I sighed in surrender. "I want you to agree that you'll stay away from me."

"If?"

"What?"

She leaned forward. Her eyes sparkled in the moonlight, and I saw the rage in there again. It was contained now, for the moment. I wondered when it would come out again. Then she sighed from irritation. "You came to me. You want me to stay away from you. I'm guessing there's something that'll come after that. You want me to stay away from you if...if what? If you come back? If you move in with David? What's the if? What do you want, darling child of mine?"

"For one, never refer to me as that again. It'll be like we're not related. Do you understand?"

"Crystal."

I winced. A knife slipped inside of me with that one word, with the chilling tone of her voice. I tried to ignore the pain. I was the one who needed to act like we weren't family. I needed to forget her, forget that she had ever been my mother.

"Is that it?"

I could hear the rolling of her eyes. I gritted my teeth against it. "I think James is a good man."

"He is."

Her dark silhouette straightened in the chair. There was pride in her voice now.

I added, "Mason and Logan will not move back in with their father unless I come too. You know that and James knows that. And you know that James wants them here."

She murmured, softly, "He loves them very much."

My teeth gritted together. She didn't get to act like she cared. "Stop. Just stop. They're not your boys. They're not your family. You are lucky to have their father love you, but they will never accept you." I drew in a shuddering breath. "They'll tolerate you, if I ask them to. Or they'll make your life hell, and after Mason heard his mom, he wants to. He's waiting for the chance to make you pay. I know the only reason he hasn't is because he's been worried about me." I leaned forward and placed my elbows on the table. It was cold against my skin. Goosebumps slithered up and down my arms. "So I have a proposition for you."

I waited as she sat there. I waited for her reaction.

"What?" She lifted her shoulders, her tone snippy.

Anger exploded in me. I wanted to reach across the table and grab her. I wanted to slam her head down, and I wanted to keep doing it until she cared. But she never would. So I sat there, and I counted to ten for patience.

When I felt something resembling it, I waited another ten, and then started, "I will move back in if you agree that there is no relationship between us. We will live in the same home, but that's it. I'm no longer your daughter. You're no longer my mother. You have no say with me, whatsoever." I tried to ignore the pounding in my chest. "When I spend time with David, you will say nothing. You will do nothing."

Her mouth tightened.

I didn't care. "When and if I go to Boston to see Garrett, you will say nothing. You will do nothing. It's as if I'm not even your child. I will only be your future stepson's girlfriend, who lives here. That's it. And you won't say a word about this to James. If you do," a layer of tears rested over my eyes. They were ready to fall, but I kept going in a hoarse whisper, "if you say a word, I will allow Mason and Logan free reign on you. They can do anything to you that they want."

As she paled, a sick darkness started in me. It grew as I continued, "They won't just hurt you. They'll take him away from you."

Her eyes closed. Her arms started to tremble so she wrapped the ends of her nightgown around her. She seemed so tiny in that moment.

Again, I didn't care. I murmured, "You know what I'm saying is true. You have manipulated everyone in your life, and you have hurt everyone in your life. There's a trail of damage behind you, to me, to David, to Garrett, to whoever impregnated you." A wall of ice was forming around my heart. "You are manipulating James. You should leave him because you're hurting him."

"I'm not," she whispered.

"He lost his sons over you. Because of you, he threw them out."

Her hand jerked up and she flicked a tear away. "I didn't mean for him to lose them. I didn't, Sam. I just wanted respect—"

"You wanted control," I hissed as my hands curled around the edge of the table. I clung to it, holding myself back. I had to keep it together until I could leave. Then I would collapse, but until then, I fought for my own control. "You wanted Mason away from me because someone else would love me."

"No," she whimpered. Her head fell down.

I nodded, to myself. A deep sob hitched in my voice, "Someone else would be there for me, and I would leave you. That's what all of this was about. Wasn't it?"

I waited. She didn't answer.

"Wasn't it?" My voice rose.

She shook her head, but she whispered, "It all went so fast. I couldn't control it. It spiraled out, and I couldn't stop it." More tears fell, and she sobbed. "I couldn't handle it. What they did to me, what I saw them doing to you. They were taking you away from me. They were making me look like the bad guy, and then David and Garrett were there. They both wanted you in their lives, I couldn't handle it. I can't lose my only daughter—"

I almost stood, but clamped down on the chair. I willed myself to remain there. I needed to hear her submission.

She kept going, broken before me. "You're mine, Samantha!" Her eyes snapped open.

I saw her madness in them, but it didn't scare me anymore.

She spat out, "No one can take you away from me. No one can touch you—"

"I'm already gone."

She stopped as she gasped for breath.

"I'm gone. I don't care about you. You've killed every last inch of love I might've had for you. You tried to make things right before, but you couldn't even do that. You called Garrett and told him about me. You were trying to be a good mother to me. But you couldn't handle it, could you?"

"You're my baby. No one can have you." Her lip wobbled as more tears streamed down. "It was wrong to call Garrett. He shouldn't have ever known about you. And David..." She sighed and looked away. "He only stayed with me because of you. He left me once, did you know that?"

I nodded.

"Dad?" I pushed open their bedroom door.

The memory jarred me, but she didn't notice. Her eyes were downcast again. Her voice sounded distant to me. "What I did to you was wrong. What I did to your brother and sister was wrong, but I couldn't lose him. He knew that I had cheated. I couldn't keep the evidence."

My eyes went wide. That's what they were to her? Evidence?

"But I couldn't think about them—they weren't like how you were to me. I knew I was pregnant so I brought it up to David. We'd been together a lot more around that time, and we were always unprotected. He thought I was on birth control, but I stopped. I wasn't thinking right." Her voice lowered to a raspy sound. "I never knew he couldn't have kids. He never told me until that night. He said that I told him in the beginning I would never want any more children, that one was enough, so he never thought about it."

It was my worst nightmare come true.

"We fought that night. Later, I walked in on him packing a suitcase. I went crazy. I started throwing things. I threw his clothes everywhere. He couldn't go. He couldn't leave me." Her shoulders started to shake. She buried her head in her hands and more sobs came out. "I couldn't lose him, but he left anyway. He said that he hadn't signed up for that. I didn't know where he went. I kept calling and calling, but he never picked up. Then I found his phone, he had left his phone on the counter in the kitchen. I had nowhere to call, no one to help me. I thought it was the only thing I could do. No one wanted me. I couldn't lose David; I was still in love with him then."

I was frozen in my chair. I couldn't look away, but I couldn't keep hearing this. I didn't want to know, even though I already did know. It was the worst night of my life, unfolding before me again. I couldn't stop it. A part of me didn't want to; I needed to know everything so it made sense. Some of it had to make sense. Some of it had to be for some reason.

As she dissolved into tears, I ripped out, "And when you came back? What then?"

She sucked in her breath and lifted horrified eyes to me. They were bleak and empty. Her makeup was smudged around her. They formed black rings around her eyes and she shook her head. Her lip trembled again, but then she bit down on it. She sucked in her breath. Her chest tightened. Her shoulders lifted, and she kept shaking her head.

I closed my eyes.

She started again in a deep voice, "I didn't know what I was doing." No. That wasn't right. I shook my head, ready to tell her that when she added, "I was wrong that night. I killed my children inside of me and you were taking care of me. I was grieving, Sam, and I was keeping it a secret. I knew what they thought. They wanted me to go to counseling, but it wasn't my life that I wanted to end. It was theirs, but then you were there and they weren't. They said if I killed you, they'd come back."

I gulped and doubled over. Scorching pain ripped through me. It was as if she threw a pot of boiling water on me, drenching me. I couldn't breathe.

Her voice sounded strangled. "I went mad, Samantha. I knew it was wrong, but I kept hurting you. I forced myself to stop. I had to. I knew they wouldn't come back, and they told me that they'd leave me again if I didn't stop hitting you."

Oh god. She *heard* them? "You talked to them?"

Her face was closed off to me. She seemed void from all emotion. "I know they weren't real. I know I was imagining them standing there. But they comforted me. They still loved me, even though I killed them. That couldn't be imaginary, could it?"

"And that's why you stopped?"

She lifted a shoulder in a shrug. It was so easy for her. Hurting her child was something to shrug about. I couldn't believe her. Who was this woman? Then I asked, gutted, "Did you ever love me?"

She frowned. "Of course, honey."

"But—what?"

Then she looked away as her eyes grew vacant. The distant expression came over her and her voice softened. "I did two horrible things to both of my babies. I hurt them and I hurt you, but I learned from both mistakes. I will never have children again. James is my life now. I am dedicated to becoming a good wife to him, the best wife I could possibly be, and I know he misses his boys. I know I'm the reason they're not with him. It's why I responded to your text message. I knew you wanted a compromise."

She was insane. I had no other thoughts. This was my mother? This was a stranger.

She nodded, satisfied now. "I'll do as you say. You can move back in. I'll stay away. I will only focus on James and being his wife. I will stay away from you, and from Mason and Logan. You're right. They should be with their father. James feels the same. He wants his boys back. He knows he can't stop your relationship with Mason. You can all live here. That's fine with us."

Madness. That was all I could think as I gaped at this woman, but then I cleared my head. I still needed answers.

"I remember being questioned by social services, but I was never taken from you." I never remembered being in the hospital. "Why not?"

Another shrug. Again. "You told them that some girls from school came to the house, and that I found you like that. I supported your story and David never knew. He suspected. I knew that, but I never hurt you again. I put it all behind me and we were fine for years after that."

"Until you started cheating on him. Again."

She nodded, but didn't respond. It wasn't worth commenting about.

I couldn't believe it. I couldn't believe her. "What about Garrett? What did you threaten him with?"

"Oh." A smile this time. For some reason, he got a smile while I seemed an after-thought to her. "I didn't say much, but I told him I would make you hate him. He didn't believe me, so I went and visited his ex-wife. I told her Garrett still loved her and he loved her when he was with me. I told her all about Helen and made her sound so evil that she'd never allow him to go back to her; therefore he wouldn't be allowed to see you. It worked." She grinned to herself and chuckled even. "I didn't think it would work, but I guess it did. He hasn't even called for you, Samantha."

A shiver ran down my spine as she said my name.

Before I could launch myself at her and do to her what she had done to me, I shoved back the chair. I couldn't feel my legs. I couldn't feel anything. I blinked and then turned away. I didn't remember leaving the house, but I stopped in the driveway. I had driven my car. James was standing beside it in his pajamas and a robe. He was frowning at my car with the morning paper in his hand. When he looked up, his frown deepened. The sun had started to rise, I wasn't sure the time, but I knew it was early.

"Mason and Logan will never move back without me." My own voice jarred me. It sounded haunted. "And Helen would make Logan leave, you know that."

His frown only deepened further.

"I fixed it. I'll move back in here with them."

His eyes grew bleak.

I kept going as my chest tightened, "I won't let them hurt her either."

He rasped out, "They won't do it."

"I'll make them do it."

Then he nodded and looked away. "I'm sorry, Samantha, I'm sorry for everything you've gone through."

I frowned. Why was he saying this to me?

"I love your mother very much and I want to help her. I can't help my family anymore, and I can't help my marriage anymore. It was my fault that Helen left me. It was my fault my family was torn apart. I won't let that happen again. I can help your mother. I really can, and I'm going to. I love her and I'm going to stay with her, no matter what."

He had no idea what he was getting himself into, but I kept my mouth shut. It was his life. It was his decision.

She'd make him miserable.

I didn't get in my car. I ran home instead.

CHAPTER
TWENTY-EIGHT

"**Y**our shift's over." Heather smacked a towel on my butt. When I turned around to glare, she gave me a crooked grin and wiggled her eyebrows. "Your dreamboat's here anyway."

Oh.

The fight in me subsided. I was ready to argue with her since it wasn't closing and I hadn't worked Friday, but when I looked over, all of that turned into a gushy mess. Mason had stepped through the door with a look of intent on his face. That made me pause. As he made his way through the tables to our back corner, I couldn't tear my eyes away. Confidence and power rippled from him. I couldn't fault the other girls who stopped and watched him as well. He was beautiful.

"Disgusting." Heather shook her head. "You're both disgusting."

"He's early. Did you call him?"

"I might've." She winked at me before she grabbed the next plate of food and put on the window, ready to be served. "But can you really blame me? It's your first day at FCP tomorrow. You're going to need all the rest you can muster when you're with that hunk-o-rama over there."

"Thanks, Heather."

She flashed me a blinding smile. "Just give me a heads up when you decide to tell them about our visitors the other night." She gave me a pointed look and I knew she was referencing the Broudou siblings.

She wanted me tell Mason now, better to get it over than deal with his anger about why he hadn't been told sooner. I had a different idea and I wanted to embark on one battle

758

at a time. Convincing Mason and Logan to move back in with their father had been a big enough battle. It took me all weekend, and I still didn't have an answer. But as he stepped closer and caught my hand, he gave me a look as if to say, 'I hope you know what you're doing.' He shook his head. "Fine. We'll move back in."

"Really?" I started to launch myself at him.

He caught my arms and held me back. "But it's only because you're right about Logan."

I chuckled. I had called it. Helen called both of them the next day. She said they had two choices, live in Los Angeles with her or she would move back to Fallen Crest. Those were her two options and when I argued with Mason that Logan living with her our senior year would leave me without a home, he started to soften. I knew he was doing it for me.

"Thank you," I murmured as I tipped my head back for his lips.

He groaned, "You're going to be the death of me. I'm doing all this nice shit for you."

I pointed to my lips, still puckered and waiting.

With a soft chuckle, he touched his to mine and I was swept up. Squealing from surprise, he wrapped his arms around my waist and lifted me high. My legs swung up and I was thrown over his shoulder.

"Mason!"

He slapped my butt. "Logan's ordered the pizza. If we're not back in twenty minutes, he won't hear the end of it. He's got it timed within the minute."

Only Logan would time something like that. I wiggled to get free. "Come on. Let me go."

"Nope." He turned around. "Can you clock her out, Jax?"

We heard from the back, "Will do! Don't make babies."

Mason shuddered underneath me. I remembered the look on his face when I told him I was late for work and giggled. He slapped my butt again. "That wasn't funny. I aged an entire year that day."

Serves him right after this. "Come on, let me go. Please."

"Nope." And he didn't, not when he marched to his car and put me inside. He even strapped my seat belt on and off when we turned into the driveway to Nate's home. When he stopped the car and rounded to my side, I jumped out before he could grab me. I started to run for the door, but it didn't matter. Mason had me in two steps, and I was slung back over his shoulder.

"Mason! This is enough."

"Logan said to carry you home so I have to carry you home. He's very excited for something."

"For pizza?"

Mason shrugged underneath me. His arm tightened around my legs as he walked over the front patio. "I have no idea. You know him. The stupidest ideas are adventures to him."

"But—"

But then he shoved the door open and swung around. A chorus burst out, "SURPRISE!" And my mouth fell open as I lifted my head to gape at the crowd in the center area.

Logan was in front with his arms outstretched. "Happy birthday, Sam!"

Becky waved from behind him. "It's a week early, isn't it?"

"Oh my god!" I pounded Mason on the back. He chuckled as he flipped me back in his arms, and then lowered me to the ground. All the blood had rushed to my head so he kept me against his chest. His hands held me by my hips, but I could only look at the group they assembled.

Becky and Raz, who had a glazed look in his eyes.

Adam. He grinned and gave me a small wave. "Can you believe they even invited me?"

I grinned but looked around some more. I relaxed as I saw most of the Academy Elite hadn't been invited, but Mark had been. I tensed a bit, just a bit, at the reminder that he thought his mom was going to marry David sooner rather than later. But then I tensed even more. They could've gotten married by now. David and my mom had been divorced, for...I wasn't sure. I hadn't asked either of them about the divorce. I didn't want to know.

Mark nodded his head towards me. "Hiya, Sam. I asked to tag along. I hope that's okay with you."

"Sure..." It wasn't like we were family...or were we? Was David still family to me? I wasn't sure anymore.

Then Lily gave me an excited wave with a smile that stretched from ear to ear. "Surprise! I bet you thought you didn't have to deal with me, but nope. Here I am. It's my night off and I'm ready for some birthday cake."

"You're welcome to my piece." Then I leaned back and asked, "Did Logan get cake?"

Mason's hand tightened around my hips. His thumbs started to rub up and down. "Of course. A birthday party without cake is a crime to Logan."

"Oh."

He grinned down at me. "You don't like cake?"

I shrugged. "It's an acquired taste."

He chuckled, shaking his head. "Pretend to eat a piece for him. I think he made it from scratch."

"I'll eat two pieces."

"Happy birthday, Sam," Nate called out as he started over.

"Hell no! I get her first." Logan shot forward and plucked me from his brother. He threw me over his shoulder and turned back to the group. "Everyone gets to spank her except Mason. He does that all the time."

He bounded to the kitchen and I looked up in time to see Nate and Mason share a grin, both shaking their heads. As Nate lifted a hand to put on Mason's shoulder, Logan turned the corner. I couldn't see anymore, but he deposited me in a stool at the counter. A large white cake sat in front of me with eighteen candles on top. None of them had been lit, but then I peered closer.

"Logan!"

"What?" He'd been waiting for my reaction, brimming with excitement. "Don't you like it?"

Those candles didn't look right. "Tell me those are not joints." Please tell me they aren't.

He started laughing. As he continued, the laughing got louder and louder. Then Becky's boyfriend bounced to the cake and pulled them out. He wiped each clean and put them back in a baggie as he gave me a sheepish look. "He thought it'd be funny." He looked like he had more to say, but then he smiled and snuck back to Becky's side.

"I'm sorry," she murmured.

Logan was still laughing. "That would've been awesome."

"Too bad you haven't gotten tested for basketball season yet," Nate noted as he and Mason rounded to the other side of the counter.

A wistful sigh left Logan. "Tell me about it."

Nate flashed him a grin and for a moment, I didn't see the tension between the two anymore. What had changed? When I caught Mason's gaze, I made a mental note to ask him, but was distracted as he gave me a heated look, dark promises in his depths.

My eyes widened. A jolt of desire burst through me, and I clenched my legs together. It was my birthday party. A private party would have to wait a few hours. I licked my lips as I thought about it.

He smirked back at me, our gazes locked together.

Then Nate spoke up, "This is also a farewell party too, a small one. Since you three are moving back home."

Logan's smirk turned smug.

And I knew why the tension had been lifted between the two. Mason was now home, with Logan and me. Nate couldn't move in with us. Though, I bet he would've.

"Thanks for letting me stay here."

"Any time, Sam. I mean it."

His words sounded genuine so my smile turned genuine as well. Maybe the old fearsome foursome would come back with the move. I had missed it.

Lily moved next to me as Logan started to cut the cake. She gave me a small hug. "Heather and the rest of the staff are coming after closing."

"That's late. Are you sure they want to do that?"

She shrugged with a delighted spark. "I think Heather said they were going to close early. She said you're worth it."

I was taken aback. That was a lot of money since the diner was full every night now. The gesture spoke volumes to me and for a moment, I couldn't speak.

Then she started giggling beside me.

"What?"

She pointed at the cake. Logan hadn't cut the cake in small sections. He cut it into the exact amount of pieces needed. There were nine people there, so the cake was cut into nine large pieces. Six of the pieces were double in size and he delivered those to the guys. The last three were smaller, but still bigger than I wanted.

Lily groaned as she took hers. "I gained five pounds just looking at that thing."

"You gotta eat it!" Logan barked before he raised his hands again. "Okay, everyone! I have an important announcement to make." He grinned to himself. "Today is not Samantha's birthday." He pretended to wave off any boos. "I know, I know. This is a shock of a lifetime to you, but we'll get over it. We'll band together and we'll make do. Raz, where are the joints?"

"Logan!"

His grin doubled and two dimples appeared. "Okay, okay. In all seriousness, we did this a week early to shock Sam's panties off her. Which my big brother will be doing tonight." He lifted an eyebrow to Mason.

"Logan."

He continued, "But anyway, I'm doing the speech because I baked the cake, with all sorts of natural goodies." He pretended to scowl. "I wasn't allowed any of the fun stuff, but whatever. We'll get over it. Peace and prosperity, right Raz?"

"Right." A fist was thrust in the air.

Logan laughed to himself, but then a somber expression came over him. The jokes were done and he lifted his piece of cake to me. "Happy birthday, Samantha. I love you. You're going to be my stepsister and maybe my sister-in-law someday, but until those days come, you already know you're family. And I think I can speak for everyone in saying, you're going to get wasted tonight!"

He lifted his cake in the air. "Salute to Sam getting wasted!"

Everyone saluted. Then they tried their best to sing the birthday song to me, which was interspersed with Logan and Mark rapping "In Da Club" in the background.

I shook my head. My throat was thick with emotion and I turned away. I wouldn't start crying, not again.

Two arms came around me, both slender and soft. Becky was on my right and Lily on my left. They gave me a hug, squeezing me with soft smiles. "Happy birthday, Sam."

"Thanks, guys." I patted both of them on their hands and looked down. I really felt the tears now.

The doorbell rang at that moment.

Logan went to answer and came back with five boxes of pizza. They were put on the table and the lids were flipped open. Steam rose from each of them. Paper plates, napkins, and plastic silverware were already on the table and he gestured to the table. "Dig in, guys."

Nate called out, "We've got beer, some soda...I think, and other drinks in the bar outside."

The guys went first. After they trailed outside to grab a drink, the three girls followed with our own plates full of food. Everyone had taken a seat around the tables as Nate turned into the bartender. He made sure everyone had a beverage. Logan hopped around to make sure none of them ran empty.

It was easy.

I hadn't expected it to be easy, but stories were shared. The guys joked and no one was ready to bite someone's head off. The guys congregated around the bar with easygoing grins. Even when Becky sat beside me, I was glad that she was there. She'd been a good friend at a time when I needed her. I hoped she would still be a friend, maybe not the one I thought she had been, but one nonetheless. Lily surprised me the most. She had a crude sense of humor with one-liners delivered at the perfect time. The rest of the Manny's staff joined us two hours later. Anne settled next to Lily and cackled together as Heather shook her head with a small grin on her face.

When Mason folded me into bed later, I grinned up at him and whispered how much the party meant to me.

He slid in beside me and pulled me close to him. He tucked his head behind me and took a deep breath. His hand flattened under my breast and he held me there, tight to him. Then he whispered back to me, his lips a soft caress against my neck, "We just love you. All of us."

"Everything will be fine," I murmured, sleepily. "You. Me. Logan. Even Nate. All of us. And Heather."

His body trembled behind me and his arms pulled me even closer to him. "Everything will be fine."

"You promise?" I smiled as I felt him kiss my neck.

"I promise."

"Even the families?"

"Even the families." His arms bulged around me and he rocked me back and forth. "Go to sleep, Samantha. We have school tomorrow."

"I love you, Mason."

He pressed another kiss to my neck, then to my shoulder blade. "I love you too. Now go to sleep."

"..o..kay..." And I did.

FALLEN CREST PUBLIC

Book 3

TIJAN

CHAPTER ONE

SAMANTHA

I woke to a hand sliding under my top and cupping my breast.

Mason!

Then I became aware of a very masculine and muscled thigh sliding between my legs and rolling me to my stomach. As he slid my tank's strap down, his lips went to my naked shoulder and nibbled on the back of my neck. Goosebumps broke out as I sucked in a breath. My legs pressed together, and a deep, strong throbbing started. It was pounding in a steady beat. As his lips moved down my spine, I gasped out loud. Arching my back for him, I was pressed against him. He was hard, but Mason didn't grunt, he didn't make a sound. Instead, his hand fell to my hip, and he pulled me even further into him. His hand caressed down my back and my tank top was bunched together into one tiny scrap of fabric. Slowly, so goddamn slowly, he pressed his chest to my back, but he was holding me up now.

I needed him now.

He slid my top up my back, trailing kisses on my spine as he did. When it was lifted over my head, I pushed up from the bed, pushing him upright with me at the same time. Enough. I couldn't handle it anymore. I needed more of him. We were now kneeling together. As the top fell to the floor, I reached behind me for him. I needed to taste him.

My hand slid around his neck to his hair, and I grabbed a fistful of it, taking a firm hold and anchoring him to me. He grunted now, grinding into me as his lips went to my ear. I could feel him smiling as his teeth took hold of it, sucking on it. Still holding me to him, one hand cupped my breast firmly while his other hand went to my underwear. They were pushed out of the way as he slid a finger inside me. Then a second.

"Mason," I wrenched out, turning my head for his lips.

A deep chuckle came from him as he nuzzled along my jawline, so achingly close to where I wanted him. I needed him inside of me. Now.

A shudder went through me.

God. I was already wet. The throbbing was pounding through me. To wake up like this, feeling him slowly rocking against me, I was almost panting.

His fingers pushed further inside of me, building a tempo, going slow. Leaning back into him, my hand fell to his and I urged him to go faster. It was building, but I needed it harder. Faster. His lips curved up as he nuzzled along my cheek. His other hand was rubbing over my breast, teasing me, and I fell against him. He was holding all of me up. I could barely kneel anymore, but I moved my head, searching for his lips. The desire was so blinding, but he wouldn't kiss me, and I growled in frustration. He chuckled as his lips nipped at the corner of my lips.

"More," I rasped out. "Now."

"More?"

A thrill went through me when I heard the thick lust in his voice. I wasn't the only one nearing combustion. He was barely holding back—I could tell—his hips were moving against me harder, faster. Then he started to bend me over. His hand left my breast and it cupped the side of my hip. He whispered against the back of my neck, "Hold onto the headboard."

Shit.

"Mason," I whimpered again. It was too much, but my hands grasped onto the headboard. My fingers curled around it, and I held on. I had no idea how. I was so focused on him, at how he was almost in me now. I could feel him through his boxers. His hand was still between my legs, but he pulled out. Instantly, I ached for him. I was too empty. I groaned in protest. "No..."

Then he was back. He had switched his angle now; he was firmly behind me. Urging my legs further apart, his fingers began pistoning in and out of me faster than before.

I was going crazy.

I needed him, all of him, and I began moving faster, riding his hand at the same time.

"Jeezus," he grunted over me, his mouth next to my ear.

A delicious shiver rushed through me as his breath caressed my skin.

"Now," I cried out, gritting my teeth.

His fingers kept ramming into me, sliding back and forth, going deeper until I wasn't sure they could go any deeper.

"Mason." I was panting now. Goddamn. "Please."

A deep guttural groan was my answer and his hand left me. His boxers were shoved down and in one smooth movement, he thrust deep inside of me.

Finally.

I closed my eyes and welcomed the heat. He was home now. We moved together, knowing each other's bodies so well. Turning my head to the side, his lips were there and they opened for me. I needed him. Sweeping my tongue against his lips, I tasted what was mine. He was mine. All of him was mine.

Bent over me, he held me anchored in place with a hand gripping my hip, but his other reached under me and took a firm hold of my breast. His thumb rubbed against my nipple. Shit. I gasped, pushing back into him so he'd go harder.

"Sam," he whispered against my lips.

I needed him to go faster. I couldn't handle it anymore and began to rock against him faster and faster.

"Shit," he gasped now, but he straightened. Both of his hands held onto my hips and he slammed into me, pushing me into the headboard now. I didn't care. My face was to the side now and I was gasping for breath. Some of my hair had fallen into my face so I couldn't see. The strands dipped into my mouth, but Mason moved them. They were tucked behind my ear and I was gasping for breath. He kept thrusting into me.

I was nearing.

I could feel it.

"Mason." A low groan came from the bottom of my throat.

I was right there.

Then, as his hands dug into my hips one last time, he emptied into me. I was right with him. My body shot over the edge and trembled as the waves rocked over me. He collapsed on my back and chuckled. His hand skimmed past my hip and he pushed off from the headboard. As our skin separated, he grunted.

I couldn't move. I hung onto the headboard, panting for breath. My body was still trembling as the waves kept coming.

"You okay?"

I shook my head. I couldn't even attempt to speak. I'd been weakened by that climax, but then he slid a hand in front of me and I was lifted into the air. Curling into him, my arms wound around his neck and my legs wrapped around his waist. His hands gripped my ass now as he moved from the bed. Mason carried me to the bathroom and tested the water before he stepped underneath. I hung onto him, clinging like a monkey as he washed his hair and then mine. When his fingers started to massage my scalp and he rinsed the shampoo from my hair, I closed my eyes. I enjoyed every last minute of his attention.

I loved him.

A feeling of contentment swept over me, and I could've hung onto him until next week. However, after washing both of us, he moved me back to the counter and I unhooked myself, giving him a rueful grin as he tossed me a towel.

When he started to dry himself off, I didn't do a thing. I just watched. My eyes drank in the sight of him.

Broad shoulders. Every muscle defined, all the way down to his abdominals and obliques. Even the muscles in his legs bulged and shifted as he bent low to dry the rest of him. A trim waist. Angular cheekbones. Luscious eyelashes that covered his emerald eyes and lips that a girl would die for. Not me. I just died to touch them and feel them against mine.

I let out a deep breath. I was addicted to him.

He grinned as his eyes darkened. He knew exactly what I was thinking or feeling. He asked, "Are you going to get ready?"

"Sure. When my legs can work again. What *was* that?"

"That," he moved closer, pulling the towel from me, "was the best way to start my last semester."

I flinched as if a cold bucket of water was dumped on me. Those words left me cold. Plucking the towel from him, I hopped off the counter and shoved past him to the bedroom.

"What's wrong?" He followed me.

"That was the best way to start your last semester?" I dried myself off and stopped to glare at him. Seriously? He was an idiot. "Screw you."

The corner of his mouth curved up. "You just did."

"Not funny, Mason."

He frowned and narrowed his eyes at me. "What's wrong?"

"You're leaving."

"Just to college. I'm not going forever."

I rolled my eyes and turned my back. *Says you, you big ass. Just to college. It's not that simple.*

"Wait, are you really mad at me?"

Ignoring him, I grabbed some underwear, jeans, a bra and a shirt. Stopping once, I glanced in the mirror to make sure I looked presentable—I'd do. My dark hair hadn't been cut so it fell below my shoulders. I'd twist it up in a braid later, but the jeans and shirt were snug. Good. I didn't care if every inch of me was on display. The jeans were washed out, but clung to me and my shirt was a simple long-sleeve white shirt. The front dipped low, giving a good view of my cleavage, and my black lace bra showed through the thin material, but I didn't care. *Mason was just going to college, my ass.* Still ignoring him, I grabbed my backpack and purse. Stuffing the purse inside of the bag, I brushed past him and headed downstairs. As I got into the kitchen, Logan was just putting the coffee pot back on the burner. He turned and stopped. Seeing me when I entered, his eyes went wide and a low wolf whistle came next.

"You're smoking, Sam." He gave me a wicked grin. "Mason must've pissed you off, huh?"

"I know I look pissed."

"Nah." He shook his head, his brown locks had been gelled to perfection. "You're smoking hot. I know you're mad because you got that cold as ice look in your eye you always get when you are, but that's not what I meant. You only come out looking hot as hell when my big bro's pissed you off." Checking his watch, he whistled again. "That was fast because I just heard you two going at it like wild animals."

Oh. Jeezus. Flushing, I ignored his comments and gestured to the coffee pot. "Are you going to start that?"

"Nope. It doesn't work."

This morning went from great to crap. "Oh."

Grabbing his keys, Logan dangled them at me. "But if we leave now, we can stop at The Quickie. I need to get gas anyway."

"Sold."

Mason was coming down the stairs as we moved past them. He was pulling his shirt down, and I tried not to watch the movement of his abdominals or how his jeans rode low on his narrow hips. He paused when he saw us. "Where are you guys going?"

My lips were pressed tight together, and Logan smirked from behind me. He shook his head. "Whatever you said must've been good. You pissed your woman off. Not a good move, not on the first day of the semester."

Wincing at how close his words hit the target, I gritted my teeth and shoved out the door.

Mason called after me, "Sam."

"What?"

He looked ready to say something else, glanced at Logan and closed his mouth.

It didn't matter. I didn't want to hear it. "The coffee pot's broken. I'm going with Logan to get some. Did you want some too? I can serve it to you, another thing to add to the 'best way to start your last semester.'" A ball of anger rolled over me.

"Come on..." An apology flashed in those emerald eyes of his.

"You said that?" Logan chuckled. "Dumb move, dipshit."

Moving closer to the door, Mason flashed a warning at his brother. "Give us a minute."

"What if I don't?"

He bared his teeth at him. "Not a request, *dipshit*." Then he shoved him and stepped closer to me. His hand fell to my arm, but he added to Logan, "March. I'll bring her."

Logan smirked at him. "We're going for coffee. Besides," he gestured inside the house, "you've gotta wait for your other girlfriend. His car's still blocked in from the party last night."

"People are still here? Where is he?"

He shrugged. "Nah, they all got rides home, but their cars are still here, and as for your girlfriend, I have no idea. Check his room. I think I heard Parker down there."

"Parker?"

"Yeah. Pretty sure I heard her voice from downstairs. I was headed down to see if he knew how to fix the coffee pot."

Mason cursed under his breath and twisted around. His hand fell from my arm. "He agreed to the exile."

"Guess it starts later today for him."

"Not helping."

"Not trying to," Logan sniped back.

"What is your problem?"

"With you? Nothing. With your other girlfriend, figure it out." Logan's eyes darkened, letting his anger show.

I held my breath. There hadn't been a lot of times when the two bickered, but I could tell that Logan was fed up. Not that I could hold it against him. I was getting fed up as well, but I knew that Mason hadn't let his friendship with his best friend affect our relationship. Not yet. As the two glared at each other, I stepped in between them. Softening my tone, I gestured to Logan's Escalade. "Let's go and get coffee."

Logan turned on his heel, his jaw rigid as he went to his vehicle.

Mason caught my wrist and held me back. "Are we okay?"

"Yeah," I sighed. I had already melted as soon as I saw his regret earlier. "It just sucks, Mason. You're leaving. You. Leaving. As in you're not going to be here on a daily basis anymore. I'm not the only one bothered by that." I jerked my head over my shoulder, where Logan had started the car and was waiting for me.

"That's not Nate's fault."

"No, but it's not the three of us or even the two of you anymore. Nate came back. This is Logan's last semester with you, but..." I gestured inside. "Your best friend gets you for the next four years, you know. You're leaving early for football."

He groaned and his head fell back. "Shit, I didn't even think of it that way."

I shrugged. "Anyway, I really want to get some coffee, and I have to talk to my coach. He said to come by his office this morning."

Mason's head lifted back up and he grinned, his eyes darkening as he tugged me close. "Coach Grath is lucky to have you. He knows that."

I was about say thanks, but then I stopped thinking. He bent closer to me. Closing my eyes, I felt his lips softly touch mine. One damn touch was all it took. A tingle began and the lust for him sparked again. I became heated as he deepened the kiss, and I burrowed closer to him.

BEEEEEP!

Jerking back, I twisted and glared at Logan, who still had his hand on the horn. He flashed me a grin, but hollered out the window, "Let's go! You can screw later."

"Idiot," Mason muttered under his breath.

"He's right. Go see Nate, see what's going on. I'll see you at school."

He nodded, but flipped off his brother. Logan's laugh was heard clearly and I gave Mason a quick wave as I got into the yellow Escalade.

Reversing the vehicle, Logan extended his middle finger in the rearview mirror and gunned the engine. He didn't pause when we got to the road. Clicking my seatbelt in place, I settled back in my seat. Logan liked to drive fast, but he had the reflexes to keep us safe, so I wasn't worried. I did comment, "All you had to do was say something to him, you know. Mason's a good brother to you."

He jerked in his seat. His face grim. "Yeah, well, it's easy for you to say. You're *supposed* to talk to him. You don't come across as bitching and whining."

"I said something."

"No."

"Yes." It was getting ridiculous. "You used to be friends with Nate."

"That was before he turned shady. I know he had Parker over last night."

"You said this morning."

"Last night. This morning. What's the difference? He still violated the exile. Mase won't forget that."

I heard the anger in his voice. It was low and underlining. Frowning, I asked, "Are you mad at Nate about something else? I thought it was just because he came back for his last semester."

Logan jerked a shoulder up, holding the steering wheel with one hand. "What does it matter? He's so far up Mason's ass, I'm surprised my dipshit brother could even hear you."

"Logan."

"It's true." But his voice lost some of the aggression. "Nate's not the same. Mason needs to know that."

"So just tell him."

"Why don't *you* tell him?" he shot back, throwing me a sidelong glance.

"Maybe I will."

Rolling his eyes, he looked back to the street. "Mase won't listen to you."

"Yes, he will."

"No, he won't."

"Mason's always listened to me."

"Things are going to go to shit. I know it."

I frowned, but the knot tightened again in my gut. As Logan turned into The Quickie, I agreed with him. This semester wasn't going to be an easy one.

For anybody.

CHAPTER TWO

When Logan turned into the gas station, I laughed when I saw who was sitting on the bench outside of Quickie's—Jeff. When we got out, a quick grin came over him and he stood up. His hands were pushed deep into his pants pockets and he rolled his shoulders back. His dark hair had been gelled, much the same as Logan's, and as he came closer, I saw the idol worship he had for the younger Kade.

"Hey."

Logan narrowed his eyes at him, but I asked, "What are you doing here?"

He jerked a shoulder up. "My car broke down."

I glanced at his phone. "Who were you going to call for a ride?"

"Not that girl I was telling you about on Friday. She hooked up with this guy Saturday." He gestured to Logan, who had started to reach for the gas nozzle.

"Me?"

"Yeah." Jeff lifted a corner of his mouth up. "No worries. I'm not heartbroken. At least I know what she's like now."

He looked ready to say more, but Logan interrupted after he started the gas, "I'm going in. You want your coffee?"

I nodded. "Thanks."

As he went inside, Jeff laughed to himself. "Man, I forgot how scary—" He stopped suddenly. His eyes darted past my shoulder and widened. I turned to see Mason's black Escalade pulling into the lot. He parked next to us, on the other side of the gas pump, and hopped out. When he came around, Jeff put a few feet between us. "Hey, man. How's it going?" His voice sounded strangled as he jerked a hand up and grabbed a fistful of his hair, making it spike even more.

Mason reached for the nozzle, but turned to me. "Logan's inside?"

I nodded. "Where's Nate?"

The corner of his mouth dipped down into a brief scowl. It was so quick—there and gone in the blink of an eye—but I caught it. No one else would've noticed it. That wasn't good. A knot tightened in my gut. "Did he have company?"

"No, but he did last night." Mason's tone was cold. I knew it wasn't because of me.

"Uh," Jeff's hand tightened on his hair, and he tried to give me a halfhearted grin. His other hand shoved down in his front jean pocket, and his shoulders hunched forward. "Maybe I should get going..."

"Did you call someone for a ride?"

Jeff's eyes darted back to Mason.

Even though he was filling his vehicle with gas and his back was turned to us, I knew he was listening. He was waiting for Jeff to leave.

"Did you?"

"Not yet, but since you're here..." His voice trailed off again. "Oh shit."

Two car doors slammed shut, but it wasn't the sound of them or the alarm that flitted over Jeff's face that sent alarms off in me.

It was Mason.

He wasn't moving. An unnatural stillness had come over him. His hand fell from the nozzle, and he stopped everything for a second. It was a small pause as he took a breath. It lasted only a second. Then his hand reached over and he flipped up the handle so the gas stopped. The nozzle was left in his vehicle as he walked forward.

Then I saw them.

Brett and Budd Broudou. They had gotten out of their car and one yelled inside it, "Hurry up, Shannon. We've only got twenty minutes and you're going to make us late."

She climbed out from the back seat, straightening her skirt so her ass didn't hang out. "Shut up, Brett. I'll take my time if I want to."

"No, you won't," Budd interjected. "Not unless you want to call for your own ride. You better piss here too. We're not stopping."

Her lips clamped shut, but if looks could kill.

Her older brother didn't care. He gave her a look of death right back. "Bitch."

"Screw you." Jerking forward, she tried to hurry inside but stopped and slowed to a casual walk. Her shirt had ridden up, showing a good dose of skin, including the top of her butt crack. Muttering under her breath, she reached up and pulled it back down. As both her brothers started laughing, she turned towards them, but stopped when she caught sight of us.

Mason was in front of his vehicle, a human wall between them and me. I knew he had done it on purpose, but I was surprised when Jeff took two steps and positioned himself in the same manner. He was facing them squarely with me right behind him.

I scooted to see what was going on, but Jeff moved with me. When I went to the right, he went to the right. "Stop. He doesn't want them to see you."

I started to protest, but remembered how Heather had acted when they were at Manny's. She'd been terrified. Heeding all of their warnings, I stayed put. If Budd recognized me from that night, he'd say something and that was still a conversation I needed to have with Mason.

Then Logan came out of the gas station. He had two coffees in hand with his head down, clueless of the Broudou brothers as he crossed the lot. There still hadn't been a word spoken between the brothers and Mason. Yet.

It was coming.

A shiver went down my spine.

Slipping my hand inside my pocket, I made sure my phone was there and pulled it out. If they made one violent move, I was calling 911. I wasn't going to risk them being hurt. Mason's future had already been threatened by Analise. It wasn't going to be threatened again.

Then it happened.

I gulped as I watched it in slow motion. Logan stepped forward, he frowned, and then lifted his head. His eyes found me first. He paused. His foot came down hard in mid-step and he glanced around. He saw Mason before he trailed his head where they were.

It was as if they'd been waiting for him to join.

Everything happened then, at the same time.

Shannon's features scrunched together in an ugly snarl. Her hands found her heavier hips and her arms pinched the sides of her breasts, making them rise from the motion. It was then when her brothers saw us too.

I jerked forward.

Mason shifted in front of his car, and Logan disappeared from my eyesight. I moved to see better, but Jeff moved with me, obscuring my view.

"Stop." I tried to push him aside.

He remained facing them, but his hand went behind him to touch my arm. "Get in the car, Sam."

"No."

He hissed, "Get in the car! Now."

"No."

They weren't going to do anything to them. They couldn't. Terror started to rise up, and the hair on the back of my neck stood up.

They couldn't hurt Mason or Logan.

Then a low baritone spoke up, "Kade."

The other one added, "Shannon, go inside and get your coffee."

"No!" she hissed. "I'm staying, Brett."

"What are you doing here, Budd?" Mason asked. I closed my eyes, falling against Logan's Escalade. He sounded in control, amused even, and a wave of relief went through me at the sound. That meant he was fully in control of the situation. "Quickie's is in Fallen Crest territory. Not Roussou."

"Sam," Jeff twisted around, his cheeks flushed from insistence. "Get inside."

"Who's that over there?"

I held my breath, and Jeff froze.

That was Budd speaking.

"What are you talking about?" Logan tried to sound casual.

One of them, probably Budd, snorted. "You're hiding someone. I heard you have a girlfriend, Mason. That true?"

"Is that her back there?" Brett added.

"You never answered my question." Mason's tone went cold as ice. "What are you doing here?"

A shrill, but cocky laugh came from them. "We don't live far from your butt-buddy's home. Remember? Quickie's is on the way to Roussou."

"That's right." Soft gravel was smashed down. Mason must've taken a step forward. His tone was full of quiet authority. "You have a farm a few miles away."

Logan let loose with a swift curse. "Forget that. This is Fallen Crest. What are you doing coming to this gas station?"

"Fuck off, Kade."

Mason spoke again, a lethal note in his voice, "This is our town. You're not welcome here."

"Last time you came around here, your cars exploded. Are you back for round two?"

I shook my head. That was enough; I had to see. I pushed forward, but Jeff caught me. His arms came around me, and he opened the door before lifting me inside.

"Jeff!"

"Stop." The serious warning in his voice made me pause. I hadn't heard that from him, not in a long time, and my eyes widened. There was a grave note in his usually jovial brown depths. They were as flat as the scowl that hadn't lifted from his face. His hand went and caught his hair, grabbing chunks of it again. "Just stop, Sam. Stay here."

I didn't say a word as he shut the door and then started forward. His hands went into his pockets and his skinny shoulders hunched down. I knew it was his 'I'm serious' walk. It used to excite me during the first year we dated, but it wasn't amusing anymore. My mouth went dry, and I sat back in the seat.

Jeff was serious. Jeff was never serious.

CHAPTER THREE

Through the car, I heard Mason's muffled voice. "Take your sister and leave."

Someone snorted. "Who's in the car?"

"Leave."

"Tsk, tsk, Mason. Your little bro is showing his cards. He must care for her as much as you do." The voice grew louder as if he'd stepped closer. "Come on, just between you and me. Your little bro loves her, too, doesn't he? At least, that's what I've heard."

Then there was silence. I had stopped breathing and clung to the car's upholstery. My fingers dug into the seat, and I couldn't move. It was like a nightmare coming to life. Then I heard a scream. That was it. Flinging open the door, I rushed out. Jeff caught me in the air. "Come on, Sam."

I heard another scream followed by a car's brakes and then a thud. Someone was on the ground. I knew it. "Let me go." I dug my nails into his arm.

"No." He cursed, flinching as I drew blood. "They left me to watch you. Stop it."

I dug harder, hard enough that he cried out in pain, and I was dropped. Scrambling up, I burst around Logan's car. Then I heaved to a stop. Mason and Logan were a united front, but Nate was there, too. All three stood next to each other, another human wall.

Someone was on the ground, and the girl cried out again, "Pick him up, Brett! You're so damn slow."

"Shut up, Shannon. Open the door."

The body was hoisted from the ground, but I couldn't see who it was anymore. A car door was slammed shut, then two more followed it. The car reversed and sped off as dirt kicked up from the tires. There was five seconds of silence before Logan threw his head back and howled in laughter. He clapped Nate on the shoulder. "I can't believe you did that."

Nate's shoulder tensed under his hand, but he shrugged. "Trying to make up. I've recently learned that I've been a dick lately."

"You have." Logan kept chuckling, turning to see me. "You missed it, Sam. Nate clipped Budd Broudou with his car."

Mason's eyes narrowed at Nate. "What were you going to do? You hopped out of your car like you were going to take a bat to him."

Nate shrugged again. A brief glimmer of regret crossed his face, but it was gone instantly. "I needed to make sure he stayed down...and to make sure that I won't get sued."

"He's down now. Don't worry, you just clipped him. Budd's a cockroach. They think a lawsuit is a pansy way to deal with a fight." Logan's hand was still on him, and he used it to push up from the ground in a semi-skip. His eyes sparked from giddiness. Before I knew what he was doing, he had rushed over to me, and I was thrown over his shoulder. "That was awesome, Sam. I can't believe you missed that. Shit. I'm horny."

"On that note." An arm slid underneath my waist and I was lifted from him. Mason slid me down his body and kept his arms around me. I wasn't inclined to leave his shelter. He spoke near my ear, a deep chuckle in his voice, "I'll be taking Sam with me to school."

"Whatever." Logan's grin widened. "I'm off then. Got something to do." He darted to his Escalade, stopping once to punch Jeff in the arm before he climbed in and took off.

"Ow! That hurt. Oh, Sam. Hey..."

I knew what he was going to ask and started to answer, but Mason beat me to it. "We'll give you a ride."

Jeff flashed a bright smile quickly before the stoic mask of coolness slid back into place. I shook my head. This would be interesting. Mason didn't wait around. He got into the front and I climbed into the passenger seat. Jeff got into the back. No one said a word as he turned onto the road leading to Fallen Crest Academy.

The irony didn't escape me—my boyfriend was driving my ex-boyfriend to my old school. A lot had changed in such a short amount of time.

"So, um," Jeff started, leaning forward, "how much does one of these cost, Mason?"

I turned to him. "Don't even start."

He frowned. "Just trying to be friendly."

"Not now."

"Oh." He remained quiet until Mason pulled into the Academy's parking lot. Just like when I went to school here, everyone looked up and saw whose black Escalade was there. They all watched like hungry vultures. It'd been a while since Mason Kade had graced my old school. I remembered their reactions then. The reaction now wasn't a surprise to me. When Jeff got out, everyone's mouths dropped open. When he hid a quick grin, I knew he loved the attention. He lifted a hand in the air. "Thanks, Mason!"

Mason ignored him and pulled away from the curb. "Why is your ex-boyfriend acting all buddy-buddy with me?"

"Because he wants to be cool."

"Is he trying to get you back?"

I snorted. That'd never happen, not even if I developed amnesia, but when he turned onto the road and drove past the front of the school, the comment died in my throat. Standing on the lush green lawn with two gym bags full of equipment at his feet was my father. Or no. David. He stared back at me, but I couldn't see his expression. Reflective sunglasses hid his eyes and his arms moved to cross over his chest. He was wearing a Fallen Crest Academy polo. I had seen him wear the same coach's wardrobe for years, but he looked different. He had bulked up. Gone was the healthy weight he kept while he'd been married to Analise and the twenty pounds he lost when she left him. The weight was back and more so.

Mason saw it, too. "Your dad looks ripped. Not bad for a guy his age."

I slunk down in my seat, ripping my eyes from David. "Whatever. It doesn't matter to me anymore."

It didn't. I wouldn't let it, but I was thankful for Mason's silence all the way to my new school.

When he wheeled into the lot, he headed to the back corner and parked in the slot beside Logan's vehicle. Strauss was rounding the back end of a rusted brown truck that was parked on the other side of Logan's, a book bag over his shoulder, where he met up with another guy. Both went over to the back of Logan's Escalade, where the others were already waiting.

I took in the crowds that were watching them. There were so many cliques. Each looked different, but they all looked the same. They were all students, but those guys were at the top. Cheerleaders. Preppies. Others dressed all in black, even black hair. A few guys lingered around a picnic table in the corner with sleeveless shirts, spiked hair, tattoos and chains.

I kept scanning the back end of the school, and saw a few girls giggling together, whispering and pointing at the books they were holding.

This wasn't Fallen Crest Academy where everyone wore the same uniforms, and the only thing that separated their image was how short the skirts were cropped or how tight the shirts were tied. The top of the food chain had been the Academy Elite, but they wouldn't have made it a day at this school.

Mason glanced over, shut his car off and leaned back. "What is it?"

"Nothing."

"Sam."

"What?"

"Look at me."

"This is my first day here." I hadn't been nervous before. I was now.

"You'll be fine."

"No." I turned to him, but I could see that all the girls had smoothed their hair back and sucked in their stomachs. If that was their response to Logan and the rest, what would it be when Mason stepped outside of his car? Or when they saw me beside him? "I was nothing before."

"Sam."

I looked away. I didn't want to see his green eyes darkened with pity. "Things aren't the same, Mason. People didn't know for the longest time that we were together, and that was only last semester. Analise and I moved in with you guys, and now I've moved out with you and Logan. Even David looks different, like he's a freaking bodybuilder or something. This isn't normal. Is it?"

I'd been a social outcast last semester. I had a feeling I'd be one here too.

I turned now to face him and held my breath. The green was sparkling at me, so clear and warm. One corner of his mouth curved up, and he leaned his head against the headrest. "Everything will be fine. At this school. At home. We're family, whether you like it or not. I thought you'd be used to it by now."

Looking through the window at how everyone was riveted by his friends, I knew I'd never get used to it. I shook my head and reached for my bag. "I'm afraid that when I get used to it, you and Logan will go away."

"We're not going away. You're not going away."

"I can't go back."

It was then a red Mazda parked close to the guys and the door was thrown open. A long tanned leg came out, followed by another. It was like in all the high school movies.

The beautiful golden-blonde emerging in slow motion like a goddess from her cliché red sports car, wearing a white shirt that flowed over her, hugging all the right curves, and falling an inch over the top of her grey skirt.

Tate had arrived.

The guys stopped talking. When she turned towards Logan, I sat upright in my seat. He narrowed his eyes and leaned back against his car as he stood in the middle of their friends.

"Did you see that?" I asked Mason.

There hadn't been much of a reaction, but I could sense the power she still had over Logan. I waited for a response, but there was none.

He was gone. His seat was empty, and his door shut just as I glanced over.

Scrambling after him, I headed for the rear of the Escalade. Then I heard the chill in his tone. "I hoped that you would've transferred after my warning."

Wariness came over her, but her eyes sought Logan again. Tate pressed her lips together as her shoulders lifted for a breath. "I'm just walking to class, Mason. I'm not here to cause problems."

He stepped close. His voice lowered as he said something to her, and her entire body went rigid a second later. The blood drained from her face, and her lips parted as her gaze was glued to him, like she couldn't turn away for the life of her. The spell was broken as soon as he stepped away, and she fled.

"Was that necessary?" Logan had come to stand beside me.

Mason turned to his brother. "Yes."

"Come on, Mason. She wasn't even doing anything."

"Why are you defending her?"

"Because you've made her life hell for two years. She's here for one semester."

Mason's green eyes switched to mine, searching if I agreed with him, but I stepped away from Logan. I didn't agree. Tate set off alarms in me. Both of them realized where I stood, and Logan snorted in disgust before he headed back to their friends, brushing past his brother who was standing in his way.

"Not to side with him, but Tate doesn't seem like too much of a threat anymore," Nate murmured lightly, breaking apart from the guys.

"*Now* you decide to be on his side?" Mason narrowed his eyes at him.

"You informed me how much of a dick I've been lately."

"You have been."

Nate grinned. "And I'm trying to make up for it." Then he swiveled to me. "Right, Sam?"

I lifted my hands in the air. The strap of my bag slipped down to my elbow as I shook my head. "Oh no. I'm not getting involved."

"Sam!"

Heather was waving her hands from the door. She yelled again, "Get your ass in here. You're going to be late on your first day. Stay away from her, Mason. I get her for the day."

Grinning, I went up to him and pressed a kiss to his cheek.

His eyes darkened again for a different reason this time. "You alright with what happened this morning?"

"Which thing are you talking about? Your comment? The Broudous at the gas station? Seeing my ex? Or just now, with whatever you said to Logan's ex-girlfriend?" I shook my head at the morning we had. "We are not normal."

"I guess all of it, but I was referring to your dad. I know that bothered you, seeing that he changed."

I shook my head. "Again. Not normal."

Hearing Heather call my name again, I was held back from answering her. Mason hooked a finger through one of my belt loops and pulled me close. "Are you okay?"

I knew he was asking about David, but I couldn't answer. I didn't know myself so I just shrugged. It was all I could do.

He nodded, getting the message and then his lips came down on mine, and I melted. Home. He was home. Logan was home. No matter all the changes, no matter where he was going, I was home for now.

CHAPTER FOUR

MASON

Sam headed inside with her friend. Watching them, I wasn't sure what to think of Heather Jax. It made more sense after meeting Monroe from Roussou. The girl wasn't a part of this school's hierarchy. That was fine, I just wasn't sure if that would help or hurt Sam. I'd have to wait and see.

"Heads up," one of the guys warned. "Hoe walking."

"Screw you, Ethan," Kate snapped. "You're showing off to get in Mason's good graces, but we both know the shoe was on the other foot last night."

Last night?

I didn't want to turn around. I didn't want to deal with Kate yet. She and her three friends had been the main companions for the guys, but that stopped when I found out about her agenda to destroy Sam. She went after my girlfriend so I went after her. Well, I tried. Sam was adamant about handling this battle on her own so I did what I could. The girls were no longer friends with our group. They were exiled, but I heard the anger from her and I knew she wasn't going to lay down and take it.

I knew about Parker and Nate, but it sounded like there was more. I wondered what else Kate was up to?

Logan laughed. "So desperate, Kate. The look doesn't fit you."

"Keep laughing, Logan. You're going on the list."

He grinned now.

I laughed to myself. She stepped wrong, and judging by the quiet intake of breath, Kate knew it as well. The easygoing air surrounding the group was gone. Knowing that look, I turned now and saw my little brother getting ready to go in for the kill. There was a certain look that came over him. His head would straighten. His eyes would narrow and roam up and down the target. No one knew what he was doing, but I did. Logan was searching for weaknesses. If he couldn't see one, he'd sense for one. It was something we learned over the years after we'd been screwed over by adults too many times. We went with our gut.

I waited for his next move like the rest.

"What list are you talking about, Kate?" Logan's voice grew soft. He was going in for the kill.

Kate seemed frozen, and the rest of her crew had varying reactions. Parker grimaced, her eyes darting to Nate's before looking away. Natalie took a deep breath and Jasmine moved back a step. All of them recognized the tone, they just weren't used to being on the receiving end.

"Come on, Logan," Kate tried to laugh it off. "I was kidding."

A smirk came over me, but then it vanished. As I watched the scene unfold, I saw Logan decide to give her a pass.

No. That wasn't going to happen. "No, you weren't."

All heads jerked in my direction. My gaze caught my brother's in a silent mocking, and a spark flared in Logan's. The message was received: Kate couldn't be let off the hook, no matter what. I wasn't surprised when I heard him add, "What list are you talking about? Come on, Kate. I'd like to know how I rate getting on some list?"

She let out a shaky laugh, glancing between us now. "Seriously, come on, guys. Mason. Logan. I was joking."

"No, you weren't."

She turned to me and her eyes widened. A glimmer of fear showed. "I came over to see if you needed help."

My eyes narrowed to slits now. "With what?"

"With Tate."

"You think we need help with her?"

She peeked at Logan before turning back to me.

Too late. I caught the slight smugness. It mingled with her fear, but I caught it. "What was that?"

"What?" An innocent mask slipped over her.

I shook my head, pointing to her face. "That. That look you gave Logan."

Logan's head straightened. His interest was piqued.

"What are you talking about, Mason?" She was growing cockier now. "I'm trying to be a friend. We used to have your backs. Remember?"

One of the guys muttered, "Oh shit."

Even Nate laughed at that. "Since when? What are you talking about, Kate?"

She turned to the rest of the guys. All of them were looking at her in disbelief. Except Logan, he was grinning widely, leaning back against his Escalade. He shook his head now. "You're digging yourself a hole. Stop talking. It might help."

Jasmine hissed behind her, "Don't you talk to her like that—"

"Like what?" Ethan shot back at her.

That stopped her. All the wind she had ready to let loose fell flat. Her eyes darted to his, and she couldn't look away.

Ethan leaned back against the car beside Logan, and shoved his hands into his front pockets. His shoulders hunched forward, but his gaze never left hers. They were dead-locked as he added, "You're going to tell us what to do? You're going to tell me what to do, Jaz?"

"Stop." Her throat moved as she visibly swallowed. "Ethan—"

"No, Jaz. You picked your side. We're not friends with you guys anymore."

Her shoulders flinched as if he'd punched her.

He nodded in my direction. "And you know why."

She didn't turn and look. She only took another deep breath before her head went down, and she shuffled backwards. Natalie touched her arm softly, and then sidled beside Kate. She whispered something to the other girl, quiet enough so no one else could hear, and Kate's only response was a heavy nod.

All the fight had left her.

I waited, watching the entire thing fold out. I didn't take pleasure in this, but I wasn't going to let Kate get a pass, not when I knew she was just starting. The chances were high that she already had a plan in place, and I wouldn't have been surprised if her next move was to go inside and say something to Sam. She'd pick a public arena, let everyone know that they shouldn't become friends with Sam, or they'd have to suffer the consequences of dealing with her.

As she jerked her head and headed inside, her friends followed behind her. She glanced over her shoulder, and met my gaze for a single heartbeat.

I saw the rage. I even understood it, but when she caught the warning from me to let it go, her rage doubled. The look only lasted a second, but it was long enough. We both knew neither of us would budge.

It was war.

Kate thought she was fighting Sam, but she wasn't. Kate was fighting me. She just didn't know it.

I became aware of Logan next to me. "What was the look she gave me?"

We watched the girls go inside. "She's smug about something. I didn't like it."

"About me?"

"I don't know." I glanced at him. "Any reason she'd be like that about you?"

He frowned and shrugged. "Not that I can think of anything, but I know she thinks she can get you back."

"I know." I didn't care about that. I wanted to know what she was thinking when she looked at my brother like that. Studying Logan, I knew he was telling the truth. He was clueless, but that made me wonder even more. Did she have something planned to hurt him? Hurt Logan. Hurt Sam. Hurt the ones around me?

I didn't know. Yet.

Logan added, "She thinks that if she destroys Sam, you'll go back to her. Doesn't she?"

"Yeah."

Logan started laughing again. "New definition to the phrase 'dumb bitch'."

My gaze lingered on the door, even after it closed behind them. Logan thought this was going to be fun, but he had no idea. It was going to get ugly. I knew it, and I was ready for it.

SAMANTHA

As soon as I was through the doors, Heather linked her arm with mine and pulled me close. Dressed in faded jeans and a loose black shirt, I had to grin when the V-neck dipped low. She didn't mean to, but she oozed sexuality. I had a feeling Heather Jax would look provocative in a grocery bag and she had no idea. Her eyes weren't clueless. They were sharp and focused as she asked, "What was that about?"

"Your ex-bestie."

She froze in mid-step, but was jostled from someone passing by and jerked me to the side for a split second. "Sorry." She patted me, withdrawing her arm at the same time. "Tate was out there?"

"She gave Logan googly-eyes."

Heather grimaced, side stepping a group of freshmen girls before swinging back to my side. "And let me guess, Mason didn't like that, did he?"

"No."

She rolled her eyes. "Tate's a bitch. I side with your boyfriend on this one. If she's already looking at Logan, who knows what she'll be capable of doing later."

"You make her sound like a villain."

"She is." Stopping at a locker, Heather wheeled the lock and opened it. Putting her books inside, she added, "Whatever Tate is saying, don't believe her. We didn't really talk about her before, but there's more to the story then whatever Mason told you."

That didn't sound good. "He told me that she dated Logan and, two years into their relationship she hit on him. There's more than that?"

A hollow laugh came from her. "Oh, a hell of a lot more. Things that Mason and Logan don't even know about."

I narrowed my eyes and moved closer. The hallway was packed. A lot of people were watching us, or me. A sudden wave of nervousness came over me. I had pushed aside the normal first-day-of-school-jitters with seeing Tate in the parking lot, but they were back now. They came back hard, but when I grinned at a few girls, they rolled their eyes and turned their backs to me. If that wasn't subtle, I didn't know what was. I was not welcome here. Glancing at a few others, they stared right back. I tried smiling at a few more, but I got varying responses. None welcoming. A few others continued to stare back as if I hadn't smiled at them, while a couple narrowed their eyes at me. The ones who turned away, bent forward to whisper with their friends. I had a feeling this was my welcome to Fallen Crest Public. I'd have to get used to it.

Heather took out a textbook and a notebook. Shutting her locker, a tired expression came over her as she faced me, but then it was gone in the blink of an eye and replaced with caution. Her eyes locked on something behind me, and I turned, my gut already knowing who it was going to be. Heather was tough and spunky, but only a few things or people could affect her like that.

And I was right. The Tomboy Princesses had arrived.

Kate was leading the pack with the three others close behind.

"I really hate those girls," Heather murmured to me.

Me too, I thought as I locked eyes with Kate. *Me too.*

All four of the Tomboy Princesses stood there. Each wore tight, ripped faded jeans. They weren't designer brands like the girls at Fallen Crest Academy wore, but they clung like a second-skin, and definitely gave off a sexy vibe. Their shirts were a variation of the same. Kate's was plain white that was snug against her tight abdominals, and it was evident she was wearing a pink bra under the sheer material. Her dark hair was swept up into a waterfall braid with the ends curled. They had a healthy glow as they fell past her shoulders. Parker glared at me, her dark eyes were hostile, and her lips were pressed together in a snarl. Unlike their leader, her black hair fell loose. It matched her black sleeveless top that rested an inch above her jeans, showing off a good amount of midriff.

Natalie and Jasmine brought up the last of their group, and they were the two that I was the least familiar with. They had similar black hair. Natalie's was a little lighter with caramel highlights showing through. She was the only one wearing a Fallen Crest Public jersey. It was red with black lettering and had the number eight on the back, the bottom of it tied around her tiny waist. Jasmine was the girliest of the group. Her black hair was pulled into a ponytail that rested high on her head, bouncing back and forth as she followed her friends. Pink lipstick, glitter on her cheeks and pink eye shadow matched her pink sweater that looked like soft cashmere and had a low neckline. Her cleavage was right there, saying hello to anyone who wanted to view the girls.

Heather cursed under her breath when the group stopped before us. She leaned against her locker as I waited. Kate said she'd make our lives hell. First day jitters and surviving my mother's recent attempt at destroying Mason's future had combined together. I was angry. I was ready to fight back. I was more than ready for whatever Kate had in store.

"Last chance, Jax." That was Kate's greeting. "You can back out now and everyone and everything you hold dear will be left alone."

"Shut up, Kate," Heather retorted, shoving off from her locker. She took two steps, sticking her face right up in hers. An inch separated them while her followers surrounded us. As a hush fell over the hallway, I knew all eyes were on us.

Still.

"I don't like when people threaten me or my friends."

"She shouldn't be your friend. She's a liability," Kate hissed back at her, breaking their stare-off to glower at me.

She smirked. "What's with you and having bodyguards? Mason. Logan. Now Jax? Don't you have balls of your own?"

I smirked back. Balls? She wanted balls? I opened my mouth, ready to show her some balls when an amused voice broke into the group, "Kate, are you serious? You're still doing the bullying thing?"

Tate stood there, books in hand, as she skimmed the group with a bored expression. She rolled her eyes, flicked some of her hair over her shoulder, and shook her head. "What are you going to do after high school, Kate? You can't bully everyone to do what you want, and why are you even doing it now?" Tate gestured to me with perfectly manicured nails. "Pushing Strattan around isn't going to do a bit of good. You know that you won't get Mason back. He's gone. He was gone the second her mom moved her into his house."

Kate sucked in an angry breath. "Back off, Sullivan. This isn't your business."

"Maybe not, but Heather used to be a good friend and since I'm all about making amends, I can't walk by." She arched an eyebrow. "Wanna hear some advice from someone who has gone against Mason and his girlfriend?"

"Go away, Tate. I mean it."

She shook her head. "Let it go."

"Can't you hear, Tate?" Jasmine stepped right in front of her, much like Heather had done with Kate. The petite black-haired beauty looked even smaller standing in front of Tate, who had model-like long legs and towered over. "Kate said to keep walking."

Tate grinned down at her, like an adult whose child tried to boss them around. "You're like a mosquito that won't die. Back up or I'll swat you down."

Jasmine bristled. "Don't talk to me like that."

Tate lifted her bored eyes again, skimming me and Heather up and down before landing on the leader again. "I've been back a week, been around the last weekend, and I already know you're losing power. You're deluding yourself if you think you can push your way around like this. Let it go, Kate. We used to be friends and this is friendly advice. Stop going down this path, lick your wounds, and find a different guy to latch onto."

Heather shifted back, refusing to meet her ex-best friend's gaze, bumping into me in the process. I sighed and settled back against her locker.

Kate lifted her top lip and bared her teeth. "We weren't friends."

"We were in the beginning."

"When you ditched Jax." Kate threw a smug look to Heather. "Remember that, Jax? When your best friend stabbed you in the back?"

Tate stiffened.

"Or didn't you tell her what you did, Sullivan?"

"Shut up."

"Oh." Kate's triumphant smirk spread over her face. "You didn't tell her? That you slept with her boyfriend at the time?"

"Shut. Up."

"What?" Heather's voice had grown quiet.

"No. You started this. You came over here and interfered. You're on the list now, Tate. I was giving Jax one last chance to get away, but it's too late now. For both of you. You're all going down, right along with Mason's latest screw."

A dry chuckle left me. It acted like a beacon and as one, the rest of the girls turned to face me. I stood from the lockers. I caught movement from the corner of my eye and glanced over. I spotted Logan watching from a distance, frowning. Ethan was with him, and they both seemed unsure of what to do. I gave him a nod and sent him an unspoken message: I would handle this.

His frown deepened.

"You got something to say, slut?" Kate mocked. "Finally?"

"Finally?" I threw back, moving closer, replacing the spot that Heather had been in. Kate was my height, so I could stare her right in the eyes. I did so now, no blinking, no turning away, nothing was going to break our stand-off. "Why break this up? I don't need television. You're entertaining enough. Please, keep going. Threaten Tate some more. I'm not a fan of hers. Or even better, try going after Heather again. Go for it." I bared my teeth. "Fair warning. She bites back."

She frowned.

I rolled my eyes. "Am I supposed to be scared that the four of you ganged up on me? Or that you're willing to threaten my friend? You're making a list? Is that supposed to strike terror in me? Anyone can make a list. I've got one, too. Does it make your knees shake?"

I heard a wolf whistle from down the hallway, followed by, "That is so hot!"

Another guy yelled out, "Girl fight!"

Kate wanted to scare me. She didn't. I'd gone against the best of the beasts: my mother. As Jasmine took another step forward and raised her hand, I shifted so I was facing her head-on. She stopped in her tracks and surprise came over her. Her hand lowered.

"You think physical violence is going to do it?"

Tate started laughing now.

I ignored her. "Go ahead and touch me. I'm not scared to take a hit, but you're only going to hurt yourself. One bruise and I can go to the principal. It's not like there aren't witnesses here."

As those words left me, Kate grabbed Jasmine's arm and shoved her back.

"Kate," she protested.

"Not yet," their leader barked. "Go to class. All of you."

Parker gasped now. "You're letting her win?"

"No." Kate turned her back to me, but I heard the warning in her tone. "It's not time."

"But—"

"Go, Parker. I won't say it again."

All three did nothing to hide their disgust with Kate as they left. Parker glowered at me for a full five seconds before she was dragged away by Natalie, the only one who hadn't said a word. My gaze lingered on her and wondered what she was like. Parker and Jasmine seemed to be the hotheads of the group. They reacted the quickest, but Kate must've been their leader for a reason.

Kate rounded back to me. She took a deep breath and shook her head. "You're not what I expected, Strattan."

Tate snorted behind her. "You haven't even scratched the surface, Kate."

Kate glanced at her. "And you have?"

"I know that Mason Kade wouldn't be in love with her if she were simple."

"Maybe."

Heather burst out then, "Go away. All of you."

"I was trying to help." Tate frowned as Kate followed after her friends.

"You're not."

For a second, the two former best friends stared at each for a second before Tate's shoulders dropped. Her head lowered an inch and she lifted one shoulder in a halfhearted motion. "Fine." She was swallowed up by the crowd that remained behind her. They were all still watching and as I scanned them, a sense of déjà vu came over me. It was like my last semester at my old school, but I didn't know these people. I hadn't gone to school with them since kindergarten. I didn't know the embarrassing stories from middle school or all the cliques.

This wasn't my school. This was foreign territory to me. That should've staggered me, but it didn't. I had endured Analise. I could endure this.

Heather fell back against her locker with a groan. "I didn't expect that."

"I did." I actually expected more.

She eyed me up and down. "I thought maybe they'd steal your clothes during gym class or something. Maybe write the word 'whore' on your locker."

I grinned at her. "And on that note, I need to go to the office to get my combination. When I registered they didn't have that for me."

Heather tried to smile, but the corners of her lips went down instead of up. She glanced in the direction Tate had gone. "Why do you think she did that?"

Because she wants to be friends again. I didn't say that, though. I said instead, "What boyfriend were they talking about?"

Pain flared over her face. "Channing."

"I'm sorry."

She lifted a shoulder and shrugged halfheartedly. She looked away. "Doesn't matter. We've been broken up for a year anyway..."

"It couldn't have been anyone else?"

Heather looked down now. "No. I've only been with him, and we were dating when Tate was my friend. It makes sense now..."

Score one for Kate.

"I'm sorry," I said again, but I knew it wouldn't help.

Kate won this round. She hurt my friend.

CHAPTER FIVE

The first bell went off when I reached the office. The final bell went off when I was given my locker combination. I would officially be late to my first class, on my first day. Wonderful. When I asked where Coach Grath's office was, the secretary informed me that he'd be gone all week. That dilemma was resolved. So with that new information, I headed back out and started my day as a new student.

When I got to my class, the teacher didn't care that I was late. A worksheet was handed to me right away and the rest of the class went fast as I began working on it. There were no Tommy P.'s in there, but there were in the rest of my classes. Jasmine and Natalie were in my second period. Kate was in my third and Parker rounded out the fourth. My mornings were going to be glorious, but the one silver lining was that my locker was still clean when I headed to lunch. No 'whore' or 'slut' decorated it. Yet.

There was no sight of Mason or Logan when I went to the cafeteria, but Heather called me over to her table. There were a few others sitting with her. The guys were friendly or friendlier while the two girls gave me a cold reception. One, dressed in all black clothing, gave me a sneer and turned her back to me.

Subtle.

The other one, wearing a white sweatshirt emblazoned with a large rainbow, gave me a shy grin. She had the softest blue eyes and palest skin I'd ever seen on a person. After we ate, Heather explained on the way to our lockers that the shy one was an albino. I'd never met someone who looked like that, but she warned me not to expect anything nicer than the greeting I got. The shy one didn't talk and Heather said that I was better off not knowing the other one's name. I didn't question it. She added that No Name Chick wasn't a fan of anyone associated with the Kades. Both girls were routine targets by the Tommy Princesses and neither cared that Kate's group was no longer supported by Mason or Logan anymore.

It wasn't until after fifth period when Logan showed up at my locker. "What was going on with those girls this morning?"

It was amazing. Logan Kade appeared at my locker and most everyone stopped to watch us. I sighed as I exchanged one book for the next one. I'd have to get used to the pull he held over everyone.

I shrugged. "It was nothing."

"That didn't look like nothing."

"Stop, Logan," I warned. "I have to take care of them. You can't do this for me."

He rolled his eyes, cursing under his breath at the same time. "We're going to have to step in. It's inevitable. Kate's a bitch."

"Logan."

"You know it, Sam. Stop fighting us and let us help you. You're going to have to at some point." A final warning was in his gaze before he took off.

As he did, all heads turned to follow him. As he went one way, Mason passed him coming towards me. The heads turned and followed him instead.

As I waited, watching him come to me, people parted for Mason. He didn't seem to notice it. His gaze was on me, but I couldn't stop from watching how people reacted to him. Logan too. They knew when Mason or Logan were around. Even if they didn't see them, they still moved out of the way. It was beginning to dawn on me how big their near-celebrity status was at this school. Everything they did, people knew. Everything they said, people heard. This shouldn't have been a surprise anymore, but it was. It was different at their school. It was more than I had experienced before.

As he drew closer, his intensity softened and he gave me a grin. I saw the love in his eyes and it warmed me. Hell, he was becoming like oxygen. I needed him.

"Hey."

"Hey, yourself," he murmured, bending down to give me a soft kiss.

I closed my eyes as the usual ache started in me again.

The whispers started around us. They grew to a low buzz, and I started to turn around, but Mason grabbed my chin. His eyes were once again the only thing I saw—everything else started to melt away. He stepped closer, his hand grew gentle on my face, and his thumb started to rub over my cheek. "What happened with Kate earlier?"

"Nothing." The Kade brothers were consistent. "It's my fight, Mason. Let me fight it."

"Sam, come on."

I felt him now. His arms brushed against me. His stomach flattened and tightened, grazing through my shirt, and his familiar heat started to pull me in. He didn't have his arms around me, but I still felt sheltered by him.

This was what Mason did. His charisma was so intoxicating, and I couldn't blame anyone from wanting what I had. I reached up to his face now, feeling the small dip underneath his lips, before it formed his chin, I couldn't look away from him. Even now, my fingers ached to explore more, to feel his lips, to trace them and then cup the side of his face.

"Hey," he murmured, stepping even closer. He was almost pressed against me. My fingers fell from his face and down his chest. It felt like a cement wall underneath my touch. My hand fell to his jeans. It caught there and I curled my fingers around one of his loops. Then, feeling desire swirling inside of me, I bit my lip and pushed one of my fingers in the waistband of his jeans.

Whatever he was about to say was forgotten.

"Sam," he groaned as he turned us so that my back was against the locker. He was against me now. As my finger tucked further down, I felt him harden. The power I had over him was intoxicating. It wasn't just him. My head fell back against the metal locker, but I didn't feel it. Everything else fell away. It was only him and me. Nothing else mattered.

My desire for him rose, and I fought against letting it take me over.

My eyelids flitted closed and I felt him bend down. His chest rubbed against mine now and then I gasped when his lips found the corner of mine. He stayed there, sucking lightly, as his other hand slid down to my hip and pulled me tighter against him.

"I feel pregnant just watching you two."

Breaking apart, Heather was standing there with her arms crossed over her chest, and the corners of her lips curved down. She looked ready to vomit. "Honestly, come up for air every now and then. The masses look ready to riot."

She jerked her head down the hallway, where Kate and the rest of the Tommy Princesses were.

I sighed, pushing Mason away. "That's her locker?"

Heather leaned against my neighbor's locker. "No, that's Natalie's. She and Jasmine are only juniors. Kate and Parker are seniors. Good riddance too. I'm ready for their entire group to ship out."

Still watching Kate and the glower she was sending our way, I shook my head. "She looks ready to kill me."

"You and me both. I'm not doing what she wanted."

Mason frowned as he deliberately turned his back to Kate, blocking her view. "She wanted you to do something?"

"She told me to stop being friends with Sam." Heather shrugged, but I caught the small look of alarm in her eyes. It flared for only a second. "She gave me the warning this morning and Tate, of all people, tried to help me."

The interest Mason held fell flat now. He straightened from the locker as he ground out, "Don't believe anything she says."

"Well, I'm going to believe Kate." Heather peeked around him, eyeing her warily. "I wonder what she's going to do."

"Nothing." Not if I had anything to do about it. I was getting more and more irritated with Mason's ex-on-and-off-again hook-up. She hadn't even been a full-fledged girlfriend. She'd been used only as a scratcher when he had an itch. "I'm not going to let her."

Mason frowned, twisting around once again.

I held my breath. There was an unspoken message there, and I knew he was delivering it to her. As she made an exasperated sound before slamming Natalie's locker, I guessed she had received it, and whatever she saw, she didn't like. Then he moved again. Kate and her group were coming towards us. I snuck a peek at Mason, whose eyes went flat, but she only hissed as they went past us, "You're going to regret this. All of you."

Her friends smiled at us, following behind her.

Heather shuddered. "Evil. They're all evil."

I agreed with her, but asked Mason, "How'd they take the exile?"

His gaze had lingered on Kate, who paused and glanced back once, but he turned back to me. "What?"

"The exile. How'd they take it?"

"Oh." He lifted a shoulder. "They took it. They didn't have a choice."

"Must be nice," Heather drawled. "You declare it and people have to follow it, whether they want to or not." She snorted, tightening her grip on her bag. "I'd like to declare something. Whoever won the lottery last week will hand their ticket over to me." She rubbed her hands together. "And voila, all my problems—poof!—gone." She eyed Mason up and down. "Must be nice to be rich."

He shot her a dark look. "That's not how it went down." He touched my arm again. "We have basketball practice. What were you going to do after school?"

"Oh." I hadn't driven to school and Coach Grath was gone for the week. I glanced at Heather. I wasn't scheduled for Manny's until Saturday so what else was there? "Running."

"You want to take my car home?"

I held my hand out to Mason. "Yes, please." I didn't care how I got home, I just needed to run.

He grinned as he put his keys in my hand. "Just don't go for hours. Please." He pulled me close and pressed a kiss to my forehead, whispering at the same time, "And be careful. Keep an eye out when you're running."

My throat grew thick at his concern, and I nodded, reaching for him again. My hand clasped onto his shirt's collar and hung there. "I'll be safe."

"Good." He pressed another kiss to my lips before he pulled away.

As he headed down the hall, Heather groaned. "I stand by what I said. You two are disgusting."

CHAPTER SIX

Running was my escape. I escaped all reality and pushed forward. I kept going. It was like a drug to me. It came with its own challenges and obstacles, and as long as I kept going, I broke through every single one of them. Tearing down a wooded trail, the bass was pounding through my earbuds and my adrenalin matched it. My heart pumped as I lifted my knees and pushed off from the ground. Power rippled up through my legs. I ducked my head and raised my hands to keep projecting forward.

I'd never tire of this.

And with that thought, I rounded a turn in the new trail. My eyes widened in surprise as Quickie's came into the clearing. I never knew this path came through here, but it wasn't far from Nate's home. It made sense. There were no cars in the lot so I raced through, but saw the clerk watching me. When our eyes caught for a second, he lifted his hand and I nodded back, but then I was gone again. The path led up a hill behind the gas station and I heaved a deep breath, pushing myself upward now.

There were no thoughts in my head. No concern. No fear. There wasn't even love. When I ran, I was just being. My nostrils flared and I kept going, flying up one hill and then another. I tore past another clearing. The trees parted below me and I braked. My chest heaved up and down, but I couldn't move away.

I was looking down on Fallen Crest.

I hadn't realized how high I must've run, but I couldn't tear my eyes away. It was breathtaking. My old school's campus was on another hill, straight from where I stood.

Fallen Crest Public was in the valley below. The massive football field was a patch of green among the rest of the town. Then I looked for the south side, wondering if I could see Manny's. It was surrounded by trees so I wasn't surprised that I couldn't. Then, without thinking about it, I glanced to the neighborhood where David's house was, my old home.

Instead of the old pain, there was nothing. I frowned, but started forward. A chill drifted over me and my blood was pumping. I needed to keep going before the cold settled in. With that last thought, I tucked my head down and pushed forward with a new burst of speed.

After my run, I showered, ate, and then fell asleep watching television in the basement. It was later in the night before the guys got home. A stampede of feet sounded above me, and the door slammed shut as I heard Logan yell, "SAM! WHERE ARE YOU?"

"Logan!"

"What?"

"You don't have to scream your head off."

"Whatever, Nate. You're pissed because you need to work for some pussy now. Can't have Parker running over anymore."

"Shut up."

The door leading to the basement was thrown open and Logan's voice grew clearer as he laughed. "Don't blame me that girls are scared of you. You're a shady, motherfucker." He hurried down the stairs, but stopped before laughing. "Sam? You're down here?"

I scowled at him before rolling back over and pulling my blanket over my head. "You're so loud. Shut up."

He chuckled before yelling upstairs, "SHE'S DOWN HERE, MASON."

I held my breath. I already knew what was coming next, but as he dropped next to me, the couch jerked from his sudden weight, and I went airborne for a second. Oomph. Oh yes. I was fully awake now. I pulled the blanket back to glare at him. "Thank you for being quiet."

He flashed me a grin, pulling the handle to the footrest next to him. "No problem." It came up and he lounged back, getting comfortable. "What are you doing down here? You're never down here."

"Resting. What are you doing down here?"

Grabbing the remote from next to my feet, he switched the channel and pointed at the screen. "Game's on."

Of course. How stupid of me.

I groaned to myself, but sat up and curled my knees to my chest. The sounds of a basketball game came next. It was only the first day of school so I didn't have any homework yet. No shift at Manny's. I already ran. I knew Mason would be heading down soon. I wasn't going anywhere. When Logan reached down and lifted a fast food bag to his lap, I asked, "You guys got food?"

He had pulled his burger out. It was half unwrapped and lifted to his mouth before he stopped and turned to me. "Did you want some?"

My stomach growled. The smell of greasy food hit me like a cement truck. Crap. The little sandwich I had after my run hadn't tided me over.

Logan heard it and one corner of his mouth lifted. He held his burger to me. "You want a bite?"

I shook my head. "No. That's yours. I'll go and find something else." Still. My stomach growled louder.

"Sam." Logan was fighting back a smile. "You can have the entire thing. This was my second one."

"No, then you'll be hungry."

"Nah." The smile won out and he grinned from ear to ear. "I can steal Nate's. He got three of them, and I know he hasn't touched them. He said we should wait till we got home." He snorted. "No fucking idea why."

"Because I was going to ask Sam if she wanted one," Nate spoke up, coming down the stairs. He frowned at Logan, before he sat down on the other couch. He had two bags with him and held one in the air. "There's a chicken sandwich in here. Sam?"

My stomach spoke up with a resounding 'yes.' It groaned, growled, and shuddered all at the same time.

Logan chuckled, but turned to Nate. "Kiss ass."

"Screw you. Mason got the sandwich for her."

"Oh." Logan frowned. "I thought you were going to take the credit."

"What's your problem?" Nate tossed the bag so it landed on the couch next to me. "You've been on my ass all day."

"Because you've *been* an ass lately," he shot back before giving me a wink. He said to Nate, "It's not every day you get knocked down a peg and take it. I have to enjoy this while I can."

Nate's frown deepened to a glower as he rolled his eyes. "Well, it's getting old."

Logan shrugged. "Not my problem. You were the shady motherfucker in the first place."

"Guys," I murmured as I unwrapped the sandwich. My stomach wouldn't stop groaning. I hadn't realized how hungry I was.

Nate glanced back at the stairs. "Your brother's being an asshole."

There was no response, but I knew who it was. I knew who was coming and enjoyed waiting for him. I sunk my teeth into the sandwich. Good gracious, I was in heaven. A chicken sandwich had never tasted so delicious to me. My stomach was doing cartwheels, but then I was being lifted in the air again. I didn't even react. I already knew where he was going. When he moved so he was underneath me, I kept eating as I got comfortable on his lap and rested my head on his chest. One of his hands remained on my leg, his fingers on my inner thigh as I took another bite.

"Did you not eat?"

I nodded, mumbling around the sandwich, "Not enough."

He grinned and leaned back into the couch.

Logan chuckled, turning the volume louder.

"Nice, dickwad."

He only got a shrug in response.

Mason held me on his lap and moved his fingers in a circling motion. It was soothing and sensual at the same time. Part of me was getting excited while the other part wanted to fall asleep. With the chicken sandwich in my stomach, and the warmth from Mason, the sleepy part won out. Then Mason's phone went off. It buzzed from his pocket underneath me, and he shifted me to the side, his arm sliding under me to grab it. Pulling it out, he opened the screen. It was a text from his father: **We would like to invite you over for dinner. When are you moving back?**

"Uh, okay." Logan was reading his phone at the same time. He put it down, his eyebrows bunching together as he said, "I know you talked us into moving back, but no way. I can't do it, Sam."

"What?" I sat forward. "You guys said you would."

Logan shared a look with Mason. I twisted around. "You agree?"

Mason didn't say anything. He didn't have to. I shook my head. "What? Did you guys come to this decision without me?"

"No." Logan shook his head and then nodded. "Yes."

A lead stone dropped to the pit of my stomach. This was my fault. I promised James and now they were changing their minds. "You guys should live with your dad for the last semester. Mason, you only have a few months before you leave."

"Sam."

That big lead stone wasn't moving. I sat up and went to the empty chair.

Nate took the remote from Logan and silenced the game.

Logan snorted. "Why's it so damn important for us to live with our dad? It's not fair to put your daddy issues on us."

Narrowing my eyes, I crossed my arms over my chest. "You can't say that to me. You have no idea—"

"No idea?" Logan scoffed. "Yes, we do. Our dad's an asshole."

"Logan."

He overrode me, "It's not going to happen." Then he stopped, and glanced at Nate.

"What?"

Logan turned to the stairs.

Nate bit out a curse. "Are you serious? You want me to leave?"

"Not to be an ass, but this is family shit."

"What am I then?"

"You're extended family shit. You're one of those long-distance cousins."

Nate looked over. "Mason."

"Just go, Nate." Logan leveled him with a harsh look. "This is family and you've been a douchebag lately."

Nate gritted his teeth at him, but turned to his best friend. "Mason, come on."

Mason sighed. "It doesn't matter what I say. You need to be trusted by all of us and you're not. That's what matters."

He pushed up from the couch and stalked out. No words were shared, and the tension in the room was thick enough to cut with a knife. I didn't dare breathe until he had left. As soon as he was upstairs and the door shut, Mason leaned back and sighed. "I hope you guys know what you just did."

Logan sent him a dark look. "Screw you."

"I already ripped him a new one this morning—"

"Not good enough," Logan interrupted him. He shot forward, his eyes stormy and lips pressed tight in a snarl. "Nate's been so far up your ass, I'm surprised you remember about the rest of us." As Mason glanced at me, Logan added, "Except for Sam. You do need to get your daily screws in, don't you?"

Everything happened so fast after that.

I gasped, but then Mason was off the couch. He had Logan pressed against the wall in the next instant, one hand fisted in his shirt and the other had pinned Logan's arm up. He snarled at him, "Are you fucking with me?"

Logan twisted, jutting his hip out to move Mason aside and then slipped his arm free.

My heart was pounding. It sounded so loud in my eardrums that I struggled to hear the rest. Everything had jumped up in me, and it felt like my pulse was lodged in my throat. It was going nuts.

Mason didn't move against him, but Logan didn't move away. They were almost touching, glaring at each other.

"I'm not screwing with you."

"You sure about that?" Mason lashed back. Every muscle in him was primed. He was ready to fight; his hands had formed into fists and were pressed against his legs. He was holding himself back.

Logan eyed him warily before sending me a furtive look. His shoulders were rigid, but they dropped a fraction of a centimeter. His jaw was still like cement as he clipped out, "I'm not, but I am getting sick of this shit. Nate's up your ass twenty-four-seven. "

"We *are* staying in his house."

"So let's move."

"And go where?" A hollow laugh came from Mason's throat. He turned to me. "Back to Dad's? Sam, there's no way I'm living with your mom again. I meant to tell you earlier, but I forgot."

Rising from the couch, I hugged myself, but spoke up, "It's not right that you guys are here. Nothing against Nate, but you should be with family during this time." My heart kept pounding, thumping against my ribcage. "And yes," I caught the look he sent to Logan, "that means Logan and me, too. I don't have a family anymore."

Mason and Logan had been eyeing each other, but they turned as one now. I was front and center once again.

I gulped. Sometimes their attention was a little much, too much at times. This was one of those times. I felt stripped and raw as I added, "My life went to crap five months ago. My mom left my dad. I found out my dad wasn't my real dad. Then my real dad came into my life, but he's gone. They're both gone and then my mom went psycho. I've got you two, and on the outside, I am so jealous of you. You have a dad. He's still here. He loves you guys—"

Mason started forward. His voice soft, "He's with your mom, Sam."

I flinched at that. It felt as if he'd slapped me.

"I love you and she hurt you. That's the math to me. If we go back there, she's going to keep hurting you." Mason was in front of me now. His hand lifted to touch the side of my face. "There's no way I can watch that and not do anything."

Logan spoke up, "We can't scare your mom anymore. She's too crazy for that, so being there and seeing that happen to you," he gestured to his brother, "I'm with Mason. There's no way I could watch that and not do anything, except this time, we'd really hurt your mom."

"It's best if we just stay away. Our dad knows the deal. As long as he has her in his life, we're out. That's the way it is." Mason's chest lifted as he took a deep breath. His touch was so tender. "He's making that decision. Not us."

A piece of me broke away. It fell to the bottom of my stomach. The sadness that washed over me was overwhelming. "I can't be responsible for you guys losing your dad."

"You're not." Logan frowned, stepping next to his brother. He didn't reach out, but I felt his concern. "It's our dad. He turned into a douchebag, too."

"Logan."

"What?" Logan shrugged, giving his brother a crooked grin. The sudden tension from before was gone. "You know it's true. Well, I guess our dad's always been a douchebag. How many mistresses did he have? Had to be twenty, at least." He whistled in appreciation. "Gotta give it to your mom. She's the one that landed him. Our dad must be really nuts if that's who he chooses to settle down with. He's stuck with her even after all the crap she did to Sam." The other half of his mouth curved up. "Maybe we should have him committed? He can go through one of those brainwashing programs, brainwash him back to being normal." He pondered that for a second. "No, he'd just pick another winner again."

"This isn't funny."

Logan shrugged. His crooked grin didn't lessen. "Has to be. Dad left Mom, cheated on her for years, and Analise is who he ends up with? She's the one that he decides to stick it out with? That's the funniest damn thing I've heard." He clapped his brother on the shoulder. "Come on. You think it's funny too."

When the corner of Mason's mouth curved up, teasing at his own grin, I couldn't believe this. "Stop," I cried out. Shaking my head, I moved away. "I can't believe you guys. You're laughing about this? You can't—"

"We can," Mason stopped me. A tender expression came over him. "Logan's right. It has to be funny. We've lived through all the other stuff. The divorce. Dad's cheating. The only good thing we got from him was you."

"I second that."

I rolled my eyes. They were missing the entire point.

"Sam." Mason reached out and took my hand, pulling me back to him. "We're not laughing to be dicks, but this is our dad. You can't judge us because we're not accepting the crumbs he's giving to us. He's not a great dad."

Logan snorted, "Try he's never been a great dad?"

"We understand what you're saying. Trust me. We do." He tugged me closer to him, but I didn't look up. I couldn't. His finger went underneath my chin, and he tipped my head up. Then I couldn't look away. His green eyes caught mine and the wall he normally had up slid away. He let me see everything—the bitterness, hurt, pain, anger—all of that was there, but it was mixed with love. I saw it. I felt it when he murmured, "I'm grateful to him for you, but because I love you, I can't accept your mother. There's no way. Would you? If you saw someone hurting me, over and over again?"

When he put it like that, I drew in a shuddering breath. "I would kill that person."

Logan started laughing. "We go from scaring to hurting. She jumps right to killing. Hardcore, Sam." He patted me on the shoulder. "It's why you're our Little Kade. On that note, I love you. I'm sorry for my comment before, but I can tell where this is going. Believe it or not, I don't get off on watching the two of you." He pressed a quick kiss to my temple and headed to the stairs. As he got to the top, he called out, "Coast is clear. Fornicate away."

Mason ignored him. "You okay?"

I nodded. My throat was too thick with emotion to speak.

"We can't move back in. We can't watch her hurt you, and he's not going to leave her, so this is how it has to be." He drew me against him and I rested my head on his chest. If the situation had been reversed, there was no way I could do it either. I hadn't been joking. If I saw someone hurting Mason and Logan, over and over again, I would do anything to stop them.

Mason bent down and dropped a soft kiss to the top of my head.

CHAPTER SEVEN

"So you haven't told them yet?" Heather popped her head out from her locker as her mouth fell open. "I can't believe you. That was a week ago. Don't you think they should know?"

"Why? They know that Budd and Brett are trying to find out who I am. They said it to their face."

She slammed her locker shut and handed me her notebook. "Hold this."

I did. "What do you want me to do?"

Heather stopped looking through her book and glared at me. A strand of her hair slipped down, blocking her face, but I could still feel the heat of her stare. "You're not a moron, Samantha. Stop trying to make me think of you are. It's an insult."

"I'm screwed."

"Pretty much." Her eyes lit up as she found her page and folded over the corner. Then she grabbed her notebook from me before shaking her head. "Look, granted, Mason and Logan did their 'run-in' with Budd and Brett. They know Budd's looking for Mason's girlfriend so that's not news to him, but you yourself saw them at Manny's. You work there. They could go there any time. It's something they'd want to know."

An outburst of giggles and yells came from down the hall, and I glanced over. Logan had arrived. He was at his locker, along with Ethan and Strauss. Both guys had smirks on their faces as they enjoyed the cheerleaders next to their lockers. Boobs galore and if their skirts lifted an inch, pussy galore. I snorted, falling back against the locker behind me.

Heather paused, mid-reach into her bag. "What?"

"Nothing."

"What?" And she turned, twisting around to see further down the hallway. I knew when she spotted them. Her back straightened. Her shoulders flattened and she let her bag fall to the floor. "Oh."

Oh, indeed. "I'm starting to get used to this school."

"Uh oh."

"What?"

"No one says they're getting used to this school. Those are the people that get a smack-down." She shook her head, trembling in an exaggerated manner. "I can't let that happen to you."

I laughed. "No, not like that. I meant that I'm starting to understand this school. Instead of the Elite, like at FCA, you guys have cheerleaders."

"And the drill team."

"Drill team?"

"Yeah," Heather nodded towards a group of girls across from Logan's locker. They were dressed in sweaters. Not one of them wore jeans. They all had on dress pants that could've been matched with a business suit. They looked professional, how I would've dressed for a job interview. I glanced over their different hairstyles, all swept down or over the shoulder to look like perfection. I understood what Heather was saying. The Tommy Princesses might've been the girls at the top because of how tough they were, but these girls would've usurped them if given half a chance. They reminded me of Miranda and Cass from the Elite.

"Do they think they're in a walking beauty ad?"

Heather chuckled. As we headed towards them, she added, "Those girls try get the boyfriends. There's a few that are always trying to land any of the guys in the Kade group, but they'd love to get Mason or Logan the most. Kate and her bitch crew were the main go-to girls for the guys. They weren't into having a boyfriend like the others and each guy kinda had their own. Mason had Kate. Nate had Parker. Ethan had Jasmine and sometimes Logan would hook-up with Natalie, though we both know he never had a certain go-to girl."

"And speaking of..."

I stopped as Tate came around the corner. She didn't give us a glance as she went straight to Logan and draped herself over him. One arm went around his neck and the other hand rested on his chest. He'd been listening to Ethan, but stopped. As she moved closer to him, his head lowered so it looked as if the two were whispering to each other. A small grin was teasing the corner of his mouth when she started talking.

"Okay." Heather bobbed her head up and down. "I now see what you and Mason are worried about."

My eyes grew wide when he lifted a hand to the side of her hip. That was how Mason touched me. It was intimate and it was his precursor move before he pulled me even closer. Logan didn't pull her closer, but his hand lingered there before moving to the small in her back. Oh yes. He was enjoying every bit of her attention, but then he looked up and caught us staring. Correction. He caught me.

My face got hot. I knew I was probably red, but what was he doing? I narrowed my eyes and tried to ask him that question without saying it.

The other side of his lips curved up and the grin was no longer a tease. He was full-on smiling at me. Another correction. He was smirking at me.

"What?" I bristled next to Heather. Both knew who that question was for.

He lifted one shoulder. It dropped lightly. He said back, "What?"

Tate turned around, a Cheshire Cat grin on her lips as Logan's hand didn't fall away. Instead of being on her back, as she turned to us, it slid around her hip to her stomach and stayed there. She was now almost in his arms.

Heather was frowning at them, but I couldn't hold it in. "Did I miss the announcement? Are you a happy couple now?" There was an edge in my voice, but I couldn't hide it. Tate was bad news. She was slimy. She was sneaky. She hurt Logan. She'd do it again.

"You can't be jealous, Samantha," she taunted me. "You're happy with Mason, aren't you? You can't have both Kades."

I growled, "And you can't hurt him again."

"Uh, guys..." Heather started.

Logan shook his head. "Sam, relax."

"No—" I stopped him.

Tate turned her gaze to Heather and a bitter look came over her. "What's your problem, Heather? I didn't know we were enemies. You don't have to have her back all of the time."

That had me seething, but I glanced around and saw the crowd that was forming. The drill team snobs were mingling with the cheerleaders. Ethan and Strauss had front row seats, leaning against Logan's locker, were grinning from ear to ear. I skimmed the edge of the crowd and saw Kate. She was expressionless, but her eyes narrowed when they met mine. A slight chill went through me. Whatever she was thinking, it wasn't good. I caught Logan's eye and gestured to her. The amusement on his face faded then, and he stepped towards me.

Tate stopped in mid-sentence. "What are you doing?"

Ignoring her, he took Heather's arm and mine, pulling us through the crowd.

"Logan!"

"Your girlfriend is calling," Heather told him.

He grimaced. "Okay, that was a joke. I can't believe you guys got so riled up." He led us into the senior hallway and quieted his voice, leaning in closer to me, "I don't have those feelings for Tate anymore. You don't need to worry. I'd have to care about her to get hurt by her. Those feelings are long gone."

Heather put on the brakes. She went pale as a group broke away from the hall. "Oh, crap."

I recognized two of the girls. "Those are your friends, right?"

"Let's hope." An apology flashed in her eyes as she started for them. "I gotta go. I'm sorry, Sam. Come to Manny's tonight if I don't see you at lunch?"

I nodded as she hurried to catch up with them. When she did, the girl who was dressed all in black refused to look at her. The tiny one gave her a half-grin. It was more like a half-hearted attempt at a grin. It only came out as being sad. As the other one snapped at Heather before stalking away, the tiny one got up and followed. She didn't say a word to Heather either. There were a few guys in their group, and the one with dark hair and a tattoo circling over his jaw slung his arm around Heather's shoulders. He looked to be reassuring her, but she pushed him away and hurried after the two girls. He called after her, "Don't sweat it, Jax."

"Who's that?"

"Uh," Logan tilted his head to the side. "Max Monroe. I don't know him that well. I think Mason might. He's friendly with the Roussou peeps here so don't get close to him."

"There are Roussou peeps here?"

"A few." Logan started to lead me further down the hallway towards Mason's locker. "I think they're cousins or have relatives over there. No worries, Little Kade. They're not going to rise up and mutiny. There's not enough of them here, and they're not really liked by everyone else. Your throne is safe."

"Do you try to be annoying, Logan? Or is this post-coital bliss from whoever you went to see this morning?"

He chuckled, throwing his arm around my shoulder again. "I'm not being annoying. I'm being charming and since when do you want to know who my post-coital bliss is from?"

"I don't. As long as it's not Tate, I don't care."

He squeezed me tight, laughing as we pushed through another crowd. Mason's locker was in the back corner. It was broken off from the main wall with four others besides his. Spotting Nate and some of their guy friends, the other locker owners weren't a big leap. When Mason saw us coming, he straightened up from the wall. Nate glanced over, but he wasn't as welcoming. Shutting his locker, he took off.

"Unlike you, I'm guessing he's not interested in my post-coital bliss either."

"Logan."

"What?" He flashed me a grin, rubbing where I'd hit him. Then he said to Mason, "Nate's still not over our family meeting?"

"Would you if we kicked you out of your own basement?" Mason grimaced as he eyed Logan's arm that was still around my shoulder. "Do you always have to touch my girlfriend?"

"What?" Logan laughed and pulled me tighter against him. He rubbed his hand up and down my arm. "I thought you'd be happy that it's not Tate I'm touching. Sam just saved me from her clutches, you know."

"Your ex is causing more trouble?"

Logan's grin fell flat "I was joking about Tate." His arm fell away and he moved back a step. "You both can let up on Tate. She's not going to be a problem."

"Logan."

He gave me a little wave as he headed off.

"Let him go." Mason opened his locker and grabbed one of his books. Then he skimmed me up and down. "You headed to school early this morning."

"I went running."

He frowned. "When you run that early in the morning that means something's up. What's up?"

I leaned against Nate's locker. Even standing in the back corner, I could feel everyone's attention on us. I still wasn't used to it. "You guys are like gods here."

He grinned. "That's a new deflection."

"No." I shook my head. "It's not meant to be. I just..." I gestured to the hallway. There were students everywhere and most of them kept glancing at us. A couple girls in the far corner huddled together. When they noticed my attention, their heads ducked down and they skirted into another hallway. The last one peeked back. Her entire face was flaming red, even to the back of her neck.

"Sam?"

"It's nothing."

But it wasn't nothing.

"Hey." His tone softened and it did what it always did. It reached inside of me, loosened the knot that had formed in my throat, and pulled me towards him. I had to grin. Mason Kade would always hold this power over me, and as he tugged me against him, all my anxiety and concerns were pushed away. "What's going on with you?"

"Nothing." I corrected, "Nothing that's important. What do you think about Tate and Logan?"

"You mean," he raised an eyebrow, "besides what he just said? We're supposed to let up on her?"

"She draped herself all over him and he seemed to like it."

"Oh."

Nothing. No reaction. Just an 'oh.' Tilting my head to the side, I studied him and narrowed my eyes. "Oh? That's it?"

He flashed a grin before pressing a kiss to my forehead. "I'm not worried about Tate anymore. Not that much anymore."

Bombs exploded. The apocalypse had arrived. I could only stare in shock as he leaned back against the wall and pulled me between his legs. Looping his arms around my back, I was firmly enveloped in his arms, but I couldn't enjoy it. My stomach had started on a loop, rolling over and over again.

He sighed, watching me. "What?"

"Come again?"

"I'm not that worried about her."

"And when did this happen?"

His eyes narrowed, just a fraction, before he caught his reaction. Then it went back to the normal mask he wore in public. I felt like I'd been kicked in the stomach. It'd been a long time since he used that mask on me and anger started churning inside me. "I think my boyfriend left his body and someone took over. Who are you and what did you do with Mason?"

"You're being funny now?" he shot back, straightening away from the wall.

His arms fell and I stepped back. There was always a chill when I left his shelter, but not this time. I was growing heated as the conversation continued. "I'm sorry. Was that role taken? Only Logan can have his one-liners? Remind me of my role. I wasn't aware that I could never question my boyfriend."

"Sam, come on."

"No, you come on." My voice rose.

He glanced around and reached for my arm. "People are listening."

"I don't care." I stepped further back and his arm fell back to his side. "I want to know when you suddenly decided Tate wasn't something to be worried about."

"It's not like that. I just..." He shook his head. "Can we talk about this later?"

"I want to know what's happened. I know there's a reason why you've decided to let Tate off the hook."

"She does go to school here—"

My voice lifted again. "Not helping."

His shoulders dropped.

I added, "Before we were even together, you hated Tate. You went to parties just to humiliate her. You whispered some mojo to her the first day of school, and I don't think that it was pleasant, and now four days later you don't care?

Logan likes her; I can tell. She's going to hurt him again. No one worries you and she worried you. That made me worried too." My chest grew tight and I knew I must've started to look enraged. Mason wasn't even fighting back. "You better tell me what's going on and do it now."

My heart was pounding. I delivered one of my best mini-rants and I stood there, waiting for his response.

My answer?

He shrugged. "I don't know what to say to you. I just don't think he loves her anymore, so I'm not that worried." Then he pushed off from the wall and left.

That—what the hell just happened?

CHAPTER EIGHT

MASON

Walking away from Sam cost me. I was lying to her. She asked me a question, point-blank, and I dodged it, point-blank. She wasn't an idiot, but I couldn't tell her the real reason. Logan said he wanted to play with Tate, fool around with her, use her. So whatever. I wouldn't run interference anymore. It wasn't the best idea. I knew that much, but this was what Logan wanted and a part of me couldn't fault my little brother. She dated him for two years. She'd been the only girl he had fallen in love with, and she hit his older brother up. The need for revenge was too sweet for Logan to walk away from, but Sam wouldn't agree. She wouldn't understand. Sam protected. She loved. She wasn't a vengeance girl.

She was good. Logan and I were not.

Dodging around a group of girls, I headed down the hallway and ignored the two that stuck their hands out. One got a good grope of my stomach and the other tried to hold me back. Her fingers curled into my arm, but I twisted it free, knocking her back into her friends at the same time. As I kept going, one cried out from annoyance and I turned around.

They thought they could grab me, there were things called boundaries. "Try it again and I'll make your life hell."

Their eyes got wide and their heads shot straight up, but the one who tried to hold me back only rolled her eyes. I could tell she was the leader. Skimming over them, I figured they were freshmen—they would be the next Kate and crew— they were tough, popular, and already oozing sex.

"Mase!" Nate called, waving me down.

He was standing at Strauss' locker. The two were lounging back and watching the girls. A group of cheerleaders were next to them. I wasn't surprised. The exile had been broadcasted loud and clear. Kate and her friends weren't on friendly terms with us anymore so there was a vacancy at the top. There was always attention from girls, but it was different since the exile. The girls had become more aggressive with the guys, and more competitive with each other. My eyes fell to the left of Strauss and saw some of the drill team. Two had seductive grins on their faces while their friends were glaring at the cheerleaders.

That was one benefit when Kate reigned. She kept the hierarchy in order.

"Hey." I nodded to Nate and punched Strauss in the shoulder. I pulled it back at the last second so it turned into a friendly nudge.

Strauss gave me a halfhearted grin, his gaze lingering on an ass that walked past us.

"How'd that family pow-wow go? Did you guys get everything straightened out?"

Shit.

Strauss glanced at Nate as well. His hostility hadn't been kept in check, but Strauss didn't comment on it.

"It wasn't like that, Nate."

"Figured I should jet, just in case it was. I wouldn't want it to be awkward." He fixed me with a pointed look.

I lifted a hand and raked it through my hair. This wasn't a scene I wanted to happen here.

"Logan!"

Turning, I saw Logan had a girl pinned up against a locker. He was grinning right in her face, and her cheeks were flushed. She lit up, smiling widely, and took a deep breath. It lifted her breasts, and Logan fixed his gaze on those. He didn't look away, and the girl squirmed again. "Logan, stop."

Strauss grunted.

The girl didn't want him to stop. She was giggling, pressing against him, and pushing her breasts out even further.

"Mr. Kade," a loud voice boomed from the end of the hallway.

Logan stepped back, dropping the girl at the same time. She squealed again, this time not from enjoyment.

"Both Mr. Kades are here. Two for one deal. Lucky me," the voice said again with the same gusto. A hand came down hard on my shoulder at the same time.

Logan glanced up, meeting my gaze with a dark look before we moved as one. I turned around, dislodging the hand as Logan took a few steps to stand beside me.

I spoke first, "Principal Green."

Dressed in a grey suit, green tie, and standing over six feet, he was at eye-level with me. The older man, in his early forties with graying hair, lifted his lip. It was an imitation of a smile, but it didn't match the resignation in his eyes.

Logan snorted.

The principal inclined his head. "Something funny, Mr. Kade?"

He rolled his shoulders back, a cocky smirk coming over him. "Nah, Principal Green, except you look ready to drop on your feet. Busy night with the missus?"

Disapproval replaced the resignation. "I am here to give you both a warning."

"A warning?" Logan locked gazes with me again. "We haven't done anything."

"Yet," someone coughed from behind them.

Nate, Strauss, and some of the others laughed at the comment. A girl added in a groan, "They can do anything to me that they want." Her friends giggled and began whispering together. Someone snapped at them, "Shut it. Stop being so annoying."

Kate.

The girls fell silent.

Principal Green surveyed the crowd in the hallway, shaking his head at the same time. "How is it that you two command so much attention in this school? I've never met another person, much less a pair of brothers that can compete with the level of power you hold over my student population."

Logan shrugged. "We're cool, an inspiration to others."

A smattering of laughter started again.

Principal Green drawled, "I highly doubt that."

"It's true. We're like a walking Hallmark card, full of quotes and bible verses. We make people feel like they've been touched by an angel."

"Oh, shit," someone laughed.

Another commented, "He makes people feel touched all right."

A third snorted, "And not from anything angelic."

I cleared my throat and everyone shut up. "What'd you come here to say?"

"I got an interesting phone call from our local police."

I glanced at Logan. What the fuck? Then I narrowed my eyes at the principal again.

"They're screwed," a guy laughed.

Principal Green twisted around. "Don't you people have classes to go to?"

A few left. Most stayed.

He sighed. "I'd rather not have this conversation with an audience. Mason. Logan. Both of you come to my office?"

It was asked as a request. It wasn't. We followed him to his office. As we were about to turn right into the main office, Sam was coming from the left. Both of us saw her and she stopped mid-stride. The arm that held her books fell to her side and her mouth opened. A questioning look came into her depths, but I also saw the hurt still there. My jaw clenched and I turned away.

Logan wolf-whistled at her.

She didn't reply. I felt her gaze burning into the back of my skull. My shoulders tensed and I gripped the handle on the office door harder than necessary. I knew Logan caught the exchange and I knew my little brother wouldn't understand.

Fine. He could explain it to her himself. Then Logan would understand.

As we took the two seats across from Principal Green's desk, Logan bumped his knee against mine.

I ignored him.

He hissed, "What was that?"

"Nothing."

"Mase," Logan hissed again.

"Okay, boys," Principal Green started.

I ignored him too. "Remember the thing you talked to me about last night?"

"Oh." Logan fell back against his chair. He let out a long breath. "She knows."

"She picked up on it. You can tell her."

"What? No way—"

"Gentlemen," their principal clapped his hands together and leaned over his desk, "am I interrupting a little spat between the two of you?"

Logan rolled his eyes and slumped down his chair. I leaned forward. Principal Green had never done anything to screw us over, but he was an adult. It was bound to happen. "What do you want? We haven't done a thing so the police stuff has nothing to do with us."

Principal Green smiled to himself, leaning back in his chair. "Always down to business, Mason. I do appreciate that. Like I said before, I received a phone call. I was going to mention it to you at some point, but when I saw both of you in the hallway, I figured I should get it over with." His top lip lifted in an attempt at a smile.

"Congratulations, Principal Green." Logan rolled his eyes. "But here's a tip. Don't give your number out to hookers. They can't call for bail the next day."

"I was called by the police station this morning."

"You know a hooker that got arrested?"

"Logan Kade."

"Or don't even use hookers. If you get a mistress on the side, buy a pre-paid phone. Make sure to use cash. The wife can't catch you and your lady friend can call you all she wants."

"Mr. Kade, you should leave before I put you in detention."

He ignored him. "Don't go on Facebook either. I wouldn't even have an account if you become a pro cheater."

"Leave or I'll give you detention. I am not in the mood."

Logan snorted as he stood up. "Detention? What will the coach say? I'd miss practice."

"Leave, Mr. Kade."

"Leaving, Principal Green." Logan flashed him a grin and lifted two fingers in the peace sign. "Remember my tip: Don't give your number out to hookers and no Facebook. It'll save you a lot of trouble."

As soon as the door closed, I stated, "We didn't do anything."

"I know. They know that, too, but someone else did. Budd and Brett Broudou. They went to Quickie's and beat up a clerk. When the clerk was questioned, he indicated an earlier incident with them this week. He said you almost fought them."

"They beat the guy up?"

"Yes, they did." He cleared his throat. "Everyone is aware of the strained relationship between the two schools. There have been past incidents and this is my warning to you, Mason. Stop it. This rivalry with Budd and Brett Broudou needs to stop. This is between them and you, but both parties have included their schools. Other students will be hurt by this. Have you considered those consequences?"

My tone went cold. "I'm aware of the consequences."

Then I left. Principal Green didn't stop me, but it wouldn't have mattered. I didn't care to listen to any more advice from him. I was more aware of the consequences than anyone else.

SAMANTHA

As the rest of the week passed, I was in an alternate universe. Logan was pissy because I disapproved of Tate, who continued to stop at his locker every chance she got. Nate was pissy...well...that was deserved. We kicked him out of our meeting. I was pissy with Mason because he didn't disapprove of Tate anymore, or because he didn't explain it to me. There must've been more to it than what he said. He didn't have some 'sudden' realization that Logan wasn't going to fall in love with Tate again. There was a reason—this was Mason—there was always a reason, and as the rest of the week wore on, I was starting to realize he wasn't going to tell me.

The conversation was avoided, and when I brought it up, he'd distract me. Of course, most of those places were distracting anyways. In the shower. In bed. In the car. The only place he didn't try was in the kitchen. The one time I raised the question again, he ate quickly and left. Some excuse was thrown over his shoulder as he headed to his car.

I wasn't happy. I wasn't happy at all.

But when Friday came around and I found myself in an empty house, I was ready to admit defeat. I had no idea where anyone was, but I had a shift at Manny's. The evening would go fast, or that was my hope.

When I got there, there was no one. Crickets.

The door shut behind me and sent an echo throughout the place. Brandon stopped wiping the counter and lifted a hand. "All hail, Strattan."

"Are you trying to be funny?"

"Not you, too." His grin vanished.

"Not me what?"

"You're crabby." He gestured inside the kitchen with a glass and towel in hand. "You and my sister. What's in the water at that school? She's been crabby all week."

"Shut up, Brandon!" I heard through the door. "Just be happy you're still getting dates." Her voice became clearer as she stood in the doorway. Her hand was in her hair; it looked stuck there. "You're almost a has-been, tending bar for a living."

"Screw you. I own this side, remember?"

She rolled her eyes, stalking past him and shoved open the screen door. When it banged shut behind her, she plopped down in one of the lawn chairs. The smell of cigarette smoke soon drifted inside.

The usual sibling camaraderie had vanished.

Following her outside, I took one of the other chairs. "What's wrong?"

Flicking the end of her cigarette, she got up and shut the solid oak door. Letting the screen door shut after it, she sat back down and took a long drag before she shook her head. Her voice trembled. "Have the Tommy P.'s done anything to you this week?"

I frowned. "What? No." And I was surprised by that. They'd been so grrr and threatening before, I had expected something. "Why?"

Taking another long drag, she reached inside her pocket and held her phone to me. "They've been sending me texts all week."

"About what?"

She snorted. "Can't you guess?"

I could, but I didn't want to. They were starting with my friend. I knew this was the beginning. The first one read: **First warning, bitch.**

I rolled my eyes at their originality and clicked on the next: **Second warning, cunt.** Again. So original. The third and fourth were the same, more warnings followed by an expletive. Then they started getting interesting. The fifth read: **Ditch the bitch or you'll be sorry.** Something new. The sixth was different: **You used to cut. The word is out. Wanna know who told?**

I paused and glanced over. Heather was on her second cigarette already. I held my tongue and read the next one: **We know about your mom. Want that out too?**

Heather told me her mom left when they were kids. I wondered what more there was to the story, but went to the eighth text: **Fire Strattan. If you don't, we'll destroy your daddy's livelihood.**

I couldn't read the rest. A sick feeling took root in my gut. "I'm sorry."

Heather ground out her second cigarette, and lit a third right away. As she settled back again, she shook her head. "Brad plays ball with Natalie's cousin. Never considered warning my oldest brother not to say a word. I'm guessing that's where she learned all that stuff." Her voice quivered.

"You used to cut yourself?"

She inhaled a long deep drag before shaking her head. "In the seventh grade. That's when my mom took off. I was an idiot. She was a horrible person, but I didn't want a dad that first year. I wanted her back. I blamed him for everything, even though she was the one that cheated, and she was the one that left us. He stayed. She didn't, but I wanted her."

There was more to the story. I heard the pain in her voice. "Your mom cheated?" Something we had in common.

She nodded, looking so bleak and defeated. The wind picked up and blew her hair back. It flattened her shirt against her small frame. She was already slender, but the material was so thin that I could see her ribs. Knowing she couldn't have lost so much weight over just this week, it still made me feel guilty.

"I'm sorry," I told her.

"For what?" She was almost done with the third cigarette. "I don't like being told what to do. That's what she used to do. Kate and the tomboy bitches are just like my mom. I hate being told what to do." She drew in another drag, cursing at the same time. "They want to tell me what to do? Tell me to drop someone who's been a better friend than most of my others? I'm starting to really hate them, Sam. I'm talking really hate them, like I want to cut them how I used to cut myself."

I didn't know what to say. Heather had stood by me, but she'd been distant all week. "You never told me about your friends? They didn't look happy with you the other day."

"Yeah." She drew her knees up into the chair and wrapped her arms around them. They were like twigs. Still holding the cigarette, she drew in a deep breath. I saw how she swallowed, grimacing at the same time. "I can't really blame Cory or Rain."

"Rain?"

"Rainbow."

"Her real name is Rainbow?"

"No." She blew out a puff of smoke. "Her real name is Ginnie, but we call her Rain. She's always wearing something with a rainbow. Always has, now that I think about it, since the sixth grade when she moved here. Rain's short for rainbow."

"You said she's an albino."

"Yeah," her voice softened and her eyebrows set forward. Frowning to herself, she grew thoughtful. "Kate was being the bitch she is, making fun of her. Cory stuck up for her and the two have been close ever since. Helps that Cory understood. Kate's been picking on her since the third grade, I think."

"No wonder they don't like me."

"It's not you." Heather shook her head, lifting the cigarette again. "It's Mason and Logan. It's not even them really, it's just because they were friends with those girls for so long. They're why Kate and the Tommy P.'s got so powerful, you know? They gave them weight or cred or whatever. No one wanted to mess with the girls that were 'friends' with the top guys."

"Hey!" Brandon banged on the door. "Game's going to be over in an hour."

Heather groaned, finished her last cigarette and put it out.

"What game?"

Both frowned at me. "The basketball game."

"Fallen Crest..." A foreboding sense of dread kicked in. "Public?" I didn't need to see their reactions.

"Mason and Logan never said anything?"

"No..."

"Don't sweat it. It's like another day at the job for them. They're more about football games, aren't they?"

"Yeah..." But it still stung. Whatever. Another shitty thing to add on to this week. "So what happens after a game? What are we in for?"

"Before your guys made this the popular hangout? Nothing. We would've gotten a few stragglers in, but now it's going to get packed. Our regulars know not to come in. Even Gus, and you know how much he loves his seat, but they know we'll get swamped. A few girls from school texted and said everyone's planning on heading here. It's going to get nuts."

Forget Mason. Forget Logan. I had a job to do. "You want me in the front or back?"

"I'd say screw it and work the front, but Frank is sick."

"So the back it is."

"That's okay with you?"

It felt like I'd been kicked again when I caught a look of pity in her eyes, but I ignored it. Tried to, but it hurt. No one said a word about the game. I didn't have any friends at school. I couldn't hear it from them, and Heather had been distant on her own. I saw her in the hallways, before and after school, but she had started leaving campus during lunch the last couple of days. I'd been distracted. Mason began waiting for me at my locker during lunch. They had an open-campus policy, so we took advantage of it and left to grab fast food. Most of the time was spent on the drive there, getting our food, and then eating it as soon as possible on the way back.

Any free moments were spent in the parking lot with a few stolen kisses and some heavy petting. He made sure his car was always parked away from the school and surrounded by his friends' vehicles, so no one could spy on us.

And thinking about other students, I said, "No one really made a big deal about the game. At Academy, there would've been pep rallies. Posters and banners would've been everywhere. I don't remember seeing any this week."

Heather pulled open the doors as we went inside and answered over her shoulder, "There were flyers, but not that much. Everyone just knows about the game. They go if they want, they don't if they don't want to. Besides, the basketball games aren't like the football games. Those are nuts."

"Are you kidding?" Brandon piped in from behind his counter. "The basketball games are nuts, too."

"I know, but she's asking why it wasn't really talked about at school."

"Oh." He nodded. "It's because everyone just knows about it. That's how it was during my days." A wide grin came over him. "I remember those days fondly. Good days. Good memories."

Heather rolled her eyes as she tied on her server's apron. "You mean, good pussy?"

"Ah." The wide grin stretched in a full smile. "Easy pussy is more like it. I didn't have to search for it. Those girls came to me. I can't imagine how the Kades have it now. Compared to them, I was nothing. They're like gods."

It felt like a knife stabbed me in my chest.

Heather made an exasperated sound. "You're an idiot." She jerked her thumb at me.

"Oh." He sounded sheepish, letting out a weak laugh. "Sorry, Sam. You know what I mean, not that I remember Mason indulging in pussy like Logan does, but—"

"Just shut it, Brandon. You'll be doing us all a favor."

I held a hand up, shaking my head. "No, you guys. Really. I am aware of their near-celebrity status. This is nothing new to me. I live with them, remember? Logan's got a new girl over almost every day." But that wasn't true. He was gone most of the time. During the week we had all settled into a new routine. Logan was usually the first to leave, or he would leave the night before and not come home. He must've kept half his closet in his car because he never wore the same clothes twice, and he was always showered for the new day. Nate was the next to leave. He'd dash out a few minutes before Mason and myself. While I'd be nibbling on a piece of toast in the kitchen, waiting for Mason, Nate would dart through, holler a goodbye, and be on the road before Mason would even come down the stairs.

As for Mason and myself, we began a trade-off. We'd ride together in the mornings, unless I went on a run. I took my own car during those days, but when I would ride with Mason, I drove his Escalade home while he got a ride with Logan or Nate. If he forgot to give the keys to me during lunch, they would be waiting for me in my locker. There wasn't a lot of time for us to talk because he had basketball practice, and I'd usually be itching for a long run, sometimes my second one of the day.

"Game's over," Brandon called out. He was looking down at his phone. "We won: thirty-two—nineteen."

"Here we go." Heather took her place behind the counter. I went to the backroom. It wasn't until hours later that I remembered I had left my phone in my car.

CHAPTER NINE

MASON

I left the gymnasium and pushed through the doors. A lot of the others had already gone. Most were headed to eat and then to Fischer's party, but I needed to go to Manny's first. Sam might not want to go and after the way I'd been dodging her question all week, I needed to make it up to her. Whatever she wanted was whatever she was going to get. My jaw clenched as I remembered the hurt in her eyes when she realized I wasn't going to answer her. Shit. I couldn't. If I did…no way in hell. I couldn't. That was the end of it.

My hand tightened on my bag as I crossed the parking lot. Logan's car was still parked next to mine. What was my brother still doing here? Nate's car was here too. Things were cold between the two, but they could joke around with each other. Still, I didn't see them hanging out together, and I hadn't seen either of them in the locker room. Coach needed to talk to me, and most of the guys were gone when I came out.

"Hey," Logan spoke up, straightening from his Escalade.

I frowned. My little brother looked tired. "You need to stop with this whole sex marathon you've got going on." Unlocking my car, I tossed my bag inside.

Logan rolled his eyes. "Whatever. I hear you and Sam going at it all the time. Don't you guys take a fucking break?"

I grunted. Nice choice of words. "I can have all the sex I want with her. Know why? Because she's my girlfriend, and I love her. I know my dick can be in her, and it's safe. She's safe. We're not going to be having little Kades running around here anytime soon. Can you say the same?"

"You're such a dick."

"A dick that cares about you. Stop all the screwing around. You'll catch something or you're going to end up with a kid."

"What's your problem?" Logan ran a hand through his hair.

"You're my problem. I mean it, Logan. Stop screwing around. Find a girl, get some feelings for her, and be rabbits." He was pissed. We both knew it, but I wasn't going to ask for the motivation of his sudden marathon. "There has to be some girl in this town that you could date who's not Tate."

Logan shot me a dark look. "Get over yourself. I don't love her, and you know it."

I narrowed my eyes, studying him before I relented. "Do whatever you want. Mom'll love being a grandmother."

My brother shot me a different look now, one filled with dark humor. "Can you imagine that? Helen quilting little booties for the kid? She'd flip out."

"If we thought she went nuts after the divorce..." I chuckled. "I've got a feeling we haven't seen nothing yet. She'd go ape-shit."

"I'd feel bad for whoever the chick would be." Logan shuddered, laughing at the same time. Then he stopped and studied me for a moment. "What are you going to do about Sam?"

The amusement was gone.

A cruel glint appeared and Logan added, "Mom's moving back to Fallen Crest. What's Sam going to do when you leave for college?"

I cursed. "That's for me and Sam to deal with. You don't need to worry about it."

"Screw you, Mason. I care about her, too. We both know Mom's going to want me to live with her. I, sure as shit, ain't stepping foot in Dad's place while he's got Psychopath Barbie with him, and I'm not letting Sam go back there. No way in hell."

"No way in hell?" An equally cruel look came over my face as my lips curved in a mocking smirk. "Look at you, already stepping in shoes that aren't yours."

"And they're yours?"

"Yes." My body jerked forward. Logan flinched, instinctually reacting to the sudden threat, but I stopped myself. I was tired of this. "I'll figure something out for Sam. You don't have to worry about her." And I would, even if it meant I'd be commuting to college. Nate would be pissed; he was excited for the whole college experience, but I had football and Sam to worry about.

"Mase." Logan snapped his fingers in front of my face.

"What?"

"Where'd you go just now?"

"Nowhere." All that crap could be dealt with another day. "What's the plan? Why are you still waiting? I thought you'd be long gone by now."

Logan shrugged, shoving his hands into his front pockets as he leaned back against his car again. One of his legs lifted and rested against it. A sudden yawn came over him as he glanced around the emptied lot. "I was. Everyone decided to go for pizza instead of Manny's tonight. I figured you'd go there before the party. Sam's working tonight, right?"

"I was going to see what she wanted to do." And how pissed she was at me.

"You going to eat there?"

"Maybe. You?"

"Thought about it. I'll probably get with someone tonight but we haven't had much family time this week."

"Yeah..." A slight movement from the far end of the parking lot caught my attention. Narrowing my eyes, I moved forward to get a better view. A person was coming around the corner, and that walk...it was Nate.

"What is it?"

I shook my head at Logan. Nate was heading towards us, his hands shoved deep in his sweatshirt's front pocket. His hood was pulled up, and he was hunched forward. I caught the little movement he made in the front. Nate moved to pull up his zipper.

I gestured to Logan, lowering my voice, "Can you take off? Don't let him see."

Logan frowned, but lowered his voice too. "Sure. Why?"

"Nate got laid over there."

"Say no more." And then Logan melted into the darkness, going the other way around his car.

I waited until Nate had almost gotten to our cars before I spoke up, much the same as Logan had done to me earlier. "I thought you'd be gone by now."

Nate's head whipped up and he stumbled in his footing. "Shit, Mason! You just gave me a heart attack, you fucker."

"Relish it."

"You're such an ass." Nate barked out a laugh as he pulled his keys from his pocket. Shaking his head, he asked, "What are you doing here?"

"Coach wanted to talk about the game."

"What about? We killed 'em, like we always do." Unlocking his car, he leaned inside and reached for his bag. Riffling through it, he pulled his phone out and straightened back up as he went through his messages. Then he cursed and took a deep breath. He turned around and I saw it. All the games were done. He handed his phone over. "I just got a text from Kate."

I got video of you and Parker screwing. Do what she told you to do, and it won't go on the internet.

"Is there really a video?" I frowned at the phone as I started looking for more texts from her.

He sighed and leaned back against Logan's vehicle. "I don't know. I've been trying to find out. Parker thinks there is, and I have no idea what to do anymore."

I went cold. "Is this why you've been a shady motherfucker lately?"

Nate nodded. "I've been scared. You and Logan have both been on my ass about not being a good friend. Then I wanted to say something that one night, but you guys closed ranks on me. I was shoved out so I thought, 'Fuck it. I'll fix it myself.'" He gestured to where he came from. "I've been keeping things up with Parker because I need her to find the tape. I have no idea where Kate might've put it, if she even has one."

"She says *do what she told you to do.* What are you supposed to do?"

Nate swore under his breath. "You're going to be pissed."

"Already getting there." And I was.

"They wanted me to drug Sam one night and take pictures of her." Nate didn't hold back the truth. He delivered without missing a beat. "They wanted her naked and put in embarrassing positions."

"Were you supposed to do anything to her?"

Nate hesitated, but answered a second later. "Yes, but you know I wouldn't have done any of it. I've been stalling and trying to fix this on my own."

Kate's fate was sealed. I was going to destroy her. "Push Parker to find out when the tape was created. Maybe we can figure out if there even is a tape before we call her bluff."

Nate flinched. "We're going to call her bluff?"

"We'll search her house first."

"Or you can pretend to be tight with Kate and get the tape from her."

"No."

"That's the only thing she wants—you. Kate's obsessed with you. She'll do anything for you, even hand over a video she used to blackmail your best friend."

"Kate's obsessed with power. She'll go through anyone to get it, even my friends." Nate looked away, and I paused. "Or has she already?"

"What?"

"Don't fuck with me."

He nodded, sighing at the same time. "Yeah, she's come on to me a few times. Parker doesn't know. I haven't told her yet."

If she had with him, she would've with the others. A new plan was forming in my head. "Don't. If Kate does it again, record it on your phone. We can use it against her."

"Hey." Logan came around the car. His eyes darted between us. "What's going on?"

"Nothing."

Logan shot me a questioning look.

"I'll fill you in later." I punched Nate in the shoulder. "Go to your woman. Keep stalling for us."

"Actually," Nate glanced from me to Logan, "I told her I'd meet up with her in the morning. She thinks I'm going for pizza and then Ethan's party."

Logan narrowed his eyes, his jaw locked in place, but he kept quiet.

I kept a wary eye on my brother. He wasn't known for keeping his temper in check. This was one of those moments so I said to Nate, "Then go. We'll see you later."

As Nate went to his car, I knew my brother was a heartbeat away from exploding. I lowered my voice. "Relax, okay? I'll tell you the plan in a second."

"Fine," Logan growled and waited for Nate to reverse.. As he did, Logan said, "He was with Parker just now, but it sounds like you already know—"

A screech of tires silenced him. We darted around my car and heard a thud, followed by metal crashing into metal.

Everything slowed.

Holy shit.

BEEEEEEEEEEEEEEEEEEEEEEEEEEEEEEEEEEEEEEE EEPPPPPPPPPPPPPPPPPP

"Oh my god," Logan breathed out next to me. We stopped, just for a moment and we stared.

Nate's car was in the middle of the intersection. Another car's front end had barreled into him and both cars were smashed together.

A sudden pause fell over me. I couldn't think, breathe, or hear anything. Then it cleared just as quick. Nate's horn kept blaring as someone screamed. Then I took off, sprinting to the accident. My heart had leapt into my throat and my feet pounded onto the pavement. I couldn't get there fast enough.

SAMANTHA

The place was packed for the rest of the night. Heather popped her head in once to warn me Kate and her Bitch Crew had arrived. When they didn't see me, she said they left right away. A different emotion flared over her face as she passed along the message, but it was gone before I could place it. Maybe fear? But no. Heather seemed to be getting pissed by them. She couldn't be getting scared. A shiver went through me. I hoped she wasn't getting scared. That would mean they were winning. That they were getting to the one female friend I had. No one else had befriended me over the past week, and I wasn't sure if anyone would.

It was later on, a few hours before closing, when I realized she hadn't told me if Logan or Mason had arrived. I was half expecting them to find me in the back themselves. Mason would've helped me, but Heather only came back to ask if I wanted to see any of my Academy friends. I didn't. Adam and Becky both had been trying to remain friends, but there was too much disloyalty and pain that came with them.

When the grill closed, I still hadn't heard a thing. Because I didn't want to make a big deal out of it, or worry Heather, I found her brother during a break. "Brandon?"

He looked up mid-pour. "One second." Finishing, he slid the drink across the counter to his customer and headed over. Wiping his hands on a towel, he raised his eyebrows. "What's up?"

I felt so stupid. "Did any of Mason and Logan's friends come in?"

He frowned. "No, now that you mention it. That's weird. You worried?"

Not helpful. I sighed. "I'm sure things are fine. I'm just surprised, is all."

I was about to go back for the last of the dishes when Brandon tapped my arm. He'd come closer and lowered his voice, "Listen, I know what you're thinking, and that's not the case. I was being a jackass earlier. No way would Mason cheat on you."

Thanks, Brandon. I am now thinking it's a possibility.

Inching even closer, he scanned the room before he continued, "Listen, none of their crew came in." He shook his head, staring at me like I was supposed to know what that meant.

I lifted an eyebrow. "And...?"

"Oh. Yeah," he shuffled closer, "I remember those days. I know what it's like. If none of them showed up, that means something came up."

"Who are you talking about?"

"The popular crowd. You know, the 'in' crowd." He nodded and patted my shoulder. "Something came up. I'm positive."

"Why are you being awkward about this?"

"Oh." He straightened and flashed me a grin. All that awkwardness was gone as he shrugged. "It's called being a nice brother. My sis wasn't a part of the 'in'. She doesn't know what it's like. You and me," lifting an empty glass, he pointed to me and then back to him, "we know what it's like."

Of course. Perfect sense. I shook my head.

"No worries, Sam. If he didn't show, something must've come up."

"What's my brother talking about?" Heather plopped her order pad on the counter and leaned over, stretching her back at the same time.

"Nothing." I needed to know what had 'come up' like Brandon insisted. Patting my pockets, I cursed under my breath.

"What?"

"My phone's in the car."

"Go." Heather waved me off. There was an extra oomph to her grin.

Narrowing my eyes, I paused. "What?"

She went still. "What?"

"What happened to you tonight?"

"Nothing."

She'd said that too fast. My eyebrow went back up. "I call bullshit."

She laughed. "Spoken like a true friend." Then she indicated behind me, and I turned to see Channing at a back table. He'd been watching us.

"Ah." It made sense now. "So the no-boyfriend-not-anymore is here and you two are going to get not-friendly tonight?"

"Something like that." She chuckled before patting my arm again. "Go. I'm serious. I'll have him finish the few dishes that are left. It's not like he hasn't worked back there before."

He had? That was new info. I started for the door after making sure my car keys were in my pocket. As I passed by her, I muttered under my breath, "One of these days you're going to have explain your situation to me."

"Yeah," she sighed. Her tone turned wistful. "Maybe one day I'll know, too."

That was weird. As I headed out, I glanced back over my shoulder. The happiness on Heather's face was unmistakable. She had turned back to Channing and struck a seductive pose. I grinned as I remembered the first time I met her and pushed through the door.

The parking lot was surrounded by trees and on most days it was peaceful. It was beautiful during the day, but at night, it was eerie. It was especially creepy when most of the cars were gone. I had no doubt there was some big party, and drawing closer to my car, I could see that my phone's light was blinking. I had messages—

"You're that waitress from last week."

I screamed at the deep voice, jumping around in one leap. My heart was in my chest, beating loudly and trying to pound its way out. A dark figure appeared at the end of my car, and I couldn't see who it was. A hood was pulled over his face, casting it in a shadow, but he was large and muscular.

I needed mace. Why the hell hadn't I listened to Logan the one time he joked about that? "Who are you?" I demanded, taking deep breaths so my heart could settle.

His hands went in the air, surrendering and he used one to pull his hood down. "I'm sorry. Really. I'm not here to hurt you. I just..." He took a deep breath and I heard his voice shaking.

It was Brett Broudou.

My eyes got even wider and my heart started racing again. His words weren't very reassuring. I started backing away. "What do you want?"

"Nothing." He held his hand out to me. "Stop. Please. I'm really not here to hurt you or scare you."

"I beg to differ. I'm scared shitless right now."

"I'm sorry."

"You're huge."

"I know," he grimaced and slunk back a few steps. His shoulders went down, like he was trying to make himself smaller. "I'm really not here to scare you. That's my brother. He's like that."

I hadn't taken much account of how he looked in Manny's the other week. I'd been too focused on avoiding them and the guys hid me right away at the gas station, but I had a better view now. He had a square face that was a little meaty from his bulky size. His nose was crooked, like he had broken it once and it never healed right. A slight scar ran down from his nose to his top lip. His lips had formed into a tentative grin. Peering closer, I tried to see his eyes better. Mason always told me that you could read a person's intent through their eyes, but I couldn't see his. It was too dark.

Again, because we were in an almost emptied parking lot that only had one working light over it. Not the best meeting place to pick.

He didn't look ready to attack me, but looks could be deceiving. My tone went flat. "Tell me what you want or I'm leaving. Next time find me in a crowded place if you want to talk, or better yet, don't." But there had been something in his tone. Regret? Maybe something else, friendliness? I wasn't sure, but my heart slowed a little and my chest wasn't as tight.

"I know." His head went down, and he made a show of taking another large step backwards. "I...um...whoa. This isn't going how I thought it was going to at all."

This? How he wanted it to go? I frowned. What was he talking about?

"Um," he cleared his throat and tried another smile. "So...you're friends with Jax?"

"Jax?"

"Heather." He gestured inside. "Channing, her on-again-off-again whatever they are, goes to my school. He's pretty cool. So's she."

"She threatened you guys."

"Well," he shrugged, shifting on his feet, "I mean, I can understand. My brother can be mean...sometimes..." he trailed off, glancing around.

Was he checking for witnesses?

"Um."

He didn't *sound* like someone getting ready to attack.

"So..."

Yes? My heart began pounding again. Thump. Thump. Thump.

"I was wondering," he stopped, and looked around once more.

Seriously. The guy was going to give me a heart attack. "I'm going to go home."

"No. Wait." His hands fell down and he cupped them together; his head lowered too. "Heather doesn't seem to like us coming to Manny's, so I've stayed away, but I don't know you. I'm figuring you don't go to our school. I was looking for you this past week." A self-conscious laugh came from him. "I don't even know your name. She might've said it, but I was just paying attention to my brother. Budd can be a jerk sometimes...Shannon too, though she's a girl. There's another name for that."

"I know. It rhymes with ditch."

The corner of his mouth curved up. It started to transform his face, from what I could see in the shadows. "Yeah. So..." His nervousness was now all-too clear.

My heart sank. I was starting to figure out where this was going.

"I was just...um...so, do you... No, that's not right. Uh..." He took a deep breath, pinning me with his gaze now. "Would you like to go out sometime?"

Yep. I saw it coming. I figured it out, but it still didn't curb the shock, and my mouth fell open. He just asked me out. A Broudou brother. Me. It all clicked with me now. He still had no idea who I was. I was just 'that waitress' who works at Manny's. "Um..." I closed my mouth. I had no idea what to say.

"Oh." He drew away from me even further. "I see."

"No," I started, but stopped. What the hell was I going to say? "Um...I have a boyfriend."

"Oh." He straightened, now filled with relief. His voice came out stronger, more confident. "I see. Who?"

"W-w-what?"

"OH!" His head flew up, and he slapped himself in the forehead. "I'm really sorry. It ain't any of my business. I wasn't going to beat him up or anything. Budd does that stuff. I don't. I mean, he gets me in trouble too sometimes, but I wouldn't do that. I think you're really pretty. The guy's lucky, whoever he is, and don't tell me. I don't want to know. I don't want you to be scared. We have a reputation. I understand and all."

He was rambling. I had rejected him, and I was beginning to feel sympathy for this Broudou brother. Hell had frozen over. The world had shifted on its axis.

"I'm going to go now." He started to turn.

"Wait," I stopped him.

He stopped.

Now I wanted to slap myself in the forehead. Why had I done that? I lowered my hand, hadn't realized I even lifted it. "Nothing. Sorry."

"Okay. Well, bye."

"Bye..."

Awkward. The whole thing had been awkward, but lucky me. Brett left in the same manner he had appeared—he just disappeared. I had no idea where he'd gone.

Brett Broudou asked me out. Me, Samantha Strattan. I nodded to myself. There was something funny about that. Then I remembered Mason—my phone. Hurrying inside my car, I grabbed it and hit the screen. The first text stopped everything.

At the hospital. Car accident.

The phone fell from my fingers.

CHAPTER TEN

The drive to the hospital passed in a blur. I was on auto pilot and somehow found myself shoving through the doors to the emergency room without a clue how I got there. Taking two heart-stopping steps, my foot lifted for another when I spotted Logan in the corner. His head was down, his arms folded over his chest, leaning against a wall. His friends were around him—guys and girls I didn't recognize—but no Mason.

My chest lifted and my lungs struggled to take a breath.

Then Logan lifted his head. It happened in slow motion, his eyes scanned the room and then he saw me. Surprise came over him before it clicked. Comprehension flared next. My foot came down hard. It was worse than I thought, but he shook his head and pushed off the wall. His movement drew attention, and everyone watched him cross to me.

"No, no, Sam. It's not like that."

I was too scared to say a word. For one split second, I considered running. If I didn't know, I couldn't lose him, but I had to know. "Is it bad?" *Tell me he's alive.*

"He's fine. The brakes were cut so he got blindsided by an oncoming car. He couldn't stop when he was leaving the lot. I would've driven onto the grass or something, not out into an intersection." Logan rolled his eyes. His arm came around my shoulder and he jerked me against him. I could feel the laughter reverberating through his chest. "He's such an idiot, but it's a good thing he drives like a grandpa sometimes."

My eyes closed and I sagged under his arm. I couldn't believe it. *Mason is going to be fine. Mason is going to be fine. Mason is going to be fine. I could breathe,* I tried telling myself over and over, but my brain and my body weren't working together. My chest was still tight, stretched from fear.

"Sam?" Logan jostled me a little, hugging me tighter into his side. "You okay?"

Mason was going to be fine.

I opened my mouth to fill my lungs. Nothing.

"Sam?"

I heard him and my eyes flew open. Mason was at the end of a hallway, frowning at us, and a rush of relief came over me. My mouth dropped, but then he was heading towards me. As he drew near, he asked, "You okay?"

A buzzing sound was in my head. I shook it so I could hear him, but then his hand was on my arm, and he tugged me from Logan. Oh my god. My arms were numb, but I wrapped them around him and tried to hold tight.

He moved us and somehow we were in a private room. Looking around, I saw a small room with some clothes lying on a cot. There was also a computer and a small TV. It looked like we were in a room where the doctors slept when they were on-call. I closed my eyes when his head bent and I felt his breath on my neck. It felt good. It felt reassuring. I tried to hold him even tighter, but he asked, "What's wrong? Nate's going to be fine."

Wait.

I leaned back. "Nate?" My voice was shaking.

He frowned at me. "Yeah."

"Nate? Nate was in the car accident?"

"Yeah."

He was still looking at me, frowning as his eyes roamed over my face. Then it all hit me and I shoved him away. "I thought it was you! I thought you'd been hurt and that I was going to lose you." I threw my arm up, gesturing to the lobby. "Logan's talking about what an idiot you are, but I thought someone had crashed into your car!"

"No." He tugged me back into his arms. "You're shouting."

I didn't care. "I thought it was you!"

"It wasn't!" he yelled over me. "Calm down. I'm sorry—"

Shoving my hand into my pocket, I pulled my phone out and checked the number. It was Logan's number. I put it in his face. "Logan texted me. Not you. I thought it was you. Why else would Logan be the one to text me? And he texted! He should've called—no!—you should've called! And why didn't you even tell me about your basketball game? I had no idea. I'm new, remember? I don't know these things, and no one talks to me—"

"I'm sorry." Mason was fighting back a grin as he pulled me against his chest and wrapped both arms around me. He took the phone from my hand and pushed it back into my pocket. The intense anger kept me stiff in his embrace, and I lifted a fist to his stomach. He said, "I knew you had to work tonight. I didn't say anything because I didn't want you to feel bad about missing the game. I'm sorry...again...I'm sorry, Sam. I am. I was the one driving. I told Logan to call you, but we were right behind the ambulance so he texted instead. I'm sorry. Next time I'll be the one to call you."

Oh shit. Next time. There better not be a next time. "Mason..." The anger left me then, and a void took its place. There was a big gaping hole left in me. I thought I had lost him.

"I'm sorry."

Mason...

I couldn't even finish that thought. I was just so relieved it hadn't been him. My knees sagged in relief. "Is Nate okay?"

He nodded, looking down at me, searching inside of me. "Yeah, he's fine."

"Logan said his brakes were cut?"

"Yeah." His jaw went rigid. "My guess is that it was Budd and Brett Broudou."

My eyes got wide. Oh holy shit. "Can you prove that?"

"Who cares about proving? We already know."

Oh. My heart started beating fast. Now would be a good time for that second confession... I took a deep breath and stepped away from him. "Mason?"

"Yeah?"

Three...

Two...

"Yo." The door burst open, and Logan popped his head inside. "The doc wants to see you. He's waiting for you by the nurse's station."

Mason moved around him and took off. He disappeared around the corner. There went one...

"You okay?"

I nodded. "Never better."

"I heard you shouting." He propped his shoulder against the doorframe and kept studying me. "I'm sorry about the mishap. I should've told you we were fine; I just didn't think about it."

"Yeah."

"Sam?"

There was a giant ball of guilt and worry in my stomach. I had to tell them about Budd and Brett. It'd been too long ago, but with Brett asking me out, Mason and Logan needed to know first. "Logan?"

"Yeah?"

"What are you guys going to do?"

He frowned, but moved inside so the door shut behind him. Same room, different Kade. "What do you mean?"

"I mean, you guys are going to do something to get even." It wasn't a question. That was a fact. Everyone knew it. "What are you going to do?"

He lifted one shoulder. "I don't know. Nate will probably make the decision. They did this to him. Of course, I'm guessing they did it because he clipped Budd with his car." His eyes turned feral. "Now I wish he'd gotten hit harder, would've put him in the hospital first."

I sucked in a breath. "Are you guys going to hurt them?" Did I want that? Didn't that mean they'd retaliate? Mason or Logan could get hurt. That couldn't happen. Maybe I could talk to Brett...no. I'd make it worse then. "They'll hurt you guys back."

"Oh." Understanding flashed in his eyes and he lifted a hand. It went to my arm, meant to comfort me, but I bolted into him. Bumping against his chest, I wrapped my arms and hugged tight. Logan was family. Mason was more. I couldn't lose either of them.

I mumbled against him, "Don't hurt them. They'll hurt you back. I can't handle that."

"Oh, Sam."

"Logan, promise me."

He stiffened under my arms and moved me back. "I can't promise you that."

I knew it.

It felt as if a hand reached inside of me and was gripping my heart.

Logan added, "I'm sorry, but they're going to do it anyway. They're looking for you. Why do you think that is?"

"For running lessons?" My voice came out high-pitched and shrill. The panic was full blown. "Why wouldn't they?"

He sighed and shook his head. As he bit down on the corner of his lip, I turned away. I couldn't see the pity there. They were going to do it anyways, no matter the consequences. One of them was already hurt. When would they be next? I knew it was only a matter of time.

I had to try again. "Please, Logan. Go to the police. This is going to end badly."

"They're hoping to hurt you. You're Mason's girlfriend. Everyone knows how protective we are of you. You're our weakness, Sam. We have to finish this before they do something to you."

I gritted my teeth. Mason and Logan would not get hurt, not if I had anything to do with it...

"Logan," Mason called from down the hall.

"Gotta go." Logan cupped the back of my head and pressed a chaste kiss to my forehead. "You okay?"

I nodded. The numbing sensation had left, but it was coming back. As he broke away and headed off, I couldn't shake the uneasy feeling. I was given a glimpse into the future. One where it was one of them, not Nate, in that hospital bed, but it was worse.

"Um," a voice broke through my reverie. I jerked my head sideways and saw a girl standing in the doorway. Her top lip was curled up in a sneer, and she was eyeing me up and down. Dressed in an oversized sweatshirt and jeans that clung to her tiny form, I figured she was cheerleader. The glitter was still on her cheeks. Tucking a strand of her hair behind her ear, she pointed at me with her other hand. "Your leg is ringing."

My leg is ringing... Oh. My phone.

It was James. I closed my eyes for a second and heaved a big sigh. I could only take so much, but I answered as I left the room and headed back outside. "Hello?"

"Sam." His relief was clear. "Thank you for answering. I can't get Mason or Logan on the phone."

"They're busy right now."

"I know. Is Nate okay?"

I frowned. "How do you know?"

"About the accident? His parents were called, but they're in New Zealand so they called me right away."

His parents? Sometimes I forgot he had them. "Uh, I'm not sure. I think he's fine. Mason and Logan are with the doctor right now."

"Yes. His parents told the doctor to release information to them. Are they okay?"

I shrugged. "I don't know. I'm sure they're worried."

He was silent. Then, he added, "No, not Nate's parents. I meant my sons. Are they all right?"

"Oh. Yeah, they're fine."

"Good." I could picture him, nodding with the phone pressed to his ear. "That's good. Do you think I should come down there?"

Oh dear god. "NO! I mean, no." There was no way I could handle Analise right now.

He gentled his voice. "I wouldn't bring her, Sam. Not to this. I know Helen was called as well. I'm sure she's heading there now."

My heart started to race again. I couldn't handle her either. "She is?" My fingers gripped the phone tight.

"Yeah, that's why I'm trying to get ahold of my sons. Could you ask them if they want me to come down? Neither have responded to my earlier text about them moving back in and dinner."

"Um..."

"I'd imagine Helen will want them to stay with her," he commented without waiting, then continued, "and I'm sure they won't want to stay at Nate's house since his parents are coming."

They are? That was not in the conversation. Had I missed that?

"Do you need a place to stay? I couldn't imagine Helen being okay with you being at the hotel with them."

"What?" I squeaked into the phone. Was it possible to have a heart attack at my age? It was pounding in my chest. A rush of heat came over me as chills went down my spine at the same time.

"Sam?"

Hearing Mason's voice, I jumped, and turned in the air. His eyes widened when he saw my face, and he took two steps to reach me. My phone was plucked from my hand and he barked into it, "Who is this?"

The fight left him when he heard his father's voice.

MASON

Glancing at Sam as I drove to Nate's house, I watched as she curled in a ball. The seat belt was restricting her from completing the fetal position, but that wasn't what sent a searing pang through me. It was the look on her face. She was lost. I recognized the look and heard her sniffle, trying to cover up the lone tear at the corner of her eye. I figured it had something to do with our upheaval. Nate's parents were flying in. The last I heard, they were in New Zealand so they'd be here in a day, but we would be booted out when they arrived. James said that Helen was coming as well. That meant she would book a suite in the best hotel, expecting Logan and me to be there.

She had a rude awakening coming. Sam was coming too.

Reaching over, I put a hand on her thigh. She glanced up, her dark eyes made darker by her misery. "Things will work out." I tried to reassure her with a smile.

She closed her eyes. Just like that, I'd been given a window to her soul, and then she took it away. Sam would never know how much that affected me. I needed to feel connected to her. Sometimes it was like air to me—I needed it to breathe. When she would pull away, it staggered me—every time. I tried again, "It will, Sam." They opened again, baring her insides to me. My lungs filled as the connection happened.

"I thought it was you," she whispered.

I frowned.

"When Logan sent that text, I thought it was all over."

Regret washed over me. "I'm sorry. I should've asked what Logan texted. No, I should've called you myself. I'm sorry." I grimaced. If I'd gotten a text like that, I would've gone nuts. My reaction would've been a lot worse than hers had been. Even considering it, the beginning of rage swirled inside of me. I don't know what I would do if she was ever hurt...

Then she sent another pang through me when she said, "I can't go back to my mom's. I thought I could before. I was willing to do it for you and Logan. I think you guys should live with your dad. It's your last semester here," her voice hitched on that last statement, "you should have as many memories with your dad that you can."

"We can't. Sam—"

"I know." She sat up and faced me.

She was now in the shadows, but the streetlights flashed over her, illuminating her for a brief second. As I watched, her eyes never changed. There was always such earnestness mixed with sadness in them. Everything in me sank. There'd always been pain in her, but it had gone away for a little while, but it was back now. It had increased. My eyebrows furrowed together. Was this because of my dad?

She murmured, "You said your mom would get you guys' hotel rooms." She bit her lip. "I can't stay with my mom, not if you guys aren't there. There's no way."

"You won't." My voice grew rough. "You're staying with us."

"But your mom—"

"I don't care about my mom. If she thinks she can push you out...there's no way in hell. You're staying with us."

"But what if she—"

"Sam." My hand gripped her thigh harder, my fingers sinking into her jeans. "I don't care what my mom says. Logan and I both have our own money. We can get our own room. Besides, even if you didn't stay with me, for some unknown reason that I can't imagine, Logan would have you in his room. He'd hide you in his suitcase or something." I grinned at her. "You're covered no matter what."

Her eyes held mine, so stricken and vulnerable.

I tried not to let it slip, but this was killing me. Sam was strong. I knew that. I'd seen it and it was one of the things that drew me to her in the first place, but she was fragile too. I could see her nearing the line of too-much. The fight with her mom had almost defeated her. I couldn't fight for her, not with that battle. It was on the inside. She was still dealing with all the emotional turmoil Analise shoveled at her.

Fuck her, that'd been my theory for Sam's mother from the beginning, but I knew she needed to put Analise behind her on her own. If she didn't, her mother would still hold so much power over Sam and nothing good would ever happen then.

Analise Strattan was toxic. She ruined everything she touched. It was only a matter of time before she'd ruin my father, but James remained with her, his eyes wide open. He knew what he was getting himself into. I would never have sympathy for my dad. He refused to leave Analise, so fuck him. She hurt Sam. I was done with my dad as long as he was with that woman.

Feeling Sam slip her hand underneath mine, I broke out of my thoughts.

She smiled at me. She didn't waver, but the sadness in her eyes would haunt me. I lifted her hand and pressed a kiss to the back of it.

"What was that for?"

I shrugged, putting our hands back in her lap. Then I took a deep breath. I was rattled. I thought my best friend had died. Now his parents were coming back. I knew they would circle the wagons. He'd be banned from seeing me. There was a lot left to handle. Parker. Whatever else Kate was planning. I had a strong feeling when my mom got here, she wouldn't be leaving for a while.

Things were about to get interesting.

It seemed to take forever to get to the house, but when we did, I held the door for her. Sam brushed against my arm, and the need to have her was sudden and overwhelming. I reached for her without thinking, but stopped. More and more waves of intense desire rocked through me. I wanted her. I wanted to be wrapped up in her. I wanted to pin her against the wall right then and there.

Holy shit.

My hand shook as I forced it to return back to my side. She paused in the door, stood on her tiptoes and pressed a kiss to my lips before moving inside.

I let loose a ragged breath. Fuck. Needing Sam had developed into an addiction after my first taste, but she had no idea how she could affect me. If I was being honest with myself, I was scared of letting her know. Marriages could be broken from that. If someone had more power over the other, they could use that love to manipulate the other. It went down the same all the time. Even with Tate and Logan. He adored her, and she didn't care. She had all the power and had used it to walk all over him.

A part of me knew that Sam was different. I could tell her, and she wouldn't use it against me, but I didn't know for certain. I was too scared to find out, so I kept quiet. She knew I loved her. She just didn't know how much.

"You okay?" Her voice carried around the corner.

I needed to clear my head. My dick twitched. I needed to clear that too. Dropping my hand, I adjusted myself before answering back, "I'm fine."

When I entered the kitchen, she had the freezer open and pulled out an ice cream carton. That was good. She was eating. Sam hadn't said a word about it, but I knew she didn't eat enough. "You hungry for anything else?"

"What?" She dug in with a large spoon.

I fell silent, leaning against one of the counters as I watched her put two big-sized portions of ice cream in her bowl before pushing the carton aside. Neither of us had bothered to turn the light on. The moonlight filtered in through the windows enough so we had no problem seeing. I liked it on nights like tonight. It helped with masking emotions at times.

"Nothing," I answered.

"You sure you're okay?" She turned from the counter, bowl in hand, but didn't lift the spoon from it. She wore a small frown and her eyes were filled with concern.

My dick twitched again. And love. Her eyes were filled with love too. I tried to reassure her with a small grin. "I'm good. You want a burger or something?"

"Oh." She glanced down at the bowl. "No, I'm good with ice cream. It's been a long night."

I grunted. That was true enough.

"Are you okay?"

This was the second time she'd asked. "I'm fine."

"Mason."

"Sam?" I grinned at her as fantasies of taking her, pinning her against the nearest counter, and pushing inside of her overwhelmed me. Sam had been through too much tonight for me to be that rough with her. She deserved better.

"You can talk about it, you know?"

"About what?"

"Nate. The car accident. He's your best friend. I'm not stupid. It must have rattled you." As she finished her statement, she sat on a chair at the table and drew her knee against her chest. Wrapping her arms around it, she lifted her bowl and spoon, but propped her chin on top of her knee. Filling her spoon with ice cream, she popped it into her mouth.

I watched how she savored the taste of it. My dick was full force again.

Enough.

Pushing off from the counter, I went to her. I didn't pause, even when her eyes got big and the bowl fell from her hands. I needed her now. I needed her any way I could get her, and I wasn't going to be gentle.

"Mason?" She squealed when I lifted her in my arms.

As she looked in my eyes, she saw the hunger in mine—I wasn't hiding it. That feeling, needing to be enraptured by her, wasn't meant to be hidden or repressed. It was meant to be shared. When her mouth opened, a soft sigh left her, and I knew she felt it too. Her hand lifted to cup the side of my face.

It was one of those touches that I savored.

Carrying her upstairs, I didn't make a sound. Neither did she. I just watched her. When I went inside our room, I lowered her to the floor, but kept her against me before I kicked the door shut. I savored that feeling, too. Bending down, my hands still on her waist, I breathed her in. She smelled of fresh air and vanilla. She never wore the fancy stuff or the expensive stuff. I'd seen her in the mornings when she would lift her body spray and use one spray. It was enough. The scent of her was embedded in me; I'd never forget it.

I'd never get enough of her.

"Mason?" she murmured again, her voice throaty.

My eyes opened and saw that she was watching me. Her hands were on my chest, but she was clinging to my gaze.

Lifting my hands, I cupped both sides of her face. Without realizing I was going to, I asked, "Do you know how much I love you?"

She shuddered before me, and her mouth fell open another inch. Her eyes got wider and a look of wonderment shone through.

She didn't know the depth of my love for her, but that was part of her magic. It was one of the reasons I loved her. She had no clue what made her special or what made her beautiful. It wasn't her trim body. It wasn't how my hands fit perfectly around her waist or how her breasts fit in the palms of my hands. It wasn't even how her dark eyes would tear up when I'd whisper my love to her, or how her perfect lips would open. Samantha was gorgeous, but she had no idea. She didn't think about looks. I watched her this week at school. She had no idea how people watched her. She thought it was because of me, but it wasn't. People watched her because she was beautiful. She had a look that no one did. It was natural and graceful. She was kind and loving. The guys could see it with one glance. All of them wanted her. I knew it, but she was mine, and the girls, the nicer girls liked her without even talking to her. The others were jealous. She had what they didn't, inside and outside beauty.

She had no idea just how rare she was.

She had no fucking clue, and I didn't have the words to tell her. Even if I did, she'd be uncomfortable at the idea. She'd fidget, look anywhere other than at me, and then convince herself that I was being dramatic. Samantha didn't know how to be loved—her mother made sure of that—so she'd never understand how special she truly was.

With that last thought, my hand fell from her cheek to her thigh. I took a firm grip, my fingers sinking into her leg, and I lifted her into my arms.

She gasped, but she wrapped her arms around my neck. Grinning, she murmured, "What's this about?"

"I'm not going to be gentle." My blood was pumping too much for that to happen. "I'm not going to be quick." God no. I was going to enjoy the feel of her body underneath mine. All of her soft curves, the little gasps she made when I was inside of her, and the feel of her hands skimming over me. I was going to make it last. "And you are going to be thoroughly fucked when I'm through with you."

I lowered her onto the bed. As she kneeled on the mattress before me, her shoulders and chest lifted when she took a deep breath. Her hands were on my chest, and she tipped her head back. Her dark hair fell backwards, and then she grinned. The look of her made my heart skip before pounding back with a renewed vigor.

In a soft husky tone, she murmured, "What's taking you so long?"

That was all the okay I needed.

I took her lips with mine. I claimed her, forcing her to open for me, and swept inside to taste every inch. That was just the beginning. I heard another soft sigh from her. She always did that, right before she surrendered to me. With that sound, she pressed against me so every inch of her was touching me and her hands wrapped around my neck. Then she pulled me down to her, and I knew I could do whatever I wanted.

So I did.

CHAPTER ELEVEN

SAMANTHA

The rest of the weekend passed quickly. Nate had a concussion, three fractured ribs, and a strained back injury. He was kept in the hospital until his parents arrived. When they did, it was with gusto. Their first point of business was banning Mason and Logan from their son's hospital room. They were good enough to be allowed information, but Mason explained later that night that Nate's parents had never approved of their friendship. It was why they moved Nate from Fallen Crest in the beginning. He was only allowed to come back for his last semester because he was eighteen. When I asked how they could even ban them from his room since he was an adult, Mason only shrugged. His reply was, "Guess the hospital has different policies for rich movie producers. I'm sure they're hoping to get a donation out of them."

In the end, he still snuck in to see Nate the next night, but it was after we packed our things and checked into a hotel. He wanted to avoid Nate's parents. Logan overheard him and when the door closed behind him, he commented, "He wants to avoid our mom, too."

That sent panic through me. He wasn't the only one. An hour later, I followed in Mason's trail, except I went to Manny's. When Heather's dad told me it was her night off, I tried their house then. While Mason was seeing his best friend, so was I. I spent most of the night on her couch. We watched movies, and she filled me in on the latest rumors about Nate's car accident. There were two competing theories: The first was that the Broudou brothers cut the wrong brakes; they meant to cut Mason's. The second was that Kate had cut the brakes to hurt Nate, so it would hurt Mason.

There were a few others, but they were ridiculous. Nate's parents owed money to the mob. Nate just wanted attention. Nate was the one that actually caused the accident, and the cops were covering for him.

The first two sent chills down my spine. I stopped asking about any more theories, and we went back to the movie. I thought about asking if she received any more texts from Kate or her friends, but I didn't. A part of me didn't want to know. I didn't want to worry about losing my one female friend.

It was late when I returned to the hotel. Slipping inside the suite, I wasn't surprised to find it empty. Logan texted that Ethan was throwing a party to celebrate that Nate was alive. Mason texted an hour after Logan saying that he was leaving the hospital and was going to the party. He asked if I wanted to go, but I declined. There'd been too much drama for me, so I enjoyed the solitude of the room that night.

My drama free night carried on to the next morning.

Helen had checked into her own room, but she was on a different floor.

When I learned that, my relief was powerful. My knees almost buckled, but I caught the table and plopped down on a chair. I landed harder than normal, but I didn't care. I ignored the smirk Logan gave me and then he gave me even better news. They were going to spend the day with their mother. Neither of them asked if I wanted to go along. They both knew I'd rather hang out with Kate and her princess bullies.

It wasn't long after that when I went for my run, but instead of running from the hotel, I drove to my old neighborhood. There was a trail from a nearby park that connected to the trail that went behind Quickie's. The scenery was too beautiful to miss. Even before I parked, I was already itching to fly up the hills behind the gas station.

Maybe it was the anticipation of pushing myself up those hills, but my run went faster than normal. It was invigorating and when I ran back, two hours later, I considered going for another hour, but I didn't. I needed my energy to start on my homework. However, when I drove past my old house, I stopped the car. I don't know why. I wasn't nostalgic about the home. There were a lot of bad memories in it, but I sat in the car and stared at it. Maybe I was more tired from the run than I realized. Maybe I wanted to avoid doing homework. Or maybe I missed the slight semblance of normalcy that the house used to give me, but whatever it was, I stayed for an hour. I didn't move from the car. I just stared at the house. No one was home, but when I saw a car that I thought was my dad's, I started my engine and drove away.

I didn't tell Mason about my run. I didn't know why. There wasn't anything significant about it, but I realized that I didn't want to tell him about my old house. When they came home and he got in bed with me, I asked about their day with their mother. As he filled me in, I kept wondering if that car had been David's. Maybe he'd been home. Maybe he saw me there.

"Sam?"

"Mmm?"

Mason grinned, tipping my head up to meet his eyes. "What's wrong? You spaced there for a second."

"Oh." I shrugged, dipping my head back down. "Nothing."

I could feel his gaze on me and knew his wheels were spinning. "I talked to my mom. She won't come up here. She knows you're staying here and agreed it would be for the best if she stayed away. Is that what's bothering you?"

"Oh." Had that been my dad in that car? Why was I even thinking about him? "That's fine. I'm tired. That's all."

Mason knew I lied to him, but he didn't push. I was thankful.

I was thankful for my social outcast status the next day at school as well. It was peaceful, but when I went to gym class,

I should've been prepared. I wasn't. Kate had warned me on the first day, but she spent the rest of the week focusing all her threats on Heather. It was only a matter of time before she turned her attention back to me.

It happened when I was done showering. All of my clothes were gone. It didn't take a genius to figure out where they were.

"Um..."

The locker room emptied as soon as I stepped from the shower. It made sense now, but there was a girl behind me. She wore a baggy sweatshirt and a baggy pair of jeans. Her sneakers might've been white at one point, but they were frayed on the soles and almost black now. She brushed a strand of red hair behind her ear, but it popped back out instantly. It was frizzy, and I knew it would've been beautiful if she would put some hair gel into it. Her eyes held my interest. There was no sympathy or warmth. She jerked her hand over her shoulder and said in a flat tone, "If you need clothes, I might have some for you."

"You wouldn't get in trouble for helping me out?"

She lifted one shoulder, but the blank face remained. "I don't really care. It's not like they'd know who helped you. They aren't my clothes."

"You keep the lost and found in your locker?"

"No." I caught a glimmer of a grin as she went to her locker. When she handed me a boy's jersey, the name on the back made me pause—Kade. "Uh...?"

"Told you." She pulled out a pair of jeans that looked like they'd been on the bottom of her locker for years. They were wrinkly and smelled musky. Then she handed me a swimsuit, which looked new. That was comforting. "The shirt and jeans belonged to a friend of mine. No one's seen them in years since she transferred two years ago, but the suit's mine. It's clean; I was going to go swimming after school, but I can borrow one of my friend's."

They'd do in a pinch. "Did they at least leave my shoes?"

"Yeah." She pointed to my locker. My shoes had been stored underneath a bench. "I don't think they knew which ones were yours." Twenty other pairs of shoes were beside them, lined up and down the row of lockers.

"Small favors, huh?" I gave her a grin, but her facial expression still didn't change. It was still blank and flat. Then she started to go around me. "Wait. Who was your friend?"

"No one you'd know." She didn't stop and continued to the door.

I lifted Mason's jersey. "I'm betting that I might. This was Mason's, wasn't it?"

"Yeah, but like I said, you wouldn't know her. She wasn't his girlfriend or anything." She paused. "And she wasn't a stalker either. They were friends."

Then it clicked. "Marissa."

That finally got a reaction from her. Her eyelid twitched and she frowned. "He's talked about her?"

"A little. I know they were friends."

"Oh."

"And you were friends with her, too?"

"She left those clothes in my locker all the time. Kate and friends did the same thing to her. She liked wearing his jersey because it shut 'em up." She took a small breath. "Anyways, there you go. You don't have to give them back or anything. It's not like Marissa still wants them."

She started to push open the door, but I asked, "Would you tell me about her?"

She let the door close again. "Why?"

I shrugged, clutching the clothes to my chest. I was standing there, dripping wet from my shower and the towel was starting to slip, but I was insistent. "I'd like to know more about her. He doesn't say too much."

She snorted. "I'm not surprised by that." The small opening that had appeared was gone. The wall was back in place. "Good luck with the Princess Bitches. See you."

I didn't move for a while after she left. Mason never talked about his friend except that she'd been bullied by Tate and Kate's group. I never pushed him for information. He'd tell me if I did, but I wanted to hear it from someone else. This girl was Marissa's friend, and in the two minutes that I had talked to her, I could tell she still missed her.

She had been kind to me and I didn't even get her name.

With that depressing thought, I heard voices outside the door and knew the next gym class would be heading inside, so I darted into the bathroom stall and changed. The jersey hung on me and the jeans were a little baggy, but they would do. The swimsuit helped underneath since my bra and underwear had gone missing as well.

When I went into the hallway, the reaction wasn't what they wanted. Mouths dropped and girls bent close to whisper to each other. At the end of the hallway, Kate was at Natalie's locker. She was furious and looked ready to march over, but Mason came up from behind me. He wrapped an arm around my waist and nudged me against my locker. His hand lifted to hold the back of my head so I didn't hit the locker, but he pressed into me.

Dropping his head, he kissed my neck. As his lips caressed me, he asked, "Where did you get this? This was my freshman jersey."

I spotted a few girls beside us, within hearing distance, and shrugged. "Just something I found in the locker room."

One girl made a sound of disgust before shoving from her locker. She stormed down the hallway, past Kate, sneering at her as well before she turned into the senior hallway.

"Who was that?"

"Hmmm?" Mason lifted his head from my neck and glanced around. "Who?"

"No one."

"Hey, nauseating lovebirds." Heather appeared at my locker. She gave Mason a bright smile and placed her hands on her hips like she was going to do a cheer for him. I caught the twinge of tension in her gaze before it slipped away. "I need to steal your gal, Kade. I need her to walk me to my next class."

His hands fell away and he stepped back, but he frowned. "You keep interrupting. When's your boyfriend transferring? I'd like to return all these favors."

"Ha, ha. We both know you're proud of your girl for landing a friend like me." She pointed to her own chest, walking backwards and looping her other elbow through mine. "I'm a hot commodity. There's only one Heather Jax in this town."

"That doesn't make you a hot commodity. That makes you expendable. No one would miss you."

She pretended to hiss, grinning at the same time. "That hurts, Kade. I thought we had something going between the two of us."

"The boyfriend and best friend never like each other."

Her eyes widened and she paused in her footing for a second, but lifted her fingers to her forehead. She saluted him. "You win, Mason Kade. You always do."

But there was no response. Mason had already turned and was walking the other way. Even now, with their little exchange, so many people had been hanging onto every word. As he passed by groups in the hallway, the girls followed him with hungry gazes. A few didn't, but the guys were almost as bad. A lot of them stopped what they were doing and puffed out their chests. Their backs straightened and most struck a cocky pose until he walked past them, without acknowledging them. When he disappeared into the senior hallway, the hallway went back to normal. The girls giggled and whispered. The guys, most of them, went back to their drooped shoulders and lounging stances.

I'd never get used to it. I don't know how he did it.

"I heard what happened," Heather brought me back from my thoughts. Her hand tightened on my arm and she pulled me closer, lowering her voice. "You okay?"

"Yeah." Waves of anger and curiosity mixed together now. One thing at a time. "Do you know a girl that used to be friends with Marissa?"

"Marissa?"

"I don't know her last name. She was friends with Mason and transferred out of here two years ago."

"Oh." Her facial features tightened and her lips pinched together. "Yeah. Red hair? Frizzy? Average weight?"

"Yeah. Who is she?"

"Her name's Paige." She grimaced. "I wouldn't get close to her."

"Why not?"

Stopping at her locker, I leaned against the one beside it and waited as she opened the combination. "Because she will never be your friend. A lot of girls lust after your boys, but there's a few that hate them. Paige is one of them. She blamed Mason for everything that happened to Marissa."

"And by everything that happened to Marissa, you mean..." I gestured to my clothes. "Getting her clothes stolen."

She grabbed her book and shut her locker, but turned to fall against it with her back. "Getting the clothes stolen is the first step. That's why I found you right away."

"How'd you know?"

"My friend Cory's in your gym class."

"The one..." I frowned, trying to remember and then it clicked. "The angry one? She wears black. She hated me on sight."

"Yeah, that one."

"And she's another one of those girls who hates Mason and Logan?"

"No, she doesn't hate them, not like Paige. She hates Kate and her friends. She doesn't like Mason and Logan because they never stopped Kate. She's been okay this semester so far, but everyone can sense she's got things in the works. It's tense around here. Don't you feel it? You're not coming into this school at a good time."

It was because of me. Everyone knew that and it was starting to make sense why the welcome wagon had been missing. It'd been doused in gasoline somewhere, waiting for Kate to strike the match.

I couldn't do anything about it. That was the hard part. "How'd you escape their wrath?"

Heather chuckled. "I don't know, but if I were to guess, it's because of Channing at Roussou. He's still in my life. Everyone knows that and he holds his own over there. If they did anything to me, he'd get even. That," her head bobbed forward, "and because I think one of those four always had a thing for him."

"One of them with someone from Roussou?"

"He's hot. People can still date between the two schools. It's not really encouraged, but it's not forbidden or anything." She laughed again, eyeing me up and down. "But that doesn't matter anymore. We both know I'm on Kate's shit list now."

The first bell rang at that moment, and everyone started to scatter.

I shook my head at the mass chaos. "I feel like we go to school with a pack of wolves. It's everyone for themselves."

Heather grinned. "Only the strong survive here."

"Yeah, well, I don't like to fight back. I will when I can't avoid it, but I'm starting to realize being proactive might be the best solution here."

"Hey." She grabbed my arm before I could go to my class and pulled me back. Her eyes grew hard. "That's why I found you. Stealing your clothes is the first step. Kate and her Bitch Crew don't do cliché pranks. You're not going to find your clothes in a toilet. They did this to Marissa a few times. They'd steal her clothes and put them on a mannequin. Natalie's aunt owns a clothing store and I think that's where they get them. They'll take pictures of it wearing your clothes and then Photoshop it to make it look like you. They'll even have a picture of your face blurred on the thing. It's really creepy how close to being real it is. Then they'll put the pictures on the internet."

"Of a mannequin wearing my clothes? They could use any clothes then."

"They use the person's real clothes. It's the extra kick in their prank. Again, they Photoshop it so it looks just like you. Same hair, same everything. Your name will be attached to it. It's scary."

"But then what? It's just a big doll that looks like me."

She gave me a 'come on' look. "Sam, think about it."

A sick feeling came over me. "What'll they have the mannequin doing?"

"If you're lucky, nothing. If it's what I'm thinking, really bad things. People won't care that it's not you. They did this to Marissa and it was bad. Guys talked about raping the mannequin, but it was like they were saying that they wanted to rape her. With you, can you imagine what all the girls will do? There's a bunch of girls besides Kate and her crew that don't like you. A lot of the drill team. Most of the cheerleaders. They'll be vicious."

The sick feeling spread all over now. "How can I stop that?"

"I know you've wanted to handle Kate on your own, but this is too much. Tell Mason, or at least Logan. They might have an idea of where they're doing this. They could probably stop them."

I shook my head. "I can't. Nate's car accident. I know Mason's going to go see him after basketball practice."

"Then tell Logan."

"He'll tell Mason. I'm scared of what they'd do."

"Are you really trying to protect Kate? She's not sitting back and hoping you'll go away. She texts me every day now, and she's making threats to me, threats to even my dad and my brother. Now this." She stopped and took a deep breath. Her eyes held mine, a plea filled them. "Please, Sam. If not Mason, then tell Logan."

"I'll think about it."

"Don't think about it. Do it."

I frowned. There was an edge to her voice.

She finished, "If you don't, I will."

"Heather."

"No." She shook her head. "Kate's gone too far. She did this to Marissa and she ended up transferring. They didn't stop once they started. I know it's going to be worse for you. I just know it. Everyone else does, too. No one wants to get hit in the crossfire, so they're all leaving you alone. Please, Sam. You've got the two biggest enforcers on your side. Use them. They can stop Kate. I know they can."

As she left, hurrying away for class, I couldn't move. The last bell rang. I was going to be late, but my feet wouldn't budge. Heather's last warning echoed inside of me. It wasn't that they couldn't stop Kate, it was *how* they were going to do it.

They had forced wine down my mother's throat. They did that to prove to her what they could do, but that hadn't stopped Analise in the end. Whatever they did to Kate wouldn't stop her. I knew that in my gut, but I had no idea what to do. A part of me was scared. If I let Mason and Logan loose, I worried they'd cross a line. I couldn't let them do anything that would jeopardize their futures, not after Mason's had been threatened by my own mother. I couldn't go through that terror again, but Heather was right. I had to do something, but I had no idea what.

CHAPTER TWELVE

I couldn't bring myself to say anything, even when Mason caught me after school. He was heading to basketball practice, and I was headed to Coach Grath's office. Heather's warning had stuck with me all day, sending pangs of terror through me, but I was still worried. Being loved and protected by Mason and Logan was like holding a loaded gun. I could pull the trigger at any moment, but the consequences could be disastrous.

When he asked if I was okay, I lied. He knew it, but I wasn't ready to tell him yet. When he pressed a soft kiss to my lips and left, I realized that was my second lie to him. Two lies in two days. What lie would I tell him tomorrow?

Meeting with Coach Grath, he told me to run on my own. There was a select group of girls he wanted me to train with, but he caught wind that I wouldn't be welcomed. I was supposed to train on my own until the time came to 'bite that bullet.' His words, not mine. He wanted me to record my times to check for improvement. That wasn't a hard thing. I was bursting from the inside. Getting to the hotel room and driving to my old park took too long for me. I couldn't hit that trail fast enough and when I soared past Quickie's, I shot past all the cars in the parking lot and hit the hills at a full sprint. Once I got to the top, I skimmed over Fallen Crest below me and kept going to the next hill and the one after. The air temperature had noticeably dipped when I finally stopped.

My heart was racing and my chest was heaving as I gasped for breath.

I'd never felt more alive.

Then it hit me at the same time. It was like a cold wind to the north decided to make an abrupt turn and crash into me. It staggered me.

Kate. My clothes. A mannequin. I gulped. Whatever she was going to do would be on the internet, probably even tonight. Then the lies. I hadn't said a word about my run-in with both Broudous. I had no idea how to tell him Brett Broudou asked me out. He didn't know that I sat outside David's house or that Kate stole my clothes. I knew why I kept quiet about some of those, but not my home. As I thought about it now, my heart began pounding again, louder and louder in my eardrums.

I didn't want to feel any of this. Regret. Confusion. Lost. So I turned around and started my run back home. The adrenalin always pushed everything away, but that didn't happen this time. My body was tired. That was all there was to it. I was tired. For once, running hadn't helped me. It made me feel more defeated than when I had started.

It was later that night when Mason texted me.

Mason: **Nate's at his house now. Going over to hang out.**

Me: **I thought you couldn't.**

Mason: **Banned from hospital, not his place. I need to talk to him about some things. You ok?**

Me: **Yeah. We should talk tonight, too.**

I waited, holding my breath. Then my phone buzzed again: **Ok. Won't stay long. Love you.**

I closed my eyes, let out a deep breath, and replied: **Love you too.**

"Was that Mason?"

I glanced up and tossed my phone to the other side of the bed. My textbooks and computer had taken up most of the bed. Logan was in the doorway to our bedroom. His hair was wet and he had on a Fallen Crest Public athletic jacket. "Did you shower here?"

"Nope. At school. Ran home to get some cash." His eyes fell to my phone. "Where's Mason at?"

"He went to see Nate."

"Oh." Then he turned thoughtful, studying me. "What are you doing?"

"Studying."

I was going to tell him that I was exhausted from the run, but paused. Logan had that look. He was thinking and that meant he was planning something. I kept quiet until he nodded to himself, some decision made. He then said, "I'm meeting the guys for pizza. You want to come?"

"Why do I get the feeling that I don't have a choice?"

He started for me, rolling his shoulders back, a cocky smirk adorning his face. "Because all you do is go to school, study, run, and have coital bliss with my brother. You need to hang out with friends and have fun."

"I do." He was beside the bed now, and I couldn't hold back my grin. "I watched movies with Heather on Saturday."

He snorted, leaning down and taking hold of my ankle. He started to pull me to him. "That wasn't fun. That was hiding from my mother. That's work. Come on." With one abrupt tug, I was jerked to the edge of the bed. He tucked his shoulder down and moved me onto it. As he stood, I was slung over him.

"Logan!"

"You look fine. Always hot, Sam. You never need to worry about that." He patted me on the back and turned for the door.

I was laughing too hard to fight back. He scooped down and handed my shoes to me, along with a coat and my bag. We headed out like that. There were others in the elevator, but Logan commented, patting my butt at the same time, "She forgot how to walk." An elderly couple was confused while someone chuckled. A little kid circled to look up at me, pointed, and said, "You look weird."

I felt Logan's reaction. His body tensed and then shook in silent laughter. When the doors slid open to the bottom floor, everyone let us go first. Logan didn't lower me until he got to his Escalade. I was deposited into the passenger seat, and he jogged over to his side.

When he pulled into Manny's parking lot, I glanced over at him. "I thought you said pizza."

Turning the Escalade off, he shrugged. "They have pizza here."

"And this has nothing to do with my one good friend that's here?"

A shrug was my only response before we went inside. Logan's friends had congregated around two tables in the back section. I recognized some of the girls from the drill team at the second table. I recognized their hostility, too. Brandon lifted his hand in greeting, and Heather glanced up from the counter. Her eyes darted from me to Logan pointedly, and I shook my head. She mouthed back, "When?" I tried to tell her to shut up with an extra oomph in my glare, and I jerked my shoulders up and down. I was going to tell Mason. That was the plan.

As it turned out, it wasn't Heather or myself that brought it up. The first pizza had already been devoured when a few of the girls scooted their chairs to our table. They did what those girls did. The displayed their boobs. They tried to be coy and mysterious. A couple had even pulled their jeans down low so they could show off their thongs. I was certain another girl went to the bathroom and took off her bra. She returned with her boobs bouncing. The shirt she wore did little to cover her nipples. There was one girl that stuck out as the leader. She started talking to Strauss. From what I could overhear, they were discussing a class assignment until I heard the word 'gym' mentioned.

A blast of cold air came over me and I turned, as if in slow motion, towards them.

She was grinning at me and nodded in my direction. Everyone else grew silent and then she asked, her voice rising above the background noise, "Did you ever get your clothes back, Samantha?"

Samantha. That was my first thought. *I don't know her, and she called me by my full name.* Then the rest of her words hit me.

Logan paused and lowered his pizza slice. He frowned at her, then back at me. "What's she talking about?"

Someone muttered in the background, "Shit's about to get reaaal."

I was pretty sure that was Heather, but when I turned she lifted her hand in a rolling motion. I got the message, let's get this going.

"Let's talk outside."

Logan was up from the table before the words left my mouth. His hand was on my arm, and I was hauled behind him. Instead of going through the entire diner, he shoved through the side door. I started for one of the chairs we used when we took our breaks, but he shook his head. His fingers tightened. "Nope. We're doing this over here where no one can listen."

He took me all the way across the alley and towards Heather's house. We were starting up her porch when the door slammed shut behind us. Heather's jaw was set and her top lip curved up, flashing us a warning as she headed towards us. "Oh no. I'm staying. She's my friend too, Kade."

"Fine."

Her arms were crossed over her chest and then both of them moved as one. I was center stage. Lovely. "Okay..."

"Kate, or one of her lackeys, stole Sam's clothes after gym class when she was in the shower," Heather beat me to it. Her eyebrow arched high. "You know what they're going to do. Stop them, Logan."

He threw her a scathing look, but turned and pinned me down. "Is that true, Sam?"

My mouth was still hanging open from my 'okay', but I shut it now. This was it. This was the moment where he went after them and I'd be at home worrying if he was going to be arrested or worse. At least Mason was at Nate's. I doubted Logan would need him for this.

He bit out a curse and hopped off the porch. His phone was pulled out a second later and I heard, "Mase? We have a problem."

That hope exploded.

"Thanks for that," I said. "Note the sarcasm."

She rolled her eyes. "You wouldn't have told them, and you know it. I don't understand why you didn't say something after it happened. It's probably too late now."

"Because I'm scared for them. I don't know what Mason and Logan are going to do."

"Oh please." Another eye-roll. Another swear word. "They're not idiots, and this isn't their first rodeo. This is Mason and Logan Kade. This is what they're known for, this is who they are. I don't know what you're scared about. Stop kidding yourself, Sam."

My head jerked back. "You just bitch-slapped me."

The corner of her mouth lifted in a crooked grin and she shrugged. "Well, that's what real friends do."

"You really think they'll be fine?" No matter what she said, the fear of Mason's future was still in me. My mom had been so close to ruining it.

""Yeah." She softened and reached over to hug me. She whispered in my ear. "I think they'll be fine. I've never seen those two more protective over someone. It's why everyone hates you at school."

I stiffened in her arms. "Quite aware of my popularity."

"Things will be fine." She patted my arm again. "They'll put her back in her place and everyone will relax at school. People will start getting to know you for you. I'm sure of it."

I hoped so. I really did, but Heather was forgetting one thing. Things wouldn't go back to normal. Mason and Logan had been quiet, but I knew they were planning their revenge against the Broudou brothers. Thinking of them... I still needed to tell Mason about Brett. He needed to know sooner than later.

It was then when Brandon stuck his head out the side door. When he spotted us, his face scrunched together. I could imagine a few curse words coming from him until he hollered, "Get your ass in here, Heather! We're swamped."

"Yeah, yeah."

"I mean it!"

Her voice rose another octave. "I said 'yeah, yeah'! I'll be there in a sec!"

His middle finger rose in response before he disappeared back inside.

"Stupid brothers." She glanced at me. "Not step-brothers, but you know what I mean."

"I do."

She jerked her thumb towards Manny's. Another crooked-grin appeared. "Don't suppose you want to work the rest of the night? Lily and Anne both quit last weekend. Lily's dad got a new job so they moved and Anne won't work here if Lily doesn't. That's the excuse she gave me, but Cory saw her working at the Fallen Crest Country Club. The tips are better over there."

"You'd be surprised at how cheap rich people can be."

"You've been there?"

"Unfortunately."

She shrugged, musing at the same time, "That place is too fancy for me. I don't speak hoity-toity."

"That's funny. You named it perfectly right there."

"HEATHER!" Brandon was glaring at us from the door again. "Come on! We're getting killed."

"I'm COMING!" We started down the alley, and she muttered under her breath, "Someone's getting killed tonight. That's for sure."

MASON

The damn mannequin was where I thought it would be—Kate's garage. She was smart, but not that smart. Since it only had a dark wig on it, and Sam's clothing were next to it, I figured they hadn't done anything to it yet.

"Fuck," Logan muttered. "Is that a dildo over there?"

Her dad had an old truck parked on one side. The other side had a yellow-stained refrigerator where Harold stored his beer. He liked to drink while he played around with his truck. He kept the 'good stuff' inside the house. Two worn plaid couches that were torn up, from the cat sharpening its claws, sat next to the refrigerator. A small table with a coffee can full of cigarette butts on top was placed between the couches. There were empty bottles lined up next to the couches Kate's uncles used to spit their chew in.

"Smells like someone died in here."

"Watch it," I warned when Logan hopped off the steps leading from the house. "There might be a dead animal in here. This is where her dad skins his kills."

"You're talking about animals, right?" Logan wrinkled his nose up before covering it with his shirt. "Man, this place really stinks."

This was Kate's world. It was fucked up and I didn't want to be there longer than I needed. I went over and got all of Sam's clothes, making sure the cat hadn't pissed on them. They smelled fine. Sam's vanilla body spray was still on them.

Logan had opened the refrigerator. "Holy shit. Why don't we party here?"

"*Used* to party here?"

"Oh yeah. You know what I meant." The smirk lingered on Logan's face as he grabbed a beer from inside. Twisting it open, he took a good swig before he pointed at the mannequin. "So what's our plan for that thing?"

"No clue, but I know where they get the things."

"Where's that?"

"Sashes and Bows."

"Say again?" Logan had lifted the beer to his mouth, but paused before he took another drink.

"Natalie's aunt. Her clothing store."

"Oh." He bobbed his head up and down. "Makes sense now."

I tried to see if there was anything else we should grab. Once Kate realized we'd been there, the extra key would be moved somewhere else. I didn't know if she would warn her parents about me or not. Her mom worked at the hospital eighty hours a week, and her dad was always gone with his buddies. When Harold was home, he was drunk. If nothing else, I knew where Kate's mom stored her purse at the hospital. Kate told me the combination.

Stupid.

"Let's go," Logan started to say, but broke off at the sound of car doors slamming shut.

Going to the garage door, we saw Kate's and Natalie's cars.

"Come on." I grabbed the mannequin and went to the side door. It led to the outside and I shoved the thing into Logan's arms and pointed to the road. Kate lived in the country. Her house was surrounded by trees, and there was a road that led around to the back of her dad's barns and property. We had parked the Escalade behind one of the barns and crossed through the woods to sneak into the house. I didn't know who was going to be here, so coming in from the north side kept us hidden. It helped Logan now as he nodded and took off with the mannequin.

I stayed behind. I wanted to hear her reaction.

"...isn't that what we're doing? I mean, come on. The girl just can't lay down and take it... Oh, holy gawd!"

The door banged against the wall, and Jasmine's voice stopped abruptly. I grinned to myself.

"OH MY FUCK! FUCK-FUCK!!"

"Calm down, Kate," Natalie drawled. Her voice fell halfway through her statement as if she'd stepped to the side. "You don't have to screech so loud. I just had flashbacks to my mom."

Someone snickered. "From last night, you mean."

"Shut it, Parker," Natalie snapped back. "And speaking of, where were you last night?"

"What are you talking about? I was with Nate. Kate told me to see him." Her voice rose sharply. "Kate, you told me to go see him. I wasn't supposed to?" Her voice was near hysteria.

Everything got quiet.

A door opened and closed. Then the truck's doors were both opened and slammed shut. A thud came next before Parker asked again, quieter now, "Kate?"

"FUUUUUUUUUUCKKKKK!"

"Kate, why are you flipping out like this? Stop screaming. I didn't give up a shift at Str8t to hear this."

"Shut up, Natalie," Kate shot back.

Something hit the garage door. She was throwing shit. That was good. I didn't think they'd look out the side door, but I tucked my head down in case. It was on the opposite side of the truck, but I didn't know for sure. I tried to blend in with the shadows as much as possible. Then I heard Kate start screeching again. Something else thudded into the garage door.

"Hey," Jasmine spoke up, "where's that whore's clothes?"

Natalie laughed. "You got rats in here, Kate? I'm sure they were attracted to her musk."

"For the last time," Kate's voice turned ominous. "Shut. The. Fuck. Up. You're not worried about her clothes?"

"Well, yeah. We need them for the whole thing. It was pointless to borrow my brother's camcorder, and I won't enjoy doing his chores for the week. Punk kid," Natalie grumbled. A smaller item was thrown against the garage door. "Little does he know that he's going to pay for that."

"You guys are pissing me off."

"Tell us something we don't know," Natalie threw back.

"What are you going to do?"

"I'm going to kill someone," Kate bit out, her voice harsh.

Natalie ignored her. "I sent all his buddies his last video on here."

"Really?" Jasmine sounded curious. "What was it?"

"Him jacking off." She snorted. "Dumb idiot. That's going viral. Douche will be haunted by that for years."

"You're so mean to your little brother. You should be nicer to him."

"And you should be meaner to your sister. She treats you like dirt, Jaz."

"Seriously, guys!" Kate yelled out. "Help me find her clothes or it'll be over for all of us."

"For the last effing time," Natalie barked back. "What are you talking about?"

"Her clothes." I could hear the venom dripping from her voice. I enjoyed it. "They're gone."

"So's the doll thing."

"What?"

"The doll thing."

I shook my head. Parker had no idea what she was pointing out.

Kate spat out again, "What the fuck are you talking about?"

"The doll," Parker yelled back. "It was here. So were her clothes."

"I put her clothes on the floor. Where'd you put the mannequin?"

"Here. I just told you. Listen."

"The mannequin was supposed to go DOWNSTAIRS," Kate screamed again. "They took it. They took it all. Oh my god. Oh my god. I'm going to kill someone."

"What are you talking about?" Natalie's voice rose in alarm. "They? You think that cunt came in here?"

"Mason and Logan. Are you a complete idiot? She told them. Shit. Fuck." Kate went through a slew of curse words. "They came in here and took them."

"Oh crap."

"Exactly."

"You think they did anything else?" Parker questioned, a small twinge of fear crept into her tone.

Kate laughed now. "Probably." It came out sounding like she was being strangled. "We're screwed. She told Mason. He's going to screw us."

"Calm down," Natalie clipped out. "Let's calm down and think about this. We're not screwed yet."

"We are. We sooo are. He's going to do something horrible to us. I know it. We're so screwed."

"No, we're not. He has no idea what we were going to do—"

"Yes, he did," Kate continued yell. "It's why he came here in the first place. I can't believe that bitch told him."

"I would, if I was her," Jasmine commented. "I mean, come on. We're mean. You can't blame the girl."

"Whose side are you on?" Kate and Natalie said at the same time.

There was silence before she replied, "Yours. My friends."

"Then act like it."

"So what?" Natalie spoke up again. "We'll be fine. They took her clothes back. Whoop de doo. We can still hurt her. We *do* have other things planned."

"I know." I could imagine Kate now. She was biting the inside of her cheek, thinking over everything that we could've done to her house. She sighed. "Shit. Fine. Come on. Let's go to Tate's and put the camcorder in place and then go to Cake's garage for the other stuff."

"Wait," Parker stopped them, "so we're not putting those pictures on the internet?"

"We can't," Kate snapped at her, her voice heavy with sarcasm. "We don't have the mannequin, and we don't have her clothes. We have nothing else on her."

"Can't we just use someone else's clothes and put her name on it?"

"Not without the fucking doll, and using her clothes is the whole point. It's the added insult that it's her real clothes. Unless one of you guys want to dress up and let us take pictures of you?"

There was silence in the room.

Kate bit out a harsh laugh. "I didn't think so."

"Let's use other pictures and put her face on it?"

"Using her real clothes is the whole point. Did you get anything from Nate's house before they moved out?"

"No. Mason locked their bedroom during the parties, and I couldn't find anything else in the house."

"Of course he does. They have huge parties."

"Whatever. Let's move on. We'll do the thing that we were planning to do next week, this week instead."

"Are you sure that's smart? You just said that we're screwed. Mason knows and now we don't have the pictures."

I pressed my ear closer against the wall. Their voices faded when Kate commented, "It doesn't matter. I'm going to beat her ass one way or another."

Their car doors closed. I turned and headed into the woods to where my Escalade was parked. When I got into my car, Logan put his phone away and looked up. "You learn anything?"

"Nothing we didn't know except that we have to put her down."

Logan nodded and lifted his fist in the air. I met it with mine. As I reversed the car, I asked, "Can you text Sam for me? Tell her we're fine, but we won't get back till late."

"Already did it."

I threw my brother a frown, but Logan wasn't paying attention. He went back to texting on his phone.

CHAPTER THIRTEEN

SAMANTHA

I had no idea what they did, but Mason smelled like smoke when he passed through our room to the bathroom. The shower turned on a second later. Getting out of bed and padding barefoot behind him, he was already under the spray when I got there. His clothes were in a pile on the floor so I put them into the laundry bin. Then I leaned against the counter, and our eyes met through the glass door. He didn't smile or say hello. He stared at me, and I stared back as he continued bathing. Lifting his arms, the water cascaded over his shoulders and down his chest. I could see every inch of him, not that any of it was a surprise anymore, but the hunger was there. Always there.

He smirked, still watching me. I licked my lips.

The wait for him took forever. I was burning up by the time he turned the water off and stepped out. The towels were behind me and he reached past me, leaning into me at the same time. His chest touched mine and he paused. His arm was stretched behind me, but as I turned to meet his gaze, he was looking right at me. Just there. Within reach. I closed my eyes and inhaled when his breath coated my skin. It was a caress of its own. Then a throaty murmur escaped me, "Mason..."

He pulled away and dried himself off.

My eyelids opened, but I was caught and held by his gaze again.

My chest lifted as I inhaled another deep breath. My breasts grew heavy under my thin top. They wanted his touch. Without a bra, he could see their reaction. It took one more second as he finished drying off before he dropped the towel again and stepped close to me.

His hands found my hips.

My eyes closed. My head went down.

Home. Finally.

"Sam," he murmured from an inch away. His lips were there, right there for me to taste.

"What?" I could barely talk.

"She won't hurt you." His hand lifted.

When it touched my neck, my heart jumped into my throat, and my blood began pumping.

He moved it around my neck and cupped the back of my head. I was held, anchored in his hand. It was strong, so sure. My heart was racing now and my chest was heaving up and down. I was struggling to breathe. The knot in me started to loosen. It always did when he made me feel like this. Safe. Then a lump formed in my throat, and I had to bite down on my lip. I would either become a sobbing mess or I'd throw myself at him. I wasn't sure which one I wanted.

He decided for me.

Mason pulled me into his chest. His arms wrapped around me, and I felt his head bend down. He rested his forehead on my shoulder, so I did the same. My hands lifted to his hips, but then with a sob, I wrapped them around his waist.

I'd been so damn worried.

He was safe. They were both safe. My heart kept pounding as the relief washed over me, replacing the desire from moments ago.

Then I peeled myself from him, just enough so I could get answers. "What did you guys do?"

"Nothing bad."

"Mason."

He flashed me a grin, took my hand in his and led me to the bedroom. I checked the door and saw it was locked, but then he bent down and lifted me in his arms. I was upright in his arms as he walked us the remaining few steps to the bed. He placed me onto it so that I remained standing while his hands kept me upright. They gripped my hips, and he tipped his head back. A soft smile gracing his features.

My hand lifted on its own volition and went through his wet hair. He closed his eyes, and I could tell he savored the small caress. My fingers grabbed a fistful of his hair and I pulled with enough force so he'd open them. When he did, I asked again, "What did you guys do?"

A slow grin appeared, and his arms tightened around my legs. That was all the warning I got before he flipped me in the air and caught me again. One hand cradled between my shoulders, and the other gripped my ass. He lowered me to the bed and then climbed on top of me in one fluid movement. It was as if he didn't even move and he was above me, holding himself up with his arms and legs.

His eyes roamed over me as he answered, "We went to Kate's." He dropped a small kiss on my throat. "Everything was still there, so we took it." Another kiss an inch higher. "Then I stuck around and watched the fireworks." The hand on my hip slid around my waist.

My heart started pounding again, and I held my breath.

The hand moved down and pushed underneath my shorts. There was no restriction. They were made of soft fabric and clung to me. As his fingers moved even further down, he slid two fingers deep into me. He moved further up until he was directly above me. His lips were so close to mine again. Watching mine, he murmured, "Kate almost spilled her plans, but her friends were too stupid to let her."

"And then?"

His fingers began moving. Oh god. He pressed another kiss to the underside of my chin.

My heart spiked, and a burst of pleasure rushed over me. I was tempted to say, "To hell with the questioning" and pull him down to me, but I couldn't. This was important. "And then?" I asked again, almost panting now.

"And then." His other hand moved to hold mine. Our fingers slid against each other as he linked our hands together. Then he lowered his body slowly, inch by inch, until he was resting on top of me. He fit between my legs, in just the right spot as his fingers kept thrusting in and out.

I bit my lip, trying to stop myself from moving down. My lips fell open and I gasped, but I kept it silent. I had to. My heart was beating so loud now. "Mason," I groaned, "just tell me."

"Tell you?"

"You like torturing me."

A corner of his mouth curved up. The grin was cruel, but his eyes hadn't moved from my lips. "Maybe." They had already darkened, but they grew black now. "Maybe you torture me, too."

I was ready to start praying for patience. "You're beginning to piss me off."

"Am I?" He moved his hips into me in rhythm with his fingers.

I gasped out loud. Lust and pleasure were rolling through me like a riptide on repeat, over and over again. My hands found their way to his shoulders, and my fingers dug in. Then he moved again. I was pushed further away from consciousness. Desire for him was making me blind. I lifted my heavy eyelids and looked at him. His gaze was transfixed on my lips, and he licked his own, thrusting against me at the same time.

"Mason," I whimpered.

I felt his silent laughter; his chest tightened and jerked before he pulled away, still grinning, but it had softened on the corners. His eyes caught mine and held them. They narrowed, and I caught a spark in them, one that I recognized. He was thinking.

"Mason, tell me."

"They're planning something, said it was supposed to be for next week, but it's going to happen at the end of this week instead."

The heat from my desire lessened. It made room for a chill. "What do you think it is?"

"Honestly?" He pulled his fingers out.

I nodded, a lump was in my throat now.

"I think they're going to hurt you. Physically."

"Oh."

"Oh?" He frowned and lifted his thumb to my mouth. He rubbed it over my lips, tugging the bottom down before his hand fell away. "You're not surprised?"

I shrugged. "Not really. I mean, that's expected. Kate's never struck me as the real smart type."

"Well, she is." The lust in his eyes moved to caution. He warned me, "You have no idea what she can do. Beating you up isn't good, but I'd be a lot less worried if I thought that's all she was going to do."

"She's been texting Heather a bunch."

His body stiffened on top of me. "Saying what?"

"She needs to stop being my friend. Heather said there were threats to her and to her family, too."

"When did this start?"

"The first day of school. She came over and made a big show about warning Heather away. That was when Tate tried to intervene."

"Against you?"

"No, against Kate. She told her that going up against you isn't worth it." I frowned. The sexual intensity was gone, and he seemed deep in thought. I reached for him, curving my hand over his shoulder to his jaw. His gaze had moved past my shoulder, but I touched his jaw. "Hey. What are you thinking?"

"That I'm starting to figure out what else Kate is doing."

"What do you mean?"

"With Tate."

"What?"

He was off the bed in a flash and pulled on his sweatpants. The bed had only settled when he disappeared through the door and hollered, "Logan!"

"What's up?"

Grabbing one of Mason's sweatshirts, I pulled it over my head and ignored how it covered my pajama shorts. It looked like I wasn't wearing anything underneath it.

Logan smirked at me as I came to the doorway. "You cold, Sam?"

"Shut it, Logan."

Mason asked, "Where are you going?"

Logan had showered. He was dressed in jeans and his athletic sweatshirt. Playing with his car keys in his hand, he shrugged. "Was going to head out for a few. What's up?"

"You going to Tate's?"

His question threw both of us. There it was again, the lie Mason never explained to me. Narrowing my eyes at him, I studied Logan at the same time. He seemed cautious now and slid his hands into his front pockets. "Maybe. Why?"

"Kate mentioned a camcorder," Mason said. "And before that Natalie had her brother's camcorder. They were going to use it to take pictures of the mannequin."

"So? They have a camcorder. So do we."

"Kate said they were heading to Tate's at the end. Sam just told me they've been sending threats to Heather. They want her to stop being her friend and Tate tried to warn them off."

Logan nodded. "She told me about that. Said it was a lost cause. Kate's gone off the deep end."

"So," Mason paused and watched him. He was waiting...

"So what?"

"Logan, I spelled it out for you."

"Threats to Heather. Camcorder. Tate thinks Kate's crazy. None of this is really new here, brother."

I sighed. Even I knew what Mason was implying. Logan wasn't dumb. If he wasn't figuring it out that meant something else was going on with him. Moving to the couch, I perched on the end and said, "I think he's saying that Kate might think Tate's on our side."

"She is," Logan snorted. "No way would she go against you. She knows what we'd do to her."

"Logan," Mason groaned.

I lifted a hand to his arm and felt his tension. My hand began to rub. "Do you think Kate would take a camcorder to Tate's out of the goodness of her heart?"

"Wha—oh shit. No. No way. You think?"

"Are you going over there?"

Logan glanced at his brother again. A resigned look came over him. "Yeah, I am. What do you want me to do?"

"Don't say anything or make it obvious, but look to see if there's a camcorder stashed somewhere."

"Wait," Logan shook his head. "You think she's in on it? We do things or we have done things in the living room. They could've put it there—"

"They were going there tonight."

"Oh." His shoulders dropped. "So what do you want me to do? You want me to grab it?"

When Mason didn't reply, Logan looked to me. I shrugged. "Mason's the mastermind. Not me."

"Mase?"

"I don't know. Maybe leave it in place?"

"I'm not going over there anymore. No fucking way, not if they have a camcorder in there. That's messed up."

"I know. I'm not saying that," Mason bit out. "But if we move the camcorder, then they'd have to change tactics again. We know what they're planning right now. Maybe we can wait to see what else she's planning?"

"Should I tell Tate?"

Mason didn't respond.

"Mase, that's not right."

"No," he sighed. "I know. Yeah, tell her, but she needs to act like she doesn't know it's there. We'll figure out the next step later."

"What about her parents?" I asked. "Should they know? They might talk about things that are personal."

Logan shook his head. "Nah. She's not here with them. Her dad lost his job so they shipped her out here to live with her older sister, but she's gone on a modeling trip. Tate said she wouldn't be back for a week or so." Then he jerked his head in a nod and started for the door. "Oh wait," he braked and gestured to me. "Did you tell her about the mannequins?"

"Not yet."

"Mannequins?"

"Yeah." He flashed me a smile as he headed out the door. "We torched 'em, all of 'em. Natalie's aunt's going to get a nice little surprise when she goes to work in the morning. On that note, I'm out." The door shut behind him, but we could hear him whistling as he went down the hall.

"You burned them?"

He nodded.

"All of them?"

He narrowed his eyes, and I got a glimpse of the cruel Mason again. "Every single one of them."

"Was that safe?"

He shrugged, turning to me with a hand on my leg. He nudged it over and stepped between them as he looked down at me. "We were safe. We took all of them to a place where it'd be okay."

"And Natalie's aunt? She won't press charges?"

"We left a note with a few images I kept from when they messed with Marissa. We let her know she could thank her niece for all of it."

I held my breath. It'd been so long since he'd mentioned Marissa, and now that he had, I wanted to ask him more about her. I wanted to understand what had happened to her, but I sensed his unease. It was like approaching a wild animal. I had to go slow and with caution. My heart started to pound again as I took that first step. My hand raised to touch his arm. The muscles were corded tightly in a bunch. He was so tense, but I had to try. "You still had those pictures?"

His arm began to tremble underneath my touch, just a tiny bit, but it was enough to take my breath away. His voice was rough when he spoke, "Did you know they did the same to her?"

The lump was back in my throat. It was big and wobbly, but I nodded. "Yes."

"Heather told you?"

"Yes." My heart was racing so fast now. He was finally talking about her. I felt the wall coming down. I needed to know so much. She was important to him. I needed to understand. "Will you tell me about her?"

"I thought I had?"

"More. You didn't say much before. She transferred because of Kate and her friends?"

He let out a deep sigh and moved away. I ached, I still needed his touch, but then he surprised me. He came back, a conflicted look on his face, and lifted me from the couch. I was curled against his chest as he sat down on the couch, with me on his lap. Then he tucked his chin over my head and began to talk about her.

"It was Tate, too," he paused for a moment, "towards the end of her relationship with Logan, and before she tried to sleep with me, when Heather had stopped being friends with her. I didn't pay attention. I didn't care about your friend back then, but I remember Logan saying something about it to me. He seemed to care, but then I started noticing that Tate was becoming friendly with Kate and the girls. Made sense. Tate was always around Logan and the girls were always around us. The guys considered them friends, you know?"

"Where'd your friendship with Marissa come in?"

His arms tightened around me, securing me in place. "That was a fluke thing. We sat next to each other in a class and got paired up for a project. My parents were going through a divorce at the time. My dad had been cheating for so many years, and I watched my mom go through that shit storm, then your mom started popping up. Anyways, I had a pretty low opinion of the female gender from Tate and other girls. I didn't even like Kate and the rest of them. Kate must've thought she was my maybe-girlfriend, I don't know what she thought, but I didn't care. I used her so I can kind of see where she got it wrong, but I didn't trust her or any of the others. They were mean."

I hid a smile.

He must've sensed it because he said, "I know. I'm not the nicest person, but that doesn't mean I'm going to choose people like that to trust. I don't trust anyone except you and Logan."

"You began to trust Marissa?"

"Yeah. We'd talk. That's it. We didn't hang out or anything. I think I sat at her table a few times for lunch. That seemed like a big deal to everyone, but whatever. I didn't want to deal with the bullshit from the girls. They're hard to handle sometimes. Logan understood. Just dealing with the divorce and the fights at home, I didn't want to deal with hearing shit at school, too. Marissa was nice. Her friends were quiet, but they didn't seem to mind me when I sat with them. Looking back, I think that's what put a target on her. It was after that when I began hearing things."

My fingers curled into his, interlocking our hands together. "Marissa never told you?"

"No, she never did, but I started noticing things. She lost weight. She looked tired all the time. I don't know. Maybe I wasn't looking hard enough. She wasn't my girlfriend. I didn't care that much; she was just nice to talk to at times. That was it."

I heard the struggle in him. He didn't quite understand. "You trusted her." It was beginning to make sense. "You never trusted those other girls. You tolerated them. They must've seen it." And hated it. The pieces were coming together. They had destroyed Marissa because he enjoyed her company. If they did that to her, what were they going to do to me? A shudder went through me at the thought. I was much more than a friend. I was beginning to realize he had no idea what they had done to her. Guys weren't told when girls tormented other girls. It was an unspoken rule, one

904

that I had broken. I gulped now. Would it be worse because I brought them in? But no. That wasn't the right thought. They would win if I started to think like that. Heather was right, it was time for me to fight back.

"Yeah, maybe." His chest lifted and lowered as he took in a deep breath. "I'm sure I don't even know half the shit they did to her, but I knew about the mannequins. It wasn't Marissa, but it looked just like her. The pictures were all over. People laughed at them, and it was like they were laughing at her."

"What happened after that?"

He started to lift his shoulder in a shrug, but dropped it. "More," he bit off the end of his word. His hold on me tightened, as if trying to guard me from it, too. "I heard little things they did, like breaking the lock on her locker. She used to ride the bus to school, and I'm sure things must've happened there, too. Towards the end, her parents drove her." His hand had a cement hold on my arm now. "You don't understand. Kate and the girls had a lot of power over all the other girls back then. They don't anymore. When they were exiled from the guys, I knew that would fracture the power they had over the rest. I see it too. The other girls aren't doing what Kate wants. They're starting to go against Kate and her friends."

He was holding me so tightly. When a slight tremor went through him, I knew he wanted to protect me. Turning my head to the side, I looked at him. His eyes were closed and his eyebrows were bunched forward, strained together. Then he said further, "I didn't stop them and I should have. I'm not a bully, Sam. I don't pick on the weak or try to make someone's life hell, but if they come after me or someone I love, then I'll go after them with everything I've got. I'll use all of their weaknesses to destroy them, but I never start the fight."

He didn't start the fight, but he finished it. I understood what he was saying. "Mason."

His eyelids lifted and the regret in them took my breath away. Then I swallowed over the lump in my throat and spoke, "She didn't tell you what was happening. She wasn't your girlfriend. Your parents were getting a divorce. You can't blame yourself for not stopping Kate. I'm betting that you didn't even know half of what they did."

"That's the problem," he bit out. His eyes growing cold. "I should've. She was my friend. She was a good person, and I didn't fight for her like I should've. What they did to her is on me. I didn't stop them when I could've. No one else could've, so it was my place to do it. I didn't. A part of me checked out, Sam. You're right. All the crap from the divorce. It went on long after Logan dumped Tate, too. She made it worse. Thinking back, it was how Tate hurt me back, through Marissa, but she stopped talking to me at the end. She had the teacher assign her to someone else and she stopped even saying hi to me. It was like we were strangers."

"Did it stop then?"

"No."

That one word came out like an ache. He was haunted by it.

I waited for him to continue, and he did, "I was grateful when she left. It stopped. She was safe."

"You started talking again after she left?"

He nodded. "She emailed me, told me that she didn't blame me for what happened. I was such an ass. I didn't even comment on it. I still have never said a word about it to her."

I didn't know what to say so I moved until I was straddling him. He fell back against the couch. His hands went to my legs, where mine rested on top of them, and he watched me from underneath heavy eyelids. His jaw clenched and some of his old wall came back in place. He was always so guarded.

He shook his head and cursed under his breath. His hands turned to lock with mine. "When she came to Nate's cabin, it's why I wanted him with her at all times. Plus, you were there, and I couldn't stop thinking about you."

"Has she emailed you since then?"

"A few times. I haven't responded. That wasn't intentional, I've just been wrapped up with you and everything going on with your mom."

I saw the struggle in him. He was the unbeatable one, the ruthless one, and that broke me. I would protect him how he protected me. Lifting a hand to his face, I cupped his cheek and leaned forward to press my lips to his. It was a soft graze, but my heart fluttered. The ache started between my legs, and I moved closer, grinding on him. Then I moved back, just enough to whisper, "We'll make it different this time." My lips brushed against his. "We'll change things this time. We'll make it count."

His reaction was instant. His hands caught my face and his lips opened over mine. His hunger had been unleashed, and it was demanding more. He stood with my legs wrapped around his waist and took us to bed. A primal need started in me as I met his ghosts that night, and as he thrust into me, that need took over. The need to protect him was more than before. I had worried before, knowing I could lose him, but now it went beyond that. He hadn't stopped Kate from hurting his friend and it still hurt him, but now I was angry that they had even put him in that spot. It should've never happened in the first place, but that was on Kate. She was going to pay for what she had done.

CHAPTER FOURTEEN

Everyone knew what happened the next day at school. I had no idea how, but the news was out: Mason and Logan torched the mannequins. The truth got stretched to the whole clothing store, and by the end of the day everyone was whispering that they were going to get arrested. Apparently, Natalie's aunt died in the blaze. Poor Natalie. Or that was what I heard a freshman telling her friend as they passed us, heading towards the bus lot.

Heather heard them too and laughed, shaking her head. "They're idiots."

Putting my last book into my locker, I took a few others out and stuffed them inside my bag. "I was an idiot, too. By the time I was a freshman, my boyfriend had already been cheating on me for a year."

She wrinkled her nose. "Were they already sleeping together? Or were they just making out?"

I shrugged. "Who knows? I don't even want to think about it. They were hooking up somehow."

"Speaking of your ex. He came into the diner last night. He was with that other guy. Adam?"

I was surprised. "He's moving up in the Academy social scene if he's buds with Adam now."

"Adam's the top dog at your old school?"

"Yeah."

"He's the guy you avoided the other night?"

We began walking to the senior hallway. Mason wanted me to stop by his locker before he went to practice. As we turned the corner, I grimaced. "Yeah. He said he was okay with friendship, but I can't handle that drama right now."

Natalie brushed past me at that moment, glaring the entire time. She took a step into me at the last second to hit her shoulder against mine. I kept going, jerking my thumb in her direction. "I got enough drama like that going on. I can't deal with much more."

Heather watched the Tommy Princess disappear in the direction we had just left. She murmured, "They've been quiet today."

"No texts?"

"Last one was yesterday afternoon. Your clothes were still there after gym?"

"Didn't shower. We only walked during class."

"I see."

By unspoken agreement, we stopped and watched Kate at her locker. She was alone. For once. Then Heather remarked, "I don't like it."

"Me neither."

"Ladies," Logan boomed in our ears before he wedged himself between us, throwing his arms around our shoulders. He squeezed us into his side and made a tsking sound. "Have I not made my wishes clear enough? When you come to greet me, I prefer cupcakes and those skirts that show off half your ass. It's pleasing to the eye and pleasing to my mouth, if you know what I mean."

Heather retorted, "Don't you get tired of hitting on your stepsister?"

"Future stepsister to you." He flashed a dimple at her, his mouth curving up. "Are you jealous, Jax? Do you only want me to hit on you? That could be arranged, you know. Cupcakes and ass-skirts. All I'm asking here."

She elbowed him in the gut, stepping out from his arm. "Whatever, Logan. From what I hear, you've got all your free time spoken for."

All traces of humor left. His arm dropped from my shoulder, but he didn't move away. He only tensed. "What are you talking about?"

"You and my ex-bestie. I've heard that you two get it on almost every night now."

He narrowed his eyes at her. "Who told you that?"

"Was that supposed to be a secret?"

His jaw tightened as he ground out, "It wasn't supposed to be public knowledge." He cast an accusing look to me.

Heather spoke up, "Nope. No way. She didn't say one word so don't blame her for that gossip. It came straight from Tate's mouth. She was bragging about it in class to Morgan."

"Who's Morgan?"

"Drill team," she informed me.

I nodded. "Enough said."

"She was bragging?"

Heather turned back to him. "Seemed like it. I think Morgan was planning to make her move on you after the basketball game Friday night. Tate was friendly about it, but made it known you've been too occupied to notice other girls."

"We're not dating. We're screwing. There's a difference."

"Then you better handle her because Tate's laying claim to you and no one's going to argue with her. You two were together for two years. It makes sense to people. She's the only girl you've ever loved. That's common knowledge around here too." Heather cast a frown at me, biting her lip and I got the feeling she wanted to add more, but thought better of it.

Logan was like stone beside me. He was standing close enough so his arm grazed mine. I frowned and asked, "Why's this upsetting you so much?"

He swung to me. "What?"

"Tate can't be the only girl who's tried this with you. Just do what you normally do." I paused and when he didn't get what I was implying, I added, "You hook up with someone else. Hook up with someone else Friday night." But he still looked upset and that confused me. Normal Logan would've laughed this off. He wasn't. "Are you developing feelings for her again?"

"Why the hell would you say that?"

"Don't talk to her like that," Heather pulled me from him.

I placed a calming hand on her arm. I could handle Logan just fine. "Because you're not acting normal. Hooking up with someone else shouldn't bother you, but I can tell it does."

"That's not—" But he stopped and left.

Mason was coming towards us with Ethan and Strauss. Logan brushed through them, shouldering the last two out of his way. Both paused, frowning at him until Mason was close enough to ask, "What was that about?"

Heather opened her mouth, but I grabbed her arm. I answered first, "Nothing. Some test that he took."

Mason swung his head so he was only focused on me. When he didn't comment, I felt a swift kick to my gut. It was another lie, but I couldn't take it back. I wasn't even sure why I lied, but I managed a calm smile. "He'll get over it."

"Sure."

"Test, my ass," Ethan griped. His face was scrunched together in a snarl. He raked a hand through his wavy sandy hair before letting it fall to his side. He was shorter than Mason, but just as muscular. He wasn't happy. "Logan doesn't get worked up about tests. I bet it's because of Tate. She could always wind him up like that. Why haven't you stopped that yet?"

"Right," Mason bit out, "because my brother *always* does what I want him to do."

"He has many times," Strauss added. "It's already started. He lost his head over her before. He's doing it again."

"And speak of the devil," Heather murmured, her gaze trained on someone down the hall. The group followed her gaze as one. Tate was standing at a locker, laughing with another guy. He wasn't one of their friends, and I didn't recognize him from any classes. He was built like an athlete. His brown hair was cut short and was spiked. When she flicked her hair over her shoulder, his gaze fell to her shirt. He moved an inch taller and a satisfied grin came over him. I had no doubt he'd gotten a good view of cleavage. Then her hand found his chest and rested there for a moment before she moved it down his stomach. As we watched, she leaned closer, and he sucked in his breath. His chest bulged out, and his stomach flattened as her fingers ran all the way down to grasp the waistband of his jeans.

Ethan grunted. "Whore. Always was, always will be." He left the group, and as he passed the flirting couple, his gaze locked with the guy's. Whatever unspoken message was relayed in his stare worked. The guy straightened away from Tate and moved her back. Before she could say anything, he grabbed his bag and hurried away.

Strauss chuckled. "Well if Tate didn't know she was getting inside Logan's head, she knows now."

And sure enough, Tate was standing in the hallway with her arms crossed over her chest, staring at us. Correction. She was studying us.

Strauss flicked her off before walking after his friend. When he drew abreast Tate, his gaze locked with hers. He smirked and we saw him say something to her before he moved past. There wasn't much of a reaction from her, but she cast condemning eyes back to us.

Mason laughed. "He said the same thing, but to her face."

Heather shook her head. "Tate's always been good at messing with a guy's head."

"You think that's what she's doing?"

"No." I was surprised at Heather's blunt response. Then she added, "For Logan's sake, I hope not." She glanced to Mason, but said to me, "I wouldn't want him to get hurt."

I had an eerie feeling something unspoken passed between the two of them, but then she changed the topic. A bright smile was forced out, and she asked me, "Your shift is this Thursday, but could you pick up a few more? I haven't filled Anne and Lily's positions yet."

"Sure. Yeah. When do you need me?"

"Tonight, tomorrow, and Thursday. We've got the weekend covered so far."

"Uh. Yeah. That's fine."

"It's only the five to nine shift." She rolled her eyes at me. I understood. Five to whenever was what it really was. The nine o'clock person rarely left at nine. I nodded. It was still fine with me.

"I'll go running right after school. See you in a few hours."

"See you." She waved at both of us before she headed to the parking lot.

Growing tired, I went with my gut. "Is there something going on I don't know about?"

Mason's eyes got wide. That was his only reaction before he masked it. "What?"

I knew there was, and I was tired of being in the dark. "Just tell me."

"What are you talking about?"

"I'm getting sick of the looks and the silent vibes. What's going on? My guess is that it has something to do with Logan. What is it?"

"Sam," he sighed, stepping closer to me.

I took a breath. Here it was. He was about to say that Logan had fallen in love with Tate again. I prepared myself for the news, but he said instead, "I have no idea what's going on. I don't. Honestly." When I pinned him with an accusing look, he held his hands in the air as if surrendering. "I mean it."

"Then what the hell is going on?"

He shrugged. One of his hands fell to my hip, and he pulled me against him. "My guess is that Logan's dealing with something. He does that sometimes. When he decides to come clean, he will."

"It's not Tate?"

"I don't know, but he seemed pretty insistent that he doesn't have feelings for her again."

It didn't feel right. None of it did, but I let my forehead drop against his chest. His hand swept up and brushed some of my hair back. I closed my eyes, savoring that little tender touch from him. The slightest touch from him sent me buzzing. I let myself breathe him in, filling my lungs, as I remained in his arms. Then I moved back. Mason gave me a reassuring smile, but it didn't reach his eyes.

I spoke before I thought about it. "So that's what it looks like."

"Like what?" He grew guarded.

"A lie. That's what it looks like from you." And then, even though I loved him so much, I turned and walked away. Mason lied to me. I knew it. He knew it. I had lost count how many there were between us now. We were headed down a bad path, and I had no idea how to stop it.

MASON

It'd been two days since Sam called me out. I still felt gutted, but it wasn't my explanation to give. Logan wanted to screw with Tate, make her fall for him and shatter her to pieces like she'd done to him. I didn't like it, but it was Logan's decision. It was his place to share the details with Sam, and I was taking the brunt of it. I was sick of it. After basketball practice, I headed to the parking lot. Sam worked the past two nights and I knew my little brother would be there. We'd been getting food there every time Sam worked and he was telling her what was going on with Tate, whether he wanted to or not.

When I tossed my bag inside my vehicle, I heard from behind me, "Can I have a minute?"

My blood went cold.

Kate was alone, her hands stuffed in her pockets, and her shoulders hunched forward. It was a meek posture, but she wasn't meek. She was just alone.

"What do you want?" I made a show of looking around. "Your friends going to pop out and jump me?"

She frowned. I knew that look. She was on a fishing expedition. "Why would you say that?"

"That's what you're going to do Sam, aren't you?"

"No."

Her arm twitched. She was lying.

"Look," she cleared her throat and her face twitched. I knew that look, too. She was biting the inside of her cheek. "Seeing you now, I don't even know why I bothered."

She turned to leave.

This was bullshit. She showed up so now it was my turn for some fun. "What do you want to know, Kate?"

She paused and then let out a sigh. "Fine. Listen. I need to know that it's done."

"What's done?"

"You and me."

I smirked at her. "There was never a you and me."

"Yes, there was. I was your girl—"

"That I fucked when I needed someone." I sneered. "You kept yourself clean and you didn't *use* to sleep around. I noticed. That's all there was to it. Nothing more."

She visibly swallowed. "There *was* more—"

"No, Kate." It was the lack of caring in my tone. She heard the truth and jerked to the side, as if she were going to leave, but stopped. Her hands tore out of her pockets and balled into fists. They raised in the air, but not high enough that they could do damage. I waited. Kate was a bitch. I enjoyed that I was hurting her. "Come on. You went after Marissa because I was friends with her. Now my girlfriend? For what? To get me back? You're pathetic, Kate."

"Shut up." She flinched with every word I said, but she swung her heated eyes back to me. "You shut up, Mason. You have no idea, no fucking idea why I'm doing this."

"For power? You lost it. That's long gone." When there was no reaction, I laughed. "Haven't you been watching? No one cares. The girls are turning against you."

"You think they'll follow her?" she sneered back.

"No, but they'll like her. No one liked you. They were scared of you, but no one's scared anymore."

"They should be."

"Why?" There it was. She was starting to show her colors. I could see inside of her now. "Are you going to go after every single girl? You don't have the time, and all you'll do is piss 'em all off again. They haven't turned on you yet, but they will. You go after every person, it'll happen."

"So maybe I'll make an example out of her? Maybe that's what I'm doing because people should be scared. They have no idea what I can do."

It would be so easy to pull everything out from underneath her. I wanted to. I wanted to see that look on her face. She couldn't match me, but I held back. "One word of advice, let it go. You've already lost power. You're not going to get it back."

"What do you know about it?"

"You have three friends right now." I saw the scorn on her face. She was thinking she had more. She was wrong. "If you keep targeting Sam, you won't. I'll take them from you."

Her sneer vanished. "You couldn't."

"I could."

She eyed me, studying to see if I was bluffing. I let her see the truth. "Here's your last chance. Drop it all and you can keep your friends. I won't destroy that for you, but keep doing what I know you're planning on doing, and I will ruin you. You'll have no friends. You'll have no allies. You won't even want to come to this school again."

A strangled laugh ripped from her and she shook her head. "Listen to you, big fucking deal here. You're not God, Mason."

"He wouldn't do these things to you." The cruel mask lifted. I let her see how lethal I could be. She saw it and shrunk back. "If you came here to make sure, one last and final time, that there's a chance of you and me, there never was. There's no chance you'll ever be friends with the guys again. I know how you liked to hang out with them. You liked being at the top of the social chain. Those days are dead."

"You shouldn't talk to me like that."

Really? She had no idea, but I fell silent. She was losing her control and I wanted to hear what else she would say.

"You have no idea, no fucking clue!" she shouted now.

Keep going, Kate. Tell me how I don't have a fucking clue. Lay out the rest of your plan for me.

"No idea," she continued to seethe. "Everyone forgets about you, but I don't. You're slumming when you go to this school. They forget about the rich daddy you've got. No one knows about the moneybags your mom has. No fucking clue, but I do. It's not fair. You've got a scholarship. You're going to college. Your life is set, Mason. Most the people at our school are going to community college. They can't afford your NCAA football school."

"That's where this is coming from? I'm going to a better school than you?"

Her chest began heaving. The fury was bright and burning in her eyes. "Haven't you seen my home? You know my folks. My dad's a drunk. My mom works all the time, but when she's not, she's just as drunk as him. You think they saved up money for me? I'm not going anywhere, Mason, not like your precious princess. I've heard about her running. Track scholarship. Isn't that what you were thinking, to get her here? You're right, too. I know you are. She's going to get a scholarship, probably at the same fucking college you go to, and you wanna know why? Because of you. They'll give her one because you asked, because that's how your life goes. You ask and people do it. I'm so sick of it—"

"You're sick of it?" My eyes narrowed to slits. "Or you're pissed because it isn't you?"

"You're such an asshole."

"Been called worse."

"This is my school. This is my time." She grew quiet, but the hatred still burned. "And you declared that we're out.

Just like that and it was done. You have no idea how much worse you made it for her."

"If you're pissed at me, take it out on me. Leave her alone."

"Oh no." She shook her head. "You're unfuckingtouchable. You know it and I know it, but your girl isn't. She's going to hurt by the time I'm done with her. She's going to beg me to stop, but I won't. I'll keep ruining her long after this year, even after you go to college. You'll be gone, Mason. I won't. My life's over after high school. My biggest problem is going to be who I'll marry, if it'll be some jackass, or if I'll win the lottery and get someone who sticks around. That's the life I've got to look forward to, but the one thing that'll give me pleasure is going to be destroying your girl. Just watch it."

"Rethink all of this," I warned. "This is my last offer. Walk away."

"No," she whispered, but her tone was murderous.

"You're not going to destroy Sam."

"Oh really?" She snorted.

"You fuck with who I love, and I fuck with you. You're no exception. I'm going to destroy you, Kate. You're going to have nothing left when I'm finished with you." I didn't wait to hear any more crazy shit from her. I got in my vehicle and left without looking back.

CHAPTER FIFTEEN

SAMANTHA

The weekend passed with little drama. There was a basketball game. I went. They won. There was a party. The only big event there was when Logan took my advice and planned on going home with a new girl, but she had a friend with the same hopes. The two got in a fight. It was full of name-calling. Someone's hair got pulled and the other girl got scratched. Eventful. And Logan? He bypassed the fight and went home with Tate. I had an entire speech ready to deliver over breakfast the next day for why he needed to stop seeing her. I had it all memorized, but the speech died in my throat when Tate showed up at the same restaurant with a different guy.

Logan didn't care. Really. I studied him the whole time to catch the slightest reaction—twitch, twerk, eye-roll—but nothing. Then it dawned on me. He really didn't care if she was with another guy. I was at a loss after that. Later that evening, Helen wanted to have dinner with her sons, but I was spared another run-in with her.

I was also spared another run-in with Kate. Mason told me she had something planned for me, but it never happened. I wondered if she'd been distracted.

When I went to school on Monday, the words 'Roussou Sucks' were spray-painted on a banner. It hung over the archway at the front entrance of the school. Heather explained it was the big rivalry game. Fallen Crest Public's basketball team was going to play Roussou High that Friday night.

Great.

Not.

She further spoiled my day when she told me Fallen Crest Academy didn't have their own basketball game that night so my old friends would be in the stands.

Double great.

Needless to say, I wasn't in a great mood during the next week. Logan noticed and brought me a latte one day during lunch. It didn't work. I still wasn't happy so he told Mason to give me a quickie in their coach's office. That certainly didn't help.

It wasn't until Friday morning when another bomb was dropped.

Helen Malbourne was going to attend their basketball game. From the way Mason worded it and how Logan started laughing behind him, I knew there was a joke somewhere. I didn't care enough to figure it out. Instead, I remarked, "I'm sure she'll have a great time."

"Heather's working." Mason gave me a confused look.

"Yeah. And..."

"And..."

Logan finished for him, "Don't you want to sit with our mum for the game? She gets box seats every time. Thinks she's a goddamn celebrity for a high school basketball game. Jokes on her. She's got to share the box with the announcer, and they won't be farting out popcorn for her."

"Logan."

"What?" He glanced at his brother. "Mom thinks she's a big-time celebrity, and you know it. I love her, but her ego's massive. It's gotten worse in the last few months. Wait." He paused, frowning to himself. "Fuck. Is she dating someone new?" Logan gestured to me. "I'm surprised she hasn't tried with Sam's other dad, David." He asked me, "Is he still dating Mark's mom?"

"Um..." I wasn't expecting the question, but my heart sank. I didn't know. An image flashed in my mind. He looked so different when Mason had dropped Jeff off at Academy. He was heavier, muscled, and looked healthy. He looked good. He looked like he was better. I jerked a shoulder up before I turned away. "I guess so."

As I grabbed my bag and headed for the door, I heard the sound of someone getting whacked behind me. Logan muttered, "Ouch. What was that for?" But I was already in the hallway and headed into the elevator.

I drove myself to school that day.

People were screaming in the hallway. Everyone wanted to murder Roussou that night. I knew Mason and Logan were both itching to do the same. Even Heather seemed excited, and she was going to miss the game. She had me sit with her friends at lunch. Since the clothes incident, her friend Cory had thawed towards me a little. I only got two glares instead of the fifteen. Baby steps. On a normal day, that would've been a big deal to me, but this wasn't a normal day.

Logan's comment about my dad had blindsided me.

Their parents were around. Their mother had come back to town. Where was mine? My mother was unfit. My biological father had disappeared back to Boston and David, there'd been no recent contact from him. I saw him the day I registered for school at Fallen Crest Public, but that conversation had been so slight, it'd been meaningless to me.

He moved on. That was the bottom line.

"Yo!"

Someone snapped their fingers in front of me, jerking me out of my daze. "What?"

"Bitch Crew Walking. Head's up."

I think that came from Channing's half-brother? Max? I wasn't sure. None of them had made overt steps towards friendship. I was tolerated because of Heather.

Kate stopped at our table, and the other three fanned out behind her. Like the rest of the school, she was wearing the school colors. She had on red pants and a black shirt. The pants were more like tights, and the black shirt was transparent, showing off her red bra underneath. Her hands went to her hips and she glared at me.

I was getting used to all the glares. I felt naked without seeing a couple a day now.

I grinned up at her. "I feel like I should be a hot-air machine. For every bad look I get, I could pop out a balloon with a smiley face." I smirked. "Bet the glares would stop then."

Heather snorted.

Some of the guys snickered.

I added, "Like right now. You'd get one in black and red." I gestured to Kate's clothes. "It'd match your outfit."

I caught a faint grin from Cory, but it was masked as soon as she saw me watching. Her eyebrows fixed and her face went blank again. I sighed. So close.

Kate's sneer turned into a snarl. "You think you're funny?"

One of the three added, "Maybe she's taking lessons from Logan?"

Another snorted. "Probably. She needs all the lessons she can get."

My smile had stretched from ear to ear now. It was genuine, too. "Is this another warning from you? I thought you moved past the cliché insults and name calling. Oh wait. You said lessons. Yes, that's referencing that I'm dumb. That's another cliché insult." With my hand in the air, I lifted a finger with each point. "I'm ugly. I'm dumb. I have too much sex. Those are the three main ones most simpletons use to insult others. The clothes and the mannequin gave me hope. I thought you were starting to progress, but then I heard that you've already done that before. It's recycled material. You guys need to find new stuff. You know what they say about comedians?" At their blank faces, I nodded. "What I expected. If they use old material, the act is boring. People move on. If you're going to keep drawing fresh fear from everyone, you need new stuff." I stood and patted Kate's head. "You can do it. I believe in you."

Logan stood by the door and held it open. Mason came

in behind him. Both found me immediately. I wondered who had notified them, but then Kate grabbed my arm. She twisted it and got into my face. Her hand tightened on my arm and she lowered her voice, "You have until the end of the day to drop out of school. This is the last warning."

A taunt rose to my tongue, but I swallowed it. The jokes were gone.

Three thoughts happened at the same time. David's image flashed again. "Fuck it," came next. Third, when I knew what I was going to do, I thought, "Let's see how this goes."

Kate's eyes widened as she watched the myriad of expressions before she saw my intent. Her hand let me go, and she started to back away, but it was too late. My hand latched onto hers instead, and I took one second to comment, "Bet you weren't expecting this," before my other hand grabbed the back of her head and used all my body weight to slam her head into the table.

Everything went silent for a moment. The only sound I heard was my heart thumping. It was calm and steady. *Thump.*

"You bitch!" someone shrieked from somewhere, but the voices were so far away. They were a slight buzz to me now.

Thump.

People screamed. I heard a few guys swear. Footsteps pounded on the floor. I kept track of all that was happening in the back of my mind. I got a better grip on her head and held her arm down while I tried to lift her head for another slam. She was yelling. I saw her mouth open and caught the flash of terror in her eyes, but then I was jerked backwards. Someone punched me on the cheek. It hurt, but it didn't penetrate the numb sensation that had taken over me.

Thump.

"You're going to get your ass beat." Someone spit on me, but I wiped it off and twisted around. I lunged for whoever was in front of me. She had black hair, maybe Jasmine? I yanked on it and then punched her face.

"Oh, shit!"

"AHHH!"

"Get her off!"

"GET HER!"

I wound up for another hit when I was lifted off my feet. Two strong arms wrapped around me and carried me away. Kicking at them and trying to squeeze out from their hold, I yelled, "Let me go!"

"It's me. Stop, Sam."

Kate was being held up by a couple of guys. I think it was Jasmine that I had hit. Natalie and Parker stood around her and both were glaring at me. One brushed Jasmine's hair from her forehead and was inspecting her face. I growled. I wanted to get them all. Fuck it. I was out for blood now.

Grabbing onto one of the arms around me, I sunk my nails into it. They protested, so I pushed them deeper. I needed to get free. The need to hurt them back was a frenzy inside of me. So many people had hurt me, I wanted to hurt them all—Analise, David, Garrett, Jeff, Lydia, Jessica, Becky, Adam.

THUMPTHUMPTHUMP

"Let me go," I yelled. My voice broke, but I didn't care. I tried again.

A litany of curses came from behind me and I heard, "Sam, it's Mason. Stop it."

THUMPTHUMPTHUMP

"SAM," he yelled in my ear.

"Get her out of here. No one will say anything."

Mason argued over my head, "Yes they will."

"Not if everyone says they're liars. We'll handle it. Get her gone."

"Fine." His arms tightened around me, and he carried me through a side door. We stepped outside before he let me back on my feet. I knew it was cold, but I didn't feel it. I was heated. Enough logic had filtered back in as they discussed what to do with me, but my blood was still boiling. The need to hurt them was so powerful. My hands shook, and my head went down. I gasped for air, trying to fill my lungs so I could think straight, but it wasn't working. The need to run back inside was aching. I *had* to go back, and I started to, but Mason caught me around the waist. He pushed me against the wall and positioned himself in front of me as a barrier.

"Stop," he murmured. He kept a hand on my stomach, but it was a light touch.

I drew in more breaths and closed my eyes. *Get it together.*

"Sam?"

I shook my head and lifted a hand. I needed a minute. Enough reason had come back, and I was starting to realize what I had done. I still didn't care. There would be ramifications. There were always ramifications. I was trying to remember why I used to care about them.

Mason's statement came back to me at that moment, *Your dad looks ripped. Not bad for a guy his age.* His statement haunted me. So did mine, *It doesn't matter to me anymore.*

It did. I thought it hadn't, but I was a fool. I was beginning to realize how much it did matter to me.

"Sam?"

I heard the concern in his voice and everything melted inside of me. Just like that. The fight left me, and I wanted to disappear. "Mason," I choked out.

He swept me up. My legs wrapped around his waist, and he turned so his back was against the wall. Sliding down to sit on the ground, he started stroking my hair back and rubbing my back at the same time. I clung to him. A minute earlier I'd been ready to tear someone apart, and now I was trying to hold the tears at bay.

"Are you going to tell me what that was all about?"

I murmured against his shoulder, "Besides Kate being a bitch?"

"Yeah," he laughed. His hand kept rubbing up and down my back in long sweeps. He slowed them down as he continued.

"You mean she didn't deserve that?"

"Sam."

I still had some fight left in me. Grinning at that thought, I pulled away enough so I could meet his gaze. "I'm kidding."

"Hey, man."

"Yo."

"Oh, whoa..."

Three guys came around the corner. They were dressed in black clothing that drowned them. They looked like skinny freshmen. All three braked when they spotted us.

Mason barked out, "Leave."

Two scattered. One lingered.

He added, "Now."

The last one took off after his friends.

"Hey."

We glanced the other way. Logan was standing outside the door. Heather popped her head past him and started to step out. He grabbed her arm and pulled her back in. When she started to push through again, he reached for the door. His arm was a barrier now.

She glared at him, but moved so she could see me better. She gave me a gentle smile. "You okay?"

I nodded. "How's it inside?"

"Okay. No." Logan stepped all the way and pushed the door closed.

"Hey," Heather protested. "Come on. I'm her friend. Let me talk to her."

"Give us a minute." It wasn't a request, and he shut the door in her face. When it started to open again, he leaned against it. "Give us a minute, Jax."

She huffed from inside, her voice muffled, "Fine. One minute, Kade."

He rolled his eyes and said to us, "I'm shaking in my boots here."

I frowned. Mason stood and lowered me to the ground. That was a prime opportunity for one of Logan's smart-ass comments. I asked, "Did it look bad in there?"

"It didn't look like you were holding hands and hugging," he griped at me. His tone was biting. "No, Sam. It didn't look good."

"Relax, Logan."

"There's blood all over the table—" he bit off his statement, clenching his jaw at the same time. "Is she okay? Are you okay, Sam?"

I started to respond, but Mason answered first. His hand tightened on my back and he held me against him, speaking over my head, "She's fine. She took one hit, but she's strong."

Logan cursed under his breath before he replied, "She shouldn't get in trouble. We don't have to worry about them calling Analise in for her."

"What'd you do?"

"They already said something, so I told Principal Green that Kate and Jasmine fought each other. Since they didn't want to get in trouble, of course they're going to blame an easy target. Everyone knows how much they hate Sam anyways."

I asked, "Are people going to back that up? All he has to do is ask a freshman or something."

"He won't." Logan's gaze lingered with Mason's. The two seemed to share an unspoken conversation before he added, "Anyone who rats us out will get hurt. They won't."

"I don't care if I get in trouble." But my stomach was protesting again. They were right. Analise would be called. I'd be forced to move back in. "If someone says anything, I'll tell them about everything Kate's been doing to me: the threats, the text messages, stealing my clothes."

Someone began pounding on the door from the inside. There were a few kicks added in and they stopped when Heather yelled, "Let me out. She's my friend, too. Logan!"

"Let her out."

He nodded and stepped away from the door. As soon as it swung open, she punched him in the gut. He didn't move. He didn't even blink, and Heather seemed taken aback. She rubbed one hand with the other before she hissed at him, "That wasn't nice. I thought I was in the trust circle. That's crap."

He ignored her and said to us, "I'm going. See you later, Sam. That was a helluva hook."

When Mason remained, Heather turned her disapproving eyes to him. His hand tightened on my side in reflex until she said, "You can't miss any classes. If you do, you'll be booted from the game. I, on the other hand, can miss all I want. I won't get in trouble with my dad. Go, Mason. I'll clean her up."

He was reluctant.

"I'll be fine." The pain in my cheek was starting to filter in, and he couldn't help with that. "I mean it. I'll talk to you after school."

He frowned, but nodded. Bending to kiss my lips, he thought better and kissed my forehead instead. When he glanced at Heather, I knew there were words he wanted to share, but didn't. An outsider was present. As he stalked through the door and it shut behind him, Heather frowned at me. Her hands went to her hips. "What the hell was all of that about?"

She meant the fight. I sighed. "I miss my dad."

CHAPTER SIXTEEN

Heather took me to her house after the fight. The bruise on my cheek wasn't too big, and it was easily covered with make-up. When she asked if I'd get in trouble for skipping, I didn't think I would. Most of the teachers didn't take attendance and the ones who did never called my name. Because I was still new, I didn't think my name even got onto the attendance sheets. She seemed okay with that answer. When we first arrived, her dad met us in passing, heading back to Manny's after taking a lunch break. She gestured to me and said, "It was those same girls." That was enough for him. He nodded and replied, "Always stand-up for yourself." Then he left.

I asked her later what he meant, and she explained that she informed her dad about everything. He knew about Kate. He knew they were sending her threats. He knew they'd threatened his and her brother's livelihood. I was surprised that he hadn't gone to the principal, but her dad was realistic. He knew nothing would be done and those girls always got away with their bullying. Heather informed me that he gave her permission to defend herself, in any way she needed, and that he would have her back.

Then she added, "My dad's not stupid. He knows there's only so much a parent can do against these types of bullies. If they get in trouble, they'll only do something worse the next time around. That's why he said I don't have to worry about getting in trouble with him."

I nodded.

I didn't know if that was the right thing to do as a parent. My own weren't stellar, but she talked to her dad. He was here for her. He would support her if she needed it. Then she distracted me when she asked, "You still going to the game tonight?"

There was no question about what game. It was the game against Roussou.

She suggested, "You could sit by my friends. You remember my friend, Max? Channing's half-brother? Dark spiky hair? Usually wears ripped shirts and has tattoos all over him? He always goes when they play Roussou. He likes to spend time with Channing, but Cory and Rain should be in our stands." I grinned at the thought. Cory was like a feral cat. Her 'warming up to me' was not snarling at me. Then she added, "But you'll have all those Academites there, too. You could see some of your old friends."

Mark would be there. His mother might be there, too and that meant...my father. And hours later when I parked outside of the school, it seemed that everyone had come for the game. There were no spots in the parking lot. There were no spots within a four block radius of the school. I finally found an empty spot near the football field and parked. I jogged over it, heading past the parking lot. When I noticed the line that snaked outside of the gym's entrance, I slipped in a side door. Some of the hallways were blocked off, but not all the way. I could slip past one of the gates, and join the mass chaos once I found one I could fit through. The volume in the building was deafening. People was lined up at the concessions, there were lines for the bathrooms, and people were packed into the entrance hallway. Instead of two people selling admissions, they should've had twenty.

I hadn't gone far when someone touched my arm.

Thinking it was Kate, I swung around with a fist already formed.

Instead, it was Mark. "Hi," he shouted in my ear, but is eyes got wide as he stared at my hand. "Uh... never mind?"

"Sorry. Hi." I gave Mark a grin in response. He was friends with Logan, but since his mother started dating David, things had been awkward between the two of us.

He leaned close again. "You like it here?"

I nodded. I couldn't help myself. I looked around him, but there was no sign of his mother. Spotting Adam in a corner, he had his arm around a girl's waist. Mark must've noticed my gaze. He yelled in my ear again, "Yeah, Adam has a new girlfriend. She transferred in this semester." He let out a little laugh. "Or he's trying to get a new girlfriend. I don't think they're official yet."

She was pretty and petite. Her wavy hair was a wheat-golden blonde color and fell to her shoulders. When Adam saw me, he stiffened. She glanced up, a frown on her face, and followed his gaze. When her eyes caught mine, they were a breathtaking green.

I waved at them. Adam jerked his head in a stiff nod back to me. Her gaze lingered on me, and I could see the confusion there. Lifting a hand to his chest, she tipped her head back, the questions already on her lips. As his jaw clenched, I knew she had asked who I was.

When I turned back to Mark, he lifted a shoulder up. "Her name is Kris. He's crazy about her."

I remarked, "That must drive Cass nuts."

"You have no idea." Amusement sparked in his eyes now. "We miss you over there."

My eyebrows went up at that.

"We do. I do. I know Adam does. Not everyone hates you over there." He skimmed me up and down with a wolf-whistle on his lips. "You look good, Sam. Public school must agree with you."

I shrugged. "Seven hours earlier and you would've *really* though that. You look good, too." And he did. Mark had always looked good, but there'd never been an attraction between us. He was six foot two inches, had muscular shoulders, dark hair and the same almond eyes that his mother had. He wasn't the golden-boy beauty that Adam was, and he didn't have the classic handsome features like their other friend, Peter, but Mark's easygoing personality and contagious smile were like a magnet to girls. Always had been. I had no doubt Mark had his pick of the ladies.

He flashed his dimples. "Logan would be proud. I'm doing that workout he was telling me about last weekend..." He trailed off. "He didn't tell you about that?"

"You saw Logan last weekend?"

"I always see Logan. Same parties, you know? But we haven't been getting invites to the public parties like we used to. A lot of people think it's your fault, like you don't want your old classmates there."

I was public enemy number one at Fallen Crest Academy. Not much had changed. Fond memories. "What'd you talk about?"

"What?"

"You and Logan. What'd you two talk about?" That wasn't what I wanted to ask him, though.

He shrugged. "What we always talk about. Girls and lifting weights. What do you talk about with him?"

My eyelid was beginning to twitch. Screw it. "Is your mom still dating David?"

"Your dad, David?"

I nodded. My heart began pounding.

"Yeah. Why?"

"You told me a couple months ago that you thought they were going to get married."

"I know." He gave me a sheepish look. "I'm sorry. I overreacted. My mom told me that your mom and dad hadn't been divorced at the time, but they are now. Aren't they?"

"Are they here?"

"Your mom and dad?"

"*Your* mom and *my* dad," I shouted in his ear. The crowd had doubled, and we were pressed even closer together. I couldn't see Adam anymore.

"Oh." He laughed at himself. "Yeah, they're here. They're with the adults. Why?"

I shook my head. "No reason."

"Oh." His frown came back. "Was I not supposed to say that? Is that a secret or something? I never know what's going on."

"No, it's fine. You're fine." I patted his arm for extra reassurance while a storm had started inside of me. "I'm going to go and find a seat."

"Wait." He tapped my shoulder again. "We heard there's a party at Fischer's tonight and Academites are invited. Is that true? Are you going to be there?"

"Probably." I waved at him again before moving away. "See you later."

"Oh. Okay." His hand jerked up, and he waved it back and forth. "Yeah. See you."

Before going into the packed gymnasium, I needed to go to the bathroom. The lines hadn't lessened and then I heard a buzz inside of the gym, followed by another deafening roar from the crowd. I'd been to enough basketball games to know the teams just left their locker rooms, which meant I needed to hurry. I didn't want to wait in line so I turned a corner and went down one of the darkened hallways. Slipping past one of the gates, I jogged all the way to the bathrooms at the opposite end of the school. No one should be in them and I wouldn't have to wait in line. I would get back by the time they finished their warm-ups.

Everything was going according to plan.

Pushing through the door, the bathroom was empty. It didn't take me long. I finished and washed my hands. When I turned from the hand dryer, I stopped. Everything stopped. In hindsight, I would realize that the dryer drowned out the sounds of their entrance, but it didn't matter. I couldn't have stopped it from happening.

Kate had come inside the tiny bathroom. Parker stepped around her, Jasmine and Natalie following behind. When the door closed behind them, Natalie reached up and locked the door.

All four of them were dressed in black clothing with hooded sweatshirts. The four reached up and pushed back their hoods as one. Each had their hair tied back in a low ponytail.

My stomach dropped.

This wasn't going to end well, but I couldn't get past them. I couldn't call for help. I tried to grin, failing miserably. "Payback?"

Kate's eyes turned feral. She lifted her top lip in a snarl. "This isn't payback. This is your punishment."

Parker sneered at me, her hands hung loose beside her. They were ready to harm someone.

I gulped.

They were ready to harm me.

Then she added, "This is the first wave."

Kate grunted, taking a step closer. "You should've quit school today. I gave you one last out."

Natalie spoke from the back, "Time's up."

The room plunged into darkness, and I had one second. The sounds dimmed like earlier that afternoon. My breathing was now deafening in my ears. My heart started to race, but the fear threatened to paralyze me.

I pushed from the sink and darted into a stall. Someone reached for me. They grabbed my shirt, but I didn't stop. My sleeve ripped off, and I used that to my advantage. As they fell back with my sleeve, I punched at them. Someone cried out, I assumed it was Kate. The other three were behind her, but I got into the middle stall and locked the door. Before I had time to think, I dropped to the ground and flew underneath to the next stall.

A foot stepped on me. I heard, "She's in this one."

Fuck.

The foot lifted in the air. It was going to kick me, but I thrust a hand out blindly. I caught it, but there was too much force behind it. It crushed two of my fingers, and I clamped my mouth shut. A scream wanted to burst out of me, but I swallowed it. Good god, I swallowed it. No sound. No tears. No cries. They couldn't hear anything from me. I wouldn't give them the satisfaction. Pushing past that blinding pain, I threw my shoulder up and into the person. It was enough. She fell back, and I heard more cries.

"Get off me, Parker."

"It was that bitch."

"Let's turn the lights on. This is stupid."

"No, someone might see. If the door's locked, they won't come in here."

"Shut up and get her," Kate barked at them.

I heard the pain in her voice. I must've hit her harder than I thought, but then I heard someone fall to the ground. They were trying to crawl in like I had. Flipping around, I kicked at them instead.

"Ouch! Bitch!"

I kicked them again, and again, and again. I kept kicking them. It was working, but suddenly two hands grabbed my arm, and I was yanked from underneath the last stall. The exit door was right there. I pushed to my feet and reached for it. My fingers hit it, but then I was pulled back again. I made for one last reach. I grunted from the effort, but I got to it. The lock moved down.

I was thrown back to the floor after that. I couldn't even turn over before fists were coming down on me.

They hit my jaw.

They hit my eyes.

They pulled my hair out.

They ripped my shirt.

They punched my stomach.

And then the kicks started.

To my side. Down on my ribs. On my head. To the side of my head. Then to my hips. They wouldn't stop. I couldn't keep going. My eyes were swollen shut by now. I lifted my hands, but only to ward off their attacks. I couldn't fight anymore. The pain was too much and I couldn't get through them. The door was less than five feet away, but it could've been five miles now.

"HEY!"

Oh, thank god, I thought for a brief second. There was a pause, and they stopped.

The door burst open and someone braked. Their sneakers screeched against the floor from their sudden stop. She choked out, "Oh my god."

"You—" Kate started, her tone menacing.

They took off.

No one moved. The door shut behind whoever it had been. Then Kate screamed, "Stop her!"

Natalie was panting. "She's gone. We should get gone, too."

"We're not done."

"She can't move. Let's go."

"NO."

"Kate, you can't kill her, and that freak saw us. We need to get to her before she tells anyone it was us."

Jasmine spoke up, a tremor in her voice, "You think she's going to tell?"

"Yes," Natalie snapped at her. "Idiot. She's going to get help for this cunt. Let's go."

She stepped over me, but kicked me one last time before shoving through the door. The rest lingered, and she roared from the hallway, "LET'S FUCKING GO!"

Each of them kicked me one last time on their way out. I couldn't fight them. I knew it was coming, but the pain had paralyzed me. This wasn't a pain that I could shut off. It didn't take me away from my reality. I was here the whole time. I could hear, and I could think, but I couldn't do a thing to stop them. When the door shut behind them, and I lay there alone, I finally gasped for breath. Even my mouth hurt. I could taste blood, and I felt its wetness all over me.

Please don't let them get Mason. Or Logan. That was my one prayer. Whoever they were getting, whoever would come through those doors again, I didn't want it to be either of them. They couldn't see me like this. They'd lose control.

They'd do something horrific, and I couldn't lose them because of this.

"In there," I heard someone yell from farther down the hallway. Their sneakers were pounding on the floor. I could feel their approach, and then their shapes blocked the light from under the door. They were right there, on the other side.

Please not them, I prayed again to myself.

When they started to open the door, I closed my eye... and then I waited.

A woman choked out, "Oh my god."

That wasn't Mason or Logan. It wasn't someone I knew. My eyelid opened, but I could only see through a small slit. They were too swollen for much more.

Gentle hands touched me as she knelt beside me. "Oh, dear. Samantha?"

The girl remained in the back, but she spoke up, "They were beating her. All four of them."

"Who, sweetheart?" The warmth in that voice washed over me in waves. She touched the side of my face and turned it to the side. More light shined on me, and she sucked in her breath again. "Oh, dear." She glanced up again. "Who did this to her?"

"Some other girls."

Wait—I knew that voice. Images of Heather's friend flooded me. It was Cory.

Then the lady asked, "Can you and your friend go find someone for me?"

"The principal?"

"Yes, dear, but I'd also like you to find someone else."

"Okay."

Gone was the goth girl from earlier, with her constant glares and venom-laced words. Cory reminded me of a little girl in that moment.

"Do you remember the gentleman that was standing next to me?"

"Yes." Her voice dipped again with emotion.

"Go get him."

"Who is he?"

The hand rested on her arm this time. It was strong and healing. I felt this woman's courage through that touch, and I drew in a shuddering breath. I needed it. I needed every bit of strength this woman was giving to me.

"Try to be quiet about this. We don't want to draw a lot of attention."

"Who's that guy?" Cory questioned again.

I drew in another breath. I didn't know why she was insisting, but it felt good. Like she was looking out for me.

Then I heard the answer, "That man is Samantha's father."

The door closed again. I felt the small draft. It was soothing against the burns from everything else. Then the woman moved so I could see her. Dark eyes and brown curls framed her face. Malinda Decraw smiled at me, though I could see the hesitation in her. She nodded, but it was as if she were reassuring herself. She murmured, "We're going to get you some help, Samantha. I promise, honey." Her last word stumbled out and hitched on a sob. "Everything will be fine."

Her hand brushed my hair back. Her fingers trailed through it, and I wondered if it was the only place she could touch me. She repeated again, speaking to herself now, "Everything will be fine..."

CHAPTER SEVENTEEN

My dad was there.

That thought was on repeat in my mind. For some reason it helped block the pain. He came with Principal Green and both of them had been quiet since they came in. I couldn't see them. Malinda kept patting my hand. I wasn't even sure if Cory had returned with them.

When they began discussing plans, and I heard the word ambulance, I tried to tell them not to call for one. My lips cracked open and blood rushed inside my mouth, but I swallowed enough so I could talk. "No." It came out as a whisper.

"David." Malinda stopped their quiet conversation. Her hand patted mine. It was so gentle. "She's trying to say something."

"Hi, honey." He stepped so he was in my line of sight and plastered a fake smile on his face. It was one of the worst I'd seen.

I tried again, "Don't call them."

"What, honey? Sammy, sweetheart." He knelt down and bent closer to my lips.

I repeated, "Don't call them. I can walk."

"Samantha," he stopped and moved out of eyesight. There was a sniffle, followed by a cough before he came back. The light from above reflected off a trail of moisture on his face, but there were no tears. He said again, "You can't move. We have to get an ambulance. There could be internal damages."

I tried to shake my head. Mason and Logan couldn't know. They'd react without thinking or worse. I felt a different pang go through me. They might assume it had been the Roussou people. That would be worse. I whispered out again, "No, please no."

"I'm sorry, honey." He lifted a hand to pat my hand, but held it in the air. There was nowhere to touch.

Malinda moved her hand. "I don't think she's hurt here."

He closed his eyes and took a couple breaths. They came out sounding jerky, but then he reached over and touched my hand in the same spot. He patted it, but it was so light it was more of a gentle graze. "Honey, Samantha, your principal's already gone to call them."

I sucked in air through my cracked lips. I wanted to protest.

"But we'll have them come through the far end door. People at the game won't see then."

The relief was overwhelming. Fresh tears came to me, and they spilled down my face, stinging as they slid over the damage.

He added, "You don't want Mason and Logan to see you right now, do you?"

I stopped trying to talk, but I shook my head. It was the smallest movement I could muster. I was trying so hard.

"We won't let this out, but the paramedics have to come and get you. We're scared of moving you."

I closed my eyes. I could breathe easier, as easily as I could. He understood. Mason and Logan wouldn't find out until later. I hoped to be the one to tell them, if I could, but when the EMTs came in with a stretcher, I was beginning to realize that it would be a long while until I could do anything for myself. When they rolled me onto the stretcher, I couldn't move. My ribs ached. My chest pounded. Sharp pangs stabbed me, shooting up and down, all over me.

As we rolled down the hallway, I saw Cory beside the lockers. She stood there with Rain huddled behind her. Their hands looked as if they were clasped together, but I couldn't be sure. When her gaze caught mine, she lifted one side of her mouth. I tried to relay my thanks. She saved me.

I couldn't see her anymore as they wheeled me the opposite direction and out a back door. I barely felt the cold air. It stung my face, but the rest of me was wrapped in a blanket. I could move my legs, even wiggle my toes, but they hurt. Everything hurt.

"Yo, what's that?"

Principal Green let out an exasperated sound. "If you two are here for the game, you should be on the other side of the school."

"Relax, dude. We don't even go here."

"Then you're trespassing. Get off the school's grounds. Wait," his voice rose, "get away from her."

"Relax..." the voice trailed off, and I saw Brett Broudou standing above me. When he recognized me, his eyes widened, and his mouth opened. The cigarette he had poised at his mouth lowered. "Whoa..."

"Who is it, Brett?"

That must've been Budd.

I wanted to look away, but I didn't. He wouldn't move. He kept staring, so I looked back at him. A storm of emotion flashed in his gaze before he demanded, "Who did this to you?"

"That's enough," my dad stepped forward. He held a hand up and moved him back. "She needs to get to the hospital, son."

"Son," Budd ground out from somewhere. There was a bitter laugh in him. "You hear that, Brett? Geezer called you 'son.' We'll show you 'son'. We'll show you a whole different meaning—"

Brett snapped at him, "Shut up, Budd." He gentled his tone and asked, "Is she going to be okay, sir?"

My dad paused, frowning at him. "Are you friends with her?"

I needed to tell him. I had to stop him.

"Sir, I met her at Manny's."

"Brett, come on." Another menacing growl from Budd. "This is fucking ridiculous. Her pussy's damaged now. Let's focus on the Kades."

That got my dad's attention. His head jerked to wherever Budd was. I could still see Brett, and I saw him flinch, before he sighed and moved out of eyesight.

"Let's go." Principal Green stepped forward. His authority came out full force, and he pounded a hand on the ambulance's door. "David, don't even bother. I recognize these two. They were banned from the game. I'll have security take care of them. You go with your daughter."

"She's your daughter?"

"Who cares? We need to go, Brett. They'll escort us out, and we'll have to sneak back in. Let's tail it now."

Principal Green stood above me now. He was watching them, but he glanced down. He gave me one reassuring look before he murmured quietly to me, "I won't tell, Sam. They won't know."

The relief was overwhelming. Again. Tears burst forth, but I couldn't wipe them away. They had strapped me to the stretcher so I wouldn't shift any bones or my insides. I was in so much pain.

"David," Principal Green said as my stretcher was lifted into the ambulance. The paramedics got me into place. "You can go with her. Malinda already took your car. She's going to meet you there."

"Yeah, okay."

When he climbed inside the ambulance, he sat as close to me as possible. The doors were shut, and it wasn't long until the engine was started. As it turned onto the street, David reached out and took my hand. I'd never seen him this sad. He brushed at a tear, but tried to smile for me. "Don't worry, honey. You'll get looked at and everything will be fine."

No, Dad. Everything wouldn't be fine.

That was the truth. I was just realizing that I still hadn't let him in on it.

MASON

When I left the locker room, only a few were still in the gymnasium. Most were heading to Manny's and then to Fischer's for a big damn party. I knew Logan was riled about it, had been during the whole game and after. When I saw him jumping up and down near the bleachers, and our mom watching him, I rolled my eyes. Logan was ready to tear into someone.

"Honey." Helen stood up from her seat and gave me a gracious smile. If Sam were there, I knew she would've been self-conscious. My mother dressed to impress. I never cared what clothes she wore, but it mattered to her what others thought. She pressed a kiss to my cheek and she patted me on the shoulder before moving to press her hair back in place. "You were fabulous. It was a close game, wasn't it?"

Logan snorted, but kept jumping up and down. He was rubbing his hands together before jabbing them into the air.

"We won by four points. It was close, Mom."

"See. I know a little about basketball."

I didn't care. "Did you see Sam here?"

She stiffened before shaking her head. "No, honey. Was I supposed to look for her? I'm sure she sat with some of her friends."

Logan snorted again, still jumping. "She doesn't have friends at this school."

"Logan."

"What? She doesn't. It's your fault, not hers."

Helen skirted between us. "Are you suggesting Samantha has no friends because of her boyfriend?"

"Yeah, Mom, I am." He stopped jumping and gave her a dead look. "Your son's the cream in a pussy's food dish. The claws come out. Bitches and pussies fight over that shit. You should be proud."

When Helen didn't respond, I chuckled. "Don't worry, Mom. You can be proud Logan's the cat's meow."

Horror flashed first as she twisted around. "Logan? She's with you now?"

Logan glanced at me. We shared a look before he rolled his shoulders back, squared his chin away and threw out his cocksure attitude. "Is this news to you? I'm hurt that you're even surprised by this."

"I... I..." she sputtered, drawing to her tallest height. "I'm not. Of course not, I'm just taken aback by the camaraderie between you two. There's no hard feelings?"

"Why would there be?" Logan asked, throwing an arm around my shoulders. He lifted up on his tiptoes so we were the same height and then he patted me on the arm twice. "She dips in both of our cream dishes."

"Logan!" We waited as she swayed on her feet, a hand to her chest. Then she sputtered again, "This is disgusting. I implore both of you to break up with this girl. If she's doing what you're insinuating, this will go down a bad road. Trust me. You both need to stop seeing her." She paused and an old flare came over her. "Her mother alone is a good enough reason to try for someone better. Horrible breeding. You both need to preserve where your semen goes. Once you've reproduced, there's no going back. That child is in the world for the rest of your life—"

I'd had enough. "Mom." I shrugged Logan's arm off me. "We're joking with you. Sam's still my girlfriend, and it's not her fault she doesn't have friends here. Some of the other girls are jealous."

"Oh."

We waited. One second.

"You two are horrible children. To joke like that? Why would you even think about something like that in the first place?"

"Relax, Mom." Logan threw his arm around her shoulders. When she tried to smooth out her shirt's collar, he said to me, "I already asked around. No one's seen her."

Heather was working. Sam knew her old classmates would be there. It made sense if she opted out. "She's probably watching a movie at home or something."

"Or she's already at the party and getting drunk."

Sometimes my brother really pissed me off.

"What?" He flashed me a grin. "It'd be awesome if she were. My sis needs to get drunk more. Last time she did, she and Tate got into it. That was hilarious." His smile turned wistful. "I'd pay money to see something like that again."

"Okay." Helen gave us a kiss on our cheeks. "I can tell where this is going so I'm going to be heading out myself."

When she collected her purse from the bleachers, Logan asked, "Are you going back to the hotel?"

She snorted. "Oh no. I'm not eighty years old. I've got plans myself. I'll see you both for dinner tomorrow night? Samantha is always welcome to come. Please extend the invitation to her."

"Wait."

She paused. "Mmm?"

"So what are you doing tonight?"

"Mason, son. I do love you, but just because *your* girlfriend doesn't have girlfriends doesn't mean every female can't have girlfriends. It's a girls' night tonight. I would tell you both not to wait up for me, but you never do. I'll just say my farewell with, 'Don't impregnate anyone tonight.' How's that?" She waved at them as she headed for the doors.

I waited until she was through the door before I commented, "Mom doesn't have friends."

"She has cousins."

"Sisters."

"Sisters-in-law."

"But no friends," I finished. We shared a look before I cursed. "She has a date tonight."

Logan groaned. "There went my pre-buzz. That's like my foreplay before partying."

"I want to get drunk tonight."

"I'm down with that."

We started for the door and as we went through the gym doors, heading for the building's exit doors, I heard my name called. I couldn't see who it came from so I kept going. We hadn't gotten far from the doors before two people stepped from the line of trees near our Escalades. As I recognized the Broudou brothers, five more followed them.

Logan gave me a pointed look. He was down for whatever happened. It was the look we'd been using since childhood. Fuck it. If this was the time, this was the time. The need to bust someone up was with me and I was done waiting to get even with them. "You put my best friend in the hospital. I thought the next step was ours."

Budd shook his head, and the skin on his neck shifted from the movement. He brought a bat out from behind him and tapped it against his leg before leaning his weight onto it. "Well, we were going to do that." He gestured to his brother beside him. "Brett wondered if that was smart. I think he said we should kick the pooch while it's down. I heard he got a few broken ribs and he's being baby-sat by his rich mommy and daddy. It was all over our school. The famous movie folks are back in Fallen Crest."

Logan narrowed his eyes. "You think we're some goddamn pooches?"

"You're a man down." He made a show of looking around. "Looks to me like no one else is around."

"We heard there was a big party," Brett added.

Logan snorted. "Aren't you supposed to be banned from our campus?"

"Yeah." Budd laughed, the sound was menacing. "They caught us twice, but we keep coming back. We'll keep coming back, you know. That's how we operate. No damn Kade is going to beat us."

"That's not what the scoreboard says inside."

The smirk vanished from Budd's face. He brought the bat up and began tapping it against his free hand.

I was done with this. I heard what Budd said, they weren't going away. They would keep coming back. It was the same sentiment from Kate. I had a plan too, but right now I didn't want to wait for it to happen. He brought the bat, but I was going to use it on him and with that in mind, I stepped forward. The movement wasn't to close Logan out, it was to seal our ranks. Our backs would go against each other. It was the same system since our first fight in elementary.

The rest of them registered the movement and they dropped their stance, ready to start fighting.

"Mason!" someone called. It was the same voice from before.

Brett threw his brother a sidelong glance. "There weren't supposed to be any others around."

"Shut up," he snapped back. "I'm aware, you idiot."

Someone darted across the parking lot. It was a girl but not someone I recognized. Dressed all in black, her clothing looked like it was trying to devour her. She stopped before us and held a hand up as she caught her breath. Then she swallowed before she said, "Kate beat Sam up. She's in the hospital."

I went cold.

Sam was hurt.

Sam was in the hospital.

Kate did it. She put Sam in the hospital. My hand jerked at my side. It ached to find her neck, wrap around it, and squeeze.

Logan snapped his head around. "What?"

"Sam?" Brett echoed.

No. I changed my mind. I was going to take her friends away first and then I was going to destroy her for good.

"Was it *just* Kate?"

Everyone went still. The threat of violence had already been in me. That was where it was going with Broudou, but this was different. Everyone sensed it. A dark need rose now. The tension in the atmosphere doubled.

Someone I loved was hurt.

The girl flinched from my savagery, but she caught herself. She didn't cower as she replied, "It was all four of them. I found her and got help. I found the first person I thought was a teacher. They called an ambulance and shipped her out." She gasped again as a sudden wind rocked against her. Some hair slipped to cover her face, but she ignored it. "She was hurt real bad. She wanted me to tell you."

"Wait," Budd ground out. "You mean—"

"Let's go, brother," Brett stopped him. He stepped forward and urged his brother away. "She's not part of this. Let's go."

"Yeah, but—"

"LET'S GO," he barked at him now. "They've got *school* problems. It's not the right time for this." With that last word, he shoved Budd ahead. He was a few inches in front of me now.

Budd opened his mouth to argue, but it only took one punch.

He was right there. I reacted. I didn't want to hear any more from him, so I punched him. I hit him across the face— one hit—and he dropped. He was out cold. I turned to Brett, waiting to see what he was going to do.

The other Broudou stepped back and murmured, "I ain't here to fight any more. You need to go take care of your woman."

It was in the back of my mind to question him. He said we had school problems, but I could see from the other goliath-sized Broudou that he knew better. I didn't care. Not then. I needed to get to Sam. That was my first priority.

I jerked my head towards my car and said to the girl in black, "Get in my car. You're going with us."

Her eyes popped out, but she scrambled around the unconscious Broudou and climbed into the passenger side. Logan was already in his and didn't wait. He peeled out of the parking lot. I sat there and waited, clenching and unclenching my fingers around the steering wheel while they moved Budd from behind my car.

One second.

Two.

They had one more second before I was going to run over him.

Brett dragged his brother clear on the last second, and I reversed, spinning around on the fourth second.

CHAPTER EIGHTEEN

Mark was alone, waiting for us in the lobby at the front of the hospital. He stood as we rushed through the door. Nothing was asked, nothing needed to be asked. He gestured down the hallway. "I was waiting for you. They're in a different waiting room. The doctor's with her right now."

Logan frowned. "What are you doing here?"

He gestured to the girl who had followed behind me. "She got my mom."

Logan and I turned to regard her.

"Uh." She wavered at our attention. "Um." Clamping her mouth shut, her cheeks got red, and she began pulling at one hand with the other. "I just found the first adult who looked." She shrugged. "I don't know why I picked her. I didn't know her."

I didn't care. I turned back to Mark. "Where's Sam?"

She finished, "She looked capable. That's why I picked her."

Logan grunted. "No one cares anymore."

"And she was standing next to the principal," she added. "That was another reason why I picked her."

"Mason."

We whipped around. David Strattan was coming towards us. His hair was sticking up, there were bags under his eyes and his Fallen Crest Academy athletic jacket was wrinkled. Blood was smeared all over it.

I faltered. There was not much that scared me, but I was scared now. I couldn't look away from the blood on Sam's dad's shirt. That was her blood. It had to be. I was gutted at what they had done to her.

"Where is she?" My voice came out hoarse. No way could I be weak. Not now, that's for damn sure. "Where is she?"

"The doctor is with her, but I've been told that it's not as bad as it looks."

I growled. That didn't make it better.

"They think," David moved to stand between us and the hallway. His hand lifted in the air in a calming motion. "They think she'll have a few fractured ribs, but most of the damage is superficial."

"What's that mean?" Logan demanded.

"It means she looks awful, but it's mostly bruising. Her face is swollen. She couldn't open one of her eyes when I was with her, but they're sure it'll heal on its own."

"Where is she?" The need to see her was too powerful. I could barely hold it in, and I looked down the hallway. I'd go from one room to the next to find her. "Where is she?!"

"She's with the doctor, Mason." Mark moved forward.

I jerked my head to him. "Who've you told about this? If that fuckhead Adam walks through here, I'm laying him out. I won't tolerate him coming in here and acting all buddy-buddy with her. Not now."

"Mason—"

"Not now, Mark," I interrupted him.

Mark lifted both hands in the air and took a step back. "I didn't call anyone. I swear. I wouldn't do that to Sam."

"Fuck this," Logan bit out before he shoved past the older Strattan. He started down the hallway and I went right after him. We weren't getting answers, not the ones we wanted. We'd find her ourselves.

"Boys," David called after them. "Mason, I really need to discuss something with you before seeing Sam."

I shoved open a door. "I really need to see Sam first." She wasn't in that one. I moved to the next.

"Mark, maybe you can take the girl to the waiting room?"

"Are you sure?"

"Yes. I'll show them to her room and then I have some things to discuss with them after. Go. I'll send your mother in a moment as well." I heard the exhaustion in David's voice.

Logan was further down the hallway. He'd open a door, poke his head in and leave. A few people came to the hallway and watched as he repeated the process, but I stopped. I twisted around and saw David at the end of the hallway. He was waiting for us and he was too patient about it. I sighed as I went back to him. "She's not in this hallway, is she?"

Logan was at the end of the hallway now. He circled and started opening doors on the side I had stopped.

"As soon as the doctors will let us see her, you'll be the first one in." David frowned as he rubbed a hand over his face. His eyes opened and closed, as if trying to focus on me. Then he began rubbing them with the palm of his hand. "I never thought I'd be here again."

"Again?" I went cold. "Again? You mean without Analise being in the equation."

David hesitated before saying, "Mason, son—"

"I'm not your fucking son. If you're going to throw the father term around, start acting like it with the one person who's still hurting because you left her."

"I didn't..." His face paled.

I watched as the blood drained from Sam's father's face. I didn't care. I was being kept from seeing her. It was driving me nuts. David knew it. Noticing a sign for the emergency room further down an adjourning hallway, I knew where she'd be. "Screw it. She came in on an ambulance. She'd go there first."

"Mason."

I hauled ass down the hallway.

David jogged to keep up. "Mason, I really do need to talk to you before you go in there."

He could talk all he wanted. I wasn't slowing down.

"Because you need to be on board before you go in there."

"Be on board with what?" I got into the emergency room section. This floor was different from the one we were just in. The walls were painted an off-white color. I headed towards the main desk, but began glancing into each room I passed.

"That's what I'm trying to talk to you about." He stopped then, but his voice lifted, "I've already talked to Samantha about it and she agreed. It would be best if you heard about it from me first and not her. She's already worried about how you'll react and this is the best decision for her well-being. You cannot go in there and make her feel guilty about this decision. I won't allow it, not after what she's been through tonight."

I had no choice. The urge to do physical damage had been with me since the Broudous showed up. It had increased since then, and David Strattan wasn't helping. "If you don't start talking, I'm going to start not giving a shit whose father you are. The two things I know right now is that Sam is hurt, and I have to get to her. Logan's still over there. He hasn't figured out that she's not in that part of the hospital. You're doing a lot of talking, but you aren't saying shit. Start talking or I'll let him loose on this department."

David didn't wait another second. "Sam's coming home with me."

"Like hell she is."

"She is, Mason."

"No."

The older man sighed. "It's really not your call. I'm trying to do my 'fatherly' duties as you enjoy throwing in my face. I'm standing here and blocking you because this is the best thing for her."

"Fuck that and fuck you."

"Mason."

"No, she's living with us. We'll take care of her."

"You haven't—"

"Better than you," I threw back. My hands jerked up, but I stopped and stepped back. "I've taken care of her when you let her go with that crazy psycho. We protected her from Analise. Me and Logan. What'd you do? You stood back and let her go with her. You're stepping up now? The crazy bitch isn't here anymore. You're protecting her from me?"

David's jaw tightened. His shoulders lifted as his chest rose. He drew in a deep breath before he bit out, "You are getting on my last nerve, boy."

"Boy?" I chuckled, but I wasn't amused. "Don't stand and puff up your chest to me. We both know where this is going. I should respect you? Because you're Sam's dad? Because you're older than me?" My eyes narrowed to slits. The same lethal intent was there that'd been since I saw Budd Broudou. It was pumping through me and it was growing the longer he kept me from her. "I've been around enough screwed-up adults to know that they don't deserve any respect unless it's earned. I've not seen a damn thing from you except now. I'm the wrong person you need to be protecting from her."

"Right now, you're exactly the person I need to protect her from. She's hurt, Mason." David's jaw was still clamped tight, but he gentled his tone. "She's going to need help all day. Are you going to be there for her? You're going to skip school? Quit the basketball team? Not graduate? I know you have a full scholarship already, but it's contingent on graduating first. You can't be there for her, neither can Logan."

"And you can?"

"Better than you. Malinda doesn't work—"

"You're going to have your girlfriend take care of her?"

"No. I'm going to be there, but I have to work during the day. During that time, Malinda will come to the house and be there. She doesn't work, Mason. Would you rather have someone else?"

"Me."

"You can't," David snapped at me. "Get that through your head. Do you have a better choice? Your mother? I'm not putting Samantha through that. I'm aware of the disdain Helen has for Sam. Analise? Is that a better choice?"

I closed my eyes for a second, pressing my hands against them. A headache was raging in me. Fuck. I was always the cold one. I remained calm when everyone else panicked, but not now. I couldn't get a grasp on that old Mason, but David was right and it was killing me. I relented, I had no choice. "I get to see her at night."

"No deal."

"That's the only deal. I sleep over."

"She's my daughter."

"She's the love of my life." My heart was pumping so damn fast. I needed to see her.

David was searching my eyes.

I let him see the truth. I needed her. That was the only way.

"Fine, but only you. Logan can't start sleeping over, too."

"He'll try."

David groaned. "You two, you just storm your way in—"

"We're family to her. We took her in when you let her go. We protected her from that woman." I was relentless. I knew it was hurting him, but I kept throwing it in his face because it was true. I forced myself to think rationally and I knew what David Strattan was saying was the best thing for Sam. Logan and I couldn't skip school to take care of her, and I didn't want her close to either mothers. I didn't know Mark's mom, but Mark was an okay guy. If Sam wasn't okay around that woman, I would stop everything. I'd hire someone, or hell, I'd take her to Nate's house. She could heal next to Nate. His mom would love Samantha.

David looked away.

I saw it was hard for him to accept. Then he nodded. "Fine. You and Logan can both stay the night—"

"Where is she?"

He lifted his defeated eyes to mine. "Follow me."

SAMANTHA

After being admitted to the hospital, they gave me pain medication that put me to sleep. It was later that night when I woke. No one was there except Mason, who was sleeping in the lounge chair beside my bed. An opened pizza box was on my tray table along with a plastic water pitcher and a bunch of plastic cups. It hurt to talk, but after reaching for his hand, I didn't need to. He woke up and offered me a smile. The worry and love in his gaze made my stomach jump into my chest. I'd never get used to it. Never. When he realized I couldn't talk, he did most of it for me.

Logan had been there earlier and refused to leave, but Mason made him go. He wanted alone time with me when I woke. He said he pulled Boyfriend Rank. It would've been nice to see Logan, but I understood. The pain medication was wonderful, but there was an ache inside of me. I felt hollow, and it had nothing to do with my physical pain. Mason was the only one that could fill that emotional void, and I needed him. I needed him badly. When I patted my bed, he hesitated. I patted it again and scooted as far to the side as possible to make room for him.

"You have two fractured ribs, a dislocated jaw, and you look like a truck ran over you. I can't, Sam." His was gruff and his throat closed off on the last word. After he took a moment, he continued, "I just can't, Sam. I'm so scared I'll hurt you."

I narrowed my eyes and tried to show him my determination. I couldn't do much else, so I patted the bed again with a hard slap.

He still hesitated.

Then I hit his arm before moving onto my back again. I had to go slow, but I couldn't stop the tear that formed and trickled down my cheek. When I lifted my hand to brush it away, my skin felt like it wasn't mine. It was an uncomfortable feeling, an unwanted one, and I needed his support even more to push it away.

The bed dipped under his weight. He paused with one foot before shaking his head and mumbling, "I'm not going to be able to sleep. I'm going to be so damn scared that I'll hurt you."

It didn't matter. None of it mattered. When he shifted to his side and then reached for my hand, I closed my eyes. I could sleep now. Everything would work out. Our hands were tucked between us on the bed. I clung to his, while he seemed scared to hold mine back. That didn't matter either. I just needed to be held, a mere touch from him. It anchored me, and as that feeling of being centered came back, the heaviness of exhaustion folded back over me. It wasn't long until I fell asleep.

The nurse checked on us, but she didn't ask him to leave. When he started to get up, I gripped his hand harder. She caught the movement and only waved for him to stay. "Looks like you don't have a choice." As she headed back out, we heard her mutter to another nurse in the hallway, "They grow them like that nowadays? Sign me up to be a cougar. Holy crapola."

Mason chuckled next to me. He had moved so his mouth rested against my shoulder and his breath teased me. It warmed me even more when he yawned. "They've been coming in every hour to check on you. You wouldn't let me go the first time either."

I couldn't talk, but I tried to smile. I couldn't even do that so I rested my head against his. Sleep overcame me again. The rest of the night was spent like that. I was in and out of it. Mason was always there. I think one of my nurses took pity on Mason. She snuck another hospital bed into my private room and lowered a rail on one side of it and one side of mine, then pushed them together to make almost a full size bed. Mason gifted her with a smile and I thought she was going to pass out in my room. When the other nurses came in, their gazes went immediately to him; it didn't take a genius to figure out that the word had spread. We even heard one comment as she checked my vitals, "They weren't kidding about the hottie."

When she noticed that we had heard, she shrugged. "Nights can be the best shift or the dullest. The girls are in a tizzy about another guy. He likes to streak naked down the halls at night. If he looked like you, I don't think the other girls would mind."

"Can you tell us that?"

As she typed something into a computer, she shrugged again. "He's due for another run soon so you're going to see it with your own eyes if your door is open. Take it as more of a warning. Don't get scared if you see a flash sprinting past your door. He doesn't go into other patients' rooms." Then she patted my other leg as she moved around the bed. "You're looking better, girly. You should get discharged in the morning."

Two minutes after she left, we heard her yell, "Stop right there, four-thirty-two! Do not go into the nursing ward. Four-thirty-two!"

A streak of bare flesh darted past our door.

Mason grinned at me. "It's like we didn't even miss Fischer's party tonight."

My nurse sprinted past our door, followed by another two.

Except there are no nurses at those parties. I tried to say that, but I couldn't. My mouth must've twitched because Mason turned sharply to me. "Are you okay?"

I nodded, sighing at the same time, except I couldn't do that either. Breathing was difficult so I took a small breath, followed by another one. I was closing my eyelids again when he said my name.

"Sam."

My heart began racing as I heard how serious he was. I frowned.

He took a deep breath. "I don't know what I'm supposed to do here. I don't know if I'm supposed to distract you. If I'm supposed to make you laugh, or if I'm supposed to be reassuring you. I have no idea what to do, so all I'm doing is just being here."

Oh goodness. My heart raced faster.

His voice grew rough again, and he added, "You can't talk back to me, and I need to hear your voice. I need to know you're okay."

I tried to squeeze his hand.

He laughed to himself, lifting them, kissing the back of mine. Then he pressed it against his cheek and took another deep breath. "I'm so fucked up right now. We were going to fight the Broudou brothers when that chick showed up. I don't even know who she is. She took off when we finally got to your room, and I haven't let anyone else in here. Logan was supposed to tell people you're fine." He broke off and cursed under his breath. "I'm so goddamn sorry." He frowned before he shook his head again. "What I'm trying to say is that everything will be okay. Kate won't hurt you again. I'll take care of her, and I'll end this thing with the Broudous. I know it's been bothering you, too. I'll take care of everything. I know you're going to stay at your dad's. That's fine. I want you to know that I'm fine with that. I made him agree to let us stay there, too, so we'll all still be together. What the hell am I saying here?"

I wanted to smile at him. I wanted to pull him into me and have him wrap his arms around me, but I couldn't do either. I couldn't even tell him to shut up because I loved him, too. That's what he was trying to say, but he was never this awkward about it. I lifted my hand to his cheek. I cupped the side of his face the same way he always cups mine, and I pulled him to me.

"Sam?" His eyes grew wide and he hesitated.

I pulled again, this time firmer.

He relented until I had moved his face right to mine. I couldn't feel it, but I pressed his lips to mine. When he pulled away, I saw him brush at something on his face before he settled back into place beside me again.

We remained like that for the rest of the night, but right before I fell back asleep, I felt him kiss my hand.

I was smiling on the inside.

CHAPTER NINETEEN

It sucked being an invalid.

I was released the next day, and it took an entire afternoon before it was decided that I'd stay at Malinda's house for the first week. I couldn't go back to school for a week, and she didn't have a job. It made sense. I would move into David's after the first week since I'd still have four to six weeks to heal. Of course, Mason and Logan followed me where I went. David already agreed, but Malinda hadn't been told of the arrangement. When she was informed, both were adamant. David leaned close to whisper, "I warned you they're protective." A bright smile was plastered on her face, and she waved him off. "Oh no. It's completely fine. The more the merrier."

She didn't know what she was getting herself into. She must've caught my reaction because she broke away from David's side and took the chair beside me. She patted my arm and leaned in close to me. "I mean it. Those two have become your family, and you are David's family so that means *all* of you are welcome in my home, at any time." Her warm chocolate eyes doubled their sparkle as she added, "I grew up with twelve brothers and sisters. You think three more kids are going to scare me?"

She really had no idea what she was getting herself into.

When I was discharged and being wheeled out of the hospital, I felt like I was part of a Brady Bunch sort-of family. All eyes were on us as we left, but most of the nurses waved to Mason and Logan. David was shaking his head when all six of us got to the parking lot. Mason had pulled his Escalade up to the circle, and I was loaded into it. Logan hopped into

Mark's car. As everyone followed behind David's Luxury SUV, which I assumed was owned by Malinda, Mason said that Mark and Logan were going to a party that night.

Malinda's house was a massive log home. Logan was shown to his bedroom, which was a guest bedroom in the basement, and we were shown our room. It was tucked into a back section of the house on the main floor, so it felt like we had our own wing. Mason had packed a few bags for me, and as he dropped them on the bed, Malinda chuckled at us. "You two are like a married couple."

Uh... I pointed to my head. "Heavy meds here. Say that again?"

She rolled her eyes. "You heard me just fine. So did you," she threw to Mason. Then she gestured to the door across the hallway. "That's your bathroom. Your father wanted you upstairs in case you needed something during the night." Her gaze lingered on Mason. "But I reminded him that you're not a single package anymore; that you come with a plus-one, whether he likes it or not."

"Thanks for that," Mason murmured, leaning against the far wall. He stuffed his hands into his front pockets, which moved his jeans down an inch. As he hunched his shoulders forward, it gave him a longer and leaner look. The tops of his black boxer briefs were visible now, and I could see a hint of his oblique muscles underneath.

I licked my lips. If only... Desire spread through me. When his jeans moved another inch lower, my body felt engulfed in flames. It was like a drop of gasoline had been added to a fire.

Malinda chuckled behind me. "I recognize that look. You got the good meds, for sure."

I was burning up. "Can we open a window?"

Mason frowned. "What?"

"He says what." She chuckled some more before stepping into the hallway. "When you get an ice pack on those loins, join us downstairs. We got couches, blankets, movies, pop, whatever you need."

Why?

Mason said it for me, looking equally confused.

"Saturday family night." Her eyebrows arched high. "Don't you two know what family night means?"

We were both silent.

She snorted. "It's a night you spend with family. Forget any plans you two might have had for canoodling. You're in my home, and you have to endure the torture. Sorry, Sam. They said you have a mild dislocated jaw, but I got lots of liquids and soft foods for you. Yogurt. Applesauce. The good stuff, but the rest are going to be forced to eat popcorn, pizza, chips, and tacos. You name it, they have to shovel it in. Bahahaha." She left, her laugh eerily close to an evil witch's.

"What just happened?" Crap. I winced from pain. I'd been talking too much.

"Mark's mom is nuts."

I gave him a pointed look. Did he not know who he was talking to?

Mason shrugged. "So's your mom, but this one...she seems nice and...genuine. I don't like it."

That earned a snort from me. A mother who was genuine and nice? It made perfect sense why he wouldn't like it. I'm not sure I liked it either.

He gestured out the window beside him. "Did you know Mark lived down the block from my dad's?"

I had forgotten, but now I wished I hadn't remembered.

"Yo. Mark's mom is hilarious. She just told me she's Queen Royale of Bitch." Logan appeared in the doorway and flashed a grin. Holding onto the doorframe from the top, he leaned forward, laughing at the same time. "You see how close we are to Dad's?"

"I know." Mason gestured to me. "I was just telling Sam that."

"Mom's going to flip when we tell her where we're staying."

"Yeah..." Mason was deep in thought. He leaned forward to look out the window and moved so he could see further up the street. "You know Nate's old house? The one he lived in before his parents moved?"

"The one at the end of the block?" Logan moved next to him. Both were studying a house through the window. "The couple that bought it from them moved, didn't they?"

Mason nodded. "They've been trying to sell it for six months. Want to bet that Mom's going to move in there?"

"No way. She won't buy that."

"Dad's is three houses down. We're in this one, and Nate's old place is three doors the other way. She's going to go nuts when she realizes how close we are to Dad's. She thought she finally got us all to herself."

Logan shook his head. "Man, most of our stuff is at the hotel. She won't think we'll want to drive there to grab anything we forgot...it'd be easier to just leave it at Dad's and grab it when we need it. Or that's what she's going to think."

Mason cracked a grin. "If she doesn't buy that house, she's going to rent it. I bet you money. Somehow, Mom's going to be living somewhere on this block."

A curse slipped from Logan. "And we're not telling her we're only staying here for a week, are we?"

"You want to?"

"No way." A smile stretched across his face. "This'll be way funnier when she learns we've moved to Sam's old neighborhood, the 'poor' community. Mom will shit a brick thinking she'll have to live there. She won't know what to do."

Listening to them and watching from the bed, a pang went through me. David lived in a poor community according to them. I knew neither cared, but their mother thought like that. It was a middle class neighborhood. People weren't poor, but they weren't wealthy. They were normal. I was normal, but I was different from them. It shouldn't have bothered me, but I was reminded of how different I was from them.

It stung more than a little.

"Hey."

Mark stood in the hallway now. He glanced around before stepping inside. As he closed the door, everyone grew quiet. "David and Mom are downstairs, so I thought it was the right time to come up and say this."

The feel of the room changed. It was like a cold blast of wind tore through it, and everyone tensed. Mark said, "I don't know what you guys have planned." He glanced at me, but everyone knew he was talking to Mason. "But I'm in for whatever it is. I know how you are with trust. You don't trust anyone except the three of you in this room. You don't have to tell me the plan; you don't have to explain anything to me. Give me a job to do and I'll do it." His gaze lingered on me before his jaw hardened and he looked away. "No questions asked. That's all I wanted to say."

He started for the door, but Mason stopped him. "One thing."

Mark paused.

"Your friends can't come here this week."

"It's already done. I told them my mom's having guests staying here. My mom never says anything, so if you guys don't say anything, no one will even know you're here. Not like it's a secret or anything." He lifted the corner of his mouth up and shrugged. "Besides, it's usually only Adam that drops by or comes over for dinner. My house is quiet compared to his, but he won't ask any questions. My mom has random visitors all the time. We had a homeless dude stay for a week one time when she volunteered at the shelter last winter."

Logan started laughing. "Your mom can't be any more opposite from ours."

Then we heard from the hallway, "MARK!"

"And she summons..."

"MOVIE'S STARTING IN NEGATIVE FIVE MINUTES."

Mark said to us, "She won't pick a comedy because she doesn't want to make Sam laugh."

That was much appreciated.

"But if we don't get down there and pick the movie first, the scariest damn movie will be starting. My mom never gets scared from horror films. I have no idea why. Her other sisters are like that, too. I wish I had inherited that gene, but she loves watching the rest of us when we're close to pissing our pants." He rolled his eyes. "You're right Logan, but my mom is not like any other mom. She's not normal. For real."

The doorbell rang.

"MARK, GET THE DOOR. THOSE ARE THE PIZZAS."

He grumbled, but left.

"If Mark wasn't a cool guy, and if your dad hadn't got there first, I'd bang Mark's mom."

If I could talk easier, I would've informed Logan my vomit was coming in three...two...one... I couldn't and it would've hurt to throw up. It hurt to do anything, so I gave him the middle finger. That would have to satisfy me for now.

Logan laughed, and for the rest of night, he flirted. Mason didn't care. I did. Mark seemed confused, and David shook his head. As we watched a movie about teen wizards, followed by a documentary about polar bears, Malinda seemed to enjoy herself. Her cheeks were red by the end of the night from her wine.

The first night passed quickly and so did the rest of the week.

Things seemed normal between David and me. There were no awkward silences or uncomfortable moments. In hindsight, I realized it was because of Malinda. She always had a quick retort for Logan, and when there was a lull in conversation, she'd grill Mark on his love life. He was mortified when she suggested getting a vibrator for his girl. "Mom!" he cried out. She shrugged. "You're not a virgin, and I'm promoting her pleasure as well. The girl will enjoy it a lot more. They don't always, you know." She scanned the rest of the table. "I'm sure you two bucks think you're the stud for all those does," she remembered me and amended, "well maybe just you and Logan, but I'm telling you. Girls fake it eighty percent of the time."

That opened a whole new channel of adoration from Logan. He wanted to know it all.

The rest of the conversation was a question and answer forum from Logan while Mark looked ready to throw up. I even caught Mason listening intently to her. He told me later that he'd be stupid to pass up information like that. When I came back from the bathroom, ready for bed, his eyes had darkened in lust. His hand skimmed over my waist, gently rubbing before he moved to cup my breasts. Curling into my side, he kissed the side of my neck and remarked, "Six weeks cannot get here sooner."

I knew what he meant. The ache lingered in me, but it was mixed with pain and stiffness. However, that ache conquered all other aches when he would get ready for school in the morning, or for bed at night, or come back from basketball practice, or being around me in general. By the end of the week, when the pain was starting to lessen even more, the ache for Mason was unbearable at times.

During the time when they were at school, it was easier, but Mason was gone. Malinda didn't hover. Thank god. I had worried she would, but she seemed to pop in at the right moments. She brought me smoothies. At first, my stomach protested at the sight of the green color, but I was reassured it was delicious. I soon craved them, so I spent hours in the kitchen watching her experiment with new recipes.

The rest of the time was spent watching movies and I napped. I napped a lot.

Mason was granted half-day practices. He could leave after an hour into practice, so he was there when I woke from my naps. Principal Green approved of his request so he didn't lose any playing time for their games. Between the two, they got all of my homework assignments for me, every day. It wasn't until the end of the week that I asked, "What's everyone saying at school?" Heather had called a few times, but she hadn't said much either. When she was vague, I let it go, but something was wrong. I wasn't stupid, but I hadn't been ready to tackle this hurdle.

I was now.

Mason, Logan and Mark were all doing homework at the dinner table. An instant hush came over them, and they stopped what they were doing. Malinda was in the kitchen, experimenting on more recipes. She loved sneaking tofu into dinner. We were having chicken enchiladas that night. The tofu was going to be covered in cheese, but she paused as well.

David wasn't there. He had an evening meeting for school.

Everyone looked at Mason. He asked, "You want the truth?"

The truth. That felt like a kick in the gut. The truth was that everyone had been pretending. This week was a haven for me. I was allowed to hide from the rest of the world, but the truth was that I had been attacked. I had two fractured ribs. It still hurt to talk and eat because of my jaw. The truth was that I hadn't been able to bring myself to look in a mirror because I knew I looked like an assault victim, but I was one. It was time I started to deal with it.

I never flinched. "Yes."

Mason narrowed his eyes, searching inside of me. He always did that when he was checking to see if I was being honest. When he saw that I was ready, he nodded. "The truth is that Kate thinks she won."

I held my breath.

He kept going, "She thinks we're friends again."

It hurt to breathe.

"She thinks she's at the top again."

An intense pressure was on my chest now; it felt as if someone was pushing down on it.

"She thinks I'm going to dump you."

I flinched as I felt someone kick me again. I heard the crack in my ribs from that night. I *felt* the crack in my ribs from that night.

He looked like a cold stranger to me as he finished, "And she thinks she's going to be my girlfriend."

I couldn't talk. It hurt to breathe. It hurt to do anything except sit there and let his words sink in. All the pain that my medication had been holding at bay flooded me. It all came back in one wave, all at the same time, and I was paralyzed in my chair. I couldn't fight any of it. "Why would she think that?"

Logan looked away. Mark's head went down, but Mason didn't turn away. He stared right back at me as he said, "Because I'm letting her think that."

CHAPTER TWENTY

I hadn't let myself think about Kate. I couldn't, not the first week. I needed to heal and get through it. Everyone had been so supportive, but now I remembered that I was going back into the lions' den. Fallen Crest Academy had different problems, but no one got assaulted there. I was tired, I was in pain, and I couldn't stop thinking about what Mason said. He was letting Kate think she had won.

It didn't matter what he said after that: he was setting her up; he had a plan; he didn't want me involved because he knew I wouldn't approve; I needed to trust him because he was going to make her pay.

He tried reassuring me over and over that night.

He failed. I wasn't reassured.

I wanted to scream at him. I wanted to pound my fists on his chest. I wanted to throw things. Everyone else had gone to bed by then, but I wanted them awake. No one deserved to sleep. No one deserved to go about their daily routines, not when mine had been destroyed by her, but I couldn't enact my revenge on those in the household. Except Mason. He stayed awake with me during the night. I couldn't sleep. The need to make Kate pay had my heart pumping. I wanted to be the one to set her up, to watch her suffer. I wanted to find her in a bathroom, but there wouldn't be three other friends with me. It would be her and me, and I'd beat her senseless. When she'd crawl to the door, I'd start again.

The rage never simmered. It kept my blood boiling, and my heart pumping the entire night. Mason drifted to sleep around three in the morning, but I was still seething at six. When he woke and glanced over, he saw I was still awake.

He leaned over to kiss me, but I moved my head aside. There'd be no kisses. No words were shared as he got ready for school. When Logan came to the door, they had a quiet conversation. Logan was advised to leave me alone, and he did. They both left at the same time. Mark left for his school twenty minutes later. He sprinted through the house, and I heard Malinda yell, "It won't matter that you're late if you're dead. Slow down, Marcus."

He yelled back, "Yeah, okay."

Peeking out my window, I watched as he sprinted for his car and then gunned the engine. I pretended that Kate had been in front of his car. She would be on the street now, laying in her blood and writhing in pain.

"He's going to get in an accident one of these days. Sleeps too late, pushes it so that he's not late for school, and I just know it's a bad recipe in the making," Malinda mused from behind me. The bottom of her white nightgown was underneath her blue robe. She retied the knot in the front before yawning. "You want some pancakes? David told me that Analise never made you breakfast before."

"She didn't, but she had their chef make me sandwiches." I missed Mousteff.

Malinda grunted, a crooked grin on her face. "Some rich folk are like that. They stop doing the little things, think it's beneath them. The only thing beneath them is not doing a damn thing."

She said more, but I wasn't listening to her. I was in my own head.

Analise. David. Jessica. Lydia. Jeff.

A stabbing pain seared through me. Each one of them had betrayed me. Each was someone I once loved. The pain kept coming. It wasn't going to stop.

"Right, Sam?" Malinda laughed.

I turned back to the window. I couldn't face her. She was another one. The same would happen, and she had no idea she'd do it until the day she left me, like the rest of them. "She's going to get away with this."

She grew quiet. "Who?"

I couldn't answer. Kate. All of them. Everyone.

"They followed me into that bathroom." The door opened, but the hand dryer was on. "I remember it now. I knew they were coming. I knew someone was there. There was a small movement from the corner of my eye. It's why I turned to leave, but..." I couldn't go further. That day would haunt me, like so many others.

I turned back now.

Malinda straightened from the doorway. Her hand dropped and slapped against her leg with a soft thud. Her eyes widened an inch, and her mouth fell open.

I didn't know what she saw in me, but she couldn't talk for a second. I could. For once, the words were there, and they were gutting me. "How do I get over this?" How was I supposed to go back to that school? She was there. Mason said they only got in-school suspension. They got a slap on the wrist and were given a holiday from their usual studies.

I couldn't. That was my truth for the morning. I couldn't go back to that school, but I couldn't afford not to. Coach Grath already said that I'd have to bust my ass to catch up to my old times. As soon as I was cleared by the doctor, he wanted to meet for individual training sessions. I needed that scholarship, I had no one to help me now. I needed to go to college. Kate would be there...

I couldn't. I just couldn't.

"What do I do?" My voice hitched on a sob.

"Oh, Samantha." Malinda rushed into the room and folded me against her. She wrapped her arms around me gently and cradled my head to her. "Oh, Samantha, honey."

At the feel of her arms, I was jerked to a different reality. This one felt alien.

This was what a mother did. She comforted. Malinda wasn't my mother. She was dating David, who was rarely at the house. It hit me then that he'd been avoiding me or maybe he'd been avoiding a moment like this. Malinda took his place and because of that I couldn't let her. I wouldn't be reassured by her. There would be a time when she'd leave me too. It was inevitable.

I moved back and tried to give her something that resembled a grin. "It's fine. I'm fine." She grimaced. My smile must not have looked like one. I tried for another and repeated, "I'll be fine. Really."

"Oh, Samantha."

I heard her stricken tone and prepared myself.

She raised a hand and tucked some of my hair behind my ear. Her touch was gentle. "I'm not like the rest."

My eyes jerked to hers.

"I know what it's like to be abandoned and left behind. I do. I know what it's like, and I'm not here to make excuses for your father. That's between you and him, but me—I'm here for you. I won't leave you. I had Mark when I was young. His dad didn't stick around." She chuckled. "His dad didn't even stick around long enough for me to say he didn't stick around. He was out the window the second he saw my pregnancy test. You know what happened to me?"

I was listening to her. There was a pull to her, and I couldn't *not* listen to her, but I didn't answer.

"I got thrown out of my family. I've been out on my own ever since. My family is full of pretentious assholes and bitches that think they're better than everyone else. Pissed my grandfather off. He didn't like not being able to see Mark, so he left me his money." Another dry chuckle. "That changed their tunes. They tried seeing me, apologized out of their asses. They sent over Mark's cousins to be friends. That one I couldn't fight. He's close to a few of them, but I could fight the rest. I was an embarrassment to them, but I became an inspiration when all those dollar signs were connected to me. Pansies. I hated my family. For years I hated them, and now I just want nothing to do with them."

I grinned as an ache started in my chest. "Didn't you hear the phrase that family means everything?"

"Not to you." There was nothing held back from her. "Not to me. Sometimes family hurts you more than they could ever love you. That's a truth a lot of people don't want to hear, but sometimes people get the opposite. They get the families that love you more than they could ever hurt you. Those people are the luckiest in the world. You know what pisses me off? Is that they probably don't even know it. They don't know how lucky they are, but, Sam, you're one of them."

I sucked in a breath. That ache was a stabbing pain now.

She leaned forward. Some of her long hair fell forward, but she ignored it as she grasped my shoulders. Malinda moved so we were eye-level. "Forget the people who've hurt you. You don't have them anymore, but you have two others that'll do anything for you. Mason and Logan would move mountains for you. I see how you are with them. You love them, but you're scared to let yourself be happy. Why? Because that's when they'll leave? Is that what you think? You've got it all wrong. Those two will never leave you." She tapped my chest. Once. Twice. "You. You're the one that's going to hurt them. You have that power, and you don't know it. You could rip those two apart in a second, and they're the ones who are scared of you. Not the other way around. You need to recognize the real situation."

"My situation?"

She moved back. As her hands left my shoulders, I was able to breathe again. My chest was lighter. She went to the far wall and leaned against it. Folding her arms, she shook her head. "You got beat up. Bones and bruises heal. Those girls didn't win because they didn't do what they wanted. They wanted to break you."

I was already broken.

"You're not broken at all."

I held my breath at her words.

She added, "Those two boys have healed you. They took you in. They protected you. They continue to love you because they're your family and both of them know it. They love you for the same reasons they don't love anyone else. You're pure. It might not make sense to you, but you don't use them. You don't want anything from them. You don't want to hurt them. Your love for both of them is pure." Then she cracked a grin. "I might come off as a batty old shithead, but I'm no dumb broad. I know it because I recognize it; it's why I snatched your father up so quick, and I made sure he had no choice but to date me. I'm not saying he's made the best choices, but your father has the same pure love inside of him." She rolled her eyes. "Doesn't mean he knows how to show it. He's dug himself a grave and instead of filling it back up, he ends up digging himself another one. He's been doing that with you all these years, but he's a good man underneath. He's a good man to me. I love your father very much, and I'd like to love you like a daughter." She brushed a tear away, giving me a trembling smile at the same time. "But I'm not here to pressure you or tell you what to do. Believe it or not, I meant to ask you about breakfast, but then I got on my damn soap box. Sorry about that."

You're not broken at all. I couldn't get those words out of my head. "Did you mean that?"

"Mean what?"

"That I'm not broken?"

"Oh, honey. You have so much strength in you. You have no idea how much." She gave me another smile, though it wavered as more tears slipped down her cheeks. "I meant what I said before. I will never leave you. Whether I'm with your father or not, you're friends with Mark or not, know this will always be a home for you. Okay?"

I could feel her love. It was that same alien feeling I felt when I was bleeding on the bathroom floor. I had clung to it then. I was scared of it now, but I nodded. "Okay."

She began laughing. "You're so scared of me right now."

"I'm not."

"You are, but that's okay. Every time you come and I open my door, some of that fear will go away. Being loved and accepting love are two completely different things. It's my job to continue to show it to you. All you have to do is accept it, little by little. That's how I finally convinced your father that I loved him. Between you and me, I still have to convince him sometimes. Being with your mother hurt him, too. That's something both of you have in common." A few more tears had fallen, and she brushed them away. "Look at me. I'm hideous. Alright, I'm off to shower and get ready. You want to go out for breakfast?"

I nodded.

"Good." She gave me a bright smile. "Pound on the wall if you need help getting dressed. I'll hear it all the way upstairs. Oh, and don't tell Mark that. I caught him with a couple girls with that secret. He still has no idea."

When she left, I could her laughter all the way to the second floor. I couldn't move, but I started to hear a scraping sound. That's when I looked down. My hand was shaking. It was hitting the cord for the blinds that was scraping against the window frame.

She said I wasn't broken at all.

MASON

Sam called me before my game. She had an unusual conversation with Malinda that day, but we would talk tomorrow. It was her first night back at her home, her old home. She wanted to spend time with David, which worked for my plan.

"You ready for this?" Logan got into the seat beside me. We were on the team bus, returning from our away game.

I nodded. My phone was out. The last text from Sam said: **I love you. Wake me up when you get here. Key's under the broken step in porch. I want to talk.**

Logan saw the text. He didn't say anything at first, but after a moment asked, "She doesn't know? You didn't tell her last night?"

"Nope."

"And she doesn't know we'll be gone all night?"

"Nope."

"This could backfire, you know."

"I know." I clutched the phone in my hand.

"She might leave you."

"I know."

"You're still sure?"

We were in the back seat, separated from the rest of the team. The guys knew a plan was in motion and I was grateful for the space. I needed to go over all the risks and calculations.

I nodded now. "I am. You?"

Logan flashed me a grin. "I'm down for anything."

"If she leaves, she's leaving you, too."

"I know." His grin vanished. "It'll be worth it."

"Okay." I nodded again as the bus pulled into the parking lot and rolled to a stop. "Let's go to that party then."

Logan got up first, and I followed him. We knew what to do next.

Kate was lying to herself. When I called her Sunday night, I heard the hope in her voice. I said all the right things: I apologized; I wanted a clean slate; I missed our friendship.

She lapped it up. Then I said what I needed to cinch it for her: I'd forgotten that she was my equal in every way. As soon as I said that, she was sobbing on other end. It'd been what she wanted to hear all along. She assured me we could move forward. She would reign in the other girls. They could all be friends again, and it'd be like nothing ever happened.

Stupid girl.

I warned her. She chose to believe my lies. That was her mistake. I didn't change my mind. I never changed my mind.

The plan had been in motion for a while, but tonight was the beginning of the end.

CHAPTER TWENTY-ONE

L ogan and I drove to the party. It was spread over a large grassy field surrounded by trees. Trucks were parked so their tailgates could be lowered. People were either leaning, sitting, or standing around them. A few had their own supply of liquor. Pony kegs and coolers were spread out and barrels were in the middle section. Each barrel had been lit so the fire heated the area. This party wasn't like normal Public parties. No Academites were allowed. No one cared about coke and champagne at this party. This was a District party, held on Frisco land. As soon as I got out, people headed over and the divide was immediate. Fallen Crest people stepped toward us, and the rest of Roussou remained on the other side of the barrels with Budd Broudou.

"Mason, my man."

A tall guy came towards us. He was lean and lanky, with a build that resembled a professional basketball player.

"Pailor, how's it going?"

"It's going, man." His mouth curved in an easygoing manner, but his eyes didn't miss a thing. They were clear and alert. As Logan came around his Escalade, he held his hand out. "Logan, my dude."

"Frankie."

"Oh." He drew back and reassessed both of them. "What are you two up to?" His hand ran over his bald head.

I threw Logan a sidelong look. "Nothing. What are you talking about?"

Frankie moved back another step, studying us before he shook his head. "See. This look you both gave me. Intense as hell. With you," he gestured to me, "I expect it, but with this one," he punched Logan in the stomach, "he's never showed up without a cocky smirk. He sure never sticks around long. It takes you five minutes to get a girl—two to pick the girl, one to grab her, and the last two to take her somewhere private. Now you show up and there's no grin, there's no quick wit," he pointed at the crowd behind them, "and you haven't even looked at the girls yet. So that's how I know you two aren't here to party."

Frankie Pailor ran Frisco how we ran Fallen Crest. We played sports against each other, but that was our only rivalry with them. Since Frisco territory touched on both sides of Roussou and Fallen Crest, much like a triangle, we understood Frankie's dilemma. He kept a friendly alliance with the Broudous as well.

"And my night just got weirder," Frankie noted as he watched another person break free from the Roussou side. "Should I run interference already?"

Channing Monroe was headed towards us. His jeans rode low on his hips, the top button loose, and his shirt hung open without another one underneath. As he drew closer, he lifted a hand to run through his hair. His other hand held a beer with four bottles stuck inside his pockets. He fished them out and handed one to me and Logan. "Boys."

Frankie moved back. His eyes skirted from Monroe to me, then Logan before his hands lifted in the air. "I give up. I thought I'd have to come over here and keep the peace. Maybe not."

Channing flashed him a grin before extending a bottle to him. "I don't want you to feel left out, Frankie."

Logan chuckled. He indicated Channing's chest. "Does that work? Showing off the pecs and shit?"

Channing shrugged. His shirt opened another inch as he lifted his arm, taking a long pull from his beer. "Like you need help with the ladies, Kade."

"Okay." Frankie had been studying all of them. "What's going on? You guys are friendly now?" He jerked a thumb towards the Roussou side. "Budd and Brett know this too?"

"We have a few friends in common." Everyone was silent after I said that.

Channing shifted so he stood closer to me and Frankie caught the slight movement. "Let me guess, Budd and Brett have no clue?"

I gestured to Channing. "I suppose that's up to him to answer."

The good-natured glint in his eyes sobered. He glanced somewhere in the crowd before turning back. "They have no clue."

"Good," Logan bit out.

Budd Broudou had been trying to find out who my girlfriend was since he heard about her existence. They asked at Quickie's and had been back one other time. I didn't think Sam's identity had leaked, but I couldn't wait any longer. The situation needed to be dealt with before it was.

There weren't many from my school that were friendly with Roussou. The fact that Samantha had friendly connections through Heather hadn't escaped me. It was ironic, but I was going to use that connection now. Channing Monroe had power over there. He wasn't friendly with Budd and Brett Broudou, but he wasn't their enemy either. If Sam got hurt, that would hurt Heather and I recognized another guy in love. Monroe would do what needed to be done to keep Heather from being hurt, and that meant siding with us.

"Is Jax here tonight?"

Channing hesitated.

Logan cursed a moment later. "She's here, Mase."

"This has nothing to do with her," Channing murmured.

He was mistaken and he knew it. I said, "What do you think they'll do to her if they find out about Sam? Heather knew who she was and she never told them."

"Oh, whoa." Frankie shot his hands between us. "You two aren't friendly? I thought you were. My mind is being blown right now. You guys are enemies? Monroe, I didn't think you had enemies."

"We're not," he snapped at him, but said to me next, "I'm aware of what will happen. Are you aware that *she* knows them?"

He wasn't referring to Heather. Logan and I got the implication. We shared another look.

"Jax?" Frankie asked.

Logan narrowed his eyes. "What are you talking about? She's never met them."

"She has, actually. They went to Manny's one night looking for you. There was a confrontation. Heather had to kick them out."

"Fuck."

Channing glanced at Logan. "Exactly."

"Wait." I shook my head. "They don't know. They were still clueless last week."

"Budd's clueless..." Channing waited.

Brett wasn't. I knew what he was leaving unsaid and I glanced at Frankie. He needed to be gone. With that thought, I nudged Logan and jerked my gaze to Pailor. Logan nodded. He understood and transformed. The cocky smirk came over him. His shoulders rolled back, his head went up, and he threw an arm around Frankie's shoulders.

"Frankie, my man. My appetite came back and I'm thinking you might have some recommendations? I don't think I've tasted too many Frisco girls."

"Oh geez." Frankie shook his head, but he couldn't hold back his smile. As Logan started to lead him away, I heard him continue, "There's too many, Logan, too many. You need to share the love. Anyone from Fallen Crest..." His voice faded as they moved to the Frisco side of the party.

I jerked my head backwards. We had parked near the edge of the party. The grass lot was surrounded by woods, which meant privacy for us. Once we were far enough away, I didn't waste time. "Sam met them?"

Channing nodded. He grimaced, but finished the rest of his beer and tossed the bottle. "At Manny's like I said. They were there hoping to run into you guys. Heather tossed them out. Brett's got a soft spot for her, and he promised they wouldn't come back to start a fight."

"They don't know about Sam?"

"No, but they talked to her. Heather admitted that she didn't make the situation better. She almost let it slip who Sam was, but Sam stopped her. She shoved Budd or something. Brett got him cooled down. It blew over after that. She sent Sam packing and kicked them out, but there's something else."

The idea of them being with her, talking to her, scaring her... My hands curled into fists. A litany of curses flashed through my mind. I wanted to find Budd and Brett. I wanted to finish this entire thing, right now, between them and me. Fuck it. Logan could help if he wanted, but I had enough rage pumping through me. I wanted both of them.

They talked to her. They *scared* her.

I didn't want to know the rest, but dammit, I had to. Sam had lied to me. "What is it?"

"Brett asked her out."

"What?"

"He asked her out." Channing raised his hands in the air, backing away.

I wasn't going to attack him. I had enough control. "Spill the rest, Monroe. Stop wasting my time."

He dropped his hands. "I don't know how it happened or when, but Brett asked Sam on a date. Budd figured it out. He's been teasing Brett all week, asking if he's going to visit her in the hospital or not."

Everything changed then. Brett Broudou liked Sam and knew she was in the hospital. Budd knew she was in the hospital. They knew about Sam. I was going to have to—

"They were waiting by the door where Sam was loaded into the ambulance. Budd keeps calling her Brett's weakling."

I stopped thinking. Everything kicked into slow motion as I heard those words in my head. They were at Manny's.

Brett asked her out. He was with her AGAIN when they saw her by the ambulance.

They saw her at her weakest moment.

It was enough. I had to end them.

I started past Channing, but he darted in front of me. "Whoa. Where are you going?"

"Move."

"No way."

"MOVE."

"No," Channing shot back at me. "You need to think, man. I don't know you, but I know your reputation, and you don't react like this. You're cold and calculated."

"They saw her when she was hurting." My tone was like ice, but my blood was pumping. I needed to do damage and I needed to do it now. Brett Broudou would be the first. "Move, Monroe or I will move you."

"We're not buds."

"I know." My tone turned lethal. I didn't want to hurt Jax's on-again-off-again whatever, but I would.

One second.

Two.

Channing's eyes flashed back at me. "I care about Heather and she cares about Sam. You mess with me, and that comes back to you. You know that, and I'm *trying* to help you." Gone was the easygoing voice. Channing straightened and the threat of violence was there. "I understand. I do. I'd feel the same way. We both know the damage Budd can do to someone. He doesn't give a shit who the person is, but you need to hear me when I say that Brett could be an asset to us."

"He went to her."

"I know."

"He was *alone* with her." *He could've hurt her.*

"Everyone at school is teasing Brett about the hospital chick. They've all heard about the girl that got jumped at the basketball game. Half of them think it's because Brett liked her. That psychotic bitch crew at your school jumped her for you. They think it's an entire Roussou/Fallen Crest thing, and they're waiting to see what Budd's going to do now."

"I don't care about any of that."

"I know. I know." Channing pointed to his head. "Think about it. Brett knows who Sam is, he asked Heather if her friend was okay."

The rage in me stalled.

He asked if she was okay... after he knew who she was.

It settled me, enough to slip back into my old skin. I began picking up the pieces. I saw where Channing was leading me. "He covered for her that night. Budd was starting to figure it out, but he stopped him. He said we had school problems."

"Because that makes sense to Budd. Someone got hurt in your school. He knows you'd want to know about it."

I frowned. "We're not that controlling."

"But Budd is, or he tries. Brett covered for you."

"I'm getting that now." It'd been something I had kept in the back of my mind, but I hadn't given it enough time. "Brett's continued to lie for her?"

She lied to me. I flinched at that reminder. It stung.

"He has." The tension left Channing, his shoulders dropped, and he nodded. "Heather was at my place earlier. He wanted to know how Sam was doing. He told her that he'd keep the secret, too. He promised that Budd wouldn't know. In fact," he took a deep breath, "that brings me to the next part of business."

I knew where this was going.

"She said that Kate's back in power. She's acting like your girlfriend and the rest of her friends too, like everything's back to normal. This isn't any of my business, but it's making her lose sleep. I care about Heather and I don't like seeing her suffer. She doesn't know if she should tell Sam you're back with the Bitch Crew or wait till you do. Either way Sam is going to find out." He touched his chest. "And that's where

I'm coming in. I'm thinking you're doing that for a reason. Am I right?"

"It's none of your business."

I kept my calm. My voice was cool, but it was the truth. I didn't care what Heather Jax was worried about. She could say all the things she wanted. My relationship with Sam was my relationship with Sam. No one else got in there.

Channing sighed. "I was afraid you would say that."

"MASON!"

Kate had arrived. The bottom of my gut dropped, and I fought against the disgust of being near her. I had two assholes to deal with, Kate and Budd Broudou.

"MASON, WHERE ARE YOUUU?" She hiccupped at the end before shrieking with her friends. All of them began calling my name.

Kate was drunk. Now was the perfect time.

I downed my beer. I emptied the entire bottle before handing it to Channing. Without a word, another beer was handed to me. I cursed before downing that one, too.

"I know what you're going to do," Channing said.

I waited. The judgment would come. I was already preparing myself for Sam's reaction.

"He's going to hurt her."

That was the point. "She hurt Sam."

Channing nodded. He didn't say anything more, but he understood. He'd do something similar if it'd been him and his girl. When I went back, Kate was in the center of the area, dancing around the barrels. Her shirt was off and she was only wearing a bra with her tight jeans. When she swung around, I saw the bottoms were ripped to show the bottom of her underwear.

Giggling some more, she tipped her head back and drank out of a Jack Daniels bottle. Her friends danced with her. Everyone was watching her. Then they saw me. They were waiting now. A group of people moved back for me. A girl lifted her beer to drink from, and as I went past, I swiped the bottle from her.

"Hey. Oh..."

She was ignored, but before Kate saw me, I glanced over my shoulder. Channing had followed me but he headed to the Roussou side of the party. He went to Heather's side. It was then when our gazes collided. Her eyes burned bright with condemnation. Channing hadn't judged me, but she was. Sam's best friend hated me.

Kate gasped, swaying on her feet, "Mason! You're here!"

I hated myself, too.

I smirked at Kate as she came over to me. She was trying to be seductive. She looked like a drunken idiot and reeked of booze. Then she looped her arms around my neck, pressed her breasts against me before sliding them up my chest as she moved into me. Then her fingers curled into my neck and she drew my mouth down. As my lips stopped above hers, she whispered, "Are you going to fuck me tonight?"

I didn't think. I couldn't.

I slammed my lips onto hers.

CHAPTER
TWENTY-TWO

SAMANTHA

It wasn't home.

That was my first thought when I walked inside. David unlocked the door, but waved me through first. Nothing felt familiar about my old home anymore. It was cold. It was dark, and there was a musky smell in the room.

"Oh, sorry." David rushed around me, and the door slammed shut in his wake. "I meant to drop by earlier and turn the heat up. I knew you were coming, but things happened at school and..." he trailed off as he stared at me.

"What?"

"Nothing." A quick shake of the head. "It's... you're here. You're staying."

"Yeah?"

"I just thought..." He shook his head again. The corners of his mouth darted up and down as he cleared his throat. "I just never thought you'd be back."

There was so much emotion in his gaze, and they were too visible to me. He hadn't turned the light on, but the moonlight lit the room up. A sudden lump formed in my throat, and I looked away.

"Oh, right." He finished with the heat and flipped the light switch. The room was flooded with new light, and I was struck with the same emotions.

This wasn't home. Not anymore.

The kitchen counter was covered with empty pizza boxes. There must've been thirty of them, and the floor had empty cases of beer scattered around. The kitchen table had mail all over it. Not an inch of the tablecloth could be seen. When I spotted a television in the corner of the room, I gestured to it. "That's new."

"Oh." He sighed, flushing at the same time. "Yes. Before Malinda, I watched a lot of the game tapes here."

"Not in the basement? You used to watch them down there."

"Yeah. I, um, got into a habit of staying up here in case..." His glanced at me, but turned away. Bumping into the pizza boxes, the pile fell to the floor. "Oh no." He dropped down and began picking them up with rushed movements. "I'm sorry. This place is a mess. I haven't cleaned since—" He stopped himself and took a deep breath.

I sensed a change as he straightened. I waited for whatever he was going to say next, and my heart began pounding in my chest.

"I don't know why I'm lying to you. You've been through enough. You deserve me to tell it to you straight."

My stomach tightened.

"I would sit up here," he gestured around the kitchen, "in case you ever came back. It sounds stupid, but I wanted to be here if you ever came back. You never did. Well, you did, but it was the day after you moved."

"Yeah." My voice was hoarse. "She forgot something and asked me to get it. I did..." And he had come home. A stabbing pain pierced me. If only I had realized how final it was going to be. If I had known he wasn't my real father then, but no. It wouldn't have changed anything. She still would have forced me to go with her.

"Like I said before, it became a habit. Sitting here. Eating here. Watching the games here. I did everything here. Even months later when I knew you weren't coming back, I couldn't stop. It made no sense to me."

I nodded, but I didn't know what to say. When I saw the broom in the back, I asked, "Do you want me to clean up?"

"What? No. Oh no, Samantha. This is my mess. I'll clean it up. You can go upstairs if you'd like to get changed or get comfortable. Maybe email or check your Twitter. Mark's always talking about that with Malinda, but I never understand what they're talking about. I'm not big on technology."

"I know." Neither was I. I thought I had inherited that from him.

"You know what?" With a garbage bag in one hand, he began stuffing the pizza boxes inside. "I bet you're hungry. Malinda asked if she should make us something, but I told her that I'd take you to dinner. Do you want to go out to eat?"

"That's okay. We can eat in."

"Oh." He frowned. "Um...I could go and pick something up. Chinese? You used to like Chinese."

"That's fine."

"Or there's that new noodle place. You want to go there?" His eyes lit up.

I gestured to my face. The bruises had started to fade, but I had another two weeks until they'd be completely gone. "I'm not feeling like going out yet."

"That's right. Your face."

"Nicely put."

"Oh," he sighed again. "I'm nervous, Samantha. I'm your father. I've raised you since you were little, but I'm very, very nervous right now. I can go and get you something from the noodle place."

"You don't have anything in the refrigerator?"

"I don't stay here often." The corners of his mouth lifted again in a quick grin. "Things went fast after my first date with Malinda, and I'm there most of the time. I use this place more for storage. I guess."

Another thing that changed. "It's nice that you've kept the house."

"Yeah, well, I had hoped you might need it someday." He frowned. "But not like this. This was a horrible way to need it."

"I know, Dav—Dad. I know."

A smile formed on his face. It widened as his eyes blinked rapidly. Then he brushed at his eye and jerked his head towards the door. "I'll go and get us something to eat. I'll be back quick. I promise."

Unsure of what to do, I began cleaning up. The rest of the pizza boxes were put in the garbage bags, along with the beer cases. All of that was taken outside to trash bins and then I started organizing the mail. He had bills from the fall. When I found one from August, it was the date we left him. My hand trembled as I stuffed the envelope underneath the rest. The magazines were thrown out—they were Analise's. She never bothered to cancel her subscriptions. The pile I moved to the side were the football ones. All the coaching newsletters went there, too. Then there were the newspapers. Most were still folded together, and I knew he hadn't opened any of them. All of them were tossed. I put what I could into recycling piles. After sweeping the floor and wiping down the counters, I skimmed over the sink. There weren't many dishes, but David never dirtied a lot of dishes. The few he did, he cleaned right away. That was something Analise could never complain about.

I glanced around. He still wasn't back, so I wandered into the living room. I couldn't bring myself to go upstairs yet. I knew too many memories would surface when I went to my old bedroom, but I took one step into the living room, and memories slammed into me anyway.

He hadn't touched a thing.

I couldn't believe it.

The couch hadn't moved. The two blankets were still folded and perched on the ends. I remember putting them there. I was going to grab them when we left, but she told me not to. She said David would need extra blankets, so I left them. He hadn't moved them. A box that I had packed was still in the corner. I hadn't been looking at what I put in there, but she didn't want it. It was filled with pictures albums, but Analise saw the wedding album on top. She wouldn't listen when I explained mine were in there, too. That was another item left behind.

I didn't turn the lights on. For some reason, I couldn't fathom the idea of sitting there with bright light cast over this room.

"Samantha?"

His keys jingled together as he took them from the door and pushed it open, the screen door banging shut behind him. "Are you in here?"

I hadn't heard him open the door. "I'm in here." As I heard him come closer, I brushed the tear from my cheek and stood. I plastered on a bright smile and he paused, frowning at me. He was going to ask if I was okay. I couldn't lie to him, so I pointed to the two pizza boxes tucked under his arm. "Were they closed?"

"What?"

"The pizza. You went for noodles."

"Oh." He glanced down, as if remembering them. "Oh, uh. Yeah. No, I'm sorry. I didn't know what you wanted so I got pizza. You used to like this, so I'm hoping you still do."

My stomach growled at that moment.

His eyebrow lifted up. "I guess you do."

The aroma had filled the room, and I realized I hadn't eaten since breakfast with Malinda. "Pizza sounds great."

"Great."

I nodded.

He stared back at me.

Neither of us moved.

"OH. Um..." He glanced around. "I...we could sit." His gaze lingered on the couch.

"I cleaned the kitchen. We can sit in there."

"Okay." He sounded relieved.

"That's your routine, right? I don't want to break you of any habits you picked up when..." When we left him. I flinched. When I left him.

"It doesn't matter, Samantha. It was something I picked up, waiting if you came back and now," he gestured to me, "we could go downstairs. That's where we used to watch television. We could watch a movie."

"You still have it hooked up downstairs?" A brief spark of hope flared in me. That was our thing. We watched movies together, and Analise stayed upstairs. She didn't like the basement, said it was like a dark dungeon. It was our haven.

He nodded. "Yeah and you didn't have to clean up. Thanks for that. I didn't mean to run out and have you pick up after me."

"It was no problem." Where did I put my hands? I had no idea anymore. I crossed them over my chest, but that didn't feel right. In my pockets? Would that be less awkward?

"Okay." A grin teased at the corner of his mouth. "Why don't you take the pizza down, and I'll grab everything else. There should be pop and water downstairs, too."

"Okay."

"I think I have chips, too. You still like Doritos?"

I nodded and headed for the basement door. Once it swung open and he headed to the kitchen, I stopped at the top of the stairs. I closed my eyes and took a deep breath. I needed one deep breath. Then I felt for the light switch and flicked it on. The stairwell lit up and a glimmer of home came back to me.

It was only a glimmer, but it was something.

Watching a movie with David wasn't so bad after that. The awkwardness or tension had lifted, and it was our spot again. When we started the movie, I closed my eyes halfway through it. I could pretend for a moment. This was before the cheating. Before the divorce. I was transported back to the time before my world fell apart. Then I heard David laugh and turned to him. His eyes were sparkling. His paused with a handful of popcorn going to his mouth as he waited for the punch line in the movie. There it was. I heard the actor say it, and David roared with laughter. His head fell back and his hand waited in the air until he was done. Then he tossed the popcorn like nothing happened and went back to watching the movie.

I felt the tears coming.

This was it. This was the moment I had been craving since Analise took us away. Home. It wasn't my old home. I knew that, but it was a new home. Mason and Logan would join this home and we'd be together. Everything would be fine. I knew it.

"Did you see that?" He laughed and pointed to the screen.

Yes. We put in the same movie we always used to watch. I had it memorized. So did he, but I laughed with him. It felt right to do so. We were still laughing about the same jokes when reality hit me. I remembered everything and stopped laughing. I stopped breathing.

"Samantha?"

"What?"

"Are you okay?"

"Yeah. I'm fine. I just," *remembered that I didn't have a mother*, "realized that Mason never texted me back."

"They have a game tonight? You didn't want to go?"

Pointing to my face again, I grinned. "Look like the walking dead."

"Oh. Right. Sorry."

I shrugged and joked, "What do you do? Life of the Bullied and Attacked, right? I should write a blog about it."

"You should."

I was struck by the serious tone from him. "What?"

"You should."

I laughed again. I must've heard him wrong. "What'd you say?"

"That's how you get your voice out? I say, do it. You have something to say, put it in a blogger. I would be proud if my daughter bloggered."

"It's," blogged and not bloggered, but I kept quiet. He was so proud, and it was because of me. I stopped for the moment. He had no idea what he was saying, but he was trying. More tears threatened to spill, and I turned away again.

I had missed him.

"Samantha?"

"I'm fine." I waved him off.

"Did I say something wrong?" He had grown quiet again.

I wanted to cry, hide, and wrap my arms around him at the same time. There was that hesitation and anxiety in him again. I hadn't heard it in so long, but memories flooded me from their fights. He would respond to a question and Analise would become enraged. I heard it so many times, but it was never him. That's what I wanted to tell him for so long. It was her. She was the problem. She ripped apart our family. Everything was her fault.

"No," I choked out. "You said exactly the right thing."

"Oh. Good."

His obvious relief sent another wave of emotion through me. Malinda had been right. "Does Malinda come over here?"

He froze.

I frowned. What had I said wrong now?

Then he said, "I don't let her."

"Why?"

"I'm ashamed."

So many emotions went through me at that statement. He was ashamed. No one should be ashamed of their home.

"This was," he stopped. When he spoke again, his voice was clearer. "This house is where I failed my family. I failed you. Malinda is a new beginning. Her home is warm and loving."

Like her.

He continued, "I don't want her to see this place. It's mine, but it's still Analise's too."

A shiver went over me. He was right. I'd been feeling her presence since I walked inside.

"I decided that I'd keep this place for you, even if you didn't want me around you. I wanted you to have a home. I can't change the memories of this place, but you can. Even if it means your," he hesitated, "new family comes with you, that's alright with me."

"You're talking like this isn't your home anymore."

"It's not. It hasn't been since she took you. It's been a shelter for me. My home will probably be with Malinda now."

I drew in a sudden breath. It was serious between them. Mark had been right, but I shouldn't have been surprised. The first time I saw them together, I hated it. I hated her. It was more change. She was taking him further away from me, but I could no longer lie to myself. "Malinda's good for you. You're lucky to have her."

His head had been down during our talk. It jerked up now. "You mean that?"

Our father/daughter moment had strayed towards deeper waters, but I couldn't pull away now. I wasn't sure if I wanted to. I hadn't realized how much I had missed him. I couldn't tell him. My throat was filled with tears and emotions, it no longer allowed me to speak. All I could do was nod.

Neither of us talked. We sat in silence. The movie had ended earlier and the credits were done. Every now and then he would wipe a hand over his face. I would do the same.

He broke the silence when he lifted a hand towards me. "Malinda's yours, too, if you want." He stopped and took a deep breath. His voice cracked before he started again, "I'm not going to be like Analise and force you to do things. You've been through too much for me to treat you with kid gloves. You're almost an adult and you're going to be a great one. I can see it already, but you've got a room there, too." His mouth curved up in a rueful grin, and he wiped at his eyes again. "I already know she told Mark that room was yours. It can sit empty for years and it'll be your room. She already loves you, Samantha." His eyes widened. "But I don't mean that to make you feel pressured or anything. It's there if you come or not. You can do whatever you need. I meant it about this place. This can be your home, too. I always meant to tell you, but I was a coward. I was too scared."

He was scared of me.

He opened the door for that talk, but I couldn't. Shaking my head, I got up from the couch. "I—" I couldn't talk. I couldn't be there. "I need to call Mason. I need to check in." Going to the stairs, my hand reached for the rail and my head went down. I couldn't see his pain. I was leaving him now. "And I have to go to the bathroom. I'm sorry."

Then I fled upstairs. I didn't feel my physical pain anymore. The emotional overrode it.

CHAPTER TWENTY-THREE

When morning came, I was pissed. No. I was livid. Mason hadn't come over, and he hadn't called. He hadn't texted, and a few hours later, there was still no alerts on my phone. It was nearing nine in the morning and I knew he was awake. He didn't sleep late. He wouldn't forget his phone anywhere, so he was avoiding me. That could only mean one thing—it happened last night. Whatever he had planned for Kate had happened and I hadn't known. I'd been left out.

I called Logan. Nothing.

I called Heather. Nothing.

Two hours later. Still nothing. From anyone

I sighed, and changed into real clothes. My face resembled a mix between a panda and raccoon. The little make-up I had on was enough to cover some of the bruising. When I was done, the panda had vanished, but the raccoon remained. I couldn't perform miracles. It would have to be enough.

I wasn't going to get sad. I wasn't going to crumble and ask the 'why me?' questions. Last night had been emotional enough for me, so I skipped over all those crappy emotions and went straight to furious. That felt better. It slipped over me like a second coat. It was keeping me warm and sheltered. That's when I found David.

There was breakfast still on the counter from earlier, but he moved it aside. He was taking out vegetables, dressings, and chicken.

"Let's go to Malinda's for lunch."

His hand jerked and he cursed, whirling around to me. "Samantha!" He pounded on his chest. "You scared five years off my life."

I didn't care. "Let's go to Malinda's."

"What?" He heard me this time. "Why? I thought this was father/daughter time, though I have no doubt Mason snuck in your room last night. He left already?"

"Let's go to Malinda's."

He paused and then caught on. "Oh."

Exactly.

"Is there something you want to tell me?"

"Nope. I want to go to Malinda's."

"All right... Are you sure everything's okay?"

"Nope. Malin—"

He finished for me, "Malinda's. Got it. You ready to go?"

I was more than ready. As soon as we got there, I said hello to Malinda and bypassed her for Mark's room. It was now nearing noon, but as soon as I pushed open his door, he flew off his bed. "Mom!" He stopped, with one leg already in his jeans and frowned. "Sam?"

"Sam?" a feminine voice squeaked from under his covers. Then a blonde head popped out, and she didn't look too pleased. "What are you doing here?"

"Cassandra?" She'd been obsessed with Adam. I snorted. "Did you give up on Adam finally? Mark told me about the new girl in his life. Must suck. You got booted. Again."

The puzzled look on her face turned to a glare, and she threw the covers back. Wearing only a thin top, half was moved to the side so one breast was exposed. It didn't take a genius to figure out Mark had been getting a handful before my interruption. She snapped back now, "Did you and Mason break up? Are you moving onto your next stepbrother? I'm sorry. Logan must've turned you down. That must suck, too."

A growl came from the back of my throat. I looked like shit. I felt like shit. I wasn't ready to deal with *her* shit. Turning to Mark, I gestured out the doors. "We need to talk."

He nodded, casting a wary glance over his shoulder.

"Are you kidding me?" she seethed at him.

As she sat there with the blankets drowning her thin frame, Cassandra straightened her shirt with one jerk and glowered at me. "Why'd you have to come back? Things were perfect with you gone."

"Cass. Stop it."

"What?" She rolled her eyes. "They were."

She wasn't my problem, but I bared my teeth. "You really want to start a battle with me knowing that I'm probably going to be Mark's new stepsister?"

She cursed at me.

"Right back at you, Cass," I threw over my shoulder as I headed out to the media room.

She yelled back, "Miranda still hates you and Logan. Just wait. Karma's a bitch, Sam. Looks like you got one dose, but you got more comi—" Mark slammed the door shut on her. She paused and then yelled through the wall, "And screw you, too, Mark."

I closed my eyes. The slam was right there. It was on the tip of my tongue.

Mark opened the door and smirked at her. "You already did. Three times. Now get out." The door was shut once again, and he glanced down the hall. "We need to hide. She's going to be a bitch when she comes out of there."

As soon as we got into the room Logan used and shut the door, his opened. We could hear her cursing under her breath as she walked past us towards the stairs. The upstairs door slammed again before either of us said a word.

"You slept with *Cass*?"

He grimaced, raking a hand through his dark hair. It stuck up when his hand fell back down. "I was drunk." He shrugged. "And she's hot."

"Are you going to sleep with her again?"

"If I get the chance." He flashed me a rakish grin. "I'm a guy and she's good in bed."

999

"I thought you were dating Amelia?"

He snorted. "Hell no. She's crazy and my mom hates her. She's dating a college guy anyways."

"A lot's changed over there."

"Yeah." He shivered and touched his bare chest. "You mind if I grab a shirt? Not that I don't mind showing off the goods, but it's cold down here and you're *taken* taken."

"Yeah, that's fine."

He flashed a grin and hurried off. This time I followed and waited in the media room. Dropping onto one of the couches, I sat where I'd been with Mason a week ago. He held me while we watched movies that night. I'd been in so much pain, but he helped. He pushed the pain away. Being with him always pushed the pain away.

"Sam?"

I jerked back to reality. Mark was standing there, one of his athletic shirts on and his jeans zipped up. He sat on the opposite couch and bent over to pull on his socks. "You okay?"

"No."

He stopped and glanced up.

I wasn't going to lie about it. "I need your help."

"With what?"

"I can't drive and that's where you come in. I need a driver for the day."

"Okay." His shoulders loosened up, and he finished putting his socks on. As he reached for his shoes, he asked, "Where are we going?"

"To find Mason and Logan."

That made him stop and he sat back up. A blank mask came over him. "Huh?"

"They're not answering my calls and I'm not going to sit around and wait. So you're going to help me find them."

"Sam," he started as we both stood up.

"Don't. I don't want to hear it. You offered to help me before. I'm cashing in on it now. Let's go."

I led the way. David and Malinda were at the table, but I veered to the door instead. Mark stopped to talk to them, so I waited at the front entrance. A quiet conversation carried between the two. David didn't join in. I was listening for him, but when he remained silent I wasn't sure if it was a good thing or not. Then Mark came around the corner and tossed his keys in the air. He caught them in a swift hand motion and flashed me a smile. "Where's the first stop?"

"Jail."

"Whoa. What?"

Too late. I was already outside. The door swung closed on him, and I heard, "Ouch," before he followed me out. "We're going to the jail?"

Going to his car, I got inside before answering him. I was on a mission, and I wasn't slowing down for it. My ribs were better after a week of rest, but they weren't a hundred percent better. They were going to be angry with me, and I'd feel their wrath tomorrow, but that was tomorrow. Everything could wait until tomorrow. For today, nothing mattered except finding Mason and Logan. I would not let myself entertain the option that they left me. I couldn't.

Gritting my teeth, Mark had barely slid behind the wheel before I asked, "Can we get going? Please."

He clipped his seat belt on and started his car. "Jail, huh?"

"I need to make sure they weren't arrested last night."

"Jail it is." He wheeled around and took off down the street. As we passed the Kade mansion, I wanted to see if their cars were there, but they weren't. I wasn't surprised. My mom's wasn't either and that did surprise me. She always had her car parked out front. She liked showing off the new car James bought her for an engagement present. What further surprised me? James' car was gone as well.

"You know Mason and Logan went to a District party last night?"

Distracted from those thoughts, I turned back to my mission. "District party?"

He nodded, taking a left out of the neighborhood. "Yeah, you know those parties."

"I don't." This was Mark. He was easygoing Mark, laidback Mark. Right now he was being too much of that, and I needed him to catch on. The urge to snap at him was too much. "Enlighten me."

"Oh, sure." He chuckled to himself. "It's the three town school. You know."

"I don't." My voice rose on the last word. Anger and more anger was roiling together inside of me. "Please. Explain further."

Another chuckle came from him as he moved onto the main freeway. "I think last night's party was at Frisco. Only the public schools can go: Frisco, Roussou, and Fallen Crest. No private schools are allowed. If they catch you there, they trash your car—slash your tires, put scratches in your car, throw eggs on the window. It's not worth it to us so no one's gone for a long time."

My stomach dropped. "Roussou?" The arrested theory was gaining merit.

"Yep, but Frisco's a good town. We play them in football and basketball. They aren't at FCP's standards, which is why we play them, but they're decent."

"Did you hear if anything happened at the party?"

He laughed some more. "Like what? Everything happens at those parties. They find some place in the woods, and the cops are told not to go out there. Anything could've happened. No one talks about it afterwards. If you're caught running your mouth, you get the crap beat out of you. So no one talks."

People talked. The right questions needed to be asked, but people talked. When we got to the police station, I found out that they weren't there. So we went to the hotel next. That was when I found out that they weren't there either. My key card didn't work, and they wouldn't give me a new one. Mason and Logan had checked out last Sunday.

That was news to me, and it was not welcomed news.

As we went back to his car, Mark asked, "You didn't know they left?"

"They joked the first day about their mom moving closer to your house, but they haven't said a word. I assumed it hadn't happened and I haven't thought about it since."

"Their stuff must be somewhere. Both of them didn't keep that much at my house."

He was stating the obvious. *Thank you, Sherlock Holmes.*

Taking a deep breath, I pushed the inner rage away and sighed. "So let's try out that theory."

"What theory?"

"That their mom is living in that house."

"The For Sale sign is still on the lawn."

"Mason said that she would probably rent it."

"Okay." He turned the car back to his home. It wasn't long until we were passing his house and slowing down to see what cars were parked at Nate's old home.

None.

Mark pulled the car over and parked in front. He leaned over, inspecting the house. "There are curtains hung. I don't remember those. Someone's in there."

I hit his shoulder. "You go up there."

"Me? Why?" Cradling his shoulder, he scowled at me. "Stop hurting me. First the door, now your fist. What's next?"

"Your car if you don't go up there."

"No way. I've heard about Helen Malbourne, and she sounds scary as hell. My mom hates her."

Malinda went up a few more notches in my book. "You go. If they're in there, then they're avoiding me. They're not avoiding you and she won't lie to you. She'd *thrive* on lying to me."

He grumbled, but got out of the car. As he rounded to my side, he hissed at me before heading up the sidewalk, "You so owe me for this."

"Yeah, yeah. Go." I waved him off.

He sent me one last glare before the transformation came over him. It was the same with Logan. The head went up. The shoulders rolled back. A confident aura emanated from him, but Mark's strut wasn't as cocky. He was also nicer than Logan. As he knocked on the door, he didn't have to wait long. The door opened, and he went inside.

While he was in there, the knot in my stomach reproduced and birthed triplets. They were like rabbits. Those produced even more and there were too many inside of me. I couldn't handle it. He was gone for a minute, but my hand was reaching for the door handle. Screw it. Helen and I could go another round. I was forcing my way in there and I was going to demand some answers. Even if Mason and Logan weren't there, she'd know where they were. They were nice like that. They tried to keep their mom in the loop. Mason said one time that she hadn't fucked them over. She didn't deserve the freeze-out that James often got.

My hand tightened around the door handle and I pulled on it. It opened. Taking a deep breath, I made the decision. I was going in.

Mark came out.

I wasn't going in.

The door clicked shut and I waited as he jogged to the car, his trademark carefree grin on his face.

As he got inside, I said, "You're perpetually happy."

He paused, but shrugged and got inside. Shutting the door, he started the engine and wiggled his eyebrows at me. "She suggested Manny's. She said they like to eat there since their girlfriend works there."

I wanted to curse. No. I did curse. "Mark."

"What?" He was turning onto the street again.

"They weren't there?"

"Nope."

"What'd you say to her?"

"That I was looking for them." He cast me a sidelong look. "Why? Did I mess up?"

"No," I sighed. I knew they weren't there either.

"What about Nate Monson? He's still recuperating at his house, right? Maybe they're there."

I shook my head. "They wouldn't both be there. Mason said his parents have been pretty strict about who goes over there. They've been allowing him over, but they'd never let Logan and him there at the same time. He explained that they called in some hotshot doctor who said Nate can only handle so much stress." I frowned. "I think it's more about Nate's parents' stress. Logan and Mason together are not parent-friendly."

Mark grunted. "You're telling me." He paused for a beat. "I'm surprised they follow the rules at Nate's house."

"I doubt they do. I doubt Nate even does, but it doesn't matter. Mason and Logan are avoiding me. Even if I go over there, he'll cover for them."

"So we go to Manny's?"

I nodded. It was the 'why not' moment. They hadn't been arrested. They weren't at the hotel. I didn't think they were at Helen's. If they were, they would've called Mark's phone by now to see if something was wrong with me. Nate would never tell me if he knew anything. There was no way they were at James'. I had no more places to try. Plan B: Heather. That meant Manny's.

When we got there, my friend wasn't there, but Mark's were. He headed to their table, and I headed to Heather's house. It was another no-go for me. Brandon answered the door. He and Heather had been banned from the diner and bar for the entire weekend. Their dad didn't want them working as much as they had been so Heather was at Channing's. I asked where his home was, and Brandon laughed. He shook his head. "No way am I giving you those directions. It's too close to the Broudou house. No way, Sam. My sister would skin me alive if you got hurt somehow." He eyed my face. "And you've been hurt enough."

It was official. I had no one now. As I began to turn away, Brandon stopped me. "Hey. Wait." He disappeared inside, and my hope flared for one second. He came back with her phone. "If you see her, here's her phone. She left it and it keeps beeping every damn minute. It's password protected, and I can't get in there to turn off the alerts or the volume."

I had no words. Those alerts were from me. "Okay, thanks, Brandon."

"Yeah. I'm sorry, but I'm sure you'll see her at the street dance tonight."

My heart paused. I'd been heading back down the porch, but stopped in my tracks. "What?"

"The street dance. Aren't you going?"

"No."

Thump.

"What is it?"

My heart began picking up speed. *Thump thump.*

He frowned at me. "It's the District Weekend, right?"

"Yeah..." *Thumpthumpthumpthump.* Whatever he was about to say, I knew they'd be there. All of them would be there. My heart was racing.

He continued to frown at me, scratching his head. "It should be in Roussou tonight. All three towns go. You've never heard about it?"

"No." *Please tell me. Please, please, please.*

"Oh. That's weird. I thought Mason would've told you. He's been going forever."

"It's in Roussou."

His eyes lit up. "Maybe you shouldn't go. That's probably why no one's said anything. Yeah, don't go. Forget I said anything, but if you go, you didn't hear about it from me."

"I know about the party last night in Frisco."

"You do?" A relieved grin came over him. "Oh good. Yeah, all three towns host something over the weekend, but it's always the same thing. The first night, the party's in Frisco. Then Saturday night, the street dance is in Roussou. They shut down one street, and a lot of people from their community go. I think it was originally meant for the town, but the District Festival kind of took over. Then Sunday, Fallen Crest has a huge bonfire in the hills behind Quickie's." He grinned. "It can get crazy there, too."

"You've been there?"

"Once."

"Has Heather?"

"She hasn't in the past, but she and Channing have been tight this weekend, so I'm sure she will. He has to go. Most of his friends go so Channing makes sure no one gets hurt, or gets in a fight with the Broudou brothers."

A party. A street dance. A bonfire. As I waved goodbye and went to get Mark, my heart was pounding against my ribcage. I had a location for the night. I was going to the street dance. There was no way I would stay away. I couldn't think about Mason's or Logan's absence. It was because of their plan. They were doing this to help me. They hadn't left me. There was no way. I wouldn't accept that.

As I pushed through the side door and inside Manny's, I collected Mark. He was laughing with his friends, more people from Fallen Crest Academy that I didn't want to be around. I wasn't laughing. Gritting my teeth, I ignored all their looks. I pretended I didn't notice their stares or the mouths hanging open when they got a better look at my face.

Yes, everyone. I had been attacked and beaten. The bruises were still with me, but I wasn't getting any more. None from them and none from anyone else. It was why I needed answers from Mason. There was a reason for their absence. There had to be.

CHAPTER TWENTY-FOUR

I went to the street dance alone.

I never told Mark about it and when he dropped me off at home, I reassured him that everything was fine. Everything *was* fine. I was going to make sure of it. Getting ready for the street dance was painful in the literal sense, but I chose a white camisole underneath a black sweater and black pants with little black ballet flats. All of it was easy to get into and that had been my main objective. My next goal was make-up. More was applied than I normally wore, and I was proud of myself; almost all of the bruises were hidden by the time I was finished. Then I swept my hair up into a high pony-tail. My hair had grown longer, so it was past my shoulders now. If Heather had been there, she would've told me it looked sleek. I didn't care. I just needed to blend in. I was going into Roussou territory.

I wanted to find Heather first, but as I parked my car and got out, my heart sank. Brandon said one street was blocked off. That was true, but he never said it was the entire main street blocked off. She could be anywhere.

I sighed and started off on my mission.

Going through the first block was easy. It was during the second that people started to look at me. A group of girls jerked together and started whispering. A few pointed at me. My heart sank again. It was already starting, so I veered into the first bathroom I could find. Checking my make-up in the mirror, I didn't see anything wrong. I looked fine. Normal even. The evening had grown dark so my face looked flawless with none of my bruises showing, but when I went back out, they were still there. There were more behind them and they were watching me now.

Frowning at them, I turned to slip away, but came to an abrupt stop.

Budd Broudou was in front of me, a leer on his face as he looked me up and down. I hardened inside. The longer his gaze lingered on me, the dirtier I felt. As they were transfixed below my waist, I shifted on my feet and snapped, "What do you want?"

He grinned and lifted his hand. A forty ounce bottle touched his lips, and he took a long pull from it before wiping his mouth with the back of his hand. Then he licked his lips and tugged at his jeans. They hung low on his waist, already baggy, but the top button was loose so they sagged even more.

I narrowed my eyes.

He chuckled as he caught my reaction. Lifting a hand to his chest, he rubbed it through his white wife-beater. His flannel shirt hung open, the ends of it were frayed and ripped with holes in them. As his hand fell back down to his pants, his finger caught on the end and tore it some more. He seemed unaware that he ripped his shirt, or he just didn't care.

My guess was both. I was getting tired of his silent leering. "What do you want?"

Another deep chuckle came from him, and he pointed his beer at me. "You already said that."

"Then answer the question."

There was a collective gasp behind me, but I couldn't take my words back. I said it. It was done. Now I waited for the consequences.

He started laughing. It was slight at first, but grew. As he kept going, he bent over and slapped at his knee. His beer jostled from the movement and he cursed, but shook his head as more laughter escaped. It took another moment before his chuckles ceased enough so his hand had stopped shaking. As soon as he could, he finished the rest of his beer. When it was empty, he tossed it to the ground. His hand went back out and someone put a new one there. When he went to open it, he kept shaking his head, watching me at the same time. His shoulders jerked up as he started laughing again.

I looked for a quick escape route, but there wasn't one. Everyone around us was watching. They had taken a step towards us and closed ranks. I had to wait.

After another sip from his new beer, he burped. "You got a spine to you. I can see why he likes you."

I stiffened.

His gaze travelled over me again, stopping on my breasts. "You got a nice rack, too. Not too much. You're damn skinny, but you got enough for a good bounce." His tongue darted out and ran over his bottom lip before moving to the top one.

It was in slow motion. I began to feel sick.

"Hmm mmm." He nodded, then took another long swallow. "You're tight." His eyes went to below my waist. "I bet you're real tight there, too. He's a lucky guy."

I frowned. Feeling disgusted aside, he thought Mason was a lucky guy?

"Too bad my brother caught you first."

His brother?

"Budd."

I turned around. Brett Broudou was behind me. He wore the same baggy jeans and ripped flannel shirt, but there was no leering. He was glowering, but not at me. He said again, "Budd. Back off."

Budd snorted. He lifted his beer again, but he stumbled to the side. The beer fell from his hand to the ground, and it sprayed everywhere, most of it on me. I jumped out of the way and slammed into Brett, but I didn't care at that moment. My ribs protested, and a searing pain sliced through me. "Shit," I whispered to myself, but then I bounced off of Brett and began to fall to the side.

The ground was coming at me. My eyes went wide. The pain was going to be paralyzing, so I readied myself for the impact.

It never came.

I had stopped halfway there and looked up. Brett caught me. His one hand held a twin forty ounce beer, but his other hand was wrapped around my arm. Our eyes caught and an apology flashed in his as he lifted me back to my feet.

"Thanks." I had no idea what else to say.

He nodded, his gaze was lidded, but he looked over at his brother. "You remember our talk?"

Budd rolled his eyes and waved him away. "Yeah, yeah."

Brett frowned. "Tink?"

Another goliath-sized guy spoke from behind the counter. "Yeah?"

"Give Budd another beer. He dropped his."

"Already?"

Budd growled. "Fuck you both. I'm fine. I can get my own damn beer." He swung around, but almost clipped a girl in the head as he did. Taking a few extra steps, he regained his balance and shoved through the crowd.

My heart was racing. It wasn't until he left that I gasped for breath.

Brett touched my hand, stopping it from trembling. "Come on."

I followed him through the crowd and concentrated on slowing my heart. It was nearing combustion; it wanted to explode out of my chest. It wasn't until it had slowed a little when I realized that Brett was taking me somewhere away from the street dance. We turned down an alley and ducked into a side door where there was another party. There were people everywhere and most clapped him on the shoulder as he went past. Girls called out hellos, but it was different than when I walked with Mason or Logan. The attention they got from girls was sexual. This was genuine. These people actually liked Brett Broudou.

He went to a back hallway. Only a few others were there, and he moved around them.

"Hey, man."

Another said, "Buddy."

Brett gave each a nod, but pressed forward until he got to the last door.

Where the hell was he taking me?

Then I found out. The last door opened to a back room. Couches were pushed against the walls, lining the whole room. A bar was set-up against the side and a couple small tables were in the middle. A few people were around them, playing a card game. A large pile of money was in the middle, and everyone looked up as we entered.

Brett jerked his hand to the door. "Move the game somewhere else."

I expected protests, but there were none. The room was silent as everyone got up and collected their cards. The dealer took the money and the rest of the chips. They filed past us, taking their chairs with them.

"They literally moved their game somewhere else," I noted. Holy hell. Was I supposed to be scared? Was he going to hurt me?

"Yeah."

"Yeah...?"

There were green couches. There was a blue one. The bar had mosaic tiles on the bottom. The stools were encased in metal—

"You're scared of me, aren't you?"

Oh, dear god. I tore my gaze from the stools to him and gulped. I wasn't expecting that from him. It sounded like raw honesty. "Um..." I stopped beating around the bush. "Can you blame me?"

"I'm not going to hurt you." He went behind the bar and reached for two glasses. "I asked you out, remember?"

As he began filling the two shot glasses with rum, I moved closer. "Do you know who I am?"

He finished pouring and put the bottle to the side, then lifted his hooded eyes back to me. "I know you were dating Mason Kade. That was a nice surprise when I put it together." He paused, frowning at me. "Are you still dating him?"

"I—" had no idea what to say.

He added, "Because he's been having another girl all over him. Did you know about that?"

The air left me, and I sagged forward. My heart dropped to the bottom of my feet and new pain sliced through me. Hearing Mason's plan and knowing Kate would think she was his girlfriend was different from hearing it was happening, and hearing it from Mason's enemy. I couldn't answer him. I felt rubbed raw from the inside out.

His tone didn't soften. It hardened. "I asked around. It's that same bitch that beat you up."

"Yeah."

"And he's letting her crawl all over him? He tossed you aside? For her?" The threat of violence was swimming in his depths. He tossed the shot down his throat and refilled it again. Nudging mine towards me, he waited for me this time.

I took it. I didn't feel a thing.

"More?" He lifted the rum again.

I nodded. I needed all I could get.

We took two more shots before I moved my glass to the side. No more for me, but he still downed two more. Then he leaned against the far wall behind the bar, and I slid onto a stool. The alcohol was beginning to work. I was beginning to feel warm again.

"You never answered my question. Are you still with the guy?"

"I don't know."

Disappointment flared over him, followed by pity. "That's too bad."

"You're not going to tell your brother?"

Pushing away from the wall, he reached for the rum again. He spoke with a savage tone, "Are you kidding me? You know what my brother does? He hurts people."

I frowned. Didn't he?

"I know what you're thinking." He held his glass towards me, the shot ready to go. "I hurt people, too, but I don't hurt girls, and I don't hurt people weaker than me. I don't stop my brother either. I can't. I tried but people only get hurt worse."

"Why are you telling me this?"

"Because my brother *really* wants to hurt you." He downed his shot and filled it again. "No, he wants to hurt whoever Mason Kade cares about. Good thing that bitch has been all over him this weekend. Budd thinks it's her that he cares about, but it's not. Is it? It's you. He almost drove over my brother when he found out you were hurt. I was too stunned. I almost let it happen. Shit."

Mason almost drove over Budd? I couldn't think about that. Grabbing my shot glass, I pushed it to him. "One more."

He grinned, but his eyes were hungry. They were angry.

I didn't care. I was starting to relax. He wasn't going to hurt me. He said it and I was beginning to trust him. "You're not going to tell your brother?"

"No." He set the bottle down. It landed with a thud and he held onto it for a second. His head hung down.

I waited.

The moment grew tense suddenly.

Then he lifted his head again; his eyes were so haunted. "I'm going to let my brother do what he wants to. I know what Kade's doing with that whore that hurt you. It's fucking genius. It's cold, too."

He pinned me down with his gaze. I glanced away. For some reason, I didn't want to see what he was thinking.

"You don't know, do you?" He tone softened. "Or you don't want to know."

I swallowed over a knot. It felt like glue, and it wouldn't go away.

"That's it. You don't want to know."

"Why do you care?" I snapped at him. I was stretched too thin. My need to keep control was beginning to unravel. "Why do you even give a damn?"

"Because of you."

I stopped. There was that raw honesty again, and I felt ashamed. "Why?"

"Because you don't deserve what Budd's going to do to that girl. That's why."

"You're lying to your brother. You're lying about Mason. I'm supposed to believe you're doing it for me? You asked me out once. You don't know me."

He let out a deep breath. His hand gripped the bottle tighter, and he shrugged, but he wouldn't look me in the eyes anymore. His went back down. "I know two things. I can't stop my brother. He's obsessed with hurting Kade's girlfriend, and he won't stop until he does. The other thing I know is that it can't be you. You're a good person. There aren't many around anymore."

Then I damned us both. "Thanks."

He looked up now and our gazes locked.

"But you're wrong," I said. "I'm starting to figure it out."

"Don't," he rushed out. "Stop thinking and go back home. You'll be safer, and the regret won't eat at you then."

I shook my head. "You're too late." It was rising in me, and it was going to eat at my soul. I felt the darkness closing in.

"Brett!" someone called from the hallway. "They're here."

"Yeah."

The door opened. I expected more of his friends, and I waited. They'd come in, or he would tell them to leave. I wasn't expecting to hear my name in a gasp. "Sam!"

I whipped around. Heather was frozen in place. Her mouth hung open, and her eyes were wide, but they darted past my shoulder and grew in size. Channing came around her. He was less surprised and waved at me. Then he nodded to Brett. "Thanks, man."

"Sam," Heather choked out again. She jerked out of her frozen state. "You're okay?"

Brett was behind me so I couldn't see him, but I heard a small growl come from him.

Channing laughed and urged Heather back out the door. "Thanks for letting us know. We'll take it from here."

"Don't let her back here."

"No problem. We won't." Channing pushed Heather the rest of the way into the hallway and came back inside. He held a hand to me. "Sam?"

Glancing at Brett again, I didn't know what to say. I wanted to see Mason. It was why I came.

"Sam?"

Brett jerked his head towards the door. "Go."

I took a deep breath. I was going. There it was. I surrendered to a battle inside of me that I didn't know was going on. There were things at play that I didn't understand. He insinuated the same thing.

Go back home... The regret won't eat at you then.

His statement haunted me, even as I took two steps backwards, and Channing grabbed my arm. I was pulled into the hallway and hurried out of there. Heather wrapped an arm around my shoulders. Her hand went to the top of my head and she applied enough pressure to force my head down. I was swept out of there, down a back alley, and away.

"SALUTE!"

I jumped as Budd's voice ripped through the air.

Heather cursed under her breath, and our pace quickened.

He yelled out another cheer, and as we kept going, his voice got quieter. It wasn't until we had covered three more blocks that we slowed down. I knew the second we passed into friendly territory. Heather dropped her hand from my head, and she let out a deep, "Thank God."

My head went up and I saw a lot of Fallen Crest people, but it was the same reaction as before. All eyes rested on me. As Channing led us further down the street, the word had spread. They knew we were coming. One by one, they turned to watch us. I felt their gazes before we went past them, and I continued to feel their gaze on our backs.

"Where are we going?"

Heather's hand tightened on the top of my arm. She pressed into me, and I knew I was supposed to shut up. When we got to a back parking lot, her arm dropped from me and she moved away.

Channing cut across the lot. A group of trucks were in the back. The tailgates had been lowered so people sat on top of them. Lounge chairs were set up in a circle and coolers were spread all over. A guy reached down into one and pulled out a beer.

"What are you doing here?" Heather asked me now in a quiet voice. She moved closer, but her arm didn't reach around me again.

I shrugged. My mind was racing. I didn't have that answer anymore.

She sighed. "We're mostly around Fallen Crest people now, but there's still a few Roussou people here. All of Channing's friends are close by, but you shouldn't have come here."

"Why?" That was the answer. That was why I came. I wanted to know why Mason hadn't called. Why Logan remained silent. Why Heather was with Channing for the weekend. Why I felt like my insides were being ripped out. I wasn't leaving until I found out.

"Holy shit."

Finally.

Logan stood behind me, a beer in hand. I turned all the way around, and when he saw my face, the beer slipped from his hand. It splattered on the ground, spraying everywhere. He didn't move. His eyes never left mine. Then his eyes bulged out before he lunged for me.

His hand grabbed my arm, and he hissed at Heather, "What the hell were you thinking?!"

"We didn't. I didn't. She came by herself."

"What?!" His eyes were fierce. "What are you thinking, Sam? It's dangerous here."

I waited for Heather to tell him the rest. She didn't. As my gaze darted to hers, her head shook from side to side. It was the slightest of movements. She didn't want Logan to know about Brett. I nodded to her, the same slightest of movements. The corners of her mouth lifted up in a faint grin. It vanished as quick as it appeared and then she started to move away.

"Wait." I held her phone out. "Your brother gave it to me. Wanted me to give it to you if I saw you."

"Oh." She ran her thumb across the screen and typed in the password. As she saw the missed calls and text alerts from me, she looked up. An apology was there.

I lifted a shoulder. I was here. It didn't matter anymore.

"Let's go," Logan growled in my ear.

"Be nice to her."

He swung back around to Heather. "Are you kidding me?"

"Be nice to her," she repeated. A different message was sent between them, and she added, "You're not seeing it from her eyes."

He stopped. Whatever she meant, it hit him. More curses slipped out before his hand gentled on my arm. "Come on, Sam. I'll take you home."

"Can you drive?"

"Yes." He looked as if he'd seen his own ghost. "I'm suddenly very sober." Then he turned and I started to go with him. It was then that I saw them.

Everything stopped.

My heart froze.

My lungs shrunk.

Everything shattered.

Knowing about it hadn't prepared me. Hearing about it hadn't prepared me, but seeing it was the worst way for it to become real.

Mason was sitting on the back of a truck. It had been pulled so it was hidden behind the others, but it wasn't the sight of him that had a dagger slicing through my insides. Kate was straddling him. Her breasts were pushed against his chest, and she had both arms around him. She grabbed a fistful of his hair as she gyrated on top of him, rubbing against him. A smirk came over him as he took hold of the back of her neck and tilted her head to the side. Then his mouth opened over hers, demanding entrance, and she shuddered in his arms.

She shuddered for him and so did I, but for different reasons.

Logan pulled me backwards. "Come on, Sam." His tone softened, and he led me away. He was trying to be gentle with me, all the way to his car and as he took me home, but it didn't matter.

I was numb again.

CHAPTER
TWENTY-FIVE

My house was cold when I went inside. Logan flipped the lights on, but I shook my head. I didn't want them on. He didn't see me and went to the counter. A note was there and he lifted it to read, "Samantha, I am at Malinda's. Please call me when you get in and I will come home. Love, David." He lowered it, a slight sneer on his face. "Gee. That's sweet of him."

"Shut up."

He put the note back. "Sorry."

Images of them flashed in my mind. Mason on the truck. Kate on him. His mouth on hers. Her hand twisting in his hair. They kept coming and I couldn't stop them. If I closed my eyes, they were worse. I was there again. When he tilted her head to the side and opened his mouth, I flinched. My eyelids flew up, but it didn't matter. They were still there.

They were all I could see.

"Here."

Feeling something cold being pushed into my hand, I looked down. Logan was holding a glass to me. He held the bottle up in his other hand. "I found your dad's secret stash. He's got good taste."

"What is this?"

"Does it matter?"

I drank it. It was like water, and I held my glass up again. "More." I needed more than more. Tonight I wanted to get drunk. All the pain needed to stop. I wanted to go back to being numb. Life was so much easier then.

We didn't talk. Logan took my glass from my hand and went into the living room. When he went to turn the light on,

I cried out, "Don't." He heard me this time and let the dark remain. I sat on one couch, and he took a chair across from me. The large windows were behind him and moonlight shone inside; no curtains restricted it. It felt warming to me. I had no idea why, maybe if the lights were on then I'd have to face reality. If the lights remained off, I could still hide.

If that was the case, I never wanted to turn the lights on again. I wanted to hide from this. I wanted to run, but I couldn't, so I asked for another drink. That'd be my escape for the night.

It wasn't until my fourth drink that I began to feel the alcohol. I drew in a shuddering breath. It needed to work faster. I thrust my glass out and leaned forward. "Again."

Logan raised an eyebrow, but he filled it. Leaning back, he tipped the bottle and drank straight from it. His glass was left forgotten on the table beside him. As he finished and tucked the bottle into the seat beside him, he asked, "You want to talk about it?"

"No." Yes, but not with him. I sighed and gave in. "Did he fuck her?"

"Not that I know."

"What do you know?"

"That he did it all to protect you."

I shook my head. That wasn't good enough. He was with her and not me—he was kissing her, touching her, tasting her—my stomach rolled over, and pain flooded back in. I couldn't get the images out of my head.

"Sam." Logan leaned forward. Resting his arms on his legs, he dipped his head down and waited.

I shook my head again.

He didn't look away.

I waved my hand at him instead.

Still nothing. He gave me a faint grin. "I'm not going anywhere."

"You did," I choked out. "You both did. You left me."

"That was for you—"

"It wasn't." It so wasn't. They did that for them. "You could've texted me or called. You ignored my calls." I was left out of the loop. Didn't they get that? No, Mason wasn't there. Didn't Logan get it? There was complete silence from them and no warning that it was going to happen.

My chest constricted. It was like before. David dropped me. So did Garrett. I had them or I thought I had them and then nothing after that. I drew in a painful breath. I couldn't go through that again, and I thought I had. Mason still wasn't here. He was still with her.

So much damn pain and Logan had no clue how it felt.

"You're lucky, do you know that?"

He frowned, but leaned back in his chair again. The bottle was lifted for another drink. His eyes were lidded, but I knew he was going to let me talk.

"Your parents would do anything for you."

Logan snorted.

My eyes jerked to his. "What's that mean? Your parents would. Your mother moved back here for you guys."

"Yeah and she did that because my dad's choosing his new psycho over his sons." He stared right back at me, without pausing or breaking stride. His tone was cool. "And my dad doesn't love your mom. You have to know that, don't you? She's his pet project. It's like he's trying to make up for all his past fuck-ups by fixing her. It's pathetic. No, Sam. We're not that lucky. We've got a messed-up parents just like you."

I drew in a breath. "Did yours slap you around?"

"Did yours tell you to fuck a colleague's daughter because she was fat and lonely?" Logan laughed to himself. His eyes were hard. "The guy didn't even care that she'd be hurt later. He said the one time would be enough for her to hold onto through college. He said he had no hope for his daughter finding a guy, and one good screw could help her out."

"You know who your parents are."

"So do you," he threw right back. Lifting the bottle again, he drank from it and tucked it back in place. "What are you doing, Sam? Tit for tat? Are you trying to make me feel sorry for you? Mason's not with her because he wants to be. He's with her to protect you."

"How?" It ripped from me. "He gave her what she wants. She won, Logan. Don't you get that? She beat me up, tried to make my friend dump me, and she didn't even get in trouble for it. That's not right."

"She got ISS."

"In-school suspension is not good enough." I shot forward.

So did he. "Stop. Your ribs, Sam."

"I'm too drunk to feel it." But not drunk enough to stop the other pain. Those images kept flooding in. I couldn't get rid of them. "Why didn't she get in more trouble? Why wasn't she arrested? She should've been arrested."

Logan sighed. "You want the truth?"

It was my turn to snort. "It's all I've ever wanted. No one tells the truth anymore."

"Kate's uncle is a cop. That's why she didn't get arrested. When Principal Green was going to expel her, he got a visit from her uncle and some of his buddies. They twisted his arm so she only got in-school suspension, and he can't let the ringleader off and expel the other three, so all four got ISS."

"It's bullshit."

"Yeah." He didn't hide from it. "That's why we don't bother with reporting shit. We learned long ago it doesn't do a thing. We settle things our way now."

Their way? "Screwing the enemy? Is that how you do it?"

"No, Sam." He stood. "Is that all you can think about? Look, Mason didn't want you to know about it. He's protecting you again so that you're not a part of it. I know you've had a rough ride, but what have we done to lose your trust?"

"He's fucking her," I cried out and pushed up from the couch. Then I swayed. The alcohol made me sluggish, but a sudden sharp stabbing had me falling to the side. Grabbing my side, I bent over again.

Logan cursed, but caught me. "Sam, stop. Sit down."

I shook my head and pushed him away. Then I regretted it. He was sturdy. He was strong. I needed his support at that moment. "Logan."

Everything crumbled inside me. A sob escaped me, but then he was there. He sat on the couch beside me and pulled me into him. A hand went to my head, pushing it down to his chest, but then it didn't matter. I was clinging to him as more and more tears racked through me.

The image of Mason with her wouldn't stop. It repeated over and over.

"Logan."

"Shhh." He began running a hand down my back and smoothing down my hair. "You can cry, Sam. You can always cry. You just can't let it stop you from fighting. That's the only thing."

He was touching her. He was kissing her. I couldn't think about it. Shaking my head against Logan's shoulder, I clutched his shirt even tighter and pressed into him.

Logan drew in a breath, and he never released it. He had gone from being comforting to being rigid.

I pressed even more against him. Mason was still touching her in my mind. Her hand gripped his hair, and she was moving over his lap in a seductive rhythm. A growl burst from me. I hated it. I hated her. "Logan." I shuddered against him.

"Sam." His voice broke and he quieted.

I clambered to get closer. Lifting my legs onto the couch, I kneeled beside him, pressing into the couch so I was almost on his lap. His hand swept down and caught one of my legs. He lifted it with me, and I let out a ragged breath. I needed his comfort. That was all I needed. Slipping my arms around him, I hugged him. My cheek went to his shoulder, and my eyes closed.

"Sam," he murmured again. His hand began rubbing on my thigh where he gripped me. "You need to stop. Your ribs can't take this."

He was right. I tried to get closer to him.

"You're going to fracture them again."

I was, but Mason was still touching her. His lips were on hers. He wanted to slip inside of her, and she let him. She savored it. I could tell. That was my place. She had replaced me. "Logan," I whispered now.

His hand smoothed my hair, running down and over my back to circle up and repeat the caress. His other hand was rubbing over my thigh.

I paused.

A small trigger went off. Mason. He was close. I felt his presence how I always felt him, but that wasn't true. It was in my mind. He was with her. Kissing her. Stroking her.

It was like his hand went into my chest and grabbed my heart. He squeezed it with every memory. He was with her. I needed it gone. Now. Anyway I could, and I felt Logan's hand then. It touched the side of my face and I turned back to him. Mason moved to the back of my mind.

"What the fuck?"

But he wasn't. I turned. Mason was standing right there. He wasn't in the back of my mind anymore.

Logan's hand jerked away, like it'd been burned. He lifted me off his lap to the couch and stood up. "It's not what you think."

Mason was there. The timing struck me, and I started laughing. He was there now, and *that* was all he had to say. Neither of them said another word. Both were silent and I couldn't stop laughing. No. I was crying now. The booze wasn't helping. I was still feeling everything, even the pain from my ribs were hurting me again. I tried to stop laughing, but I couldn't. The couch had imprisoned me. I curled to my side and stopped laughing enough so I could draw in a deep breath.

Shit. My ribs were really hurting.

"Is she drunk?" Mason asked now.

That struck me as even more hilarious. High-pitched laughter peeled from me. Then I begin giggling in between, alternating between the two with a sniffle every now and then. Nope. I sobbed now. More laughter, giggle, sobbing. I couldn't stop.

Logan's voice lowered. He was cautious. "She saw you and Kate."

"I know," Mason whipped at him.

The rage was there. He was barely holding it back. I recognized it, but I couldn't say anything. I was able to stop the laughs so only giggles came from me, but then I realized I didn't want to stop. It would hurt again once I did. He'd been touching her.

"Sam."

I held a hand out to stop him and buried my head into the couch. It muffled some of my hysteria.

"What the hell did you do to her?" he growled.

Logan snapped back, "What do you think? She saw you with Kate."

"I told her—"

"She saw you, Mason! You're ready to beat me up because I was *comforting* her. You were *making out* with another girl. Put two and two together."

"I am."

"You're not. She's hurting, like a lot, and not just from seeing you and Kate. She's drunk as hell, but her ribs have gotta be killing her."

Mason cursed.

My laughter had subsided to soft chuckles now, but I still couldn't stop them. So much damn pain was slicing through me. I couldn't move so I stayed there, curled into the couch, my head pressed against the cushion. It hid the tears that I couldn't stop either.

I was a mess.

But they were there. Both of them. This was what I wanted. I needed to know they would come back. Someone sat beside me and the couch shifted underneath me. Another burst of fresh pain went through me. This time it was like a knife had been stuck deep into me. It was pulled back out and back in, over and over.

"I'm sorry, Sam." Mason touched my arm now. It was so gentle, so tender. It brought a new wave of tears. He tugged on me.

"Be gentle with her."

"Can you leave us alone?"

He wanted to talk to me, but I couldn't talk to him now. What had I done? No. What had I been about to do? Another image of Kate straddling him flared again and I stopped crying.

"Sam," he murmured again as a door shut somewhere in the house. His arms slid underneath me on the couch, and I was lifted in the air a moment later.

I froze. He was going to jar everything again, but he didn't. He moved me in the exact position I was in. No new pain went through me. Then I was lifted to his lap instead. It felt wrong. All of this was wrong. Gritting my teeth, I pushed past the pain and stood from him.

"Sam." He stood with me.

"No."

"Yes."

"NO." Everything was muddled in my head, but he touched another girl. That wasn't okay with me. "You shouldn't have done that."

"Sam." He reached for me again.

Slapping his hand down, I seethed, "You shouldn't have. You fucked her."

"I didn't."

"You did." He must have. That was how she was kissing him, as if they had...

"I didn't. I swear." The disgust was clear in his voice. "I only touched her when Roussou people were around. I had to, Sam. I had to do it. It saved you, and it hurt her. It will. I didn't cheat on you."

"You were kissing her."

"Because I had to," he ground out. "I had to. Don't you see that? He had to know about her. He was looking for you the whole time. It was only a matter of time before your name was slipped. I couldn't let him hurt you. I couldn't."

I stopped to breathe. One moment, that was all I needed. My head was pounding. A stabbing pain kept overwhelming me, over and over again. I held a hand out for him to stop. I needed another moment.

"Sam," he choked out.

"Stop."

"I can't."

"Please."

"NO... no."

"Mason," it left me in a whimper. He went away for only one night and day. That was all it took for me to become a mess, for my world to crumble. I swung my gaze to the couch. I'd been there before with—I shook my head. Standing there, I was hurting and all I wanted was to be in his arms. I wanted all of it to go away, but it wouldn't. I shook my head. It wouldn't. I knew too much. "What's he going to do to her?"

"I don't know."

"Couldn't you stop him some other way?"

"Not Budd Broudou. He hates me, Sam. He's going to hurt me the worst way he could, and that's through you. Do you see what I was doing now? He wanted my girlfriend, so I gave him a girlfriend. I spent an entire week with her touching me, but it wasn't until last night that I kissed her. I swear. He had to be there, and he needed to see us tonight, too."

"Is it going to be enough?"

He lifted his hands in a helpless gesture. "I hope. Once Budd sees something for his own eyes, he doesn't go against it. He won't trust what other people tell him. Besides, something tells me that there are people close to him who won't let him know about you."

I felt the extra kick behind his words. He knew. "Brett."

"Yeah," he bit out.

Hopelessness hit me hard then. There was so much distance between us now. Brett had been...what lie? I couldn't remember now. "I meant to tell you about him."

"It would've been nice to know my girlfriend was on a first-name basis with one of them, or when you first ran into them?"

I flinched from the accusation in his tone. "You lied to me, too."

"When?"

"Don't play that game with me."

"When? I told you what I was doing with Kate—"

"With Logan," I cried out. My heart started pounding again. It was racing. "You lied to me about Tate, and why you stopped giving a crap if they hooked up or not. Why, Mason?! Why?"

"Because he wants to screw with her," he threw back. His green eyes were heated, but he was holding back.

That wasn't why. I jerked my head in a nod, but began looking for that bottle again. "You just lied to me. Again."

"What are you talking about?"

It wasn't in the chair. I rounded to the couch and felt under the cushions.

"What are you looking for?"

"Alcohol."

"You don't drink that much."

A harsh laugh ripped from me. "I do tonight. I'm going to keep drinking a whole shitload tonight." My insides were churning, and the hysteria was starting to rise again.

"Sam."

I stopped. His voice broke and I heard his defeat in my name. I turned from the couch, my heart paused and my breath held. He had fallen against the wall and was leaning against it now. His green eyes were stricken as he hunched forward.

Whatever tension that was between us was gone.

I didn't speak. I didn't dare. I felt something coming. It was the old Mason, before the lies got between us. I felt him coming back, and I wanted it so badly. I wanted *him* so badly. *Please...*

He slid down the wall to the floor and sat there. His eyes never left me. They were usually so intense and powerful. They could pierce through all my walls. He had since the beginning, but it was me this time. I pierced through his and he surrendered to me. I took a step towards him. My heart began beating rapidly. I missed him so damn much. "You touched another girl."

"It was the only way, Sam. I know it hurt you, and I'm sorry for that. It was the only way. She hurt you. I can't let that go. No one hurts you and Budd wanted to. I've stopped that too now."

What could I say to that? I had no idea, but I took another step. I saw it then. He was sorry. As I closed the distance and stood above him, his head tipped back. There was agony inside of him, but determination too. He would do it again. That knowledge slammed against me, and I stumbled back a step.

"Sam." He reached for me and caught the back of my leg. His hand cupped me there, and he pulled me back to him. "Please."

"You lied to me."

"Because I see that it's already getting to you. He's going to hurt her. I didn't want you to know. I didn't want that on your conscience."

"But it is now."

"Yeah. It is now."

I drew in a sudden breath. He was right. He was right about everything. He touched her, but it was for me. He lied to me. I lied to him. I was so tired of it all, and I just wanted him again. Mason had been my shelter for so long. The world hurt when I wasn't with him. Folding my knees, I bent, and he caught me. He pulled me onto his lap like I had never left.

I was home again. Cradling my head in his hand, he took a deep breath. I felt his relief because it was mine, too. Our old connection was coming back, but I couldn't forget what Brett had warned.

"Go back home... The regret won't eat at you then"

Mason's arm slid around me, and I was moved so my back rested against his chest. "What's Budd going to do to her?" I asked.

She had kissed Mason. She ran her hands over him and pushed her breasts against him. Anger clawed at me. She wanted to take what was mine.

"I don't know." His arms tightened around me. His tone was soothing once again. "But it's not you. That's all I care about. Better her than you."

He knew my lies, but he still held that one truth from me. It took root inside of me, and it was going to grow until it would take over us. I was too weak to fight for it now. He evaded, but he was here. He was mine. That would be enough...for now.

CHAPTER TWENTY-SIX

"Hey." Logan came back from the back porch, the bottle in one hand, his phone in the other, wearing a dark frown. "Not to interrupt, but I just checked my phone."

Mason stiffened underneath me. "Yeah?"

"Yeah." That didn't sound good. "We have a problem."

Of course we did.

"Just say it, Logan. Stop beating around the bush."

"Tate called me. Actually," he lifted the phone as if we could see her calls, "she called me ten times and texted another seven times."

Mason stiffened underneath me. He leaned his head back against the wall. "What about?"

"Uh..."

"Logan."

"Okay." His shoulders lifted when he sucked in a deep breath. "So when you shooed me out of Sam's room when she was in the hospital, I wasn't thinking clear, and I needed to get my mind off things..."

"Spill it."

"Yeah." The hand with his phone went to his hair and he grabbed onto some of his locks, pulling at them so they stuck up. His other hand tightened around the bottle. His shirt rode up, exposing the waistband of his boxers. His jeans slipped down an inch, but Logan wasn't aware. He shook his head. "I forgot all about it."

He stopped again. Seriously.

"Yeah, so I went to Tate's that night, and we were in the living room. No one else was there. There was a time when she went to the bathroom, and I was looking through her magazines."

"Logan, tell us what happened."

His hand dropped from his hair. "They have video tape of Tate giving me a blow job."

"What?"

I began to giggle again. This night couldn't get any worse.

"Like I said," Logan's head went down. His shoulders drooped. "I can't believe this. I wasn't thinking that night. Now Tate's freaking out. She thought I covered the camcorder. She never knew where it was, and I stopped caring. I thought it would've ran out of batteries, but I guess they fixed that somehow."

"How'd they get the camcorder back?"

Logan groaned.

Mason cursed. "Just tell us."

"It's because of you." His hand jerked up and gestured to Mason. "Tate was freaking out because she thought you and Kate were tight again. She said they came over this afternoon to get ready for the street dance together. She let them in. She figured if they were tight with us again, she didn't want to be on Kate's shit-list anymore."

More curses spewed from Mason. He was like cement underneath me. Lifting a hand to his chest, I felt his heartbeat going off like a stampede. His eyes caught and held mine, but I couldn't share in his misery.

They got Tate giving Logan a blow job. That was karma.

He explained the misery. "I have to kiss Kate's ass again and get all those copies from her."

"Yeah." Logan came into the room and collapsed down on the couch. His elbows went to his knees, and he leaned forward. The bottle and phone were left on the cushion beside him, and he covered his face with his hands. They slid into his hair again and he tugged once more on his strands. "This blows."

Literally.

I snorted at the joke, but stopped. Neither of them were amused.

Another curse sounded from Mason, and then he asked, "What do they want from Tate?"

"Huh?" Logan glanced back up. His eyes were glazed over, and I wondered how full that bottle had been in the beginning. There were only a few droplets left inside.

"Tate."

"Oh. Yeah. Uh, she needs to find out where Sam's living now. Guess you weren't too sharing with Kate over the week, huh?"

"Are you kidding me? She's still looking to fuck Sam over?"

"I'm sure Kate thinks she has free reign since you two are hooking back up again. Probably hopes you won't find out until after she finishes whatever she has planned. That's what I'd do." He caught the glare from Mason and corrected, "At least that's what she thinks, that you two are good. Not that you are, not from your side, but whatever. She's a hateful bitch. Let's go blast her. I've had enough dealing with them all week."

Mason groaned as his hand curved on the inside of my thigh. His finger rubbed between my legs in a smooth motion as he started to lift me back to my feet. I gave him a lopsided grin when he stood next to me, and his hands found my waist once again.

I was still drunk. A bit.

He shook his head, but the corners of his mouth curved up. Pressing his lips to my forehead and then to my lips, he whispered at the same time, "I love you. You need to know that."

I did. As they headed off and I stayed back, I continued to know that. Then I grabbed my phone and dialed Mark's number. When he answered, out of breath, I told him, "You need to come pick me up again."

"What? Come on—"

"You said you'd help."

He grew quiet, then groaned. "Fine. Be there in a little bit. I'm in the," he hesitated, "middle of something."

"Again?!" someone screeched in the background.

It was a screech that I recognized, and I couldn't hold back a smirk. "Cass? Really?"

"Yeah," he grumbled. "Hold on. I'm getting clothes on. You're at your dad's?"

"Yeah."

"Alright. See you in a few."

Yes, I knew Mason loved me. Yes, I knew he was doing all of this to protect me, but I wasn't a sucker. I was going to be at that confrontation. Nothing was going to stop me from being there with front row tickets. When Mark pulled into the driveway twenty minutes later, I was glad that I hadn't changed out of my clothes or washed my make-up off. He gave me a quick perusal and nodded in approval. "Can't see the bruises anymore, but you smell like booze."

My day was complete. "Thanks. Just what every girl wants to hear."

He grinned. "Where to, boss?"

Where would Kate and her friends be? Or the better question is, where would they go after sending Tate a blackmail message? I shrugged. "Where's the party tonight?"

"Ethan Fischer's having a big one."

"Isn't there supposed to be a bonfire tonight?"

"That's a no-go. The only way back there is next to Quickie's, and they shut it down. I guess the clerk keeps getting beat up by the Broudou brothers, so they've been banned. I heard police were even going to be there, and if the Broudou's can't go, no one from Roussou's going. Hence," he flashed his dimples at me, "there's a Public party at Fischer's. I was there earlier."

It was perfect. "That's where we're going."

He didn't move. In fact, he turned the engine off.

"Mark?"

"You sure about this?"

"What do you mean?" There was something in his gaze that made me uncomfortable. As he continued to stare at me, the more I wanted to run. Then it clicked. Pity. He felt sorry for me. "I know."

"You do?"

"About Kate and Mason?"

His eyes widened.

"I know. That's why I'm going."

"They weren't there before."

"Let's go, Mark." They were going to be there. *She* was going to be there, and so was I. I wasn't going to miss this for the world.

MASON

"They're late."

I glanced at Logan as he checked his phone for the fourth time. We were waiting in my car, parked outside of Ethan's house, and I was tempted to punch my little brother. "We've been here five minutes. Relax."

"You relax," Logan shot back. "We need to get in there and get that video back from Kate. If it were Sam in it, you'd go steal the video from Kate's house."

"I wouldn't."

"You would too and we both know it."

"You're not pissed about the damn video and we both know it."

Logan didn't comment on that, not that I expected him to, but I rolled my eyes and sighed as I leaned back in my seat. Twenty people were running around Ethan's front yard in rhythm to the bass from inside. Drunken idiots. The entire night had been fucked up. The hurt in Sam's eyes wasn't something I'd forget any time soon, but I shoved that memory aside, for now.

"Finally." Logan pressed a button and his window went down.

Ethan, Strauss and Derek broke away from the crowd and crossed the street. A few from the front yard watched them, but no one followed.

"Yo." Ethan led the way around to Logan's side. He held onto the Escalade's top and leaned against it. "What's the plan?"

Logan glanced at me.

I leaned forward. "You guys got all your things ready to go?"

Ethan looked to the other two, and they all nodded. "Looks like. That was the plan we hashed out at Nate's. I didn't know it was going down tonight."

"It is."

"Okay. Sounds fine to me." A cruel grin came over him. "I love butchering little shits."

Derek snorted in laughter. Strauss nudged him out of the way, hitting his shoulder into Ethan's harder than necessary.

"Ouch, man."

Strauss ignored him and addressed me, "I thought you were waiting another day."

"This idiot," I pointed at Logan, "got caught getting a blow job on camcorder."

Ethan and Derek burst out in laughter. Strauss grinned, but reached inside and punched Logan's shoulder. "Should I congratulate you or call you a moron?"

Derek snickered. "Depends on who the girl is."

A fresh burst of laughter came from Ethan. "Did she deep throat you?"

"Could she?"

They kept laughing.

Logan cursed and slammed his hand against the car door. "Shut the fuck up."

"Shit." Derek straightened away from the vehicle. "I thought this was a topic we could laugh about. You would be if it happened to one of us."

"You better run, Streeter," Logan threatened, his hand going to his door handle. "I'm going to beat your ass until—"

"Enough." I stepped out and slammed my door. As I rounded to their side, I asked Ethan, "Kate's inside?"

"Not yet. You called her?"

"Yeah. I told her to bring everything."

"You think she will?"

I shrugged, glancing at Logan from the corner of my eye. "She knows I hate Tate."

Derek snorted. "And she thinks the two of you are tight again."

"Yeah."

Strauss slapped his hand to Derek's chest and pushed him back a step. He moved in front of me. "Kate stopped sniffing around us when she thought the two of you were good again. Is that going to be a problem?"

"No. We just need proof she was coming around before that."

"We got that."

Logan got out of the Escalade as I told Strauss, "You and Derek stay up top. We'll do this downstairs."

"I cleared it out when I got your text," Ethan added.

"Good." I glanced at Logan. "Where's Tate?"

He checked his phone. "She's inside. I'll tell her to hide in a room downstairs for now. You know Sam's probably headed here too."

Everything was falling in place, except for that.

As we started for the house, I told Strauss, "Sam will figure out where we're at. She's got too many buddies from FCA here. Don't stop her, just let her through. We'll have Tate play interference when she gets into the basement." I didn't like it, but she was coming no matter what. "And don't let anyone touch her. She's still hurting. A lot."

Strauss asked, "What about the other girls?"

"Kate and Parker can come down with us right away. Hold Natalie and Jasmine back."

"But what about the stuff? They need to hear it, don't they?"

"We'll text you when to let them hear. Ethan, give yours to Streeter. He can play it for Jasmine."

Swapping phones, Ethan smirked at the other guy. "Good luck with that. She's going to go nuts on you."

Derek paled, but jerked around to me. "What do we do then? He's right. They're both going to flip."

"Then let them through."

Logan remarked, "That's the whole plan, dumbass."

When we crossed the street, people stopped what they were doing on the front lawn. A tackling game paused. Conversations halted. People looked up, but no one said a word as we walked past them. It was the same effect inside. The music continued playing, but the partying halted until we were downstairs. As we descended the stairs, I glanced around to find the best room, but Logan tapped my arm and pulled me into a corner. Ethan got the gesture to stay back and he did. Tate came down the stairs a second later, but he pulled her over to him.

Logan waited to make sure she wouldn't head to our corner. He lowered his voice then, "What are you going to do if Kate goes to Broudou? She's going to get mad. She could tell him the truth about who Sam is."

I shook my head. He was right, there was a chance. "There's people in Broudou's camp that are covering for her. He saw Kate and me. We both know he doesn't trust other people's word, just what he sees for himself."

"And when he does whatever he's going to do?"

"Channing said he'd let us know. We'll call the cops."

"She won't go to the cops. Kate hates being the victim."

I flashed him a grin, though my eyes were dead. "We'll make a personal call to her uncle. We both know how protective he's been."

"He's going to hurt her bad. We're okay with that?"

Thinking about what Kate did to Sam and knowing it could happen again, but by Budd Broudou reaffirmed everything for me. I didn't care what he did to her. I was too dead inside to care. "He was going to hurt Sam. All we're doing is giving him a different target. You know that."

Logan nodded with the same darkness coming over him. "Okay."

"Okay?"

"Yeah."

Another look passed between us. An image of Sam in that hospital bed flashed in my mind. It haunted me. All the bruises, dried blood, how frail she looked in that bed would haunt me for the rest of my life. This was what I needed to do to make sure it didn't happen again.

I headed to Ethan's rec room and went to the far wall. Logan filled Tate in on her part of the plan. She disappeared into a separate room. Then he came to stand beside me while Ethan took position next to the pool table in front of us.

The door was left open, but it wasn't long until I heard Kate's voice.

It was go-time.

SAMANTHA

Cars were lined around the block, as well as the next block over. When he pulled into a back alley, there were a few hidden spots open behind Fischer's house. Cutting across the backyard, a lot of people waved at Mark. I recognized a few people from Academy spread out throughout the yard, but when we went up the back porch, the Elite had taken their spots. From how they were sitting, with everyone beneath them, it looked like they were perched on their thrones, reigning over the lower class. All of them were there: Miranda was on Peter's lap; Amelia; Emily; even Adam was sitting with them. When I turned to go inside and make my way to the kitchen, Cassandra was pushing her way out. Both of her hands held cups of beer. A sneer came over her when she saw me. "You really need to get over this stepbrother thing. It makes you look like trash, but then again, you are trash."

"Does Adam know that you finally gave up your obsession with him? Or is it not public knowledge you're stalking Mark now?"

Mark laughed from behind me.

Cassandra sucked in her breath, and her hand raised. I was waiting for it. It wouldn't be the first beer thrown at a party.

Adam swooped in. His hand covered Cass's and he took the cup from her. "Thanks, Cass. I owe you."

"Yeah," she said, raking me up and down. "You sure do." Storming past me, she would've rammed her shoulder into mine, but Mark stepped right next to me. She would've ran right into him, but growled as she was forced to go around him instead. I waited. She rammed her shoulder into his. Mark's laugh was cut off, but then he started chuckling again.

Turning to us, he rubbed at his shoulder. "The girl can hit. If she can do that with her shoulder, I'm excited to find out what else she can do in bed when she's angry."

Adam frowned, but shook his head. "I said it before, and I'll say it again. Are you sure you know what you're doing?"

"Screwing Cass?"

"Dating Cass."

"Oh, come on. It's not like that."

"You will be. Before you know it, you will be."

I was still wondering what happened with Amelia, but I caught a glimpse of Logan. He was walking past the kitchen door. "I have to go."

"Sam," Adam started.

His hand caught mine, but I shook him off. "I'm fine."

"Sam."

"I am," I reassured both of them before turning and following Logan.

Kate walked past the kitchen door, too. The rest of the Tommy Princesses followed behind like ducklings, but there were too many people between us. I couldn't get to the living room fast enough. When I did, it was full of Fallen Crest Public people, but no Mason. All the people I wanted to see were nowhere to be seen.

"Sam?" Jeff stood up from a couch. His arm had been around a girl, and he grabbed her hand, pulling her with him as he crossed to my corner. "What are you doing here?"

A light bulb was flickering as I stared at his girl. She looked familiar—wait. Adam. Basketball game. "Your name is Kris. I saw you at the basketball game last week."

"Oh." A faint smile came over her small lips. Her hand was pulled from Jeff's, and she wrapped her arms around her petite frame. "I didn't see you there."

Jeff threw an arm around her shoulder and pulled her against his side. He announced to me, "She's friends with Jessica and Lydia, but I'm trying to make her see the error of her ways." He sent her a pointed glance. "Sam would know. They were best friends with her and..." he flailed, closing his mouth. "Never mind. So you've met Kris, huh? Quinn's trying to court her, too."

She gasped, and her head jerked down.

I gestured to the girl. "You embarrassed her."

Her shoulders stiffened, but she didn't correct me.

Jeff's smile was blinding as he squeezed her again. "It's like you 2.0, except I have a clean slate and I'm hoping without the Kade part. I can't hold up against your..." He cringed. "I need to stop talking tonight."

"Yeah, you do." Kris nudged him with her elbow.

He laughed, squeezing her again.

I sighed. "Young love. Too bad you're going to get screwed over. It's inevitable."

Jeff dropped his arm from her shoulders and they watched me with pity. I could detect that look from a mile away now. He asked, "You okay, Sam? I tried getting my 'friends' to help you, but they all said you were handling yourself fine."

"Uh. Yeah." I pointed to my face. "It's not porcelain skin underneath all this make-up."

"I know." His mouth dipped down. "I meant that I tried, you know. I told you at Nate's party that I'd try to get them to help."

This conversation was going to a bad direction. He was talking like I had died, and I still had fight in me. I needed to find Kate. I had a whole lot more fight in me. "Where'd they go?"

"Who?"

I snorted. "You're a bad actor, Jeff. You might've been able to lie to me before, but I'm smarter now and I hang out with liars who are in the professional league. Tell me where they went."

"Sam, don't do this." He reached for me.

My arm swung away from him. "Don't."

"It's not going to end well. We heard about it."

"Where are they?"

"She's been all over him this week. Even if it's not over between you two, it's," he hesitated, "it's over, Sam. He's back with her."

I was getting really sick and tired of hearing this. "You tell me where they are, or I'm going to give a character reference to your new girlfriend." I bared my teeth at him. "And it won't be a good one, if you know what I mean."

"They went downstairs. That door right there." He pointed at a door behind me. It was closed with Jasmine and Natalie guarding it. Strauss and another guy stood with them, but I marched over anyway.

"No. No way—" Jasmine started to say, raising her hand at the same time.

Strauss caught it and twisted it behind her back. The other guy opened the door for me and stepped so he was blocking Natalie from me. I sailed behind both of them without breaking stride. As the door closed behind me, I heard Jasmine cry out, "What?"

As soon as the door clicked shut, I stopped on the other side of it. The stairs were in front of me, but I grabbed the railing and held onto it. I couldn't move. Everything in me was trembling. I felt them kicking me. Hitting me. *Shut up and get her.* Kate's voice came back to me. Images flashed in my head, and I flinched with each one. I felt every hit and every kick all over again. I was back in that bathroom. It was dark, like it is now. They were coming for me.

"Hey."

I cried out, shooting my hand out. They wouldn't hurt me. Not again.

"Bitch," someone hissed at me.

My eyelids flew open—when had they closed? My hands jerked up, ready for an attack. It never came and I was staring at Tate. She was pressed against the far wall, rubbing at her throat. She cursed at me. "You hit me. That hurt."

"Oh."

We stared at each other, and no one said a word. She snorted then. "Of course you're not going to apologize."

Waves of anxiety were still crashing over me, but I wouldn't have even if I was fine. She knew it. I knew it. Why lie about it?

"I'm in this mess because of you, you know."

"How?"

"Because I backed you in the hallway."

"You backed Heather, not me."

"It doesn't matter to Kate. Once someone crosses her, she doesn't let it go. So thanks for this."

"You blew Logan when you knew a camcorder was there."

"I thought he covered it up. We don't make noises when we do things like that."

"Why in there then?"

She shrugged. "I don't know. He looked stressed. I was giving him a treat."

A bitter laugh came from me. "I don't get you two. You guys just hook up now? There's no feelings anymore?"

She smirked. "Wouldn't you like to know?"

My smile matched my tone. Brittle. "Just don't screw him over again."

"Hard to hurt someone who doesn't give a flying fuck about you anymore."

I paused.

As she started down the stairs, she added, "And he doesn't, you know."

"What? Give a flying fuck about you?"

"Care about me like that. We're friends, only friends."

I followed her to the bottom, but no one was around. "You didn't come back to be friends with him."

"No." She jerked her head to the right. "They're down there. Logan said you'd be coming, so I came to get you. They need to get the tape first."

"You didn't come back to be friends with him," I pressed.

"I didn't. You're right. My parents shipped me out here so I thought it was my second chance." She skimmed me up and down. Her top lip curved up in a sneer. "It didn't take me long to catch on that I was wasting my time."

Pausing outside a door, she reached for the door handle, but stopped. "You ready for this? Logan told me a little of what they've been planning. It's going to be brutal."

"Besides setting her up for Budd Broudou?"

"What?"

"Nothing."

"Okay. Showtime." She flashed me a grin and opened the door.

I held back. Mason had more planned? Then I heard Kate's shrill voice. "What is that whore doing here?"

CHAPTER TWENTY-SEVEN

MASON

Kate had dressed for me.

Her jeans were ripped in the crotch area. She'd worn them before, always with a skimpy thong underneath. Kate thought they turned me on, but they didn't. They never had. Those jeans were her signal that she was down for anything. I knew I could have her anyway I wanted and some of those times, I'd take her up on the offer. That was all Kate had been to me. I had an itch, and I used her to scratch it.

I regretted it now.

She came in with no question, no regret, no doubt and she came straight for me. I didn't do a thing. Someone normal would've reacted. She was coming into a trap for slaughter, but I wasn't normal. She was going to touch me and I wanted to shove her away. I didn't do that either. She ran her fingers over my chest. The tips of them trailed down to the front of my pants, and she rubbed there.

I turned it off. This was Sam touching me. This was Sam in front of me, pressing against me. I did what I had done all week. I pretended. "You have a present for me?"

"I do." Excitement lit up her face and she held up the camcorder.

I took it from her and saw she had the video ready for me to watch.

There was no sound, just an image of Logan on the couch and Tate kneeling before him. His eyes were closed as he leaned back on the couch. His hand was tangled in her hair as her head moved, sucking on him.

I passed the camcorder to Logan.

"Hey—" Kate stopped herself.

There it was—doubt. I caught it and it was the first time it showed all week. Then she stopped and it was shoved aside. Desperation flared for a moment before blind trust came back over her. She gave it so readily to me.

I told her, "He doesn't care. He just wanted to see the evidence before it goes viral."

"Oh." Relief flashed over her face.

"You have other copies?"

"Just what's on there."

"And this." Parker held up a USB drive. "We'll keep it safe."

Ethan snatched it from her hands. "I don't think so."

"Hey!"

"We'll keep it safe," I said.

Parker cast Ethan a sidelong look, but quieted.

Kate's hand grew bolder as she continued to rub on me. She was more insistent. "So what's next?"

"Did you email this to anybody?"

"Just Tate. I'm sure she's freaking out."

I glanced at Logan, who nodded. His thumb hit a button. The video was gone. With that done, I texted Nate and then nodded to Ethan. Without hesitation, Ethan took off the case, pulled the chip out and tossed the case to Logan. Then he left the room.

"Hey!" Parker cried out again. "What the hell?"

Kate frowned. "What's going on?"

I waited a minute. They needed a head start. "That was Ethan destroying your USB drive."

"What—"

"I knew we shouldn't have trusted these guys. You're an idiot, Kate," Parker snapped as she started for the door.

"It's already gone," I stopped her. "It's pointless to go after him."

"You're such an asshole."

She had no idea. "There's more to come, some of it you'll want to see."

Kate grabbed the camcorder from Logan and started searching through it. We waited, and her eyes widened the more she searched.

Logan grinned. "It's gone."

"You wiped everything."

"You're the dumb bitch who handed it over."

"Not to you," she seethed. "To Mason. I trusted him."

He rolled his eyes and laughed. "I don't even feel bad for you. You're so stupid."

She jerked back. "Mase?"

There it was again. She still didn't believe it. "I agree with my brother."

It was at that moment that she started to get it. I watched as each piece of the puzzle began to fit into place and she stumbled back a step. When she ran into the pool table behind her, she choked out, "It's on my computer. It's in my email. You're going to regret this."

I lifted my phone. "Both of those are gone. Say goodbye to your email."

My phone beeped.

"What's that?"

Parker whispered from behind her, "Oh no."

Logan began laughing. "You guys are so screwed. Getting it, Park? Did you get a text, too?"

Kate whipped around. Parker had gone pale, and she showed her phone to Kate. "It's Nate."

"Nate?"

"Yeah, Nate, you fuckheads." Logan shook his head. "He might be injured, but he's not out of action. He hasn't been the whole time. We knew about your plans for Sam. You wanted to drug her, have him make a sex tape with her?"

"Oh my god." Kate lifted stricken eyes to me. "You knew?"

Logan started to say it, but I shook my head. I needed to do this. Everything was cold inside of me. I'd been hiding it for the past week. They should've known better. Smarter people would've, but Kate wasn't sane. She was desperate so I used that to pull her back in. She saw what she wanted, but she couldn't mistake it this time. I let her see my loathing. I let her see the cold calculation and when she did, she began shaking. The blood drained from her face, and I knew she was going over everything in her head. I waited and when she gasped, I knew she remembered.

"You should've listened to me that day."

"No." She shook her head. "No. You dumped her for me."

"Did I?"

"You—"

"She hasn't been in school since we attacked her," Parker said.

Kate's mouth clamped shut and she began to turn away. "No, no, no, no... No. It can't be."

Parker growled. "It is. Get with the program. They played us. They all played us. Nate just sent me a text. It's done between me and him."

"What did you do?" Kate turned back to me. She cried out, "What did you do?!"

"Nate sent me a text just now, too." I would spell it all out for her. "He went to your home, Kate. I told him how to get in. Your dad's at the VFW, and your mom's working a double shift tonight."

She paled even more, stumbling back another step.

I continued, "That's what you told me earlier. Your mom won't be back to the house until seven tomorrow morning. You had a gift for me, and we'd have your house to ourselves for the entire night. Your dad would go to some whore's house after closing. Those were your words."

"So? I mean..." She looked to Parker, who rolled her eyes and moved away. Kate shook her head. "This can't be happening. Nate can't do anything. He—all of you guys are here. I mean..."

Logan snorted. "You're too slow to deal with us. You never should've tried."

"Nate was at your house. That was him texting me. I gave him your password, sexcontrolsthemall. You never changed it. You told me it last summer. You laughed about it. Did you forget that? You should've remembered telling me. You should've changed it when I brought Sam around."

"Sam," Kate spewed out. "Her. This is all about her, isn't it?"

"Yes." Logan hit his palm against his forehead. "Are you seriously only now getting that? He worked you, Kate. You went after the woman he loves. He TOLD you he was going to fuck you over. You didn't listen. Listen now!" He laughed to himself. "You might pick up a few pointers for the next time a guy screws you over, and it'll happen. You're dumb enough to think you're smart, but you're not. You need to be smarter to realize how stupid you are."

"Hey," Parker started, but stopped.

Logan cut his gaze to her. When she couldn't say anything, he nodded. "Exactly."

"Stay out of this Logan," Kate cursed at him. "This has nothing to do with you."

An exasperated laugh ripped from him. "You took a video of me getting a blow job? AND you beat up my stepsister. Sam's not loved by only Mason, you know. I care about her too. Any of this filtering in that thick head of yours? I can't believe how you're not shitting your pants right now. He hasn't even gotten to the good part. Parker, grab a bucket. Stick it between her legs. Shit's going to fall any second now."

"ENOUGH." Parker jerked forward a step and pulled Kate back to her. She glared at him. "She's getting it. The guy she loved just stabbed her in the back. Let her figure it out without all the insults."

"No."

Logan opened his mouth, but stopped. All three turned back to me.

I said it again, "No. You don't get to think like that. I'm not the guy she loved who turned out to be an asshole. I've always been an asshole, and I've never cared about her. I used her for sex. That was it. You don't get to spin it how you're doing it. I've been honest about that with her. I told her it was just sex with us. No girlfriend/boyfriend status. No lovers title on us. Sex. That was it."

Parker glared at him. "We were your friends."

"The group of you hung out with us, but you were never considered friends on my part. You kept the other girls away. That's the only use I enjoyed from you. You were deterrents. That was all."

"You're such an asshole." Parker wrapped her arms tighter around Kate. "It'll be okay."

"No, it won't."

"Would you stop?" Her eyes were heated now. "We got it. Nate broke into her email—"

"And put a virus on her computer," Logan added. He began chuckling again. "You guys have nothing now."

"We're getting that, too."

I nodded to Logan. It was time the rest joined the party. He sent another round of text messages to the guys, and I said, "Kate." I knew each guy would share their own recording with her friends.

She lifted her head from Parker's shoulder. It was tear-streaked, but I saw the resolve there. She was hurt. I knew that, but she would come back. She would garner the strength and support she needed from her friends and she'd launch another attack. I couldn't have that.

I shook my head "Now's not the time to act like a victim. Everyone in this room knows what you can do."

Her chest lifted as she took a deep breath, but the acknowledgement was in her depths. I baited her just now. I called her weak and Kate wasn't weak.

I was right. Everyone in the room knew it too.

She stepped away from her friend's shelter.

I smirked at her. Good. It'd be the last time that shelter would be offered. As the door opened, I asked, "You remember what I said to you at my car?"

Tate led the way. She came in first.

Kate saw a new target. "What is that whore doing here?"

"Kate," I brought her attention back to me, "do you remember?"

I felt Sam's presence and gestured for her to come to me, and she did. Kate sucked in her breath when my hand reached for Sam's, and she took it. I pulled her behind me now and Logan moved closer to shield her from the other side.

"Do you remember, Kate? You have three friends. I told you that I'd take them away." I paused for a beat. "Hey, Parker."

"What?"

She wanted to murder me, but I was going to change her mind in the next second. "Right before Nate told me what you guys wanted to do with Sam, he told me something else."

She froze. Her chest stopped moving as she stopped breathing.

Kate started under her breath, "Nononononononon—"

My voice lifted over Kate's protests as I told her friend, "There's a reason why Nate wanted to be the one to go to Kate's house. He told me about the video Kate said she had. That video of you two. That bluff started this whole thing."

Kate's voice rose in volume. "Nononononon."

"Oh my god," Parker was connecting those dots too. Her eyes were glued to Kate as she started trembling. Then her phone beeped again. Her attention was torn away as she checked it once more. When she hit a button and noises came over the room, this was it. It was a matter of moments before the rest exploded into the room.

"What is this?" Parker asked as her eyes got even bigger. They were bulging out of her face as she thrust the phone at Kate. "What the HELL IS THIS?"

She pressed a button, and the volume rose so everyone could hear.

"Come on, Nate, Parker doesn't have to know. Come on. I'll make you feel good."

"Get away from me, Kate. I know you've been going to the other guys, too."

"Only you. You help me. I'll help you."

"You can help me by telling me where the video is."

A seductive laugh came next. "There's no video, but there could be. Of you and me. If you'd like."

"There's no video?"

Her voice grew louder, as if she had taken a step closer to him. "You're hurting. I know Parker hasn't come to see you since the accident. I'll make you feel good."

"There's no video?"

"No—"

The recording stopped after that, and Parker remained holding it in the air. Her hand gripped it tightly as her chest lifted up and down. She was seething as she stared at her friend. A strangled laugh came from her next. "Were you with him? Nate's mine. MINE. You went to him and—" she choked off again.

Kate jumped back, as if expecting to be attacked. She hissed first, "I needed help. I had to find it from somewhere. I had to *create* it. We had nothing. I didn't think beating her up was going to be good enough. We needed something to make sure she stayed away. I did it for us. I needed him to help us get something on her. We needed to destroy her." As she said the last word and her lip curved in a snarl, she looked at Sam. Everyone knew who she meant. "She took him away from me. She took all of them away from us. I had to do something. We were nobodies in school again. I did that for you, too."

"You bitch—"

"He didn't believe you about the tape. He wasn't going to help, but I needed help from somewhere. It's the only reason I went to Nate. I promise. That was it. You would do the same thing..."

A door banged shut in the hallway.

They were coming, but I said first, "You did it for power, Kate. Don't delude yourself. You wanted to make Sam's friends turn on her so I did it to you first. I just used what you were already doing. I didn't blackmail you. I didn't have to threaten you, drug you, or video you. I didn't have to do any of that. You handed it to me on a silver platter."

"What else did you do?"

She snarled at me. She shouldn't waste the energy. She would need it to run from her friends. "You went to each of the guys: Nate, Ethan, Strauss, even Derek. You tried it with each of them."

"I didn't do anything with them."

"But you tried, even after they reminded you about your friends. Nate hooked up with Parker. Ethan and Jasmine used to do the same. I know Natalie's fond of Strauss. You went after their guys."

"They weren't exclusive."

I grinned at her. "I doubt they feel the same."

Then the door flung open and Jasmine stood there. She locked gazes with Parker, who said heatedly, "She hit on Nate. She hit on Ethan too?"

"Yeah," Jasmine clipped out.

Ethan stood behind her, a Cheshire Cat grin on his face. "It was a nice little recording."

"Guys." Kate began to back up.

The two joined forces and started after her.

Kate continued to back up. Her hands lifted in the air. "Come on, you guys. I needed their help."

"NO," Parker barked out. "It's just like Mason said. You wanted power and you went crazy for it. Fuck you, Kate. You lied about the video and then you hit on him? Did you suck him? You made sure to tell me to do that. You said it'd make him do whatever I wanted. That he'd be wrapped around my little finger. It didn't work, did it?"

Her voice rose on the last statement, but it didn't matter. Kate shoved past them, past Ethan and up the stairs. The two took off after her.

The room remained in silence for a beat. Then Tate started laughing. She stood next to Logan and hung on him, bending over as more laughter spilled from her. Shaking her head, she tried to calm down, but couldn't. More and more kept coming until Logan was holding her up. She clung to him and then took a deep breath, tears rolling down her cheeks from the laughter. "Oh my god. I can't believe that happened. You just ruined her life, Mason. Holy shit."

Yes. I had.

Sam's hand tightened around mine and she moved closer to me.

Glancing down into Sam's eyes, I'd do it again.

CHAPTER TWENTY-EIGHT
SAMANTHA

Mason took me home that night. He parked in my dad's driveway, but there were no other cars. I knew there wouldn't be. I texted David to stay at Malinda's and that I'd be with Mason. We were there, and it was time to go in, but I couldn't bring myself to open the door. So many emotions and thoughts were swirling through my head.

"What is it?"

There were no back lights on so we were in complete darkness. The moon shone down, casting a soft glow over us. It matched his soft tone, but I couldn't get what he'd done out of my head. He'd been ruthless and knowing what more was coming to Kate, I didn't know what to think anymore.

I glanced at him. He was watching me. He was always watching me. I was coming to realize it would never be the problem if he wasn't going to be there for me, but what wouldn't he do for me. I said, "I'm very lucky."

A grin appeared over his face. "What makes you say that?"

"You're willing to ruin someone for me."

The grin vanished. "That's not it, Sam."

"Can you explain it to me?" I didn't get it. I really didn't. "You took away her friends, and you made Budd believe that she's your girlfriend. She has no power. She has no support, and he's going to do something horrible to her. It's like you gutted her and threw her into the ocean for a hungry shark to devour."

"The choice was you or her. I lined things up so that it wasn't you. I'll never let it be you. That's what I did."

I drew in a breath until my lungs hurt. A tear slipped from my eye, and I brushed it away. Jeezus. What was I doing? He was right. Budd Broudou was a serious problem. He saved me from him.

"You're not remembering what she did to you."

"What?" I looked at him again.

He was so beautiful—tall with broad shoulders, a trim waist, and emerald eyes—but it was his angelic face that held me spellbound right now. Mason wasn't an angel. That was obvious, had always been obvious, but when he loved, he truly loved. It was beautiful, and it was something that I'd forgotten the past couple days.

He leaned back, but he watched me. I caught the wariness in his eyes.

He was always so cautious and on-guard. He was scared of me right now. This man that could render so much power was fearful of me. The irony was not lost on me. "I'm not remembering her the right way?"

"She wanted Nate to drug you, Sam."

I sucked in my breath. "I didn't know that."

"He was supposed to get you naked and then he was supposed to take pictures of you. He was supposed to do worse things, too."

Nate. My ribs were in flames now. Everything was screaming from pain inside of me. Nate... I couldn't believe it.

Mason added, "Heather and Tate."

My mind was reeling from Nate, what they wanted him to do. I frowned. "What about Heather and Tate?"

"Heather stood against them. Tate did it once, but it was enough." He paused a moment. "Kate wanted to take your friend away and I think she wanted to make Tate your enemy again."

He was right. He was so right. I sucked in another breath. Why did it hurt so much to breathe? I shook my head and pulled my shirt away. I needed to breathe, but I couldn't forget. "She sent Heather text messages threatening her."

"They were going to go to Manny's tomorrow night."

An invisible hand went to my chest. It began pushing down on it, pushing down on me. He was saying...

"They were going to break in and destroy as much as they could before anyone woke up in the house. You said they sleep with loud fans because they're all light sleepers. Think about how much damage they could have done before someone woke up."

I turned away. I didn't want to hear any more, but his voice had a soft beckoning to it. I couldn't look away. His eyes darkened, but I couldn't tell if it was from pity or regret. I didn't want to know. They were going to hurt my friend.

He continued, "She wanted to take your friends away and Tate would've turned against you too. I know what kind of person she is. She would've blamed you for that. Heather would've eventually grown leery. She wouldn't have turned on you like Tate would've, but she would've distanced herself. She would've done it to keep her family safe unless she knew a way to handle Kate, but there's no way to handle Kate. It's why I had to gut her. It's the only way to take care of Kate. I removed any power or support she might've gotten."

"I took everybody on at the Academy. I didn't have any friends there."

"You can't do it alone at our school. This is a school where you can get jumped in a bathroom."

I flinched as I was transported back to that room. The door closed, but they were already there. All four of them. They chased me into the stalls. They crawled underneath to grab me. I'd been so close to the door, but they pulled me back in.

Mason was right. Kate had to be destroyed. He had done it for me. He had done all of this for me. "Thank you." The words wrung from me.

"Sam?"

"Mmm?"

He had turned away, and his hand gripped the steering wheel tightly. "Next time you're pissed at me, can you do me a favor?"

"Yeah?"

"Don't go to Logan." His eyes moved to mine and held them captive. My mouth dropped open as he stole my breath away. That hand went back into my chest and squeezed, but it was a different pain this time. It was from the pain I caused him.

I nodded. "I'm sorry."

"He's my brother. You're my other half. I can't…"

When he struggled for words, I reached for his hand. I started to go to him, but my ribs protested, so I gripped his hand as tight as I could. "I won't ever do that again. I promise."

He nodded, but I saw that he couldn't say anything.

"Mason," I whispered.

"What?"

"I'm sorry for that."

He nodded again, exhaling a deep breath at the same time.

"That must've looked," *horrible* "not good."

A harsh laugh came from him. "Probably the same as you seeing me with Kate."

The anger began to flood back in, but I didn't want to think about it. I felt bad for her, but he was right. Kate got what she had coming to her, and whatever else was going to happen, it wasn't me. Mason took care of me again. The magnitude of everything that had happened over the last few weeks rushed in, and I grew overwhelmed. "Let's go to bed."

As we went inside, the lights were left off, and I took his hand, leading him to my room.

I hadn't taken full inventory of my room my first night back, but taking Mason to it made me look at it through new eyes. My desk was covered in old pictures: Jeff. Lydia. Jessica. All four of us at various events and Jeff's football games. Jessica and Lydia were both on the cheerleading squad our freshman year. I was the only one not in a uniform. I hadn't cared then, but now it struck me. Had I always been the odd one out?

Mason went to sit on my bed, and I held my breath.

My quilt was patched together with different patterns and colors. My grandmother made it before she died, and it was an item I was surprised Analise let me keep. As she handed it over to me, her jealousy had me clutching it close. I had come home every day for a year wondering when she was going to ruin it. She never did, but as Mason stretched over it, it looked too old-fashioned for him. My entire room was too old-fashioned.

"What's wrong?" He followed my gaze as I studied my old books. "*Babysitters Club*?"

"I used to read a lot." I used to do a lot of other things, but that seemed so long ago. I sat beside him and felt him take my hand. "I'm seeing everything through your eyes. It must seem so..."

"This was your home, Sam."

I ended with, "Childish."

"Why do you think that?"

Gesturing to my desk with my old books, my old CDs, the pictures, even my old backpacks. "Analise told me not to bring a lot of my stuff. She said it was pointless. That none of my stuff would fit in at the Kade house. Your place was too modern and wealthy. My stuff would remind everyone of how poor we were."

He laughed, tipping my head up to his. "I never thought you were poor."

"You didn't? You could've. I forget sometimes that you come from money."

"Why does that matter?"

"It doesn't." But it did.

"Then why'd you look away just now? Sam," he brought me back to face him, "money is just padding. It can be used to shelter you from some things, but there's no sheltering from other things like love and kindness. Money has no effect on the real stuff."

"Is Helen going to buy that house? Nate's old house?"

"Wait. Where'd that come from?"

Money was important to her. Helen Malbourne would never approve of me; she didn't think I was good enough for Mason. "I know she's there. It's another thing you didn't tell me this past week."

"Oh." His hand fell away from my face. "You don't trust me now?"

After all he had done, that was the last thing I should be feeling. "No. I'm sorry."

"Sam."

I sighed on the inside. Would I ever be secure enough?

"Sam."

"What?"

"Look at me."

I refused, glancing at my hands. Twisting them in my lap, I looked again after he gently nudged me with his shoulder. He smiled at me. Seeing the tenderness in his gaze, I melted inside. Then he murmured as he drew closer to me, "You have baggage. I understand. Your mom betrayed you. Both of your dads left you. Your two best friends and your ex screwed you over. I start keeping secrets, and you see me kissing another girl. I get it. I'm sorry for making you doubt me."

"This week sucked."

He laughed, capturing my hand again and bringing it onto his lap. He held it with both of his. "The past couple weeks have sucked."

"Is it done?"

"Who knows?"

I cracked a grin. "That's not very reassuring."

"Whatever else happens, we'll deal. We always do." Turning to me, he lifted me onto his lap and scooted back until he was resting against my headboard. For some reason, sheltered in his arms in my old room gave me a peaceful feeling. My old and new had combined and somehow that was all I'd needed. He pressed a kiss to the side of my head. "You don't believe me?"

I did, but words weren't coming to me right then and there. My throat swelled and a big knot lodged in my chest, but it was the good kind. For once.

"Sam," he whispered, his breath caressing my skin, "I love you."

I clasped my other hand over his and squeezed with as much force as I could. I loved him. I just couldn't say it. The knot had doubled, so I tried to turn around so he could see it. I needed him to see my love. Tears and all, they were shining within me, and I wanted him see it all. He always saw everything.

Then he groaned, "Do you know how hard I am right now?"

A laugh broke free. My ribs hated me, but I kept laughing. It wasn't until later that night when the lights were off and we were in my bed that I was able to speak over the pain, "So your mom really is buying that house?"

His arms tightened around me. "Yeah, I think so and especially after last night."

"What else happened?"

He stiffened underneath me. "I got a call last night from my dad, and I didn't even think about it until now, but you should know something. Your mom had another freak out. My dad had to call the cops on her."

I didn't know what hit me first: fear or hope.

He added, "She was admitted to the hospital and she's under a seventy-two-hour psychiatric hold. My dad says that your mom has a disorder or something. She's going to some treatment center."

"For how long?"

"He's hoping for as long as it takes."

"Takes? For what?"

"I don't know. For her to get better, I guess. Maybe just for her to deal with things before bringing her back. The bottom line is that they're going to be gone for a long time. My mom hasn't said anything, but I'd be surprised if that doesn't seal the deal. She'll buy that house or another one in the same neighborhood."

"To be close to your dad's house?"

"Because of you."

I lifted my head from his chest. "What?"

"Because of Malinda Decraw. It's where she lives."

"What are you talking about?" I sat up and leaned against the wall, gazing down at him.

He grinned at me, reaching for my shirt and pulling down on the top so he could graze against my breasts. He captured one in his hand. "Your dad's going to marry that woman, and you'll be there from now on."

"We could go back to the old house, your dad's."

"Nah." His thumb rubbed back and forth over my nipple, and I sucked in my breath. A burning sensation was going through me, the kind that I couldn't do anything about. "I'm not dumb, Sam. You moved back in with your dad. You can't leave him, not when you just got him back, and that's his woman, so I'm guessing we'll be spending a lot of time going between Malinda and my mom's houses."

"What about this house?" I just got it back, too.

"You really want to stay here? We can if you want."

But he was right. This home was cold now. David was right. This was Analise's home. There were too many bad memories here. Malinda's was warm. Loving. Caring. She was the future for my dad. I sighed out loud and laid back into his side. "Well, that'll be interesting."

"What will?"

"Going between Helen and Malinda's houses all the time."

"Yeah." His voice dipped and he shifted to his side. His arm tightened around me and he slid his hand down the length of my side. When he stopped and began to rub my thigh, he said, "I know you can't do much, but maybe I can make you feel better."

His hand inched down and began to rub between my legs. I closed my eyes and laid there as his fingers dipped inside of me. Later, as he moved down between my legs, and I felt his lips on me, I opened my eyes and gazed at him. His lips were sending me over the edge, but it was the sight of him that sent a burst of desire through me. His back was sculpted. All the power was there, but he held himself so he wouldn't hurt me. Even now, he protected me. Then his tongue swept inside and I was gone.

CHAPTER
TWENTY-NINE

Kate dropped out of school. Heather told me the rumor was she was going to get her GED, but I didn't care. I was happy she was gone, although in her absence Natalie became the new leader. She appealed to Mason and promised they learned from Kate's mistakes, but it didn't matter. The guys were done with them. The bathroom beat down finalized the decision for each of the guys, which I was thankful for. School was easier when I returned. People were friendlier.

Once I healed enough, Coach Grath had me running with a select group of girls in the mornings before school. There were five of us, but there was only one that was competition for me, or she was the closest thing I had to competition. When real practices started, I was still leery about running with so many others, but I went at my own pace. I shut it all out. The guys. The girls. The people who were talking with each other, the girls who gossiped, the ones who complained about practice. All of it. Half way through the season, after a few scouts started coming around, my status changed again.

I was one of the best.

I was also becoming popular. Slightly.

Heather snorted when a few of the drill team girls hurried to open a door for me one day. She said I was now the prime target—get close to Samantha Strattan meant getting close to Mason and Logan Kade. They didn't care that I was Mason's girlfriend, they were lining up to be his next one or Logan's go-to girl since Tate had stopped his all-access to her.

When I asked Heather if it was because they felt sorry for me, she started laughing. "Are you kidding me? People don't give two shits if someone gets hurt or not unless you're their friend. You weren't friends with anyone. They're being nice for two reasons: you got Kate out of here and they want to use you to get in with the Kades. It's a good thing I don't give a damn about either Kade."

My eyebrow arched up at that. "You going to finally talk about Channing?"

Heather kept her lips sealed tight about that relationship, but I wasn't blind. Channing was at Manny's more often than not. He now had his own stool right next to Gus and they kept Brandon entertained during the slow nights. Logan and Mason joined them after their basketball practices, and all five of them had become friendly. Logan mentioned going running with Gus since the guy had a beer gut that was bordering on becoming a bear gut.

He even invited Gus to family dinner at Helen's. That didn't go well.

Nothing went over well with Helen.

Mason had been right and wrong. She didn't buy Nate's old home. She bought land at the end of the block. She was going to build her ultimate dream home. Since James and Analise were gone, she moved into their house until it was done. I moved into Malinda's home, and that seemed to be the official move in day for David as well. He reassured me he wouldn't sell the old house. It would be there for me if I ever wanted it. Mason spent the nights with me while he 'lived' with Helen in the old house. Logan came over for almost every breakfast and they were around most of the time during the weekends.

This was another arrangement Helen didn't like, neither did David, but neither of them could say anything—it was going to happen whether they wanted it or not. We'd already fought one parental unit about our relationship. They knew we would've done it again, but it didn't mean Helen didn't make things uncomfortable at times.

Today was one of those days.

It was a Saturday, and Mason had spent the night, but so had Logan. Helen didn't like that. He and Mark came back to the house after a party and played video games all night. He fell asleep on the couch, and Helen started calling at eight that morning. She called both of their phones, and then she began calling the house phone. When she asked for her son, Malinda knocked on our door and gave the phone to Mason. Wrong son. When he sat up and I heard her yelling on the other end, I rolled out of bed and grabbed my running clothes.

Helen was a saner version of Analise.

It was time to run.

I headed towards my favorite path. Instead of driving to my old neighborhood and jumping on it from the park, I found another trail that connected to it from behind Malinda's house. When she learned where I ran the most, she pulled out a map of walking trails and showed me new trails, but I kept with the one that ran past Quickie's and into the hills behind it. I could get lost back there and today was a day I needed that. It was when I came back that I noticed something was wrong.

The clerk was pacing back and forth outside the side door. He would stop, wring his hands together, shake them out, and return to pacing. After a few moments, he stopped again, took a deep breath and peeked around the back corner. Jerking back, he shook his head and started twisting his hands together again.

I made my way down to him. My heart was pounding so I pulled my earbuds out and silenced the noise. As I got to the bottom of the hill, I took a few breaths so I could talk and not pant through a conversation. He was turning around again in another sharp circle when he saw me, and his eyes bulged out. I recognized the same clerk from all the other times I'd been around here. I saw him through the window the first morning when the Broudous showed up for a pit stop and a few times when I've run past here.

"Hey," I murmured, "are you okay?"

He jerked his head in an abrupt movement. "No."

"Okay." I frowned at him. When he didn't say anything more, I leaned my leg against the building and started to stretch it out. "Can you tell me what's wrong?"

"Ahh-hmmmggbbb—"

"What the hell?" I whipped around. It sounded like someone was being strangled. I started to step towards the back, but the clerk grabbed my arm.

He held me back. "Don't." His voice was trembling, as was his hand. The longer he held me, I realized all of him was shaking.

A foreboding sensation started in me. "What's your name?"

"Ben."

I nodded. This guy was about to piss his pants and I glanced down. He hadn't, but he was close. Reaching up, I started to remove his hand from my arm, but his fingers tightened. He hurried out, "No. You can't go over there."

"Okay." I let his hand stay in place. "Where?"

"They're on the other side of the gas station, by the back."

I nodded. He looked ready to bolt. "Why?"

"AHHHHHHHHHH! No..." The last ended on a whimper. A girl's whimper.

I started to turn again. The girl was in trouble, and it wasn't because she was crying to cry. She was crying in fear, the kind that comes from deep inside a person.

"No." Ben pulled me back, firmer this time. He had stopped shaking so much. "You can't go back there."

"Okay, but why?"

His mouth closed and his lips pressed tight.

"Ben, you have to tell me or I'm going to kick you in the balls so I can go and see who that is."

He winced and tried to cover himself with one hand. I snorted. *That wasn't going to help.*

"Ben," I started again.

The girl cried out again, but it was hushed by someone else. A male someone. The foreboding sense kicked into full gear. Disgust was next. I had to go. Whether this clerk was going to let me go or not, I was going. "I mean it. Let go or you're never going to have children."

"You can't."

"Why?"

"You just," he faltered. "You can't."

Slap!

I started around the corner, dragging Ben with me. My blood was still pumping from adrenalin. I hadn't gone numb like I usually did when I run. I was going to help whoever was back there. I'd been hurt. Someone came to help me. I was going to do the same.

"You can't," Ben grunted as he held me back. He was scrawny, but he was stronger than me. I was hauled back and then shoved towards the front of the gas station. "Budd Broudou is back there."

I stopped. Ice cold water filled my veins, and I couldn't move.

That was Budd.

So that was Kate. This was it, this was what he would've done to me if Mason hadn't manipulated everything.

"Nnoo... AH! Wha—"

"Shut up," he hissed at her.

I flinched. I could imagine him slapping his hand over her mouth. Then he continued doing whatever he was doing.

"Oh my god."

"See." Ben yanked me the rest of the way. "You can't go back there. He'll hurt you. She told him that you were Mason's girlfriend and not her, but he didn't believe her. You can't go back there. He might not care and hurt both of you."

"Call the cops."

He stopped, and I ran into him. Shaking his head, he started trembling again. "Yeah, right."

"You have to."

"No."

"Ben."

"NO. No."

"He is hurting her." It didn't matter. None of it mattered. If she hurt me, if she hadn't. What he was doing—I didn't even want to know, though I had a good idea—was wrong. Revulsion swept through me, but I shoved it down.

I'd been hurting. Someone helped me. That kept running through my head. I had to help her, no matter who she was.

"We can't call the cops."

"We have to. Do you have cameras? Anything? Her uncle is a cop."

"He is?"

I nodded.

"Okay." He still looked ready to piss his pants. "We have two cameras, no—three. We have three cameras."

He stopped. Nothing.

I asked, "Where are they?"

"Oh. One is pointing towards the front. One is where they are and the other is inside."

My heart sank. "So none on him?"

He shook his head and pushed up his glasses. They began sliding down right away, but he didn't notice. His eyes were glued to me and his hand went back to his hip, his very tiny, scrawny hip. I sighed. What the hell was I doing?

"His truck is over there."

"What?"

He pointed down the road where his truck was hidden in a copse of trees. It was far enough away from the gas station and surrounded by healthy trees. If...a plan began to form, but as I went over it in my head, I couldn't. There was no way.

"HELP—"

He slapped her again. It was followed by a thud.

I closed my eyes. He hurt her again.

That sealed it. Looking at Ben, there was uncertainty, but panic mixed with trust. He was trusting me, but I had no idea what I was doing. I did, but I held no promise it was going to work. It had to. I pushed all the fear down, and I remembered everything that had made me angry.

Analise.

David leaving me.

Jeff cheating on me.

Jessica and Lydia stabbing me in the back.

Adam lying about me.

Becky believing him.

Kate and her friends. She wanted Mason back. All of them hurting me.

And now Helen. I knew she didn't want me to be with Mason. Everyone knew it. It was another obstacle in our relationship. I felt it coming, so did Mason, but neither of us knew how to stop it before it began.

By the time I remembered everything, all that old anger had mixed with the adrenalin from my run. I was heated. I was sick and tired of being hurt, being shoved down, being pushed around, being punched, stabbed, and being replaced.

"Ben." My voice was firm.

He settled down and nodded.

"Turn your cameras off in the front. There can't be any evidence of me."

"There won't, but," he hesitated, "what are you going to do?"

"I'm going to distract him."

"Okay." Another beat of hesitation. "What do you want me to do?"

"Wait until I light it before you call the fire station."

"Okay." He rushed back inside.

I waited a second.

He rushed back out. "Light what?"

I took a deep breath. "I need some gasoline."

His eyes popped out, but he went inside and brought back two full red containers and handed them over without a word. This was the time when I was making the decision to help someone else. This could cost me my life. I had no idea, but he was hurting another girl, and I couldn't let that happen. There was no way I could walk away from it without losing a piece of my soul, so I took the two containers of gasoline Ben gave me, and I carried them to Budd's truck. It was hidden, and I had no doubt that he was going to use the running trail to slip past the cameras and drive away.

That pissed me off even more. I had no idea why, but he wanted to get away with it, using *my* trails. Everyone got away with screwing people over.

Not this time.

I didn't touch the truck, but I doused the entire thing with gasoline. When I was done, I heard Kate cry out again. He was still doing whatever it was he was doing. I closed my eyes and pulled my sleeves over my hands. I wiped down the containers. Ben told me to do that. He said they could maybe get my finger prints off of them. I had no idea what he was going to say when the police would come. He said he would turn the cameras off. He was an accomplice, but he told me not to worry about it. He had my back. Apparently, he had my back the entire time. Budd kept coming back to the gas station and questioned Ben about Mason's girlfriend. He never told him, not once. I could only imagine what Budd must've put him through.

I'd never come to Quickie's again without being thankful.

"Oh...God..." Kate moaned, but not the good kind. It was the kind that reached inside a person's darkest parts and took root.

I moved far enough away before I flipped the lighter and bent down. Grabbing some old branches, I put the flame to them and waited. My heart was pounding in my chest and everything went to slow motion then.

I was going to do this.

I kept hearing her cries.

You should've quit school today. I gave you your last out.

My thumb slipped off the lighter, but I couldn't move. I remained crouched down, the lighter to the tree branch and my hand never trembled.

This isn't payback. This is your punishment.

She wanted to destroy me, but she had only hurt me. I fought back. When I was down, I got back up. She hadn't destroyed me.

Shut up and get her.

I dropped the lighter. My hand jerked as I felt their first hit, their first punch, their first kick, and when I dropped to the ground. I felt them again. They were closing in on me. I'd been so close to escaping.

You can't kill her. Let's go.

When would she have stopped? She had wanted to do more damage that night. Her friends stopped her and he was hurting her now, but it didn't matter. He was killing her on the inside. I heard her cries and I knew that agony. It had been me, but at her hands.

I reached for the lighter again. This time there was no wavering and I waited until the branch was burning before I tossed it towards the truck. Then I ran.

When he saw the fire, Ben was supposed to call the fire station and the cops. I wasn't going to wait and see the fireworks. I needed to leave. As I sprinted across the road and over to the next running trail that would take me back to Malinda's, I froze for a second.

Kate saw me. Even from this distance, I could see the pain in her eyes.

They were right there, pressed against the side of the wall. He had taken her near the dumpster, but I could see them. A passing car wouldn't be able to, and I knew that was why he chose that spot. Only someone walking or running by would see them.

He had a hand to her throat and another hand between their bodies. I didn't know what he was doing, and I didn't want to know.

BOOM!

The explosion had enough force to it to push me back, but I didn't look away.

Budd let her go, and he ran around the side of the gas station. "What the hell?!"

Kate pushed herself up, but she didn't look away from me. Her hair was matted, and she had scrapes over her face. It was red from where he had slapped her. Her throat was already bruising, but she mouthed, "Thank you."

She knew.

I jerked my head in a nod. She had hurt me and I had saved her. The irony was not lost on me, but I didn't wait to see what else happened next. I took off. As I pushed up another hill, just nearing the trail to Malinda's, I heard sirens in the distance. I couldn't help myself so I stopped and looked down. There was a tiny opening between some trees so I could see Quickie's. The flames had lifted high in the air, but that wasn't what I cared about. Budd was pacing back and forth.

I laughed to myself.

He tried to get inside the gas station, but he couldn't. The doors were locked. Ben and Kate stood inside and watched him. He kept trying, but when he heard the sirens, he started running.

He wouldn't get far enough. I heard him yell, "FUCK!"

I turned and started walking now. The need to run had left me. I wanted to savor this. He'd gone after Mason. He'd gone after Logan, put Nate in the hospital, and terrorized way too many others. Budd Broudou was going to jail. I knew it, and he knew it. It was a day that I would enjoy for a long time. Maybe Mason was right. Maybe taking control into your own hands was the best way to serve justice?

I remembered Kate's whimpers and my conscience was clear. I did more for her than she had done for me. It was good enough for me.

CHAPTER THIRTY

THREE MONTHS LATER...

Budd had been arrested for trying to rape Kate. Her uncle was first on scene, and they arrested him right away. He hadn't gotten far down the road, and there was enough evidence to send him to prison. As for Kate, she moved in with her uncle. Heather heard through the rumor mill that he hadn't been happy with her parents for years, and with so many problems happening at the same time, he had her move in with him and his wife. Her mom and dad never fought the decision so as everyone else was finishing up their spring semester, Kate was working on getting her GED through the alternative school.

I was just happy that I never saw her again. I was also happy that no one knew who set Budd's truck on fire. Ben and Kate kept quiet. I was relieved, and I wasn't going to start questioning her motives. If she talked, I'd set her truck on fire, too. I was done dealing with her.

"You got a visitor."

I glanced up from the register. Heather had a tense smile on her face. She was standing with her back to where the guys were. Mason, Logan, Channing, and Gus were all lined up on barstools in front of Brandon. A baseball game was on the television, and Logan was goading Gus into betting against his favorite team.

"Who?"

"Ssh." She leaned closer and rolled her eyes to the back of her head. "You have a visitor."

There was a message in there somewhere, but I couldn't decipher it. Mason was leaving in a few months, and I was already dreading his graduation in a week. All emotional energy was spent towards that, not figuring out cryptic messages from my friend.

"Spell the name," I said instead of guessing. I wasn't going to go and see. It could be Kate, or worse, one of her friends trying to apologize again. I wasn't having any of it.

"Just go," she hissed before expelling a frustrated sound and grabbing my hand. She pulled me through the side door, and announced as she passed the bar, "Smoke break. No boys allowed." No one moved, but then we were through the doors before anyone had the chance. Before the screen door could slam shut, she caught it and reached inside for the main door. Both were pulled shut.

I glanced around the alley, but no one was there.

Heather dropped down in a chair and pulled out her cigarettes. I started to sit as well, but she waved me away. "No. Go."

"Where?"

"Oh." She glanced around and frowned. "Where'd he go?" Then her eyes lit up, and she pointed to the back end of Manny's, right next to her house. "There. I see him."

Uh... I was putting my trust in my friend as I started to the back. When I got there, I relaxed. Slightly. "Brett."

He was leaning against a tree with his hands stuffed inside his front pockets. As he stood, his goliath-sized body unfolded and grew again in front of me. If he hadn't asked me out and if he hadn't protected me from Budd, I would've been pissing my pants. All I did was wipe my hands off on my pants and give him a relieved grin.

He grinned back, but grimaced. "I'm sorry for not doing this earlier."

Oh whoa. That wasn't what I expected to hear. "Do what?"

"Come to apologize."

"Apologize? For what?"

"For my brother and what he must've put you through. For me too." He glanced down as his shoulders lifted when he took in a deep breath. "I should've stopped him a long time ago, but I didn't. I never had incentive to, and I guess it was easier to let Shannon get in his ear. This all started because my sister told us Mason Kade used her for sex. I know what she did wasn't right."

"Shannon?"

"She lied all those years ago."

Oh, whoa again. "You knew?"

"Not then, but I found out the truth a few months ago. I never told Budd." He shrugged, reaching up to scratch his face. As he did, his arm doubled in size, and I gulped again. It was the size of a tree trunk. Then he added, "My brother doesn't work like that. Once he hears something, it's it in his mind. Your man knows that, too."

I flushed at the memory. The image of Kate writhing on top of Mason had my stomach churning, but I shrugged it off. It was over and done. He had his revenge. She got her due. I helped her out in the end. My conscience was clear when it came to Kate.

I cleared my throat. "What do you want, Brett?"

"Just to extend an olive branch, I suppose." His jaw hardened, and he glanced to the side. Lifting his arms, he folded them across his chest. If it was possible, it made him look even bigger. "And to let you know that the beef is over between my town and this one. As far as I'm concerned, we got no problem with Fallen Crest folk anymore."

"Oh."

"Is that right?"

I stiffened, but I couldn't deny the relief that went through me. Mason came up behind me and stood next to me. He didn't touch me or pull me against him. For some reason, I was thankful.

Brett stiffened too, but he jerked his head in a nod. "I was telling your woman that I consider the rivalry done. Budd's in jail. Whoever set his truck on fire made that possible."

"You make it sound like you wanted him in jail?"

He frowned at Mason, and the two engaged in some unspoken message between them before Brett slowly lifted his head up and down. "My brother was hurting a girl. He needs to take the punishment for it. That's all I'm saying."

Mason didn't respond. The two continued to stare at each other.

I shifted next to him, unsure of what to do. The air had filled with tension when Mason spoke up, but I didn't feel that it was nearing any violence. I hoped not. "So," I gave each a forced smile, "Brett came to say that Budd's in jail, and Shannon lied all those years ago. We've made progress, I think."

Faint grins came over both of them, but disappeared instantly.

Mason spoke, "You know Shannon lied? That I never slept with your sister and used her?"

Brett jerked his head in a nod. "I do. Her best friend told me the truth. She came onto you and you rejected her." His gaze lingered on me. "I know you could have your choice of women so it never felt right, my sister's story, but she's kin, so we did what we did."

"If someone rejected my brother, I wouldn't force her to date him." Mason's jaw had hardened. "It's an extreme response."

Brett lifted his head, and his shoulders rolled back. As his arms fell back to his side, my eyes widened. His hands turned back as if they were going to form into fists, but they didn't. I let out a small puff of air, and then he replied, "We're old fashioned. Big brothers look out for their little sisters."

"Your sister's a bitch."

I closed my eyes in frustration. Logan had the worst timing. Ever.

He strolled to the group, his eyes narrowed and lethal as he added, "And she's a viper. There's no way in hell you have to look out for her."

Brett's head lifted even further, and I saw the storm brewing.

"Okay." I stood between them and shooed Logan away. "Get out of here. You're not helping."

"Not going, Sam."

"Go. I mean it."

He ignored me. His gaze trailed past me to Brett, and he asked further, "What are you here for?"

I lifted my voice, "He came to make peace, so get out of here before you blow it."

Logan's narrowed eyes turned to me in disbelief.

My eyebrow arched high, and my hands found my hips. "I mean it. Go," but I stopped as Mason's hand curved around my waist, and he pulled me against him. His fingers slid under my shirt and pressed against me. I got the message. I shut up.

Logan stepped next to me now so that all three of us stood in a line. As he did, I understood Mason's message. The three of us were together, no matter what. I'd forgotten the rule, and it felt good. It felt like home once again.

Brett skimmed over us and nodded to himself. It was a faint nod, but I caught it. He gave me a small grin before he moved back a step. "I came to see how Sam was doing, but to say what I already said. Budd's in jail, and he ain't getting out any time soon, so I run Roussou now. As far as I'm concerned, there's no beef between us anymore." He paused a beat. "And Fallen Crest is closer to our farm than Roussou, so I'm also warning you that I might be grabbing a bite to eat every now and then at Manny's."

Mason narrowed his eyes.

Logan raised his chin. "You put our buddy in the hospital. We never got even for that."

"You had a hand in putting my brother in jail. I think that evens the field."

Oh boy. That can did not need to be opened. I nodded. "That's fine with me."

The two glanced down at me as I stood between them. I ignored them. Heather would be fine with it. She'd be happy even. If Brett stopped by for a bite that meant the rest of Roussou could come, too, and that meant Channing's friends. They had stayed away because of the rivalry. He'd been the only one to come around, and had started an odd friendship with Mason at the same time.

"Okay." Brett nodded to himself, and then gestured to me. "It's nice seeing that you're better."

I told Mason what Brett had done for me at the street dance, and I felt him relax beside me. I gave Brett a small grin. "Thanks for coming."

He lifted a finger to his forehead in a slight salute to me, but it was his farewell. Turning, he headed back around Manny's. It wasn't long before we heard his truck leaving the parking lot.

"Well, shit. Who do we prank now?"

Mason grinned. "What do you mean? I think we owe Principal Green a few times."

Logan flashed a smile. "You're right. We never got him back for not expelling Kate in the first place." He asked Mason, "Where's Nate? I thought he was supposed to be here by now?"

"He's got a new girlfriend. Relax," Mason chided, but pulled me close and pressed a soft kiss to my forehead.

As he moved back, his eyes caught mine and held them for a second. A shiver went through me at the heated promise, but I caught the underlying message, too. Brett was in the past. So was a lot of other stuff. I caught his shirt and pulled him back for a real kiss. As his lips covered mine, the need for him began inside of me. Logan groaned. "Come on, guys. You've been going at it like rabbits since she got all healthy." His phone beeped. "Thank god. That's Nate. He's done with the girlfriend, so let's go."

Mason pulled away, but not before giving me a tender kiss.

I shook my head. Every part of me was trembling. No matter the distance and no matter the obstacles, he'd always have this hold over me. As he stepped back, his eyes never left mine. I caught another message. I was his. I sent one of my own to him. He was mine, too. When the corner of his lip curved up, I knew he read it loud and clear.

"You guys were going to prank Roussou tonight?" I asked hoarsely. They had never told me.

"We need to do something. Graduation's in a week." Logan threw an arm around his brother and pulled his head down. He tussled his hair before Mason shoved him off. "We got two more months with this guy. We need to make memories, and that means we gotta do some damage." He let out a loud whoop. "Let's go, Mase. I'm in the mood to get in trouble tonight."

He pressed a quick kiss to my forehead. "If we don't come home tonight, check the jail first, Sam."

As he disappeared around the corner, I asked Mason, "Is he serious? You're going to get arrested tonight?"

"Nah," he paused, "I don't think so."

"Come on, Mase!"

He grimaced. "Maybe."

"Mason."

He shrugged before giving me another kiss on the lips, then he whispered against them, "We'll be fine. We always are."

He started to pull away, but I grabbed him one more time. He caught the need in my eyes and took over. I was lifted in the air and pushed against the wall. He pressed into me, and it was a long time before he pulled away. When he did, both of us were panting. The rest of the night was going to be uncomfortable. I knew I'd be walking with this ache between my legs, and it wouldn't go away until he got home. He flashed me a rueful grin and smoothed a tender hand down the side of my face. As he tucked some hair strands behind my ear, he asked, "Are you okay?"

"I'm hot and bothered."

"No," he chuckled, but stepped close again. His hips pressed against mine, and I felt his own need as he ground it into me. "I meant if you're okay after seeing Brett Broudou again?"

"Oh." Some of the desire lessened, but he moved into me in a rhythmic motion, and it came back again. I struggled to think over what he was doing to me. "Uh...yeah. I guess." My head went against the wall, and I gasped as he moved even closer. "Are you okay?"

"I will be," he murmured under his breath. His gaze was on my lips. "I will be." Then his hand went to my pants, and I felt him grab for my zipper.

"No." I caught his hand. Shit. Then I shoved him back. Logan had been right. Since I was given a clean bill of health, we'd been insatiable. Another second longer, he would've slipped inside of me, and I would've let him. "Tonight."

He nodded and stepped closer once more.

"Mason," I warned softly.

A grin appeared as he kept his hips away, but rested his forehead on mine.

I sighed a breath of relief mixed with bitter longing. He was leaving. I knew that was the reason for this need that had become so overwhelming, and I didn't want to control it anymore. He was leaving. I couldn't get enough of him until he left for college. Logan had been right. Two more months was all we had with Mason.

I closed my eyes as my hands went to his jeans. My fingers caught a loop on the waistband, and I struggled. I wanted to pull him back to me. I wanted to forget where we were and forget where we were going. I wanted all of it to go away, but I couldn't.

"MASON."

He chuckled softly against my skin and pressed another kiss there.

How many had there been? I needed so many more.

Then he stepped back. "I'll see you tonight."

"Do not get arrested."

He flashed me a grin. "I won't. Promise."

Then he was gone, and I was left to collapse and pick up the pieces. I had a feeling this was my future. I'd be picking up the pieces every time he left. Tonight. We had tonight, and we had over sixty more of them before he left early for football practice.

It'd be fine. I'd make sure it'd be fine.

When I was able to go back, I stopped again as I went around the corner.

Tate was in one of the chairs Heather and I sat in when we took our breaks. As I came closer, she readjusted her legs, throwing one over the opposite knee and doing it again before she realized I was there. Her fingers had been tapping on the chair in an impatient motion, but she stopped all of it and threw me a forced smile. "I should've figured you were there. Your two men took off a second ago."

"Yeah." I frowned at her. "What are you doing here?"

Since she got the blow job video back, Tate had melted into the background. I rarely saw her at school. She called everything off with Logan, no longer hooking up with him when he wanted. If she was here, it was because of Heather and that had me worried.

She sighed, rolling her eyes. "Don't worry. I'm not here to mess up your holy trinity with the two gods. I'm here to see Heather."

"Like I said," I clipped out, "what are you doing here?"

Mason had told me what he thought would've happened with Tate and Heather if Kate had done everything she wanted. I agreed with him about Tate. She would've turned against me, but I didn't agree with him about Heather. He thought Heather would've distanced herself from me, but she wouldn't have done that. If they destroyed Manny's like they were planning to, Heather would've torched Kate's house like I torched Budd's truck.

I knew she would've reacted like that. I told her Kate's plans, and she exploded. Natalie and Jasmine had been at their lockers at the time, and she tried to head over to them.

I held her back, but the two caught the commotion and scurried away.

They were smart. I'd been touched by Heather's loyalty. She wouldn't have pulled away from me. Because of that, my protective side was coming out. Tate had hurt Heather too much in the past. I wasn't going to let her do it again.

When Tate flicked her hair over her shoulder and ignored my question, I yanked her chair towards me. She was trapped by me now, and I repeated my question. "What are you doing here?"

She rolled her eyes. "Seriously. You're mama bear now?"

"Violence doesn't scare me. You should remember that."

She started to roll her eyes again, but stopped at my words. Her shoulders dropped in surrender. "Fine. I finished all my classes. I'm out of here tonight, and I have no wish to stick around for graduation. This school has been nothing but a pain in my ass." She gestured inside, but the movement was halfhearted and it fell in her lap. "I came here for two reasons. Heather and Logan. I can see now that both reasons were stupid. I'm an idiot."

My eyebrows went up, and I moved back as she stood up. "Does Heather even know that you're out here?"

"No, and it doesn't matter. I'm wasting my time. I'm going to go."

That was odd, but I wasn't going to stop her. I agreed. She should go. Heather wasn't going to forgive her. Ever.

She went a few steps, but stopped and swung back. "You know what? Fuck it. I don't give a shit. He can't hurt me anymore."

What the hell?

She gave me a bright smile. The renewed zeal behind it had me holding my breath. That wasn't a good look, not on Tate. Then she said, "My dad lost his job, and when he said I could move back with my sister, I had no problem with it. I was an idiot before and because of it I lost two great people in my life: Logan and Heather. I thought I could come back, grovel for a while, and both would let me back in." She gestured to Manny's. "You can see that's not happening. Heather will never forgive me, and I know it. I just haven't wanted to accept it, but not with Logan. I got it through my thick skull a month after I moved back."

She grew serious and a knot formed in my stomach. This wasn't going to be good.

"Logan was never going to love me again, but dumb me. I still tried. It was useless, and I know why."

It loosened a little, but I knew she wasn't done.

Tate took a breath, shook her head at me and a bitter smile flared for a second. "Mason hated me. I thought it was going to be the same as last time. I thought he was going to humiliate me at every chance he could, but he didn't. That threw me for a loop. For a while."

"Why are you telling me this?"

She shrugged. "I have no idea. Maybe to piss him off one last time? Maybe because I'm the only one who'll actually say it to your face? I don't know. I don't care. I'm done with high school. I'm off to college, and Mason Kade can no longer fuck with my life."

That sounded worse than the first part. The knot doubled, and I was starting to struggle with breathing.

"Has he told you that Marissa's going to Cain University too? That's where he's going, right? He and Nate. They're roommates."

He hadn't. A part of me sank inside.

Then she laughed some more, the same bitter sound from earlier. "I started to suspect a while back, but it's beyond me why no one else has. I was at Fischer's party earlier, you know. The one where Mason relished ruining Kate's life. Guess who I ran into there? Miranda Stewart. I heard that she dated Logan for a little bit, but I never thought about it. Who would? He goes through girls like beer. He chugs one down and throws the can away."

This wasn't going where I wanted it to go. I knew where it was going, but I didn't want to know. I didn't want to hear the words and I began to shake my head. Things were good. Things were better than good. The three of us were united again. Mason and I were together. I needed him.

She kept laughing. "Miranda has no idea what happened. From what I heard, she got all judgment on whoever slept with Logan, then he turned the tides on her and seduced her. She dumped her long-time boyfriend for him, only to get dumped by Logan a month later." She nodded. "She told me about that night at the party. She told me that she had words with Mason and Logan and that was when he seduced her. It was that night. It was because of Mason, wasn't it?"

Dread began to form in me. It went deep, all the way down, and I couldn't answer her. I started to turn away.

Tate kept going, as if she was enjoying this. "You see, Logan rarely does something without a reason. Not a lot of people know that about him, but you and I do. So does Mason. I was curious, so I kept asking her more questions. She explained everything, how she was a hypocrite to her friends." Tate paused and drew in a ragged breath. She bit out, "She has no idea. That's the beauty of everything. She has no fucking clue."

"No, no, no." I shook my head. I knew what was coming, and I didn't want to hear it.

"And she didn't even say anything. It was all in her look. She told me how she was so confused. She thought you were dating Logan, but then Mason stepped up and set her straight. She couldn't believe it, but that was all that was needed. Mason saw it. Didn't he?"

This couldn't be said. It would make it real.

"She saw what he already knows." Tate kept going. Her voice was so goddamn cheerful. "And I love it because it sent him into a tailspin. It wasn't that he couldn't lose his brother, it was you. He couldn't lose you. I don't know what he did, but I'm not stupid. I know how Mason works. He was behind Logan dating her and dumping her, wasn't he? I love this. I love that I'm the one that's going to spill it."

I held my breath. My hands were in fists now, and I pressed them into my legs.

"He wanted to silence the one other person that caught on, and she might've said something. Too bad she never figured it out, but she is dumb. Quite dumb, though she acts like a princess." A hollow laugh came from her. "She saw the same thing. She saw why Mason stopped giving a damn about me this year. That's what she saw and why she was so confused that you were with Mason."

I continued to hold in my breath and kept my eyes closed. *No, no, no, no...*

"Mason didn't get that video of me sucking off Logan out of the goodness of his heart. He didn't even get it to help Logan. This is Logan. He doesn't give a shit if someone watches him getting a blow job. Oh no. Mason got that video because he was hoping it'd keep my mouth shut because he knows I figured it out." She snorted to herself. "He didn't want me to tell you what I know. And like I said before, I no longer give a shit. You want to know what Miranda saw all those months ago, even though she never connected the dots?"

I shook my head. I couldn't lose them.

Tate continued to laugh as she started to back away. "Logan couldn't love me because he's in love with you. It's finally out there now." She paused and an abrupt laugh came from her. "Logan's in love with you."

She kept laughing all the way to her car, but I couldn't move.

Logan was in love with me.

Fuck.

Keep reading:
Fallen Fourth Down
Fallen Crest University
Fallen Crest Home
Fallen Crest Forever
Logan Kade
Crew
The Boy I Grew Up With
Crew Princess

ACKNOWLEDGEMENTS

Thank you for reading the first four books in my Fallen Crest Series! Please read on and continue with Heather and Channing's book (*The Boy I Grew Up With*) and also Channing's sister who inspired her own series. You can read TBIGUW as a standalone, but it does technically start one week after the timeline of *Crew*. *Crew Princess* needs to be read only after reading *Crew*!

I have to acknowledge the incredible readers who have loved and supported all things Fallen Crest to me! Thank you guys! It has meant the world to me.

Head to my website for a few more bonus scenes in the Fallen Crest universe, along with a new *Mason* bonus scene!

www.tijansbooks.com